Mine, always

Koko Heart

Happy reading!
All my love
Koko ♡

Published by Koko Heart 2022
Edited by: Eliza Ames
Cover design by Shower of Schmidt

MINE, ALWAYS

Created with Vellum

Glossary of words:

This book uses British and Irish slang words. A list of some are below:

- Mammy: Irish dialect of the word mummy/mommy
- Eejit: Irish dialect for idiot
- Wean: Irish term for baby
- Scared the bejeezus out of me: Irish dialect of saying 'you scared the life out of me.
- Fecking: Irish dialect for fucking
- Ye: Irish dialect for You
- Tis: Irish dialect for It is
- Treacle: British term of endearment like sweetie/sweetheart
- Numpty: British slang for Idiot
- Knob: British slang for dick
- Me old mucker: British slang for my old friend.

CONTENT NOTE

Just to advise you that this book contains discussions of violence, depression and panic attacks. It also has parental abuse - parent to adult and past parental abuse as well.

Prologue

"Open ya eyes and look."

I looked up at the tall, beautiful woman standing next to me. Her long dark hair blowing gently in the breeze. Her face tilted up a little so the freckles sprinkled across her nose were glittering in the sun. She looked down at me with eyes as blue as the sky and I smiled. I smiled a smile I knew mirrored hers exactly. I knew my eyes matched hers and my freckles did, too. My hair, not as long as hers, but just as dark, was secured in a ponytail with a large blue bow. We stared at each other for a few seconds, a mammy gazing at her daughter and a daughter admiring her mammy.

We didn't speak for what seemed like ages. We just stared at each other and then silently back at the view with the sea expanding forever before our eyes. Standing on the beach of our little town looking out across the sea was a favourite thing for my mammy and me to do. As I looked around and saw the un-spoilt empty beach I laughed. I knew what my mammy was going to say.

"Promise me, Darcie," her Irish accent thick, strong and filled with love. "Promise me ye will leave. Ye'll go and never look back. Explore the big wide world, Darcie. Go to New York, or London. Oh, Paris and Rome." She had that faraway look in her eyes that I'd come to expect whenever we came here and a little smile on her lips. She continued looking out to the sea.

"Live ya life for ye and enjoy every second of it. Get as far away from here as ye can. Never settle for second best in life. Never tink ye aren't good enough. Don't let a man treat ye as if ye are. Ye are my everyting. Ye deserve the world and not the shitshow I brought ye into. I'm sorry."

The loving, faraway look in her eyes had changed and I felt myself take a deep breath. She always urged me to travel, to embrace adventure but she'd never told me the other things. Her smile twisted into a grimace, and she closed her eyes, as if she were willing the thoughts to leave her head. I stared up at her waiting, as I hoped she'd snap out of it as quickly as she went into her trance. She didn't look down to me with twinkling eyes as she normally did. She didn't tell me she was being a silly sausage like normal. Instead, she raised her hand to touch the side of her face and my eyes followed. I could see the bruise on her cheek, the concealer she applied not quite concealing it. I grimaced as her finger traced over her swollen lip and watched as she sighed. The marks from last night were evident on her beautiful face but I wasn't shocked, it was normal for me to see my mammy hurt. Hurt by him. The anger and hatred bubbled inside me when I looked at her face again. I wanted to cuddle up to her, kiss her and make it all better like she did for me when I fell over, or when I was sad.

"Mammy?" I asked innocently, my eyes pleading with her to come back to me. It wasn't enough to break her out of her thoughts. "Mammy," I said with more firmness and a shake of her hand. She snapped her head to me and bent down so we were at the same eye level. She grabbed the tops of my arms with urgency and held them tightly.

"Darcie," her beautiful sky-blue eyes were as clear as ice, and the fear inside of them scared me.

"Promise me if anyting happens to me, ye will run, run as far away from here as ye possibly can and never look back. Never come back, for no reason, do ye understand? Never come back!" The fear in her voice and the way she held me made me speak through my fear.

"I promise, Mammy. I promise." As I stared into her eyes, I hoped I was saying the right thing. I wanted to see the blue eyes that reminded me of the sky on a clear day. I wanted her beautiful face to go back to the smiling one that made me feel like everything was okay. That I was safe. I wanted my mammy to look as happy and carefree as she had when we'd arrived at the beach. Our beach, our spot. She smiled and kissed me on top of the head.

"Good girl, Darcie, always remember. Now let's go paddle." She took my hand and led me down the beach, towards the water's edge. The sand tickled my toes and the water made me jump with how cold it was when it lapped at my feet. My mammy laughed as we walked along, and I looked up at her and took a mental picture in my mind. I wanted to keep this image of her forever. Laughing and carefree, no sign of the fear and desperation etched across her face a moment ago. I looked at her and I vowed I would do as she said. I'd live my life for me. I'd never let a man treat me the way he did and if she wasn't here for whatever reason, I'd run and never look back. I'd live a happy life and I'd make her proud.

Chapter 1

Darcie

Tis May and warm. Unseasonably warm, as I open the windows of my wee flat. I sigh, "Not that it makes a difference, no bloody breeze." My accent, still thick and clear, rings through the emptiness. As I look over the remnants of my twenty-four years, I can't help but feel a twinge of sadness.

"Not much to show for a lifetime is it, eh?" I turn my head towards my little brown bear who's propped up on my pillows. She's tatty and old and has seen better days, but she's one of the only things I have from my childhood and from my mammy. I smile as the memories of when she gave her to me come flooding in.

"Darcie, she needs ye to look after her; she needs ye to love her and keep her safe for all of time; can ye do that?"

I remember looking up at her with my big blue eyes, hopeful and happy. "Of course, I will mammy. I will love her for always." I was so happy; I took her from my mammy's hands and spun her around in my outstretched arms and then hugged her tightly to my chest. "I love ye, Sheila, I always will."

I remember how my mammy laughed when I said

'Sheila', her blue eyes twinkling. I wasn't happy about her laughing at me, and my face told her. She threw her head back and belly laughed at my sour little expression and even though I was still put out at her laughing at me, I liked to see her happy. I didn't get to see her happy a lot of the time, so when I had these glimpses, I savoured them.

"Fecking scruffy ting. What've ye given her that for? Spending my money on shite." My head snapped around and found him standing in the doorway. My mammy's laughter stopped abruptly and her whole demeanour changed. She looked scared and sad, and I was ushered into a room with the door closed...

I shake my head violently and banish the memories to the back of my mind.

"Right, Sheila, what should I wear for my first day on the job, eh?" I walk over to my wardrobe and run my hand over the clothes rail. Tisn't a lot, or filled with designer clothes, but they're mine, paid for by me and me only. I found work easily when I first came here. I arrived in London a year ago, with the intention of travelling around the world. I had nothing but some clothes, money I'd saved up since I was wee, and, of course, Sheila. I fell in love with the city. The big buildings, the busy roads, the history around every corner, I love everything about it. I love blending into the crowds on the morning commute and I love that no one expects ye to stop and have a chat or knows anything about your life. I may not have gotten extremely far with my adventure around the world, but I now get to call London my home. Tis a stark contrast from my little village in Ireland where everyone knows everything about everyone that lives there. I shake my head again to banish the dark thoughts looming in my memory and shoot an exasperated look at Sheila. "What is wrong with me today?"

I roll my eyes and go back to staring at the clothes in the

wardrobe. I opt for a pair of light blue, skinny jeans and a white top with a knot at the front. I look in the mirror and assess my reflection. I look grand. I don't really have any major hang ups about my body or anything and I don't really care what anyone else thinks. I've been told I'm beautiful and asked out by men but I'm not interested in all that. I'm a twenty-four-year-old woman and I've never had a boyfriend but I don't care. There hasn't been anyone worth exploring the whole relationship business with and I don't want to settle for just anyone. I saw what happened first hand when you settle and I won't be that woman. I promised mammy, I wouldn't.

I pop my feet into my trainers and head to the front door. I pick up my bag and make sure my phone is in there and call out, "Bye Sheila, wish me luck." As the door closes behind me, I pull my chin up from my chest, exhale loudly and whisper to myself. "Let's do this Darcie."

The bus isn't too bad this morning - a couple of overly friendly people but nothing I can't handle. One guy is apparently, "Mesmerised by my insanely beautiful eyes". Another man, "Could listen to my voice all day long." Insert eye roll here.

Then, a wee old lady says, "Ye are the most beautiful Irish girl I've seen in a long time."

Well, that one I don't mind because she's the most adorable old Irish lady I've seen in a while too.

I could probably walk to work from now on though – less people to have to deal with first thing in the morning. I look down at my watch and realise I'm fifteen minutes early. Well rather be early than late, eh? I look up at the huge town house in the middle of Chelsea and wonder whether I should go straight in or if I should wait. Before I can make my mind up, the front door opens and standing in the doorway is someone I didn't expect to see there. Feeling confused, I rack my brain back to when I had my interview here last week.

I met Mr. and Mrs. Blanc and their three children, Isaac, Isabelle and Isla. Isaac, the eldest is six and the identical twin girls are four. Mr. Blanc, Daniel as he asked me to call him, a sophisticated man, was dressed in a suit but with his tie loosened around his neck. I put him in his mid thirties. He was handsome enough. However, Mrs. Blanc, Rebecca, now she was stunning. She had blonde hair, which she wore in a bob, with highlights of all different shades of gold running through it. Her face was exquisite, and she could easily pass for my age. I knew she was older though, when she looked at my resumé and saw my date of birth, she laughed, a beautiful wistful laugh.

"Oh, to be young again eh, Dan?" She gazed adoringly at her husband.

He smiled back at her, making his green eyes twinkle with love and affection for her.

It made me feel something seeing them together. A sort of tightening in my chest, but I couldn't put my finger on what, and before I could, the feeling was gone. As Rebecca stood up, I noticed how tall she was. Then again, anyone who's over five feet is tall to me, but Jesus, Mary and Joseph, Rebecca was very tall. She had legs that went on and on and on. Raking my eyes over her figure I noticed how slim she was, too, even after having three children. It made me wonder if she were a model in her younger days. It would explain how they managed to have such a nice house in such an expensive area of London. But then again, I didn't know what Daniel's occupation was, so it could have been all down to him. I watched them together for a moment. Rebecca's green eyes shone as her husband put his arm around her and kissed the top of her head. Smiling, she gave him a gentle nudge in the ribs with her elbow.

"You sentimental old fool."

I looked at them and I couldn't help but feel a pinch of longing. I wanted that; the love and trust they had between each other, but I doubted I'd ever find it. It seemed rare these days to see anything of the like. I mean, all I'd been shown growing up was heartbreak, violence and love looking a lot like a man controlling ye. There was a little part of me that still looked at couples like Mr. and Mrs. Blanc and wondered if I could ever have that.

I shoved the notion of happily ever after into the back of my mind and scolded myself, telling my brain they probably hated each other, and all of this was just for show, but deep down the little voice didn't believe that at all.

After the interview portion was over and they'd offered me the job, they introduced me to their children. Isaac was the loveliest little gentleman ye'd ever meet. He was a mini version of both his parents physically, but ye could see his father was his idol. The way he carried himself and the mannerisms he had were exactly like his father's in every way. I couldn't help but smile when I noticed them. Isabelle and Isla were stunning little girls, all blonde hair and dimples. They looked like angels, but they had an air of mischief about them that Isaac didn't have. They questioned me about everything.

"So, are you gonna be da new lady looking after us?" Isabelle inquired.

"Yes, if ye'll have me." I replied with a smile to her.

She looked me up and down and whispered to her sister. "I like her voice, how 'bout you, Isla?"

Her sister turned her face to me and gave me the exact

same look her twin had just given me and whispered back to Isabelle loudly, "Me too, I fink we should keep her."

The whole time Isaac was shaking his head and giving me his best 'I'm sorry about those two' look which I think he probably did a lot more than he would want to admit. I laughed at all three of them and put my hands on my hips in my most matter-of-fact way.

"Right, well I'm very glad you've decided to keep me, and I'm looking forward to working for ye three." I ruffled Isaacs's hair and gave him a wee wink. I turned to the girls. "Now I know ye two are the bosses really but let's not tell Isaac, eh?" They squealed in delight and hugged my legs tightly and turned their faces towards Isaac and gave him the exact same smug look. He grinned up at me like a Cheshire cat. I knew then I'd be happy here with them and we'd probably have a lot of fun together.

My heart is racing as I drag my eyes up from the exquisite shoes on this strangers feet. My gaze skims up his body hidden by his navy suit and I note how beautiful the aqua tie looks against his white shirt. Heat rushes to my cheeks and flashes through every fibre of my being as my gaze meets his perfect ice blue eyes. A shiver wracks my body as I stare at him and an electric current courses through me. I'm staring openly at him and I don't know how to look away. I release my bottom lip, which I hadn't even realised I was biting down on, and continue to stare. After what seems like forever, he looks away. And whilst I'm relieved, I notice there's also a glimmer of disappointment within me. I glance at his mouth. A smile tips his lips up and I gasp out loud. Surely, he can't know what I was feeling from up on the top step? Did he notice the heat that went from the tips of my toes all the way through my body and came to settle as a bright red blush across my cheeks?

An internal panic spreads through me. He can't know my underwear is soaking wet from just looking at him, can he?

I physically take a step back as I realise he's moving toward me. He runs a hand through his jet-black hair, and I catch a glimpse of what might be a tattoo on his hand. He gives me a dazzling smile full of confidence that makes my insides jump. That heat, the one that engulfed my body, is once again making me glow red. I hate the fact that just seeing him has made me feel vulnerable and open. I'm mad at him for making me feel like this and mad at him for smirking at me as if he knows what's going on. I force my head up, put my phone in my bag and square my shoulders off ready to face him. I turn my blue eyes towards him and I'm just about to give him my deadliest look when he walks straight past me and into a car waiting shortly behind me that I hadn't even noticed was there. I stand on the pavement staring at the car dumbfounded as it leaves; I can't help feeling disappointment and sadness. I shake my head and scold myself for being so stupid. It's got to be the heat of the unusually warm weather I tell myself and walk up the steps of my new job. No matter how much I try, I can't shake those eyes from my mind.

Chapter 2

Denny

"Are you okay?"

I drag my gaze up to meet my driver's eyes in the mirror and say, "Yeah, I'm fine. I'm fine." I don't know why I say it twice, maybe I'm trying to convince myself I am because I've no idea what that was all about. That woman completely knocked me for six and that's never happened before. I'm used to seeing beautiful women, but there's something different about her. I don't know what, I can't put my finger on it. She's absolutely stunning with her long dark hair and beautiful curvy body. She's tiny, like a real-life Polly Pocket, the dolls Isla and Isabelle love to play with, and I certainly wouldn't mind putting her in my pocket at all. It was the way she looked at me that really confused me though. Like she hadn't seen a man before in her life. She had this innocence about her which I'm putting down to her age. She looked young, maybe early twenties, but her eyes were filled with lust and want mixed in with a hint of confusion, all of which looked alien on her beautiful face. Her icy blue eyes, just like my own, made me feel like I was standing before her naked. Vulnerable and open. Two things I didn't want or need to be with anyone.

She was beautiful though. She stirred something inside of me. Hope? Want? I don't know. The way she looked at me made me want things I have no place wanting. I rub my hand over my face and through my hair, groan and shake my head. What is wrong with me? It's not the first time a beautiful woman has looked at me with lust in her eyes. I know I look good on the outside, the inside is a whole heap of mess but she made me feel differently about myself. Like the inside could match the outside for a change. I don't know if I'm going to be able to work out what or how she made me feel like this but when her eyes locked onto mine it felt like a connection was there. I shake my head again. I don't connect with women. Ever. What's wrong with me? I stick to my rules. I avoid emotions and feelings. What happened to throw me so off track today?

This morning and everything about it was ordinary. I woke ten minutes before my alarm went off. I stretched out over my handmade, extra-large bed and stared up at the high ceiling of my suite. The white walls reflected the sun and the gold accents around the room added to the warmth. I stroked the headboard and sighed. My bed is by far my favourite item in my room, custom made for me and my large frame. I spent a small fortune on it, but it was worth it. I hate sleeping in any other bed now. I rolled and smiled as the view of London greeted me through my windows. I fucking love this city. My hometown. My London. I love everything about it, even when it rains nonstop. Today was, however, another beautiful sunny day. Once I was finished in the bathroom, I threw on one of my suits and went down the two flights of stairs, only to be greeted by shrieking and yelling.

"But it's mine. Why you always gotta take MY fings. I hada live in mummy's tummy wiv you, now you take my stuff. Mine!"

"Uncle Denny, tell her, she has to share!"

As I got to the bottom step, both of my nieces were staring at me beseechingly, only one niece's expression was pleading for help and the other's could only be described as a fiery look of "don't-you-dare." I looked over at them and saw their brother Isaac standing in the door frame looking exactly like a mini version of my brother.

"I'm not getting involved, my little Princesses. If you're looking for someone responsible to help, we all know you should be asking Isaac."

With that comment, Isaac's eyes lit up and he strode over to the girls. "Uncle Denny is right; I am the most responsiblist person here. Isabelle, you have to share your toys with Isla, those are the rules." He folded his arms over his chest.

"Not FAIR! I'm telling mummy. MUUUUUUUMM-MMMMMMMYYYYYYY!" The twins ran off into the direction of the kitchen.

I looked at Isaac and shrugged my shoulders. "Women eh?"

He rolled his eyes and stalked behind his two little sisters.

I chuckled to myself as I walked over to the door, opened it and felt like I'd been struck by lightning. Approximately five feet of lightning.

Leaning my head back onto the plush leather seats in my car, I pull my phone out of my pocket and dial my brother.

After a couple of rings, he answers. "And what did I do to owe the pleasure of your call, brother dearest?"

"Nothing, Dan. Listen, as I was leaving for work this morning there was a woman outside. Do you know who she was?" I try to sound nonchalant about it, but I'm not sure I'm successful.

"Why do you want to know who she was? Did you finally get turned down by a woman? Did you ask her who she was, and she ignored you?"

I can tell in his voice he thinks he's hilarious, but he's probably the only person in the world who thinks that. Well, him and Becs actually, she finds him hysterical. How he got her to marry him I will never know but they are definitely a match made in heaven.

"Funny, you arsehole. Do you know who she was or not?" I ask, getting more and more irritated.

He chuckles on the other end of the line. "Den, I'm going to need a bit more than that to go on, mate. There are literally millions of women that could have been outside our house."

I sigh and rub my hand over my eyes. "Well, she didn't look in place, not like your typical Chelsea bird – sorry – lady..." I flinch at the words I used. My brother is a stickler for political correctness and I know my terminology frustrates him. Normally I would do it more to wind him up, but it's not smart when I need something from him. I know how to play ball. I quickly carry on so he can't lecture me about women not being called birds.

"She had long dark hair and piercing blue eyes, a banging body and she was tiny; I could fit her in my pocket." Just describing her is making me hard and I look down at the bulge in my trousers.

"DENNY! Are you there?"

Shit, I wasn't listening to him. "Yeah, sorry, go on."

"I think it was Darcie, the new nanny. I forgot she was coming today. Shit, I hope Becs remembered. Remember I told you about her. She's Irish and strictly off-limits Denny, you promised me and Becs. We can't keep replacing nannies because of your 'any hole is...' I can't even say it, it's wrong on so many levels. Off limits, baby brother, do you hear me?"

I can't help but laugh at him for not being able to say, 'any hole is a goal' – it was my mantra through my adolescence and Dan has never been able to say it out loud. Even though I never use that term anymore because I've grown up and I'm no longer an arsehole like I was when I was younger, he still throws it in my face all the time.

"It's yours and Becs's fault. You keep hiring fit birds and they keep swooning at my feet. What am I supposed to do?" Okay, maybe I'm not entirely grown up yet. But I'm getting better.

"That's exactly what we don't want you to do, Dennis. No seducing Darcie. Leave her alone and find someone else to play with. Don't you think it's time you stopped being a man-whore and settled down now? Don't you want what Becs and I have?"

I take a deep breath and close my eyes, preparing myself for the lecture I've heard a million times before. I press my fingertips to my closed eyelids and sigh. Yes, I want what he and Becs have but I can't tell him that. I can't let him know it's what I want more than anything. I can barely admit it to myself let alone say it to him.

"You know me brother, I'm not made for monogamy. I'm more of a no strings attached kind of fuck, not the settling down kind..." I'm glad there isn't anyone around that would judge me for saying that shit, but I said it for a reason. I know he won't like it and will hopefully change the conversation away from me and my happily ever after.

"Jesus, Denny, I hope to God my girls never get treated by a man the way you treat women..."

For a moment, I'm speechless. The angelic faces of my two little nieces flash through my mind. I can't really think of them as grown, and certainly not in the position he's suggesting, but the idea of them being treated badly makes me rage. "Anyone ever treats those girls with anything less than fucking respect and I'll beat them to within an inch of their lives, let them recover and then beat them all over again. No one will ever hurt them, and no one will ever upset them. I'll make damn sure, don't you worry." I take a breath to try to shake the anger from within and blow it out again before continuing. "Anyway, the women I see get treated very well, they get the experience of a lifetime and I'm always up front about no commitment, so they know what they're getting into with me." I'm still raging at the idea of the girls being treated badly, even though they aren't my kids, they ARE my heart.

"Jeez Den, calm down. No one's going to do anything to the girls. I was just trying to make a point. I just want to see you happy and in love. It's the greatest feeling in the world and you, more than anyone, deserve to be happy."

My anger dissipates and is replaced with fear and guilt. I don't deserve to be happy. I don't deserve anything except punishment, but my big brother doesn't see it like that.

"I'll leave the love, marriage, and a baby in a carriage to you. You do it so well."

I hear him sigh and say, "I'll take the love and marriage but please no more babies in a carriage. The twins are more than enough, thank you very much."

With that comment, we both laugh. We love the twins and Isaac more than anything, but my God those girls are a force to be reckoned with.

"And on that note, I'll speak to you in a bit."

As I look outside, the world goes by in a whirr of blurry buildings; I can't help but think about what my brother said. 'I deserve to be happy...' I can't expect to be happy, ever. I don't deserve it. My past is dark and twisted and I can't let anyone into my life to get sucked into that darkness with me. I'm better off alone. It's the only way for me. A promise I made to myself a long time ago.

As I put my head back onto the headrest, I get a flash of her piercing blue eyes staring at me. I try to picture something else but all I can focus on is her. Her legs, the curve of her hips and her arse. Her tiny waist, the swell of her breasts - she has certainly been blessed in that department. Her beautiful pale skin; I'm salivating at the idea of her taste. I noticed the little catch in her breath as she spotted me. And when she chewed on her bottom lip, a jolt of desire shot straight to my dick. I wanted to go over to her, grab the ties out of her hair and run my fingers through it. I wanted my hands all over her body, to show her how much I desired her. I wanted to take her lips and taste that beautiful mouth, trail kisses along her body...

"Denny, are you okay my boy?"

I open my eyes, look up and find Joseph looking at me in the mirror and realise we've stopped.

I clear my throat and say, "Sorry, Joseph, I don't know what happened there. I'm okay. Thank you." I give him a reassured smile, and he tips his head to me. Joseph has been my driver for years but is also family, not biologically but still family. He doesn't need this job but likes doing it to be close to Dan and I. He drives with me more than Dan though; he's keeping an eye on me. I don't mind because Joseph is one of my favourite people in the world.

As I step out onto the pavement I look up at the building. I've worked my arse off to be able to have a company in a building like this. In the middle of central London, the heart of the business empires, our little corporation is thriving. Dan and I started out with nothing and literally worked our way up to the top. We landed a big client early on and it helped to sky rocket our little operation into the successful business it is today. It's amazing what word of mouth can do when it comes out of a very influential businessman. Our buildings certainly speak for themselves but the recommendations from him helped to put us on the map.

As I make my way through the entrance, I greet the front desk and security staff. I'll never be the kind of boss who sticks his nose in the air and thinks he's better than others. Outside my office is Gloria, my beautiful assistant and Joseph's wife. One of the reasons I enjoy waking up and coming here is to see her. I love my job; creating a building on paper and then watching it come alive onsite is amazing, but Gorgeous never fails to put a smile on my face. No matter what kind of a shitshow my life is, she always makes things brighter with that smile of hers. Pictures of me and Dan, Becs and the kids and of course Joseph adorn her desk. A cup of coffee, made to perfection awaits me as I sidle up to her.

"Good morning Gorgeous, how are we on this beautiful, sunny Monday?" I bend down and give her a kiss on her cheek, and she swats me away with a playful slap on the arm.

"Oh Denny, you rascal, you shouldn't be kissing married, sixty-year-old women. You should be finding a nice young lady to give your kisses to every morning."

She always tells me this and I always reply with, "Gloria, if I can't have you, I won't settle for anyone else, you are the love of my life, lady." I give her a cheeky wink and she laughs at me.

"Rascal," she says through her giggles.

Gloria has been with me from the very beginning, and I'd be lost without her. Not just at work either. I've told her and Joseph they should be living in the countryside and enjoying their retirement but Gorgeous always tells me, "We'd be bored senseless. Besides, we'd never see our boys and grandbabies. And I like organising your chaos, Denny."

I enter my office and banish all thoughts of the blue eyed siren, Joseph and Gorgeous from my mind. I spread a drafting sheet over the table, grab a ruler, protractor and pencils and get my head down to do some work.

I plough through the morning like a madman before I realise it's lunch time and I'm starving. "Gorgeous, what you up to for lunch?" I call through the doors.

"I'm going out with a few of the girls; you're more than welcome to come, I'm sure they wouldn't mind." She gives me a knowing look and I smile back at her.

"Nah, you're alright, Gorgeous. Enjoy yourself. I'll see what my annoying brother is doing." I pick up the phone and dial his extension.

"Dan, fancy lunch?" I ask.

"Denny, you do remember we have a client meeting at one, don't you? Did you bring the plans with you?"

SHIT!

"Dan, I've left them at home. I'll call and get the meeting pushed back till two and I'll swing by and get them. Good job you're the brains and I'm the beauty, eh?" I laugh at his exasperated sigh.

"I'll call them now. You go and get the plans." He says through a grimace.

Even though I know he's pissed off with me, I can't help but smile. He knows this deal is done and dusted and this meeting is a formality, but he is such a stickler for rules and regulations. We couldn't be more different if we tried.

I call out to Gloria and tell her I need to run home. She waves her hand at me as I run past her to the lifts. She knows the way Dan and I work.

I spot Joseph pulling up to the curb and smile as I jump into the car. He shakes his head at me and smirks and I settle back into the seat when realisation hits me. The new nanny. She'll be there, and I'll get to see those eyes up close.

A nervous burst of energy shoots through me. What the hell? I don't get nervous about women but this is no ordinary woman. This one has me rattled. Her eyes felt like they could see straight through me. And she's off limits. I run my hand through my hair, take a shaky breath and squirm in my seat as my dick twitches at the thought of her. Off-limits, I remind myself. Fucking off-limits.

Chapter 3

Darcie

"No, I'm not giving in. Ye can look at me all ye want with those big puppy dog eyes, but ye know tis not right to hit your sister over the head with a doll. No matter what she said to ye. Now ye will sit there and think about what ye did."

Isabelle is sitting, pouting on the bottom step, whilst Isla is dramatically holding her head and swooning on the floor as if she may pass out. The little drama Queen.

"Isla do ye feel okay enough to come into the other room whilst your sister does some thinking on the step?" I ask her tentatively.

She jumps up and gives me a nod and then glares at her sister who sticks her tongue out at her as she passes. Just what I need on my first day – a fight between the sisters where weapons were used. I roll my eyes and follow Isla into the lounge.

"Now show me where the doll hit ye, sweetie." She offers me her head and I examine it thoroughly and am very relieved when I see there's no blood. Just a little red mark that will hopefully fade before their parents come home. Of course, I'll tell them, but I'll feel better calling from home and not the hospital for a doll related incident. Rebecca was in a rush this morning, and I didn't see Daniel at all as he'd left to take Isaac to school for before I arrived. I had no time to have a conversation about anything, including the man mountain that stood in the doorway. Sweet baby Jesus, the way my body reacted to him was a joke. I shake my head to clear the image of him from my thoughts when I hear the front door open. I jump ten feet in the air when I hear a man's voice.

"Hey Princess, what's up?"

I fly into the hallway and stand in front of Isabelle, still sat at the bottom of the stairs, and turn to see who's come into the house. I freeze on the spot when man mountain himself is standing right there in front of me with his sexy blue eyes locked onto mine. My whole body alights with warmth, but the girls' safety comes before anything else, and I have no clue who this man is.

"I'm sorry but who the hell are ye and why are ye walking into people's houses in the middle of the day? Leave now or I'll call the guards. I mean, the police."

A grin spreads across his face but before he can respond, Isla comes running in from the lounge and straight over to him squealing and throwing herself into his arms.

"Uncle Denny, Isabelle hit me on da head wiv her doll and it REALLY, REALLY hurt. Darcie put her on da naughty step but da step ain't naughty. It didn't do anyfing wrong. It's just called dat cause you sit dere when you naughty."

He chuckles as the words spill out of her mouth and I'm still trying to come to terms with the 'Uncle Denny' reference when he speaks. His voice makes my heart beat faster and my breath comes out harder. I have to stand straighter to try to hide it.

"Well Princess, that's not okay, is it? I'm glad – Darcie?" He looks at me and raises his brows.

I give a slight nod with my arms folded over my chest, not wanting to let on how affected I am by him and his deep, silky voice.

"Has told her off and put her on the naughty step – the one that hasn't done anything wrong." He grins and my knickers are ruined.

She hops from his lap and skips over to me.

"Darcie, can Isabelle come off da step now? I'm bored and wanna play wiv her."

I gaze down at her and smile, then turn to her sister. "Isabelle, do ye have something to say to Isla?"

"Sorry sissy, I won't do it again, but if you make me really mad I will."

They both laugh and run upstairs to the playroom. As I watch them go, I'm very aware I'm standing in the hallway alone with the man mountain or 'Uncle Denny' as the twins called him. I turn around slowly, and my eyes are met with him staring at me. His mouth tips up a little as he runs his hand through his hair.

"Sorry, I assumed Becs, or Dan would have told you this is my house, too. I live on the top floor. I'm Dan's brother, Denny." He holds out his tattooed hand to me and I step forward to shake it. As our skin touches, I feel a tremor go through my whole body. It starts when his fingers first touch mine and goes up my arm like an electric shock. I pull my hand away quickly, hoping he doesn't notice my odd behaviour. What was that?

"I'm – I'm Darcie Quinn. Erm, your brother or Mr. and Mrs. Blanc didn't mention ye lived here, hence my confusion when ye just turned up. I'm sorry. I'm the twins' new nanny." I'm jabbering and feel like I'm sweating buckets.

I'm so affected by him; every inch of my body is practically screaming at him to 'take me now' and tis all very new and strange to me. I've never had a reaction this strongly to a man before. I'm sure tis clear for him to see what's going on with me and I don't like that one bit. Tis like I'm hypersensitive to him in every way. When he speaks my knickers get damp. When he smiles, my knickers get damp. And when he touched my hand, it felt like there was a flood down there. I think I had my first mini orgasm from just that little touch and I'm terrified he knows. How embarrassing for my body to betray me like this in front of this Godlike mountain of a man. I don't want him to see these reactions. He'll think I'm a silly little girl and I don't want him to think like that of me. I've never cared what a man thought about me before but with him, everything's different. I force myself to remember to breathe. Being in his presence is making me dazed and I don't like it. I need to leave so I can gather my wits together, but I can't leave the house as the twins are upstairs. I can leave where he is though. I back away to head upstairs and I'm just about to make my excuses when his voice beats me to it.

"Darcie, are you okay? Have I upset you in some way?"

I turn back around to face him and the look in his eyes nearly tips me over the edge. He looks uncertain, sad and the minute my gaze meets his, his pupils dilate and a flash of something else is there – lust. I've seen it enough times in other men's eyes, but instead of feeling bored or annoyed by it like I have before, it makes my heartrate pick up and my breath catch in my throat. Why does knowing he wants me make me feel so differently than I have before? I swallow hard and realise I need to try to get this under control, as I'll be seeing him all the time, if he lives here. That thought excites but terrifies me. I'm a walking contradiction.

"No, no ye haven't. Not at all Mr. Blanc. It was just a shock, having what I thought was a stranger standing in the house and it made me on edge. I'm sorry if I offended *ye* in any way, that wasn't my intention. You've a lovely home and I've loved spending time with the twins today." I smile at him, a full megawatt smile to try to show there are no hard feelings and I'm comfortable with him now. Comfortable isn't the right word though, because with my soaked underwear, rock hard nipples and throbbing core, comfortable is the last thing I feel right now.

He stares at me for a couple of seconds with that look on his face again, but then shakes his head and smiles right back at me. That smile causes an eruption in my knickers and I dig my nails into the palm of my hand to stop myself from jumping on him. What in the hell is wrong with me? Twenty-four years I've gone without experiencing anything like this before.

"I'm sorry I was staring, but your accent is mesmerising. I could listen to you talk all day. What part of Ireland are you from?"

Tis my turn to look a little blank and startled. I don't want to talk about Ireland. I don't want to tell people where I'm from. I want to stay aloof and vague but before I know it, I'm talking.

"Erm, thank ye, I guess. I'm from a little village in Donegal. I've lived in London for about a year now and I absolutely love it. The only ting I miss is the beach. Back in Ireland we lived near one and it was my favourite place to go to with my mammy." I freeze. In just over a year, I haven't dropped the h in "thing" or "think", and I've never mentioned where I was from or my mammy to anyone apart from my best friend. I've never even thought to talk to her about our beach. I don't know what happened. I suddenly have the urge to run, to get as far away from the house and this man as I can. I need to escape. I can't risk anyone back home knowing where I am. What am I doing talking to him about that? It just came free falling out of my mouth. I bite my lip and fiddle with the knot on my top. I can't think, I'm just frozen. I jump a bit when he speaks.

"Your accent is beautiful. I'm glad you love London. I do too. It amazes me every day. I think it's the best city in the world, but maybe I'm biased." He smiles at me and it instantly puts me at ease. "You're right though, it is missing a beach. Do you go back and see your mother a lot?"

The sound of his voice took my panic away but his words have put me back on edge. I feel like I'm on a roller-coaster the way I'm up and down. I look at my hands fiddling with my knot and mumble, "No, I haven't been back since she died a year ago." My eyes remain low as I stare at my fingers. I can't bring myself to look up. I don't want him to see the pain and vulnerability in my face. I feel like I can't hide anything from him and that scares the bejeezus out of me.

I'm normally so good at putting on a mask and hiding my feelings from anyone, even my best friend, but not with him. Panic shoots through me. I can't be telling him the ins and outs of my life like this. I need to put some distance between us. He goes to speak to me again and I smile and cut him off.

"Anyway, was there a reason ye are here during the day, Mr. Blanc? Or is this a normal occurrence?" I wipe my sweaty hands on my jeans and take a step up the stairs.

He grins at me and runs his hand through his hair and shakes his head, "I forgot some plans that Dan and I need for a meeting." He checks his watch, whistles and motions with his head to the stairs. "I need to grab it and get back to work. And, erm, Darcie, please call me Denny. And I'm sorry about your mum. Darcie."

He smiles kindly and walks past me. Our arms brush each other and a zing of electricity zooms through me. I look at his departing back and a frown crosses my face. What is it about this man? I wait for a few beats and head up after him to check on the girls, knowing I have some time before Isaac gets back from school.

Chapter 4

Denny

Sitting in the back of my car, I can't help but laugh and say out loud, "Fucking Darcie."

Joseph looks at me, amusement in his eyes, "What's so funny boy?"

I shake my head at him, still smiling and go on to tell him all about the Irish siren that goes by the name Darcie. Joseph knows me. He raised me from the age of eight. I trust him with my life so I know he won't say anything to anyone, especially my brother.

"I don't know what's come over me. I can't seem to shake her from my mind and I need to because Dan has made it abundantly clear that she's off limits."

Joseph chuckles and shakes his head at me, "Can you blame him? After the last fiasco? They've been without a nanny for weeks because of you, my boy."

I take a deep breath and slink into my seat, "I know. I should never have gone anywhere near her. And I didn't for months. I still don't know how she knew I'd be at that bar that night but she did, and alcohol is an evil little fucker. The kids didn't like her anyway. And Dan told me they were getting rid of her." I try to defend myself but I know it's no use. I ruined their little set up. I put more pressure on Becs because I couldn't keep it in my pants.

"Don't worry, Joseph. I won't repeat the same mistake twice. Even if she is ten times more beautiful and appealing." I wish I could though. Darcie has an elegance about her that calls to me. Yes, she's very pleasing to the eye. But her voice? That's another story altogether. When she spoke, it hit me somewhere deep inside. Her accent, her tone and the way she carries herself just added to the package. When she mentioned the beach in Ireland she went to with her mum, her eyes lit up and a peace came over her. I wanted to bask in that peace. I wanted to reach out and touch her, pull her into my arms and kiss her... but she's off limits. I can't chase her. It's a shame as I'd enjoy a little cat and mouse game, but I can't do that to my brother again.

Joseph looks at me and shakes his head. "What aren't you telling me Denny? Did something already happen between you two?" A frown mars his face.

I roll my eyes at him. "No. Nothing. Even I'm not that quick Joseph. It's just she's... Ignore me. I'm being stupid."

Joseph's eyes twinkle in the rearview mirror at me and he smiles. "Maybe you could try talking to her and get to know her, maybe date her and see where that goes. Dan said no seducing her. He didn't say you couldn't date her. Just a thought, son."

I stare at the back of his head with my mouth slightly open in shock. Joseph knows what my deal is, and he's never said anything about me dating or settling down.

"What the hell, Joseph? Where did that come from? You know I'm married to my job. I don't need any other complications."

Joseph's laughing, actually howling at me.

"Boy, I know what you've told yourself and everyone else over the years, but I didn't think you actually believed it. I've seen something in your eyes today, son. Something I haven't seen in all the years I've known you. This one can be different if you want her to be. You could be different."

It's my turn to laugh, but it isn't a belly laugh like Joseph just had; it's scornful. "Joseph, I have the utmost respect for you, but you, my friend, are a crazy man. You and I know the only lady I will settle down with is Gorgeous. When are you going to leave her and pave the way for me, eh?"

He chuckles and flashes his eyes in the rear-view mirror at me, "Not till the day I die son. She's been my everything for over forty years now. She saved me from a life... Ah nicely done boy. Divert my attention to my lovely wife and change the subject, eh? She's right about you; *you* are a rascal." He laughs and carries on driving.

His words ring in my head and resonate with my soul – what has he seen that's different? It scares me how perceptive he is because when I look at her, I know she's different, too. I envy Joseph; he has the best relationship with Gloria. Between them and Dan with Becs, I've seen what true love looks like. Deep down I've always longed for that closeness with a woman, but I know I'll never have it. There isn't anyone out there for me like that. The darkness of my past would consume them. I can't let someone else deal with that. Especially someone as light as Darcie. It's bad enough Dan, Becs, Joseph and Gloria know. I don't need anyone else to find out and change the way they see me. Or be consumed with it like I am. It's better the way it is. The women I'm with never have any complaints. They have a night or two of uncomplicated fun and I get no strings attached, no-emotions-involved sex. I'm always up front with them and they know they aren't going to change me or fix me. Some have tried. It's laughable that they think they have any power to help me when I can't even help myself.

No, the way I am is the way I'll stay. It's better for everyone that way.

I'll stay away from Darcie. She was good with the girls today and I'd hate her to leave because of me. I can't be the reason another nanny leaves, why everything is ruined again. But I've never felt that spark with anyone before. Never had that connection when I touched someone before. Never wanted someone as badly as I want her. Maybe, just maybe... I shake my head. No. No matter how appealing she is to me, I'll leave well enough alone. I won't repeat mistakes when they'll damage the people I love the most.

It's after six when I get home from the bar. I came home alone so Joseph could go straight to Gorgeous. As the cab pulls up to my house I'm torn. Half of me wants Darcie to be there so I can see her again, but the other half never wants to see her again. I don't like the effect she has on me. After some serious reflecting at the bar where I'd had dinner with Joseph, I realised, I can lie to myself as much as I want to, but I want more with Darcie than I'm comfortable with admitting. After one meeting with her, I know she's different. She makes me want to break all the rules I've set for myself, and I can't do that. Those rules were put in place for a reason. No emotions, no feelings and no commitment. That way there's no chance I can ruin anything. No chance of her getting attached and leaving when she wants more than I can offer. The kids like her and Becs deserves someone who's good with the kids. I can't put Darcie in a position where she'd be uncomfortable working for them because of me. I've already established in my head that I can't just fuck her once either - it'll never be enough - so I conclude, I'll avoid her and eventually she'll become like part of the furniture.

I head inside and straight upstairs to my room. I can hear the laughter and chatter as I walk up the stairs and pause on the landing for a second to hear her voice. Her accent floats through the air to me and I can't fight the smile that finds its way onto my face. I let it rest there as I walk the rest of the stairs to my room. It's been one fucking day and she's made me smile more today than I have in the last month. Fuck!

Chapter 5

Denny

For two weeks I've been cooped up in my room after work, instead of freely spending time downstairs. Two weeks, I've been tortured with hearing her voice, smelling her scent and wondering about everything that makes up Darcie Quinn. It's the strangest reaction I've ever had to a woman, and I don't like it. But I also love it. It makes me feel alive knowing I can feel this way, but it terrifies me at the same time. Feelings leave you open and vulnerable and I can't be that. I've turned down every invitation to go out, every offer to work late at the office, even though it would've made my life easier because I like being near her. I like knowing she's just downstairs. Knowing her light, her goodness is down the hall from me helps to keep the shadows at bay. I've devoured every snippet of information I've been able to garner from the kids, Dan and Becs. Everyone's in agreement, she's perfect and they all love her. I did the right thing staying away. It's been torture though. In a normal situation I'd have asked her out, told her up front it was a fling and we would've had a great time together. But this isn't a normal situation. She's too entwined with the family and I won't be the reason they're hurt or things get ruined again. My phone rings from my desk and I see Becs's name flash up on the screen. "What's up?"

Becs's frustrated voice rings in my ear. "I'm running late Den. Can you go down and relieve Darcie please. She's only meant to be there until six. Please?"

I blow out a frustrated breath. "Becs I'm swamped with work, can't you call her and ask her to stay on for a bit, Dan will be home soon anyway." I don't want to go downstairs and make small talk with her.

"He won't, he has a meeting with the accountant, remember? Please Denny." Normally, I'd jump at the chance to spend some time with the kids but not when I'm avoiding their nanny. I can't say no to Becs though either. She's been my best friend since we were kids and I've never been able to say no to her.

"Fine, but you owe me." I hang up and run my hand through my hair and blow out a breath. It's not a big deal. I'm just going downstairs and telling her she can go home. No big deal.

I head down the stairs, head dipped down, ready to avoid eye contact with her, when I hear a crash. I freeze mid step for a second and then in a flash I'm in the kitchen doorway. The sight that meets me nearly knocks me off my feet. Darcie holds a crying Isabelle, in a loving, protective hug, and is rocking her backwards and forwards, softly singing to soothe her. "Tis alright, you're grand. You're grand, I've got ye baby."

The image rocks me. If I were a cartoon, I swear you'd be seeing giant hearts where my eyes should be. A lump rises in my throat, and a vision of her flits across my mind - a vision where she's holding a little boy with dark hair and eyes as blue as ours. I watch an image of myself, kind of like an out of body experience, come up behind her and engulf them both in my arms. The smiles on our faces are of pure happiness and bliss. The entire scene is filled with light, no darkness to be seen. I blink away the image and swallow several times as my mouth becomes drier than the desert when Isaac notices me.

"Uncle Denny are you okay? You look weird."

Out of the mouths of babes, so they say. Everyone's eyes are on me and I suddenly feel really uncomfortable.

"Ahem, yeah, yeah of course I am." I ruffle his hair which I know he hates, and he gives me his father's 'stop it right now' look.

"What's happened here? I hate seeing you upset, Princess." I walk closer to them so I can see Isabelle, and Darcie turns ever so slightly so Isabelle is between myself and her. I'm grateful for that small action as I fight every urge I have to not touch her. Isabelle reaches out to me and I take her from Darcie's arms. I take a deep breath and inhale her scent. Not because she smells of my beautiful Princess but because she smells of Darcie.

"I climbed up dere and fell down." She pouts her little mouth at me and points to the countertop. I bury my face in her neck and blow a big raspberry on it. She squeals with laughter, and I know my job is done.

"Now Princess, what were you doing on the counter? Mummy and daddy are always telling you about climbing, aren't they?" I ask her gently.

She nods and looks down whilst playing with my shirt collar.

"Darcie told her to get down too and she didn't listen." Isaac tells me whilst looking at Darcie adoringly.

As I cast my gaze at my nephew, I smirk; the boy has taste. I'll give him that.

"Did you not listen to Darcie, Princess?" I ask her.

She lifts her chin up and fights to stop her lip from wobbling with emotion. "No. Sorry, Darcie."

She gives Darcie a little smile and I follow Isabelle's eyes. I shouldn't have; the look on Darcie's face makes my heart stop. She's so beautiful. Her eyes aren't icy or cold but are filled with love. Her smile's genuine and happy, with a look of contentment on her face. I can't tear my eyes away from her as she looks at Isabelle. "Tis okay honey, did you hurt yeself at all?"

The little girl in my arms shakes her head, "No. I got scared. Can we go play til dinner's done? Pretty please?"

She laughs at Isabelle and it's music to my ears. "Of course, ye can. It won't be long though so when I call ye, wash your hands and come right away please, all three of ye."

With that Isabelle has wiggled out of my hands and she, Isla and Isaac all run out of the kitchen.

There's an awkward silence as we stand alone. I run my hand through my hair and blow out an exaggerated breath. "You were really good with her. You calmed her down straight away. That's something Becs normally has to do. She doesn't normally calm down as easily, even for her own dad."

"Tis my job, she just needed a cuddle." Her voice is softer than usual, almost timid like. "Ye were surprisingly good with her, yourself. She idolises ye; they all do. All I've heard for the past couple of weeks is about Uncle Denny, the superhero. Tis nice to see an uncle have such a strong bond with his nieces and nephew." She looks up at me with hooded eyes and my cock rises to attention.

I gulp and then force a smile back at her, a genuine smile, and tell her, "Those kids are my heartbeat. They're like my own. When Dan told me they were having Isaac, I-I wasn't in a good place. That little man, he brought me back to life..." Woah, where did that come from? Why am I telling her information about myself? I don't speak to anyone about my shit. Not Dan, Becs, Joseph or Gorgeous. So what the hell is all the divulging about? I look down at my hands and see they're shaking. I shove them into my pockets and focus on breathing. What the hell is going on with me? This woman has cast a spell on me or something. Once I calm down, I look at her and see her eyes staring at me with wonder in them.

"Well children tend to do that; they don't know the magic they have. My mammy always said that to me, and I genuinely think she was right about that."

She smiles at me and I have to take a step back from her as my nerves are shot. I don't trust myself not to reach out and brush her hair back from her face. And she's off limits.

"That's twice you've mentioned your mother to me and twice I've seen you look so happy. It's a good look on you, you should talk about her more." I smile at her and turn to walk out of the kitchen completely forgetting the reason I came down here. I need to get away from her before I tell her my life story. I've never wanted to talk to anyone about my past, but with her, I want to tell her everything and that's dangerous. I can't risk her knowing. I step into the hallway when I hear her call my name. I stop dead in my tracks and turn around slowly. Hearing my name on her lips sends a shot of desire through me and I close my eyes and take a deep breath before I turn to find her hungrily looking at me. Her eyes running up my whole body and finally meeting my gaze. She is fucking stunning. The caveman in me wants to rip her clothes off and take her in the kitchen here and now but instead I answer softly, "Yes, Darcie?" I stare at her, silently urging her to come forward and stake a claim on me. If she makes the first move it won't be my fault.

Instead she asks, "Do ye, erm, do ye want to... Oh

jeyzus, spit it out Darcie. Are ye having dinner with the kids? There's enough food if ye'd like too. I mean if ye haven't already eaten. Ye know what, ye probably already have. Don't worry about it, ye go about your business now. Don't mind me."

If I wasn't so enthralled by her, the deep red blush that's taken residence on her cheeks, her beautiful accent singing each word to me and her rambling on showing me just how affected she is by me, I would've been laughing my head off.

Instead, I smile back, "What are we having?" The way her eyes light up with those four words is everything I didn't know I needed. I don't care if I was supposed to send her home, I'm not refusing her after that adorable rambling.

"I've made lasagne and salad. Well I'm in the middle of making a salad." She holds up a cucumber and a peeler both of which I didn't notice before.

I walk towards her and take the cucumber out of her hands. "Allow me the honour of making the salad, please."

She blushes a deep red and I feel bad for embarrassing her, but I'm glad she's as affected by me as I am by her. She gives me the peeler and starts to chop the tomatoes up.

"We haven't seen a lot of ye. The kids I mean. The kids haven't seen a lot of ye. Ye must be busy. Ye and Daniel, Mr. Blanc. For god's sake, Darcie." She blows a breath out and rolls her eyes.

I smirk as I continue to peel the cucumber.

"Do I make you nervous, Darcie?" I watch as the blush creeps up her neck and takes pride of place on her cheeks.

"Erm, ye do a little bit, Mr. Blanc."

I smirk at her and can't help but flirt with her a little, surely that can't hurt. "Why do you think that is?" I shuffle a little closer to her and brush our arms together on purpose as I reach for a knife to chop the cucumber. The bolt of electricity that surges through me takes me by surprise a little but also confirms to me what I already knew. This woman is different from the others.

She clears her throat and stares at the place our arms touched. "Sorry Mr. Blanc, I don't know why that keeps happening. Static electricity or someting..." She blows out a frustrated breath, "Thing. Something."

The whole time she speaks she looks down at the tomato she's chopping. I smile when she corrects herself, she must be trying to lose a bit of her accent. I don't know why, I fucking love the way she sounds.

"Don't apologise, Darcie, and please call me Denny?"

She nods at me but still looks down at the food she's preparing.

"Have you managed to get out and about in London, Darcie?" I watch carefully as she shakes her head.

"No boyfriend wining and dining you?" I ask casually but desperate for her to say no.

She blushes so hard I think her head might explode. She's chewing on her bottom lip and it's all I can do to stop myself from reaching out and taking it in my lips and soothing it with my tongue. But I can't. She's fucking off limits. So instead I grab the lettuce and start chopping.

"No, Mr. Blanc. I don't have a boyfriend. I used to go out with my best friend but she moved to France a little while ago."

Sadness takes over her beautiful face and it makes the breath stutter in my throat. I don't want her to be sad. What the fuck is wrong with me?

"Would you like to? Be wined and dined that is?" My head's screaming at me to walk away but my feet stay rooted where they are, with my hands making a damn salad.

She turns her hooded eyes towards me, and I stare right back at her.

"I suppose that would depend on who was doing the wining and dining, Mr. Bla..."

"DENNY." I say firmly, cutting her off. "Denny, please. Call me Denny." I say softer.

"Denny." She lowers her lashes and licks her lips and all I can think of is kissing her. I don't do it but I fucking want to.

"And what if it was me asking you out, Darcie? What if I wanted to take you out to a nice restaurant? Give you flowers and chocolates. Would you want that? Would you let me walk you home and give me a goodnight kiss at the end of our date?" I don't know what I'm doing. What I'm asking or why I'm doing it. She's off limits and I promised Dan... But she's also calling to me like a siren of the sea.

She blinks a few times and wets her lips again and shakes her head, emotions flitting across her face. She wants me as much as I want her but she's cautious too. "This is inappropriate, Denny. You're practically my boss and I don't even know ye. I haven't even kissed anyone before..."

I'm staring at her hard, shock and confusion clear as anything on my face. "Did you say you haven't kissed anyone before?"

She brings her gaze firmly to mine and says, "No, I haven't been kissed before."

I feel like she's just knocked the air right out of me. How's that possible? She's fucking gorgeous. Beyond fucking gorgeous. There isn't even a word to describe her, that's how fucking gorgeous she is. I'm shaking my head and I'm just about to ask her how that's possible, when the front door opens.

Becs calls out. "Hi, I'm home. Denny, where are you?"

Becs comes into the kitchen whilst I'm still chopping the lettuce. She sidles over to me and kisses me on the cheek, eyeing me suspiciously whilst she puts her camera equipment down, and then turns to Darcie. "Sorry I was late, the shoot overran, and I was boxed in and couldn't get my car out until everyone moved. It was a nightmare. Were the kids okay? Any dramas? I didn't expect you to still be here, Darcie."

She shoots me a suspicious look again; this bloody woman's like a bloodhound. I listen whilst Darcie gives a breakdown of her day with the kids and note she included the incident with Isabelle. I have to rate her for her honesty. Whilst they speak, I finish off the salad and tell them I'll get the kids. I call up the stairs and all three come bundling down.

"Mummy's home. She's in the kitchen."

They sprint away and give her the biggest hug whilst she laughs and tells them, "I take it you guys are happy to see me then. What smells so good?"

Isla is the first to answer. "Me, Darcie and Isabelle made asana for dinner. I'm having cucumber salad cause I hate leaves."

It's a good job I know my niece as I've already chopped some cucumber and left it separate for her, and when I show her the bowl she squeals excitedly.

"Well, if ye don't mind, I'm going to head home. I'll see ye all tomorrow."

I smile as Darcie makes a dash for freedom knowing full well Becs isn't going to let her go anywhere.

"Darcie, if you think we're going to eat the food you've prepared without you eating with us, you have another thing coming. Sit down and eat with us and then Denny can drive you home. You can take my car. I won't hear another word about it!"

I chuckle as the kids all yell, "Yeah!"

Darcie tries to open her mouth to protest but I lean over and whisper in her ear, "I wouldn't. She's like a dog with a bone and you won't get her to change her mind at all."

She gasps at my proximity to her and I inhale her scent again. She's like a drug to me. I need to smell her or hear her to get my next fix.

"If ye insist but I don't want to impose."

Becs has already laid a place at the table for her and is motioning for her to sit. And from the looks of things Darcie takes my warning about Becs seriously and sits down.

Dinner has been very uneventful. I'm not sitting close enough to Darcie. In fact, I'm on the other end of the table from her, in between Isabelle and Isaac, who I haven't failed to notice has wrangled the seat next to Darcie. He looks incredibly happy about it too. I'm going to have a word with him later. Looks like we're both after the same woman. Shit, where did that come from? I'm not after anyone, I remind myself.

Darcie talks with Becs about general stuff and whilst she does, I watch her carefully. I find it ludicrous she's never been kissed before. I'm assuming if she's never been kissed before that would also mean she hasn't had sex before. To know I could be the first one to touch and taste her, that I could make her mine, nearly makes me come in my pants at the dinner table. I need to talk to her; I want to know more. I want to know everything even though I know it isn't fair. Even though I know this changes nothing, I need to know. I want to know why she's saved herself for so long. Why hasn't she been kissed? Why doesn't she have a boyfriend? I mean she's seriously fucking hot. I feel a kick under the table and realise Isaac's responsible.

"What the hell dude?" I ask him quietly.

He motions with his head for me to lean in so I can hear him.

"Stop staring at her, it isn't polite."

Is my nephew warning me off her? I couldn't be prouder of this kid if I tried.

"You stop staring too, I've seen the way you're looking at her. Good taste, my man."

He smirks at me and rolls his eyes. My nephew is a fucking legend. Laughing to myself I stretch my arms up and groan quite loudly to signal for us to wrap this shit up. The ladies look over.

"Tired are you, Denny? Don't forget you have to drive Darcie home."

"Tis okay. I'm grand with getting the bus. Honestly, I've already imposed enough."

"Nonsense, you're not an imposition at all. You're in our house, looking after the kids for us. You're going to be just like family soon and we look after family, don't we, Den?"

I smile at Darcie and shrug my shoulders and say, "Afraid so; you're not getting on the bus. Isaac would never forgive me if I allowed that."

Isaac's eyes nearly bulge out of his head as he throws me a dirty look.

He smiles sweetly at Darcie and tells her, "It would make me worry about you if you got on the bus."

She smiles down at him, gives him a cuddle and ruffles his hair, and he doesn't bat an eyelash. This boy has moves. I may need to bow down to him soon.

After she says goodbye to everyone, we step outside into the cool night air. I motion for her to follow me towards Becs's car but she stops on the pavement.

"Ye really don't have to drive me home. Tisn't that far and I don't mind getting on the bus."

"Darcie, if I walked back in there now, Isaac would kill me, so please just get in the car."

She gives me a nervous smile and relents.

Once she's buckled in, I close the door and walk round to the driver's side. I take a deep breath before I get in and ask her to program her address into the GPS. We drive for a few minutes in silence. We're so close I can smell her shampoo – coconut. I inhale a little and I can't wait any longer.

"Darcie, about what you said earlier. Did you mean it? You've never been kissed before?" I look at her briefly and can see the embarrassment written on her face.

She is staring out of the window, keeping her eyes from meeting mine and she softly says, "Aye, I meant it."

I blow my breath out and ask, "But how is that possible? I mean, shit, sorry, I didn't mean it to come out like that. What I meant was, you're beautiful. How have you got to your age, I'm guessing twenty-five, without someone kissing you? I wanted to kiss you the first day I met you. I don't get it."

She turns to look at me, cheeks going red at my last comment and takes a breath, "I had people try, but I didn't want them to. I've never wanted to, until..."

I turn to look at her and see the lust in her eyes again, "Until me? It's okay to say it, Darcie. I'm attracted to you, too."

She seems to relax a bit. "I'm twenty-four, not twenty-five. Ye were close though."

"Very close. I take it you want to know how old I am?"

She shrugs her shoulders in a noncommittal way.

"Okay, I won't tell you then."

"Tis grand by me. I don't need to know. Ye can drop me here and I can get the bus from over there. Tisn't far."

Is she serious? She went from relaxed to furious in a

split second. "Darcie, I thought we'd established you're not getting the bus. We're in the fucking car, so I'll drive you home."

"Don't swear at me please. I don't like it!"

I glance at her. Her arms are folded and anger is written all over her face, which just makes her look even more adorable. I soften my tone before I speak to her.

"Darcie. I wasn't swearing at you. I was just frustrated. I swear a lot, but now I know that you don't like it, I'll try to curb it. I'm sorry." This woman has got me apologising left, right, and centre.

She takes a deep breath and turns to me with a little smile. "Thank ye. I didn't expect that if I'm honest. I'm sorry. How old are ye?"

I glance over to her and she's staring at me intently. "I'm not telling you."

The shock on her face is a picture.

I can't keep it going for much longer though. "I'm sorry I couldn't help myself." I say, laughing as she pouts at me. "Thirty, Darcie. I'm thirty. Don't hate me."

The pout softens and she turns to face the window again.

"Oh Darcie, don't deprive me of seeing that beautiful face and those gorgeous eyes. I've spent two weeks avoiding you. Look at me please." Nothing, she still faces the window. We pull up outside her building.

She turns her head to me and says, "Well, you're getting on a bit aren't ye, Mr. Blanc?"

"You cheeky..." I laugh at her sass and shake my head in desperation, "Please, for the love of God woman, call me Denny." Before she can reply I lean over and brush the hair from her face and gently tuck it behind her ear.

Her breath catches in her throat as she quietly asks, "Why were ye avoiding me, Denny?"

I smirk at her and blow out a breath. "Because you call to me like a siren, Darcie. You make me want things I shouldn't. I can't give you what you need, but it doesn't stop me from wanting you."

She tilts her head at me, "What do you think I need?"

"Not me, Darcie. Not me." I tell her with a grin and watch as her eyes flash defiance at me.

"I don't think that's your call to make, Mr. Blanc. I decide what I need, not ye."

I smirk and realise I want this woman more than I want to honour my promise to Dan and Becs. Maybe I can do both.

"Darcie, can I take you out for dinner tomorrow night, please? Just dinner. I'd like to get to know you better."

She bites her lip and her eyes flit from side to side. "I don't know. I want to, but I'm worried. You're basically my boss and I don't want to date anyone, Denny. I'm sorry."

She looks unsure of her answer so I push a little. "It's just dinner, Darcie. We could discuss our attraction. I don't date either. This could be the perfect solution for both of us."

A frown crosses her face when I say I don't date and she chews on her lip furiously.

"What's the point of going out for dinner if we don't want to date each other? I don't think I can. I'm sorry Mr. Blanc... Denny..." With a little smile she hops out of the car and in a flash is in her building.

"SHIT!" I fucked that up. I put my head on the steering wheel and grip it tightly in frustration. "Fuck this. Stay away, Den." I start to drive away and stop when I look over at the passenger side and see Darcie's bag in the footwell. Great, now I have to find out where she lives to give her back her bloody bag. I could leave it and give it back to her tomorrow but if I go home with it Becs is going to want to know why I didn't take it back to Darcie now. Then I'll have to let her know I asked her out. That I ruined everything again.

Before I know what I'm doing, I'm out of the car and into her building. There are three floors and three flats on each floor. I'll have to knock on every motherfucking door I come across to find her. I walk towards the lift and thankfully the doors open. A woman, I'd guess in her fifties, steps out dressed in very tight trousers and a low cut top.

"Oh my, what a specimen you are!" She looks at me appreciatively.

I fight the urge to roll my eyes and tell her it's all superficial and inside where it counts I'm ugly as sin, but instead I smile at her.

"Oh Jesus." She moans out loud.

I chuckle under my breath and ask her, "Hi, I wonder if you can help me. I just dropped my friend off outside and she forgot her bag in the car. I know she lives in the building, but I can't remember what number she lives at. You don't happen to know her, do you? She's called Darcie and has a beautiful Irish accent." I flash the smile again and I swear I see her buckle a bit.

"Oh yes, she lives in 3B next door to me. She is a lovely young thing, incredibly quiet though. It's nice to see her have such a caring *friend*."

I thank her and make my way to the lift. Once I'm on the right floor, I walk down the narrow hallway. Standing outside her door, I knock abruptly. I listen to her footsteps as they get closer. They stop and I hear a catch of breath. I look up and into the peephole.

"You left your bag in the car, Darcie. We can talk through the door if you want, but I would love to talk to *you*, apologise and ask you not to leave. Becs and Dan like you and the kids adore you. I'm sorry if I upset you."

The locks turn and slowly the door opens. I keep my face calm and try to make my breathing steady. I want her to see the cool, calm, confident man I normally am. Not the one who's shaking and nervous. When the door fully opens, her nervous eyes meet mine and there's confusion on her face. I don't want her to be confused but I love the notion that I'm making her feel something. I want her to feel. I want to be the person who makes her feel. I hold out her bag for her and look straight into her eyes.

"Tis a grand apology, but do ye have to make it loud enough for all the neighbours to hear? What's wrong wit ye?" She whispers at me.

"You are what's wrong with me, Darcie. For two weeks you've been what's wrong with me." I blow out a frustrated breath and run my hand through my hair. "I came to give you your bag back and apologise. I've done both, so do you want me to leave?"

She's frowning at me, but she moves to the side and motions for me to enter. Once inside I do a quick scan around. It's small and compact, very tidy. There isn't a separate living room to her bedroom, it's all open planned, with little personal belongings. I look over to her bed and spot a teddy bear, I smile at the endearing thought of her cuddled up to it. I rake my hand through my hair again and turn back to her.

"Firstly, let me clear something up. I. AM. NOT. YOUR. BOSS. I didn't hire you. I wouldn't have hired you. I'm too attracted to you to hire you. Whatever we have or do will not affect your job if *you* don't let it."

She blows out a breath and walks over to her bed and sits on the edge. "Denny, just because we're attracted to each other doesn't mean we should do anything about it."

I put my hands in my pockets and nod my head at her. "You're right, of course. But I can't seem to walk away from you. I've tried for two weeks, but I haven't been able to shake you from my thoughts. Now what did you mean? You don't date?"

Her shoulders bunch up and she wrings her hands together in her lap. She shakes her head at me, "I don't want a relationship. I don't want to have to answer to a man. I'm living my life for me. I'm not going to settle for a mediocre relationship for the sake of it."

I nod my head at her, realisation kicking in, "You haven't been kissed, so it's highly likely you haven't been in a relationship before, so that tells me you've been hurt by someone other than a boyfriend. Care to elaborate?" Standing in her bedroom/living area I fold my arms over my chest. The place feels small, but I'm a big guy, so I'm used to places feeling smaller than they are. Trying to hide my nerves by being over cocky I raise my eyebrow at her, whilst she stares at me mouth agape. She shakes her head at me to say no and lowers her gaze.

"Am I on the right track? Just answer yes or no and I won't push further." I soften my tone and relax my arms. I want her to open up to me. I don't know why I need to know what's going on with her, but I do. She nods her head and turns slightly away from me, her guard is well and truly up and the need to run is as clear as day. It's like looking at a mirror image of myself. She's hiding something, just like I am.

"So, here's the thing, like I said in the car a minute ago, I don't do relationships either, Darcie. I don't do love or feelings; it's too risky for me. I have secrets just like you do. You don't have to lock yourself away from men just because you don't want to date."

She brings her head up and clashes her eyes with mine, "What makes ye think I'm locking myself away from men?" She folds her arms over her chest and stares at me.

I frown at her, "You're twenty-four and have never been kissed, Darcie. It's not a ridiculous assumption to have."

She raises her eyebrows at me and laughs, "Okay, I'll give ye that but tisn't accurate. I haven't locked myself away like some damsel in distress, Denny. I choose not to date and to not be in a relationship. I don't want to kiss someone or sleep with them for the sake of it. No-one's floated my boat enough to get me interested. Ye on the other hand, have probably felt the need often and definitely aren't as fussy about who ye keep company with either." She smirks at me, the pink tint staining her cheeks.

I like this feisty side of her. I smirk back and tell her, "I have sex, Darcie, good sex but that's it. When I'm with a girl, I take her out. We do 'normal' things together but there are no emotions. I'm up front with them so they know where they stand. It's about sex and company. Yes, there have been a few, but none I've had to avoid for two weeks because of my insane attraction to them." I pause to let that sink in to her and then look at her intently when I say, "You can have sex with someone without falling in love with them. You can enjoy someone's company without being indebted to them. I want to have sex with you Darcie and I also think you want to have sex with me, too." I lean against the little desk and watch her. She takes a deep breath and stands up. She's facing me and staring straight in my eyes. I smirk as she takes a slight step forward and keep my gaze fixed on hers.

She gently licks her lips, and her breathing is a little faster, "And what if I do want to have sex with ye? What happens then, Denny?"

I swallow the lump that's clogging my throat and tell her, "I know you haven't had sex before, well I'm assuming..."

She nods at me, "And?"

Everything inside of me is screaming at me to kiss her, but I can't. She's inexperienced. I won't take advantage of that, but fuck I want her. "That's up to you."

She smiles at my answer, and tells me, "Ye wanted to take me to dinner but that sounds an awful lot like dating to me."

I grin and take a step closer to her. The bravado slips on her face, slightly. "Dating without emotions. No need to worry about anyone catching feelings. I've told you I don't do love and complications and you've told me you don't want that anyway."

"Just dinner?" She asks as she steps even closer to me.

I take a deep breath and nod at her, not trusting my voice right now. She's too close. I reach up and drag my hand through my hair.

She chuckles at me, "Do I make ye nervous, Denny?" I recognise my own words from earlier and laugh as I nod my head at her. Her eyes shine like blue crystals and behind them I can see the need.

She reaches her hand out and tentatively touches mine and those sparks shoot off throughout my body again. She shakes her head, as confused by them as I am.

I entwine my fingers with hers and her breath catches in her throat. "If I asked ye to kiss me right now, Denny, would ye?"

The breath catches in my throat this time. I can't break my gaze away from hers. I lick my lips and watch as her eyes greedily take the movement in. I nod at her, unable to speak. She takes the final step towards me and presses her body up to mine. The air whooshes out of me and she smiles.

Her cheeks are stained red but determination flashes through her eyes, "Will ye be my first kiss, Denny?" She whispers to me.

"Fuck yes, Darcie." I bend my head, place my hand in

her hair, and I pull her into me. A moan escapes her lips as I lower my mouth onto hers. I kiss her fiercely, passionately and hungrily. I lick her tongue with mine and gently nibble her lower lip and then suck it ever so slightly. I can feel her rock-hard nipples against my chest. I want to bend down and bite them, lick the sting away and suck on them until she's begging me for more. Her scent is overwhelming, and it's like I'm being attacked by every sense. The little moans she makes, the way she tastes, the smell of her and when I open my eyes to see her, I'm blown away. I have to stop, or I won't be able to, and I really don't want to scare her away. I pull back but keep my hand in her hair to keep the contact between us, not wanting to let her go. I can't walk away from this feeling, not yet.

"Wow, Denny."

"Yeah, wow." I can't bring myself to say anything else. My mind is on overdrive with her. She's in my arms, still pressed against me, and all I can hear is a voice saying, "Mine." I stroke the side of her cheek and lose myself in her eyes as I continue. "You deserve for all of your firsts to be magical and I think we have a bit of magic about us. Don't you?" She stares into my eyes and her sparkling blue pools are screaming yes at me but I wait until her words match her eyes.

"Aye I do. Denny, what if, would you..."

She pauses and I hold my breath whilst I wait for her to gather her thoughts enough to finish her sentence. "I want to go to dinner with ye. I want to kiss ye again and maybe ye can help me spread some magic on my other firsts too."

She whispers the last part and I smile at her and rest my forehead on hers. I lower my mouth to her lips briefly as I need to be able to walk away. But I know if I keep kissing her like this, I won't be able to.

I take a step back and let her go. My arms feel empty

without her in them so I rake my hand through my hair whilst blowing a breath out. "Darcie, I want nothing more than to do that but I have to make sure that you're absolutely clear about what I can offer you. I'm not the relationship kind of guy. I can't offer you more than friendship and sex. Are you sure you want to go out with me?" Darkness clouds my thoughts and I take a few shaky breaths as she ponders my question. She bites on her lip as the shadows chase the light her kiss gave me away.

"Denny, I don't want a relationship but I do want to kiss ye again. What better way to experience my firsts than with someone magical who won't fall in love with me? Like ye said, tis the perfect solution. Unless ye don't want me like that."

The self doubt crosses her face and within a second I have her in my arms, reassuring her. "Darcie, I've never wanted something more than what you're offering right now. For some strange reason I need to be with you. I've yet to work out in my own head why. You bring me something no-one else has been able to, and because of that, I can't be the reason you're upset, and I can't risk you leaving the kids."

She steps back and puts some distance between us and tells me gently, "I won't need to leave because ye won't upset me as this is no strings no emotions dating, isn't it?" I nod at her and she grins back at me. The grin slides off her face and she brings her gaze to mine and asks, "Why me, Denny? Why did ye need to do this?" Her beautiful face is marred with confusion.

"I'm not one hundred percent certain of the answer myself, Darcie. There's something between us. I don't know what it is or why, but I didn't have great firsts, and the idea of you not having great firsts upsets me. I can't explain why because I don't know why. I can make sure your firsts are magical. Why you? I can't answer that either. I've been attracted to a lot of women, but I've never been as attracted to them as I am to you."

Her breath catches in her throat and she looks surprised by my words.

"Full disclosure, Darcie. I can't stop thinking about you and I've never felt like that before. Your light speaks to me and the good you have inside of you is calling to me. I want you but I don't want to hurt you." I stare at her, trying to hammer home my point because I don't think I could live with myself if I were the reason for her to be in pain. Something about this woman makes me want to protect her, look after her and make her happy. I can't have her hurt because of me. I won't ruin her.

"I don't want a relationship with anyone. I won't fall in love with ye either, Denny. That's something ye don't have to worry about." Her voice is loud and clear. "But I do want ye to be my first everything. I've never been as attracted to anyone before and now that I am with ye, I want to explore that."

Keeping my eyes neutral to hide the fact my heart is singing right now; I smile at her and pull her to me. As she rests her cheek on my chest, I kiss the top of her head and ignore the fact that this is the most intimate I've been with any woman before. Yes, I've fucked women, but I've never held them like this. I've never kissed their heads and stroked their cheeks and I'm shocked at how much I like it; how much I crave it with her. I shut it down. I can't think like that.

I step away from her and reach into my pocket as I tell her, "Dinner tomorrow night, I'll pick you up at seven thirty from here." I pull out my business card and hand it to her. "All of my contact details are on here, call me if you need to."

She nods and walks over to her bedside cabinet and opens the drawer. She writes on a piece of paper and hands it to me. I look down and see her beautiful handwriting with her mobile number and email address on it. I kiss her briefly on the lips and walk to the door.

"Tomorrow. Seven thirty. Dinner, yes?" Reaffirming more for myself than she needs to know. She nods and looks down at the floor. I bring her chin up so she's looking at me again and whisper to her, "Don't hide those beautiful eyes from me Darcie, please." I kiss her head again and turn and leave before my restraint snaps and the voice in my head shouting 'mine' gets louder.

Chapter 6

Darcie

I'm shell shocked and sitting on the bed for what seems like an eternity trying to grasp what just happened between me and Denny. One minute I was normal Darcie, the one who hadn't liked a man enough to kiss him, let alone consider doing other things with him. And now, I'm kissing a man I barely know. A man I'm so insanely attracted to that my knickers are soaked through. A man I WANT to sleep with and make magic happen again and again. Instead of being panicked or worried about it, I'm excited.

I flop down onto my bed and can just see Sheila out of the corner of my eye. Tis times like this I wish Nat, my best friend, was here instead of being millions of miles away. I sigh and reach out to Sheila and look her in her eyes.

"Sheila, what have I gotten myself into?" I hug her tightly to my chest as I've done so many times throughout the years when I had to pretend I couldn't hear mammy's screams. Before my mind can dive down the rabbit hole of my memories, my phone beeps from across the room. Still clutching Sheila, I stand up and walk to it to see who's messaging me. An unknown number shows up and I push my fear away over who it could be. After I open it, I quickly store the details into my phone.

Denny: You've made an old man very happy Irish x

I can't help but laugh out loud - he's not old, he's thirty. I want to reply straight away but I know better, after watching way too much TV and all my late-night talks with Nat. I know ye should always wait before texting back so as not to seem too keen, even if ye really are keen and just want to message back. Gah! I force myself to put my phone back on the bed and walk into the kitchen to get a drink of water. I casually touch my lips and remember the way Denny kissed me not long ago. They're still tingling from his touch. I bring the cup to my mouth but stop when I hear another beep. I practically run to my phone.

Denny: Are you waiting to reply to me so as not to seem too interested? If so, I think that ship has sailed Irish x

This man is so bloody arrogant, but I can't help but smile at the fact he knows my game. I type out a reply and hesitate a second before sending it. What am I doing? Should I reply? What would Nat say if she were here? I close my eyes and listen for her voice. As clear as day, I hear her scolding me. "He wants you, Darcie. No feelings, no relationship, it's perfect. Make some bloody magic, Darce." I shake my head to clear my best friend's voice away as I don't want to start a conversation with her in my own head. That's a therapy bill I can't afford. I take a deep breath and press send.

Me: Irish? Is that my new nickname? Original old man. You double texted me, you broke the rules of texting BTW x

Nervously waiting for him to respond, I grab Sheila and

cuddle her again. The little bubble with the three dots appears that tells me he's typing, and my tummy flips over.

Denny: I think your nickname is better than mine. Tell me about it, Irish, I have a feeling I'll be breaking all my rules for you... x

I take a deep breath and stare at my phone for a couple of seconds. He'll be breaking his rules for me. What does that mean? He told me he dates women, but he lets them know what he can offer them. He told me no emotions, no feelings, so what rules is he breaking for me? I want to ask him, but I know I can't. If I delve into him and his rules he's going to want to do the same with me, and I've already told him more than I like to share. With anyone. Not knowing what else to put I opt for an easy reply.

Me: Me too x

He's typing again, and I chew on my bottom lip whilst clutching Sheila to my chest.

Denny: It'll be worth it, trust me. Remember, for some unknown reason I have to chase you, so there's no point in running and cancelling on me now x

A shiver runs up my spine, not one of fear but excitement. He's really chasing me. He wants me. Why? I don't know. I mean I've had offers from men before, but once I've turned them down, they've given up and haven't given me a second thought. I told Denny I wouldn't go out with him and instead of turning the other way and finding someone else, he came after me. Yes he gave me my bag back but he still pursued me. He told me he isn't like this with other girls but is that just a line? No, I've seen my fair share of liars and I know Denny isn't lying to me. He's been avoiding me for a reason these past couple of weeks. There's something between us. I don't know what it is, or how long it will last, but it's worth exploring. I felt it instantly on that first day. I quickly type out a tongue-in-cheek reply.

Me: I hope so. You're a lot older than me, Old man. Are you sure you'd be able to keep up. I'm not cancelling... yet x

I can't believe I sent that. I wish I could delete it before he sees it, but he's already typing back. Dammit. Will he know I meant keep up as in chasing me and not keeping up during anything else? The innuendo is there staring me straight in the face and he'll definitely see it too.

Denny: I'm laughing so hard right now. Challenge accepted, Irish. Age is just a number. I'll show you how much stamina I have. I'll have you begging for a break, you mark my words young lady... No yet x

I blow a breath out I didn't realise I was holding, and before I get the chance to reply another message comes through.

Denny: Go to bed and get some rest. You've got some amazing kids to look after tomorrow and a date with a handsome man to look forward to as well x

The mention of our 'date' makes me feel the most turned on and the happiest I've ever felt in my life. If that kiss is anything to go by, I'm in for one hell of a date. My nipples are straining against my top and the throb between my legs is aching to be touched. I bet Denny could make the ache go away. My lust is giving me confidence and my sass is coming out to the forefront. *'Filthy whore.'* A voice flashes through my head but I shut it down firmly.

Me: Is that what I am to you, a challenge? Has anyone ever told you how arrogant you are? I can't wait to see the kids tomorrow; I'm sure

they'll be the highlight of my day. Telling me to go bed so you can get some shut eye, old man? It must be very tiring at your age. You double texted again. Goodnight x

With a smile on my face, I go to place my phone down, but I see he's typing and wait anxiously for his reply. I try to slow my hammering heart down. No emotions. No feelings. No attachments. They are the rules, Darcie, stick to them.

Denny: The best kind of challenge and one I can't wait to complete over and over and over again. The kids WILL be a highlight because they are adorable like their uncle, but not THE highlight, trust me on that. I think your auto-correct replaced handsome with arrogant in your text, you should get a new phone. Tomorrow. 7:30, dinner and kisses. Goodnight Irish x

Denny: Oh and by the way I don't care about double texting, get used to me texting and calling when I want to, I don't play games, beautiful. Sleep well, Irish x

I read and reread those texts repeatedly. I try to reply but I can't. There isn't anything I think of that can come back to those. The idea of kissing him again excites me. Just the thought of it makes me giddy. As I get ready for bed, I have the silliest grin on my face.

My two weeks at work have been pretty eventful. I've spent the days with the most wonderful little kids I've ever looked after. They've told me all about their amazing Uncle Denny. I feel like I've made a friend in Rebecca and that's a good thing, as I've very few friends.

My only real friend, Nat, she isn't even in the same country as me anymore. Apparently Paris is a much more enticing offer than living with me. I'm happy for her; I really am but I'm also sad I don't have her with me anymore. She'd be able to make sense of all of this and make the craziness in my head go away.

I try to call her to tell her all about Denny, but she doesn't answer. It sucks not being able to run things past her, but I know she'd encourage this. She's the only person who knows I'm a virgin. She wasn't shocked by that information but she was shocked by the fact I'd never taken matters into my own hands, so to speak. In fact, she was so outraged I'd never had an orgasm that she went and bought me a vibrator. My eyes when I opened it were wider than saucers. A few months later she was thoroughly disgusted when she was searching through my wardrobe for a pair of shoes to borrow and found it still in its packaging unused. She had a few choice words for me that day. Smiling at the memory, I shake my head. God, I miss her.

Four forty-five am, my phone glares at me when I check the time. I can't sleep and can't lay in bed any longer. Forty five minutes is my limit. I throw the covers off and decide to get ready and have a stroll around London for a while. To anyone else that'd seem like a ridiculous idea but it's my go-to when I have things on my mind. Nat thought I was mad until I took her with me one day, and ever since it was her go-to as well. I shower and dress in record time. Grab my bag and phone before I leave.

I walk around for a while and end up on the banks of the Thames. I love walking around the Thames. It gives me a sense of peace. Maybe tis the water that reminds me of the beach back home with my mammy. I've tried to avoid thinking of her all night as I don't want anything to make me change my mind about Denny. I've always backed away from sex because I don't want to prove *him* right.

"Ye'll turn into a filthy slut whore, giving it up to any fecker who'll take it." I close my eyes against the onslaught of pain I feel hearing the memory of my so-called daddy spit venom at me. I was five when I heard it for the first time, and I'd no idea what the words meant but I knew they were bad. I tried to reassure him I wouldn't but that just made him laugh. I didn't, and don't, like people laughing at me. When I told him that, I got my first taste of the back of his hand across my cheek. My whole face felt like it'd exploded as the pain shot through it. My mammy flew in front of me and screamed, *"NOOOOOO! Ye hit me, take it out on me. I haven't taught her properly. Tis my fault, punish me not her." She pushed me into the other room where I listened to my mammy get a beating from my daddy because of me. When I heard the front door open and shut again, I opened the bedroom door a crack.*

"Mammy?" I saw her on the floor, and I tried to go over to her, but she stopped me.

"No Darcie, get back to ya room. Mammy's grand. I promise." She tried to sound happy on that last bit, but her voice cracked. I went into my room and sobbed. The next day her beautiful face was bruised, bloody and swollen but she was still there serving him breakfast with a smile on her face. Even at that young age, I never understood why.

A vibration shakes me out of my memory, and I look down at my phone, tis six am and Nat's calling me.

"Why are ye up so early? Did ye wet the bed again, Natalie?" She laughs and I can't wipe the smile off my face at hearing her laughter.

"Very funny, Darcie. I fell asleep super early last night, slept all the way through and have woken up at ridiculous o'clock so thought I may as well phone me old mucker for a chin wag."

Just hearing her voice makes me so happy and replaces the fear and self-loathing I felt thinking of my past. Nat is an original London girl, and when I first came to live here I was so shocked everyone didn't sound like Dick Van Dyke in Mary Poppins. Nat thought that was hilarious. Every now and again she'll resort to some sort of 'cockney talk'. Tis always notoriously bad, but it never fails to make me smile.

"So, treacle, what did you call me for last night?"

Oh Nat, where do I begin? With a deep breath I start at the beginning.

"Woah, that's insane Darcie. Firstly, you got wet just from looking at him? That must make him a fucking God-like creature! He managed to melt the ice queen. Literally! Thawed you right out."

She's such a bloody eejit tis unreal.

"Secondly, you kissed him! Like actually played tonsil tennis with him, tongues and everything. And thirdly, you agreed to go out on a date with him? This is fucking mega, babe! I didn't think you had it in you. I'm impressed. You thinking about your mum and that scumbag?"

Nat knows bits and pieces about my daddy and my mammy; she knows about the abuse and why I ran away after my mammy got sick.

"Yeah, I am, what he's asking of me is no strings attached, no feelings, no love, he just wants me to have great firsts. Am I proving him right?" I need to hear her reassurance.

"Darcie babe, you shouldn't need to worry about what he thinks of you. You could go and shag the whole fucking

British army and he wouldn't be worthy enough to comment still. You're twenty four, Darcie. Your mum wanted you to live your life for you, remember? So, go live it. Enjoy every kiss. Enjoy every orgasm. And come for me a couple of times will you? I haven't had a fuck for ages."

I laugh so loudly the homeless man from across the way jumps out of his skin. I put up my hand to motion sorry to him and he smiles at me.

"Natalie, ye bloody eejit! I miss ye so much. What time do ye finish tonight? My date is seven thirty. Will you be able to help me with clothes?"

"I'll facetime you at six your time. Darcie, honestly, I'm so happy you're finally living a bit. Don't chicken out or I'll get on a plane and kick your fucking arse."

When I hang up with her my mood is certainly lifted. I walk over to the coffee stand that's just opening and order two teas, a coffee, a blueberry muffin and two chocolate ones. I take the tea, coffee and muffins over to the homeless man I startled earlier and crouch down next to him.

"I didn't know if ye would prefer tea or coffee so I got ye both. I also got some muffins for ye for breakfast, my way of apologising for making ye jump earlier. I've given the guy on the stand some money so if ye get cold or hungry or need something to drink go to him please."

He thanks me lots of times and after a few minutes of conversation with him I make my way home. It's seven forty-five, and I still have an hour before I have to be at the Blancs' house. I have a quick scan of my clothes for dinner tonight and groan at how boring they all are. I lift out my best three options and hang them on the outside of the wardrobe. I linger over the pale-yellow halter top that makes my boobs look amazing, but I'm not sure if it's too promiscuous. I hate that my brain questions that but growing up in a house with a man like my daddy puts these thoughts into my mind. Instead, I opt for a simple summer dress, white and floaty. Tis so comfy and versatile. With some heels and jewellery, I can dress it up. I hope Natalie agrees with me later. I check the time again and it screams at me eight fifteen. I grab my bag and phone and run out of the door.

Chapter 7

Darcie

As I rush outside of my building I freeze on the spot. Denny is standing on the curb next to a big black car. My jaw must hit the floor because he laughs and walks over to me.

"Good morning, Irish." He plants a kiss on my lips and pulls me in so I'm pressed up against his body. He's as hard as steel and is poking me in the top of my stomach. I feel my face blush bright red. As he pulls away from me, I hear a little groan and am surprised to realise it's come from me.

"Later Irish. I promise. I wanted to see you before tonight, make sure you were alright. We'll drive you to work if that's okay?"

I look up into his eyes, there's heat there but there's something else. Vulnerability? Sadness? Tis gone before I can grasp it though. I shake my head, still unable to believe this powerful, handsome, experienced man wants me enough to wait outside my home to take me to work. I'm so confused by how comfortable I feel around him, up against him, kissing him. It feels so strange but so right.

I roll my eyes at myself and tell him, "Ye are a mad man. Ye are telling me ye got up early and drove over here so ye could drive all the way back over there to drop me off? That isn't doing a great deal for your carbon footprint, old man."

He laughs at me. A full, throw your head back laugh. And if hearing that doesn't send a tingle of excitement through my body... I can't drag my eyes away from him. This man is the handsomest man I've ever seen, and I still can't believe he's interested in me.

Realisation dawns on me so I ask him, "Ye said we?" I look around to see who is with him.

Denny must have sensed my nerves as he chuckles at me. "This is Joseph. My driver."

My eyes widen.

Before I can speak, he tells me, "And my right-hand man. Joseph has known me and Dan since we were little. He's basically like our dad."

I'm staring at him in amazement and confusion. The way his voice softened when he mentioned Joseph told me exactly how he feels about this man. I shift awkwardly whilst still in his arms.

In a flash Joseph is standing in front of us.

"Good Morning Miss, it's lovely to meet you. Don't let this one get away with anything, you hear me? And if he gives you any trouble, you tell me, and I'll get my wife on him." His eyes twinkle when he smiles.

The kindness pours out of him washing away any awkwardness, making me feel safe and relaxed – tis not a feeling I'm used to experiencing around strange men, but I'm used to trusting my gut and my gut tells me Denny and Joseph are good people.

"Tis lovely to meet you too, Joseph." He holds out his hand and when I place my hand in his he raises them and kisses the back of mine.

"Yeah, yeah, alright mate, or I'll tell Gorgeous about you."

I look up at Denny suddenly and a little bit of hurt flashes in my eyes.

I try to shoo it away but he must have seen it. He sidles up closer to me and tells me, "Gorgeous Gloria is Joseph's wife and my assistant, and the only woman alive that terrifies me. She and Joseph have been married forever and have both known us since we were young. They're our only family, besides Becs and the kids obviously."

He lowers his head and his breath tickles my ear, sending a shiver through my body as he whispers, "Don't worry, Irish, I only have eyes for you. Just you. By the way, you look and smell divine. You're playing havoc with this old mans dick this morning." He brushes his lips over my cheek as I gasp in shock at his comment, which he chuckles about quietly.

Joseph opens the door for us, and Denny leads us into the car. I sit back in the seat and put my seatbelt on, as Denny does the same. He reaches over, takes my hands and laces his fingers with mine. I turn to him and smile as he asks, "What you grinning about, Irish?"

"Nothing, old man." I turn my head to stare out of the window when I suddenly realise Rebecca or Daniel might see me getting out of his car. Panic rushes through me.

"Denny, have ye told Rebecca and Daniel about this? I don't tink they'd approve and they're going to see me getting out of the car and tink horrible tings about me..."

Cutting me off, he calmly tells me, "Irish, stop panicking. When you get worried or angry you drop the h's in your words. It's bloody adorable. I haven't told them anything. Not because I don't want to, I'm not ashamed of this." He hesitates for a brief second and then continues.

"They kind of told me to leave you alone before I'd even met you. I'm going to drop you around the corner, so they won't see us together."

Feeling a bit of relief, I relax a tiny bit but can't help but panic still as I ask him, "Why did they warn ye off of me?" My heart is racing, and I feel my palms get sweaty. They probably didn't think I was good enough for him and they wouldn't have been wrong, would they? I mean he's gorgeous personified and I'm just me.

I feel him take a deep breath and watch as he sighs. "That came out wrong, Darcie. Erm, I may have slept with their last nanny and she may have turned into a bit of a stalker when I finished sleeping with her and they may have been super pissed off at me about it. They all love you and they don't want me to ruin everything. Again."

I chew on my lip, wanting to speak but he carries on.

"My only consolation is the kids hated her, and they were planning on looking for a new nanny anyway. They told me about their new nanny, you, being perfect and how the kids had taken to her and how I wasn't allowed anywhere near her. I didn't think about it again, once bitten and all that. Then when I saw you standing outside the house, you knocked me on my arse with those ice blue eyes of yours, I phoned Dan up to ask if he knew who you were. I was hoping you were a new neighbour. But once I described you, he warned me off and explained you were the new nanny." He grips my hand tighter and turns his body towards mine as much as the seatbelt will allow. "I had no intention of doing any of this. But then when I came home for those plans that first day, you blew all of my ideas out of the water. I tried to avoid you and stay away but I couldn't. The kids would tell me how amazing you were. Becs would bleat on about you too. And every time I was in the house I could hear your voice through the walls and I was intrigued. You've done a number on me, Darcie."

He's staring at me intently and I don't know how to respond. I'm in shock and awe that this beautiful man was so taken by me. I look down at our hands entwined, take a deep breath and bring my head up to look him square in the eyes. "Ye knocked me on my arse too, old man."

The look of relief that floods his face sends a shot of want straight to my ladybits. This man genuinely wants me as badly as I want him. I feel my stomach flip and I cross my legs to try to stop the sudden dampness in my knickers. I choose not to focus on the fact that he has form for doing things like this because I'm not going to fall for him and turn into a crazy stalker like the last nanny. This is just about my firsts. Not finding a happily-ever-after.

"You've not changed your mind about us?" The look of relief has turned to anxiety and his blue eyes are searching mine, seeking reassurance.

How can I need to reassure this man? He's a God and I'm a twenty-four year old virgin. "No, I haven't. I was never stupid enough to think ye weren't experienced, Denny. And ye told me yesterday ye were always up front about your situation with women. So if she couldn't hack it then tis on her shoulders not yours. Ye shouldn't really poo on your own doorstep though."

He laughs his beautiful laugh and another tingle takes over me. "Irish, I don't think I've met a woman who genuinely makes me laugh before. So, if I shouldn't, as you say, 'shit on my doorstep', should I cancel our dinner tonight, seeing as I'm taking you to my doorstep and I wouldn't want to shit on it again."

My cheeks flash red and I drop his hand, all tingles gone and replaced with anger. He's laughing at me. Mocking me and our arrangement. Swearing at me, when he knows I don't like it.

"Grand by me, Mr. Blanc. If ye would have your driver pull over, I'll walk the rest of the way." My face is flushed and I'm fuming he'd laugh at me like that after I was so bloody understanding. I'm halfway to unclipping my seat-belt when he growls at me.

"Irish, what the hell? You can make a fucking joke, but I can't? We go from old man to Mr. Blanc in a matter of seconds. I've been nothing but up front with you. And I told you before if you run, I'll chase you. So why the fuck are you running now?"

My hand freezes on the seat belt clasp and my eyes are lowered, but I still see him rake a hand through his hair and let out an exasperated sigh.

"I'm sorry," I say, still looking down at my lap, "I thought ye were serious and were looking for a way out and I thought ye were laughing at me. And swearing at me. Please don't swear at me again, I really don't like it." I try to keep the tears in, but I can't hold them back.

He catches my chin in his hand and lifts it up so I'm forced to look in his eyes. "Shi... Sorry Darcie. I'm sorry. I didn't mean to make you cry. I wasn't swearing at you, it's just a reflex of mine and I should've remembered you didn't like it. I'm sorry. I wasn't laughing at you. What you said was funny and it made me laugh, but I'd never laugh AT you. Please don't cry, I can't take seeing you sad." He wipes my tears away with his thumb and strokes my cheek.

"I got frustrated, that's all. I was just joking. I'm seeing this through, Darcie. I need to. I don't know why but I need to. I will poo all over my doorstep for you."

I laugh through my tears. I'm an absolute mess. He probably regrets ever looking at me the way I'm up and down with him.

"I'm sorry. I'm all over the place. It was my fault entirely. I guess I'm just a little bit surprised by your interest and I'm waiting for ye to realise I'm a really boring person and ye'd not want to do this anymore. Plus, I really don't like it when people laugh at me. Even when I was wee, I hated it."

He chuckles, "Irish, you're the least boring person I know. And you're still wee."

I roll my eyes at him, and he leans in closer so only I can hear him again. The intimacy of it takes my breath away and I'm beginning to question everything I've ever thought.

"I've already been your first kiss. I *will* be the first person to have sex with you, Darcie, if that's what you want. It's what I want, more than anything. Take my word for it." He puts his lips onto my neck, and I melt under them. He gently kisses up to my ear and nibbles on it. I gasp out loud and can feel his grin against my skin.

"Irish, I have to leave you now. I don't want to, but I have too. Tonight. Dinner. Seven thirty, yes?"

I nod, the only thing I'm capable of doing.

He straightens up in his seat, grabs my hand, and gives it a squeeze. Denny turns to me and repeats, "Seven thirty, tonight."

I nod at him again and get out of the car, waving my goodbyes to Joseph. Unable to speak through my lust addled mind. When they're no longer in sight, I let out a huge breath and pull out my phone to check the time. I'm still early. I put the camera mode on and flip it around so I can see what I look like. My eyes are a bit puffy but other than that I look presentable. I walk around the corner and head up the steps of Denny's house. I jump when my phone rings with an unknown number. I answer it but there's no one there. I put the phone back in my bag and sigh as I enter the house. Only a few more hours to go.

Chapter 8

Denny

"Well Joseph? Am I royally screwed or what?" I catch a look at Joseph's eyes in the mirror and can see the crinkles that his smile is causing. He knows this woman has put me on my arse, and I've known her less than a month. I can't stop thinking about her. She's like no other woman I've ever met before and although I'm scared shitless by it all, I'm also excited.

"Boy, I think she's delightful. Don't, as you would say, fuck this up, son."

I look at Joseph's eyes again and the crinkles are gone. He's deadly serious. I'm gobsmacked. Joseph doesn't swear. Ever. And I've not only been warned by him, but I've been sworn at too.

I can't help the laugh that bellows out of me as I tell him, "You're going to be in so much trouble. I'm telling Gorgeous, and she's going to kill you for swearing at me."

I pause as he shakes his head at me, and I take a deep breath before I quietly tell him, "I've told Darcie that I don't do feelings and emotions." I stare out of the window not wanting Joseph to see my eyes as I know he'll be able to see every emotion I'm feeling right now. He's known me near enough my entire life after all.

"Did you tell her why?" He asks me tentatively.

"Fuck no. She doesn't need to know." No one needs to know besides the people that already do. I won't tell anyone else. I'm surprised Joseph's even asking that.

"Maybe not yet, but one day you'll tell her, you mark my words. She's a keeper, son. Your very own Gloria. Just tread carefully."

My eyes swing to his in the mirror again and all I can see is honesty, so I scoff at him. "Joseph, you're an old romantic. Some people aren't destined for true love like you and Gorgeous or Dan and Becs. Some people are meant to be single."

Joseph's eyes lock with mine. "Well, I had you down as a lot smarter than to believe that bullshit son. Be happy for once in your damn life and don't ruin it."

My mouth hangs open as he swears again. With nothing to say back to that, I stay silent.

Work goes by in a flash and before I know it, it's time to clock off and go home. My phone vibrates and I feel a little sick, worried it's Darcie calling to cancel our date. Checking the screen anxiously, I see it's just a message from one of my clients about work. I give Gorgeous a big kiss on the cheek, and she throws me a sly look – Joseph tells her everything and I know he's told her about Darcie. I roll my eyes at her and blow her a kiss as she calls out, "Be happy, son."

As I make my way around the office, I wave at a few of the people that work for us and get a few offers to join them in the pub. I take a rain check. I never wanted to be the type of boss his staff didn't like, so I've always made a conscious effort to be friendly with them. For the most part it's been okay. There have been a few that have tried to take the piss, but I just gently reminded them I was still their boss and they soon started acting in the right way. I round the corner to Dan's office to see if he's ready to go and he's just grabbing his jacket.

"What are you looking so happy about? Oh, let me guess, you've got a hot date lined up where you're guaranteed some action? Are you bringing her back to ours?"

I laugh at him and shake my head. "Oh, big brother, when are you going to learn? I don't bring women to our home. I didn't even fuck the old nanny at our house, and she worked there and served herself on a platter to me. Our home isn't where I fuck random women. You're right about the hot date though." I wink at him and he rolls his eyes at me.

"So, I take it you don't fancy settling down and giving my kids some cousins to play with then? You know it's okay to do normal things, don't you? You can't let her win and by..."

Punching his arm I shout, "DAN, Shut the fuck up! Let me enjoy my happy mood without you getting all womany on me for fucks sake." I know I shouldn't but it's the only way I know how to shut him up. Throw a curveball by suggesting he's acting like a woman by being concerned, then his political correctness OCD won't let him leave it and he'll change the conversation.

"So, because I dare to show a bit of concern for my baby brother, I'm being womanly? What the fuck does that even mean? You really must think before you speak..."

I watch as the penny drops and he realises what I did.

"Do you know what? You're an arsehole. A genuine fucking arsehole."

I'm laughing so hard I can't stand up; I have to grab hold of the sides of his desk to stop me from keeling over.

"I'm sorry, Dan, it was too easy, and you needed to shut up. Come on, let's go home." I sling my arm around his shoulders, and he shrugs it away. I laugh even more, give him a big kiss on the cheek and wrestle him into a headlock. Dan may be the older brother but I'm the bigger one and I've always been the better wrestler. We grapple about like this as we walk past Gorgeous.

"Oh, you two are nothing but a pair of silly boys. You stop that right now or I'll come over there and knock your bloody heads together."

We both roar with laughter and shout back at her, "Gorgeous, we love you," as the lift doors close, but not before we see her smirk at us.

Seven thirty on the dot. I knock on her door and hold my breath. I feel like a nervous kid going on his first date, not an experienced man. I take a deep breath and try to get it together. My palms are sweaty and my heart's beating so hard I swear you can see it through my shirt. She opens the door and it feels like the air is knocked right out of me. **She is fucking beautiful**. She has her dark hair down and it frames her beautiful face, which only has a hint of makeup on. Just mascara and lip gloss; I like that a lot. Her eyes are as clear as the Arabian Sea. She wrinkles her nose a little and her freckles dance. She's wearing a white summer dress with a pair of strappy heels. God damn it, even her feet are beautiful. The dress skims just above her knee and hugs her tiny waist. It's low-cut enough to show off her beautiful breasts. I picture myself kissing them, one after the other, tasting her nipples, circling my tongue around and nipping them until she's crying my name out. My dick is rock solid, and I shift on the spot to try to relieve some of the pressure but it's no good. Realising I've been standing here for a few seconds without speaking, I force my words out.

"Wow, you look amazing. Maybe too amazing." I shift awkwardly, continuing to try to relieve some of the pressure off my erect dick. I look at her and catch her sneaking a little peek at my erection and I can't help but smile when the look of shock and surprise sweeps over her face.

She looks back at me with hooded eyes and licks her pink lips which makes my dick lurch forward for her. I'm so affected by this bloody woman.

"Ye know, in all of the romcoms I've watched, never once has the guy told the girl she looked good by motioning to his erection. Ye could have just said 'wow'." She's smiling and the smile goes all the way up to her eyes. I like being the reason for that smile.

"Sorry Irish, but 'wow' just didn't cut it. I tried to be subtle, you were the one looking."

She blushes a deep red and looks down at the floor.

"Irish, look at me. Don't get embarrassed. You're beautiful and I've never been this affected by a woman before. I'm glad you know how bloody crazy the sight of you gets me. It's nothing to be embarrassed about. Believe me."

She looks up at me and I walk the few steps toward her so our bodies are touching, and kiss her like my life depends on it. This kiss isn't for her, this one is all for me. I kiss her possessively but gently. I want her to be mine but I have to go slow with her. Her taste is like an explosion on my tongue that I know I'll never get tired of. She moans when I nip her lips with my teeth. Spurred on by her reactions I let my hand dip lower and stroke her arse. I feel her legs buckle when I suck her tongue and I know I have to stop this now or we'll never make it to dinner. Our lips break apart, but our bodies remain as close as they can and I look down into her eyes. Pride swells in my chest when I see them filled with need and desire. I did that. I made her want me just as much as I want her. I try to show her with my eyes too. Try to convey just how much this means to me. We stand in her doorway for what seems like an eternity, just breathing heavily and staring into each other's eyes, when Darcie's next-door neighbour, who happens to be the same lady I spoke to at the lift, comes into the hall. She pokes her head into Darcie's front door.

"Is everything alright, Darcie? Oh, I see everything is very alright." She cackles to herself and walks over to the lift. Darcie groans and hides her head in my chest. I chuckle at her as I pull my body away from hers. I grab her hand, it's only been a second, but I miss the warmth of her body already and that terrifies and excites me at the same time.

As we walk into the restaurant, I can see eyes on Darcie. The men are watching her greedily and I have to fight every one of my caveman instincts to pull her into my arms and grunt 'MINE.' Instead, I place a gentle hand at her lower back and glower at the men so they know she's taken. Damn, I like the way that sounds. She's taken. By me. She's mine.

She's completely oblivious to it all. As we make our way through the restaurant, I move my hand from her back and instead take her hand and intertwine our fingers together. When we're seated at our table, she tries to let go but I hold on tightly, not only because I want everyone to know she's with me but also because I need to touch her. The feeling of needing her throws up a few uncertainties in my mind, but the urge is too strong to fight. The way our connected hands feel is like a magnetic pull on me. We sit opposite each other, and I notice the waiter watching her. The cheek of the man, but also fair play to him because she is stunning. I pull her hand up to my mouth and kiss her fingertips. She lets out a little shocked gasp when I gently nibble on one and then proceed to suck her finger. A blush creeps up onto her beautiful face and I look pointedly at the waiter who smirks at me. I smirk back. "Game on" flashes through my mind. If he wants a full-on pissing contest I'm certainly game. He steps closer to the table and smiles down at Darcie, who smiles politely back. Rage flares through me when I realise he's looking straight at her exposed cleavage.

"Would you like to look at the wine menu, madam?" His sleazy smile is making me want to rip his face off. I've never felt this possessive before. This is definitely not my usual way.

"Yes, we would." I raise my voice an inflection, making his smile falter a touch but not enough. This kid is brave and goes for what he wants, I'll give him that. He can afford to though; he doesn't have the darkness I have following him. He can date, laugh and love without the shadows engulfing him. Reminding him that he doesn't deserve happiness. I shouldn't be here, doing this, but just for a little while, I want to be free from the shadows and Darcie gives me light. She makes me happy. I need to warn this man off what's mine. There's that word again, mine. It spreads a warmth through me, makes me feel whole but scared shitless as well. If I'm this attached already...My thoughts are interrupted by him clearing his throat and I look adoringly at Darcie.

"Would you like some wine, Irish?"

She lowers her lashes and tells me, "No thank ye, Denny. I actually don't drink alcohol. Can I have a sparkling water, please?" She directs her order to the waiter who smiles down at her again and leans closer to her.

"Your accent is beautiful, much like you are. What part of Ireland are you from?"

Anger surges through me and before she can answer I'm standing up and grabbing the waiter's elbow, tighter than I need to.

"Listen, she's with me. Stop flirting with her and get our fucking drinks. Send another waiter to serve us too, yeah?" The waiter looks gobsmacked. I divert my gaze to Darcie and wince when I see the shock on her face. As the waiter stalks off, I know I'm going to have to make it up to her, explain to her why I reacted like that, but how can I without explaining everything?

Sitting back down, I blow out a breath.

"I'm sorry about that. I didn't like how he was looking at you. Flirting with you. It made me territorial." I give her my best smile but with her face like thunder and her blue eyes ice cold, my smile isn't working. Her arms are folded across her very ample chest and I know the night is over already.

"This was a mistake, Denny. I'd like to go home please."

"Darcie, please, I didn't mean to lose my rag. He was pissing me off, staring at your tits. He was challenging me. He thought he could flirt with you in front of me and I was just going to ignore it." It's not a lie but it's not the whole truth either.

Her face turns angrier, and it actually scares me a little bit. "So what if he was flirting with me. I'm not yours. I'm allowed to flirt, talk and do whatever I want. I'm not stupid, Denny. I know he was looking at my cleavage and tis no worse than what you've been doing for most of the night. I'm no one's to be claimed, Denny. I belong to me and me only. This was a mistake. Tank ye for the offer, Mr. Blanc, but I'm going to have to decline." She stands up and leaves the restaurant and I can feel everyone's eyes burning into me. Fuck! That didn't go as planned at all. I jump up from the table and chase after her.

"Darcie, wait please. Let me at least take you home. Please." She stops on the pavement, hand in the air as a black cab pulls up next to her. She puts her hand on the door and looks at me.

"Goodbye, Mr. Blanc." She hops into the cab and it leaves before I can stop it.

I drag my hand through my hair and shout, "FUCK!" loudly into the darkness of London. I fucking blew it. Ruined everything again. I stand and watch the taxi drive off into the night, rooted to the spot. I don't even move when it starts to rain. "Fuck." I whisper this time, defeat and darkness closing in on me.

Chapter 9

Darcie

"No Nat, he acted like he owned me. It was okay for him to look at me like a piece of meat but not for the waiter. And then, then he acted like I was too stupid to know he was staring at my boobs. I mean, come on. I've carried these tings around with me for years. I know how men stare at them." I take a breath and hear my best friend chuckling down the phone at me.

"Well, you do have a beautiful pair of tits, Darce. Sorry babe, I know you're royally pissed off, you saying tings instead of things is an indication of that, but don't you think you're overreacting a little bit?"

"OVERREACTING? Are ye for real, Natalie? I was better off as I was. No relying on men, no needing men, and no sex with men. I was grand as I was. I don't know why I agreed in the first place."

I hear Nat sigh and I know I'm in for a lecture. "You were not fine as you were, Darcie. You agreed to this arrangement with Mr-gorgeous-enough-to-get-you-wet-with-a-look because he did just that. And you've spent twenty-four years not giving a shit about any guy anywhere.

Guys do this crap, Darce. They act like cavemen and get all possessive with their partners. It's just who they are."

I roll my eyes at Nat, even though she can't see me. "But that's just it, Natalie. I'm not even his partner. It was meant to be like a business arrangement. He'd give me my magical firsts, no strings or emotions, that's it."

She chuckles again and I'm getting bloody sick of that sound.

"Darce, come on. You're overreacting. He likes you, you like him, and he didn't like someone looking at what was his, even if you're only his temporarily. How would you have felt if it was a female waitress doing that to him in front of you?" My mind flashes to how I felt earlier on in the car when he mentioned Gorgeous, before he told me who she was, and I frown at the valid point she's making.

"Okay fine, yeah I wouldn't have liked it, but I wouldn't have reacted like that."

"No, you wouldn't, because you're a woman and he's a stupid, arrogant man. Look Darce, I have to go in a bit, but please promise me you'll think about giving him another chance. Please? For me?"

I sigh, "I hate it when ye do that. Ye know I'd do anything for ye, but he won't even get in touch, so I don't have to worry about that." I ignore the heavy feeling that sits in my chest at the thought he hasn't texted me or phoned and listen to my best friend.

"Darce, you run, he'll chase, trust me. You've totally gotten under his skin. Just promise me, WHEN he contacts you, you'll hear him out and think about giving him a second chance, please?"

"Fine" I mumble at her and I can hear her eyeroll down the phone.

"Love you, you pain in my Darce."

"Love ye too, Nat." I throw my phone onto my bed and

strip off my dress and put my pjs on. I head into the bathroom and clean my teeth, wash my face and head back over to my bed, ready to snuggle in with a book. I pick my phone up to put it on my nightstand when I look down at the screen and see a message from Denny.

"Son of a..." hearing Nat's voice in my head, "for me" I roll my eyes and open his text.

Denny: I am so sorry. I was an idiot. You make me crazy x

I stare at my phone, and I know he's waiting to see that little bubble with the three dots appear, but I don't want to message straight back. I click out of the messaging app and place my phone on the nightstand. I grab Sheila and place her next to me, but her judgmental eyes are boring into me, so I turn her away to face the pillows. I grab my book to read, but by the time I've read the same line over and over again, my phone has beeped another three times. Heaving a sigh of frustration I pick it up, if only so I can focus on my book.

Denny: Please don't ignore me, Irish. I know I was a fool. You're not a possession and I shouldn't have acted like you were, but I won't apologise for liking the idea of you being mine, even if it was temporary x

Denny: Darcie, can I have a do over please? I'll take you out again but this time I'll do it right. Please. Just think about it. Help a foolish old man out x

Denny: You really shouldn't ignore your elders, you know. You should respect them and always make allowances for their idiocy. We're old, we can't help being fools x

My lips curl up and a giant smile takes pride of place on

my face, but I shake my head, "No, I'm not being won over by some silly texts". Great, and I'm talking to myself again. I log out of the messaging app and switch the Do Not Disturb mode on my phone, put it on the nightstand, and turn off the light. I know I won't sleep but at least I won't have to fight the urge to make allowances for the elderly's idiocy.

———

After an awful night's sleep, I wake up before my alarm to knocking on the door. Dishevelled and anxious, I step silently closer to the knocking. I peek out of the peephole and see a delivery man standing there holding a massive bunch of flowers.

"Can I help ye?" I ask through my closed door.

"Er yeah, I'm looking for Darcie, 3B."

Sighing I open the door slightly, "I'm Darcie of 3B." The man grins at me and hands me an iPad to sign my name to and then proceeds to hand me the rather large bouquet of flowers. As I watch his back retreat, I step into my flat and close the door. I look into the bouquet and find a card, but I already know who they're from. I open the card anyway:

To Darcie, I'm sorry. Please forgive me for being an idiot. I promise the next time a man looks at your boobs I won't get mad, well I will but I won't show it ;-) Call me or text me please? From the old (idiot) man x

He must've spent a fortune getting these to me this early. I have tears welling in my eyes as I read the note for the third time. I take a picture of the flowers, the note and screenshots of the messages and send them all to Nat, hoping she sees them before I have to head to work. I've just managed to put the flowers into some water when she messages back.

Nat: Well fuck me sideways and call me

cupid, did I or did I not tell you he would contact you? Fuck a duck Darce, the man means business. They must've cost him a small fortune. Please tell me you've responded to him now?

Darcie: No, I haven't because none of this changes the fact I shouldn't be doing anything with him.

Nat: Sometimes I wish murder wasn't illegal. I mean for God's sake Darce, you've got to be shitting me right now. The only man you've ever been attracted to, wants to have hot and heavy 'firsts' with you, with no strings attached and no emotions involved, thus helping you to not break your 'stupid and idiotic' no dating policy and you don't want too? Stick a fork in me cause I'm done. Do what you want but I think you're mad for passing this opportunity up. Go out with him again and just see what happens. Do it for me! PLEASE?

Darcie: I thought you were done? I don't know. I'll think about it, okay? I'll message to say thank you though because I do have manners.

Nat: Fuck a duck... Manners, jeez. Just go out with him, love you.

I decide not to message her back and I also decide not to message him to say thank ye either. Manners be damned. I take one last look at the flowers and head into my bathroom to get ready for work instead.

Chapter 10

Denny

Stubborn, bloody woman. She hasn't replied to my messages, she hasn't acknowledged my flowers and note, which was witty as fuck, so now she's going to get a house call. In person. See if she can ignore that.

"Can you run me past the house, Joseph? I forgot something." I avoid his gaze, as he's always been able to tell when I'm lying, and stare out of the window. Why can't I shake this woman from my brain? Why do I want her so much? Is it just because she's untouched? Nah, that's just an added bonus. Even before I knew she was a virgin I still craved her badly. She won't get out of my fucking head.

"Something troubling you, son?" Joseph's voice yanks me out of my thoughts and I look at his eyes through the rear view mirror.

"No, I just forgot something."

He chuckles at me, "Yeah you said that already. You sure you aren't stopping to see a certain someone?"

I roll my eyes at him and sigh. "Fine, yes, Joseph. I'm going to see Darcie, but please keep your mouth shut around Dan and tell Gorgeous that too. I know you can't keep any fucking thing from her."

"Scouts honour. What's happened then? What did you do?"

My head snaps back to catch his crinkled eyes which tells me, again, he's smiling at my reaction. "What makes you think something is up? Couldn't I just be going to see her?"

"You could be, but your face and mood tells me a different story. What did you do?"

I sigh and rake my hand through my hair. I can't get away with not telling him so I suck it up, ready for him to either take the absolute mick out of me or rip me a new one. "I took her out last night and acted like a caveman when another man looked at her. She's nervous, Joseph."

Again, he chuckles and then stays silent.

"You going to say something or what?"

"Are you asking for my advice here?"

Getting agitated I reply, "Yes, I fucking am. So, talk."

He sighs, "Denny, she isn't your usual type, you can't play the usual games. Be yourself, not the self-assured, cocky bastard we all know and love. Treat her like I treat Gloria and you'll be fine, my boy."

I slink back into my seat and mumble thanks and watch the world go by my window. Is he right? Being myself is dangerous, it leaves me vulnerable. But I think that might be what I need to do to get Darcie back in my favour.

I call out to Darcie as I enter the house but no one answers. I search in the kitchen and living room but there's no sign of Darcie and the girls. I head up to the playroom with the sounds of squeals and laughter peeling from it, letting me know where they are. I open the door slightly. Sitting around a little table is Darcie, Isabelle and Isla, all wearing feather boas and tiaras. Isabelle is wearing long white gloves and pearls, on the table is a little teapot and teacups. I watch enthralled as Darcie raises her teacup, with her pinkie finger stretched out and takes a sip of the imaginary tea as Isabelle beams in delight.

With a smile on my face, I say quietly, "Knock, knock, ladies, I'm sorry to interrupt..."

Isabelle squeals, and Isla jumps up and rushes over to me so I pick her up and cradle her to my chest.

"Uncle Denny, come, join us." Isabelle tells me as she drags another little chair over to the table and places it right next to Darcie. She grabs my hand and pulls me over to sit down. Isla jumps off my lap and scurries over to the toy box. Excited, Isabelle joins her, both talking quietly and hurriedly.

"Darcie, I wanted to apologise in person for my behaviour last night. It was unacceptable. Please give me another chance." She looks down at her teacup and sighs, but before she can respond the girls are back and giggling, thrusting a feather boa and a plastic tiara in my face.

"Uncle Denny, you're not dressed right!" Isabelle tells me bossily.

I catch Darcie's smirk. She doesn't think I'll wear these things for my girls. She doesn't know me at all.

"Anything for you, Princess. Can I have some pearls too, please?" I take the feather boa and tiara and put them on as Isla giggles at me.

"You so silly, Uncle Denny. We have pearls for you **and** Darcie. Dere you are." Isla hands me the necklaces together.

I reach up and place mine around my neck. "May I?" I ask Darcie, who is openly staring at me. I hold out the necklace to place it around her neck. She nods her head slightly and I lean next to her. Thankful that she's allowing me to do this. She gathers her hair off her neck and the scent of it catches me off guard. I inhale deeply and am instantly turned on.

I lean next to her ear and whisper, "You look so beautiful sitting there, playing with two of the most important people in my world. I'm sorry I blew my chance with you. It's something I'll regret forever because I think we would've been magical together, Irish."

A sharp inhale of breath comes from her beautiful mouth. I rest my head against hers for just a second and then sit back in my chair. For the next five minutes, we sip pretend tea and I make Isabelle and Isla laugh at my conversations with their dolls.

"Right, you three beautiful ladies, I have to go back to work. I only snuck home because I missed you all." I hug the girls goodbye, take off the pearls and feather boa, and head for the stairs. I stand at the street door and sigh as I reach out to open it. I stop when I hear her call my name softly. I look up and meet her gaze with mine. Our eyes are locked together as she walks down the stairs towards me.

Once she's in front of me, she tells me, "One more chance, Denny. Tonight at seven p.m., pick me up at home."

I nod my head at her and give her a full megawatt smile, but instead of saying anything I lean down and take her hand in mine. I bring it to my lips and kiss the back of her hand. I turn to leave and she calls me back again. This time, full of swagger I reply, "Yes, Irish?"

Darcie steps towards me and I'm confident she's going to kiss me. I lick my lips. She leans in. I close my eyes and I'm slightly startled when I feel something being taken from my head. I open my eyes and see her smirking in front of me. Her eyes are dancing with amusement as she lifts the plastic tiara for me to see. She turns away and walks back up the stairs, laughing the whole way.

Well that certainly took my swagger down a notch or two, which is probably for the best seeing as I've another chance to do things right this time.

It's six fifty-five and I'm standing outside of Darcie's flat trying to work up the nerve to knock, but kind of wanting to wait until bang on seven o'clock. I don't want to do anything to rock the boat with her tonight. I take a deep breath and rap my knuckles three times on the wood. She opens the door way too quickly.

"I see ye plucked up the courage to knock then, Denny?" She's smirking at me again and I want to shove her up against the wall and kiss her so thoroughly she forgets all about her smugness. Instead, I swallow and smile sheepishly at her.

"I was trying to wait for seven o'clock on the dot. I want tonight to be perfect for you, Darcie."

She sighs, "There's no such thing as perfect, Denny. Let's just forget last night happened and start again. Deal?" She holds out her hand to me.

I smile back at her. "Deal, Irish. You look beautiful tonight." She's wearing a similar dress to the one she had on yesterday, except this one has little flowers on it. I let go of her hand and let her go back inside to grab her purse and we head out of her building together. I take a deep breath and blow it out hoping I don't do anything stupid like I did yesterday.

Sitting across from each other in a different restaurant, I offer my hand to her and to my surprise she takes it. I entwine our fingers together and she blushes which makes me smile at her.

"I like it when you blush, Irish." She rolls her eyes at me and gives me a small smile. A waitress, I could fucking scream with how happy I am that we have a woman serving us, comes over to take our drinks order and this time I know to order her a sparkling water and order myself a beer.

"Yes sir, would you and your wife like a moment more before you order your food?" Her question should have me correcting her quickly and letting her know I'm not married, but I don't. Instead, I find myself simply nodding and telling her that would be perfect. I notice Darcie's raised eyebrows at me as she leaves, but instead of saying anything I just smile at her again. I should be running for the hills with the way my brain is thinking, claiming her as mine and not worrying about people thinking we're married. I have to keep myself from thrusting my chest out and strutting around like a proud peacock because everyone thinks she's mine. That I'm good enough to have her as mine. And there's that word again. The word that should be raising alarm bells in my head, but isn't, because I like the sound of it too much.

"So, old man, seeing as I actually know very little about ye, why don't ye tell me about yourself?"

This breaks me out of my own head space. I raise my glass of water to my lips, take a sip and reply. "What do you want to know, Irish?" I place the glass back down and lean onto the table, looking her straight in the eyes whilst still holding her hand.

"Hmmmm, well ye obviously like to keep your cards close to your chest with your 'let's answer a question with a question' tactic, so let's start with what ye do for a living?"

I laugh. She's observant and I like her sassing me. When

she does, she gets this look of triumph in her eyes, and that is one of my favourites to see in them.

"I'm an architect. I design the buildings and Dan deals with the business side of things. We started out as a small company working out of Becs's studio and have worked our way up to be one of the most successful firms in London." I can't help the pride brimming over in my voice. My business is the greatest achievement in my life, and I could talk about it forever. I watch her as my words come out. I want to see her reaction. I watch to see if the pound signs show in her eyes like they have in so many other dates I've had. I never take my eyes off her and her face goes from curious to impressed. No pound signs, just respect, and that makes me even prouder of myself for once.

"Wow, that's something to be really proud of. I'd assumed ye'd come from money and had just built off that. I mean, ye have a driver, and your house is very impressive. I would never have guessed ye'd had to graft for your success now." I squeeze her hand a little. She doesn't realise how far from the truth her assumption is.

"The house is actually Becs's. Her aunt died when Becs was just finishing uni and left it to her as she was her only niece. Her and Dan moved straight in and gave me no choice about living with them. I'm glad they did. Joseph's only my driver because he wouldn't work in the offices and wanted to be close to all of us and Gorgeous. They won't retire, no matter how much I tell them to." I smile thinking about my family and she squeezes my hand gently this time.

"Well it's still kudos to ye, old man." Her eyes twinkle and she grins at me.

"You carry on with that sass and you'll be in so much trouble later." The smile on her face disappears and hunger returns, she bites her lower lip, and my dick is straining under the table to get to her.

"Jeez, Irish, you keep looking at me like that and my dick's going to explode. And I don't want the first time you make me come to be in my trousers." I run my hand through my hair and guilt washes over me as she looks like a rabbit caught in headlights.

"Darcie, I'm sorry. I'm sorry. I won't talk like that again. I just wanted to let you know you're driving me wild." She lowers her head and before I think, I blurt out, "Fuck. Shit sorry. I wasn't swearing at you. Jeez. I'm screwing this up again, aren't I?" I rake my hand through my hair again and put my head in both hands.

"Hey. Hand." I look up and she's motioning to her upright hand that, until a moment ago, was being caressed by my own. I put my hand back where it was.

"That's better. I liked what ye said, Denny. Yes, it scared me a little. But more than that, it turned me on. Just like this turns me on, too." Her face is the colour of crimson and she's tracing the tattoo that's on my hand with her fingers.

Although I can see she's uncomfortable talking like this, I need to hear what she wants to say. I smile at her to give her the encouragement to carry on, and she does.

"Ye drive me wild too. And if ye could see the state of my underwear ye'd understand that. I don't mind swearing, if it's not *at* me. I can't help looking at ye like that because, well, it's the way I look. If I didn't want to be here, Denny Blanc, I wouldn't be. I've turned men down before because I didn't want them. You're different. I want ye."

I didn't think her face could get any redder than it was, but as she finishes, she's glowing crimson and takes a big gulp of water. My mouth gapes open at her but a second later a ridiculous grin tips the corners of my lips up. I stand up, walk over to her and kiss her so passionately I know everyone is watching us. And I don't care. I break our kiss and gaze into the windows of her soul.

"Fucking beautiful." I give her a quick peck and go back to my seat.

———

"I don't think I could eat another thing. I'm stuffed."

I look at Darcie with admiration, "Girl, you can eat. How can someone so tiny eat that much food?" She shifts in her seat, squirming under my gaze.

"I must have hollow legs or something, I've always been a big eater. I wish I wasn't. Well my arse wishes I wasn't." She rolls her eyes and I shoot her down before she carries on.

"Now Irish, I don't want to fall out with you on our first date, but if you're going to talk shit about the most perfect arse I've ever seen, then we will have trouble." I give her a serious look and she holds her hands up in a 'I surrender' gesture.

"Beauty is in the eye of the beholder and all that jazz," she rolls her eyes at me as I chuckle.

"You better believe it, beautiful, and that arse is pure class. Ha I didn't mean to rhyme, I promise." She laughs out loud and it's becoming one of my favourite sounds. I wonder what other sounds will come out of her mouth that'll be making it into my top set?

I get the check and we stroll hand-in-hand out of the restaurant. As we stand on the pavement, she reaches up and puts her hands around my neck and kisses me, ever so gently.

"Thank ye for the best first date."

I look down at her and smile back.

"The first of many firsts I'll be making with you, Irish.

And, besides, the date isn't over yet. Do you want to take a walk? London at night is my favourite." She nods eagerly and I wrap my arm around her shoulders and tug her into me. She fits next to me like the perfect piece of puzzle I didn't know was missing, and I wonder how I'm going to walk away from her when her firsts have been ticked off.

Chapter 11

Denny

We stroll along the river and chat about endless things; favourite music, tv shows, books, tattoos, the normal stuff people talk about on dates. I haven't done this before though. Normally I take a girl to dinner, flirt, then go back to hers to fuck. I'm not interested in their stories or likes and dislikes, but with Darcie it's different. I'm like a sponge absorbing every little piece of information about her. I'm drawn to her. And it terrifies me. Will I be able to walk away so easily like I have with everyone else? I shake my head a little to clear those thoughts as I can't go there tonight. As sex is taken out of the equation, it frees me up to find out about her. And I think even if sex were on the table tonight, I'd still be as interested in her as I am now. We end up outside the London Eye and her surprise is evident when I move past the long queue and head straight to the front, much to the disgruntled noises of disgust from the people waiting in the line. I give the guy at the front my special boarding ticket and he motions for us to get onto one of the pods. I had to pull all the stops out after the disaster of last night. The doors close and before we know it, we're alone hovering over the Thames.

"How did ye manage that? Not only did we not have to line up, but we have this all to ourselves?" Darcie's astonished face turns to look at me.

"A magician never reveals his tricks, Irish. Stick with me baby and I'll show you the time of your life." It was supposed to come out smooth and sexy, but it didn't. "Jeez I sound like a knob." I put my hands over my face as we both laugh. In my head, it sounded a lot better than 'I designed a building for someone who had particularly good contacts and was able to swing it for me.'

"I wanted to do something special after the wreck I made of last night."

She shakes her head and puts her hand over my mouth and I kiss her palm. I'm rewarded with a smile back from her.

When we're halfway up, I turn to her and say, "You haven't told me anything about yourself before you came here. I know you came from a tiny village and your mother passed away but nothing else. Why?" I watch her closely. I know there's something she's carrying with her, but I can't pinpoint what it is. Most girls who come over to London looking for work go back and visit relatives or friends, but she said she hasn't been back at all. When she mentioned her mother and the beach, she looked so happy. But then the happiness turned to fear, which struck a chord with me. I don't want her to fear anything. I want to protect her from everything that scares her. She shifts from one foot to the other and looks around as if she's looking for an escape route, which is one of the reasons I waited until we were on here to spring my question.

"Erm, well, I don't know what else there is to tell really." Her voice is a higher pitch than normal, and she sounds rattled.

"How did your mum die?" I push her a little trying to

figure her out. Her eyes cloud with pain and it takes everything for me not to go over and kiss the pain away from her face. But I want to know everything about this woman. This is a first for me and I can't let it go.

"She was sick for a while, cancer. We found out it was terminal, and she went downhill very fast and, in the end, they said she didn't even know who was who and what was what." She has her eyes closed and hugs her body tightly. The pain evident in everything she says and does.

I lean a little closer to her. "'They said'. You weren't there?" I question gently.

She shakes her head, "No I wasn't. I'd already left. She made me. When she found out she was dying she made me. She made me escape whilst I could. She wouldn't let me stay."

Silent tears are streaming down her face. In a flash, I have her in my arms whilst she sobs. I kiss the top of her head and I ask her gently, "Escape from who, Darcie? Why did you have to leave her?" I know I have no right in pushing her, and I know she's already so upset, but there's a burning desire deep in my soul to know everything about this woman. And protect her.

She opens her eyes and looks up at me, the vulnerability achingly exposed in her beautiful sad eyes.

"From my daddy. With her gone he'd never have let me leave him alone, and she was terrified I'd be stuck with him forever without her to protect me. He wasn't - he isn't - a nice person." She buries her face in my chest.

I push the building anger and hatred down and shush her. I tilt her head up to face me. "I'm sorry, Darcie. I shouldn't have asked. I'm sorry. I know how painful it is. I'm so sorry." I kiss her everywhere. Her mouth, her nose, her eyelids, all over her cheeks, trying desperately to erase the tears and replace them with my kiss.

"No. I feel better. I've finally said it out loud to someone other than Sheila. Nat knows a little bit but not everything."

I look at her confused. I know who Nat is, as Darcie spoke about her over dinner, but she didn't mention a Sheila.

"Sheila?" I ask, shaking my head.

"Oh, don't laugh at me, okay. I don't like it, remember? Sheila's my teddy bear. I've had her since I was a wee thing, and I talk to her all the time. Does that make me crazy?" She wrinkles her nose and puts her head down into my chest again.

I chuckle and raise her head to me and mutter "Fucking brilliant, Irish," before I brush my lips over hers. I kiss her mouth expertly for a few seconds and then trace a trail of kisses all over her face, wiping away any sign of tears I come across. I turn my attention back to her mouth and slide my hands on to her perfect arse, pulling her closer to me as I deepen our kiss. As her mouth opens to groan a little, I slide my tongue inside and trace a line along her tongue. I deliberately keep the kiss slow and lingering. I can feel my dick straining against my trousers as it pushes up against her. I move one of my hands from her arse up to her breast and feel her already pebbled nipple get harder under my caress as I roll my thumb over it. She moans loudly. It's enough to break me from the trance I'm in and let our lips come apart from each other, but I rest my forehead on hers so every part of our bodies are still touching. We breathe deeply for a few seconds before either of us can speak.

"Is it always like this, Denny?" She whispers to me.

I feel a tug at my heart and reply honestly. "No, it isn't." A frown furrows on my brow and I break our bodies apart and run my hand through my hair. I step away from her and take a swig of the champagne that's been left out for us. I look around and realise we're on our descent back down.

"We nearly missed out on the view." She turns around, but before she does I can see the confusion on her face. I suddenly feel extremely hot and claustrophobic. Who thought being trapped on this thing was a good idea? I'm freaking the fuck out and I need to get my wits about me. There's something about this woman that does strange things to me and if I'm not careful my rules will be out of the window. Would that be such a bad idea? Being happy would make a nice change. I banish the thought from my head before it even has a chance to settle.

She turns around to me with a smile and asks, "Everything okay?"

I look at her and see concern in her gaze, but a smile of hope plastered on her face. I smile back and tell her, "Everything's perfect, Irish. I had to take a minute there or I wouldn't have been able to control myself, and I certainly don't want your first time to be on the London Eye for everyone to see. I want that pleasure all for myself." She flushes red again and smiles at me as I take her hand. We slip back into pleasant conversation as before. It's so easy talking with her. Everything is easier with her.

At the end of the evening I walk her back to her place. I don't hesitate in going inside her tiny flat and sitting on her bed. She stands over me with a glint in her eye.

"Ye said no sex tonight, Mr. Blanc, have you changed your mind?" I smirk up at her.

"No, I haven't actually. I said no sex, but I didn't say no orgasms, did I?" I look her straight in the eye and she stares back at me. I silently curse myself for making that stupid declaration earlier at dinner. "Do you want me to make you come, Darcie?" I pull her down, so she's sitting next to me. She looks unsure so I reassure her.

"You don't have to do anything you don't want to, Darcie. I won't hold it against you. We can finish the night here and look forward to our next date. It's all your choice."

She turns to look at me and then looks at her hands in her lap. "I want to."

I reach over and cup her face. I stroke my hand over her cheek, and she leans into my hand. I angle closer to her and kiss her. Deep and slow. I move my hand from her cheek, down past her shoulder and on to her chest. I find her nipple through her dress and trace my finger around it in small circular motions. She groans against my mouth; she's so responsive and I love it. Kissing, sucking and nibbling at her tongue and lips. I release her mouth and slowly trail soft kisses along her jawline, down her neck, until my mouth has replaced my hand working her nipple. She gasps out loud as I take it between my lips and suck hard enough to make her gasp again. I raise my head and maintain eye contact with her as I move over to her other breast and repeat my movements there. She closes her eyes, rolls her head back and groans again.

"Do you like that, Irish?" I ask her.

She murmurs her pleasure to me. I stop what I'm doing, and her eyes shoot open and look at me in shock.

I chuckle and say, "We need to lose some of these clothes if we want you to feel really good."

Her perfect mouth, swollen with our kisses, forms an O as she understands what I'm saying. I expect her to be shy, but she stands up before me, slips her dress off and stands in front of me in just her heels, and her matching lace white knickers and bra.

I growl at her, "You are perfect, Darcie. Abso-fuckinglutely perfect." She bends to take her shoes off, but I stop her. "Leave them on and I'll handle the rest from here." I remove my shirt and stand as proud as anything when she runs her eyes hungrily over my body. I notice her eyes track the shadows of my tattoo, portraits of the kids. Becs and Dan's names. The initials, 'G and a J' intertwined together. The numbers eleven and thirteen and a hand of cards - a royal flush of hearts, are interwoven on my arm. They go from my hand all the way up onto my chest. I watch as she licks her bottom lip in appreciation. I kiss her hard this time, passionately and fiercely. I walk her back to the edge of the bed, and we fall onto it, with our lips still pressed together. I slip my hand around her back and unhook her bra. A growl escapes from my throat as I look down at her.

"You seriously are the most perfect woman I've ever seen in my life." She flushes red and before she can say anything, I wrap my mouth around her beautiful little pink nipple and skim my teeth over it. I'm rewarded with a moan. I swirl my tongue around it and she wriggles and groans.

"Tell me if you like it, Irish. This is all about you and what you need, so you have to tell me if I'm doing something you don't like." I circle my thumb over her nipple and suck on the other one and she cries out.

"Oh God Denny, tis all good. Tis so good."

I smile as I let go of her nipple with a pop and move my kisses down her stomach. I hitch my thumbs into either side of her knickers and pull them down. I stare at her completely naked except for her heels and I'm frozen. I've never seen anyone look so perfect and for a moment I'm lost.

"Denny?"

Her pleading voice snaps me out of it and I tell her, "You need to tell me what I can call... you. I *really* don't want to offend you right now as I know you don't like me swearing." She looks up at me with hooded eyes.

"What do you normally call it?"

"I've never seen anything like this before, ever. Yours is different. It's wonderful, perfection, exceptional...I would go on, Irish, but I've got other pressing things I need to get back to." I grin down at her and she shrugs at me. "The only word for it then. Darcie, I'm going to taste your perfection now, is that okay?" She bites down on her lip and nods. I grin down at her and move lower.

My head is screaming at me 'what are you doing? We don't do this! It's too intimate an act. We never do this. Stop! Think about the rules!' but the need to taste her is all consuming. I can feel the heat off her and it's almost too much for me. As soon as I taste her, I know I'm going to want to do this over and over again. She cries out as my tongue touches her. She whimpers as I lap at her. She cries out again as I devour her. She starts to shake as I pull her clit in between my teeth and I feel her hands grab the sheets underneath her as her climax builds.

"Denny," she chokes out and I know she's close now; I replace my mouth with my hands. I want to watch her come apart for the first time and I can't do that with my head between her legs. I lean over her and rub my finger over her clit. She's writhing beneath me and I insert my finger into her. Her eyes shoot open, her gaze locking with mine. I'm as hard as I can be and she hasn't touched me. If I feel like this watching her and making her come, how am I going to feel when my dick is buried inside of her? I have to stop my thoughts, or I'm going to make a mess in my boxers. One final move of my hand, and she comes apart in front of me, with our eyes locked on each other and her screaming my name. I know my life will never be the same again after watching that.

Chapter 12

Darcie

Jesus, Mary and Joseph! What in all that is holy was that? I can't breathe properly; I feel like I'm having an out of body experience. I'm vaguely aware of Denny saying my name, but all I can do is try to breathe. Taking oxygen into my body, greedily filling my lungs with it. I try to open my eyes but they're too heavy. My breath is ragged, and I focus on breathing in and out. Once I have it under control, my senses come back to me.

"Darcie, are you with me? Darcie?"

I put my hand up to his face and lazily stroke his stubbly cheek, almost like my limbs are too heavy to move fluidly. "Ye are amazing. Tank ye. My God, what happened there?"

He chuckles and lays on his side next to me, slowly tracing circles on my stomach with his finger.

"I like it when you drop the h in words, Irish. Just to be clear, was that 'My God what happened there' as in 'my God' is my new nickname? Because I've got to say I prefer that one to old fucking man, let me tell you."

Regaining some of my composure, I whip my head around so I can see him, and I'm met with a very smug and amused look in his beautiful blue eyes. "No, there was clearly a pause in between me saying 'my God,' and the question. Your nickname is still under consideration though."

He pouts at me and I shake my head and roll my eyes at him.

"I still don't know what happened though. One minute I was here and the next..." I trail off trying to find the right words when Denny speaks.

"I think you blanked out a little bit. Which is ironic considering my last name and all." The smug and satisfied look on his face is all it takes for my 'perfection', as he called it, to twitch. I bite my lip as I feel my arousal build again and a shudder goes through me. This man has completely captured me. I've gone from not wanting anyone, to wanting this man to make me come again and again. I smile at him shyly.

"I think ye mean blacked out." I look down to avoid his gaze and ask, "Will that happen every time?"

He chuckles and lifts my head with his hand under my chin. "Maybe. Sometimes you'll come quickly and hard, sometimes soft and slow but I'll guarantee you one thing, beautiful, you will come every time when you're with me. That's a promise. Even if it's just so I can watch you again because to see that pleasure on your beautiful face was heaven for me."

He's staring intently at me, eyes meeting mine and holding them there. I feel my cheeks flush red, and I can't help but feel stupid for being embarrassed after what we've just experienced together. But I'm also hot and ready for him, as his words promise endless orgasms and my body is screaming out for them. I fight the urge to look away for as long as I can and then break our gaze with a smile.

I look down at his amazing body. Taking in every inch

of him, my gaze is held on his chiselled chest. He has the body of a Greek God so a new nickname could be on the horizon for him; he certainly doesn't look like an old man. He looks like an Adonis, but I won't be telling him just yet. I already knew his face was beautiful, but his body is extraordinary. Especially the V that forms at the bottom of his taut stomach and goes lower into the waistband of his trousers. I bite my lip and realise I want to see him standing naked in front of me. I want to feel him, taste him and have him inside of me.

Instinctively my hand reaches up and strokes his shoulder. I lower it down and let it dance all over his chest. My hand goes lower and lower, hesitantly, as I don't know if any of this is what I should be doing, but I know tis what I want. Lower and lower it goes until my fingers glide along the top of his waistband where I gently tug at it. He raises his eyebrows suggestively and I bite my lip and nod. He stands up from the bed and, in one swift movement, removes his trousers and boxers and is standing in front of me naked and very God-like.

My breath catches in my throat and my eyes are instinctively drawn to his rock-hard shaft. I'm amazed by how beautiful it is. Never in my wildest dreams would I have thought I'd look at a penis and think it beautiful, but Denny's is a work of art. I look away nervously; tis huge! There's no way that's going to fit inside me, but I find my eyes right back there again.

"Irish, you're killing me with your eyes."

Denny's strained voice interrupts my thoughts and before I know what's happening, we're kissing again. Our chests, naked and rubbing against each other, cause me to moan with delight. I feel his erection touch me in my most sensitive area. I lift my hips up so I can press against him, but he moves away instead of into me.

"Irish, I said no sex tonight and believe me, it's taking all of my strength to say and do this, but no sex. Not tonight."

Feeling embarrassed and frustrated I pout at him, and he infuriatingly smiles at me.

He brings his mouth to my ear and whispers, "Soon enough."

He dips his head and kisses me quickly and hard on the lips before turning his attention down to my hardened nipples. I groan in pleasure as he circles his tongue around and around my nipple and then lifts his head and repeats with the other. I snake my hand into his hair and pull gently to tell him I want him to kiss me. He responds by placing his mouth on mine with a smile on his sexy lips. This man could bring me to my knees with a kiss and I'm loving every second of this. I can't believe I've waited this long to feel this alive. I wonder if it would be like this with everyone and jump when he responds.

He growls, "Mine. Just me and just mine," against my mouth as he bites down on my lower lip.

I realise I must have voiced my question out loud. I open my eyes and blue ice stares back at me. There's a flicker of something there but in a flash, tis gone. As he lowers his head to trail kisses all over my body, I sit up.

"Denny, are ye okay?" He doesn't falter and carries on kissing and biting all over me, frantically. I grab his head and kiss him hard on the mouth, letting my hands trail down his body so I can reach him. My hand clasps around his erection and I hesitate as I realise, I have no idea what I'm doing. I just know I want to give him pleasure too. He must sense my hesitancy as he moves his hand over mine and slowly moves our hands up and down together. Once I have my rhythm he lets go and continues his relentless kissing of my mouth, face and neck. He moans and thrust his hips into the rhythm of my hand. My confidence rising,

I break away from our kiss and slowly lower my head down.

"Irish, you don't have to..."

My tongue is licking the tip of him before he can finish his sentence and instead, he groans. I slowly put him in my mouth and suck on him hard. I haven't done this before so I'm going on instinct, and his sharp intake of breath tells me he's enjoying what I'm doing. I carry on, moving my hand up and down whilst licking and sucking on him, and he reaches down and thrusts his finger into my wet sex. I gasp around his erection and he pulls his finger out and thrusts two fingers in, making me groan around him.

"Darcie. You're so perfect. So beautiful. Absolutely amazing."

I moan as I feel my climax build inside of me. I completely forget what I'm doing as my imminent orgasm takes hold. I move my mouth away from him but continue to move my hand up and down, faster and faster without a conscious thought, and I can feel him building too. I'm seeing stars behind my closed eyelids, and when he flicks his fingers one last time inside me and his thumb rubs my clit, I explode into a million pieces shouting his name as I come. He takes over from my hand and what seems like seconds later I feel something hot and wet on my breasts and stomach.

He shouts "Darcie!" as his orgasm spills onto me.

We both fall back onto the bed, our breathing ragged and shallow, and stare at the ceiling. Denny moves first, walking into the bathroom and coming back with a wet cloth. He wipes the cloth over my stomach and breasts and when I look down at him our gazes meet and he looks sheepish.

"Darcie, I'm sorry, I had no intention of doing that on

you... tonight." He gives me a cheeky wink and I laugh at him.

"Well, it was kind of my fault. Ye told me I didn't have too but I wanted to."

He's staring at me intently. "Why?"

His question catches me off guard and I stutter back, "W-w-ell ye made me feel amazing and I wanted to do the same for ye." Looking down, embarrassed I continue, "I know I'm probably not as good as the other girls you've been with but..."

He silences me with his lips and then tells me. "Darcie, you're nothing like the other girls I've been with."

Feeling dejected I turn my head away, but he grabs my chin and gently brings me back to face him.

"And that's a good thing. Trust me on that. Thank you for thinking of me."

He genuinely looks touched and it makes me sad to see the vulnerability on his face. *Thank you for thinking of me.* Tis such a loaded sentence with so many interpretations. Do people not think about him? How's that possible when all I can do is think about him? He looked so vulnerable when he said that, so far away from the confident and cocky man I've seen before. I don't have a chance to carry on with my thoughts, as judging from the cheeky glint in Denny's eye, confident and cocky Denny is back.

"Well, I must say, you gave as good as you got, seeing as this was your first time. I thoroughly enjoyed being in your mouth. You can do that again whenever you want, Irish."

I feel my cheeks go red and cover my face with my hands.

"Oh God, stop it." He laughs and finishes cleaning me up. Throwing the cloth on the floor, he lays back down, laces our fingers together and kisses the back of my hand.

"So, was that good for you?" He's grinning from ear to ear and I swat his shoulder with my other hand.

"I may be a virgin but even I know that's a crappy, cheesy line. And I think ye know it was more than good, old man."

He grimaces in a mock hurt kind of way.

"What happened to 'my God'? That one was good. Much better than 'old man'. Come on, Irish, I just gave you two orgasms, and you passed out from one of them. It was that good and you're still going to call me 'old man'?"

I can't stop myself from laughing at his pretend shock mixed in with his arrogant pride. Tis more than I can take. "Okay, how about I call ye 'Denny' and 'old man' when ye annoy me?" I counter trying to take away the fake pained expression on his face.

"Deal, I suppose. But I have a feeling you're going to call me 'old man' more than 'Denny'."

I grin up at him whilst resting my head on his shoulder.

He kisses the top of my head and says, "Listen, I'm sorry I said no to having sex, but I wanted to show you when I promise something to you, I mean it. I'm going to try my hardest to never hurt you, Darcie. I want you to know that."

He looks down at our joined hands but not before I catch the conflicted looks in his beautiful eyes. I want him to open up to me and explain why he's conflicted. I want to know why he's so surprised by me thinking of him earlier, but I know he likes to keep his cards close to his chest. I also know what it's like to not want to talk about old wounds. I won't push him. Not yet anyway.

I lean over and give him a quick kiss on the cheek.

"Thank ye for saying no. Even though at the time I wasn't happy, I am now. I respect ye for honouring your promise and I'll try not to hurt ye, too, Denny."

He smiles at me and says, "I don't think you have it in you to hurt anyone, Irish."

I put my head back on his shoulder and sigh. I can feel my eyelids slowly closing and no matter how hard I try to keep them open I can't. Just as they close, I hear a whisper.

"Mine. Mine, always."

A light kiss brushes my head and I can't find anything in me that wants to disagree with that.

Chapter 13

Darcie

"And then when I woke up he was gone. There was a text on my phone that said, 'I'm sorry, Irish. I had an early morning meeting, but I'll phone you later. I fully expect to be called old man because of this but I promise I'll get you to call me 'my God' again,' with a winky face. Yes, Nat he actually put a winky face emoji."

I woke up at ridiculous o'clock again and after finding Denny gone, I couldn't go back to sleep. I decided to go for the same walk I'd done the day before. I called Nat as I knew she'd be chomping at the bit to hear all about last night, and I wasn't wrong.

She answered the call in two rings and the first thing she said was, "Please tell me you came and please tell me he was fucking brilliant in bed."

After confirming the first and explaining I still didn't know about the second, she set about decoding the whole evening.

"Oh, come on, Darcie, now you must know why he did what he did on the first date? He was making it clear to the waiter and every other Tom, Dick and fucking Harry you were his. Kind of like a dog marking his territory when they pee up everything."

I snort in disgust at her, "Natalie Wilson. That is disgusting. I'm not some sort of possession he owns." She cuts me off before I can finish scolding her.

"Cut the bullshit, Princess, did you like it?"

I make a noise in the back of my throat not wanting to admit to her that I did, but not knowing how to lie either.

"I'll take that awkward little noise you just made as a yes. What the fuck was that about by the way? Anyway, you liked it and he got to show off his manhood. What's the big deal? I'd give my right arm to have some fit as fuck fella suck my bloody fingers in a restaurant, let me tell you." I laugh at her and shake my head at the same time. She's certainly given me food for thought. I continue to fill her in on every detail and she waits for me to finish before she's speaking again.

"Fuck me, Darcie, he sounds like he has it bad. Are you sure he said no commitment and no feelings, 'cause his actions are saying something else? Not that it's a bad thing. Having a guy focussed on giving you mind blowing orgasms and committing only to you is never a bad thing."

Hope flutters in my heart at the idea of Denny wanting me forever but I force myself to stop it soaring because it's not what I want. I think.

"Nat, stop being ridiculous. He said himself no feelings, no commitment. Tis grand. Once he's finished giving me my firsts, he'll probably run for the hills." The pain that thought evokes in my heart is too much, so I stuff it down and remind myself **I** don't want a relationship. This is purely to get the firsts out of the way and scratch this itch I have for Denny Blanc. That's it.

Changing the subject, I casually question my best friend.

"Anyway, why are ye so, how should I put it, frustrated? Ye haven't found any hot Parisian men to pursue?"

She sighs sadly. "French guys are hot, but I just haven't fancied any of them enough. I don't know, maybe I'm in a slump. I'm coming home in a few weeks. I'll get my fix of a nice cockney lad. Maybe one will make me scream 'oh my God' at him, too."

My face flushes red and I shout, "NATALIE WILSON!!!"

She's laughing on the other end of the phone and I can't help but join her. I'm so excited for her to come home. As we chat for a wee bit, something I said earlier is niggling at me. I haven't had a conversation with Denny on how this is going to go after he's given me my firsts. I don't know if it's going to be a wham, bam, thank-you-ma'am one of a kind thing, or if he'll want to do a casual sex kind of thing. The first option has my stomach tying itself in knots at the thought of not being able to see him. And that terrifies me. How will I cope at work every day? Will he ignore me? Parade other women in front of me?

To rid myself of the worrying questions careening through my mind, I think of Nat and how she's always told me that comparing any relationship I might have with that of my parents is unfair and unrealistic. She's always been quick to point out Mammy should've got up and left the abusive, alcoholic dick that was my daddy - her words not mine - and saved me from living through that hell. She thinks my mammy was weak for not running away with me. I wouldn't have witnessed the awful things he did to her if she had. It's easy for Nat to think like that though. Her mam and dad are still together and love each other. Her mam is one of the strongest women I've ever seen, and they don't live in a tiny village where marriage is cherished above everything else. Catholic people take vows of marriage very seriously. The thing is my mammy tried to leave him so many times when I was a wee girl. Once, we even managed it, getting all the way to Dublin before he tracked us down, told her a sob story and convinced her to go back with him. As soon as we got in the house, he beat her so badly we had to pretend she had the flu for a week and a half whenever someone visited the house so they couldn't see she was black and blue. Natalie shouldn't judge my mammy. She did what she had to do to survive. Yes, I wish we could've gotten away from him a long time ago, but I don't blame her for staying. She didn't know any better. She fell in love with someone who treated her appallingly and that wasn't her fault. I'm sad that was all her life was about. I wish I could've saved her and not left her to rot away there with him.

"Hi."

I jump ten feet in the air and give a yelp, but as I look up I see the homeless guy I scared the other day smiling back at me.

"I'm really sorry. I didn't mean to make you jump. I just wanted to say thank you for the tea, coffee and muffins. I really appreciated it."

I smile at him. He has kind eyes.

"I guess we're even now on the making-each-other-jump stakes. No need to say thanks. It was the least I could do for waking ye up."

We sit on the same bench I sat on the other morning whilst talking to Nat and chat for a few minutes more. He's smart and articulate, and he sets my enquiring mind into action.

"I hope ye don't mind me asking but how've ye come to be homeless? Ye seem intelligent. I can't smell alcohol and ye are too coherent to be on any kind of drugs. What happened?"

He gives me a sad smile and blows a breath out.

"I fell in love, that's what happened."

His answer shocks me to my core. Tis as if he has been sent to remind me of what love can do to a person.

"What do ye mean?"

He goes on to tell me he'd fallen in love with a girl from London. He moved down here against his family's wishes and moved in with her. After a few years they had a baby and he'd lost all contact with his family. When he found out she was cheating on him, he confronted her and she kicked him out. She stopped access to his daughter and because his wages were low, he couldn't afford the rent on his room *and* to be able to pay child maintenance to her, so he ended up out here. He lost his job shortly after and his life has been on the streets ever since. I reach out and hold his hand in mine.

"I'm so sorry. Couldn't ye call your family, I'm sure they'd be relieved to hear from ye, even if it's after all this time."

He shakes his head sadly and the pain that reflects in his eyes is heart breaking.

"Too much time has gone past now."

My phone rings and I look down and see tis Denny. I clear his call and ask the man his name and where he used to live.

"George Matthews. I lived in Dorset. Aside from my daughter, I should never have come here. My mum, Lina, she was the kindest person on the planet. I should've known there was something wrong with my ex when mum said she didn't like her. She loved everyone; it was her nature."

My phone rings again, and I clear the call once more.

"Sorry, I'll leave you to get back to everything, I just wanted to say thanks again. It's nice to have someone see you and not look through you when you live out here."

He goes back to his 'spot' on the pavement and I walk over to the coffee stand and get him muffins, coffee and tea and take them over to him. I smile and tell him the conversation and his time was payment enough. I want to help him reunite with his family, and hopefully Nat will be able to help me.

By the time I get back to my flat I have six missed calls, all from Denny. I tap out a text to him.

Me: Sorry, Old Man, I was out for a walk and was talking to Nat and didn't hear my phone as it was on silent. You should have woken me this morning. Can we talk later? x

I hit send and call Nat.

"Hey Nat, do me a favour please and go on your face-gram thingy and see if ye can find a Lina Matthews from Dorset." I fill Nat in about George and she instantly sounds cagey.

"Darcie, this isn't a good idea. I mean what if he's lying and he's psycho and there's a reason they aren't in contact anymore? How would you feel if someone tried to reunite you with your long-lost family, babe?"

What am I thinking? She's right. I'm hiding out in London because I don't want to be anywhere near my daddy. "Okay, okay. Ye have a point. I just feel really bad for him though. I mean he lost everything because he fell in love. Tisn't right. It made me think though, Nat. This ting..." I huff as I realise I let the h drop from thing again and correct myself as I continue.

"This THing, with Denny has got to stop. I can't afford to fall for him." I hear Nat scoff.

"I hate to be the bearer of bad news babe but you're already halfway there."

I'm not halfway there am I? I can't fall for him. I don't want a relationship. Being in love leaves you open and vulnerable and I don't want to be like that with anyone.

Nat's voice takes me out of my thoughts and brings me back to our conversation.

"I'm kidding, Darcie. Please, for my sake, just keep going with it. Please, Darcie, just see what it feels like to be happy for a while."

I know she isn't kidding and I should be running for the hills right now, but the idea of calling it off with Denny makes me feel sick to my stomach. So I'll just agree with her for now and let future Darcie deal with the fallout.

"Okay, but only if ye promise me that if ye see me falling, like proper falling, ye'll pull me out."

"Deal. Sorry, Darcie, I've got to get ready for work. Call me later. Love you." She hangs up before I can respond and when I check the time, I realise I need to haul my arse into gear, or I'll be late. I throw the phone on the bed and quickly run a brush through my hair again. I run out of the house, grabbing my keys and bag as I go, and slam the door behind me.

Chapter 14

Denny

"Mine. Mine, always." I can't help but say it aloud as she falls asleep. I'm fucked. Looking down at her I already know I'm in deeper than I've ever been before. I thought I'd be able to ignore the little voice in my head that kept saying things like 'mine' and 'always'. Ignore the future I pictured with her. Silence the voice asking what if? Now after being with her and sharing another first, I can't shake that voice away. I let myself hear it. I let it shout from the rooftops - we want her, not for a while but forever. What if everything I'd been told when I was younger was wrong. That I could have someone love me. That I was worthy of it?

Images of us together assault my mind. Standing at our wedding, her in a beautiful white gown and me in my tux. Us on a balcony together watching the sunset, my hands wrapped around her rounded belly as I kiss her head. Holding a beautiful little boy, hair as dark as hers and eyes blue as ours. A single tear escapes my eye and trails down my cheek. I rub it away hard and rub at my temple. This is stupid. This beautiful, amazing, girl, has in no uncertain terms, told me that this isn't what she wants. She doesn't want commitment, or feelings, she wants to be free. I can't blame her after the little information she's given up about her waste of space father and mum. What is it with people having kids and then fucking them up? I mean, her mum had the perfect reason to leave. As soon as she knew she was having Darcie, she should've been brave enough for the both of them to get out of there and then she wouldn't have had to live a life of fear. I shouldn't be blaming her mum though. The blame lies at his feet and I swear I'll make him pay. One day.

I blow out a breath and rake my hand through my hair. She stirs against my chest, her face looking up at me whilst she sleeps, and I sweep my hand over the loose strand of hair that's covering her cheek. I want to stay like this forever. Her in my arms with all the worry wiped away from her face. But I'm a realist. We can't stay like this. She'll wake up soon enough and the fear and worry will be there. My own pain and fear will wreck my brain as it always does. I close my eyes as a memory envelops me.

"Come here Daniel, give mummy a kiss and a cuddle and make sure you're good for your daddy."

Daniel nods his head energetically. He turns to me and squeezes me tightly and whispers, "I'll be back before you know it, stay out of her way, yeah?"

I nod ever so slightly, and he leaves with his dad. I try to turn away quickly, so she doesn't see the tears in my eyes, but she grabs my arm.

"Look at them, you little shit. You're the reason Daniel can't be with his dad every day. You ruined everything. You think Daniel loves you, but he doesn't. No one could love you, look at you. Your own mother can't love you so why would you think anyone else could?"

She grabs me by the arm and pulls me into the house. Once the door is closed, her verbal onslaught against me continues. "Useless. Waste of space. Ruined everything. Should never have had you. HATED! Unlovable. Unwanted. HATED! Unloved. DISAPPOINTMENT. Regret. HATED!" Just a few of the words I'm used to hearing spewed from my so-called mother's mouth.

Darcie moves from my arm and shakes me out of my trance. I look down at her and grimace at my earlier thoughts. I have to get out of here. I unwrap her arms from around me and slowly get off the bed. I get dressed and look around for a pen and paper to leave a note but can't find anything. I look over at Sheila, her bear, and mutter, "Don't look at me like that."

I take my phone out of my pocket and send her a text saying I had to leave. She'll probably be annoyed at me, but I have to get out now. I'm panicking. The darkness threatens to take control of me. I grab the door handle and open the door. One last look at her makes my heart constrict and I force myself to close the door behind me. I let the darkness cloud over me. I lean against the cool wood and close my eyes tightly, willing the pain and panic away. I can't let her be a part of this. After what she went through in her life, she deserves someone good, someone who can give her everything. Someone who can shine a light on her demons, not cast their own onto her as well.

Once I'm outside, I try to gather my thoughts and form a plan. I've promised her all the firsts and to make them great. I've ticked off first kiss and orgasm, I can even tick off first blow job as well. All that's left is sex. Maybe once that's over with, I'll be able to go about my normal shit and be able to fuck women without feeling like this. I throw my head back and sigh up at the sky that's in between night and day. I want her more than I've ever wanted a woman before in my life, but I know keeping her is impossible. Once she sees through me, sees the real me, she'll realise I'm a disappointment. Or I'll do something to ruin it like I always do. If I were to hurt her it'd do more damage to me than I think I can take. I can't walk away though, not yet. I have to see this firsts business through with her. At least then when she goes off and meets the man of her dreams, she'll always remember me. That thought cuts through me, but I know what I have to do. I'll keep her as mine for now but it can't be forever, no matter what that little voice in my head says.

My meeting's over and I check my phone for what must be the millionth time. I've still had no contact from Darcie. I texted her, phoned, left voicemails and nothing. It shouldn't be bothering me as much, but it is. Panic starts to rise in my throat. What if somethings happened to her? What if she's had an accident on the way to work? I dial the landline number for home but there's no answer so now I have to find out if she turned up for work without making it obvious to Dan. God dammit. I stalk out of my office and knock on his door.

"Yo Dan, you got a minute?"

My brother looks up from whatever boring spreadsheet type paperwork he's looking at and says, "Yeah, what's up? You look like shit bro." I look at his concerned face and shrug my shoulders at him. I try to flash him a grin, but it doesn't have its usual finesse.

"I didn't get much sleep last night."

Concern flashes through his features and I flinch when he speaks.

"It doesn't normally bother you, not getting any sleep. There's something different about you today. What's the matter? You do realise you can talk to me about anything right? Joseph told me you've met a girl. Is this about her?"

Shit, that fucker has told him about Darcie. Fucking Joseph. He can't have told him it was Darcie or I would've been on the receiving end of a major telling off for going anywhere near her.

"Joseph has a big mouth and an imagination to match. I saw a girl last night, not a big deal at all. I see girls most nights for fuck sake." I rake my hand through my hair.

"So why are you getting all agitated? You always do your stupid hand through your hair thing whenever you're stressed or nervous." Dan smiles smugly at me.

"No, I don't." I lie back to him but roll my eyes in my mind because I know he knows I'm lying. I sometimes hate that he knows me so bloody well.

"I know you see girls most nights BUT you don't normally go all out taking them to dinner and then cashing in on a favour to sort out a private, no queuing, trip on the fucking London Eye, Den. Who is she and why are you getting your knickers in a twist? It's okay to admit you like someone, baby bro." His voice softens at the last bit.

I silently curse Joseph for giving him all the details of our date. I need to get to the point and find out if Darcie has turned up for work.

"Okay, Dan, you're right. I met someone who I like and actually went out on a date with her. Not a 'I'm going to get a fuck out of buying you dinner' date but an actual 'I want to get to know you date.' Are you happy now and can I get back to why I came in here?"

Dan's face is a picture, half shock and half happiness.

I've never gone out on a date to get to know a girl before and I can see wedding bells flashing in his eyes.

"Wow, Den. Are you serious about her? Not that I'm saying you shouldn't be, but it's only been one date. Are you going to see her again? Where did you meet her? What's she like? Tell me! What did you want anyway?"

Jeez, he's spent far too much time with Becs and her love of asking fucking questions.

"For God sakes, she's absolutely gorgeous. I want to see a lot more of her. I met her in a bar, and she is the sweetest woman you'll ever meet, happy? Now is Da... nanny at work today? I have some plans I need and wondered if she could send them over, so I don't have to go back home?"

I can see his brain still trying to ingest the information I gave him about my mystery woman and hope that means he hasn't picked up on me nearly saying her name.

"Da nanny? Really, Denny?"

I shrug at him and grin. "Just trying to stay in wid da kids ya know."

Dan slowly blinks at me and shakes his head muttering about me being an idiot. After a few seconds of him shaking his head at me and me sweating under his gaze, he speaks again.

"She's at work today. Becs said she got there a bit late. But Denny you can't expect her to run around after you when she has the twins to deal with. Sorry brother, you'll have to go and get it yourself if you need it. Now about this woman, what's she called? Denny? DENNY!"

I'm already out of his office before he has a chance to call me back. She's at work and hasn't had an accident. I feel a moment of relief wash over me. I get back to my desk and pick up my phone and call her again, still no answer. FUCK. The relief is gone. I'm now stuck between frustrated and fucking fuming.

I look over at Gorgeous who mouths, "Are you okay?"

I shrug my shoulders up to her before deflating in my chair. Before I know it, she's in my office, pulling the blinds closed and locking the door behind her.

"Now is this about Darcie? My hubby told me all about her and that nonsense you spouted off to him as well. What's going on? Has something happened?"

Of course, Joseph's told her. Feeling utterly dejected I look into her eyes and blow out a breath, ready to tell Gorgeous all about her.

"Gorgeous, she's amazing and I think I may have fucked up already."

She tuts at me and tells me, "How many times do I have to tell you, don't swear, it doesn't become you, Denny." I chuckle at her and she reaches over my desk, grabs my hand and holds it tightly as I tell her everything, apart from the thoughts of me and her settling down and being normal, because I know she'll tell me to pursue those and I can't.

"Oh, you silly boy, she's probably embarrassed. She isn't used to all this sex malarkey. Go home and see her face to face. I'm sure there's a perfectly reasonable explanation, son."

Feeling defeated and out of my depth I ask her, "What if she doesn't want me anymore? Sh...I mean, shoot, it's only been one night, and we haven't even had sex. What's wrong with me?" I grab my head in my hands.

"If she doesn't want you then she's fucking mad. Don't be afraid to feel, Denny. For me, please, don't be afraid. Don't let that woman ruin anything else for you." I lift my head up with my mouth wide open.

"Did you just say fucking? Gorgeous that's both you and Joseph that have sworn at me in the past few days. Bloody hell." I let my head fall back on to my chair as laughter echoes around my office from the both of us. After a while she gets up and walks around my desk to give me a kiss on the cheek.

"Go and speak to her, less sex and more words."

Chapter 15

Darcie

Tis one thirty and the twins have just eaten their lunch and are busy playing dress up in the playroom. Tis been a lovely morning of fun and laughter. Now I'm in the kitchen doing the boring job of washing dishes when I hear the front door slam. I spin around to find Denny stalking through the hallway at me, his eyes on fire.

"Why haven't you responded to any of my calls? I've called you like a hundred times, sent texts, left voicemails. What the actual fuck, Darcie? I texted you this morning to explain why I left and thought you might have been pissed, but not enough to ignore me all fucking day. I was worried sick something had happened to you. So much so I had to ask Dan if you'd turned up to work and when he confirmed you had, I came straight over. What's going on?"

I'm stunned into silence. I shake my head a wee bit and walk over to the counter to get the cloth to wipe my hands dry. I find my bag on the side and dig through it.

"I texted ye this morning. After I'd gotten off the phone with Nat, I texted ye. If I could find my bloody phone." I mumble as I search through my bag a few times and puff an exasperated sigh out of my mouth.

"I must've left it at home. I got side-tracked by Nat and then after talking to George, I was running late so I must have left it on my dresser or my bed or someting. Some*thing*. I'm sorry I worried ye. I'm sure I texted ye though. I said I was on the phone and asked if we could talk later. I'm really sorry if that didn't go through and I worried ye." Finishing my nervous ramble, I look up, desperately hoping to see him looking more relaxed and happier, but he looks angrier than ever and his eyes are so clear they're almost crystal like.

"Who's George?" He demands.

My mind is racing. "A-a friend of mine." I don't want to tell him about George. He's entrusted me, and I don't want to betray him. Judging by the look in Denny's eyes, murderous, I don't want him to do or say anything to George.

Pain rips through his eyes and is replaced with despondency as he asks me, "What did you want to talk about?" His tone is off. He sounds almost robotic and it throws me for a loop.

"C-can we talk about it later on, when I'm not supposed to be at work, please?" I stutter back, feeling nervous but not scared.

"No. What did you want to talk about?"

I stand in front of him and even though he's seething with rage, I can feel the crackle of electricity in the air between us. I want more than anything to reach over and touch him, but I'm also scared of his reaction. I'm not scared of him. I know he wouldn't hit me. I don't know why I'm so trusting of him, but my gut tells me he wouldn't hurt me. Maybe tis all those years of living with my so-called daddy. Denny doesn't have that nasty, evil glint in his eyes that my daddy had. No, I'm worried he wouldn't let me touch him and that'd be worse.

"Denny, please. I don't know what's wrong with ye right now." I plead with him, trying to break through the anger.

"What did you want to talk to me about?"

I open my mouth to speak but I'm interrupted.

"Darcie?" Rebecca's voice calls from the hallway. "The shoot wrapped up early, so I thought I'd come home and rescue you. You can head out if you want." She walks into the kitchen whilst fiddling with her camera equipment and laptop. She places them on the counter and looks up at us. "Oh, hi Denny, what are you doing here?" Her tone is suspicious as her eyes dart back and forth from both of us.

"I needed to get some prints I left upstairs this morning and when I came in Darcie was a bit upset as she couldn't find her phone. Now you're here I'll leave her in your capable hands. Ladies."

He turns and leaves and I bite the inside of my cheek to fight the tears away.

Rebecca looks at me and gently asks, "You've lost your phone? D'you want me to call it?"

I shake my head at her, willing my voice to work and sound normal. "No, tis okay. I was in a rush this morning and I tink, think I left it at home."

Rebecca smiles at my wee slip up and stares at me intently. I know she can sense something else is going on.

"Do ye mind if I go? My head's killing me, and I want to make sure my phone's at home before I cancel my contract and everything?"

Without giving her the chance to respond, I grab my bag and practically run out of the house. I get outside and let the tears flow down my face. I rub them away as I notice Joseph at the bottom of the steps. He smiles his kind smile at me, and I wave back. I run in the other direction from him because Denny will be joining him as soon as he can and I need to avoid him at all costs.

I run blindly until I come to a tube station. I duck inside and jump onto a train. My head's spinning. I don't know why he's so angry with me. So, I missed a few of his calls, big deal. He's acting like I'm his property. Like he has a right over me or something. My mind flashes back to last night, "Mine. Mine, always." He said that when I was falling asleep and then again when I voiced my question out loud. Oh God, what if the reason he doesn't commit is because he gets too attached. I've already had to run away from one overbearing, control freak. I don't think I have the energy to run from another one. What was I thinking doing this? Why didn't I listen to my head instead of what was in my knickers? Now I'm going to have to leave my job and I love those kids.

I'm snapped out of my thoughts when the train doors open at my stop. I jump off and walk up the stairs to the exit. As I come outside, I take a deep breath. I turn around the corner and stop dead in my tracks. It can't be. No, I must be mistaken. He looks so angry to see me. Why's he here? He starts towards me; my head tells me to run but my feet are rooted onto the spot. He reaches me in seconds and as soon as he's near enough to me, I can smell the alcohol on him. It sends me spiralling back to being a wee girl and fearing that smell because it meant we were in for a beating. I shake my head and try to run this time but he grabs my arm.

"Darcie, I've been looking for ye, ye wee fecking slut. When that old bitch finally died, I went tru her stuff and found ya address. Did ye really tink I'd let ye escape? Fecking stupid. Tis your job to look after me like ya slut of a mammy did before she fecking died."

I close my eyes; Mrs. O'Donnell is dead. When I was eighteen my mammy convinced my daddy to let me work in the wee post office/corner shop in town. Mrs. O'Donnell and her husband had run it for years and when he died earlier that year, she was all on her own in there. She was the sweetest, wee old lady I'd ever met. After working with her for so long, I'd come to think of her as my grandmammy, seeing as I hadn't met my own ones; they'd died before I was born. She was the one who helped me save money from my wages. And she was the one who helped me escape from him when my mammy had gotten ill. She knew he was a monster. I didn't have to tell her. I ache for the loss of her, but my fear grips me. What's he going to do to me? He grabs my arm tightly and walks me towards my flat. He was waiting for me. He knows where I live. I can't ever escape him. I wish Nat were here, or Denny.

"Can't be talking to ye on the street with all these people here, can I?" He snarls into my ear. I should fight him; I should struggle but I can't. I'm frozen in fear. If Nat had been here, she'd be punching and kicking and would fight with all her might, but I'm not strong like her. It feels like I've been transported back to being a wee girl again, except this time my mammy isn't here to protect me. Once we get inside, he throws me to the floor. He looks around scornfully and laughs, spit flying out of his mouth.

"Ye've really done well for yourself, ye wee slut. What? Ye bring men back here to feck all the time, do ye?" He kicks me in the stomach so hard my vision goes blurry. He pulls me up by my hair and slaps me across the face. I fall to the floor and curl up into a ball just like my mammy taught me and how I'd seen her do a million times before. His blows rain down on me and I think 'this is it; this is how I'll die. I won't get to see Nat again – or Denny.' The thought of him fills me with pain. I want to see him again. I don't want to die with him being angry at me. A knock at the door halts his assault. I'm thankful for the reprieve as he bends down to me and whispers. "If ye make a sound, I'll kill ye, ye filthy whore." I know he will, so I stay silent. There's another knock.

"Darcie, are you okay? I heard a noise but maybe you're in there with that handsome man from last night."

Tis my neighbour, the one who saw me with Denny. I stay silent but a look of disgust flashes over his face and chills me to my bones. Neither of us moves for a few seconds waiting for her to leave. The silence is deafening and then tis broken by my phone ringing. He walks over to the bed and looks at the caller display.

"Denny? Is he one of ya wee boyfriends?" I go to speak but he puts his finger to my mouth and shushes me as he answers my phone.

"Hello? Who are ye and why are ye calling my girlfriend's phone?"

"Noooo! Denny! Help me. Please." I can't help it. I scream out even though I'm terrified of him killing me, but it hurts me more to think Denny could hate me. If I'm going to die, I don't want him to think I was a lying cheat.

My daddy screams at me in rage. "Filthy whore." He drops the phone on the floor and between his blows I can very faintly hear Denny shouting my name through the phone. I try to call back but I'm too weak. The blows rain down on me and then everything turns black.

Chapter 16

Denny

As Joseph parks the car outside of my house, I feel sick. What if she doesn't want to speak with me? What if an orgasm was enough for her? I take a deep breath and blow it out. She enjoyed herself last night and I'm not just talking about the foreplay; the whole night was perfect. So why is she ignoring me this morning? This crap isn't meant to be happening yet. We still have so much to do and loads more firsts to get through. I thought up lots of firsts to tick off before I have to give her up. She isn't doing this right now. She's meant to give me more time.

I'm angry and sad now, not a combination I like being. How can she just disregard last night? I race up the steps to my front door and charge through the house. I need to see her, to get my fill of her skyblues and her beautiful face. I can see her at the sink in the kitchen and storm over to her. She turns to face me and there's apprehension on her face.

"Why haven't you responded to any of my calls? I've called you like a hundred times..." Her eyes are confused, and she looks at me warily as I continue. I take a quick breath and she shakily speaks.

"I texted you this morning..."

She's saying words but I'm trying to calm the rage that's built up in me. I'm angry at her for trying to get away from me so quickly. Has she seen in me what my mother saw all those years ago? After one night she's had enough. She walks over to her bag and is rifling through it, and then spins some line about forgetting her phone at home and speaking with Nat. That I believe. On our 'date' she talked about Nat incessantly and I liked her even though I haven't met her. It makes sense she would have called her after last night. I calm a little.

"...after talking to George I was running late..." I don't hear what she says after, all I can focus on is the name George. She hasn't mentioned a George to me at all. She told me about Nat. She even told me about Sheila the fucking teddy bear. But no George.

"Who's George?"

She looks flustered, "A-a friend," She is lying, there's something she's hiding about him.

"What did you want to talk about?" I'm not angry anymore, I'm deflated. She's seen past the smokescreens, my looks and money, and she's seen the real me. The worthless, unlovable mistake. That's what I am to her, a mistake, and I'm a fool for thinking this could have been anything more.

I ask her again what she wanted to talk about and I stare straight at her as she speaks. I need to hear it now, not hours later when she can make up some bullshit story.

"Denny, please I don't know what is wrong with you right now, talk to me." How ironic. That's exactly what I want her to do. To tell me she doesn't want me and I'm just a regret for her., Like I've been my whole life.

The front door opens and Becs calls out. I drag my gaze away from Darcie and rake my hand through my hair. Becs comes into the kitchen and her eyes sear into mine. I look away from her. Becs has an unnerving gift at being able to see through me, and I swear on several other occasions she's even read my mind. It comes from knowing someone nearly all of your life. I dismiss myself from the conversation and go upstairs to get my imaginary prints and take a few deep breaths. As I get to the top of the first flight of stairs a door opens. Isla walks out and when she sees me, she runs into my arms. I scoop her up, needing the comfort from her more than she needs it from me.

"Hey Princess. You okay?" She buries her face in the crook of my neck which I know means she's upset.

"Hey, what's the matter, my beautiful Princess? What has Isabelle done now?" She sniffs and rubs her nose all over my neck. Normally I wouldn't be happy about having someone wipe their snot on me, but anything these little ladies do is fine by me.

"She said I was stoopid. Dat mummy and daddy only wanted one baby and cause she's older dan me, dey wanted her."

My heart breaks that she feels unwanted for even a second. I know what that feels like and I wouldn't wish it on my enemy, let alone on one of the people I love more than anything in the world.

"Isabelle is wrong, Princess." I tell her and get a small grin in return. "I've known your daddy all of my life..."

"Dat's cause he's your brother, Uncle Denny." She rolls her eyes at me and a chuckle escapes my mouth. The sass on the girls is out of this world.

These kids are fucking brilliant and are all I need in my life.

"Right, I'm his brother, so I know him inside out. He always told me when we were little, he wanted three children, a boy and twin girls. He got his wish. You were never unwanted, Isla. All of you were wanted and have always been loved, even before you were in mummy's tummy and

Isabelle took up all of the room." I put my finger to my lips in a 'shhh, don't tell her motion'. She nods and winks at me and I wink back. She squeezes me tightly and I savour the feeling of being needed, wanted.

"Uncle Denny, how many babies do you want?"

The question causes a lump to form in my throat. I look down into her perfect little face and dare to dream for just a bit as I see Darcie holding our little dark haired boy with her belly rounded with another baby.

"I want as many as I can have, but that's a secret between me and you. Now let's go tell your sister to be nice, shall we?"

As I come down the stairs, I know she's gone. I know she's run. Normally she sets my hairs on end and I can sense her before I see her. Right now, there's nothing. I heave a sigh out, knowing I'm going to have to chase her again, even if it's just to hear her tell me to leave her alone, but Becs's voice stops me in my tracks.

"Denny, come and talk to me please."

I let out a sigh and drop my head in frustration. Becs knows, she always knows everything. I've known Becs longer than Dan has. Funnily enough she started out as my friend before she was anywhere near interested in Dan. In my younger stupid days, I resented them getting together. I felt like he'd taken something that was mine and made me share it. I never had anything that was mine throughout my childhood, and everything I did have was because Dan had shared with me, so I wasn't really in the right place to feel resentful towards him. But I was. After seeing them together I realised I wasn't losing anything. I knew they'd be together for the rest of their lives and I'd have Becs as a sister forever. As I walk into the kitchen, I know the blood-hound in her is in full effect.

"Den, I'm not beating around the bush. You and

Darcie? Spill!" She raises her head, so her chin sticks out pointedly to signify she isn't going to accept my bullshit.

"Did Dan call you?"

She shakes her head, "I haven't spoken to Dan since this morning before he left for work, and if you tell me not to speak to him about this I won't. I'm your sister, Denny, always have been and always will be. Now spill."

I slump on the chair and tell her everything. Even the bit about dreaming about a future with her, but not being able to have it because it isn't what she wants. I'm not what she *needs* either. I don't want to look up and see her, so I keep my head down.

"Denny, do you smell that?"

I look up confused.

She looks straight in my eyes whilst sniffing around, "It's bullshit, and it's coming from your direction."

I shake my head at her. "Funny Becs, you should give up photography and take up comedy, NOT. It's not bullshit, it's just the damn truth." I lean back in my chair and put my hands behind my head and lace my fingers together.

"Denny, you are the most genuine and caring man I've ever met. The way you love on the kids. The way you love on Gloria and Joseph. The way you love on Dan and me. You have so much love to offer and so much to give to someone. The only person stopping you from having all you want is you. I don't think Darcie wants to just have her firsts with you, Den. A girl doesn't wait this long to give up her firsts to just a random, believe me on that one. She's got her own issues to deal with, but she can deal with them with you. You've got to put in the work. Gloria is right, talking is key. You guys have gone from zero to one hundred in the space of a couple of dates and it's enough to terrify the sanest of people, let alone two people that have commitment issues. Don't force it, but talk. Talk as much as you can and don't get scared."

I look at her like she has grown two heads and is a stranger in front of me. "Becs. Please, be real. I can't do any of that because she has another fucking bloke lined up to replace me. George, the prick." The venom spills from my mouth as I speak his name. I wonder what he's like. Probably not scared of settling down and helping her through her crap, unlike me.

Laughter catches me off guard and I whip my head up to see Becs howling at me.

"Oh Denny. You Blanc men make me laugh. Jealousy runs right through you both. You remember when Dan and I first started seeing each other and he was seething with rage every time I mentioned Miguel. No matter how many times I told him he was just a friend and someone I worked with, he wouldn't have it. Until he met him and realised Miguel had no interest in me whatsoever."

I laugh at the memory. "Yeah, he wasn't interested in you because he was too busy chasing me around. He was fast as well. I still go funny when I see cut up pineapple." I shudder remembering all too well him trying to force feed me pineapple slices whilst chasing me around the large makeup table in Becs's old studio.

"What did she tell you about George?"

I mumble, "He's a friend."

She tuts her disapproval at me and shakes her head. "Phone her and ask to talk and explain you're not a nut job but you just have some stuff going on. Believe me when I say she's as into you as you are into her."

My startled eyes turn to her.

"The looks you two have been putting out since yesterday are seriously hot. And that little charade at dinner the other night? You weren't fooling anyone, bro." Becs grins at me and winks as she turns away. Damn this woman is good.

I try her phone again and no answer. I walk outside and Joseph points me in the direction Darcie fled in. I'm fairly certain she's heading home. Her stubborn arse probably wanted to prove she'd left her phone there. I jump in the car and tell Joseph the address. We're about five minutes away when I try to call again, figuring she's had enough time to get home and get her phone by now. Preparing myself for the onslaught of her words as the phone rings, I take a deep breath.

"Hello? Who are ye and why are ye calling my girlfriend's phone?"

My brain doesn't have a chance to register anything as I hear a chilling scream.

"Noooo, Denny..."

"DARCIE? DARCIE?" I scream into the phone.

I hear a deafening crack and a man's thick Irish accent rings out. "Filthy whore." And all I can hear are thuds.

"FUCKING LEAVE HER ALONE! DARCIE! Joseph drive fucking faster." The urgency in my voice is as clear as anything as Joseph manoeuvres between the traffic.

He's swerving all over the place and then he speaks. "Ambulance and police please. We were just speaking to her... I don't know if she's been attacked or what, but someone needs to get there. We're a few minutes away. Thank you." Whilst he's driving like a mad man, he's also called 999. I can't put the phone down and I'm screaming into it.

"I will find you! I will fucking kill you!" I can hear the grunts as he hurts her, and the rage is too much to bear. I look ahead and see the traffic lights are red, so I jump out of the car and run the rest of the way. I fly down the street like a mad man and climb the stairs of Darcie's building as

I can't wait for the lift. I get to her door and I see her, a crumpled mess of blood and bruises. Her beautiful eyes are closed, and her perfect face is unrecognisable. I bend down on my knees and lean over her to feel for a pulse. I don't realise I'm holding my breath until I find one and exhale.

"Darcie, darling it's me, I'm here. I'm so sorry. I'm so sorry. Irish, come back to me, sweetheart. Open your eyes. Please open your fucking eyes, Irish..." Sobbing, I stroke her face, willing her to wake up.

Her eyes flicker and she opens them a tiny bit and manages a whisper. "Don't swear at me, old man. Ye know I don't like it."

The relief that washes over me is immense. I'm so happy. I grab her hand and squeeze it tightly.

"Darcie, baby. I'm so sorry. I'm here, I'm not leaving you. Tell me who did this? Who the fuck was it?"

She winces as she tries to move and manages to whisper. "My daddy. He found me." Before I can say anything, her eyes roll back into her head and she spasms. I look around, searching for help and when I see the paramedics coming through the door, I scream at them.

"Help her, please fucking help her." They move me away from her and do whatever it is they need to. Joseph is next to me, holding me up. I swear if it wasn't for him, I'd be collapsed on that floor next to her. It feels like my heart is breaking into a million pieces.

"We're taking her to hospital, sir." The paramedics inform me.

"Can I come with her? Please?" Desperation dripping with every word. I need to be with her. I need her to know I'm here.

"Only one of you can come, we don't have enough space." I nod my head and leave Joseph to follow us in the car. Gripping Darcie's hand as we get into the ambulance my thoughts keep circling back to the word 'mine'.

I'm by Darcie's side and holding onto her hand for dear life. It's where I've been for the past two days and it's where I'll be staying too. The doctors have sedated her to help her body deal with the swelling and pain, especially with her head injuries, which was the cause of her seizure. It's been two days and I'm begging her to wake up. The doctors have said it could happen at any time. I've been waiting and waiting and still nothing.

"Denny?" Becs asks tentatively, "You need to get some rest. Why don't you go..."

"No. I'm not leaving her. When she wakes up, I'll be here."

There's a look passed between her and Dan and I know it's due to the fact I haven't slept or eaten anything since the attack happened. The police don't know where her dad is, and I'm not going anywhere whilst that madman is out on the loose. It broke my heart having to tell Nat what had happened. She was absolutely devastated. She's working on getting her things in order to come over earlier than she'd planned so she can be here for her, and she made me promise I'd be there for Darcie as well.

I made Joseph go back to her place and pack everything up and take it to my house, once the police were through with it. She isn't going back there ever, and I need her to be somewhere I can take care of her. I've set her up in the downstairs guest room, so she won't have to climb the stairs, and I made sure there was a space in there for me too, whether she likes it or not. Until that piece of scum is picked up by the police, I'm not leaving her side.

I get up to grab Sheila and put her on the bed with her.

"Who the fuck keeps moving her?" I grumble to no one and everyone in the room.

Dan and Becs are here and Joseph is outside waiting to update Gorgeous who's looking after the kids at home. I feel a movement and look down at Darcie's face, her beautiful perfect face covered in bruises and cuts. Her eyes flutter and Becs runs out to get a nurse.

"Darcie, baby, you're okay. You're in hospital. The nurse is coming." Her eyes open slowly, and she turns her head to me and smiles a little smile.

"Ye are still here. I'm sorry I left my phone at home." I look at her, stunned for a second by the sheer goodness that she is.

"Darcie. Baby, you have nothing to apologise about. I'm the one who should be sorry. Had I not made you uncomfortable in the house that day, you wouldn't have run home, and you wouldn't be..." I can't finish, the anger that's rising isn't just for her scumbag father, but it's for myself as well. I drop my head, so she won't see the anger, shame, hatred for myself in my eyes.

"Denny, no. Tis not your fault. Please don't tink..." She sighs and rolls her eyes as best as she can. "Bloody accent. Please don't THink it is. I shouldn't have run from you. You saved me. Thank you."

I kiss the back of her hand, one of the only places that's bruise and cut free.

"I told you before, if you run, I'll chase you and I'll catch you every time, Darcie. I will always be there; I promise you with everything I have. I'll always be there. Until you don't want me anymore." Our eyes are locked onto each other's and I can feel my breathing coming in short rapid breaths. I mean every word I just said to her. I'll be there until she doesn't want me. There will come a time when she sees through me, and when that happens it'll be torture, but I can't and won't let this woman go. Not now. The nurse comes in and breaks our gaze as I step away from Darcie so she can run some observations. Shortly after, a doctor follows. They ask for space and I let Darcie know I'll be just outside. I tell Joseph to go home to Gorgeous and to take Dan and Becs too. They all bid me farewell but before they disappear, I call Joseph back.

"Joseph, thank you. You kept me strong when I needed to be and, without your quick thinking to call the ambulance or police, I dread to think of what could have happened. Thank you for always being there for me." I bring my arms up and around him and embrace him in the tightest hug. I've only ever hugged him once before and that was when he came to tell me my mother was dead. I hugged him then because I was relieved and sad all at the same time. I hug him now for always being there and for saving me from a life of hell. And for saving Darcie. When we pull apart, I can see the tears in his eyes that I know are in mine too.

We look at each other for a second and then he says, "My boy." whilst holding my chin. It's like a dam has broken and I can't stop the tears from flowing. He takes my face, kisses my cheek, and turns and walks out. That man saved me and his quick thinking saved Darcie too. I will forever be in his debt.

I take a deep breath and wipe my tears away just as the doctor comes out and says I can go back into Darcie. When I open the door, she's holding Sheila and smiles up at me.

"Thank you for bringing her here."

I run my hand through my hair and smile at her.

"You don't have to thank me for anything. Are you feeling okay? Are you in pain?"

She shakes her head at me. "The nurse took care of that.

Denny, I'm sorry. He found me. He found me." She breaks into sobs that wrack her whole body.

I run to her side and put my arms around her as gently as I can. I move her hair out of her face. "Shh baby, don't cry. You're safe. He won't find you again. I promise you. When I find him, I'll make sure he's never able to come near you again. I swear, Irish, I fucking swear."

The police come and take her statement. Watching her relive it is too much for me to take. I do take it though, as she has my hand in a vice-like grip and I couldn't leave her even if I wanted to. The police inform us that it doesn't look like he's in London anymore as he boarded a ferry back to Ireland. They've contacted their colleagues over there and that's all they can do for now. A warrant has been issued for his arrest, but that's it. In other words, they aren't doing fuck all. When I voice that to them, Darcie gives me a look that tells me to shut up, so I do, begrudgingly. I breathe out a sigh of relief when they go and get Darcie some water.

"Did he use to hurt you when you were younger, too?" She lowers her head and shrugs her shoulders.

"Not all the time because my mammy would be there to step in. He seemed to like having that power over her, knowing she'd take the beatings that were intended for me gave him a kick I suppose. He'd always tell me I would grow up to be a filthy whore and would be a slag like my mammy. The ironic thing is she was a virgin when she met him and until the day she died he was the only man she'd been with. I doubt he could say the same thing though."

I stand up and walk over to the sterile white walls of Darcie's room and look out of the little window in her wooden door.

"Is that why you never kissed anyone or had sex? Because he made you think if you did you'd be a whore and you wanted to prove him wrong?" I carry on looking out of the door as I don't want her to see the pain and anguish on my face.

"Yes and no. I didn't want him to be right. No matter how many times Nat told me differently. I still believed me doing the normal things like kissing would make me a whore, but I also never met anyone I wanted to do those things with either, Denny. Until ye. Please look at me, I know my face isn't a pretty picture right now..."

I spin around to face her so fast I almost lose my balance. "Irish, don't you dare say a bad word about that beautiful face. You. Are. Perfect. You always have been and always will be." I'm at her side holding onto her hand for dear life.

"Then why were ye looking away from me?"

I sigh and hear Gorgeous and Becs's words in my ears, less sex and more words.

"I was looking away because I didn't want you to see me upset. I keep thinking back to how I pushed you to go out with me even though you tried backing off and then after our date, what I did to you, must've made you feel awful. I'm truly sorry about that." My blue eyes meet hers and I know in that moment she can see the pain in them.

"Listen to me, old man. Ye kissed me because I wanted ye to. After our date I couldn't have been happier with how things went, the first time AND the second time. The whole time I've been with ye, you've made me feel special and wanted. Nothing like a whore at all. Might I remind ye it was me that wanted to go further that night and it was ye that was being very gentlemanly and kept to your word. D'ye know how that made me feel?"

I look down, not wanting to look into her eyes. "Embarrassed?" I offer.

She laughs at me and shakes her head softly. "No, ye bloody eejit. It made me feel special. Like ye didn't just want me so ye could break my cherry."

I stare at her in bemused shock.

"Did you just call me a bloody eejit and quote Goodfellas at me?"

She nods and smiles at me.

"Aye, I did. Ye are acting like an eejit so I called ye an eejit and tis my favourite filum."

I take her face into my hands and very softly put my lips on hers. Holding her there I tell her, "I've never wanted you more than right now, that film is my favourite. I love the way you say 'filum' too. Could you be any more perfect, Irish?"

I kiss her gently. She sighs and opens her mouth. I softly touch her tongue with mine. She grimaces a bit and I pull away.

"No, don't stop, Denny." I have to fight everything in me, but I pull away from her pleading pout.

"We've got plenty of time for that, Irish. We have to get you better first."

Chapter 17

Darcie

After a week and half of being in the hospital, I'm allowed home. Well, I say home, I'm not allowed back to my flat because Denny, Rebecca, Dan and Nat have forbidden me from doing so. Of course, I tried to argue with them, but they aren't letting me win on this one. I've gone along with it as I know I need a wee bit of TLC seeing as I'm contending with two broken ribs, a fractured collar bone and several cuts and bruises all over my body. When I saw the state of my face for the first time, I was absolutely devastated. There was a part of me, albeit a ridiculously small part, that thought maybe he wouldn't hurt me as badly as he did. After seeing the state of my face, I know now that had Denny not called at that point, I would've been dead. I look over at Sheila sitting on top of my holdall. "We'll be safe at the Blancs' house, ye will see. We'll be grand, Sheila."

She gives me her ever-knowing look. I take it to mean she agrees with me.

Denny walks in the door at that point and everything goes blank - ironically seeing as it's his last name. All I can focus on are his striking eyes and the wee beard he's been sporting for the past week. The man was a God before but with that wee bit of a beard on him he's turned into an Adonis before my eyes. I'm not the only one to notice either. Nurses are falling at his feet, their knees going weak with his smile, but his eyes are always focused on me. He watches me to see when I'm in pain. He notices every grimace, every flinch. His gaze has been so unwavering, he noticed when my jealousy took over and my fingers curled into my palms, my nails digging into my flesh to stop from scratching the nurses' eyes out for daring to look at him the same way I do. He smiled and took my hands into his and entwined our fingers together. He raised them to his lips and gently placed his mouth onto them. Letting not only the nurses, but also me, know that he's interested in no one else. Just me. Tis scary and intense but tis swaying me and urging me to believe this man wants me for more than just firsts. Firsts I can't wait to complete with him. If our first kiss and first others are anything to go by, I'm in for the time of my life with my bearded Adonis.

"You ready to go, Irish? Baby, earth to Darcie," Oh my, he's caught me staring at him again. I bite down on my bottom lip and instantly wince.

"Well, that's what you get for looking at me like that when there isn't a thing I can do to help take that look off your face." He walks over to me, softly brushes his lips on mine and helps me up. I'm wearing a pair of black leggings, flip flops and a vest with a denim coat thrown over the top. He bends down, close to my ear where I can feel his breath tickling me, and a shiver runs through my body.

"You're absolutely fucking beautiful and because of that look on your face, I have to walk out of here with a raging hard on. I hope you're happy with yourself, Irish." He kisses my cheek and I smile up at him.

"Ye are really tall when I'm wearing flats."

"I'm not that tall, you're just really short. My very own Polly Pocket." He chuckles back at me.

I can't help but roll my eyes at him because like I haven't been called that before. He grins mischievously down at me, and I can't fight the smile that sweeps over my lips. Nor do I want to. As we make our way to the car, I spot Joseph standing with the back door open for us. This man is another one who has gone above and beyond for me. A sudden gush of emotions threatens to overwhelm me, but I smile and swallow it down. Without him and Denny, I wouldn't be here right now, and I'll be forever grateful for that.

"Afternoon, Joseph."

He tips his head at me and smiles. Our gazes meet and I try to convey every bit of gratitude I feel. The slight twinkle in his eyes lets me know he sees it. Once we're in the car, I sit back and try to relax.

"Are you okay? Do you want us to pull over?"

I smile up at Denny, his eyebrows lowered and pulled together as his eyes scan over every inch of my body in concern.

"No, no, don't be silly. I'm not in pain, just uncomfortable. The sooner we get home the better. Well, the sooner we get to your home the better." Tis his turn to roll his eyes at me now.

"I've told you how many times? Just call it fucking home and be done with it. It's going to be your home for the foreseeable anyway. Nat should be getting into London soon."

I sigh and smile at him but stay quiet because I'm not having this argument with him again. We've gone back and forth about my living arrangements since Denny told me he moved all of my belongings out of my flat and into his house. Not asked me, mind ye, just told me I'd be moving in with him. I put up a protest, to save face of course, but if I'm honest with myself I'm so bloody happy tis unreal. Not only do I not have to go back to where it all happened, but I'll be in the same house as Denny. I don't want to be apart from him. He makes me feel safe. He's held me during my nightmares and promised to keep me safe no matter what, and I believe him. I need him right now. Having your daddy beat ye to near death will help to put everything into perspective, and these past two weeks have proved Denny is someone I **can** rely on. As scary as that is, and believe me, tis terrifying, I had no choice but to rely on him when I was at my most vulnerable. And he certainly stepped up.

My phone vibrates in my bag and Denny leans over to reach it for me. A smile stretches across my face when I see Nat's name on the screen.

"So tis true, Natalie, if ye talk of the ass, tis sure to appear." I breathe through my smile at her.

"Did you just call me a fucking ass, Darcie? What the hell?"

I laugh so hard and instantly regret it as a sharp pain shoots through my ribcage. "Ow don't make me laugh, Nat. Where are ye?"

"Well serves you right for calling me a donkey. You and your bloody Irish sayings. I'm just at Kings cross, I'll meet you at yours and Denny's in a little bit. I can't wait to give you a hug."

I smile even harder. "Me too, just don't squeeze too hard please. I'll see ye soon."

"That you will, treacle, that you will."

I hang up and turn to Denny. "She's going to be here in a bit. I can't wait for ye to meet her. Ye will love her. I know ye will. Everyone does. She's the best person on the planet." I tell Denny and he looks down at me and smiles. I'm so glad I'm sitting as I'm sure that smile of his made me go weak at the knees.

"I already love her, Irish. I feel like I've spoken to Nat more than I have my own friends in the past week. Is she sure she wants to stay in a hotel? There's plenty of room at the house and she's more than welcome to stay."

I'm so happy I could burst. Not only is this gorgeous Adonis of a man the most kind and caring person ever, sitting next to me, holding me and caring for me, but he's also adoringly talking about my bestie like that. Could he be any more perfect?

"No. Nat likes her own space and besides her company is paying for the hotel so she may as well stay there. I love that ye offered though so thank ye." He takes my hand out of my lap and laces his fingers in with mine, bringing them up to his lips.

"Anything for you."

As I walk up the steps to the house it feels different from the other times I've been here. I'm not here in a professional capacity anymore. I'm here as Denny's... I don't want to finish that sentence as I don't know what we are. We've had loads of conversations. We've talked about my mammy and my reluctance to date. He understood my situation a lot more after that. Even though I've opened up to him about my demons, he's still closed off to an extent with me. He's tried to explain why he freaked out when I didn't respond to him but it doesn't really add up. I haven't wanted to push him on it though. I can see that this 'problem' he has runs deep and he isn't ready to share and open up those old wounds yet. I can be patient. I can wait. I didn't have the chance to hide my secrets. They all came flooding out when my daddy turned up. I think that helped me understand it was okay to want to be close to a man. I wasn't weak for it. That was a big revelation for me.

Denny gently squeezes my hand as our footsteps come to a stop and I blow out a shaky breath. I'm worried about the kids seeing me. I don't want them to be scared of my bruises and cuts. Standing outside the door, I tighten my grip on Denny's hand and clutch onto it.

"Denny, what if they get upset? My heart won't take it." He bends towards me and kisses my forehead.

"Irish, the kids will be okay. They may be a bit taken aback, but they'll see it's still you. If they don't, I'll help them. Trust me."

I take a deep breath and nod at him. No hesitation. I trust him with my life. He's saved it once already so why wouldn't I?

I close my eyes and let Denny guide me inside. When I slowly open them, I see they're on the stairs waiting for us. I lower my head, instinctively letting my hair fall over my face. I don't want them to see me like this. My breathing picks up and I can feel the panic rise in my chest. I'm just about to bolt back out of the door when Isaac walks over and cuddles me ever so gently.

"I'm so glad you're okay, Darcie."

I squeeze his wee body as tightly as I can and wipe the tears that are falling from my eyes as he steps back and motions for his sisters to come over too.

Isabelle bounds over and points to my face and boldly asks me, "Does dat hurt? It looks like it hurts. When I fell off my bike, my knee hurt and dat was just one teeny cut. You gots loads." Exuding confidence, she rocks back on to her heels and puts her hands in her dungaree pockets.

I can't help but laugh at her, and when I hear Rebecca scold her, I shake my head at her.

"Please, Rebecca, she's grand." Smiling, I turn my attention back to Isabelle who has turned to face her mammy.

Isabelle says, "Yeah mummy, I'm grand."

Rebecca gives a look that tells her not to push it, but I see the twitch of a smile on her lips too.

"It does hurt a wee bit, Isabelle but not too bad. I bet your leg hurt worse."

She nods her head at me and then shrugs her shoulders and walks off towards the foot of the stairs. I seem to have staved off any more questions from her, but I notice Isla clinging to her daddy's legs. Denny steps forward and picks her up.

"Hey what's the matter, little Princess? She's still the same Darcie. She just has a few ouchies on her. Can I take you closer to see?"

She buries her face into his neck. She's clearly upset and I don't want to make it worse for her.

"Denny don't force her, please. I don't want her upset. Tis okay, Isla." I can feel tears filling my eyes at the thought of her scared of me, and my lip trembles as they threaten to spill down my face.

"Hey, Irish?"

My gaze meets Denny's and he tells me with his eyes to suck it up. I nod at him, and I force the emotion down. I take a few deep breaths as he bends his head to Isla's ear and whispers something none of us can hear. Slowly, she looks up. He walks over to us and she looks at my face. Her angelic blue eyes looking straight into mine. She leans forward, still in Denny's arms and kisses my cheek. Our gazes meet again.

"You look da same here." She points to my eyes and smiles at me.

She squirms out of her uncle's arms and Isabelle grabs her hand.

"Come on, let's go play doctors and nurses. You be Darcie. I'll be da doctor dat fixded her."

I watch transfixed as they run upstairs and then chuckle to myself.

Rebecca asks, "Denny, how did you do that? She's been scared all day and kept saying Darcie wouldn't be the same. I tried everything to get her to understand it was all superficial and she was indeed the very same Darcie as before."

Denny grins like the cat who's had the cream.

"A magician never reveals his secrets." He winks at Isaac and ruffles his hair as he walks past him and receives a stern look and an even sterner "Seriously?" from him.

He chuckles again as he leads me over to the guest bedroom, his hand on my lower back, stroking softly to reassure me everything is okay. Tis those sorts of wee things he does that's made opening up to him so much easier.

As the door opens, I stand in shock. This 'room' is bigger than my flat. I stand in the doorway looking inside in awe. Tis absolutely beautiful. There's a huge white framed wooden bed in the middle of the room, and across from that there's a single bed set up too. We walk inside and Denny points out the single bed.

"I'm not leaving you in the night in case you need anything, and I didn't want to roll over and hurt you whilst I was asleep, so I got a spare bed put in here."

I look up at him and smile. I seem to be doing that a lot now. His thoughtfulness is endless. He genuinely cares about me. I continue looking around and turn to him when he speaks again.

"That's the en suite through there. I would've had you upstairs in my room, as it's bigger, but the stairs are a no go at the moment."

As soon as the words 'had you' come out of his mouth I feel myself blush. I lower my head, so I'm looking at my feet, as I'm very aware my current employers are standing right next to him. I don't want them to think ill of me and I'm fairly certain they won't, but that wee voice in my head, my daddy's voice, is still there.

"Denny, will you and Dan go and make us some tea. I'll help Darcie settle in for a bit."

I could kiss Rebecca for that. She must have noticed my embarrassment and gave me a few moments to gather myself. I concentrate on keeping my breathing level and remind myself I've done nothing wrong by exploring my attraction with Denny.

"Darcie, do you want a cup of tea?" Denny asks, worry lacing his words. I nod at him with my head still lowered. I know my face is still bright red and I don't trust my voice to come out normally.

As he and Dan walk out, Rebecca comes over to me, picks up the bag Denny discarded and walks over to the bed. "You know you don't have to be embarrassed with Dan and me, Darcie. Even if Denny wasn't crazy about you and this had happened, I would've made you move in anyway."

I raise my head to look at her with my eyebrows raised to my hairline in shock.

She continues, "Who wouldn't want a live-in nanny, Darcie? Childcare twenty-four/seven. Heaven." She rolls her head back and clasps her hands in front of her chest as if praying and laughs.

I laugh with her, and just like that my embarrassment is gone and my daddy's voice is banished.

"I'm so sorry, Rebecca. I don't know what came over me. I was just very aware my bosses were standing there whilst their brother was talking about having me upstairs and I couldn't fend off the shame of it all." Rebecca's laughing again and I count to ten in my head to stop the anger bubbling inside of me. I hate being laughed at.

"Oh Darcie, just think of us as friends. I really mean that. You can start by calling me Becs." She looks me in the eyes and squeezes my hand. "And if Denny comes on a bit strong, just remember his heart is always in the right place. If you need me to though, I'll kick his arse from here to Timbuktu."

Laughter fills the room, and I unpack the stuff in my bags as Becs shows me where my belongings from the flat have been put. All the clothes are hanging in the walk-in wardrobe, and my laptop is on the wee desk on the other side of the room. Just as I take the last of my things out of the overnight bag I had in the hospital, Denny and Dan walk in.

"Becs, why are you letting her carry things? The doctor said she had to take it easy." Anger and worry flashes over his face and Denny rushes over to me, places my tea on the nightstand and takes the handful of clothes from me.

"Oh, shut up you bloody moron. It's a few bits of laundry and Darcie is more than capable of knowing what she can and can't do. Try to remember that or you'll stifle her to death." Becs looks at me and gives a wee smile of reassurance.

"Well, that put me in my fucking place, didn't it?" Denny is dragging his hand through his hair and I note the grin on Dans face that's not too dissimilar to the one Denny gives too.

"You've known her long enough to know she won't take your shit, Den. That's on your head, brother." He chuckles as he stalks over to his wife and places a kiss on her cheek.

Denny shakes his head and mutters, "Pussy whipped motherfucker."

"DENNIS BLANC!" I shout at him. Spurred on by Becs telling him off and unhappy with the words he uttered about his brother, I continue to admonish him. "He isn't what ye said he is. He's just in love with his beautiful wife and taking her side as ye were being a rude eejit to her. I'm perfectly capable of holding some clothes and I don't want ye being an arse to Becs again. Do ye hear me?" I use my best authoritative voice I normally use on children that are misbehaving, which means my accent got a bit thicker too. I lift my chin and look him square in the eyes to make my point clear. I can hear Becs and Dan snickering behind me, as Denny pouts and avoids my gaze.

"So, is this how it's going to be? You three teaming up to bring me down?" He grips onto the back of his neck and continues, "I think I might go and take my chances with Isabelle and Isla." He shoves his hands in his pockets and looks at the ground clearly sulking. It makes me want to kiss and coddle him. I don't, because the nanny in me tells me to stay where I am to assert my dominance. But my God, tis hard.

Dan and Becs shuffle toward the door, but she gives me a hug and whispers to me, "Handled nicely, Darcie. I'm going to love having you here. If you need me just shout." She looks over at Denny and sticks her tongue out at him which gets her a smirk back. Their sibling-like relationship is lovely to witness. Growing up as an only child I didn't have this banter or someone to go to bat for me. Dan waves at me from the door and I smile back at him. As the door closes Denny and I are finally alone.

"So, are ye going to sulk all day or what?" I ask him.

He looks up at me with a sullen face.

"That depends. Are you going to be on my side next time? They already have each other. I brought you here for me." He looks down at the floor, sticks his hands into his pockets again and kicks at the carpet.

The nanny in me subsides and the girl who wants to kiss him so badly is at the forefront of my mind, screaming to let her at him. I walk over to him and lace my hands around his waist. "Bend down and kiss me, old man. I can't reach ye all the way up there."

He gives me a sly grin letting me know he'd been playing me all along, but before I can voice my protest about it, his lips meet mine. My mouth is still sore, but I've waited too long for a proper kiss from him. He's gentle and slow, and his lips massage over mine, almost as if he's helping them to heal. As our tongues caress each other, his hand moves around my waist and very gently, pulls me to him. I can feel his erection on the top of my stomach. My nipples are straining against the material of my bra and even though we're fully clothed I can feel the heat from his skin. I faintly hear a knock at the door and break our kiss away, much to Denny's groan of disappointment.

"Darcie. Look what you do to me!" He gestures down to his groin area, and I laugh at his very apparent erection.

I walk over to the door and squeal with delight when I see Nat. I'm so happy I don't quite grasp why she's looking so horrified. It suddenly dawns on me as she grabs me for a hug, and I wince slightly.

"Shit, Darcie. I'm sorry, babe. I forgot. Are you okay?"

I nod at her as best as I can with her arms wrapped around me still, when I hear her chuckle.

"Well, hello sailor... You seem very happy to see me. I'm assuming you're Denny?" I turn around to see Denny scurrying behind the bed trying to hide his erection. Giggles escape from my mouth, which makes him groan at me as he ducks down and out of our sight.

"Natalie! Stop it. Denny, this is Nat. Nat, that was Denny." I can't stop laughing at him. He looked like a rabbit caught in headlights.

He mutters, "Hi," to Nat from behind the bed and rushes into the en suite to calm himself down.

As my eyes meet Nat's, we both break into fits of giggles again. And when he appears a few minutes later we're still laughing like school girls.

"Stop laughing at me. It's your bloody fault, woman." He points at me and shoots me an accusatory look. I hold my hands up in defence. Nat clears her throat and pretends to hit an imaginary glass in a mock toast kind of way.

"I would just like to say, congratulations, Darcie. Once you're all healed, you, me old mucker, are in for a fucking treat from what I saw." She wiggles her eyebrows at me.

Denny collapses into laughter as my face flushes bright red.

"Oh, Nat, I fucking love you, I do." He grabs her into a hug and then walks out mimicking her.

"Me old muckers, I'll leave you to catch up."

Chapter 18

Darcie

Minutes turn into hours and we've only been disturbed by Denny bringing us cups of tea and biscuits.

"Blimey, you've got him well trained." Nat says, laughing as Denny brings us another cup of tea and my painkillers.

"Well, I had to find a replacement for my last nursemaid as she abandoned me for bloody Paris. How is it over there?" I narrow my eyes at her because I know something isn't right.

"I bloody hate it, Darcie. The people aren't as nice as I thought they were going to be and I miss everything about London, especially you. I'm thinking of handing my notice in. I don't know where I'd live or what I'd do but it's a thought. A serious one too." She grimaces at me and I grab her hand and squeeze it tightly.

"Natalie, if ye are miserable, ye come home right away do ye hear me? We'll sort something out. We can go and look at flats and can find ye a job, no worries. Just come home. Life's too short for ye to be miserable." My voice breaks with emotion when I say that to her, and she gives a wee laugh.

"Hark at you. A month ago you were as miserable as sin, had been for years, and now, well look at you." Her eyes shine with pride for me so I motion to my face.

"Aye, I'm positively glowing if cuts and old bruises are your ting, that is?" I lower my face as she shakes her head at me and nudges me with her foot.

"No, you giant numpty. You look happy. Denny makes you happy, doesn't he?"

I nod at her and bite my bottom lip gently.

"I don't even know him though, Nat. Of course he knows all about my charming daddy, but I don't know anything about him. We walked into this as two people that didn't do emotions or feelings and certainly didn't do relationships and now, I don't know what the hell's happening. I don't know if he's doing all of this because he feels obligated to or what. Tis all a bloody mess and I don't want to approach it because I don't want to ruin it all. When I'm with him, I do feel happy. And more importantly, safe." I look down at my hands in my lap and tears spill out.

Nat is up in a shot and cuddling me gently so as not to hurt my broken ribs. "Oh Darcie, you're so new to all of this, sometimes I forget. Communication is key in any relationship. Talk to him. He's a good guy. Believe me, I can tell. I've kissed enough frogs for the both of us to be able to spot a Prince Charming among them."

She kisses me on the cheek and goes back to her chair by my luxurious bed Denny insisted I get into after I'd taken my pain killers. Even though I grumbled and fought him on it, I'm glad he did as I can feel myself getting sleepy. I try to stifle a yawn, but it ends up coming out.

"And that's my cue to leave, I'll see you later sleeping beauty."

The darkness I wake up to confuses me. I normally sleep with my wee light on. Trying to clear my sleepy head I figure the bulb has probably gone out in the middle of the night. I reach over to get my phone, but I can't find it on my nightstand. I try to sit up and wince.

"Ow Jesus, Mary and Joseph." And with that sharp painful reminder of where I am and why I hurt, everything comes crashing back to me.

"What's the matter? Are you okay?"

I jump and let out another hiss as pain sears through my side.

"Ye bloody eejit ye scared the life out of me." My eyes are trying to scan the room but haven't adjusted to the darkness when the room is illuminated by what seems like a million lights. I squint and look over at the door which is firmly closed. When I look over to the left my breath catches in my throat as I see my Adonis, dressed only in a pair of briefs. I forget all about the blinding light trying to burn my retinas off because Denny is a sight for sore eyes anyway. I try to get my breathing under control and bite on my bottom lip and wince. The pain from my lip doesn't stop my knickers from dampening instantly though.

"Denny. My God, ye look like an Adonis." I utter.

The look in his eyes goes from anxious to liquid desire in a flash. He lets out a cross between a growl and a groan as he stalks over to the bed.

"Don't call me that, Irish. And certainly don't look at me with eyes screaming sex when I can't touch you. Do you know how hard this is for me?"

I can't help it. My gaze travels the length of his body and settles on his erection. I giggle and nod at him. He shakes his head and walks the rest of the way to the bed. I need to touch him so badly, but I also know I won't be able to physically take any kind of touch from him right now. Tis been too long since that first time. He gets onto the bed and kisses me tenderly.

"You're a very naughty girl, Irish." He kisses my nose and leans back against the headboard. He sits upright with his hands behind his head. His legs are fully stretched out, his erection very visible. I scoot closer to him and kiss him on the cheek and let my lips explore his face with my kisses. I gently bring my hand to his erection and wrap my fingers around it.

He groans and shakes his head. "Darcie, you should be resting, not doing this." He tries to move away but I hold him tighter.

"Denny. Please let me. I'm grand." He looks into my eyes, and I move my hand up and down along his shaft. He moans loudly. The sound sets a fire inside of me but suddenly he stops me for a second time and jumps off the bed. Rejection and humiliation flood through me as he runs into the bathroom. I don't have time to do anything as he dashes back into the room clutching a cloth. The confusion etched on my face slowly disappears as recognition dawns on me. I smirk at him.

He shrugs his shoulders at me impishly and asks, "Are you sure?" I nod my head at him. He quickly rids himself of his boxers and my mouth waters at the sight of him standing naked before me. My Adonis. He gently climbs onto the bed and brings his lips to mine, kissing me hard. I don't care that it hurts the cut on my bottom lip, I need to feel his lips on mine. He releases my mouth and lowers his head toward my nipple.

"Tell me if I hurt you. Please." He looks up at me,

begging, and I nod to him. He lifts my vest top down and takes my nipple in his mouth as I groan in delight. My hand reaches out to grip him again. As I move it up and down on him, his tongue swirls around, and his teeth graze my nipple causing me to shudder. He lifts his head and takes the other nipple into his mouth, continuing his onslaught. His breathing gets deeper and more ragged. He pulls my nipple deeper into his mouth, the sensation becoming more intense. I can feel myself building to an orgasm simply from nipple stimulation and from the feel of him in my hand. He changes positions quickly so he's straddling my legs without putting any of his weight on me. His erection is easier to get to now and I'm able to grip it tighter. I squeeze my hand around him and glide the silky skin, up and down, faster and faster until he throws his head back and cries out in ecstasy.

"Fuck, Darcie." I watch him as he comes. He's mesmerising. His head's thrown back in pleasure and his whole body tenses up, making his chiselled physique look even more sculpted. Pride emanates from me, I did that to him, and my smile shows him how happy I am.

He looks down at me and gives me a kiss on the top of my head.

"I'm sorry you didn't... Let me go get cleaned up and we can sort that out. I'll be back in a minute." Confusion sweeps through me and he motions with his head down. I follow his gaze to see he's holding the cloth over himself. I bury my face into my hands giggling like a schoolgirl.

He waits for me to finish and I tell him, "Sorry, go. But we probably shouldn't do anything more, it'll hurt too much." He nods at me sadly and dashes off to the bathroom. After a few minutes he's back.

"Sorry, Darcie. I didn't want to come all over you again, it didn't seem right..."

He looks down and away from me which makes me furious.

"Why? Did I tell ye I didn't like it?" I'm angry with him for thinking the way he is. He thinks that act would make me feel cheap and dirty, like a whore, and would remind me of my so-called daddy, but he can't be further from the truth. Tis bad enough I have that man's words in my head, I don't want them in Denny's as well.

"No, you didn't but I thought– Well I thought– Shit. Darcie, why are you mad at me?" Confusion marring his perfect face.

I sit up straighter in the bed, wincing as I do. "Don't ye dare try to help me, Denny Blanc. I'm too fecking pissed with ye," I shoot at him when he jumps to offer help to me and I note the shock on his face when I swear at him.

"I didn't tell ye I didn't like it because I didn't not like it. Wait, let me start again – don't ye dare laugh at me, old man, now's not the time."

He raises his hands up in apology and the smirk forming on his face is soon gone.

"Now ye listen to me, Denny Blanc and ye listen good. Nothing ye have ever done or said has made me feel like a whore. If it did, I would tell ye. In fact, I did like it. There I said it. I don't know what that makes me, but it made me feel – it made me feel like I was yours." I say the last bit quieter, running out of steam and slightly confused as I really hadn't meant to take it in that direction. I have now and tis out there, and he's just looking at me with his mouth open and his blue eyes hidden under a hooded look. My sass and anger fades away and regret fills the silence. I look down at my hands in my lap and curse silently at myself.

"It made me feel like that too, Darcie."

He speaks so quietly I almost miss it.

"I don't know if it's the basic animalistic urges in me or

not, but it felt like I'd marked you in some way. That other people would be able to know you're mine. I've never wanted a woman to be mine before and it scares me."

I look up at him. The usual mischief that dances in his eyes is gone and replaced with vulnerability. This makes him even more attractive to me. He's opening up to me.

"I feel the same, Denny. I'm more than a wee bit terrified that if I commit to any kind of relationship, with anyone, I'll end up like my mammy. I can't end up like her."

I hear him sigh. "Darcie. I would never physically hurt you, EVER, and I hope you know that. That's not to say I wouldn't hurt you, emotionally, and that's what scares me. That I'll eventually ruin everything like I always do."

His face is shrouded with guilt and sadness. I want to take it all away from him, but I also want to know why?

"Denny," I say very tentatively. "Why do ye say that? What happened to ye for ye to think that way of yourself?"

His head is bowed down, and his breathing is slow and steady, like he's controlling it on purpose. He swallows and drags his hand through his jet-black hair, the sadness and vulnerability that's etched onto his face makes my stomach feel nauseated. I know something bad's happened either to him or by him and I desperately want to know what. But I'm also scared tis something that will alter the way I'm starting to feel about him.

I wait for him to speak but no words come. Instead, he gets up and goes straight into the en suite. I can't do anything but sit in the bed, feeling confused and worried. I don't know whether to go after him or to wait it out. I decide on the latter as I don't want to push him before he's ready. Again, tis like he gives a wee bit of himself to me and then retreats back even more. A wee while later the door opens slowly. Denny comes out and walks over to the bed.

"Darcie, it's time for your pain killers. Here."

I look up at him, my eyes burning with anger, and I'm just about to rip into him when my icy stare meets his. The desperation in his haunted eyes is enough to make me stop. My anger disappears. I take the pills from his hand and place them on the nightstand. As he retreats, I grab his wrist.

"Denny, I won't push ye. I don't want ye to feel pressured into anything. Just like you've been patient with me, I'll be patient with ye. But listen, old man: if ye run, I'll chase ye. And when ye feel like ye can, talk to me, please." I stare up at him and he drops to his knees at the side of the bed and hugs me. He holds me as tightly as he can without hurting me, and when he releases me, he places his hand on my cheek and I lean into him.

"Darcie, when I'm ready..."

I nod at him not needing anything more. I pat the empty space next to me in the bed. "Come on, let's get some rest."

He looks at the space and then to me. "What if I knock you in the night or roll over onto you? I don't want to hurt you. I'll sleep in the single bed."

I give him my sternest look and use my nanny voice again.

"Denny Blanc, either ye get your backside into this bed, or I'll come and join ye in the wee one. The choice is yours, but I think there's more chance of ye rolling on top of me and hurting me in that one."

He shakes his head and grins at me. It's not the full-on mischievous grin I'm now so used to, but tis a grin nonetheless.

"Okay, you win. But only because the first time I roll on top of you I want you to be writhing in ecstasy, not agony." He kisses me on the lips faintly and jumps into the bed. I lay next to this Godlike man and can't help worry about what he's holding back from me. I want him to trust me enough to tell me and I want to trust myself enough to not run from it too.

Chapter 19

Denny

"Denny, tis been four weeks now. My bruises are barely visible anymore and the cuts have all but healed. My ribs are sore, but nothing compared to what they were like before. I'm grand and want to go back to work."

I pace around the room, uncomfortable and agitated.

"What if Isabelle falls and needs to be picked up or – or – Isla's crying, and you need to bend down to her?" I ask her. I'm trying to think of the worst-case scenarios and those are the best two I can come up with. And they are, I must admit, weak. Her eyes are laughing at me, but her face remains straight. Her poker face is getting better and I blame Nat and Becs for that.

"Denny, ye are being crazy. I'd literally be going outside of my bedroom door to look after two of the sweetest wee girls ever. And ye know Isaac won't have me doing anything that could put me at risk when he's home. The girls understand I've had my 'ouchies' and they know I can't pick them up. I've basically been working for the past four weeks anyway as I'm in the house with them and Becs. At least with me 'working' properly, she'd be able to go back to her job and I wouldn't feel like a massive burden on everyone. Plus, I need to try to make some money so I can look at flats, as I can't go back to my old place. Not that I'd ever want to."

My head flies up at the mention of her leaving, panic rising through my body and etching itself across my face. I don't want her to leave. In my stupid head, when she was healed, she would move upstairs and into my room. She obviously isn't thinking along those lines. I thought she was in the same place as me when it came to us. I know we haven't had a conversation about what we are, but she's admitted on several occasions she's mine and I'm hers. They're normally words spoken when we've been 'getting to know each other better,' but still. I thought they meant something. They did to me. Trying to hide my upset, I clear my throat and turn away from her.

"Fine. I'll cave on the work thing but please wait until the end of the week. It's only two more working days so I'm not being unreasonable. Please?" I turn back to look at her and see her nodding her head. I kiss her with my gratitude and because I desperately want to feel close to her. I don't like the idea of her slipping through my fingers. I need to come up with a way of making her stay.

"Go and take a nice hot bubble bath and enjoy your last days as a lady of leisure." I tell her with as much normality in my voice as I can muster and head out the door.

Once I'm in the hallway, I blow out a ragged breath and squeeze my eyes shut. I don't want her to leave. I need her with me. I fall asleep cuddling her, smelling her hair, fucking spooning the shit out of her and now she wants to leave? I push myself off the door and head into the kitchen where Becs is cleaning up after the kids' breakfast.

"Hey Becs, I need your help."

She stops wiping the table down and gives me a dirty look.

"Morning to you too, Denny. No, no I don't need any help. Please, just come in here and demand things of me seeing as I don't have three children and a husband doing that already." She scowls, throws the cleaning cloth at me and stomps over to the sink.

"Holy shit, what crawled up your arse this morning?" I chuckle at my quick wit but then firmly shut my mouth when the look she shoots me makes me shiver to my soul. I raise my hands in surrender and her death gaze relents slightly.

"Den, I'm sorry. This morning has been an exceptionally challenging one. The girls were being she-devils, and your brother is a pain in the arse and can't say no to them ever, and to top it all off, work called. They're really struggling with me working from home. Only so much you can do when you're needed to be on location taking the pics rather than at home editing them. The sooner Darcie comes back to work the better. How is she?"

I feel like shit. Here, Becs is struggling and a mere few minutes ago I was trying to get Darcie to never go back to work again.

"Well, that's what I wanted to speak to you about. Darcie wants to come back on Monday." I tuck my hands into my pockets and shift on my feet so my back is facing the door. She looks at me suspiciously but I carry on.

"I've had my doubts, obviously after what she's been through, but she put up a very convincing argument so I can't moan anymore. So, Monday morning she's here to work. Take the pressure off you a bit." Becs smiles at me and sighs a happy sigh, but then shoots me a quizzical look.

"So, what did you need help with?" I look down and kick at the floor, trying to think of the right words to tell her my concerns.

"The thing I have an issue with is she wants to go to

work so she can find a new flat and I don't want her to leave, but I'm too fucked up and stupid to tell her to stay. Can you offer her a live-in role instead?" I lift my eyes to look at her and I'm a little bit shocked to see Becs staring at me with an insane grin on her face. I mean, I knew she'd be happy Darcie was coming back to work but surely not this happy.

"Erm, sure, Denny. I would absolutely love for Darcie to be living here permanently. I've said it before and I'll say it again, childcare twenty-four/seven sounds like a dream come true. Although, I think you'll find she's pretty perceptive. Probably already knows you don't want her to leave and even knows you're here speaking with me about it too. My advice is to talk to *her* and tell *her* how you feel. Communication is key and all." She stands there grinning inanely at me, and I blow an exasperated sigh at her.

"No shit sherlock. Speaking to her would be the ideal choice to make but I can't. I've tried and the words won't come out. Plus, if she's looking to get out maybe she wants away from me. Maybe George is waiting for her. I don't know, Becs. I just don't want her to go." I sound desperate and pathetic, and I don't even care. I just need her help to get Darcie to stay. Becs tips her head to the side and smiles at me like a big sister, then motions with her head behind me and an overwhelming feeling of someone being there takes over me. I spin around quickly and see Darcie standing in the doorway, looking at me with an expression I can't quite understand on her face. Without saying a word, I turn back to Becs.

"Shit, Becs. Really? You're meant to be my sister for fucks sake." I give her my best dirty look but she just shrugs at me and smiles sweetly. The woman is infuriating and if I hadn't known her for forever, I would be seriously pissed off at her. I turn back and catch Darcie walking straight back to the bedroom. I run my hand through my hair and tug on the ends. I hesitate, unsure of what her reaction will be.

"Denny Blanc, I'm waiting."

Instantly I'm turned on. She sounds like a schoolteacher and I'm about to get a telling off for being a naughty boy. What the fuck is wrong with me? The woman's pissed off with me and all I can think about is a kinky schoolboy fantasy? I try to hide my grin, but as I walk to the bedroom door, I hear Becs giggling. I shoot her a dirty look and then wink at her.

She shakes her head at me and rolls her eyes, she knows what I was thinking. Bracing myself at the door, feeling a little bit scared but still aroused, I walk in and find Darcie standing with her arms folded across her chest and her foot tapping the floor. My grin is gone, and my anxiety creeps back in. I keep my gaze down on my feet and I try to talk but find myself stuttering all over the place.

"Darcie, I– I don't– I can't– SHIT!" I throw my head back and pull at my hair. Why am I so tongue tied? I take a deep breath and make my eyes meet hers. "I don't want you to leave. I understand if you don't want to stay in my room with me, but I don't think I'd be okay if you left the house. I like having you here. I like knowing you're safe. I like falling asleep next to you and being able to reach over in the night and touch you or smell your hair. I know you don't want to stay here, and we were supposed to be a temporary thing, but please think about staying." I look down for the last words, unable to handle the rejection in her face when she tells me she doesn't want me anymore. I can't face it. I was rejected by the one woman who was *supposed* to want me, and that didn't hurt half as much as I think it will if Darcie doesn't want me too.

"Denny, look at me." Her voice isn't as stern as I expect, and I slowly raise my head to look at her. "I never said I didn't want to stay, did I? I didn't know it was an option. I like being here too. I like falling asleep next to ye too. I like feeling safe and I like exploring what we have going on here... but I'm scared." Her head dips and it's my turn to speak.

"Of what? Me?" I hold my breath. I don't want her to say yes and I'm terrified she will.

"Yes and no."

My head slumps down and it feels like I can't breathe. She's scared of me. It didn't take as long as I hoped it would. The darkness envelops me and I grab the back of my neck.

"Shit, Darcie. I would never hurt you. I'm so sorry. I've ruined it all like I knew I would. Listen, I'll help you find a flat and I'll stay upstairs from now on. I'm really sorry. You're scared of me?" I can feel the hatred for myself wash over me as I turn on my heel and walk the few steps to the door. The shadows that were kept at bay when I met her are sweeping over me now that I've lost her. Her light is evaporating and my darkness is closing in. Feeling dejected and fuelled with self-loathing, I grab the door handle.

"If ye walk out of this room without finishing this conversation with me, I'll be so fecking mad with ye, old man. Bloody listen, will ye? Ye infuriate me sometimes. Argh!"

As I start to open the door something hits me in the back. Stunned by Darcie shouting and swearing, I turn around and see a pillow on the floor at my feet.

"Did you just throw a pillow at me?" I ask as a grin spreads across my face. I bring my head up to look at her. Her face is pale, and she looks like she's about to collapse. I'm by her side and she's in my arms in seconds, as I stroke her face.

"Darcie, what's the matter? Baby, talk to me." I desperately want to make that stricken look on her face disappear and never come back. I stroke her hair and try to soothe her.

She mumbles, "I'm so sorry. I'm so sorry." She covers her face in her hands and sobs in my arms.

"Are you okay?" I stroke her cheek and take the glass of water from her grasp. My other arm is wrapped around her shoulders pulling her into me so we're as close as we can be. She nods at me and leans into my side.

"I'm sorry. I should never have thrown anything at ye. I got so angry with ye for not letting me finish what I was saying and the next thing I knew I was throwing something at ye. I couldn't help it."

I smile down at her and try to reassure her. "Darcie, it was only a pillow. Don't worry about it. It didn't hurt. And I shouldn't have been running. I was just upset and disappointed to hear you're scared of me. I'd never hurt you. I wanted you to know that. I thought you did." My voice is as sincere as I can make it, willing her to believe me.

She sighs at me. "It doesn't matter it was just a pillow, Denny. I let my anger get the better of me. I won't be like my daddy. I won't hit or throw things in a fit of rage. I can't be like him." She cries again, and it all makes sense to me.

"Darcie, are you for real right now? You are sweet, kind, caring, honest and tender. The nicest woman in the world. The best person I've ever met. You're nothing like him. It's my fault. Apparently, I'm enough to bring out the worst in anyone." I force a chuckle out and try to make it sound like a joke, but know I've failed when I hear how upset my voice sounds.

With that little admission her head flies up and searches

my eyes, but I manage to shield them from her by hugging her closer to me and carry on quickly.

"Like I said before, I shouldn't be leaving, and I should've had the balls to talk to you about our living situation and not go running to Becs. I'm sorry. I just didn't want you to go. I panicked. I didn't think you'd stay for me, but I knew you'd stay for her and the kids. I was being a selfish bastard and I'm sorry for that." I loosen my grip on her and let my arm drop away from her shoulders. I put my hands in my lap, not knowing what else to say.

She reaches over and takes my hand and entwines our fingers.

"Denny, I would've stayed for ye. When I said yes and no to being scared of ye, what I meant was, no ye don't scare me physically as I know ye would never hurt me like he did, EVER. I trust ye. The way you've looked after me, and not just whilst I was healing but the way you've looked after me since ye first met me. Not many men would have been so patient."

She nudges me and I look at her, not really believing what she's saying but desperately hoping she means it.

"But I am scared of ye, though. I'm scared because I want ye so much. I promised myself I'd never become dependent on a man and living here with ye, and giving up my independence, scares the bejeezus out of me. Especially when we haven't known each other for very long."

I try to speak but emotion clogs my throat, so she carries on.

"I'm scared by living here, I'll want more than what we originally planned and ye won't. I'd be heartbroken AND homeless. I'm scared after we've shared my firsts, ye won't want me anymore. And I'm bloody scared I'll lose my job and not see those wee faces anymore."

She's fiddling with the hem of her top as I just stare at

her. The immense amount of courage it must've taken for her to speak those words is a true testament to how strong she really is. It terrifies me, though. What if I do break her? I'm not good enough for her. She's too good, too pure. I can see the anguish on her face deepening, and I know I need to say something. I want to tell her to run from me and find someone who deserves her. Someone who can promise her everything I can't. She deserves someone good, someone who isn't shrouded in darkness. Someone who doesn't have demons from his past that he has to face daily. But I'm a selfish bastard and I can't let her go. I need her. Her lightness. Her voice. Her smell. Her.

"Darcie, I'm scared too. I'm scared I'm not good enough for you. I'm scared I'm going to ruin this because I'm a major fuck-up and have been my entire life. I walked into this telling myself it was just going to be a fling, just get the firsts done and that's it, but I never genuinely believed it. From the very first time we kissed, I knew you were mine. I'm not saying I know what's going to happen because this is all new territory for me too but..." My palms are sweating, and my hands are shaking. I take a deep breath.

"I really fucking like you, Irish, and I want to see what this is that we have. I want you to stay but I want you to feel comfortable. Would you consider staying in the guest room whilst I went back upstairs to my room, please?" I don't have to wait long for an answer as she nods her head shyly.

"I don't want to take your independence away from you, ever. If you decide you don't want to be here anymore. I'll find you a flat in your price range and in the location you want. You wouldn't be homeless..."

She interrupts me. "George is a homeless guy I met whilst I was on the phone to Nat talking about ye. He isn't another option or anything, by the way."

I blink a couple of times and then laugh; I can't help

myself. I throw my head back and belly laugh. It isn't the information she's given me that's made me laugh but the way she told me. Just blurting it out in the middle of my sentence. Her eyes are flashing a warning sign at me and I hold my hands up to apologise.

"I'm not laughing at you, Irish. I swear I'm not. And I'm not laughing at George's situation at all, just the way you came out with it. I'm sorry." I try to gain my composure whilst watching her intently and I see her eyes soften a bit.

"Ye know I don't like to be laughed at. He told me some personal information the day after we – well I didn't want to break his trust by telling ye about it so that's why I said he's just a friend. Had I known that ye had it in your stupid eejit head that we were romantically linked, I would've told ye sooner. Why haven't ye mentioned this before, Denny?"

She turns to face me head on and the smile vanishes from my face.

"I didn't know if I wanted to hear the truth. I thought he was a potential boyfriend. Becs told me to talk to you. To stop being jealous and communicate. And I was going to. Then all hell broke loose, and it just never seemed like the right time." I look at her with a small smile on my face asking for forgiveness for being such a jealous and arrogant fool.

She nudges me in the side and shakes her head.

"Can ye please listen to Rebecca a bit more? There's nothing going on with George at all, apart from me buying him muffins and hot beverages."

I reach down and take her hand and kiss the back of it. She's the kindest person I've ever known, and I was a jealous let down. If I'd just asked, and spoken to her in a calm way that day, she wouldn't have run out of the house and straight into her dad. She wouldn't have been hurt. It's all my fault. I caused it all. I need to let her go. The darkness creeps over me. I drop my head, defeated.

"Darcie, maybe you shouldn't stay here. I want you to, but I don't think I'll be right for you. You deserve someone better, someone good. If you stay and get hurt again because of me – I don't think I'll survive it. I'm sorry." I drop her hand and get off the bed. She grabs my wrist and puts her hand back into mine.

"My childhood. I had everything decided for me. Manipulated into thinking things about myself that weren't true. By him. I can even see my mammy should have done things differently in my life for herself as well as me. Ye, Nat, Becs and Dan have shown me that. She *chose* to stay there and I *had* to stay because of her decision. Please let me make my own choices about whom I have MY firsts with and whom I share a house with. I want to stay here in the guest room. I WANT YE, DENNIS BLANC! I'm doing what *I* want for a change. Please don't stop me. Denny, what happened wasn't your fault. He had my address. If I hadn't left at that time, he would've been waiting for me whenever I did go home. The only person to blame is him. Not ye. Please believe me."

She reaches up and touches my face and I kiss her hands, the darkness retreating as it always does when she touches me. She kisses my lips tentatively and I kiss her back, firmly and possessively. She's staying and she's mine. For now. That's all I can ask of her. I'll enjoy my time with her and savour every second of it until the time comes for her to know about my darkness and regret everything about me and her.

Chapter 20

Denny

A few days turn into a few weeks. The happiest weeks of my life. Darcie has stayed downstairs in the guest room and I've slept over with her some days. I made myself stay upstairs away from her as well, so she didn't feel like I was taking her independence. We've gone on several dates and all of them have ended with us exploring our bodies and me giving her endless orgasms. I've made her blank out a few more times, which I've now labelled 'the Blanc move', much to Darcie's annoyance. We haven't had all her firsts yet. I'm planning something special for that. Nat is officially back in London now, she's found a little place around the corner from us, and tonight, we're going out to celebrate with everyone.

This is a massive first for me. I've never been out with Becs, Dan and a girlfriend of mine, ever. I've never had a girlfriend before. Is that what Darcie is? My girlfriend? I suppose she is. We haven't had the talk about our relationship, but we're doing everything boyfriends and girlfriends do, so...

As I look over my appearance in the mirror, I take note of the nerves that are shining in my eyes. I laugh at myself and shake my head as I step out onto the landing. I can hear chatting and laughter from downstairs and realise Joseph and Gorgeous are here already. I look over at the playroom and send a silent thank you that the kids are with Becs's parents for the night. Isabelle and Isla cornered me earlier and I could do with a break away from those two, who have inherited their mothers bloodhound abilities and unrelenting questioning.

"Uncle Denny." They'd started off so sweetly. "Do you love us?"

I was really suckered in. Without hesitation I replied, "More than anything in the world. You two and Isaac are my heartbeats."

They looked at each other and then turned back to me, mischief in their eyes.

"Would you do anyfing for us?"

Again, without missing a beat I replied, "Anything. What's going on with you two?"

They giggled and then Isabelle asked very sweetly, "Do you love Darcie?" Her eyes narrowed suspiciously.

It was like looking at a mini Becs and I could never bloody lie to Becs.

"Erm, well it's complicated, Princess. I don't know what love really feels like. I care for her a lot though." My eyes darted away from her so she couldn't read anything in them. I'm telling you; MI5 should employ Becs and the girls to interrogate people, they're that good.

"What's compo-cay-ted?" She shrugged her shoulders and Isla told me, "You know what love is cause you love me." She batted her eyes at me and I smiled down at her.

"You love Darcie, too." Isabelle told me as her bossiness washed over her. She put her hands on her hips to really emphasise her stance.

I found myself staring down at my nieces with a look of

shock on my face. I swooped them up in my arms and looked at their identical beautiful little faces.

"When did you two get so grown up and clever, eh?" They squealed in delight and when I put them down, I was hoping I'd avoided any more questions. Isla rounded on me, they were tag teaming me and they knew Isla's sweetness was my weakness.

"Uncle Denny?"

She looked up at me and I could already feel myself go weak at the knees. The only other girl who could make me turn to mush besides these two was Darcie.

"We like seein you happy." Isla smiled up at me.

Isabelle then took over from her, making me bat my head back and forth to look at them as they each took turns to speak.

"We like seein Darcie happy."

Isla continued, "We fink you two look like a Prince and Princess togever."

I looked at Isabelle, expecting her turn.

"We fink you love her, and mummy and daddy fink it too."

"Even Isaac knows." Isla informed me.

"I don't fink it's compo-cay-ted, Uncle Denny." Isabelle said and placed her hands back on her hips.

"You love da Princess. You can live happy ever after in our castle-home." Isla clasped her hands under her chin and sighed out to me.

"We know dat's gonna happen. You know it, Uncle Denny." Isabelle huffed out on a different kind of sigh than her sister's.

Isla nudged her and sweetly asked me, "Will you try to know as well?"

My head felt like it was going to explode, just like it always does when they double act me. They were both stand-

ing, one on each side of my legs, and stared up at me with their angel faces. I swooped them up, one in each arm, and turned my head to look at each of them in turn.

"I will try to know it as well." They snuggled into me and I hugged them tightly. These two beautiful, intelligent little bloodhounds had just made me realise I was in love with Darcie. I thought I was falling, but with a little help from them I realised I fell a long time ago and kept falling more and more. Now that I knew I loved Darcie, I wanted to tell her, but I was terrified of her not loving me back.

Instinctively, as if they'd read my thoughts, Isla spoke.

"Da Princess loves da Prince back, Uncle Denny." She giggled.

Her sister grabbed my cheek and turned my face to look at her. She nodded her head and told me, "Yep, she does."

I laughed with them and kissed them each on the head and put them down.

I shake my head to try to rid myself of the memory but find myself asking questions. What if she did love me back? Could she have fallen for me as easily as I've fallen for her? She couldn't, she doesn't know me properly. She doesn't know the darkness that follows me everywhere, I remind myself bitterly. Fairy tales don't happen in real life, not for me anyway. I don't deserve them, but it was a nice thought, living happily ever after and all that.

I stalk into the kitchen and over to Gorgeous to give her a big kiss on the cheek and stand behind her as she sits on a stool, my arms wrapped around her tightly.

"Hello, my Gorgeous, you smell divine today." I nuzzle my head into her neck and smell her dramatically.

She giggles at me. "Rascal, I like this smile on you, keep it on your face."

"Do you want to let my woman go now?"

I turn my head to see Joseph looking at me and laugh whilst squeezing her tighter. "Nope, she's mine, all mine." I feign horror and pout at her as she swats at my arms. "Gorgeous, I thought I meant something to you." She rolls her eyes and tuts at me through a smile.

"Any other man had his hands on her, and I wouldn't be responsible for my actions. It's a good thing I like you." Joseph's grinning at me, but I notice how he steps closer to her and places his hand on her lower back.

Smiling at him, I'm just about to respond when a movement from the kitchen door catches my eye. As my eyes focus, I see a vision. A fucking amazing one. My Darcie. Her dress is wrapped around her like a bandage that stops just above the knee. It hugs her body deliciously. It's so tight I can see every curve on her. And the colour, sky blue, makes her eyes look clear. She's styled her hair into loose waves and has them swooped over one shoulder. Her make-up is barely there, which I love as I get to see her face and her beautiful freckles. She finishes the outfit with strappy heels that show off her sexy little feet. There's a part of me that wants to take her back to her bedroom, rip the dress off and ravish her all night long. But there's the other part that wants to take her out on my arm and show the world she's mine.

"Do I have to find myself another date for the night, old man?" Her voice gives away the nerves she's trying to hide behind her statement.

I'm a little confused until I realise she must have seen me draped over Gorgeous.

I grin at her and motion towards Gorgeous and Joseph. "Unfortunately, this one's taken so I'm afraid you're stuck with me, Irish." I wink at Gorgeous and stalk over to my love. I like hearing that. My love. My eyes burn with desire and lock on to hers which mirror exactly what I'm feeling. I put my arms around her waist, locking them together so she can't escape, and pull her up against my body. Still staring into her clear blue eyes, I can't break our gaze.

"You look fucking unbelievable. Like a Goddess."

She blushes.

I move my mouth to her ear and whisper so only she can hear. "I'm going to have to get through tonight with a permanent hard on. I hope you're happy, Irish." I nip at her earlobe and revel when I hear her intake of breath. She smiles up at me, her face still flushed, but the look in her eyes is screaming desire at me.

"Alright put her down for God sakes, will you. Or are you going to hold her all bloody night, Den?" Becs says.

Coming out of my lust filled stupor, I relax my arms but only let her move a fraction away from me and turn my head in Becs's direction. Becs is grinning at the both of us.

"Now that's an idea." I grin back at her, wiggling my eyebrows suggestively, and she laughs and slaps my shoulder as she walks into the kitchen. Darcie's face is getting redder and redder as she tries to put some distance between us, but I won't let her. I watch her with a smirk on my face.

"I don't think so, Irish, you can't come in here looking like that and expect me to stay away from you, it's impossible. Becs has the right idea."

Becs looks over to us, rolls her eyes and throws out, "Don't worry, Darcie. I'll rescue you in a bit."

She shakes her head at me and Darcie giggles next to me.

"Not going to happen I'm afraid," I tell her. "I'm going

to be by her side all night and you're going to have to lump it, sister. You look gorgeous by the way."

"Hey, I didn't know you said that to all the ladies. I thought I was special." Gorgeous feigns sadness and then grins at all of us.

"There is only one Gorgeous Gloria." I blow her a kiss and she giggles back at me. Joseph swoops down and plants a kiss on her lips and looks up at me pointedly.

"He can blow kisses all he wants but only I get to give you a proper one."

Laughter erupts from all of us and I bow down to Joseph.

"I bow to the master. There's only one man I would trust Gorgeous with so you're lucky."

He smirks back at me and puts an arm around her shoulders. "I'm the luckiest man in the world."

The women "aww" at him and I nod my head in admiration at how smooth he is. Dan comes into the kitchen at that point and looks over at the scene, me holding Darcie tightly to my side, Joseph snuggling up to Gorgeous, and he walks over to Becs and puts his arm around her shoulders and brings her to his side.

"I didn't want to be left out and be the only man not holding his beautiful partner."

A lump forms in my throat. I've never been this happy before and I'm so scared I'm going to ruin it like I always do. I want this forever. All the people, bar the kids, that I love in my life are all here, together, and happy. This is what I've dreamt of but never allowed myself to acknowledge. All I've always wanted was to love and be loved. My mind skirts back to my earlier conversation with the twins and my eyes dart to Darcie. She's smiling up at me and the love I feel for her constricts my heart. I try in vain to get the words out and tell her how I feel. I implore my eyes to tell her. I want her to know but the words won't form.

I kiss her softly on the lips and murmur, "Mine," against them.

She murmurs back, "Always."

It's enough. It's what I need to hear. I may not have been able to say it, but I'll show her how I feel all night long. And for once I'm not thinking about sex.

Chapter 21

Denny

Nat's arm flies backward and forward at us waving frantically from outside the restaurant. Darcie runs over to her and gives her a hug as I stand and watch. Becs sidles up beside me with Dan still attached to her and Joseph and Gorgeous are walking behind.

"Suits you, Den, being happy. Let go of the fear and enjoy the happiness, please."

I look at her in wonder.

Dan laughs. "We know you Den, inside and out. She's for you. She's your person, brother. Don't be scared about what might happen, just be happy and trust her."

Again, I'm lost for words. I stop in the middle of the street, unable to move as I'm overcome with emotions for these people who love me regardless of everything.

"Gloria, let's leave the guys for a bit." Becs takes her hand and Gorgeous strokes my arm as they walk past us and over to Nat and Darcie. Gripped by my emotions, I just stand where I am. Joseph puts his arm over my shoulder and holds me tightly.

"My boy. Everyone here tonight loves you. EVERY-

ONE. And I think you love everyone here as well?" His eyes are burning into mine.

I nod at him, still trying to get words to form in my mouth but failing.

"I know what you went through and I'm sorry I didn't get to you sooner. I should have, it was – No one should go through what you did, but that doesn't define who you are now. Please don't let her have another inch of space in your mind, or your present, and certainly not your future. What happened to her was not your fault, it was hers and hers only. You and Dan were a blessing to me and Gloria, and we thank God for you every day. We love you and we don't regret having you in our lives at all."

I can't speak so I grab him. I hold him so tightly and then I grab Dan into the hug too. Hearing those words from him, knowing he means them, is everything to me. We stand there, three giant men embracing on a street in London, and no one bats an eyelid. We come apart from each other and clear our throats. We awkwardly fidget and shuffle our feet as men do after they've expressed emotions. I look at both of them. The two men who know me inside and out, who love me and accept me, who saved me. I shake my head and clear my throat again.

"Thank you. I love you both, very much."

Dan's eyes fill with tears and Joseph's mouth forms an O shape with his shock. I've never said that to them before. Even though they know that, they aren't going to make a big deal of it. Dan squeezes my shoulder and blinks his eyes a few times and Joseph clears his throat again. We walk across the road to the restaurant where the girls are waiting and as we look at each of them, we can see tears in their eyes. I look to Joseph and Dan, who both smirk at me, and we each in turn laugh at the emotions pouring out of everyone. The girls give us exasperated looks and shake their heads at us. It clears the air and releases the emotional tension.

I motion for Darcie to come over to me and she slides up to my side. She fits so perfectly next to me, her arm around my waist and her hand on my chest. I take a deep inhale of her scent and she looks up at me with concern.

"Are ye okay, Denny? Ye seem different tonight."

I smile down at her and kiss her head.

"I've never been better, Irish." I kiss her softly on the lips and murmur "Mine." I raise my head from her, but her hand comes up to my cheek.

She presses gently to focus my gaze back to her, looks me straight in the eyes and says, "Always, Denny. Always."

I stare at her with my mouth open. A smile tips the corner of my lips up and I stroke her cheek. She knows I love her. She knows I'm telling her that with every 'Mine' and she's saying it back with 'Always'. I just hope she means it and when she finally does see the real me, she still means it. She breaks our gaze and smiles at me.

"Come on, old man, I'm starving."

I grin down at her mischievously. "So am I but I don't think they'll serve Darcie's perfection on the menu."

"My God..."

And before she can continue to scold me, I kiss her again.

"That's definitely better than old man, Irish."

Chapter 22

Denny

"I'm not complaining or anything, and you guys know I love you all like mad but, seriously... I need to find me a man and I need to get fu...sorry Gloria." Laughter fills the table and Nat shrinks down a bit more, mortified by what she was going to say in front of Gorgeous.

"Natalie don't be embarrassed, I'm quite partial to a fuuu myself you know." Gorgeous winks at her.

I spit my drink everywhere, whilst everyone laughs raucously, and Joseph sits a little taller next to her with a proud smile on his face.

"What can I say? She's insatiable, and I aim to please." He smirks as he lifts his glass to his lips. Nat sits upright and looks at Darcie.

"Sorry, Darcie, you're out girl. Gloria's my new wing woman. Spill it treacle, how do I get myself a Joseph? Do they make them at a factory? I mean Dan is a Joseph. Joseph is a Joseph and Denny is a Joseph, are there any left?"

I zone out during Gorgeous's answer because I certainly am not a Joseph. Dan is. He loves Bec's more than anything and wouldn't do anything to hurt her. I'm not so certain about myself. I force a laugh out when everyone else does but I feel lost. I excuse myself to go to the bathroom and leave them at the table, my mood as far from what it was outside as it can be. I'm distracted and angry with myself for going from happy to hateful in the blink of an eye. As I walk across the restaurant, I can feel eyes burning into the back of me. I turn around expecting to find Darcie staring at me, but she's still engaged at the table. I shake the sensation off, feeling even more annoyed, and carry-on heading to the bathroom. Inside I splash some water on my face and look at myself in the mirror. There are four ice blue eyes staring back at me. I spin around and find a man standing in front of me.

"Can I help you?" I bite out aggressively. The man continues to stare at me, and I can feel my anxiety mixing with my anger. The look on his face doesn't look intimidating or angry. Hoping to shift my anxiety about him, I try for a joke.

"Look I'm flattered. I am, really, but I have a girlfriend and you're not really my type."

Laughter fills the room as the man throws his head back like I'm the best comedian he's ever seen. I shake my head at him and turn towards the door, not understanding a thing that's happening. It wouldn't be the first time I've been propositioned in the men's room, but it is the first time anyone has laughed like that at my response.

"Is your name Denny?"

I stop dead in my tracks, turn and stare at him.

"Who are you? How d'you know my name?" I look over the man in front of me and take in his appearance. He has jet black hair like mine, except he has some greying at his temples, and piercing blue eyes, also like mine. He has a scar on his left cheek but other than that his face looks kind, and somewhat familiar. He's wearing a designer suit and expensive shoes, so he obviously has money behind him. I stare at him, eyes locking with his. A vague familiarity fleeting through me. I wait for his answers, but none come. We stand and stare a few beats more until he breaks the silence.

"Do you know who I am yet?" He looks hopeful that I do but I shake my head at him. Before either of us can say another word the bathroom door opens, and Joseph walks in. His face turns the palest shade I've ever seen a human being go.

"Lewis."

Joseph knows him.

"Hello brother, it's been a long time." This guy, Lewis as Joseph called him, is holding out his hand to him as if he wants him to shake it. Joseph grabs his hand and pulls him into an embrace.

Confusion rips through me as I stand there, staring at them both, I raise my arms and ask, "Is one of you two going to tell me what the fuck is happening here and who the fuck Lewis is or what?" The two men pull apart from their embrace and stand side by side where I can now see how similar they both look. Lewis's face looks a bit harder than Joseph's but they both have the same eyes and the same smiles. Lewis goes to speak, but Joseph puts his hand on his arm to stop him.

"Denny, son, Lewis is my brother... and your dad." My world spins, the air rushes out of my lungs. I look at Joseph and then at Lewis and shake my head at them. Anger filling my senses. A red rage descends upon me, and I lunge at Lewis. I grab him and we fall through the door and spill into the restaurant. I hit him in the face and as I'm about to do it again, I hear Darcie screaming my name. I look up and her terrified face, eyes pleading with me to stop, catches me off guard and makes me freeze. I release a roar from deep inside of me. I get up and walk out of the restaurant. The darkness is smothering me. It's boxing me in. I can't fight my way out. My breathing's shallow, and my heart's racing.

"DENNY! Denny, wait for me, please! If ye run, I'll chase ye, so fecking stop. I'm wearing heels ye bloody eejit!" She screams and I stop instantly. She grabs my arm, twines her fingers into mine and urges me forward. The darkness releases its hold on me and her light shines through. I cling to her hand as she chases the shadows away.

"Right now. We'll go together."

We walk in silence for what seems like hours. We find ourselves at the Thames and sit on a bench. Darcie has her hand firmly linked with mine still and her knuckles are white where she's holding on to me so tightly. I lift her knuckles up to my mouth and give them a kiss.

"Denny, what happened?" I sigh and roll my head back so I'm looking up at the sky.

"I've been lied to my whole fucking life, Darcie. By two of the people I thought I could trust more than anything. I don't know what's real or fake anymore. I should've known, everything was too good to be happening to me. I always find a way of ruining everything." She snuggles closer to me and her brows furrow together.

"I hate it when ye talk about yourself like that, Denny. Ye are the kindest and gentlest man I've ever met. Ye have so much good inside of ye. Why ye believe ye would ruin anyting is beyond me. Ye have a successful company, a family that idolises ye, and ye have me – always."

I bend my head to hers, our foreheads touching and tell her, "Mine. All mine." It's become our way of saying so much more without saying those three little words that we're both terrified of.

"Denny, who lied to ye? I'm sorry, but I'm kind of playing catch up here and I can't help ye if I don't know what's going on." She gives me an encouraging look and rubs little circles on my hand.

I take a deep breath, knowing the time has come to reveal the darkness to her. To let her see the real me. "Darcie, I'm going to tell you everything and I'm really fucking praying you're still sitting here at the end of it."

She kisses me. "Always, Denny."

And I pray with everything that I am, she means it.

"Daniel and I don't have the same dad. Our mum was married to Daniel's dad, Richard Mortimer. He was wealthy, came from old money, and there was nothing our mummy liked more than money." I give her a tight smile, squeezing her hand and she squeezes mine right back. I close my eyes to shut out the world as I continue to speak.

"They lived in a big house in Hampstead. To the outside world they were the perfect couple. He was a loving and attentive father, and she was the ever-glamourous mum who adored her family. Looks can be deceiving though, Irish, as you know." I open my eyes and look down to see her listening intently, still wrapped around my arm, holding on so I don't run. I urge her with my whole being to still be clung to me soon.

"Our mum was cold and horrible. She was an alcoholic and a drug user, coke being her chosen tipple as she would say. She would drink every day, but as soon as Daniel's dad would leave for business, she would go off on a coke binge and wouldn't care about Daniel at all. There were so many times before I was born that he was left alone to fend for himself, bearing in mind he's only four years older than me."

There's a sharp intake of breath and I see the realisation in her eyes and watch as they glisten with tears. I manage to untwist her from my arm, put it around her shoulders and bring her into my side. She fits so perfectly in my arms. *Please stay with me, Darcie.*

"Daniel's dad was away for business a lot and he was left alone a lot; he's always told me being alone didn't scare him half as much as being left with her. When she fell pregnant with me, she told Dan's dad I was his. He had no reason to think any differently. As far as he was concerned his wife was a drunk, but he hadn't heard of any infidelities. He must've been worried about it on some level, as they had a prenup which stated she got nothing if she cheated. His name went on my birth certificate, everything continued as it was until I turned six. I thought we had it pretty grim up until then, but it was nothing compared to what we had in store. Somehow, I don't know how, Dan's dad found out I wasn't his. I remember hearing a lot of arguing and I heard her blaming me for ruining everything." I pause to wash away the pain of her words.

"Fecking bitch. Sorry, Denny but she's a fecking bitch. How could she blame ye? Sorry, carry on please."

I grin at her sadly. "Richard moved out and because of the prenup we were kicked out of the big house in Hampstead and were forced into a two-bed council flat in Hackney. It was so small, but I liked it better there. Dan and I shared a room. It was our safe space away from her and the steady stream of men she had coming back to the flat. I dreaded every weekend when Dan would go with his dad. He'd come and pick him up and completely ignore me. This man who'd been Dad to me for six years suddenly just ignored me as if I didn't exist. Dan would feel guilty about leaving with him. He knew what I'd have to go through when he wasn't there. As soon as Dan and his dad were out of earshot and she'd tried all the begging to get him back, she'd turn on me – 'It's your fault Daniel isn't living with his father; you ruined all of our lives.' I'd try to argue back and tell her Dan loved me, and he didn't blame me, but she just laughed and told me, 'You aren't capable of being loved, Denny. If your own mother can't love you no one can or ever will. I hate you. You're a vile little cretin who'll never be loved, only hated by me forever.' When you've heard it enough times it becomes your truth."

I take a deep breath. I can't bear to look at Darcie, so I continue with my eyes closed.

"After a couple more years, I was eight, Dan twelve, Dan's dad stopped coming to get him on the weekends. He'd got remarried and his wife didn't like the fact he was tainted with a child, so he stopped coming. It hurt Dan a lot, he idolised him. And it turned our mum even colder and more dangerous. We were so used to men coming and going in the flat that once we locked ourselves in our room, we didn't bother going out again. One day someone barged into the room. He was drunk and high and thought it was funny to drag Dan out into the front room. He was holding him by his neck and throwing him around the room while our mum was slumped on the sofa. She told him to leave Dan alone and he lunged for her. He started to beat her up and Dan tried to get him to stop. He hit Dan a few times but Dan must've caught his legs or something, and he managed to wrestle him to the floor. He overpowered Dan and was on top of him, pummelling his face. Punch after punch. All I could see was blood over Dan's face. I couldn't let him keep hurting him. He was going to kill my brother. I picked up the first thing I could grab, which happened to be this big, heavy ashtray, and hit him on the head with all of my strength. He stopped hitting Dan and laid on the floor whilst I sobbed. My mother came over, felt for a pulse, looked me square in the eyes and told me, 'well I hope you're happy you little mistake, you've killed him.'"

I keep my eyes closed still but I hear her gasp. I turn my face away from her. I can't face the hatred and disgust in her eyes that I see in my own every day. I move my arm away from her shoulders and get up to leave. The darkness has a hold of me, and I know this time it won't let go. I've lost my only source of light.

A tug on my sleeve stops me and then her fingers lock into mine.

"You're a hero. Ye saved Daniel's life, Denny. Ye saved him."

Tears flow down my face. I turn to look at her and her light almost blinds me. I slump on the bench next to her and shake my head. "I'm not a hero. How the hell did you get that from what I did?"

She rolls her damp eyes at me and shakes her head in disbelief. "If I'd killed my dad when I'd seen him hurting my mammy what would ye think?"

I swallow hard and without hesitation tell her, "You were justified, and you should have done it sooner."

Her stare penetrates mine as if trying to will me to see something. When I've obviously taken too long, she shouts, exasperated, "Tis the same ting. Ye didn't mean to kill him. Ye just wanted him to stop hurting your brother. Ye killed him after he beat a twelve-year-old boy whilst your eejit of a mammy did nothing to protect ye both. I'm glad ye killed him, because if ye hadn't, ye and Daniel mightn't be here now. And the world is better with ye in it. MY world is better with ye in it. Jesus, Mary and Joseph, Denny. Your mam was wrong, ye aren't a mistake. Ye aren't unlovable or incapable of loving people. I see the love ye give to the girls and Isaac, to Dan, Gloria, Joseph and Becs. Even the way ye care for Nat is amazing."

Before I can speak she's continuing, "Is this why you're so closed off and ye don't do relationships? Because ye tink you're unlovable and can't love back?" Her breath is coming out fast and her cheeks are red from her anger, but I close my eyes and nod at her.

"Well, I hate to break it to ye, old man, but you're wrong. Ye couldn't be more wrong if ye wanted to be. Ye are more than capable of love. I've seen it and God damn it I've felt it. I don't care if ye haven't said it to me yet. I feel it from ye every bloody time we kiss and when ye looked after me when I was hurt. I've felt it from ye every day and ye bloody eejit, I love ye more than ye will ever know. So your stupid witch of a mammy was wrong. Ye love me, Denny Blanc, and I bloody love ye too, ye big eejit."

She's panting as if she's just run a million miles. And I'm staring at her with my mouth wide open in complete shock. The darkness is gone, obliterated, and her light is swirling around the both of us. We sit there for an eternity, just breathing and looking at each other.

"I'm sorry I got so angry." She looks down at her feet.

I run my hand through my hair. "At least you didn't throw a pillow at me this time." I grin at her, and she nudges me in the stomach. She's still looking down at her feet.

"Darcie, I've never had someone be so protective of me before. I liked it, a lot."

She raises her eyes to look at me and I smile at her.

"I realised I was in love with you today, with a little help from the twins, and I've been trying to say the words to you all day. I felt guilty because I know I'm not good enough for you and you deserve nothing but the best, but I do love you. You're mine."

She looks straight into my eyes and shakes her head. "That's not good enough, Denny. Try it again, without putting the man I love down, please." She crosses her arms over her chest and gives me that stern teacher look.

That look really turns me on. I grin at her and reach forward to tuck a piece of her hair behind her ear and cup her cheek with my hand. "I fucking love you, Darcie. YOU. ARE. MINE!" On every one of the last words, I slide a little bit nearer to her until I'm so close I can feel her breath on my face.

"Much better, my Adonis. I love ye too. Always." We reach toward each other, our bodies as close as they can be, and kiss. Not a desperate kiss, but a slow, loving kiss that almost takes my breath away. She knows my darkest secret and she hasn't run away. She's chased away the darkness and only her light remains. She's still here. And to top it off she bloody loves me as well.

"Where does Joseph fit in your story, Den? When ye said ye were lied to, I'm assuming it was by Gloria and him." Darcie is holding me tightly, her arm wrapped around my waist and her hand laying on my stomach as we walk along the Thames.

My arm is wrapped around her shoulders and before I speak, I kiss the top of her head. "After what happened, our mum phoned someone, and we were told to go into our room and not come back out. I was panicking and Daniel tried his best to calm me down but he was in a pretty bad way. I kept saying, 'I'm going to prison. Dan, I'm sorry,' and he just kept trying to reassure me but he could barely speak. Dan's poor face was covered in blood and his eye was swollen so much it was closed. I stood next to him whilst he laid on the bed and held his hand.

After a while, the door opened, and a man stood there. I thought he was a policeman and I burst into tears and told him, 'I'm sorry, he was hitting my brother and I just wanted him to stop, I didn't mean to kill him, I didn't mean to...' He came over to me and held me by the shoulders and told me it was all going to be okay. He packed up our things. We kept asking where we were going and where Mum was, but no one answered us. He lifted Dan up and my brother grabbed my hand and weakly told him he wasn't going anywhere without me. When we went out into the front room, it was empty and clean. No blood, no alcohol, no drug remnants. He took us to another house and that's where we met Gloria. She cleaned up Dan's face and she hugged me so tightly. All night long she hugged me, Darcie. I'd only ever had a hug from Dan before that."

She squeezes me tightly to her and snuggles her head into me. "That man was Joseph, wasn't it?"

I nod once, acknowledging the identity of the man who saved us. "We never left their house. No questions were asked. We were just grateful we were safe, and we didn't want to say anything in case they sent us away.

A couple of years passed, and everything was normal, which was a welcome relief, believe me. When I was ten and Dan was fourteen, we knew something was going on as Joseph and Gorgeous had been whispering a lot. They asked to talk, and I blurted out, 'Please just send me away for ruining it and keep Dan here.' Gorgeous cried and told me neither of us were going anywhere. Joseph told us our mum was dead from an overdose. He hugged us and asked if we wanted to stay... and the rest is history.

When I turned eighteen, Daniel and I decided to ask Joseph if we could change our surnames so they matched his and Gorgeous's. He was so overwhelmed. That's how we became Blancs. I asked him a few years later if he knew who my dad was. He said no.

Now I find out my dad is his fucking brother and Joseph is my fucking uncle and I don't know what to believe anymore!" I stop walking and drag my hand through my hair. I'm so angry and scared but I'm overwhelmed at how hurt I am. I was lied to by two of the people I adore.

"Denny, I believe those two people love ye more than anything, and whatever they did, whether it was right or wrong, they did it for ye and what they thought was right. Joseph had reasons and I know it's a shock, but you'll need to talk with him to find out what those reasons were. Don't throw a lifetime of support and love with Joseph and Gloria away over this. Please, Denny." I stare down at her and I'm blown away by how amazing she is. I throw my arms around her and pick her up and hug her to me tightly.

"I don't deserve you, Darcie, but I promise I'll do everything I can to make sure I never bloody lose you, ever. Never leave me, Irish; you're mine, yeah?"

"Always, Denny. I'm going nowhere. You're stuck with me forever and always." I take her lips fiercely and the groan that emanates from low in my throat tells her how much I'm enjoying it. My tongue rolls over hers and I nibble on her bottom lip. I open my eyes with her lips still locked onto mine and the look on her face nearly tips me over the edge. I want her. My erection is so hard it hurts and I feel like I'm going to explode. My hands are on her arse and are pushing her into me. I break the kiss and drag some air into my lungs.

"Irish, I need you baby."

She looks up at me and grins. "You've got me, Denny. You've had me for a long time, ye just have to take me."

I growl at her, lift her up and over my shoulder, one hand on the hem of her dress to make sure no one sees her arse and the other wrapped around her legs. Her squeal of delight turns to laughter as I hail a black cab and jump inside, not caring what anyone thinks, just immensely happy I have what's mine and I can finally be hers, too.

Chapter 23

Darcie

As we sit in the back of the black cab a nervous, yet excited energy washes over me. Denny is stroking my hand and kissing the back of it, mumbling mine after every gentle kiss. The driver doesn't try to converse with us, I think he can see we're only interested in each other. As we pull up at home, I feel a wee bit disappointed. I thought he was going to take me to a hotel and rid me of my last first with him.

"Denny? Home?" I'm so taken aback at being here I can't utter any sentences, just words.

"Where did you think I was taking you?" He's paying the driver, out of the car and round to my side before I can answer.

"I just assumed we'd go to a hotel for the first time." He smiles down at me and whispers in my ear, his breath tickling me as he speaks.

"Darcie, I've never slept with anyone in MY bed and I want you to be MY first."

I swoon. I literally, in real life, swoon at his words. My knees give out a wee bit and his arm comes around my body and grips me close to him to stop me from stumbling over. After a few seconds of steadying myself, I grab his hand and I pull him up the steps to the front door. He wraps his arms around me from behind and nuzzles into my hair. As the cab driver watches us with a smile on his face, I wonder if we seem like an ordinary couple in love. Not a couple that were so scarred from their parents they were terrified of commitment and just had the best and worst night in the history of saying those three little words. We walk into the extravagant hall, arms around each other and staring into each other's eyes, when a noise from the kitchen makes us turn our heads. We freeze when we see Joseph and Daniel hugging.

The euphoric, blissful happiness that's surrounding us turns to ice cold rage within seconds as Denny bellows, "Are you fucking kidding me? Why the fuck are you all back here? For fucks sake. This night keeps fucking me over!" He pulls my hand towards the stairs, heading up to his bedroom.

"Denny, please?" Gloria's pleading with him and as I look down at her I can see the devastation in her eyes. I can't bear to see her in pain.

"Denny...Ye need to hear them out. We've all the time in the world. I'm not going anywhere. Always – remember?" I gently tug his hand so he'll follow me back downstairs, and with a heavy sigh he does. As we pass Gloria on the way to the kitchen our eyes meet. She smiles a sad smile at me, and mouths thank you. I smile back but grip Denny's hand tighter.

When we step into the kitchen Becs is busying herself making coffee and tea, and Joseph and the man I now know is Denny's dad are standing against the counter, almost a mirror image of each other. Daniel is hovering near Becs, as if he needs her close by him. For once, I completely understand why. He needs her to give him strength and help him, and I know this because I feel the same sense radiating from Denny. I squeeze his hand tighter, and he gives me the smallest of smiles. My attention is caught by movement in the corner of the kitchen, away from everyone, and I look over and see Nat sitting in one of the chairs. I smile at her and try to give her an 'I'm sorry I left ye in the restaurant on your own with all of this craziness going on and I'm sorry your welcome home meal has gone to shite,' look, and when she smiles at me and nods her head, I know she understands. We all stand in silence, nervous eyes all on Denny, who in turn is eyeing his dad and Joseph, anger and hurt burning in those ice blues of his.

"Denny? Can we talk? Me and you? Brother to brother?" I look over at Dan and then to Denny who's nodding his head slightly. Dan walks over to him and puts his arm around his shoulders. Joseph takes a step forward too.

"No, just me and Denny. I want to talk to my brother on our own. Please?"

Joseph lowers his head and steps back. Dan tugs Denny's shoulders gently and when Denny doesn't move, his brother looks down at our hands. I follow his gaze and realise it's my hand holding on to Denny's so tightly, not wanting to let him go, that's stopping them from leaving.

"I'm not going to hurt him, Darcie. I promise you. He'll be okay with me." Dan's reassuring smile hits me and puts me at ease a fraction, but I need Denny to tell me tis okay to let go.

"Darcie, it's okay, baby. I love you."

I slowly let go of his hand and stroke his cheek. "I love ye too. Always." I watch him go and turn back to the room. All eyes are on me and I suddenly feel very self-conscious. When Denny was here it felt like no-one else existed, just me and him. And now he's gone, I realise I'm standing in a room full of people who are all looking at me. I fiddle about with my hands and before I can say or do anything Becs has rounded on me and is embracing me so hard. Slightly taken aback by her hug, my mouth drops open when I realise she's crying.

"Darcie, he said he loves you. He's never uttered those words to a girl before. I've only ever heard him say them to the kids. Thank you. Thank you for allowing him to love you and thank you for loving him."

Happiness floods through me and I hug her back and cry my own tears. The ones I've been holding back for the young Denny who'd been starved of love his whole childhood. Tears for the Denny who hadn't had a hug from anyone but Dan for most of his childhood. Tears for the Denny who was ignored by the people who should've loved and protected him. Tears for the adult Denny who has always believed he wasn't enough.

As we pull away, I lock eyes with Joseph. He lowers his gaze in shame and I can't help but go over to him. This man has shown me nothing but kindness and compassion. He helped save my life. I won't judge him.

"Joseph, please don't feel any way towards me. There isn't any judgement here. Ye took two wee boys into your home and ye loved and protected them, both of youse." I glance over at Gloria and smile at her.

"I don't know all your reasons for not telling them everything, but I know ye made the decisions based on love and to protect them from harm. I understand that, but ye have to make Denny understand. Because now he feels betrayed by the two people who he trusts most in this world. He's hurt, BUT he loves ye both dearly and he'll forgive ye because of that. Just tell him everything now though, because I don't think he'd take anymore lies. Okay?" Joseph nods and holds on tightly to my hand as Gloria walks over to cuddle me. She kisses me on the cheek and then walks into Joseph's open arms. I slowly walk past Lewis and avoid his eyes. I don't know him or his story yet. I reach where Nat is huddled in one of the dining chairs, sit next to her, and just put my head on her shoulder.

"Sorry." I whisper to her, and she shakes her head and holds my hand while we all wait in silence.

After what seems like an eternity, the brothers walk back into the kitchen. They stand side by side as Denny's eyes search for mine. The moment he finds them the anxiety and stress disappear and a calm comes over him. He holds his arm out for me to go to him and I do, knowing he needs to feel me next to him. I snuggle into his side, and I can feel the tension lift a little. His gaze is fixed on Lewis. And when he looks up, their eyes lock, the air suddenly charged with electricity. Not the same electricity Denny and I experience, that carnal need for each other. This is a mixture of hatred, rage, regret and hope. Joseph steps forward, he looks like he's aged ten years over the space of the night, and I desperately want to give him a hug. I don't. I stand firm next to Denny, Daniel still at his other side, and I realise Becs is standing next to him as well. The two brothers are so similar in some ways and so far apart in others.

"Can I explain as best as I can please, boy?" Joseph's eyes are begging Denny to give him something, but as soon as he hears Joseph speak, he tenses up again. I'm worried Denny's going to dismiss him without hearing him out when Gloria speaks quietly.

"Denny, please let us explain." His stubbornness subsides with her kind and friendly voice that's filled with emotion. He drags his gaze to her, and his face crumples when he sees how hurt and upset she is.

"Fine. Explain."

With those two words the atmosphere in the room changes. Expectation and hope fill the air as we all wait for Joseph to speak. I wrap my arm tighter around his waist, willing him, with everything I am, to know no matter what happens, I'm here. I'm not going anywhere. Denny is everything and I know he'd never hurt me like my daddy did. He'd never trap me with him. Would never make me feel like I couldn't be on my own. He makes me safe and loved, cherished, and fills me with so much confidence in myself.

I look up at him and flinch at the pain searing across his face. I stand on tiptoe to kiss his cheek just to remind him I'm here. I whisper 'always' into his ear and he turns his head to look at me. His eyes nearly destroy me. They're so raw and scared, but I can see his love for me in them too. I reach up and kiss him on the lips, holding onto his hand and arm for dear life, hoping he knows I'm here to stay forever.

"I'm sorry. I should never have lied to you, Den. When you asked me if I knew who your dad was, I should've told you. I felt like I had to lie to protect you."

A scoff comes from behind Joseph, and everyone turns to Lewis.

"If you've got something to say then say it," Denny bites out through gritted teeth.

"You're not the only one who was lied to, just know that." Lewis turns on his heel and walks out of the kitchen into the lounge.

We all watch but no one follows, all wanting to hear what Joseph has to say, rather than the petulant stranger. He clears his throat and starts again.

"Like I said, I thought it was safer for you not to know who your dad was. You were a very fragile and damaged boy and finding out who he was and what he did... I was scared you'd go down the wrong path and become like him. Like how I almost became. I wanted more for you. You remember I told you when I was younger that Gloria saved me from a life not worth living?"

Denny nods his head, his eyes barely blinking as they bore into Joseph.

"I was working as security for one of the top gangsters in London. I started off working his doors, doing bouncer jobs for his members only clubs. Worked my way up to his personal security very quickly and was one of his closest people. I drove him around and kept him safe. I kept out of the dodgy business, turned a blind eye when he was having his meetings, but I knew what he was up to. I just never acknowledged it." He looks at me and explains, "We weren't a rich family when I was younger, Darcie. My dad died when I was young and it wasn't like what it is now. Women didn't go out to work. I had to become the provider for the family. That's why I took whatever jobs I could. Before that, I worked three, four jobs in a day and night. I landed on my feet when he said I could work the doors; good pay and I could still work during the day as well. Anyway, I never found what I was doing easy going and I struggled with it. My conscience took a beating every day.

Then one day I met a girl and fell in love. I had no intention of giving up my work until I came home one day beaten and bruised. She flipped out, and gave me an ultimatum. I either went straight or she'd leave. Scared the life out of me, the idea of losing her. I quit, but when I was getting out, I didn't realise Lewis was in. And he was in a lot deeper than I'd ever been."

"A bit of an understatement there, brother."

I jump and swing around shouting. "Jesus, Mary and

Joseph. Ye scared the fecking beejezus out of me, ye bloody eejit."

Laughter erupts around me. I look at each of the people in the room, all laughing at me. And instead of getting angry at them, I laugh along with them. We all need the laughter a lot more than the anger that's been the theme of the night.

"All this backwards and forwards is giving me whiplash! Can you just sit down and tell the fucking story together so no one else scares 'the beejezus' out of Darcie and makes her call anyone else a 'bloody eejit' again please?"

I nudge Denny in the side as he puts on my accent with the word's beejezus and bloody eejit. He motions to the table and chairs over where Nat is sitting and walks over. Nat shuffles down to the last chair and then gets up.

"Guys, this is a family thing. I'm going to head out. Darcie, Den, call me if you need anything." She takes a step but Denny firmly stops her.

"Sit down, Nat. You're Darcie's family and that makes you mine as well, so stay. Please. Besides, it'll save the conversation in the morning when Darcie phones you anyway. I want you here. Please sit." He smiles at the last bit and she inclines her head to him.

"If you want me here, then I'll stay." She takes the chair next to me and I grab her hand. Once everyone is sat and comfortable Lewis speaks.

"I was more than in with them as Joey said. I was in debt to them. You see, when you work with people like them and you know their business and you see what they do, how they do it and with whom they do it... Even if you claim not to notice, they don't just let you walk off into the sunset with your beloved. That's not how this life works. They like power and control over you. The choices you make aren't really a choice at all. He wanted out and they didn't want to lose a man. Joey had something worth leaving for, I didn't. Well, I thought I didn't." He looks at Denny, who looks away from his dad, and Lewis's eyes show the pain of his rejection for merely a second. I don't know if anyone else saw it, but I noticed it. Maybe I'm so used to reading Denny's eyes I can see the emotions in his father's mirror image of them.

"I offered them a trade. I told them I'd pledge my life to them if they let Joey go. I was showing a lot of potential and made them a lot of money. I fit the role better than my big brother ever did, so they agreed. I cut all ties from Joey and went it alone. I didn't want to put him or Gloria in any danger, so I did as they asked."

Joseph slams his fist into the table, his anger radiating. "God damn you; you shouldn't have done that. Why didn't you tell me? I would've found another way."

Lewis chuckles. "There was no other way, Joey. Only this way. If you'd known you would've got us both killed. This way at least one of us was free. I just wish you'd have told me about my son." Lewis pushes his chair back and stretches his legs out, putting his hands behind his head.

I can't help noticing the familiarity between him and Denny. He's like an older, rougher version of him. I glance around the table to see if anyone else is seeing it and my eye catches Becs's who's nodding at me as if she sees it too.

"How did you know my mum? Did you sell her drugs?" Daniel's voice sounds strange to hear after he's been quiet for so long.

"No, I didn't. I first saw her in a bar in Hampstead. She was telling me about her husband and how he'd been cheating on her. She was a sad, incredibly attractive woman drinking alone in a bar. I offered her a shoulder to cry on. We chatted and one thing led to another. She was nice to me and I was nice to her. We started seeing each other regularly," he looks over at Daniel and says, "She never mentioned she had a kid."

I watch as the pain flickers over Daniels's face. "Figures, she probably forgot she had one." Daniel replies bitterly and Becs cuddles into him.

"Yeah, I get that. She was self-absorbed, but so was I. One day she told me she couldn't see me anymore. Said her hubby was getting suspicious and if he found out she'd cheated she wouldn't get a penny of his money. According to her she'd earned every penny and was entitled to the lot. I wasn't devastated about it. Sorry if that sounds harsh, but we were warned about being honest by freckles over here." He motions his head at me.

I feel a deep flush spread over my cheeks as all eyes are on me again, but instead of lowering my head in embarrassment, I hold it up and lock my eyes on his. "Well, I'm glad ye listened. The truth is always better, don't ye tink?"

I'm rewarded for my sassiness by a chuckle from Denny followed by a whisper of 'Mine' in my ear. I'm certain my face is as red as a tomato, but I don't care. I don't even care I dropped my h in think. Lewis inclines his head at me in agreement.

"That was how I left it. For near on eight years. I never thought about her again until I got a call from her one night asking for help in getting rid of a body."

I hear Nat's sharp intake of breath and feel Denny's shoulders sag, so I steer the conversation away from that revelation.

"So where did ye come into it, Joseph? How did ye end up rescuing Denny and Daniel that night?"

My eyes plead with him not to mention the body and skip over it. Thankfully he must've known what I was doing as he speaks.

"I got a call from Lewis in the middle of night saying he

needed help. When I got to the flat I was told there were two boys who needed a place to stay. They told me what had happened, and one look around the room, all the drugs in it, I knew I couldn't leave them there with a clear conscience. I took them home with me. That night, Lewis came to see me and asked if I thought Denny was his. He looked so much like him I knew he was, but I lied and told him he was her ex-husband's.

You have to see my point of view here. I hadn't heard from my brother for eight years. I'd heard he was in with them, and was in big, and the next time I saw him he was helping to clear a... Well, it wasn't an ideal reunion. The boys had been through enough and needed guidance and love, not someone who was going to lead them into the organised crime world. I'm sorry Lewis, and Denny. I'm sorry I took away your right to know your son and your right to have a father." Joseph's voice cracks at that. Tears stream down his face. His shoulders heaving up and down as the sobs rack his body.

Gloria gets up to go to him, but both Daniel and Denny reach him first. I watch with pride filling my heart as Denny grabs him by the shoulders and Daniel places his hand on his back.

"I had a father," Denny says. "You were my dad. You still are my dad. You and Gloria saved me. I don't care if you lied, you saved me. You chose me and I chose you, too. I love you both." He's hugging Joseph and Daniel joins in on the hug too.

Tears are falling from everyone's eyes and I reach over and hold Lewis's hand. He looks at me curiously, then lets his guard down and holds my hand but lowers his head so I can't see into his eyes.

Hours have passed and we've been in the kitchen talking into the early hours of the morning. Lewis informed us he's no longer indebted to anyone and he took over from those who used to be in charge. Worked his way up, to quote him, and was now enjoying retirement, which was code for 'I'm not physically involved in the dodgy dealings, I run my club, but I'm still very well connected.' He asks Denny about his job and Denny tells him, reluctantly, but he can't help the excitement in his voice when he talks about his baby. He's thawing to Lewis a bit which is a relief for everyone.

Gloria yawns and Joseph, being the ever-caring husband he always is, stands up and announces to the group, "I think we all need some rest. It's late, or early, however you want to look at it. We need to sleep." We nod our agreement, and everyone gets up and says goodbye. Nat and I are left at the table as Denny and Dan walk them to the door.

As Becs cleans the cups, I look over at my bestie. "Nat, I'm so sorry your night out was ruined."

She scoffs at me. "Don't be stupid. We can go out anytime. I'm back in London now so it's no biggie. How are you after all the revelations? You and Denny finally said what we all knew to each other I see."

I giggle and notice Becs's head whip around to us.

"Oh, wait for me and be quick before they come back." She runs over to where we're sitting and plonks herself down, washcloth still in her hand.

"God ye two, after he told me about his past, I couldn't keep it in anymore. I really didn't expect him to say it back, but he did. We were coming home to, well ye know. But ye guys surprised us by being here." I give them both the stink eye but get shot down.

"Surely you would've known we would come home, Darcie." Becs says.

Nat gives me a 'well duh' look. Trying to sound defensive, I argue back. "I said the same thing, but Denny said he's never slept with anyone in his bed and wanted *me* to be *his* first so that's why we came home." I don't look at Becs just in case she tells me it isn't true. Nat's swooning over him wanting to have his first with me and Becs reaches over the table and clasps my hand.

"Darcie, he's never had a girl in the house, let alone in his bed. He's strangely obsessed with his bed. He was telling the truth."

She smiles at me and I stutter trying to cover myself. "Oh, I was – never mind."

Nat and Becs exchange looks and roll their eyes at me.

"Christ, they're coming back. We'll talk more tomorrow."

"Maybe there'll be more to talk about too." Nat's wiggling her eyebrows at me and we can't stifle our laughter.

"What's funny?" Daniel asks.

We all shake our heads and giggle more when we see the guys give each other confused looks.

Daniel holds out his hand to Becs and she stands and takes it. "We're off to bed. Nat feel free to stay over, Hun, it's too late to go anywhere."

Nat protests but Denny cuts her off. "You can stay in the guest room Darcie was using, she can stay with me."

I look at him as a sudden flash of desire crosses his face, and I'm instantly aroused by it. I grab Nat's hand and pull her up off her seat before she can protest to staying.

"Come on, I'll grab my toothbrush and pjs, ye can borrow what ye want of mine." I practically drag her down the hall with Daniel and Becs heading upstairs. Once inside the room I grab her by the shoulders.

"Nat, what do I do? Is it wrong to do anything after all

that's happened tonight? I'm so bloody nervous. What if I'm shite and he thinks tis the same as having sex with a wet fish?"

Nat laughs at me. "Darcie, stop it. How would he know what having sex with a wet fish was like anyway? See now my brain is having some serious image problems when I should be focusing. Right, you and Denny have the most amazing chemistry together, you love each other. Whatever happens tonight, just enjoy it, don't stress. And certainly, don't do this, trout pout."

She pouts her lips at me, and we burst into giggles again. After having a hug and retrieving some pjs, a toothbrush, and some clean clothes, I head out into the hallway. Denny's waiting on the stairs and as our eyes meet, I can see the hunger in his. I lower my gaze so I can force myself to move. We walk up the stairs and into his bedroom in silence. His bed is amazing. Tis big enough for a giant and takes up a lot of the space in the room. And that isn't a small feat as the room is huge too.

"Denny, this bed's impressive. I don't think I'd ever leave it if I had this. Tis amazing." I sit down on the bed and I look over at him to see his beautiful smile as he leans against the doorway with his legs crossed.

"You look damn good on my bed, Irish. Kind of what I thought you would look like. Except, somethings wrong."

He takes the clothes from my hands and places them on the side. His mouth crashes down onto mine. Our lips starved for each other's. Like we hadn't kissed in forever. He's kissing me hard but slow at the same time. My core is exploding and screaming to be touched. I moan into his mouth when his tongue caresses mine. It feels like we're frozen there for eternity, just kissing, slow and hard. He moves his hand to the side of my cheek and runs it down, all the way past my arm. It curls around my waist and sits at the small of my back. He pulls me up from the bed and into him. As our bodies collide, I hear a growl emanate from his mouth. I lose all sense of time. We could've been kissing for a second, a minute or an hour. Christ, we could've been there for a whole week for all I know as I've no idea about anything, except this gorgeous man and his mesmerising lips, kissing me. I moan into his mouth and his hand moves lower. He's holding me as close as he can, and I'm loving every second of being this near to him. My hand comes up to fist his hair and he gives another growl. These growls are something else.

His lips trail down my face and he smothers me with kisses, all the time murmuring 'beautiful, gorgeous and mine.' When he finally pulls away and looks into my eyes, he tells me, "Darcie, I love you."

I melt against him and kiss my response back. I trail my hands over his shirt and fumble with his buttons. The urgency has disappeared from earlier, replaced with love and need. As I slide his shirt off his shoulders, I place my lips on his chest and he shudders against them. He reaches around the back of my dress and unzips it and I let it fall to the floor, pooling at my feet. I step out of it and lower my hands to Denny's trousers. I unbuckle his belt and undo his fly and button. I pull his trousers and underpants down over his hips and past his engorged erection. I want to reach over and put him in my mouth, but I need him naked and inside me more. Denny unhooks my bra with ease, and I have to push back the thoughts of how many women he's practised that move on. I don't want anything to spoil this. He may have had experience before, but I'm the one in his room. I'm the one he loves. And that's all that matters. I keep repeating that to myself and it seems to calm the wee voice in my head.

His fingers brush down my arms, and over my chest,

skimming my nipples. The further down they go, the faster my breathing becomes. His fingers reach my knickers and, hooking into the sides of them, he slides them down my legs. Finally, we're both standing in front of each other naked - well I still have my high heeled sandals on.

Chapter 24

Denny

Words aren't forming in my brain. I want to devour her. I want to consume her. I want every part of her to be filled with me. I want to own her body. Her lips screaming my name. Her hands raking over me. I need to touch her, but I can't. Not yet. I need to get my self-control in order, so I can go slowly with her. This is her first time. I have to make it good for her. I'm struggling to breathe; she looks that good. I take a deep breath in and blow it out, again and again. I slowly reach forward and let my hand go to the back of her neck. She notices my trembling hand as I twine my fingers into her hair and gently bring her mouth to mine. I kiss her slowly and steady, taking my time with her mouth. I inhale her scent into me. She smells like coconut and Darcie. My other hand rests on her hip and she steps closer to me. But instead of bringing her up against me, like I know she wants, I keep her body slightly away from mine. I need to gain control, or this'll all be over too soon. I want this to last forever.

I slowly walk her to the bed, our mouths still joined. I feel her legs hit the edge of it and lower her gently. Laid out naked and beautiful, her hair fanned out against the covers, looking like a damn angel. I stand above her, admiring her and trying desperately to get words to form in my mouth. But I can't. All I can do is appreciate her and worship her. I bend towards her and trail kisses all the way down her body. Her gentle moans spurring me on. I get to her ankles, undo the straps of her sandals and take them off her beautiful dainty feet. I've never had a thing for feet, but I'd do anything for these. Once I have her shoes off, she scoots further onto the bed, resting on her elbows. I stand up and look down at her, a smirk on my face, finally able to form a sentence.

"There, that's better. Now you're exactly how I imagined you'd look on my bed. Naked, beautiful and ready for me to give you the best damn experience in the world." I climb on top of her, and she grins up at me.

"Ye are so arrogant, Denny Blanc, for such an old man."

"I'll let my actions do the talking, Irish. We'll see what you're calling me afterwards." I wink at her and kiss her lips. She moans in pleasure and then groans as I pull away and open my bedside drawer. I place two condoms on the bed. Darcie looks down at them and bites her bottom lip as nerves fly over her face. Worried she's having second thoughts, I grab them and throw them on the side.

"Darcie, we don't have to do this. We can just go to sleep. As long as you're in my arms that's all that matters to me. We can do this when you're ready."

A slow smile curves on her beautiful, full, pink lips and I furrow my brow in confusion at her.

"We won't be needing those, Denny. Well, if ye want them we can still use them, but when I was in the hospital, I asked the doctor to put me on birth control. Tis over four weeks now, tis in full effect. If ye still want to wear a condom, well that's grand, but I didn't want anything to be between us when we, ye know." She lowers her eyes and looks down at her naked lap whilst I stare at her in amazement. She constantly blows me away.

"Darcie, I'm not wearing one of these if I don't have to. I want to feel everything when I'm inside you. Just you and me and nothing in between. Another first for me though Irish, I've never had sex without one. Thank you for trusting me." Her head flies up and I can see the shock in her eyes my little admission brought.

"I'm breaking all of my rules for you, Darcie, because I love you." I kiss her nose and take a deep breath.

"I love ye to. Rules were made to be broken, old man."

Our eyes lock together as I climb onto the bed and settle next to her. My hand travels down her body. I hesitate over her perfect nipples and then lower my thumb, and gently skim over them. Her low throaty moan spurs me on but I force myself to go slowly. I want her to savour every second of this and I need the time so I don't embarrass myself.

I replace my thumb with my mouth, and she groans underneath me. I grin around her nipple and lower my hand to find her soaking wet sex. My fingers work the sensitive little nub, the way I know she loves. She gasps and slowly rocks her hips into the rhythm of my hand. As I place a finger inside of her, her eyelids fly open and our gazes lock. I quickly follow it with another finger and press the heel of my hand onto her clit causing her to cry out in pleasure. She bites down on her lip, her cheeks flushed and her hair fanned out behind her. She looks at me through heavy lids.

"Denny." She whines like she's in pain but all she needs is for me to make her come. "Denny, I want ye inside me, please."

The desperation in her voice is matched by my own erratic breathing but I manage to tell her in a huskier voice than normal, "Darcie, baby. I need you to be ready first. I don't want to hurt you." I'm not sure if she understands what I mean or not, but I can't explain it now. I kiss her belly button and swirl my tongue inside it and then lick all the way down to her mound until I reach her heat. I run my tongue everywhere but avoid her clit. My fingers are still inside her, working her into a frenzy. The anticipation is driving her mad and her head is thrashing from side to side. Her moans are becoming more desperate but instead of going faster I take my time. I inhale her scent again and mumble, "fucking beautiful."

She says my name on a breathy moan and I can't hold back any longer. I devour her. My tongue is relentless against her clit. She's gasping and moaning, begging me to take her, but I carry on. I need to feel her come against my tongue before I can get inside her. I curve my fingers and find the perfect spot inside whilst sucking and nipping at her clit. With one last nip of my teeth, she comes crashing around my fingers and screaming my name. I don't stop. I move my head up and trail kisses all over her, nibbling and sucking as I go. I find her nipple and place my mouth over it and bite it hard enough to make her gasp and then soothe it with my tongue when she cries out. I bring my fingers out and grab my cock and rub the tip of it up and over her soaking centre making her groan and beg again.

"Please, Denny. Please. Be my first and last, please."

"Mine." I growl, a deep noise from low in my throat, and I kiss her on the mouth as I lower the tip of my throbbing erection into her. I pull my mouth away from her and look into her eyes.

"Darcie, it might hurt. I'm sorry, but I'll do everything to make it less painful for you, baby, but please listen to me. Okay?" She nods and bites her lip. I inch in a little bit more and keep going until I feel her barrier.

"Denny, why aren't ye moving?" She's begging, pleading with me.

"Trust me, baby. Just let me make you come like this." She nods and closes her eyes, my thumb kneading into her clit gently and I feel her getting close. I wrap my lips around her nipple. Slowly working her into a frenzy again.

Being inside of her and not moving takes every bit of my self-control, but this isn't about me. It's about giving her the best experience for her first time and making sure I keep her pain to a minimum. My thumb works her harder and faster and it takes her higher as I build her orgasm up again. Sweat is dripping down my face. The restraint it's taking for me not to move whilst feeling her clench around me is taking its toll. I know we're on the cusp as she tightens her muscles and screams.

"Denny, I'm coming."

Just as she climaxes I push my way through the barrier, watching her face intently, and when she barely even flinches, I feel myself relax. I move my hips in a round motion, trying to stretch her out, and as she comes down from her orgasm I push myself into her fully.

"Did I hurt you? Are you okay?" I'm scanning her face for any signs of pain or discomfort but can't see any.

"Denny, I'm grand. Twas perfect. Please stop talking and make love to me now."

I don't need to be told twice. I grind my hips around and thrust deep into her. She feels so good. She feels like mine. She was made for me and me alone.

"Darcie, I fucking love you. You're perfect. You're mine." She's chanting my name like it's a mantra and I'm thrusting deep into her until she grips my shoulders and screams again.

"Denny. My God. My Adonis!" Her muscles gripping onto my cock and hearing her scream my name is too much for me to take and it tips me over the edge. I cry out "Darcie" and have the best damn orgasm of my entire fucking life.

"Are you sure you're okay?" I ask her again, just to be sure. She rolls her eyes at me and smiles as she traces circles with her fingers on my bare chest.

"For the one hundredth time, aye, Denny. I'm grand. I'm more than grand. I'm absolutely fantastic. Now stop asking me."

I laugh at her and with a mischievous tone in my voice I ask, "Do you remember when you called me old man and questioned my abilities due to my increased age, Irish?" She covers her face in her hands and groans whilst trying to stifle a laugh.

"Aye. I do."

I take her hands and pin them above her head. She's trapped underneath me, as I straddle her stomach.

"And do you remember, I told you my actions would prove my abilities and we'd see what you're calling me after?" I grin down at her, pride flowing through me as she looks me in the eyes and nods whilst biting her bottom lip.

"And, my beautiful Darcie, do you remember what you screamed out in ecstasy when I made you come, for the third time, I might add?" I kiss her neck and shoulder, going up to her face and kissing her everywhere but her mouth. One hand still holding her wrists together, I let my other one slide down to her breast and cup it. I swirl my thumb over her nipple again and again.

"Denny, my God, my Adonis!" She says breathlessly, her body writhing underneath me and her mouth pouting, desperate for my lips.

"Hmmmm now that sounded pretty clear to me. You

were calling me your God, your Adonis, but let's clarify. Am I your God or your Adonis?" Still teasing her with my mouth, I lick along her bottom lip and trace along the outline of her mouth with my tongue. She moves her head to gain access to me, but I lower my mouth to her jawline again.

"Denny, ye have always been my God and you are definitely more Adonis-like in the bedroom, but if you don't kiss me right now, I'm going to–"

Before she can finish her sentence, my mouth is on hers, kissing her, licking her, nibbling and sucking on her tongue. I break our kiss off so I can taste the rest of her again. Still holding her hands above her head, I kiss and lick my way to her perfect breasts and go to town on her nipples. She's so sensitive and responsive and it drives me wild. One lick and she writhes beneath me.

"Darcie, I'm going to let go of your hands but you're going to keep them where they are okay?" She nods at me, too wrapped up in the pleasure she's receiving from me working her nipples. I let go and trail my hand lazily down her body. Feather light touches tickle her as I place my lips everywhere I touch. As my mouth lingers above her breasts, her eyes open and give me a pleading look to carry on and I smirk at her. I take her nipple into my mouth and suck hard on it, all the time looking into her beautiful, sky-blue eyes. They're filled with love and desire, and they're driving me wild. I bite her nipple and watch as she cries out in pleasure. Her face is beautiful.

I turn my attention to her other breast, which is just as sensitive and responsive and her cries urge me on. I kiss my way down her belly. I trail my tongue all the way down, past her little mound of dark hair until I taste her. Once she's in my mouth I can't stop. It's like I'm an inmate on death row, and she's my last meal. I grab her legs and swing them over my shoulders and lift her arse up, so she's thrust right up to me. She's crying out loud and telling me not to stop and I want to assure her I have no intentions of stopping but I'd need to stop to do that. Instead, I grab her clit with my teeth, tug on it gently and then suck as she comes apart in my mouth, my name falling from her lips again. I lap up her juices. Savouring her sweetness. I let her legs go and kiss her from her ankle all the way up to her mouth.

"Tank ye. Tank ye. Tank ye."

I laugh and kiss her mouth and rub our noses together. "No need to 'tank' me baby." I fucking love her accent. "Are you sore?" I need to know whether I can get inside her again. I'm desperate to be inside her and feel her around my cock, but if she's sore, I'm not going anywhere near.

"A wee bit, but I'll be..." I shake my head and place my fingers over her lips to silence her.

"Darcie, we have all the time in the world. I'm not going anywhere. Every day, for the rest of our lives I'm going to be here with you and inside you, but not when you're sore." I kiss her again and roll off the bed.

"Where are ye going?" She looks me over as I stand naked before her. She bites on her lip and the look on her face is pure sex. She's insatiable.

"Irish, stop looking at me like that. I'm going to run you a bath. It'll help with the tenderness. Then once we're clean, we're going back to bed."

She gives me a waggle of her eyebrows and I laugh.

"Carry on, Irish, and I'm going to spank that beautiful behind of yours."

I wink at her and laugh when I hear her say, "Promises, promises, old man."

I hear her teasing as I head into the bathroom. I've created a monster and I fucking love it.

Once inside the bathroom I turn the taps on, pour some

bubbles in and wait for it to fill up. I look at myself in the mirror. I note the worry's gone, the guilt has subsided, the darkness has been obliterated and I look... happy. I chuckle. Finally, at thirty years of age, I've seen myself happy. And it's all thanks to that beautiful woman in my bed. I think back to what I just said to her, 'every day for the rest of our lives.' There's no anxiety or dread about being with her forever, just hope and excitement. I turn back to the almost filled bath and turn the taps off. I call her in and as she stands in the doorway, completely naked, she takes my breath away. Again. She looks like my Darcie, but she has that just been fucked glow about her. Her beautiful big breasts jiggle as she walks and the way those full hips sway is hypnotising. I grab her tiny waist and pull her to me.

"You're fucking gorgeous, Darcie. If you weren't sore, I'd bend you over the sink and fuck you so hard until you were calling me your Adonis again." I see a slight bit of shock flip through her expression but it's quickly replaced with anticipation. I kiss her hard and feel my dick shoot straight up. I pull back, take a deep breath, and lift her up and into the bath.

"What the feck, Denny? Some warning would be nice ye flaming eejit."

I smile when her anger fades away as she realises I'm getting into the bath with her.

Chapter 25

Denny

As I open my eyes the next morning, I have a ridiculous smile on my face. It could be the amazing sex Darcie and I had last night or that I slept for hours. Or it could be I'm waking up, wrapped around my beautiful girlfriend, the love of my life, in my bed, which happens to be another great love of mine. It's definitely the latter. Darcie is facing me, our legs entwined together, and my arm is laying over her waist. She looks like an angel sleeping, her dark hair spread out around her head and her beautiful freckles dancing on her nose as she breathes deeply in her sleep. Her pink full lips pucker slightly, and I can't resist bending my head and having a little taste of her.

She stirs and I whisper, "Morning baby, sorry I woke you. I couldn't resist kissing you."

She smiles at me whilst her eyes are still closed tightly. "Morning, my Adonis. What time is it?" My grin turns into a full-on smile and I grab her around the waist and roll over, so she is on top of me. I look over at the clock on my night-stand and tell her it's ten am.

"Gosh we slept for ages. Poor Nat, she's probably been

awake and uncomfortable downstairs with Becs and Daniel." She goes to swing off me and out of the bed, but I catch her before she can. I hold her against my chest and laugh when she tries to wiggle out of my embrace.

"Excuse me, Irish. Even though you just called me your 'Adonis' – which I think I prefer to 'my God' by the way - you can't leave the bed without giving me a kiss and opening your eyes properly so I can see those gorgeous blues."

She smiles at me and opens her eyes wide, then laughs and brings her lips to mine, hard but fast.

"There, can I go to the bathroom now?" She rolls her eyes at me.

I reluctantly let her go, but I smack her arse as she gets out of the bed just to let her know I'm not happy about it. She gasps and turns around to face me. Biting my bottom lip, a bit worried about her reaction, I look at her through squinted eyes.

"Oh really, old man?" She picks up a pillow and swats me over the head with it.

Completely shocked and thrown, I sit on the bed stunned. When she swats me again, I can't help the belly roaring laugh that comes from me. I grab her and throw her onto the bed. Pinning her hands above her head, I stare down at her. She's so beautiful, and it takes my breath away. Every time I see her, I'm blown away with just how beautiful she is. Her genuine smile and love for me pouring from her face honestly knocks me for six.

Regaining my composure, I tease. "Now what am I going to do with you, Irish?"

She rolls her eyes at me and pouts. "Nothing, you're going to let me go." She's very matter of fact about it.

"I am, am I?" I question her with a raised eyebrow.

"Aye, because ye love me."

I smile down at her, just those words coming from her mouth and knowing she knows how I feel about her makes me the happiest man alive.

"Damn straight I do. Go to the bathroom and then we'll head downstairs for some food." I kiss her quickly on the lips and she sways that arse over to the bathroom. It takes everything in me to not go over and spank it again.

"Morning."

We walk into the kitchen, arms wrapped around each other, and come to an abrupt stop with all eyes on us. Seriously, six eyes staring at us. It's enough to make us both squirm.

"What are you all looking at?" I ask them, trying to make my voice scolding but it comes out happy. I can't help how this woman makes me feel.

Dan and Nat divert their eyes instantly. Dan focuses on his tablet like he hasn't just been caught staring at us, and Nat pretends to be really busy reading a magazine. Becs on the other hand stares straight at us, and laughs.

"Morning love birds, get much sleep?" She waggles her eyebrows at us and smirks mischievously as Darcie turns a lovely shade of red.

I kiss the top of her head trying to get her out of her embarrassment.

"Yes, we managed to get a few hours," I say as I glare at Becs and motion to Darcie with my head, telepathically telling her 'I can't believe how insensitive you're being. You know it was her first time'. She seems to receive my psychic message and as the penny finally drops, I watch as mortification sets in on her face at knowing she's embarrassed Darcie.

"Do you want some coffee?" She asks hesitantly as I steer Darcie over to the table to sit with Nat whilst I walk back to the breakfast bar where Becs and Dan are.

I hiss at Becs, "What is wrong with you, embarrassing her like that. I expected more from you." A look of shock and hurt crosses her face, followed by anger.

"I'm sorry alright, I forgot and– oh bugger off." She walks over to Darcie and after a second, she hugs her and sticks her tongue out at me over her shoulder.

"How the fuck do you put up with her, Dan?" I laugh and clap him on the shoulder.

"There are certain benefits, brother." I almost spit out the coffee I'm drinking and the girls look over at us, me spluttering and coughing and Dan laughing his head off.

"Are you okay? What's so funny, Daniel?" Becs asks, eyeing us both with her arms crossed over her chest, making it abundantly clear she's pissed off with us.

"Went down the wrong hole. I'm fine." I say back to her. She raises an eyebrow at Dan who in turn blows her a kiss, which seems to relieve some of the anger on her face. I smack him on the back and join the women. As I sit down next to Darcie, I catch Nat's eyes.

"Morning Nat, I want to apologise for last night. It was supposed to be a celebration of you returning to London and instead it turned into a mighty fine mess. I just wanted you to know I'm sorry." I lower my gaze, ashamed of everything she heard last night about my druggie mum and my crappy upbringing. She even heard a mention of dead bodies. My head hangs in shame and my hands are laying on the table when Nat reaches over and grabs one.

"Hey, like you said last night, you're Darcie's family which means you're mine too, so don't be sorry. It just means you owe me a do-over night. But instead of just a welcome home meal, we'll be searching for my own version of a Blanc man, which means I'll have to have my girl Gloria there, as you know she's my wing woman, now, right?"

As I laugh, feeling gratitude and relief for another amazing woman in my life, Darcie clasps her hand to her heart and feigns shock. "Natalie, how dare ye? You've replaced me so quickly."

As quick as anything Nat replies, completely dismissing Darcie's fake shock. "Let's be real, Darce, you were never very good at being my wing woman. And now you've found your version of Joseph, you're not going to have any time to help me. I need to get Gloria on the case. Plus, I think she'll be a brilliant fucking wing woman."

I'm relieved and glad Nat brought Gloria and Joseph up as I wasn't sure how I'd react to them today. Even though I understand the reasons behind their actions, I'm still a little upset with them. I'm glad I don't feel any anger or hate. Just a little sadness about the situation overall, rather than just for me. I'm sad Joseph missed out on having a relationship with his brother and he felt guilty about everything. Hell, I'm even sad about not having had the chance to have Lewis in my life. But I don't regret the way it all panned out. If it had worked out differently, I might not have met Darcie, and she trumps everything and everyone.

"As long as there are no other long-lost relatives anyone has hidden, I think a do-over night is just what we all need. What time are the kids back?" I look over at Becs, who's been staring at me intently throughout my conversation with Nat.

"About twelve-ish. Mum and dad said they'll drop them off as they're heading out for lunch with some friends." She gets up and walks over to the sink and I follow her, quickly kissing Darcie on the top of her head as I get up. I've known Becs for too long to not sense when something's up with her. She's my best friend and my sister (in-law but we never mention that), and I know something's bugging her.

"Hey, what's up?" I whisper to Becs who's standing near Dan. She shakes her head and tries to walk away from us, but I grab her hand and stop her.

"Becs?" She also knows me well enough to know I'm not going to let up until she spills. She sighs and looks me square in the eyes.

"What're you going to do about Lewis, Den? I'm not sure if I'm comfortable with him being around the kids, seeing as what he does for a living and everything."

I let out a long breath. "You had me worried there. I thought you were going to say something really bad, you muppet."

Her eyes are blinking in shock at me as she hits me in the arm and tells me to shut up.

Rubbing my arm, I continue, "I don't know yet and that's the honest answer. I'd never bring anyone here and around the kids you were wary of so don't worry about that. I'd never put them in any kind of danger, you know that."

She rolls her eyes at me and goes to speak but I cut her off.

"I'll let you all know when I decide, but at the minute, I have no fucking clue what I'm doing. I do know I'd like to spend some time with my beautiful girlfriend today though." I say that last bit way too loudly, just so she can hear me, even though I know she's heard every other word Becs and I've been saying. Her head shoots around, and she raises her eyebrows at me.

"Your girlfriend would love to spend some time with her boyfriend too. What do ye want to do?"

I raise my eyebrows up at her, give her a suggestive grin, and enjoy watching the colour rise in her cheeks. I feel another blow on my arm and look around to see Becs standing beside me. "Oh, you give me bollocks for embarrassing her and guilt trip me, but it's okay for you to do it? Fucking dick."

Becs can definitely pack a punch and rubbing my arm again, I scowl. "Ow, by the way, you realise I could have you done for assault, don't you?" I glance over at Dan for some moral support, but he keeps his eyes fixed on his tablet even though he's smirking his bloody face off.

She rolls her eyes at me and speaks to Darcie. "I thought we were going out for lunch this afternoon? Me, you and Nat? Or are you ditching us for this big lug over here?"

She stands with her arms crossed, looking at Darcie, so I do the same, copying her stance exactly and look at Darcie too. "So, Darcie what's it to be?" I ask her with a wink, to let her know I'm okay with her going out but I also really want her to stay with me.

"Sorry old man, sisters before misters and all that. Let me go and get ready." She jumps up off her chair and comes over to me, kisses my cheek and runs out of the kitchen.

Nat is getting up too and Becs turns to look at me with a smug smile on her face.

"Cock blocker." I tell her and jump out of her way to avoid another punch in the arm. "Will you do something and protect me from that crazy arse, you call wife, please?" I stand on the other side of Dan, putting him between me and Becs.

"Nope, I'm not getting involved. You two will have to fight it out I'm afraid. My money's on you, sweetie." He lifts his head up from his tablet for a kiss from her.

I mutter, "Pussy whipped" as I walk out behind Nat.

Becs shouts after me, "I'm telling Darcie you said that again."

She laughs as I curse loudly. "Fuck, now I'm in trouble."

"Are you sure you want to go out for lunch when you can eat here and be with me?" I don't want her to go out. I know I thought it was okay when I was downstairs but now, I want her to be here with me so I can make love to her again. I want to smell her, taste her, feel her and watch her face as she comes again and again. But I also don't want to be that whiny annoying guy that doesn't let their girlfriends breathe. I've never felt like this before and it's confusing the life out of me. Laughing, she looks over at me. I'm pouting whilst laying, fully stretched out with my hands behind my head, on the bed. She leans over so her face is directly above mine.

"Denny. I'll be back in a few hours. I want to go and get some female perspective on everything. Don't be grumpy. When I get back, we can see if ye can get me to call ye my Adonis again?" She looks at me with sex in her eyes. She bites her bottom lip and I can feel my control slipping away from me. I can't help it. I growl and grab her, quickly rolling her underneath me, pinning her hands by her sides and kissing her hard. I pull our mouths apart and groan at her.

"You can't say things like that, whilst looking at me like that and whilst biting down on this." I pull her bottom lip with my teeth and nibble on it. "And then expect me not to want to do this." My hand cups her breast, finds her nipple and works it around and around. I love that her nipples are so sensitive. That she's so responsive to me. She groans at me and whispers my name. I lower the strap of her dress and pull the cup of her bra down and take her nipple into my mouth. My hand reaches up under her dress and into her knickers. Before my hand has even touched her, I know she's ready for me. She's always so wet for me. I push her knickers to the side and my fingers slide up and down her slit. I push a finger into her, and she cries out.

"Denny!"

"Do you want more, baby?"

She nods at me and I slide another finger inside as she groans her appreciation.

"Tell me what you want, Darcie. Tell me what you need." My eyes bore into hers. Hesitation flickers in them but is quickly replaced with fire as her need takes over.

"I want ye, Denny. I want ye to make love to me again. I want ye inside me. I want ye to make me come. My beautiful Adonis." I don't hesitate at all. I bring her knickers down and undo my trousers. I bring my lips to hers and moan against them.

"This is going to be quick, Irish, but I swear you'll enjoy it." I thrust into her hard and we both cry out with the intensity of it.

"Are you okay, baby?" I need to know before I carry on.

She looks up at me with fire in her eyes and breathlessly replies, "Yes, my Adonis. Yes. Please, Denny, move." With that I thrust into her.

"You're so beautiful, Darcie. Fucking perfect. I love you." She's so tight it takes all my strength not to come straight away. She feels so good wrapped around me, her eyes glassed over in pleasure and her beautiful tits bouncing with each of my thrusts. Her pussy tightens around me and I know she's getting closer and closer. I can feel her on the edge, ready to come all over my dick so I reach down and circle my thumb on her clit. She screams my name loudly, followed by, 'my Adonis', over and over again as she shatters with her orgasm. Feeling her muscles clench around me, milking my dick, and hearing her scream my name is too much. The tingling sensation starts off in my balls and shoots through my whole body as I come straight after her. I roll us over, still buried inside of her, and let her collapse onto my chest.

"Fucking hell, woman. You're going to be the death of me, you know that don't you?" I kiss her on top of her head and snake my arms around her, holding her tightly to me. After a few minutes she moves, and I groan when she pulls herself off me which means we aren't connected anymore.

"You suck, Irish." I grin at her.

"If you're lucky after lunch I might." She wiggles her arse as she walks into the bathroom and I groan and pull the pillow over my face and bite into it hard. This woman is fucking everything!

Chapter 26

Darcie

If someone had told me a few months ago I'd be in a serious relationship with an Adonis-like man, deliciously sore down there and happier than I've ever been, whilst sitting in a little Italian restaurant with my two best friends in the world, I'd have called them mad. But here we are and I can't fight the smile off my face for love nor money. And I don't want to either. The three of us take a little booth with Nat and Becs sitting opposite me. Strategically done on their parts so they can fire off questions about last night, no doubt. I'm not bothered by it. I want to scream from the rooftops that Denny and I made passionate love to each other, but I think I'd be frowned at by the other diners and the owner, and I don't want that to happen as the restaurant is lovely. It reminds me of what a traditional Italian restaurant would look like. With walls an off-white colour and artwork of landmarks from Italy adorning them. There are arches instead of doorways which I think is a Mediterranean style in itself. The waiter comes over and takes our drinks order, wine for the girls and a water with lots of ice for me. As the waiter leaves to collect our drinks,

Becs and Nat are both scrunching their noses up at me in a disgusted way.

"Water with ice? I don't know what's wrong with her." Becs states matter of fact but with a wink and a grin at the same time. She looks so much like Isabelle when she does it that I can't help but giggle.

"Becs give up. I've tried for some time to get her to drink more but other than a handful of times I haven't succeeded. Although I must say she isn't one of those girls that's boring and no fucking fun if she isn't drinking. She's been out with me loads of times and is always the last one on the dance-floor and acts like a twat with me, all whilst sober."

I know she means it as a compliment, but she just called me a twat and insinuated I act like a drunk person on my normal nights out. Christ, the cheek of her.

"Thanks for that, Natalie. I tink I need to re-evaluate my friendships, ye know."

She throws an eye roll at me. "Oh, shut up you, it was meant as a compliment and it's think not tink, you twat." Laughter erupts out of me at the same time Becs guffaws.

"God Nat, if that was your idea of a compliment then jeez." We're laughing uproariously when the waiter comes back with our drinks. He places them nervously on the table and backs away quickly saying, "I'll give you a minute more." The poor guy looks terrified of us.

Once we've gained our composure Nat's the first with the questions.

"So, Miss Darcie, you need to spill, and you need to spill now. How was last night? How many times did you come? Was it as big as I said it would be after I saw him excited that time..."

"Lalalalalala, please stop. That's my brother. I'll listen to how good it was, as long as it's not too graphic, BUT I don't want a full description of his parts puhlease." Becs is covering her ears and Nat looks at her in mock disgust, her nose scrunched up again and her eyebrows drawn together.

"Becs, you're ruining it. I want the details."

Becs rolls her eyes and takes her hands away from her ears. "Fine, let's order and then I'll go to the bathroom, and you can give her the details about his bits and bobs."

She shudders and gags a little when she says this, which elicits giggles from Nat.

"And then you can wait for the rest until I'm back, but please try to get all of your questions answered before I get back Nat, you beast of a woman, you."

Laughing and holding her hands up to admit that Becs has a point about her being a beast, she summons the waiter over and orders our food. Becs vacates our booth and heads to the bathroom as Nat rounds on me instantly. She doesn't even speak, just looks at me.

"Twas wonderful, Nat. He made sure I came as many times as I could, and he's so beautiful..."

She rolls her hand to tell me to carry on and I giggle knowing what she wants to hear.

"Yes, Natalie. He's bloody huge and perfect." She throws her arms in the air dramatically and holds them there like she's at a football match and has just seen her team score.

"I knew it! Mazel Tov, Darcie."

Laughing again we clink our glasses and Becs returns from the bathroom with her hands over her ears.

"Have you finished?"

I nod at her.

She asks, "So how was it? Did it hurt? I remember my first time, it hurt, but me and Dan were just kids. It's gotten a hell of a lot better since then, though." Her eyes twinkle and her cheeks flush red as she bites her bottom lip. She's clearly thinking of a 'fun' time she had with Daniel recently.

Before I can answer her, Nat pipes up.

"Hold up, are you telling me you've only ever been with one person in your entire life?" She looks at Becs with her eyes as wide as saucers and her mouth gaping open. Becs simply nods her head in response.

"You lost your V card to Dan and you're still with him. You lost yours to Den and will be with him forever. And I'm just 'Mrs. Shags everyone and can't even remember the name of the boy who took her V card'. I'm never going to find my Dan/Den/Joseph." I shake my head a wee bit as I watch my best friend put her head in her hands and groan at us. Becs's eyes flit between mine and Nats lowered head, worry flashing in them.

"Nat, you're worrying Becs."

Her head shoots up and she grabs Becs's hand. "Sorry, chick, ignore me. I'm overly dramatic, don't you know?" She wiggles her eyebrows at her and Becs gives her a playful smack to the hand. "So, you really haven't been with anyone apart from Dan? Do you ever think 'what if'?"

I want to scold Nat, but I'm also so curious to hear what Becs has to say about that. I don't plan on being with anyone else other than Denny and I want to know if she has any regrets. I don't think it'll make a difference to me as I'm not leaving Denny for love nor money, but I'm curious, so I keep my mouth shut.

"No regrets, Nat; Daniel is my everything. He's the most generous lover, the perfect partner, and the most amazing daddy, ever. He's always showing me and telling me how much he loves me, and I love that only he has known me in that way. My only regret is..." As she hesitates a flash of pain stalks her face, and I know what it is.

"It's stupid, we were here to talk about Darcie, not me."

She looks down into her lap and I reach across the table at her.

"Dan's been with someone else, hasn't he?" She looks up at me startled.

"How did you know?" She locks eyes with me and I give her a gentle smile.

"Because I feel the same about Denny. I love that he'll be the only one to know me like that, and whilst I've shared a couple of his firsts it guts me that other women have had that side of him. I know how ye feel Becs, but *you've* got Daniel and he loves *ye* and ye have your beautiful kids. I guess we can't have everything perfect, can we?"

She looks up at me smiling and thanks me just as our waiter brings our food. Before we've put a morsel of food in our mouths Nat puts her cutlery down on the table with a bang.

"I have to know Becs, how's he been with someone else? You two have been together since you were young? Did he cheat on you?" She points her finger at Becs and shakes her head. "Actually don't. Don't tell me because I don't want to hate the fucker. No, tell me, but if he did, I'm going to rip his bollocks off."

I kick Nat under the table and give her a thunderous look, but as she cries out in pain and rubs her shin, Becs smiles.

"Nothing like that, Nat. He slept with someone in college. It was frustrating as hell as it was only a few weeks before we got together but..." Becs pauses and a sad smile flits across her lips.

"He still apologises to me and although it kills me sometimes, I think to myself it happened the way it was supposed to. Like you and Denny. And like you and your Dan/Den/Joseph when you meet him, Nat."

I smile at them. I love how Denny's family have embraced me and Nat into their lives. I've gone from having no family to having Nat and now this amazing set of people.

"So, you're not going to rip Dan's bollocks off are you, Nat? I'm not sure I'm finished with them just yet."

We erupt into another fit of giggles and the waiter turns away from us, thinking twice about clearing our plates. My phone rings in my bag and I answer it without looking at the caller display. Giggles still leave my lips as I say hello. I expect to hear Denny but there's nothing. I look at the screen and seeing the withheld number, I disconnect the call and go back to my giggles and friends.

We decide to take a stroll seeing as we're in no rush to get back. I'm having so much fun with the girls, even though I'm missing Denny like mad. They've become such an important part of my life since the incident with my daddy, spending time with them makes me feel happy. I'm enjoying the girl time.

Nat sighs loudly and gains our attention as intended.

"I need a job. Becs d'you need a new nanny by any chance?" My head snaps around so I'm looking at her.

"Hey, ye stop trying to take my job away from me."

Laughing, she grabs me around the shoulders. "You don't need it anymore. You can be a lady of leisure and spend the day with me whilst I look after the twinnies." I shake my head at her, just about to tell her no again when Becs interrupts me.

"That's not a bad idea, Nat."

I can't help the shriek that comes out of my mouth, "WHAT!"

Becs laughs whilst Nat and I look at each other confused as anything.

"No, I didn't mean about you being a lady of leisure. I meant spending the day with Nat whilst I work. Instead of you spending the day with her, I could. I need a PA and you would be ideal, if you don't mind being my slave that is." There's a playful twinkle in Becs's eyes.

Nat shrieks and jumps on top of her shouting. "Do you mean it? I'll be your slave, oh beautiful mistress. Whatever you need of me I will do, even sexual favours if that's what you're into." She wiggles her eyebrows at her and Becs bursts into laughter. "Honestly though Becs, are you serious because you could have just saved me from having to crawl back to my mum with my tail between my legs."

Becs nods and beams at her. "Honestly, I need a PA. And I know you're good at what you do, or you wouldn't have been headhunted to bloody Paris. Come in with me on Monday and we can sort the bits and bobs out. But I won't be needing sexual favours, Nat, I have Dan for that."

I put my arms over both of their shoulders and tell them I love them both. My attention is dragged away from them to across the road where I see two men taunting and hitting someone. With no regard for my own safety, I run over and shout at them to leave him alone. I can hear Nat and Becs shouting at me to stop, it's too dangerous, but I can't stop, I have to help. I know I'm running into the face of danger but I can't stand by and watch someone get hurt, not anymore. As I get closer I can see the two guys are young, probably late teens, and when they see the screaming woman running toward them, they run in the opposite direction.

I reach the man who's now on the ground. "Are ye okay? Did they hurt ye?" He turns to face me, and familiar eyes meet mine.

"George? Are ye okay?" His nose and mouth are bleeding, but he manages to smile at me.

"Darcie, thank you. I'm okay. Perks of sleeping rough I'm afraid." He looks away, sadly and I crouch down so I'm in front of him. His beard is longer than the last time I saw him but not so long that he looks like a wizard or anything. His kind brown eyes shine at me and I grip his hand tightly.

"Will ye let me clean that up for ye? I can..." Before I finish the sentence, I stop. I was going to offer him to come to mine, but I realise mine is actually Becs's and she doesn't know who George is, and probably wouldn't want a homeless stranger in her home.

"Nat, will ye see if ye can find a chemist or something we can clean this up with please?" I frown at Nat who's staring at me and George intently and I have to say her name again to snap her out of it.

"Sorry. There was a chemist open up the road, I'll go and be back in a minute." She turns and runs off like a whippet.

Becs looks down at me, a quizzical look on her face. "Darcie, do you two know each other?"

Briefly I tell Becs about the time I met George and about his story, with his permission of course. Becs has a worried look on her face.

"George, the one who Denny thought... shit, Darcie. Call Denny and tell him about this now."

I draw my eyebrows together whilst looking at her and shake my head. "No, Becs. I told him about George. He knows there's nothing going on or anything like that."

"I know the Blanc men, trust me. Phone him now and save yourself the drama later." Something in her eyes tells me to listen so I reach into my pocket and pull out my phone.

After a couple of rings he answers. "Hey, Irish, you

coming home yet? I miss you and yes I'm aware I sound like a whiny, needy, baby right now."

I smile to myself and quickly interrupt him. "Denny, we were walking back, and I saw George getting beaten up. Well, I didn't know it was George. I ran over to help him and I'm just waiting for Nat to come back so we can clean him up and make sure his cuts aren't too bad. Becs thought I should phone ye..."

Before I can finish my sentence, he's cutting me off. "Where are you? I'm coming now." His voice is full of anger and he sounds cold.

I don't argue and just tell him where we are. He hangs up and Becs gives me a sad look.

"Once he gets here, he'll see and will be okay. Trust me, Darcie."

I can't argue with her about his ridiculous reaction as Nat's heading back to us. She's carrying a bag of supplies and when she reaches us, she bends down and speaks to George.

"I've got some antiseptic wipes. They may sting a bit, but I don't think you need stitches or anything. Did you know those jack arses?" She opens the wipes and is gently cleaning his nose up.

"Nah, they came over acting like twats and then one of them hit me. I hit him back but the other one joined in and I stood no chance."

She curses but carries on cleaning him up. I stand next to Becs with my mouth flapping open like a fish. I've never seen Nat do anything like this before.

Becs looks at me and mouths "What the fuck?"

I mouth back "I don't fecking know!" at her. A few minutes later I feel a hot sensation running down my spine, tingling. I turn around and see my Adonis heading towards me. I walk to meet him halfway and can see the anger in his ice blue eyes. It should make me scared or worried but instead it turns me on. He's created a wanton woman in me for sure. As he spots Nat on the floor tending to George, the anger disappears a bit. He looks at me with raised eyebrows. I raise my shoulders trying to convey I haven't the foggiest about anything. He grabs me and pulls me off my feet, lifting me so we're face to face.

"You ever put yourself in danger again and I'll, well, I don't know what I'll do, but I'm pissed at you." He kisses me.

I smile as I think he can't be that pissed at me if he's kissing me, but keep myself from saying it.

"I'm sorry, Denny. I just can't stand by and watch someone getting hurt." My eyes glaze over, as he hugs me. He puts his lips to my head and shushes me. He lowers me gently down and we walk over to Becs, Nat and George. I'm relieved to see Nat's done a fairly good job at cleaning him up. I'm also relieved he hasn't been hurt any worse.

George stands up and looks down at the ground. "Thank you, all of you. It's nice to see there are still kind people."

Denny looks over at him, with his head cocked to the side.

"Do I know you? You look familiar?" George looks up and smiles at him.

"You probably don't recognise me properly looking like this," he sweeps his hand over himself and looks thoroughly embarrassed. "I used to work for you, Mr. Blanc. I was in the mail room, but after my ex kicked me out I didn't have anywhere to stay or wash, so I was let go by Dave and I ended up here." I look over at Denny and note the devastation on his face.

"I didn't know that, George. I would never have allowed that to happen. I would've tried to help. I'm so sorry you were treated like that by one of my staff. I'll be speaking to Dave personally about it."

I squeeze his arm tightly. I believe every word he says because I know him, and I know he's the kindest and most caring man on the planet. George looks over at him and smiles, inclining his head in thanks, too choked up to speak.

Nat however isn't. "That's all well and good, Den but he doesn't have a job now because of that dick."

I shoot Nat a 'what is going on with ye look' but she ignores it and stares Denny down. He shifts uncomfortably on his feet. My bestie is a force to be reckoned with for sure.

"Erm, well I'm sure I can find a position for you, George. In fact I will find a position. George, come and have a chat with me, I have an idea. Ladies, will you be okay to make your own way home, without getting into any more trouble?"

He directs that last bit at me, so I poke my tongue out at him. Nat narrows her eyes at Denny as Becs smiles like she has some insight into what's happening. We all nod and watch Denny, dressed immaculately in his designer jeans and jacket, drape his arm over George's dirty and ripped clothes like they've known each other forever. I'm so curious as to what he has planned but I know tis going to be brilliant because that's what Denny is. Brilliant, amazing and mine, always.

Chapter 27

Denny

Anger and fear burn through me as I turn the corner and spot Becs. My gaze wanders, desperately seeking out my love, my heart racing. As I spot her black hair blowing in the breeze I relax. Instead of running over to them I slow my pace down and stalk. I want to watch for a bit. I want to see how Darcie is with this bloody George for myself. As I prowl over and try to control my breathing at the sight of her, my whole-body tingling from seeing my girl, she turns as if she can feel me there and our eyes lock. Ice cold blue meets ice cold blue. She doesn't break our gaze, she smiles at me and her eyes go from icy to blue fire in a beat. As I get closer, I can make out Nat tending to a homeless man. Shocked is an understatement at seeing Nat being the caregiver here. I mouth 'what the fuck' at Darcie. All of my jealousy has disappeared, and I'm now filled with curiosity. The anger's still there, but more so because she was reckless going over and intervening in a fight in the first place. As I reach where she stands, I grab her and lift her up, her feet dangling inches off the ground, my little Polly pocket. Her face is so close to mine I can feel her breath on my lips.

"You ever put yourself in danger again and I'll, well, I don't know what I'll do, but I'm pissed at you." I hadn't thought that through properly and can see the amusement in her eyes before I cover her full lips with my mouth. I look over at the scene that stands before me. A busy Chelsea street, people around us, coming and going, and Nat on the ground sorting the man, I'm assuming is George, out. Once Nat is satisfied she's finished, and he's able to stand, she allows him to get up off the ground and she does the same.

As George looks sheepishly around, I notice there's something so familiar about him. I know him from somewhere. As soon as he mentions working for me, I can place him immediately. He was always so happy and cheerful when he was delivering the post to us. How could I have not seen the change in him? Why didn't I notice he wasn't there one day? I've always prided myself on being a good employer and that's obviously all bullshit. If I'd known what he was going through I would've helped him. Well, I know now, and I'm going to help him whether he likes it or not. All my earlier jealousy has dissipated, mainly because of the vibes Nat and George are throwing off to each other. His eyes haven't left hers once. He isn't interested in my Irish at all. I grin as a plan forms in my head. I tell the girls goodbye and put my arm around George, I know this man's going to be alright.

Once I've heard George's story it forces thoughts of Lewis into my head. He was stopped from even knowing he had a son. He seemed genuinely upset about that. Maybe I need to reach out to him. Become friends at least. I shake my head and bring my focus back to George.

"The woman's a joke, doing that to her own daughter!

Makes me fucking sick. Every kid deserves to know their dad." I can't hide the pain in my voice but as George looks at me hesitantly, I rein it in and change the conversation. "I'm going to get you another job in the company."

We round a corner, "And I've secured you a place to live in here as well. Rent free for the next six months as part of a compensation packet for what you've had to go through because of one of my employees. And I'll be giving you a sum of money, so you can source some clothes and stuff for work. Then once we've done all of that, I'm going to get the company lawyers to source a family lawyer for us to use to get you access to your daughter." Walking full steam ahead into the building Dan and I own a couple of flats in, I turn around expecting to see him next to me but instead I see him standing on the pavement with his head down.

"George, are you okay?" I ask tentatively.

He looks up at me, tears brimming in his eyes. "Why are you doing this?"

Emotions threaten to spill out of me too, so I clear my throat and put my arm around his shoulder.

"Everyone deserves some help every now and again. I also think every kid deserves to know their dad if they're a good man, and you, George, are a good man. You've just been unlucky, that's all. I was unlucky for a long time, and it sucked, and someone helped me, so I'm just paying it forward. I want to help you. Hell, I'm going to help you, so we can either stand out here gabbing like a couple of old washerwomen or we can go inside and start the next lucky chapter of your life. What d'you say?" He takes a deep breath, says thank you and we walk into the building together.

I notice the concierge's face when he sees George and I enter. I walk over confidently to him whilst George hangs back a bit.

"Good afternoon, Mr. Blanc. Is everything okay?" The concierge asks, clearly concerned about George standing behind me, dishevelled and looking like a broken man.

"Everything's fine Bill, flat thirteen's empty isn't it?" I ask the concierge.

"Yes sir, the previous tenant left a couple of weeks ago." He responds with a questioning look on his brow.

"Excellent. This is the new tenant. I'd appreciate it if you made him feel very welcome. Did you arrange the welcome basket as instructed?" Bill nods at me. His face is no longer curious. Shock is written on his features and I can't hide my displeasure at his lack of professionalism and basic human kindness. I've schooled my face into an intimidating stare and I glare at Bill. I hate the way he's looking at George. I glance back at him standing behind me with his head down, staring at the floor. I hate seeing him like that, broken and with no self-confidence. I know what it feels like to feel worthless, and after months of having to endure living rough what do I expect him to be doing? Exuding confidence?

Bill quickly reads my glare and dips his head in apology. I take a step towards George, put my hand on his shoulder, and guide him towards the stairwell. Slowly we make our way upstairs to his new flat. I want him to digest all the new information I've thrown at him, so I keep quiet and let him have some peace with his mind.

"George, welcome home." I clap him on the back and open the door. Stepping to the side, I let him look around. The place is a good size, two bedrooms, one for when his daughter comes to stay. Neutral tones have been used throughout the property, white walls and cream carpets open the space up and make everything look clean and sterile. It's fully furnished so there's a sofa in the front room and beds in the bedrooms. I watch him look around and notice how he holds onto his bag tightly, looking uncomfortable.

"Erm, Mr. Blanc, I don't belong here. It's all lovely and clean and I'm, well, I'm not." Again, he puts his head down and steps toward the door. I walk over and take his bag and walk into the bathroom motioning him to follow.

"Dan asked the concierge for a welcome basket to be put in here, there's toiletries in it. Run a bath and sort yourself out, there'll be clothes waiting for you when you're done. Then we're going to my house for dinner. You can meet Dan again, my brother, and we'll explain about the job offer we have for you. Hear us out." I can see he's overwhelmed but, I also need him to get over it because this is something I'm doing. And once my mind's made up, that's it.

"George, you deserve a break and I'm giving it to you. Take it with both hands and let your pride be damned. Please."

He looks me in the eyes slowly and the vulnerability in them almost tips me over the edge. This man has been through hell and back. He deserves some good to happen to him. He tentatively offers me his hand and I take it and smile at him encouragingly. As he walks into the bathroom, he stops in the doorframe, his back still to me.

"Thank you, Mr. Blanc. You and Darcie are amazing people, perfect for each other. I'm honoured to call you friends and I'll forever be in your debt." Before I can respond he's closed the door and I hear the taps being turned on. I blow out a deep breath and get busy on the phone to Dan.

"The girls back?"

"Yeah, they are, and they told me what happened. How could Dave do that to him?"

I'm glad to hear that Dan's as furious as I am. "I know,

we'll discuss it with him, don't worry. I need some clothes for him, Dan. Can you sort it and bring them over." As I tell Dan my plan, he's on board instantly, like I knew he would be. Not only will he figure out how to get some clothes here ASAP, but he'll get HR to sort out a contract for him as well. By the time he's finished in the bathroom he'll have a new life waiting for him. My phone buzzes and I check the screen and see a text.

Darcie: Denny, where are you? What's going on? Are you still annoyed at me? I'm sorry if you are. I didn't mean to put myself at risk, I just had to help. Forgive me, old man? xx

Darcie: I shouldn't have called you 'old man' when I'm asking for forgiveness should I, lol? Even though you were angry at me, you looked sexy as anything striding towards me earlier. I love you, Denny. Always, my Adonis xx

Me: You double texted, I thought that was against the rules for you young uns? I'm never going to be okay with you putting yourself in danger, Irish, but I get why you did it. I will always forgive you. You are mine, after all xx

Me: I like seeing that I'm your Adonis in writing, but I love hearing you shout it out more. I hope you're ready for later, Darcie... I love you xx

Darcie: Us young uns are learning from you old uns, and double texting doesn't seem like that bad a thing anymore. I'm ready and waiting for you and I cannot wait to shout my Adonis out to you in our bedroom later. Always and forever yours, my Adonis xx

Darcie: Stop sexting and tell us what's going on 'old man.' You've got to teach me old mucker to have a better poker face. I could tell what you were sending from her bright red face LMAO. This is Nat by the way, Darcie's making us tea x

Darcie: Oh my God, Denny. I'm so sorry. I'm going to kill her xx

Well, that's a lot to take in, in the space of five or so minutes. Laughing, I call Nat's phone.

"You are in so much trouble, woman." I can hear Darcie telling her off in the background.

"Don't. She's so not happy with me. Can you hear her? She has her 'nanny' voice on and she knows it scares me when she does it. Shit, now she's giving me evils. Denny, you should really control your woman better. Well, that went down like a lead balloon. She isn't making me tea anymore because I'm a bloody eejit. Anyway, what's going on? Is George okay?"

I notice the slight change in her voice when she mentions his name and I chuckle.

"What's so funny, Blanc?"

I laugh more. Nat only calls me Blanc when she's pissed off with me.

"Still laughing at you texting me off Darcie's phone and then her not making you tea as a punishment for telling me to control her. Anyway, I better go–" I can hear her saying 'no, tell me,' before I hang up.

Nat likes George, that bit's clear. And I have a raging hard on just hearing Darcie scold her friend. I can picture the evils she's giving to Nat as well and, fuck, I'm rock hard. Just from an image in my head, like a fucking teenager. Football players, old football scores, and Dan are what I'll be thinking about for the next few hours to help calm myself down. Until I get back to Darcie and she can take care of my very big problem.

The girls are sitting in the downstairs living room and I assume the kids are upstairs in the playroom as I don't have Isla wrapped around me like she normally is when I step in the door. Dan walks over and practically sits on top of Becs. I roll my eyes and smile at him. Before I met Darcie, I would've had two thoughts about that. First, what a pussy whipped fucker he was. Second, I want that. I wouldn't have let that last one fester in my head for too long though. Since I've found Darcie, I understand him better than ever. I know the reason he does that is because they're in a room full of people, and he can't be inside of her and that's what he wants to do. Not for sex or for an orgasm but to have that connection, to feel like he's home. I know this because it's how I feel about Darcie.

I tear my gaze away from them and find blue eyes focused on me, eyes that are filled with love. She bites down on her lip and I feel my dick twitch. We move to each other without communicating at all. My hands wrap around her, I place my mouth over hers and kiss her like I'm starved of oxygen, and she's the air I need to breathe. It's more passionate than I intended in front of everyone, but I can't help it. I break away when I hear a shuffling of feet and remember poor George standing at the doorway.

"Sorry, George." I motion for him to come into the room and give him an apologetic smile. He steps in wearing a pair of new dark blue jeans and a crisp white t-shirt and trainers, also white. We've taken care of his hair and beard, and apart from a slight cut near his top lip, you would never know he'd just been beaten up and was living on the streets.

"Guys, George is our newest recruit at work and our newest tenant in one of our flats around the corner."

He smiles sheepishly and waves hello to everyone.

"George, I'm so happy for ye." Darcie is choking back tears and heading over to him. She reaches up and hugs him and my hands clench into fists. I have to restrain myself from tugging him off her. My inner caveman isn't far from the surface when it comes to Darcie and I really have to keep him in check, especially after the way Darcie reacted to him the last time. I thought that was going to be our first and last date.

Becs catches my eye, and she shakes her head at me while Dan gives me a sympathetic look. When I look over at Nat, she has the same look on her face I have on mine, but I would bet my bollocks her possessiveness isn't about Darcie. I smirk at her, and she looks away from me, embarrassed.

"Alright, alright I've let you hold her for long enough now." I say pulling Darcie over to me in a joking way but also, so I have my hands on her, *mine*. I peek a glance at Nat and see relief wash over her face at them being apart too. The grin on my face is firmly stuck there whilst Nat frowns over at me again. I bite my cheek to hold back a full-on laughing fit at her and judging by the evil look she throws my way she can tell. I motion for George to sit down and strategically manoeuvre him so he's in front of Nat.

He nervously strokes the back of his head. "Er, Nat?"

She looks at him, trying to be nonchalant, and in her defence, she does a surprisingly good job of it. But I catch the little hesitation in her eyes mixed with the desire that's causing her to blush slightly. Nat has it bad.

"Thank you for your help today. I really appreciate it.

You were kind to me. It means a lot." He reaches over and takes her hand.

You can almost see the sparks fly when they touch. I look around and notice no one else is paying them any attention. Dan and Becs are engrossed in a tv show and Darcie's walking over to the other chair. Unbelievable, Becs the bloodhound managed to sniff out me and Darcie but is sitting there oblivious to George and Nat. I watch them for a few seconds and smile to myself. I head over to Darcie and sit down next to her. Not as close as Dan and Becs because I want to give her space in case she needs it, but she instantly scoots over to me so that she's pressed up against my side. I kiss the top of her head and inhale her scent and she places her hand on my chest, over my heart, and looks up at me.

"Ye are the very best of men, Denny. I am in awe of ye. I'm so proud to be able to call ye mine. Always."

My throat constricts a bit and I have to swallow hard to rid the lump that's formed there. I take her hand off my chest and raise it to my lips and kiss the back of it. I smile down at her and we just sit there for a while. Content in each other's arms.

Chapter 28

Denny

Monday morning comes around too fast for my liking. I'm not happy about being away from Darcie all bloody day, but I also can't convince her to come and work for me at the office, so it looks like I'm stuck without her. All day! As we step into the kitchen for breakfast, the girls are already arguing. Isaac has left for school, Dan dropped him off, and Becs is talking to Nat at the kitchen work top.

"Girls, knock it off right now." Becs's warning is firm, and it makes them both stop and pay attention more.

"So, I'll get you to shadow me for a week and teach you the basics with my calendar and everything and then it'll be 'throw you in at the deep end,' I'm afraid. If my old assistant hadn't been a fu-fudging poop head, they could've trained you but unfortunately–"

She shrugs her shoulders at Nat who in turn informs her everything's going to be fine. The girls get rowdy again and this time Darcie steps in.

"Isabelle and Isla, your mammy has had to tell ye once already and now I'm having to as well. This behaviour needs to stop. Now go upstairs and brush your teeth, please. I'll be checking, so do them properly, Isabelle."

The girls straighten up and listen better than soldiers do to their commanding officers. Once they're upstairs, I stand behind her, snake my hands around her waist and pull her into me so she can feel my hard-on press against her, and I whisper in her ear.

"Is it wrong, you going all sergeant major just then has made my little soldier stand to attention? It was fucking hot, Irish; you may have to speak to me like that in the bedroom." I nibble her earlobe and she lets out a breathless sigh.

"Your soldier is anything but little, old man, or should I say my Adonis?" She turns her head so she can brush her lips over mine.

"Hellooooo, people standing right here you know. Jeez, surely you got enough last night and probably this morning too."

Our kiss ends and I look at Nat and give her a look that confirms we had indeed been at it all morning too.

"See, I bloody knew it." She laughs as Darcie nudges me in the belly with her elbow.

"Darcie, quick word about the girls."

Darcie heads over to Becs and as they talk, I turn my attention to Nat. Well half of my attention as I can't devote all of it to her with Darcie standing in the same room as me.

"So how are you, Natalie?" I smirk at her.

"Fine. What's up with you, Denny? Not enough blood rushing to the head on your shoulders?" She smirks back.

"George will be here in a minute; I'm giving him a ride into the office." I watch in glee as the colour rushes to her cheeks and she bites onto her bottom lip. And then, as quick as a flash, her lip is released, and she shakes her head a tiny bit looking defiantly into my eyes.

"Oh?"

That's it. I laugh a deep belly laugh and notice Becs and Darcies eyes on me. Their eyebrows pulled together suspiciously. I walk over to the counter and grab an apple off the side and smirk as I take a bite out of it. Nat rolls her eyes at me and walks out of the kitchen.

Darcie comes over to me with her arms folded over her chest. "What are ye up to, old man?"

I shrug my shoulders nonchalantly at her. "Nothing. Just winding Nat up. I think she likes George. What happened to Adonis? Why are we back to 'old man' after this morning?"

Darcie rolls her eyes at me and chuckles.

"Ye picked up on that did ye? She blushes every time someone says his name." She gives me a cheeky grin and continues, "And as to ye being an Adonis..."

I wince, waiting for the insult to come so I can return with a witty comment as per our usual banter.

"I couldn't have said it better myself. Ye, Denny Blanc, are my Adonis and I will worship ye and be indebted to ye until the day I die. Then I'll be sitting up there on my cloud looking over at the big man, thinking 'this God has nothing on my Denny.'"

The smile on my face is so big it's hurting. I kiss her because I have no words for her and as our lips brush each other tenderly I whisper 'Mine. Always mine' against them. We're interrupted by the doorbell. As I walk to let George in, I pass Nat who's checking her appearance in the hallway mirror.

As I walk past her, I lean close to her ear. "Relax, you look beautiful." Giving her shoulder a squeeze, I open the door.

"Morning boss, thanks for driving me in..." As his eyes wander past me and find Nat, he loses all train of thought and stops mid-sentence. I grin at him as I close the door and think to myself, the poor bugger has it all to come. I'm so glad I'm over that with my Darcie.

My stomach starts to flutter as I head down the steps towards my car. This is the first time I've seen Joseph since all the drama on Saturday night. I've spoken to him and Gorgeous on the phone and they reassured me everything is fine as I did with them, but seeing him is another thing. I'm glad George is here with me so we can't talk about anything too hard or personal, mainly my so-called dad, as I still have no idea what to do with that situation. I know Joseph feels guilty about the sacrifice Lewis made for him, but I can't force myself to do anything just yet.

"Morning, Joseph, Gorgeous okay?"

Joseph nods at me and motions his head to George.

"Sorry, Joseph. This is George, our new employee. George, this is Joseph, he's my driver and uncle but is more like my dad. It's a complicated story. He and Gorgeous, my assistant and Joseph's wife, raised me from the age of eight. They're basically my parents."

I notice Joseph's reaction to me calling them my parents. The pride, sadness and love all rolled into one that emanates from him. I could never deny him and Gorgeous. They saved me at a time when I needed it the most and gave me a family. We fill the ride to work with office chatter and go over where he'll be working again. As we pull up to the building, Joseph asks me if he can have a word. I nod my head at him, and I ask George to wait outside for me. I sit forward in my seat and Joseph turns around to face me. I'm nervous, worried and anxious all over again.

"Everything okay?"

He looks at me carefully and speaks quietly. "I just wanted to say, my boy, I'm so immensely proud of you. You're an amazing man, and I'm proud to call you my son. I'll never push you into a relationship with Lewis, but I'd like you to try to get to know him just like I'm going to try to do. Is that something you'd think about for me?"

That damn lump is in my throat again and I have to swallow hard to get rid of it. I'm turning into an emotional wreck. I clear my throat and nod my head at him.

"Thank you, Joseph. I'll think about it. I promise." My voice sounds thick with emotion and Joseph reaches over and grabs my hand and squeezes it. For a moment we just sit there looking at each other with appreciation and love between us. He smirks at me and I grin back at him, shaking my head at the amount of emotional moments we've had over the past few weeks. I shuffle out of the car and walk into the building with George and note the darkness is nowhere to be seen.

Chapter 29

Darcie

"Calm down. No, I don't think Denny will say anything. No, I won't tell him that. Because tis threatening the man I love, Natalie. No Nat, seriously, calm down."

With the phone resting between my ear and shoulder and my hands full of a combination of toy dinosaurs and baby dolls, I'm trying my hardest to get Nat to calm down. Becs, who's next to her on the other end of the phone, is doing the same thing. Tis tedious but as Nat's normally the cool, calm and collected type, I'll indulge her for the time being. I've never seen or heard Nat so wound up about liking a man before. I'm used to her being the cocky one in the dating world, not nearly hyperventilating because she thinks someone's hot. She must really like George. I think back to not so long ago when Denny and I were in that beginning bit of a relationship and how nerve racking it all was. I'm so much happier to be where we are now.

After hanging up and dropping the toys into the girls' toy hamper, I plop myself down on the floor and I look over to see the twins playing together at the toy kitchen in the far corner of the playroom. They've been so good today,

I'll leave them to play for a while longer. My phone rings again and I pick it up, expecting to see Nat's name but frown when I see an unknown caller on the screen instead.

"Hello?" Silence is on the other end and before I can speak again the line goes dead. "Bloody computers calling random numbers." I sigh out and decide to leave the tidying for a bit and text Denny.

Me: You know you winding Natalie up this morning has given me a headache all day x

Denny: What? Why? x

Me: She's stressing out thinking you're going to tell him she likes him. You didn't do that did you?

Denny: I'm not answering any questions you have, until you correct the abomination of that last text. No kisses are a big no-no, Irish. Tut Tut xxx

Me: I'm sorry, my love xxxxxxxxxxxxxxxxxxxxxxxxxxxxxxxxxx better? x

Denny: Much. To answer your earlier question, I may have wound her up about it but I didn't say anything to George. I know he likes her too, though it might be a bit soon for him to make a move x

Darcie: Look at the great and mighty 'no feelings involved' Denny Blanc being all considerate about other people's relationships x

Denny: Just to be clear, the Denny Blanc you speak of, the no feelings involved one? He died the day he met an Irish beauty and was reborn as Denny Blanc the one whose heart walks

around outside of his body and is called Darcie, just an FYI xxx

My hands tremble as I read his text. How perfect is this man? The fact he's mine just makes my heart sing. He's given me the freedom to be me and to love and be loved. He saved my life and has always chased after me. Instead of getting bored of waiting for an emotionally scarred virgin's broken bones to heal, and running off to find someone else, he reassured me, he cared for me, he loved me. He made me feel treasured, and cherished. After years of never letting my guard down, I've finally been able to open up to him. To let him see the real me. The one that's craved to be looked after since I was a wee girl but didn't dare to say it out loud. The one who just wanted to be loved for who she was and wanted to love someone back so fiercely. Denny has given me so much. He's taught me tis okay to love and be vulnerable with the right person. Tis okay to fall for someone because the right person will catch ye when ye do. And now he's sat there texting me things like that on a Monday morning. I can't cope with how happy I am. I want to burst into song and have little animals from the forest join in, but I can't sing for shite and I really don't want to scare the two four-year-olds I have in my care. Besides, imagine all the bird and squirrel poop I'd have to clean up. I shake my head at my crazy, jumbled up thoughts and instead of singing, I reply to him.

Me: Well, that took my breath away, Denny. You are my heart too, you are my everything. I can't wait for you to get home tonight. I love you. Always and forever more xxxxxxx

---

"What are you two doing home so early?" I'm in the kitchen preparing lunch for the twins when Becs and Nat saunter in. I slap Nat's hand away as she tries to steal a carrot stick and she sticks her tongue out at me.

"The model threw up everywhere. I think she'd been out on the piss last night. It's so fucking unprofessional. She's set us back nearly a whole day. I've already told her agent I'm not using her again."

Becs is fuming. She's speaking so fast tis hard to keep up and I direct my gaze to Nat who's grinning inanely at me, clearly very happy to be finished early. More time to moon over George. Well, that's what she thinks. No mooning on my watch.

Nat and Becs sit down at the table, Becs still ranting on about schedules and models. I finish making the girls' lunch and take it up to them in the playroom. Becs doesn't mind them eating in there and I don't want little ears around when Nat, Becs and I are chatting.

We migrate over to the front of the house and sit in the living room whilst drinking tea. This room is my favourite. The windows are big and wide, so the room is always swathed in light. The walls are a light cream with flecks of gold glitter in the paper. I love how the light catches it every now and again. Tis like the paper is twinkling at me. We snuggle on the large sofa and put the world to rights. I love doing this with them. I've finally got sisters who'd do anything for me and me for them.

"Denny told him, didn't he?" Nat's question catches me off guard.

"No, he didn't. Are ye cross about that?"

"No, I'm not fucking cross. Are you mad? I'm relieved. It's too soon for him to be thinking about dating anyone. The man has been through hell. I didn't want him to be uncomfortable, that's all."

"I still can't believe I didn't spot the little looks she threw off and Denny did. I'm losing my touch." Becs looks downhearted as Nat chuckles at her.

"Nah, you were too busy trying not to fuck Dan in front of all of us to notice."

I spray my tea everywhere.

Becs nods her head. "Damn straight, have you seen my husband?"

I laugh at them both and turn to look at Nat as she speaks.

"I love you Becs, I'm so glad I know you."

Becs raises her cup of tea at her in a toast. "Right back at you sister."

I smile at both of them.

I'm lost in the moment so I miss it when Nat nudges Becs and screeches loudly.

"Darcie!"

"Ye fecking eejit, ye made me jump out of my skin. Jesus, Mary and Joseph." I'm clutching at my chest whilst Nat and Becs are laughing at me and I don't even care that they are.

"I love it when you go full on Irish at us Darce. Fecking eejit." Becs mimics me and I roll my eyes at both of them. My phone rings again and I grab it off the side and see another unknown number calling. I silence it and put it back as Becs looks at me, her bloodhound abilities in full force.

"Another one?"

I nod my head at her and ignore the worried looks that flit between them when I say, "Tis a glitch in some computer system. Nothing to worry about."

They both frown at me and I raise my tea to my lips trying to believe my own words. Nothing to worry about.

Chapter 30

Denny

"Are you sure you can keep this to yourselves?" I'm outside a nondescript building in the middle of Hatton Garden, the top diamond place to go to in London, with Natalie and Becs. They both nod at me and Nat rolls her eyes, but Becs puts her hand into mine.

"We won't say a word to Darcie. I've already told Dan though because you know I can't keep anything to myself around him."

Nat rolls her eyes at Becs this time and she responds by sticking her tongue out at her. These two have become quite the double act in the short time we've all known each other. I chuckle at them. Even though I'm anxious Darcie will discover my surprise, I'm really happy to have them here with me. The door opens and I'm quickly shaking hands with a member of staff and telling them my name and appointment time. From the outside you'd never know it was a jewellery shop or it was one of the best in London. There's no window display, nothing tells you what's inside. You only get to see the interior by appointment. It's all very cloak and dagger but I want only the best for my Darcie. Once we step inside it's a different story. It's decorated in natural tones with gold aspects everywhere. Obscenely large chandeliers hang from the vast ceiling space and draw your eyes away from the sparkling glass cabinets forming a U shape on the shop floor. Various pieces of jewellery are scattered in them, diamonds twinkling under the lights like stars at night.

"What's the saying about judging a book by its cover? Jeez this is surprising." Nat mutters to me, I smirk back at her.

"Were you worried about what kind of ring Darcie was going to get when we were standing outside?"

She brings her hand up and puts her thumb and forefinger together to signify a little bit. I roll my eyes and shake my head at her. An older woman approaches us and glances at Nat, offers a polite smile at her and holds out her hand which Nat takes politely.

"Pleasure to meet you Miss, do we have an idea of what type of ring you'd like, or would you like me to get a selection out for you to give you a feel?"

Nat shakes her head fervently and stammers as she tries to get words to come out quick enough whilst still holding the ladies hand. "N-n-nooooooo. Me and him? Nope. Nu uh. No way, Jose. Nada. It's not for me. I'm just helping out."

Becs saunters over and puts her hand on Nat's shoulder, tugging her hand free of the brutal handshake that lasted for way too long. She turns towards the lady.

"What she is so eloquently trying to say is the ring is for our dear friend, and we're just here to offer our support today."

She takes a second to glance at Becs and Nat and her mouth forms an O.

"Say no more. I'm so sorry if I offended you and your wife. I understand why she was so adamant it wasn't for her now. I'll just pop next door and get the selection I've put aside for you today."

As the woman saunters off, I take a look at Nat's face and I can't contain my laughter any longer.

"She thinks I'm your wife, Becs, why would she think that?" A look of shocked horror is frozen on Nat's face whilst Becs pouts at her.

It just makes me laugh even harder.

"Why is the idea of being married to me so bloody repellent to you, Natalie? If anything, you should be thankful she thinks you could get someone as hot as me to marry you." She crosses her arms and looks at Nat with a smug smile on her face.

Nat's forehead furrows in retaliation and a sly smirk forms on her mouth.

"Erm firstly, I just wanted to know why she would assume we were married; I'm not wearing a ring. And secondly Becs, don't kid yourself, if I wanted you, I could have you, trust me. I'd do things to you that would make you forget all about that handsome husband of yours. You certainly wouldn't be pouting when I was done with you, baby."

Becs turns herself to face Nat, hands on her hips and her head slightly tilted. "Really? Do tell me what these things are you'd do to me, put your money where your mouth is, babe."

Nat grins at Becs, her eyes twinkling mischievously. "You'd certainly know where my mouth would be, darling, trust me on that. There'd be no doubt about it when you're screaming my name and not Dan's."

They stare at each other for a second and then both laugh.

"You two are fucking nutcases. I'm telling Dan about you."

"No, you're not telling Dan, or we'll tell Darcie where we've been today." Nat raises her eyebrow at me. "I still don't get why she thought we were married though."

I smack my hand to my forehead and turn to her. "You were so against the idea of the ring we're here to get being for you, she assumed you didn't do men and with Becs's arm around your shoulders thus showing her wedding ring off, she concluded you were gay and was with Becs. It's not hard to figure out."

I blow out an exasperated breath and hear Nat mutter about me being a dick. I can't respond as the lady comes back with a tray of rings and diamonds in different cuts and quite frankly I've had enough of dealing with Nat and Becs's shenanigans.

As we admire the diamond rings, Becs and Nat ooh and ah but nothing I see screams Darcie at me. The lady looks at me and can clearly see the disappointment on my face.

"Clearly none of these are doing it for you, Mr. Blanc, tell me about your girlfriend. Just a few little bits that can give me an insight into what she might like."

I sit back in my chair and think about Darcie. "She's the gentlest person you'll ever meet, but she won't hesitate to put you in your place if you do something wrong. She sees the good in everyone with those ice blue eyes of hers and she's loyal to a fault. She'll go above and beyond to help anyone and is the most caring person in the world. I trust her with my life. Without her, my life would be empty. She's Irish, beautiful, funny, smart, sassy and fiercely passionate. I want the ring to be perfect for her, to show her she's perfect for me. If that makes sense."

I look at each of the ladies in turn and they all have the same dreamy look on their faces.

"I must have said something right judging by the looks on you three."

Becs gets up and puts her arms around me.

Nat punches me in the arm softly saying, "Denny, my man. Darcie is fucking lucky."

"Nah Nat, I'm the lucky one." A thought jumps into my head and I suddenly know what I'm looking for.

"Do you do blue diamonds?" I ask, looking at the lady and she nods her head eagerly. She disappears into the back again and comes out a short while later. She has a tray with some rings and stones on it. I look at the rings and dismiss one instantly.

"The blue's too dark, her eyes are more like mine. Just like that." I find a ring with a stone that matches her eyes perfectly. That's Darcie's ring.

"Ah, the aquamarine. Excellent choice, Mr. Blanc." I nod slightly at the lady and pick the ring up and show it to Becs and Nat. Nat places it on her finger and I approve. The stone isn't too big, it's subtle but the tiny diamonds around the band make it sparkle in the right light. Nat holds it up to my eyes and smiles.

"Yours and Darcie's eyes are near enough identical and this ring is perfect, Denny."

Two weeks later:

I've planned everything about tonight with precision. I've booked the venues. Invited the right people and I've picked out a beautiful full length pale blue dress for Darcie to wear. The only problem is, she's refusing point blank to wear it and I've got Becs and Nat trying everything to convince her otherwise.

"I just don't understand why you're making a big deal about this, Natalie?" Darcie's standing in our room with her hands on her hips and refusing to wear the dress.

Give the girls their due, they really are trying.

"This is my do over night, you pain in my Darce. We're meant to be celebrating me being home. I'm wearing a bloody formal dress because dammit, I want to and so is Becs. Why d'you have to be so bloody stubborn? Denny got you that dress over two weeks ago and you haven't even so much as looked at it since then. It's stunning and you should get to wear it once in its little dress life."

I snicker from behind the door and wait to hear Darcie's response.

"I just don't understand. We're going to a restaurant, not the fecking Oscars. Sweet Jesus and the wee baby donkey, do I really have to wear it?" She whines at Nat and although I don't hear Nat confirm it, I do hear shuffling which sounds like she's getting dressed. I walk down the stairs and into the kitchen where George, Dan, Joseph and Gorgeous are waiting for me.

"Is she wearing it?" George asks me and I nod my head at him.

I'm glad he agreed to come tonight. Over the past few weeks I've grown closer to him and I want to help him as much as I can. He's a good man. Plus I love watching Nat squirm when he's around.

"I think so, she isn't happy about it though." I smirk at Gorgeous and go and give her a squeeze.

"Thank you for being here tonight."

"I wouldn't be anywhere but." She winks at me and straightens my tie.

"You got the ring?" Dan asks me for the millionth time, and for the millionth time I check my pocket, even though I know it's there and nod at him. I can hear the girls coming down the stairs and turn in time to see Darcie walking into the kitchen, she takes in everyone and what they're wearing, the frown forming on her face replaced with a roll of her eyes.

"Well, I'm glad I bloody wore the dress now. Where are we going tonight?"

She directs the question to me, and I shrug my shoulders and nod my head and look at Becs. I can't talk. Darcie's breathtaking. A thief who's stolen my breath away every time she walks into a room. Becs glares at me for putting the pressure on her to answer. She gives Darcie a flippant look and turns away from her.

"It's a nice restaurant we're going to, and they require their guests to dress formally. Besides, I think it's nice to get all dressed up once and again. You'll appreciate things like this when you've got three kids running rings around you and a husband that's more like a kid as well, believe me."

I give her a stern look at the mention of husband, and she flinches, realising her slip up.

"Well, they've years before they need to worry about kids and marriage." Nat shudders for effect and I notice the slight wink she gives me.

"Oh, ye be quiet. There's nothing wrong with marriage and kids if you're with the right person." Darcie speaks up and looks at me with love and admiration in her beautiful eyes. I shrug nonchalantly.

"I agree, but Nat's got a point. We have all the time in the world, Irish, there's no need to rush anything."

She looks down and simply says oh and I feel like the biggest wanker in the world. I hate making her doubt us. I almost get to my knees and ask her there and then to be my wife, but restrain myself and keep the bigger picture in my mind.

"Right, let's hit the road then guys, we don't want to be late."

Becs is being the bossy mum of the group and I couldn't love her more for it right now. We all file out two by two and Darcie and I bring up the rear.

"You okay?" I kiss her bare shoulder and pull her into my side. She looks up at me, her eyes filled with angst and concern. She goes to say something but shakes her head slightly.

"I'm grand, are ye okay?"

She smiles, but it's not a full smile and I know she's worried. She thinks I've been distant the past two weeks and I have a bit because I don't want her to sense anything about tonight from me. She can read me like a book, one look and she would've known something was going on. I've been staying late at work and trying to avoid her. Not the greatest of things to do but I need tonight to go perfectly. I know from talking to Becs and Nat that she's asked them on more than one occasion whether they think I'm seeing someone else, which they've both denied massively of course. It kills me she thinks that, but I can't blame her with my past and all. Once this night is over, she'll know once and for all she's it for me. I pull her close so that her body is pressed up against mine and look into her beautiful but sad eyes.

"Darcie, I know I've neglected you these past couple of weeks and I'm so sorry. I love you and I'll make it up to you. You have nothing to worry about. Mine." Finally, she smiles a proper smile at me. All the sadness is gone from her eyes, but the worry is still lingering as she says "always" back to me. I kiss her softly on the lips, forcing myself to break away from her even when my body is crying out with need for her.

"We have to go or Becs is going to put us on the naughty step."

Laughing, we walk out of the house and my nerves get worse.

Chapter 31

Darcie

Two weeks earlier.

"Something isn't right. I'm telling ye guys. I might be being a fecking eejit here, but I tink Denny is seeing someone else." I can't hold back the tears anymore and I howl. Becs and Nat are by my side in a second with their arms wrapped around me.

"Darcie, that's the most ridiculous thing I've ever heard in my life. Denny loves you, probably more than I've ever seen anyone love anyone else before and that's coming from me."

"She's right. I mean her and Dan are pretty disgusting with all the lovey dovey shit they do, but you and Denny are ten times worse. He'd never cheat on you. He loves you, Darcie."

They're saying all the things I want and need to hear but I can't shake the feeling he's keeping something from me. They cuddle me a little bit more and I pull myself together and go upstairs to wash my face. I've cried more the past few days than I have in my entire life. The emotions are pouring out of me, mainly from my eyes. I walk out of the kitchen, noticing we spend an awful lot of time in that bloody room. As I look back in, I watch Becs talk quietly on the phone and I'm pretty sure she said my name, but I can't be certain. God, I hope I can trust her. She's Denny's sister-in-law, more like sister, after all. I know Nat wouldn't betray me so if Nat's saying the same to me as what Becs is, I'll be okay. As soon as I get in our bedroom, I grab my phone out of my pocket and send him a text.

Me: Hey old man, are you working late again? I miss you x

Denny: I am, I'm afraid, Irish. Dan and I have to stay behind for a meeting, and this was the only time they could do. I'm sorry. I miss you too x

Me: I'm scared I'm losing you x

I hate that I'm feeling insecure but I can't hold it back from him. I need to tell him. I need him to reassure me. I need him.

Denny: Never. Mine x

Me: Always? x

Denny: And forever. Stop worrying x

Even though he's just told me his way of saying he loves me and to stop worrying, I'm worrying even more. I know he's at work with Dan and isn't out with another woman. I'm not worried about that. Well I am but tis more than just cheating. When he's at home, he's distant, something Denny hasn't ever been with me. Tis like he's here but he isn't. Tis so frustrating. Becs doesn't get it and keeps trying to convince me tis where I'm not used to relationships. And Nat just said the honeymoon period has faded a touch and twas normal, but it feels anything BUT normal to me. It feels like he's purposefully holding himself back from me.

That breaks my heart because we've always been so open and honest with each other. Well not at the beginning, but after that we have been. Something just feels wrong and with this added stress on top of the annoying phone calls, I have this overwhelming sense of foreboding. Hopefully I'm wrong.

Present day:

I'm standing in my robe in our bedroom with my arms folded over my chest, pouting. I don't want to go anywhere tonight, and I certainly don't want to put on a fancy dress and get dolled up either. I want to stay indoors and spend the night with Denny and try to get us back on track. I'm miserable and desperate and if he's about to dump me, I certainly don't want to spend the night out with other loved up couples. I don't say any of this to Natalie and Becs. I flounce about instead, knowing full well I'm being unreasonable and a bit of a brat. If one of the kids acted like this I'd give them a time out, but no one pulls me up on it, which is odd for Nat. She normally calls me out over everything.

Everyone is acting weird, and I really don't want to put on this gorgeous pale blue gown, but Nat and Becs aren't budging on this. Tis a stupid argument and after a huge lecture from Nat and a massive guilt trip too, I reluctantly put the dress on. I feel slightly relieved when I step into the kitchen and see everyone else is just as glam. They won't tell me where we're going. Becs seems to have that piece of information stored in her head and isn't giving it up for anybody. As I moan again about being dressed to the nines, she casually tells me I wouldn't complain when I was married and had kids. I smile at her, picturing myself and Denny getting married and having beautiful babies of our own. I have that warm fuzzy feeling in my tummy, but when I look at Denny he's glaring at Becs. Nat spouts out some rubbish about waiting to be married and shudders at the thought of it, and I can't help but tell her marriage is grand if you're with the right person. I look to Denny expecting him to back me up, but he shrugs nonchalantly.

"I agree but Nat's got a point, we have all the time in the world, Irish, there's no need to rush anything."

I lower my eyes so he can't see the pain in them and try to force the tears back. I bite on my cheek to hold them in and wish for the ground to open up and swallow me whole. I know he didn't say he didn't want to marry me ever, but this is Denny. The man who took me on amazing dates, rescued me from my abusive dad and moved me in with him all within a month or so of meeting me, and now he's talking about having all the time in the world. Something isn't right and I can only think Denny I-don't-do-feelings-and-relationships is back. He's having second thoughts about us. I feel like the stupidest woman alive. I did what I promised myself I wouldn't. I fell in love with a man and relied on getting his love back and now tis all going to end. And I'll end up broken, desperate and miserable.

Becs gets everyone moving, but Denny holds me back a bit. I don't want to look at him. I don't want him to see the desperation in my eyes and the need to have him still, but I can't resist when he brings me up against his body. I don't know how much longer he'll be mine, and I want to get my fill of him for when he's gone from my life and all I have left is the memory of him. When he speaks, I only half-listen, trying to capture every part of him to memory.

"Darcie, I know I've neglected you these past couple of

weeks and I'm so sorry. I love you more than ever and I'll make it up to you. You have nothing to worry about. Mine."

I smile at him, not because I believe him but because he reminds me of my Denny. And even if he isn't going to be mine for much longer, he's mine for now. And he'll always be mine even if tis only in *my* heart. Always.

Chapter 32

Denny

As we pull up to the London Eye, I grab Darcie's hand. I watch her face as recognition of where we are hits her and her eyes light up. But there's still a sadness to them. I kiss her hand and push the urge to tell her everything to the back of my mind because in a little bit she'll get it and that sadness will disappear forever. We'll be engaged. God, I hope she says yes. My stomach's in knots and my mouth is as dry as the desert. I try to swallow, to rid the nervous lump that's in my throat, but there isn't any saliva in my mouth. Standing outside of our car waiting for the rest of the gang to pull up in theirs, I grab Darcie around her waist and pull her into me, her back against my front. I sweep her beautiful dark hair from her shoulder, place my lips on her neck and whisper 'mine' into her ear. I feel her tension shift a bit as she leans back into me. When the others join us we head to the front of the line again, much to the annoyance of everyone else. There's a nervous and anxious tension in the pod. I feel sick to my stomach and force myself to take a couple of deep breaths. Nat's managed to get Darcie away from me and they're looking out over the breath-taking view of London, my city, each holding a glass; Nat's is full of champagne and in Darcie's is orange juice. As I speak with my brother a sheen of sweat covers my forehead. I lift the champagne to my mouth and stop when I notice my hand trembling. He must notice it too as he asks for the millionth time tonight if I'm okay.

"Not really, what if she says no? She's been so aware of my distance over these past couple of weeks, what if I've ruined it?" I voice my fears to him, hearing those words that are naturally ingrained into my brain. Denny equals ruined.

"Den, shut the fuck up, will you?" He laughs at me and puts his arm around my shoulders. "She loves you and once you ask her, the stress and distance will be a thing of the past. You'll go back to practically screwing her in front of everyone again. Don't worry." He smirks at me, and I grin back. George and Joseph step closer to us to let me know it's almost time. I stalk over to Darcie and Nat. I've never felt so nervous in my life, but I also feel so right. I put my hand on her elbow and as I do, I realise I'm still shaking. Darcie must feel it too as she looks at her elbow and then at me.

"Are ye okay, Denny?" I smile at her always caring about other people, and I reach into my pocket with my other hand and take out the little square box. I'm vaguely aware of Becs snapping pictures, but I don't think Darcie has registered it, which is a good thing. I kiss her on the head before I drop to my knee and show her the ring box.

"Darcie, I never thought I'd find anyone to love, didn't think I was even capable of it, but you made me realise that not only am I capable but that I could love someone so deeply it actually hurts. You've made me the best version of myself. You believe in me and most importantly, you love me so fiercely I can feel it in my soul. I fell in love with you the first time I saw you, outside on the pavement. Then you showed me those beautiful ice blue eyes and I sank right into them. I love you with everything I am. You are mine, forever and I am yours, always. Will you marry me?"

I hold my breath.

She's crying but I can't tell if they're happy tears or not as her beautiful emotive eyes are shut. It feels like an eternity before she whispers, "Mine, always. Of course, I'll marry ye."

I jump up and grab her off her feet, pull her face against mine and cry happy tears with her. I can hear the pod erupting into clapping and when I look above, the pod of people in there are clapping and cheering too. I'm the luckiest man alive as I kiss my beautiful fiancée.

Becs says, "You haven't even looked at the ring. I want to get pictures of your reaction so come on."

Laughing, I open the box and show her the ring I picked for her. She gasps and her eyes shoot up to mine.

"Tis beautiful. It reminds me of your eyes, Denny."

Laughter erupts from everyone else in the pod and she shoots an angry glare at them.

"Why is everyone laughing at me?"

I grab her hand and kiss it to reassure her. "They aren't laughing at you. They're laughing because when I went to pick the ring, I told them I wanted something that reminded me of your eyes. This was perfect. It's the same clear blue as yours. And obviously mine too."

She smiles and whispers to me, "Twas beautiful before but now tis perfect. Can I try it on?"

I nod at her and put the ring on her finger.

Becs calls out to us, "Show me."

She turns to face her and holds her hand up, beaming a beautiful smile as Becs snaps away. I'm quite content watching my fiancée pose with her ring until Becs scolds me and tells me to get closer to Darcie and be in the shots. She doesn't have to tell me twice to get closer to my love. I don't acknowledge Becs or the camera once I have Darcie in my arms. I don't care about anything else, just being as close as we can be. It feels like an eternity since I had her in my arms and was this close to her.

The rest of the trip on the Eye goes by in a blur of talking to everyone and drinking champagne. It feels like I didn't get any time with Darcie on our own, so I'm grateful to be back in the car with her, driving to the restaurant. My arm around her shoulder as she snuggles into me, and her left hand placed on my chest over my heart.

"I'm sorry I've been distant. I didn't want you to find out. I wanted it to be a surprise. I nearly told you the other day when Becs phoned me saying you thought I was with someone else." I grab her hand and she tilts her head up to look at me. "There's no one else Darcie, only you. Forever. You're mine. I'm sorry I made you feel like that." She looks at me and smiles.

"I knew she was on the phone to ye. I shouldn't have questioned it, Denny and I'm sorry I did. I'm glad now that ye didn't tell me. Thank ye for making my life complete. Ye were the piece I never knew was missing. I'm sorry I doubted ye. I did genuinely tink ye were with someone else, and I feel so bad about it, Denny."

I laugh at her little slip with 'tink'. "Don't feel bad, Irish. I can see why you'd think that. Just know that you're it for me. I tried to avoid you, walk away from you, keep my distance. But nothing stopped me wanting you."

She sits up straighter and looks me in the eyes, patiently waiting for me to carry on.

"The day I saw you the first time, I was so affected by you, I didn't understand it or like it. I was, erm, ridiculously hard let's say."

Her eyes twinkle with amusement and she looks down at my lap. "No change there then, eh?"

Laughing I pop a gentle kiss on her lips.

"Around you? No, no change there. I went out for dinner with Joseph that night and swore to ignore you and forget all about the out-of-bounds nanny."

Laughing at me with a twinkle in her eyes she asks, "How did that work out for ye, old man?"

I shake my head and roll my eyes at her. "Like I ever had a chance."

She sighs contentedly at me and asks, "What made ye change your mind? Ye spent two weeks avoiding me, then asked me out, chased me every time I ran?"

I smile at the memory and tell her, "When I came into the kitchen and Isabelle was in your arms, crying because she was scared. You were rocking her, and I had this vision of you holding our little boy in the kitchen and me coming over to you to hold you both. It was then that I knew I was fucked."

She stares at me intently and smiles. "I've had thoughts of us with children too. I never knew whether you wanted them or not. I'm so happy to hear you say that." She scrambles up so her face is level with mine and kisses me hard, so hard I don't want it to stop. But just my luck, the driver pulls over and speaks to us through the intercom to tell us we've arrived. We both groan loudly and grin at each other and head out of the car.

"I honestly thought she was going to dump your arse the other day." Whilst Becs is retelling the story of Darcie thinking I was cheating on her, I'm sitting here wishing I'd done this differently. By differently, I mean on our own. I slide closer to Darcie and when my mouth brushes her ear a shiver runs through her body.

"I should've done this alone. All I want to do is go home and make my beautiful fiancée scream my name whilst she's wearing nothing but that beautiful ring that tells everyone she's mine!" I nibble on her ear lobe and she gasps and turns her face to me. The blush that creeps up over her cheekbones sends an electric current straight to my dick and I groan as she bites her lip. She looks up at me through heavy eyelids and I want to throw her on the table and fuck her there and then. A bright light flashes in front of us and Darcie and I flinch back from its assault on our eyes. Once we can see again, I focus on Becs, camera in hand, grinning from ear to ear.

"Sorry, guys, I couldn't resist, it was such a beautiful and intense picture I had to grab it."

"Plus, it cooled you both down. Any hotter and you would have been screwing on the table." Nat receives a short gasp and a tut from Gorgeous and she lowers her head and apologises to her.

"I forgot you were here G, I'm sorry. You have to admit they were hot for each other though, weren't they?" She swigs her wine and smirks at Gorgeous who winks and smirks back.

Those two are a fucking duo I wouldn't go against if my dick depended on it.

The restaurant Becs chose for us to go to is lovely, and once everyone has eaten we head downstairs where they have a live band and a dance floor. It's nice to hold Darcie in my arms and sway to the music. I look over at the people I love more than anything in the world and I feel genuinely happy. Happier than I ever dreamt possible. I notice Dan looking at me. He dips his head to me, and I do the same.

He dances closer to us and asks, "Darcie, can I dance with you, my new sister, please? I never thought I'd be able to say those words." Dan's ear to ear smile has been unwavering all night.

Darcie walks over to him and shoots a look back at me. "Now don't be getting all jealous on me, dancing with another man and all." She gives me a mischievous grin and I smile back.

"It's not me you have to worry about." I motion over to Becs with my head and get a punch on the arm in return.

"Ha bloody ha, Den. Like I'd be jealous of Darcie dancing with Dan." She rolls her eyes at me, then points two fingers to her eyes and turns them at Darcie in the universal sign for 'I'm watching you'.

Darcie holds her hands up in surrender and crosses her heart. They smirk at each other, as Dan leads Darcie away, swaying to the music. I bow to Becs and ask for the dance and she glides into my arms.

"I'm so happy for you, Den. I never thought I'd see this and I'm so glad I did."

"Me too, Becs. You sure you're going to be able to let another woman near me, you have had us Blanc men all to yourself for God knows how many years now." I grin down at her and she shakes her head at me. "You really are beautiful, Becs. The twins look just like you and I'm so proud to have you as my sister. I've watched you grow from a girl to a woman, and you are the best mum and wife ever. Thank you for loving me and Dan. And thank you for being my best friend."

As she wipes her eyes, she clings to me, and I can hear her little sobs. I let her cry it out and before I can blink Dan is by our side, like he has some sort of Spidey sense when it comes to Becs.

"Hey, what's with the tears, what did this arsehole do now, angel?" Dan looks at me with a frown.

I laugh in his face. "I was being nice. I complimented

her and thanked her. But thanks for the vote of confidence."

Becs lifts her head and shakily giggles at me as she turns to Dan. "He really was being nice. He said some beautiful things to me, and it made me very emotional, that's all."

"Oh God, you're not pregnant, are you?" All the colour in Dan's face drains and I grimace at what he just said. Becs and Darcie both bring their eyebrows together and let their mouths gape open in shock.

"I cannot believe ye, of all people, just said that because she said she's emotional, Dan." Darcie speaks first, using her stern teacher voice, and once again I can't help but be a little turned on, even if I do feel bad for Dan.

"I didn't mean it, it's just the last time, and the girls are young, and fuck. I'm sorry, angel." Dan is digging his grave and is busy putting one foot into it when Becs speaks.

"Actually, Dan, I am. I didn't want to say anything because I didn't want to steal Denny and Darcie's thunder." Her face is deadly serious and I want to jump for joy at the idea of having a new niece or nephew.

Dan's face has turned green, and he's sweating profusely. Poor man looks like he's going to throw up. He's stammering and trying to form a coherent sentence when Becs laughs, an uncontrollable laugh that catches all of us off guard.

I shoot a curious look over at Darcie and she shakes her head at me just as confused.

"I'm sorry but the look on his face was too much, he looked like he was going to pass out and be sick at the same time. No, you, prick, I'm not pregnant and it won't be likely for me to get pregnant again because I won't be sleeping with you for a loooong time." Becs storms over to the bar and Dan runs after her as Darcie and I stand there staring at each other.

"Damn, I was excited about being an uncle again. They'll be okay in a little bit. Dan'll grovel and Becs'll make him wait a while, but she won't be able to keep her hands off him just as much as he won't with her."

Darcie holds out her hand to me and tugs me towards the bar. We sit on the other side, opposite from Dan and Becs, and Darcie shoots Becs a look, but I didn't catch it. I do manage to see the sneaky wink Becs shoots back at her and then Darcie's smile.

"Do you two have a secret girl code that involves eyes and looks and winks or something?"

Darcie laughs and it brings my dick to attention. "I was worried, but it seems ye were right."

I snake my arm around her waist and put my mouth on her neck. "Can I take you home now, the future Mrs. Blanc, and make love to you, please?"

She leans into me and whispers, "Yes, please."

That's all I need before I practically drag her outside.

"Right, who had between ten thirty and ten forty-five?"

The fuckers placed bets on what time we'd leave. I laugh to myself and wonder who won, but then Darcie strokes my arm and all thoughts of everyone else disappear from my head. All I can think of is getting my woman home and devouring her.

Chapter 33

Darcie

Every Sunday us girls go for brunch to that little Italian restaurant; we eat and chat and put the world to rights. The guys stay at home and look after the kids and hang out together as well. Of course, Denny always moans about me 'leaving him' but I think he enjoys the bro time especially as George has become a permanent member of our group too. Sitting in what has fast become our booth, Nat, Becs and I order some drinks. They have wine and I have water again, and once the waiter has left, I round on them.

"So, for two weeks ye knew what was going on and yet ye both let me believe he was seeing someone else! For shame on ye ladies." I tut at them and shake my head, but they can see the grin on my face, so they know I'm playing with them.

"Darcie, you have no idea how hard it was watching you break your own heart and not be able to say anything." Becs grabs my hand and looks genuinely upset.

Nat scoffs at us both. "Oh, come on. She's mad if she genuinely thought Denny was seeing someone else. The man is obsessed with you. His distant is everyone else's normal. You were acting crazy, and only one thing makes you crazy like that, Darcie. PMS. Or are you preggers?"

I laugh at Nat and shake my head. "I did believe he was. Or at least he didn't want me anymore. Ye should have my back more." I give her a fake scold and grin when she sticks her tongue out at me. "I'm not hormonal. Or pregnant either, thank ye very much. I had my period..." I stop to do some quick period math and my face freezes.

"Uh oh, Darcie. That face doesn't look good. I was only joking about being hormonal or pregnant, but could you be?"

I can't get my mouth to move to push my words out.

"Darcie, do you think you could be pregnant?" Becs is looking at me expectantly and I shrug my shoulders at her.

"I'm on the pill." I whisper at them.

"When was your last period, Darcie?"

I honestly can't remember. I got the contraceptive pill from the hospital when I was getting my painkillers and haven't had a proper period since before then. I pull my phone out and google how effective the pill I'm on is, something I probably should have done before I had wild passionate sex.

"Look it says tis 99% effective if taken every day at the same time so I should be okay. Right?" I ask them both hoping they say yes.

Nat nods and Becs looks down, avoiding my eyes.

"That's only if you've remembered to take them at the same time and every day. Do you think you could've missed any?" She smiles at me, and I put my head in my hands.

"It wouldn't be so bad, Darcie. You and Denny are in love and we're all here to help." Becs is trying to reassure me, and it works a wee bit. She's right. Yes, tis fast but when have Denny and I ever done anything slowly?

"Let's just find out if there is anything to be worried about, shall we?" Nat stands up and grabs her bag.

"I'll go to the chemist and pick a couple of tests up." She's out of the door before I can protest, and tis just me and Becs in our booth.

"I fell pregnant with Isaac when I was on the pill and he was the best thing to ever happen to me and Dan, Darcie. It'll be okay. You and Denny would be amazing parents and a little baby would be so loved by all its aunties and uncles and cousins. It won't be the end of the world, I promise you." She's holding my hand tightly and I squeeze it back. I mouth 'thank ye' at her as tears spill down my cheeks.

"Are you that sad about it, Darcie?" She asks me and I shake my head.

"No, I'm happy at the idea and I'm nervous I'm not now." Becs smiles at me, and I smile back. We sit there holding hands as Nat comes back in just as our food comes.

"What are you going to do?" She asks me between fork-fuls of food.

"We're going to eat this and then we'll go home and do this test with everyone and see what the feck is going on."

We all nod our heads at each other. The other two eat whilst I move the food about on my plate. My hand rests on my belly and I think to myself, I hope you're in there, wee one.

"Pregnant? B-but you're on the pill." Denny is on the sofa in the living room. When we got back to the house, I asked him to follow me in here so I could tell him on his own, but I made sure Dan, Becs, Nat and George stayed in the kitchen in case I needed moral support. Or in case he fainted.

"I'm on the pill Denny, tis not 100% effective though. No contraception is." He looks up at me amazed.

"Seriously, even condoms?" I can't help but giggle at him. Here I am with one sexual partner under my belt schooling Mr. I've-shagged-everything-that-moves about contraception.

"No, Denny. Not even condoms are 100% effective. I suppose the only way to be certain is abstinence, but I can tell you there's no fun in that at all." I grin at him, and he grins back. He grabs my arm and pulls me down to sit on his lap.

"How do you feel about it all, if you are, I mean?" I look into his eyes and search them to see if I can gauge his feelings. There's fear, anxiety and happiness. I smile back at him.

"Don't judge me, but I'm hoping there is a wee one inside of me. A part of ye and me. I hope that doesn't make ye feel trapped." I lower my eyes, and his hand comes under my chin, tilting it up so I'm looking at him.

"I do, too." He kisses the tip of my nose and smiles at me. "So, do you need me to go buy one of those test things?"

I shake my head at him. "Nat has two in her bag. She went to the chemist for me."

"Let's go then."

"How long's left, Becs?" Nat is pacing behind me and Denny, whilst we sit at the breakfast bar in the kitchen. Dan is standing close to Becs, and George is in the corner, deep in thought.

"It's time now." Becs looks up at us and Nat stops pacing.

I turn to Denny and tell him I love him. He replies with

"mine," and together we turn over the stick. I look at Denny who has the biggest smile on his face, and I mirror it back to him.

"Ye are going to be a daddy."

Nat shrieks behind me about being an auntie and Becs and Dan are hugging. George has walked over to us too. He claps Denny on the shoulder as he stares at the test, smiling. I squeeze Denny's hand as he looks at me, and the look on his face is beautiful. The shock has worn off and there is just pure and unadulterated happiness. He kisses me hard then cradles me to his chest, and I realise he's crying.

"Thank you, Darcie. Thank you for everything." The room disappears around us and it feels like tis just the two of us, well three of us. Denny holds me and puts his hand on my belly, and we're brought out of our little haze by a blinding light. Becs has her camera and is snapping away again.

"Sorry, guys but you'll thank me tomorrow when I have these all printed off." After she takes a few more shots of Dan, Nat, and George hugging us, she puts the camera down and cuddles us both. When another flash goes off, we look around confused and see George standing in front of us with the camera.

"Sorry, but I thought it would be nice having Becs in this one." He places it down carefully, looking embarrassed as Becs gives him a cuddle in thanks.

Dan grins at me. "You need to phone Gorgeous; she'll be over the moon at being a gran again."

I look over at Denny. When a frown appears on his face, I touch his arm tentatively. "Denny? Are ye okay?"

He sighs and nods at me.

"I'm so happy and of course I want to tell Gorgeous and Joseph but what do I do about Lewis? He gave up everything for his brother, and I get that because I'd have done the same for Dan. Especially as I believed I could never have the happy ever after like he believed he couldn't either. He didn't know about me, but as soon as he found out he was here. He wanted to know me. I don't know what's right?"

He lowers his head, and my heart breaks for him a little, he's so hard on himself all the time.

"Ye have to do what ye feel is right, Denny. If ye want to get to know him, tis okay, and if you don't, tis okay too."

"She's right, Den," Becs says, and everyone's eyes shoot to her in surprise as she's been the most outspoken in her concerns about Lewis and his 'career.'

"He's your dad. You have the right to get to know him. I shouldn't have said what I did before. I know you wouldn't ever put us at risk, and after speaking with Joseph and Lewis I don't think they would either. Please don't hold yourself back for me or the kids."

As she's wrapped in Dan's arms he looks down at her. "You've spoken with Joseph? And Lewis?"

She nods up at him and explains. "After he turned up and I voiced my concerns, I had to find out more. A few weeks later I asked Joseph and Gloria to meet me for lunch and we talked. Halfway through, Lewis turned up. Joseph said he'd called him so he could answer for himself. He's so much like Joseph it's unreal. I was wrong to judge him, Denny, and I'm sorry if you've put off meeting with him because of me." She looks down at the ground.

Denny speaks to her softly. "It wasn't just you, but thank you for telling me and for meeting him. Joseph has asked me a few times to meet with him and talk and I keep putting it off. I think now's the right time, if that's okay with you, Irish?"

I smile at him and kiss his cheek. "Anything for ye, old man."

He picks up his phone and calls Gloria to share the news. Her screams are so loud I can hear her from where I'm sitting, and then I hear Joseph talking to Denny. I get up, leaving him to it, and walk over to sit opposite George and Nat who are chatting quietly together.

"We wanted to give you guys a minute, family stuff and all that."

My head snaps up and I look ferociously at Nat. "Natalie Wilson." She bolts upright at the use of her surname and stares at me. "Look around and tell me how many of my family members do ye see? Hmmm? Let me tell ye, I see one and one only. The one person who's been by my side day in and day out since I came to London. The one person who knows me inside and out and has cuddled me when I've cried and laughed with me when I've mucked up. She isn't my friend, she's my sister and my only family. My wean's auntie. Please don't dismiss her as my family. It makes me angry."

She stands up and bear-hugs me and whispers in my ear. "I love you, Darcie, and my little niece or nephew. Thank you." She kisses me on the cheek and goes back to her seat.

George puts his hand on top of hers, squeezing it gently, then looks around embarrassed, clears his throat, and walks over to the fridge.

Nat smirks at me. "He'll get there slowly."

I raise my eyebrows and smile at Nat. She shrugs her shoulders back to me and casts her eyes over to George who's talking to Dan. When my phone rings on the table next to me, I glance over to see an unknown number, again, and silence it. They've been happening more and more but I'm hoping if I ignore them they'll stop soon enough.

I can sense Denny behind me before I see him, and he

sits down next to us as Dan and Becs appear too. We all huddle around the table and wait for Denny to speak.

"What? I only spoke to Joseph and Gorgeous, they're ecstatic by the way and are coming for dinner after work tomorrow. So, George, Nat, dinner tomorrow?" They both nod at him and he dips his head back.

"I've texted Lewis and told him about the baby and asked if he wants to come too. When he responds I'll let you all know." He shakes his head and looks at me, grinning.

"It's going to be a boy, I know it is."

"What's going to be a boy?" A small voice asks.

"Is someone having a baby?" Another small voice asks.

"It's not you, is it, mum?" Standing in the doorway are three sets of blue eyes staring at us.

I look at Becs and Dan and they grin back at us.

"Nah, it's not your mum who's having a baby, guys." Denny tells them and waves them over to us.

Isla and Isabelle jump onto Denny's lap and Isaac stands next to me. I put my hand around his shoulders and bring him closer to me.

"Yesterday, I asked Darcie if she'd be my wife and she said yes." Denny starts the conversation off but is quickly interrupted.

"I told you she loves you." Isla exclaims.

I laugh at her. "Today we found out you guys are going to be big cousins. Darcie has a teeny tiny baby in her tummy."

Isla squeals in delight, but Isabelle folds her arms and scolds him.

"Uncle Denny, You did it wrong. You upp-osed ta get married and den have da baby."

She shakes her head at me as I stifle a chuckle.

"And it's a boy one?" Isabelle has a look of disgust on her face as Isla brings her head out of Dennys neck.

I shake my head and tell her tis too early to know for sure.

"I think it's a boy. He can sleep in my room with me. When he gets bigger though, cause babies make a lot of noise." Isaac pulls a face and looks just like his dad, then turns to me with a look of happiness.

"Darcie, I'm happy you're marrying Uncle Denny and having a baby with him because now you'll never leave us, and you'll be our auntie forever."

He hugs me tightly and I sob lightly onto his little man shoulder. As he pulls away from me, I ruffle his hair and kiss his cheek. "Ye, Isaac, are my favourite nephew and I love ye so much."

His little cheeks flame red, and he smiles and dashes off to his mum and dad to give them a cuddle. I grab Isabelle and squeeze her tightly and then Isla.

Isla asks me shyly, "Can I call you Auntie Darcie now?"

I laugh and cry at the same time, kiss her cheek and tell her yes.

They leave the kitchen and head upstairs together arguing over who the wean is going to love more. And my heart soars.

Chapter 34

Denny

"Congratulations Denny. I'm really happy for you."

He holds his hand out in front of me, and I swallow hard, reach out and shake it. "Thanks, Lewis, I appreciate it."

He slides on to the chair opposite me and places his hands on the table. As we sit in awkward silence, neither knowing where or how to start the conversation, a waitress approaches to get our drinks order. She looks at Lewis and smiles. A lazy smile spreads across his face. My eyes roll in my head as the waitress turns to look at me. Her smile gets bigger and I shift in my chair, uncomfortable by her gaze.

"Wow, you can tell you two are related. Those eyes you both have are amazing." Her head turns to each of us as she speaks and we both smile at the same time and, I notice, in the same way. No DNA test needed with Lewis and I, anyone can see I'm his son. Even the damn waitress.

"I take it you're his dad." She gestures to me with her head whilst talking to Lewis and he nods at her.

"Yep, that handsome bugger's my son, gets his looks

from his old man. I had him very young though." He winks at the waitress.

Her face turns red and I can't help but laugh at his shameless flirting, seeing as she's younger than me. She turns her attention to me and I'm not a fan of the look in her eyes. "Is he always this brazen when he's flirting?"

I shrug my shoulders at her nonchalantly. "You'd have to ask him that, I'm just here for the food." I run my hand through my hair and smile up at her curtly. I don't want to flirt with her, and to be honest I don't want to sit here and watch Lewis do it either. I'm here to get to know this man as my father, not watch him flirt his way into her knickers.

"That's a shame. You flirting, I could deal with." She smiles and then bites her bottom lip suggestively.

I roll my eyes and give her a tight lipped smirk. "Sorry. I'm off the market."

She grins at me and fiddles with a lock of her hair that's come loose from her ponytail. "You could always come back on the market for a one night special."

I don't smile at her this time. In fact, I stare at her coldly, trying to get her to understand I'm not interested in her at all. Nerves flit across her face when she takes in my expression.

"For that ridiculous pick up line? No, thanks. Now can you get us two beers please? Actually, make sure you get another server to bring them over as well."

I don't look at her again. I stare at Lewis, not really seeing him and trying to control the rage seeping out of me. I know she's just trying her luck, and before Darcie, I was the same- saw a pretty face and tried it on- but it's different now. Not only am I head over heels in love with Darcie, but we're getting married and having a baby. There's no way I'm going to ruin it all by flirting with some woman who I'm not even remotely interested in.

"Jeez Den, you could've cut her some slack. She was only flirting." Lewis's eyes are on me. My anger is bubbling up again.

"Do you know what Lewis, how about I get the fuck out of here and you can go chase pussy all you want because, believe me, I'd rather be at home myself. Nice chat." I push my chair back and get to my feet, but he reaches over the table and grabs my wrist.

"Denny, please."

My eyes meet his and I can see the desperation in them so I sit back down. He leans back and runs his hand through his hair, and I fucking hate how alike we are. I mean it's bad enough we're a mirror image of each other, a before and after for fucks sake, let alone our mannerisms and quirks are the same as well. I clear my throat and keep my gaze down, waiting for him to speak first.

"I'm really happy about the baby, Denny, and the engagement. You're a lucky man and you deserve every bit of happiness."

I look up at him slowly to see if this is genuine and I'm shocked by the raw emotion I can see in his eyes.

"If I had known, Denny, I would've tried to do something. I didn't know. I didn't fucking know." He drops his head and avoids eye contact with me now, shielding himself from me.

I clear my throat again and this time I force words out of my mouth. "Let's leave that part of the past where it belongs. Tell me about you and your work."

Well, that certainly got his attention. His head shoots up and he eyes me curiously. "What do you want to know? Let me guess, am I putting you and your family at risk by being here with you?"

I nod at him and before he can answer, our drinks are

being placed in front of us by a male server. I thank him and tilt my head at Lewis to continue.

"You're not as scary as your sister-in-law, you know. She asked me the same questions and I'll tell you the same thing I told her. You're at no risk whatsoever, boy. The enemies I made are dead, and I always had more 'friends' than enemies anyway. I'm retired, so I'm reaping my retirement. Hopefully, I'll get to know you more. You're all I have."

He looks me right in the eyes when he says that, and it hits me in the chest. I shift on my chair. "Becs is enough to scare anyone, especially when it comes to what's hers." I pause and take a sip of my drink. "You never had any other kids? Why?"

"Denny, the kind of life I led, you didn't want to have anything that could be used as leverage against you. Nothing someone could take that'd make you lose control and lose your head over, because then you would've lost the advantage and that would've lost you your life. So no, I never had any other children, that I knew of."

I stare at him, trying to let his words sink into my brain. The waiter comes back over. We haven't even looked at the menus, so he leaves and gives us a few more minutes. Lewis picks his menu up and studies it and I do the same. Confusion's swirling around in my head. In one breath he's telling me there's no threat to my family and in the next he's telling me he never had children for fear of someone exacting revenge on him with one of them. Using them as leverage, as he called it. I want to know what he could've done that would've made someone so mad they'd go after his family, but I also don't want to know. I just want to get to know my dad so I can have some sort of a normal parent. I envied Dan so much when he'd go to his dad's house every weekend, and not just because he escaped the cold-hearted bitch we had to call mother. But because he had a dad. Someone to watch football with, to muck about with and be a boy with. I told him this when he got with Becs, and he laughed so much as the time he spent with his dad was nothing like I imagined. But I didn't know that back when I was a kid. Now, I just want to know what it feels like having that with one of the people that made me.

"So how come you retired? You have enough of quick cash and your pick of women?" I ask him because I want to know what he's been doing, but I don't want to seem too interested.

"Now who said I still wasn't making quick cash and didn't have my pick of the women, eh?" I chuckle at him and his unashamed attitude.

"I made some very legal and healthy investments when I was younger, and I'm now reaping the benefits. I passed the business on to the young one's and they're running with it. I can finally say I'm officially legit. Like I said before, my enemies are gone, my debts repaid, and I'm free."

I look over and sense the relief wash over him, but then his eyes turn ice cold again and the vulnerable look disappears. I nod at him silently and the waiter appears again, this time we order our food and sit back.

"What do you expect from this?" He asks me, bluntly and to the point.

I shrug my shoulders at him. "I honestly don't know. I just want normal. I finally find myself in a place I didn't think I'd ever be and now I just want peace and normality. I sound like a fucking woman. If Dan were here now, I'd be getting a bollicking for that comment." I laugh to myself, and he laughs with me.

"Is Dan one of these new age types of men? He doesn't get his eyebrows waxed, does he?"

I shake my head unable to speak through the laughter that image conjures up for me.

Still chuckling a bit, I manage to explain my comment. "No, he doesn't do that but he's very politically correct. He got worse when he found out he was having twin girls. Becs is very pro-women and believes in equality in all things and I think she's rubbed off on him over the years. Big Spice Girls fan was our Becs." I smile at the memory of a young Becs dressed as Geri from the Spice Girls, Union Jack dress and dyed ginger hair.

"You know your eyes give you away. They tell me more than your words do. It's something I had to learn to hide. It's scary how alike we are. It's like looking at myself when I was younger."

I nod my head again not knowing what to say. "You like football?" I ask him just to cover the silence, feeling awkward.

"Of course I bloody do. Massive Arsenal fan over here. We used to live round the corner from Highbury when we were kids. Match day was always magical. Broke my heart when they moved to The Emirates stadium, but what a fucking stadium, eh?"

I smile up at him and shake my head in amazement, the awkward feelings dissipating. "Can't believe you're a Gooner. Dan's been an avid Chelsea fan all his life and from my earliest memory, I can remember saying to him I supported Arsenal. Don't know why. Used to drive him mad, he wanted his little brother to follow him, but I was adamant I was a Gooner. Do you go to many games?"

His eyes smile at me, yet his face remains blank. I see what he means about your eyes giving you away now.

"You didn't do that good a job with your eyes then mate, they told me more than your face did."

He erupts into laughter and finally it feels like we've both relaxed.

"It was good, he answered all of my questions and we're going to an Arsenal game together."

I have all eyes on me. Darcie, Dan, Becs, Nat, George, Joseph and Gorgeous. They've been waiting for me and when I got back from my lunch with Lewis, they ambushed me. Huddled in the kitchen, again, I tell them about lunch.

"I told him I wanted to get to know him, as a friend. I already have a dad in my life." I bring my eyes pointedly up to Joseph.

He dips his chin at me and Gorgeous dabs her eyes with her sleeve.

"Did he tell you about what he used to do? We're all safe?" Nat asks me with anxiety lacing her voice.

I nod at her. "Whatever crap he was doing before is over with. He has enough money to be extremely comfortable so he isn't after that from us. And anyone that would've caused him trouble is dead, so we're all very safe from the life he used to lead."

She smiles at me. Darcie looks at her watch and then at me again. "We need to go old man, if we're late, they won't see us."

She stands up and walks over to the island. Grabbing her bag, she checks to make sure her phone is in there even though she's just put it in there. It's a little quirk of hers I've noticed she does every time she has to leave the house. She'll check again before we leave as well. I grin at her, and she knows what I'm grinning about and smiles back at me.

"Make sure you get some good pics of my niece please." Becs says to her as she kisses her cheek.

"Or my nephew, thank you very much." Dan swoops in with a kiss and a cuddle too.

Darcie laughs at them and assures them we will.

"Hell, just get one we can make out. I've never been able to see anything on those pics, it's all blurry lines and grey fuzz to me." Everyone turns to Nat, and she shrugs her shoulders. "I'm just being honest."

George chuckles as Nats cheeks turn pink.

"Don't worry Nat, I'll point out what's what in the picture for you." George steps closer to her and places his hand on her shoulder.

The blush on her face goes a shade darker as she stutters out, "Th-thanks."

A grin snakes its way onto my face, knowing these two are going to be so happy together one day.

I stalk over to Darcie and take her hand. We walk into the hallway and stop by the front door. I chuckle at her as she checks her bag again, whilst grabbing her waist and pulling her into my chest. She smiles up at me and her eyes tell me just how happy she is.

"Are ye ready to go see our wean?"

I let my eyes answer for me and dip my head down to press her lips into mine.

As we stand in the hospital hallway staring at the pictures of our baby, my emotions get the better of me and tears fill my eyes. I look at Darcie and my heart constricts so tightly I worry it might stop working altogether. This woman has changed my whole outlook on life. She's made me believe in the good and not focus on the bad. She chased the darkness away and filled my life with light. She makes me believe I can be loved and give love and that I'm worthy. And now she's giving me a baby. A family I didn't think I deserved. I owe this woman my life. My throat is clogged with emotion but I manage to speak through it.

"Darcie, I don't want to wait to marry you. I want you to be my wife from yesterday. I love you so much. I don't want to go another minute without you being Mrs. Blanc. What d'you say to a quick wedding?"

She looks up at me, her bright blue eyes burning with happiness. "I say hell yeah, Mr. Blanc. Let's do it."

I pick her up, spin her around and kiss her hard.

"You've made me the happiest man alive, Darcie. Let's see how quickly we can get this shit organised. I love you so much and I cannot wait to make you mine officially."

She throws her head back and laughs as my heart sings.

"You're such a caveman, Denny, but I can't wait to officially be yours as well. Always."

Chapter 35

Denny

Four weeks later...

Standing in a little chapel in Gretna Green, I wait nervously for Darcie to come down the aisle. I'm dressed in a new suit, new shoes and tie and have Dan, Isaac, Joseph, George and Lewis at my side wearing matching suits. I look at each man in turn and I'm glad I have them in my life.

When we got back from the hospital after our scan and told everyone we wanted to get married right away, there was no judgement. None. No one told us we were mad or we needed to wait, they just jumped on the bandwagon with us and helped us plan. Becs, Nat and Gorgeous went straight into wedding mode and discussed locations and dresses and flowers and I don't even know what else as I stopped listening after a while. Until, that is, Darcie said no to everything.

"I don't want a big fuss. I want us and that's it. No one else. I want a nice dress but nothing fancy. I'd be happy to go to Gretna Green and get married there."

As soon as she said it, I knew that's what we were doing. I walked over to her, in the kitchen as always, bent down to her and told her, "If that's what you want, Darcie, that's what we're doing. I just want you and me and these bunch of dicks to be there. Oh and my beautiful nieces and nephew of course."

With her face alight with happiness she turned to the rest of them and spoke in that strict teacher voice of hers. "Right, ye heard the man. Let's find somewhere to get married, ladies and gentlemen."

They worked tirelessly, and their hard work has paid off as we stand waiting for them to come in. First comes Isabelle and Isla, wearing beautiful pale blue dresses, their hair in little blonde curls falling around their angelic faces. My heart is bursting with pride looking at them. I turn to look at Dan and laugh at his soppiness when I catch him wiping his eyes, but swallow hard to rid the lump in my throat that's formed by seeing it, too.

Next comes Gorgeous who looks just that. I watch Joseph's chest swell when he sees his lady looking mighty damn fine. I even catch him giving her a sly little wink and again laugh to myself. I hope Darcie and I are as happy as those two are after all the years they've been together. Becs is next and she looks absolutely stunning. She gives Dan a wink and mouths 'she looks amazing' at me. A grin worthy of a mad mans adorns my face.

The wedding march comes on and the doors open one final time. My gaze falls on Nat, who I know is at Darcie's side looking gorgeous in her bridesmaid's dress. I leave my gaze on her for a second and take a deep breath before I let my eyes wander past Nat's feet and over to where my bride is next to her. I start at the bottom, working my eyes up the beautiful white full lace skirt of her dress. My eyes graze up over her stomach, where our little baby is growing inside of her, over her beautiful breasts that are again covered in white lace, but the swooping neckline shows her ample cleavage. My mouth waters just thinking about them but I focus my attention on Darcie and reserve those dirty thoughts for later. My eyes slide up her neck and rest on her beautiful full lips I'm desperate to kiss. I almost walk right over to her and claim her mouth, but I stand frozen to the spot, knowing I have to let her come to me. My eyes slowly work their way off her lips and find those clear cool blue eyes, and as our gazes lock together, I smile. A full beamed megawatt smile. I can see the urgency in her eyes and feel it within me. I need her beside me, and she needs to be beside me. It feels like forever for her to get to me but once she does, I hold onto her tightly.

"Are you sure you want to be shackled to me forever, Irish?" I whisper.

"Always." She whispers back and we turn to the officiant and make our vows.

Chapter 36

Denny

The ceremony is finally over. Darcie is my wife. Mine. Forever. The darkness is gone, banished by Darcie's everlasting light. And I can't wait to start married life with her.

She looked fan-fucking-tastic walking down the aisle towards me. I don't think Gorgeous has stopped crying the whole day and I even caught Joseph and Lewis wiping their eyes a few times. Darcie and I are married, and I can't wipe the smug smile off my face for longer than a second. I stand outside in the garden of our reception to take it all in. I'm married. I'm in love and I'm loved back, and we're having a baby. I'm going to be a dad. I shake my head at how incredible that all sounds.

"Not bad for a worthless mistake that ruined everything, eh?" I say out loud to myself. I chuckle at the thought of my so-called mother being royally pissed off with me for not turning out how she wanted me to.

A noise distracts me from my thoughts, and I turn to see Isla at my side. My beautiful little angel.

"Hey Princess, you okay?" I crouch down next to her, and she jumps into my arms and clings to me whilst burying her face into my neck. A sure sign she's upset. From when she was a tiny, little newborn she'd always snuggle into my neck when I had her up on my shoulder, burping her or rocking her to sleep. As soon as she could hold her own head up, if she was upset and in my arms her face would head straight there.

"What's the matter, my Princess? Is Isabelle being mean again?" She shakes her head against my neck, and I sit us down on the stone steps.

"I can't help you if you don't tell me what's wrong, my angel." I unhook her arms from around my neck and put her on my lap, so she's facing me. She has her eyes closed but tears still manage to stream down her little cheeks. I wipe her face and tilt her chin so I can see her properly.

"Hey Princess, open your eyes for me, please, and tell me why you're so sad. It's breaking my heart seeing you like this."

She sniffs a bit and lets out a little sob. "I-I d-d-don't want you t-to leave me." She sobs again. Big, fat, gut wrenching sobs and my heart aches for her. I stroke her hair and shush her.

"Why would I leave you? You're my Princess. Is this because Auntie Darcie and I got married?"

She nods her head and sniffs some more. I smile down at her.

"Baby girl, I would never leave you. You, your sister and your brother, and even your mum and dad, are my family. Why would I leave you?" I give her a kiss on the head, and she finally calms down enough to talk to me.

"People do dat when dey get married. Dey move away. I don't want you and Auntie Darcie to leave. You gotta stay so you can tell Isabelle to stop bein mean to me. And... and I'll... miss you!"

She lets the last words out on a wail and throws her

arms around my neck, burying her face again. I try to stifle my laugh and hear her scold me.

"Not funny, Uncle Denny,"

This just makes me laugh a bit harder. "I'm laughing because you're all upset when there isn't anything to be upset about. Yes, when people get married and have babies, they normally move out, but that's my home just like it's yours and your mummy and daddy's. We're lucky we have enough room in that big old house for us to stay there and have our baby there too. I want to live there with you guys and so does Auntie Darcie. Besides if we move out, who will look after your cousin for us when they get bigger? Don't tell Isabelle, but I think you'll be the best babysitter in the whole wide world." She looks up at me, her big blue eyes wide open and a smile tugging on the corners of her lips, sniffling away her sadness.

"You stayin wiv me? I can watch da baby?"

I nod down at her. "Once the baby gets a bit bigger you can play with them and teach them and help us when we need it. How does that sound?"

Her smile says it all, and as if a switch has been flipped, her face is alight with happiness. She kisses me on the cheek and states matter of factly, "When I get big, I'm gonna marry someone just like you, Uncle Denny."

Swallowing the lump that seems to have found residence in my throat again, I force a frown on my face. "You're not allowed to get married, ever! Remember? Me, you and Isabelle had a deal. No boyfriends, no princes, no marriage. Nothing."

I tickle her and she giggles then jumps off my lap and runs back inside shouting, "You funny, Uncle Denny."

As I stand back up, I notice George watching us with a smile on his face, but his eyes look sad. I motion for him to come over. Standing next to me I can see something's bothering him, but I don't want to force it out of him.

"The wedding was lovely, Den, thank you for including me in such an intimate event. For the first time in a long time, I feel like part of a family."

He takes a sip of his drink and the sadness in his eyes shines brightly.

"George, you thought about reconnecting with your mum? I know you've been dealing with the legal side of seeing your girl but what about your mum?" I sense his apprehension, and he takes a deep breath and sighs.

"I've been chatting to Nat about it all but it's a lot, you know? I feel so guilty. Mum raised me and she raised me well, and I chose someone else over her." He shakes his head and takes a gulp of his drink, knocking it back in one go.

"We'll all support you no matter what you decide. We're your family now as well. It's just I know you feel bad, but she won't be here forever. And sooner or later it'll be too late."

He grabs the back of his neck, clearly uncomfortable with this talk, so I wrap it up; not wanting to upset him but also not wanting him to miss out on an opportunity as well.

"I'm not trying to force your hand or anything, just being honest. Think about it and let me know."

He nods at me, and we stand in silence for a bit. We turn back towards the inside of the venue and see Nat and Darcie dancing together.

"Look at our girls." I say to him nodding towards them.

"Nat isn't– Is it that obvious?"

I laugh at him and shake my head.

"She deserves the best, Den, I can't give her that." He looks down.

I put my arm around his shoulders. "Yet. You can't give her that yet."

He lifts his head and smiles at me.

We head back inside and I grab Darcie around the waist and pull her into me.

"Mrs. Blanc, you are gorgeous." I kiss her head and she sighs as she melts into me.

"I thought that word was only reserved for Gloria?"

As she looks up at me her eyes twinkle with happiness and I laugh down at her.

"I'm sure she won't mind sharing the moniker with my wife. Hmmm I like that. MY wife. Mine." I bend my head down and kiss her softly on the lips.

She whispers "always" into my mouth.

I moan, lips still touching hers lightly, and feel myself harden against her. "Darcie," I groan. "We have a situation that needs a wife's assistance."

She grinds herself against my hard-on and giggles.

"We have a room full of people that are all here to celebrate us and I really don't think we can leave yet." Still pressed tightly against me she licks her bottom lip and then puts it in between her teeth.

"Right, that's it. We need to go now, Irish."

Heat and desire shine through her eyes, but mischief's there as well.

"Sorry old man, we can't leave yet. Don't worry though, we have forever to take care of that." She presses herself hard against me and stands on tiptoe to kiss me on the cheek whilst her hand lowers and strokes my extremely hard erection.

I move my hands from gripping her waist to cup her face, but she steps to the side of me, out of my grasp, and dances away, laughing at me standing in the middle of the room with a hard-on. I shake my head at her and mouth 'You're in trouble.'

She blows a kiss to me and winks.

That's it. I'm going to spank her beautiful arse for that. I step to go after her, but I'm stopped mid step by a slap to my shoulder. I inwardly groan, shift my legs to try to subtly rearrange myself and turn to find Dan laughing at me. Fucking great!

"I feel for you brother, that looks uncomfortable." Dan hands me a drink and I grumpily accept it.

"Thanks, the little witch did it to me on purpose. She's in so much trouble later." I smirk at the thought of Darcie bent over the dresser in just her heels and stockings...

"Gross brother, gross. That's my sister now, man."

I almost spit my drink out at his words.

"Are you fucking for real? Becs is my best friend, has been for forever, and I've had to watch you paw all over her for how many years? And you're offended by me talking about having sex with my pregnant wife on our wedding night?" I run my hand through my hair, and as I blow out an exasperated breath I catch the grin on his face and punch him in the arm. "You fucking dick."

He grabs me in a headlock and ruffles my hair. "Oh, little brother, did I upset you?"

Pushing him off me, I call him a dick again and he blows a kiss at me.

"Boys..."

We both stop dead in our tracks and look over our shoulders to find Gorgeous standing at the bar with Darcie, Nat and Becs. She puts two fingers to her eyes and points back to us to tell us she's watching us, and we both shout "sorry" over to her. The girls are bent over laughing at us as we hang our heads and turn around so she can't see our faces. Standing in front of us, Joseph and Lewis smirk at us being reprimanded by Gorgeous too.

"Don't you two start. It's bad enough the girls are laughing at us being told off, let alone you two as well." I say.

"And Denny has to deal with a bad case of blue balls thanks to the hard-on his wife put there," Dan teases.

Both men wince at me, and I punch a very smug looking Dan in the arm again only to hear Isabelle ask.

"Why's Uncle Denny gots blue balls, Daddy?" Dan's eyes are wide and his mouth gapes open in horror.

I laugh and smile smugly at Dan as I tell her, "Go and ask mummy, Isabelle."

"Shit, Denny. You fucking idiot. ISABELLE COME HERE!"

Joseph and Lewis are howling, and I'm laughing so much I have tears streaming down my face. My wedding day is the best day of my life... so far.

Eight weeks later

"You don't have to do anything you don't want to baby. If you want to know, that's great and if you don't, that's great too. It's your call, Irish." I tell Darcie as the technician scans her belly.

"I want to know. Let's find out if we can." She tells me.

I squeeze her hand and ask if she's sure and she nods, smiling through her beautiful blue eyes.

"We're in luck, I have a clear shot that tells me what you have. Have you decided?" The technician looks over at us with a grin.

Darcie nods at her. "We want to know." Her face splits into a smile and she turns the screen to us.

"Congratulations, you're having a baby boy."

Darcie instinctively looks up at me, her eyes twinkling with happiness and awe. "Ye were right. Ye said it was a boy from the beginning."

I grin down at her, smugness written all over my face. "I told you. I had a vision of you holding our little boy in your arms in our kitchen, and when you said you were pregnant, I knew it'd be a boy. I'm going to have a son. A little boy. I love you, Irish."

Still beaming like an idiot we step outside into the hospital corridor, and I pull Darcie tightly against me. I look down at her and brush my hand over her lower back.

"Thank you, Darcie. You've given me everything."

She smiles up at me lazily and brings her hand up to nuzzle my cheek as I lean into her touch.

"Right back at ye Denny. I love ye."

I kiss the top of her head and squeeze a little tighter when I feel something. I look down at her in shock and she smiles up at me.

"I think your son wants some attention, old man."

I drop to my knees in the middle of the hospital corridor and put my hands and my head on her stomach. "I love you too, my boy. You and mummy are mine, always." I kiss her belly and feel another little movement. I smile up at Darcie and shake my head in wonder at how I got so lucky. Her head is swathed in light and she smiles down at me, looking like an angel. We stay there, me on my knees with my hands and head on her stomach and her smiling down at me for what feels like forever.

Chapter 37

Darcie

"So, what's it like walking around with a penis inside of you permanently, me old mucker?" Nat is smirking at me whilst drinking a big glass of wine in our usual booth in the little Italian restaurant.

I roll my eyes at her and grin. "How do we put up with ye? I don't know why George likes ye, ye know"

She shrugs her shoulders at me. "Must be my impressive brain."

"Don't ye mean your impressive rack? Ye aren't known for your massive brain, Natalie Wilson."

She puts her hand to her heart, feigning shock and horror, and points to me. "How dare you, my brain is extremely big, thank you very much. I'm shocked and appalled at your words, Darcie. I think those Blancs are a bad influence on you, you know."

Becs splutters her wine and punches Nat in the arm. "Excuse me, I'm one of those Blancs and I'm also your boss, so watch it, bitch."

Nat gives her a kiss on the cheek and grabs her in a bear hug. "Sorry, boss. Have you thought of any names yet, Darcie? Have you told Lewis, Joseph and Gloria?"

I shake my head. "No, not yet. Denny wanted to do it face to face and Lewis is away until tomorrow morning, so they're going to come over for lunch and we'll tell them then. I can't wait to see their faces. I have a few names to be honest with ye. I like Dexter, Dex for short. and Daegen, Dae for short, and Dillion but I don't like that one shortened."

I haven't told Denny about any of the names I like, or that I want it to start with a D like him and Dan. Since we found out about the baby being a boy yesterday, we've been so busy beaming and telling our loved ones that we haven't had a minute to sit and discuss things. As soon as we came home from the hospital, we had Becs waiting in the house to see whether we'd found out. And as soon as she knew that we knew, she was a relentless bloodhound. We wanted to tell everyone together so no one could moan or accuse us of giving preferential treatment, but with Lewis being away until Sunday morning, Becs was insistent she couldn't wait and had been on at us non-stop. She even phoned Dan on a group call, made us get in on it as well, even though we were in the kitchen with her, and got Nat on it so we could tell them all together. When I mentioned Joseph, Gloria, Lewis and George were absent they pulled faces and moaned. Dan shouted out of his office for someone to get George there ASAP and within minutes he was a floating head on our screens as well. We couldn't fight them off any longer and told them with strict instructions not to tell Joseph, Gloria or Lewis until we did.

I grin at the memory that overtook my thoughts and can't help but smile at Nat and Becs who are sitting together on one side of our booth whilst I'm stretched out on the other. I look around and notice the restaurant is a lot livelier than it is on a typical Sunday.

Nat speaks up, "So, I have a favour to ask you two, and

Denny and Dan actually, but they aren't here so I'll ask you and you can ask them. Or whatever. I can ask them. I don't mind. It's up to you, you know, you're married to the guys..."

"NATALIE WILSON. What's wrong with ye? You're babbling incessantly right now." I shoot a shocked look at Becs who's looking as bewildered as I feel.

"Shit, I know. I'm nervous. George contacted his mum the other day." This is a huge deal. George hasn't spoken to his family for so many years and tis been weighing on him heavily more recently.

"Oh my God, how did that come about?" I ask Nat.

"He put it down to something Lewis said to him at poker night, apparently it resonated with him and gave him the kick up the arse he needed."

I look over at Becs who has her eyebrows raised into her hairline and all I can think to mutter is "wow."

"I know right? Anyway, he tried the landline, can you believe people still have landlines, and, get this, she still has the same phone number since when he was little!" We both shake our heads and thank the waiter after he drops off our orders.

"And how do ye know all of this when Denny doesn't?" I ask Nat curiously whilst Becs smirks knowingly.

"Because pain in my Darce, we've been talking. A lot. Texts here and there and on the phone, too." Nat retorts huffily at me and I smirk back at her.

"Anyway, he phoned her, and they spoke for hours. She was so happy to hear from him, she thought he was dead, the poor thing." She shakes her head.

Becs puts her arm around her shoulders as I reach over and squeeze both of their hands.

"She's invited him down to stay for a few days, and since this is such a big deal for him, I was hoping we could all go as moral support. I suggested it last night to him and he was really excited about having everyone there. George was saying how he feels like he has brothers in the guys and I think he'd genuinely be more relaxed about it if they were there too. It could be like a little babycation. What do you two think? I know if you say yes, the boys will follow." I look at Becs sitting opposite me and shrug my shoulders at her.

"Count me and Denny in. Are Joseph and Gloria coming? Denny'll probably want to invite Lewis if that's okay?"

"Of course it is, he's the one that got him to phone in the first place."

We look at Becs and she's frowning. "We don't have to stay with his mum, do we?"

Nat snorts obnoxiously. "God no woman!"

"And we can have our own hotel rooms as well?" Becs questions.

"You can do what you want, you're bloody paying for where you stay. Oh, I see where you're going with this, you little minx. You want a little nookie nookie without having to be all quiet in case you wake the sprogs up. Becs, you are one dirty Mumma. I knew I liked you for a reason." Nat throws her arm around her shoulder and high fives her as Becs laughs.

"Yeah, alright you got me. I'd have to check with my parents to see if they can have them for that long though, when were you thinking?"

Nat and Becs throw some possible dates together and Becs pops outside to phone her parents.

"Darcie, between me and you. Am I being stupid spending all this time helping him and supporting him when he clearly isn't ready for anything with me? I mean what if he doesn't even like me like that?"

She's staring into her food, so I get up and slide in next

to her. Natalie is always so self-assured and hearing her doubt herself is a shock to the system, but like she's done for me so many times before, I give her a pep talk. She needs to remember she's a bad arse woman who's perfect for George.

"Natalie, ye listen to me and ye listen good. George likes ye. He looks at ye like how ye look at your vibrator, Nat. That's serious."

She laughs and starts to talk but I cut her off.

"No, I don't want to hear it. Ye are amazing and if it hadn't been for your support and help, he wouldn't be where he is today. When he's ready, he'll come for ye, Natalie Wilson, ye mark my words."

She looks at me with wide eyes and nods her head slowly at first and then with more vigour as if my words are sinking into her head finally.

"Fuck yeah, Darcie, you're right. I'm a fucking catch and he'd be damn lucky to be with me." Nat's voice has risen a few hundred decibels and some of the other customers are looking our way. I put my hand on her arm and shush her whilst grinning like a Cheshire cat. The old Nat's back.

Becs walks in and gives us an enquiring look. "What's the matter with you two?"

"I'm fucking awesome that's what. And George would be fucking lucky to be with me."

Becs looks at Nat and screams back. "Fuck yeah girl." I can't keep the burst of laughter inside of me and howl. Becs joins in and Nat too. Our usual waiter comes over and asks if we're alright and we nod back at him still giggling.

"You girls make my day when you come in. Oh, and by the way, you are fucking awesome." He winks at Nat and walks away.

Laughter erupts from all of us again. Nat grabs her phone and sends a text to George to tell him a hot waiter is hitting on her and her phone rings instantly which just makes us laugh even harder.

As we lay on our massive bed, tangled in the sheets, sweating and breathing hard after our morning love making, I turn my head to look at Denny. He looks beautiful. His hands behind his head, his dark hair falling onto his forehead slightly. He has sweat glistening on his hard body and his face looks happy and relaxed. The only problem is his eyes are closed, and I can't see his beautiful blue pools. I'm just about to reach over and snuggle into him when my phone vibrates on the dresser next to me. I groan and roll over to see who it is, thinking it may be Gloria or Joseph to ask about our lunch later that day. I grab the phone, annoyed it's interrupted me, and frown at the unknown number. I stab the green answer button on the screen but there's nothing. No one on the other end. No words, just nothing, until the line goes dead. I sigh in frustration and throw the phone onto the bed.

"Another one?" Denny's propped himself onto one elbow and is facing me looking concerned.

"Yep. I'm sure tis nothing to worry about though. I think it's probably a computer-generated call and tis glitched somewhere along the way. It'll stop soon."

Denny gives me a look that says he doesn't agree, but he doesn't offer up an explanation. I don't want to push it. I've had a lot of these calls recently and I know Denny's worried about it and who he thinks is behind it, but I don't want to have to stress out about it all. Tis just a phone call and it can't hurt me, so I don't care about it. I try to take Denny's mind from it and change the subject.

"So, what do ye really think about all of us escorting

George to his parents' house then?" I'd told Denny about Nat's idea last night and he told me George had already phoned him to ask if we would go as well. I love the relationship the guys have and how they embraced Joseph and Lewis into their circle as well. It really does feel like a family, and that's something I'm grateful for.

"I think it'll be a good idea. George'll feel more at ease, which will make the visit go smoother. Plus, I get to have you all to myself in a hotel room, and that's something I'll never complain about, Irish. Are you sure you're okay?"

I know by the look on his face, all concerned and frowny, he isn't talking about whether I'm okay about the trip. He's circled back to the phone thing, but I play dumb.

"Yeah, I agree with ye. Tis a grand idea. I was shocked when Nat said Gloria and Joseph were coming as well, but I guess I shouldn't be seeing as Gloria has become mammy to all of us. I hope Lewis says he'll come when we see him later. Tis our first family trip." My hand instinctively rests on my stomach. Denny's eyes follow it and then he nudges me onto my back and rests his head on top of my hand.

This has become his new favourite thing to do, put his head there and talk to his son, and I love it. He doesn't speak this time. He simply places his lips on my now rounded stomach and just leaves his head there. My hand strokes his hair as we lay content and in silence.

"Denny, I was thinking... What would ye say if I said I wanted his name to start with a D like yours and Dan's?"

He takes his head off my belly, just enough so he can flip onto his other side, and puts his head back on it whilst facing me.

"I like that idea, follows his daddy and his Uncle and his mammy." He smiles his megawatt smile on the word daddy, and I smile right back at him when he mimics my accent on mammy.

"I've been toying with a few names. Do ye want to hear them?" I ask him, knowing he will be chomping at the bit to hear.

His eyes shine and he nods his head at me.

"So, I like these but if ye don't for whatever reason, we'll keep thinking, obviously. The first one is Dexter, or Dex for short. Then there's Dillion, but I don't like that one shortened at all, so no Dill, Dilly or any of that. This last one is a bit out there. Tis an Irish name and means dark haired, because I'm assuming he'll be dark seeing as both of us are. Daegen. Dae for short, spelt D-A-E." I peek at him to gauge his reaction. He's frowning but not an angry frown, more like a concentrating frown. His eyebrows drawn together and his lips pursed in thought.

"I don't like Dillion, there was a boy in school called Dillion and he was such a numpty."

He pulls a silly face when he says numpty which makes me chuckle.

"So, no Dillion then. That was my least favourite anyway and ye know someone would end up calling him Dill and would drive me mad."

"Dexter. Dex. I like Dexter and Dex. That's a cool name, that's a maybe. Daegen. Dae. I really like that. I like the Irish connection and I like the meaning behind it. We should probably wait until he's born though because it'd look a bit silly having a real blonde kid and calling him a name that means dark hair?"

I laugh at his seriousness; he's genuinely worried about that.

"I don't think anyone would know what it meant to be honest, unless they searched for it, but tis a good idea to wait. We can look at others too."

He grins up at me and shakes his head. "No, I think we have his name, Irish. Dae, if he's dark, which he will be because my vision seems to be spot on. Dexter if he's fair." He brings his face to within inches of mine and kisses me on the lips, a quick fast kiss.

"Can he have middle names?" He's looking all Mr. Serious again and I smile at him.

"Of course, he can. We can give him whatever we want, seeing as we made him. How many were ye thinking?"

"Well, seeing as we're naming him a D name, we could say was for Daniel, then give him his two grandfathers' names." I look at him confused for a second or two and then I smile as realisation hits me.

"Joseph Lewis or Lewis Joseph?"

He smiles back at me and shrugs. "Maybe we let them decide the order."

After lunch, with our bellies filled with food and our hearts happy with the news of us having a little boy finally shared with everyone, I'm content and happier than I've ever been. My phone rings, and I glance down at it and inwardly sigh when I see a withheld number. Not wanting to draw attention to it or make Denny worry more, I decide to ignore it. Less than a minute later, another call comes through. I ignore it again and switch it off.

Nat looks over at me, worry in her eyes. "They still happening, Darcie?" She looks concerned.

I nod but tell her tis nothing to worry about.

Lewis looks over at us fiercely. "What's up freckles?"

I roll my eyes at Nat and throw her a glaring look as she mouths "sorry" at me.

Denny fills Lewis in as I'm busy glaring at my now ex best friend. "Darcie's been getting dodgy phone calls for a while now. She thinks it's nothing, but I don't agree."

Lewis frowns at him. "Why not?"

Before Denny can reply I grate out. "Jesus, Mary and Joseph. He tinks it's my daddy. He's done it before, but he can't hurt me, tis just a call. There's no reason to panic." I sit back in my chair with my arms folded, completely over this conversation.

"Why would he want to hurt you?" Lewis looks angry now and I don't want to rehash all the business with my daddy again. I sigh and look over at Denny.

"Can ye? I don't want to go over it all again. Full disclosure with him, I don't want secrets from my family now, do I?"

Denny nods at me, winks at the 'my family' comment and he and Lewis head into the front room.

"So, childbirth eh? I bet that fucking kills." Nat says and then flinches as if waiting for a smack from Gloria.

A giggle falls from my lips, and I give Nat a thankful look for the reprieve. I suppose she can be my best friend again now. She gives me a wink and unfortunately for her, she misses Gloria get up, stand behind her and give her a smack on the back of her head. "Ow, son of a..."

Nat howls and laughter erupts from the rest of us as Gloria tells her, "Stop swearing, Nat. It doesn't become you."

Normality resumed and I couldn't be happier about it.

Chapter 38

Denny

"I'm going to need his full name, address and date of birth. I'll get this sorted, son." Lewis is pacing around the front room and, as much as I know the right thing to do is to tell him this isn't necessary, I give him the information he asks for. I need Darcie's dad to be gone. I don't know what I want him to do but I want the constant worry to be done with. I don't want her looking over her shoulder in fear he'll come back and try to finish the job he started. Maybe a little scare tactic from some of Lewis's acquaintances will warn him off.

"I don't want you to do anything if it's going to drag you back into that world, dad, or get you sent down. I just got you in my life, I don't want to wreck that. Not with the baby coming."

I'm afraid to tell him I want him around for me, so I make sure to mention the baby. He won't leave the baby, but he might me. In the short time I've known Lewis, I've come to rely on him. He's a support to me, and a friend. I finally feel like I'm one of the normal ones, having a family, including a dad, a wife and a kid on the way, and as much as

I want rid of that scumbag for good, I don't want to jeopardise what I have to achieve that.

"Son, I have a lot of favours to call in and this'll be one of them. Don't worry about me. I'm surprised you haven't taken care of it already if I'm honest. I'm not judging, just saying."

I look down at the floor and sink onto the sofa. I blow out a deep breath and rake my hand through my hair. "I've wanted to, believe me. When I saw Darcie on the floor of that shitty flat and for that split second, I thought he'd killed her, I could see it. I could see myself with my hands around his neck and squeezing. I would've found him, and I wanted to kill him, and then reality hit. I can't be responsible for ending another life. I don't think I can come back from that. Even if it is a fucking oxygen thief that completely deserved it. I just wouldn't cope. I know, I know, I'm a weak pussy eh?" I give a little laugh of disgust in myself and hear Lewis shuffle closer to me.

He sits down next to me and throws his arm over my shoulder. "Son, you aren't to blame for what happened to that junkie when you were a kid. You saved your brother. I know what that must've done to a kid though and believe me, I don't see you as a weak pussy at all. I'll deal with it. He won't mess with my family again." He pulls me into an uncomfortable man hug and kisses me on top of the head.

We stand up and head back into the kitchen. Side by side we walk over to Darcie and embrace her in a three-way hug. She laughs and then sighs and rests the back of her head on my chest and wraps her arms around Lewis's waist. He kisses her on the top of head, just like he did to me a minute ago and walks out of the kitchen to make a call. As he heads outside to the front of the house, Darcie looks up at me.

"What's he doing? Where's he going" Concern flashing through her eyes.

"Nothing baby, just seeing if he can trace that scumbag so we can hand him over to the police. That's all." I smile down at her and squeeze her tighter to me. I hate lying to her but technically Lewis hasn't told me his plans so for all I know that could be accurate. That's my story and I'm sticking to it.

Chapter 39

Denny

"This place is amazing. Literally right on the beach and the weather's alright as well. Becs, you did a brilliant job at finding this little hidden gem." I high five her as we look around the foyer.

We're staying in an old manor house that's been converted into a small hotel, and it captures the essence of being at home when you're away perfectly. The beach is only a stones throw down a winding pathway that leads you there from the garden. It's perfect for our little babycation.

Darcie opens the door to our room and it's just as beautiful as the rest of the hotel. We have a beach facing view and as I look out of the window, I can see the water stretching out in front of us until it touches the sky. The room is dominated by the huge bed, not as big as my bed back home but it'll do, with a beautiful headboard that looks like it's been hand carved in a lightly stained wood. The rest of the room is very sparse, in a good way, with just a wardrobe, bedside tables and a tv on the wall. I'm impressed, and when I look over at Darcie, I can tell she is too. Just as I'm about to grab her, her phone rings and the dread in my stomach knots together. I note the brief grimace on her face when she glances down at it, and then the relief when she smiles is palpable.

"It's Nat." She beams at me.

As I step into the bathroom, relief washes over me, and I make a mental note to check in with my dad about the anonymous phone calls at some point this weekend. Darcie comes into the bathroom after me and puts my wandering mind to rest.

"We have thirty minutes to get ready. Nat said George is taking us out to let us know how it went today. Can ye get ready in that time?" She grins at me mischievously and I pull her over to me. When she's in my arms the world feels right.

"Are you implying I need longer to make myself gorgeous?"

"No, my Adonis, ye are always gorgeous, but ye do take longer than I do to do your hair, so ye better get cracking." She stands on her tiptoes, kisses me on my lips and turns to walk away.

When I smack her arse she turns her head to look at me over her shoulder and blows me a kiss. She closes the door on my growl, and I hear her laughing from the other side of it.

"My mum kept holding my hand and kept telling me she loved me. I kept saying sorry, but she wouldn't hear it."

George is filling the gang in about his visit with his family and I couldn't be happier. He's a good guy and deserves all the happiness in the world. I'm proud of Dan and I for being able to help him. I smile at George and glance over at Nat who has her hand clasped firmly over his on the table, her eyes are transfixed by him. I chuckle to myself when an image of Nat's eyes turning into cartoon hearts pops into my head. I turn my head to study my Darcie. Her eyes are staring straight ahead at her best friend, but she leans into me to let me know she knows I'm watching her. I pull my chair a little closer to her and wrap my arm around her shoulder and catch a piece of her hair in my fingers. I place it between each finger and play with it without even thinking. I seem to find some sort of inner peace when I'm touching her. It's strange but she calms me in a way I never dreamt possible. She leans into me, her head on my shoulder and her hand on her rounded belly, the sight making me content and humbled.

Lewis's phone rings and he excuses himself from the table and heads towards the bathrooms. I notice his head slightly tilt at me, telling me to follow him. Pretending I'm going to the gents, I stalk after him. He's at the back of the restaurant, near the kitchen doors, and is still on the phone when I find him. He sees me heading towards him and nods for me to wait until he's finished. My whole being is on edge. How can I go from completely blissed out to frantically anxious in the space of a few seconds? I take a few deep breaths, knowing from the look on his face and tone of his 'yeps, nos and fucks' something's wrong. After he hangs up, he looks at me and his eyes are crystal blue, almost clear and diamond-like, which I know from my own eyes isn't a good sign.

"Dad? What's happened?" I ask him, even though I'm not sure I want to hear what he's going to tell me.

"That was a mate of mine. He went to see Freckles's, her, well that fucking waste of space, piece of shit scumbag, but he wasn't there. Looks like he hasn't been there for a couple of days now. He's sending me some pictures of his place. I'll keep on it, Den." His phone alerts him to a message which I assume has the pictures attached.

"FUCK!" I look at my dad's face, twisted in anger and his eyes flashing pure rage. I take a step closer to him and he moves back.

"Den, you don't need to see this. I'll handle it, son." His face is still angry, and he's trying to put his phone back into his pocket, but I need to see what's on that phone and what kind of threat we're facing.

"Dad, show me. NOW!" I try to keep my emotions in check, so he'll show me the phone. The darkness is swirling around my head, reminding me of the last time someone I loved was under threat. Pulling me back into the despair I felt when Dan was getting beaten. I try to push the thoughts away. I try to shield my eyes so he can't see the anguish in them. This is it. My happiness was never going to last. The darkness was always going to win. Her light is going to dim because of me. Darcie's going to be taken from me. My son. Fuck! I have to see what's on that phone. I know it's going to tip my rage over the edge, but I can't walk away from this. My everything is on the line. He lifts his hand with the phone in it back towards me and asks if I'm sure.

I nod back, unable to trust my voice to not give away just how scared I am. I look down as he places the phone in my hand and can understand my dad's violent reaction instantly. The picture is of what looks like her dad's bedroom. There are photos all over the walls of Darcie, taken from afar. Some of them I'm with her, and some are with Nat and Becs. He even has some of the kids on there. In the middle is a photo of Darcie as a child, clinging onto Sheila her teddy and holding her mother's hand. Her mothers face has a big black X through it and around Darcie's face he's drawn a target. On one side of it there's a piece of paper that has writing on it saying, 'Filthy whores get what they deserve.' On the other side is a photo of Darcie stepping out of our house, hand on her rounded belly, looking into her bag, probably checking for her phone for the millionth time. He knows she's pregnant. He knows where she lives, he knows who she loves, and she's his target. Fuck. I feel sick. I don't know what to do. I want to run back to her and take her home and keep her protected, never leave her side, but I can't. She won't let me. I can't take this to the police, I don't know where he is. I'm useless. I look up at my dad who looks furious still.

"What do we need to do now, Dad? Whatever it takes, and this time I mean whatever. I have to keep everyone safe. I don't care about before or what'll happen after, they have to be safe." He takes two steps toward me and embraces me in a bear hug.

"They will be son, don't you worry. No one will hurt my family. I'll sort it. I'll keep you updated. Now come on. We have to keep this normal. We don't want them all panicking. I'll find him and I'll deal with it. Trust me. Try not to worry. And for the sake of Freckles and your son, try to be normal. Stress isn't good for the baby. I've been reading up on it."

That last bit of information shocks me and has me tilting my head at him with a slight smile on my lips.

"Yeah, yeah, I know, I'm going soft."

I laugh a little bit to cover the sheer volume of emotion that has spiked through my very being. This man loves me too. He's choosing to stick around and wants to be a part of my life. He's my dad. A proper dad. One I'm fucking proud of.

"I'm glad you're my dad." I tell him, letting him see all the emotion in my eyes. He doesn't speak, just nods at me, but the look in his eyes says it all. We go back to the table together and I sit as close as I can to Darcie. I can't rest properly; the rest of the night is awful. I keep trying to act normally but I can't. Darcie asks me a million times if I'm alright and all I can say back is yeah, I'm fine.

It's our last day on our little babycation and I can see Darcie's frustrated with me. I'm distant with her, less touching and kissing. Not because I don't want her, but because I'm scared she'll see through me. I know she can sense I'm hiding something from her, so I keep my distance like I did when I was planning to propose. When she looks into my eyes, I look away. I can't let her see my worry and fear. I have to protect her from that. The curiosity in her eyes soon turns to fear and then anger, until she can't hold it in any longer.

"Talk to me Denny, please. Stop shutting me out. Always, old man, remember?"

I take the few steps that stand in my way to reach her and tuck her into my arms, holding her tightly, I inhale her scent. God, I've missed her so much. I'm an idiot for shutting her out. "Mine Irish, always mine. Forever, both of you. I'll do everything I can for both of you. Please never doubt that." I kiss the top of her head and smell her hair again.

"Denny, tell me what's going on. We're a team. I can handle it."

I sigh a deep sigh, torn between my promise to deal with everything together as a team with her and keeping them both safe.

"Your dad's missing and knows you're pregnant. We think he's targeting you. I've got to keep you safe, Darcie, both of you, at all costs. He had pictures..."

She takes a deep breath and cuts me off. "Thank ye for telling me. We need to tell the others, so we all know what we're dealing with here."

I nod at her and squeeze her tighter. I feel a prod from her stomach and smile. I part from her slightly so I can put my hand on her belly.

"I'm sorry son. Daddy'll fix everything. I promise you."

I look at Darcie for the first time in days and she smiles at me. "Well, hello there. Tis been a while since I saw ye, old man."

I kiss her quickly on the lips and round up the troops on the phone. Darcie's right, we need safety in numbers.

"I'm not sure about this. Can't you just stay here?"

Nat rolls her eyes at me, and Darcie puts her hand on my chest over my heart.

"Denny, we'll be grand. I'm with the girls and Joseph's driving us. We're only going into town to do some sight-seeing and shopping. I promise ye, we'll be okay."

I'm still uneasy about it; I haven't left Darcie's side since I saw that disturbing photo. I may've been distant, but I was still right next to her. Today's different. Lewis needs me and Dan to stay at the hotel and strategize about what our next move is regarding Darcie's scumbag of a dad.

"Stay with Joseph. Please, Darcie. Humour me. No matter what, stay with Joseph." My eyes plead with her, and she nods her head, biting her lower lip at the same time.

"Darcie, don't do that. Unless you want me to take you upstairs, lock the door and fuck you senseless."

Her beautiful blue eyes widen in shock but flash desire and need as she smiles at me.

"I'll stop doing it now, but to be sure, I'll do it later on. Make sure ye keep up your end of the bargain, old man."

I growl at her and kiss her hard on the mouth. I gently

tug on her bottom lip with my teeth, and she moans into my mouth.

"Put her down, Blanc. We're leaving now!" Nat's standing near to us and tugs her away from me.

I hold onto her tighter and give Nat a scowling look. "Cockblocker."

She throws her head back and laughs at me. "I think your cock has seen enough action, Blanc. She's already pregnant for fucks sake. Shit, where's Gloria?" She looks around to see if Gorgeous is anywhere near, but she's already in the car, so her head is safe from a smack.

"I'm telling her you swore." I grin at her smugly.

"I'll tell her you did too," she smirks back at me.

Before I can respond, Darcie's strict nanny voice rings out.

"Children, enough now. Don't make me put ye both in time out." She points her finger at both of us in turn and we guiltily look down.

"I fucking love that voice. It turns me on so much." I whisper into Darcie's ear and nip her lobe. She smiles back up at me, a dreamy look on her face, and my heart nearly stops at the thought of losing her. She takes a few steps towards the car, and I mouth 'Joseph' at her, and she nods back at me. I catch Joseph's eyes from the driver's seat, and he nods at me too. He knows just how important it is for him to keep them all safe. Dan comes over to me and flings his arm over my shoulders and turns me away toward the hotel.

"They'll be fine, Den. Joseph wouldn't let anyone hurt any of them and those women can handle themselves. Don't worry."

I nod at him but stay silent. I want to rage at him, tell him it's easier said than done to not worry. To scream at him that my whole world is sitting in that car. My life, my heart, my reasons for breathing are being put at risk, but I don't say anything. Deep down I know Dan knows it all anyway. I don't need to say it out loud to him, he knows.

We meet Lewis in the reception and take the stairs up to his room to discuss the situation. As I walk up the staircase, where only a few days ago I'd been admiring the artwork on the walls and was blissfully happy, I notice the contrast of how I feel today. Sick, that's how I feel now. Gone are the pleasant thoughts about the pretty pictures, all that's running through my head now is Darcie. Images of her bruised and battered body come into my mind, and I want to hurt someone. I don't know what to expect as I walk into my dad's room. Do I want him to tell me they've found him, and he's no longer a threat? Or do I want him to say he's no news at all? One makes me complicit in someone else, no matter how much they deserve it, being hurt or killed, and the other leaves my whole family at risk. We step inside my dad's room and I briefly look around. It looks like mine and Darcie's, just smaller. I look at my dad, but he's avoiding my gaze.

"Boys, here's where we are. We haven't been able to locate him yet. I've got eyes on the kids at your mother-in-law's house, Dan. Everyone else is here, together and safe. I've got a couple of men on standby that are local too, just in case. When we get back to London, I think he'll come out of the shadows, and once he shows himself, we'll be waiting." He looks at me nervously, expecting some sort of a reaction but I don't say or do anything.

Dan shifts from foot to foot, clearly anxious and agitated. "So what? We just have to sit around and wait? That's bullshit. We make ourselves sitting ducks for this psycho and wait for him to attack? We need to be doing more. Can't you get someone else on it?" He's pacing backwards and forwards like a caged tiger as he speaks, and I feel so guilty he's in this situation because of me. If I'd left Darcie alone, she'd never have been on the street the day he found her, and everyone would've been okay. Instead, everyone's a target because of me. It's all my fault again, just like when I was a kid, everything's my fault. I slump down onto the bed and rake my hand through my hair. The darkness surrounding me, forcing me back under its spell, welcoming me in like an old friend. I tug on my hair as my mind is assaulted by images. Dan getting beaten up in our old flat. I pick the ashtray up and swing it as hard as I can. Thud. The sound of it connecting against bone. I look down and I can see the body laid out on the floor and then it twists and disfigures itself into Darcie. My beautiful Darcie, her body twisted and battered. Her face covered in bruises. Her round belly deflating before my eyes. I can't breathe. I can't stop the darkness as it covers me...

"DENNY! DENNY! LOOK. AT. ME. DEN!" Dan's voice comes from a far away place and I can feel hands tugging on my wrists. I force my eyes open and see Dan's face in front of me. He's talking to me but it sounds like he's a million miles away and I can't hear what he's saying. I take a deep breath and my lungs scream at me to release it and with a whoosh I can hear him again.

"Denny. You're okay. You just had a panic attack, it's okay."

I take a few seconds to breathe and clear my head. A few minutes later, I've got myself under control but I avoid Dan's gaze as I tell him, "It's not okay, Dan. This is all on me. I should have known I couldn't be happy. I don't deserve it. I've put you all in danger and I'm so sorry. This is all my fault..." Before I can finish my sentence, my dad is stalking over to me.

"What's your fault? Falling in love with a fucking fantastic, smoking hot woman who loves you back just as much? Or is it your fault Freckles had to grow up with that fucktard as her dad? Or that her mum couldn't see a way out for herself and had to waste her life with that fuck?" Every word he spews out takes my mind away from the pity party I was throwing myself, and closer to total rage I've never felt before.

"Oh, wait a minute, it's your fault he likes to hit, and abuse women, isn't it? I forgot you made him do that, didn't you? It was you that made him batter Darcie's beautiful face, wasn't it? I fucking forgot that was all on you, Denny." My dad's words are dripping in anger and sarcasm, but my blood's boiling.

"Fuck you!" I scream at him, unable to contain my anger any longer. "It's his fucking fault he's like the way he is, not mine you fucking prick. And if you call Darcie smoking hot again, I'll dig your fucking grave myself. She's mine, do you hear me?" I know my anger is misplaced but I can't hold it in anymore. As I stand there seething, I look at my dad and he smirks and raises one eyebrow at me. I frown at him, half ready to rip his head off and half curious about what the hell he's doing. He winks at me and carries on smirking.

"Welcome back, son. By the way, Freckles is fucking hot, I'm proud of you."

I lunge at him, but he dodges me – he's surprisingly quick for his age. He laughs and winks again. I should be madder at him, but I can't fight the laughter that bubbles up inside me and bellows out of my mouth. I see past his tactics and appreciate them. The fucker riled me up to remind me what we're facing and to stop me wallowing.

Dan, who's been standing in the same spot for the whole of our interaction, just shakes his head and mumbles about us being fucking crazy.

"Daniel, to answer your earlier concerns, yes, we have

to wait and be patient. No, I can't get someone else on this as there aren't a lot of people I trust, and the more people that know what we're looking for, the more risk there is that he'll know what we're planning. Also, my guy is the best. Don't doubt me or him. I'll find him, and you'll all be safe."

Dan, still rooted to the spot, nods his head at Lewis.

We've spent the past two hours going over our strategy for when we're back in London. Lewis has shown us the men who'll be 'watching us' and has explained about sticking to our schedules and not diverting off them. The girls and Joseph have been gone for too long now and I'm getting really anxious. I'm pacing restlessly and I'm so worried I can't eat any of the food George brought us back for dinner. My dad, George and Dan are eating and casually talking when my dad's phone rings. He answers it and I can tell from the tone of his voice something's wrong.

"Ok – you're sure? This morning? Clean up's a possibility, I'll let you know for certain after. Cheers."

Before he can hang up, I round on him. "What's going on? What does 'clear up' mean?"

My dad turns and faces me, but his eyes are closed off, void from any emotion, guarding me from seeing him.

"My guy traced him to Dorset, he knows we're here. Don't panic. He doesn't know we know, so we have the element of surprise. I'm trying to figure out how he knew though. None of you put anything on social media like I asked you not to, did you?"

I shake my head as does Dan, but George hangs his head and drags his hands through his hair.

"Shit, Denny, Dan, I'm fucking sorry. Lewis, I didn't even think. I posted some shit yesterday with my mum. She was so happy I was back, I didn't think. I'm so fucking sorry." George looks gutted.

I feel bad for him, he just wanted to share the good news that he was reunited with his family, but I'm fuming too. My dad explicitly told us not to let our whereabouts be known, and George gave him all the information he needed.

"George, don't stress, it'll be okay." Dan tries to console him as I look at my dad whose eyes are as clear as ice. He's furious. I shake my head at him, and he turns away, clearly trying to control his anger.

"I'm going to call Becs and tell them to come back straight away. Agreed?" Dan is asking the group and we all nod at him.

Lewis turns to face him and advises, "Don't panic them, just tell them there's been a development and we need them back here. The last thing we need is poor Joseph having to deal with four hysterical women on his own."

I can see the tick in Dan's jaw twitching at his wife being described as a hysterical woman in the face of a crisis but he, like my dad before him, is trying to keep his temper in check.

"Hi baby, there's been a development and we need you guys to get back here ASAP. We'll explain it when you're here. I know baby but Lewis doesn't want to make you, and I quote, 'hysterical women for Joseph to handle'..." He holds out the phone. "She wants to speak to you, Lewis."

Dan hands the phone over to Lewis who's shooting a murderous look back at him, but Dan doesn't care, he just smirks at him. I can hear Becs shouting at Lewis through the phone from the other side of the room and can see his anger dissipate before my eyes at her words. If I wasn't so wound up, I'd have found the whole thing extremely entertaining. As he hangs up and hands Dan his phone back, he shoots him a filthy look. A look that if it could have, would've killed him, or at least maimed him badly.

Ten minutes pass and my phone rings. Before I can look at the screen to see who's calling, I know something bad is going on. The darkness is back and circling again.

"Joseph, what's wrong? What do you mean? How's that possible?" I'm shouting so loudly I'm sure they can hear me back in London. My heart's thudding in my ears, and I can hardly make out what he's saying. I grab George's keys and head for the door, followed by George, Dan and my dad. Lewis takes my phone off me and Dan takes the keys muttering something about me not being in a fit state to drive. Once inside the car Lewis speaks.

"He has Darcie. She went into a shop because she needed the loo and said she didn't need anyone to go with her. She didn't come back. Den, can you track her phone?"

My fog-addled brain clears, and I nod my head.

"Yeah, she has locations turned on. I downloaded an app on her phone recently in case she went into labour and I wasn't at home, and she couldn't direct me because of contractions or whatever." He hands my phone to me and tells me to track it.

"George, pull up the maps on your phone, so when Denny gives you the location we can head straight there. I'll phone Joseph so he can head there too."

I manage to navigate my way through the app I've only browsed after I synched her phone and details into it. I thought I had more time to be more thorough with it before the baby was born. The thought of my son sends a shiver of fear through me. If he hurts him I'll... My phone dings and interrupts the dark thoughts I started to have. I give the location to the guys and George types it into his phone whilst Lewis is on the other line to Joseph.

"Guys, this is a cliff point. It's not far from here but it's a notorious place for suicides."

My heart feels like it's going to explode in my chest. The fuckers going to kill her and then himself, I know it. I don't need it confirmed by him, I just know. The darkness threatens to close around me and I force it back. I roar, an animalistic sound screaming from me. I feel like a caged animal. I want to get out and do something, but I need to stay in the car and get to Darcie and our son as quickly as possible. I didn't notice the rain when we left earlier, but I do now. It's dark and wet. Darcie and our son are in the hands of a monster. God help me, I need a miracle tonight.

Chapter 40

Darcie

"Guys ye really don't have to guard me like this. I'm sure nothing's going to happen here of all places. Denny and Lewis are just being overly cautious." I try calling off my bodyguards, aka Nat and Bec, but to no avail.

"Who said we're guarding you? My nephew is precious cargo in there and I'm guarding him." Becs rubs my stomach as she speaks.

Nat joins in. "What she said."

She raises an eyebrow at me, daring me to question her but I shake my head as laughter bubbles out of me.

"Oh, let's go in here, please?"

I look at Nat and then at the shop she's heading us over to, and that laughter flows out of my mouth, again.

"We can't make poor Joseph go in here with us, tis not fair." I look around to see Joseph's eyes go very wide in his head as he takes in the adult themed shop, and then watch as he grins down at Gloria.

"I'm game if you girls are. One rule though, I don't want to see what any of you are buying or what you try on, except you." He finishes his sentence by popping a kiss onto Gloria's nose and she swats his arm playfully.

"See that's what I'm talking about. Get you a guy that looks at you like Joseph looks at G. Simple really." Nat has a faraway look in her eyes.

"You mean like George looks at you." Becs sniggers at her and Nat gives a sly grin and winks back.

"Well until George is ready to take our relationship from looks to everything else, I'm going inside here to get myself a new bob."

I giggle as Becs high fives Nat whilst curiosity takes over Gloria's face.

"What's a bob?" She asks as my hand flies to my mouth and Becs snorts in laughter.

Nat doesn't miss a beat. "Your battery-operated boyfriend, B-O-B. Your vibrator. G, I'm shocked you didn't know yours was called bob."

Gloria hides her shock well, but ye can see she's thrown by that one. Just as she's going to speak, Joseph cuts in. "Well, my dear, she doesn't know about that because she doesn't have a bob. She has a BOJ, body of Joseph, to take care of her 'needs.' And she doesn't have to worry about running out of batteries either." Joseph winks at Becs and I who are staring at him with our mouths wide open.

Gloria is the colour of beetroot and once Nat has recovered, she laughs and smacks Joseph on the back. "I fucking love you, will you please adopt me?"

She's still laughing when Gloria smacks her upside the head and tells her it doesn't become her.

"Sorry, can I use your bathroom please?" I motion down to my stomach and the lovely cashier smiles warmly at me and points towards the back of the shop. I seem to need the loo all the time at the moment. I quickly look over my shoulder and see the rest of them waiting for me in the car and waddle faster toward the back of the shop.

As I leave the bathroom, feeling empty and anxious at what's waiting for me at the hotel, I see a door on the opposite side open. I freeze. He's here. Before I can scream or shout or do anything, he grabs me and pulls me outside. The door leads to an alley behind the shop, right next to where we originally parked the car. He's probably been watching us all day. Goosebumps stalk all over my body, and as I look down to my belly I catch a glimpse of something shiny. I look closer and see he's holding a big kitchen knife to my bump. I can't do anything. I can't fight. I can't run. I have to do as he says. Once again, I'm under his control. I look up into his eyes and search for anything, any kind of familiarity or paternal feelings, but there are none. Nothing. Just pure hatred for me. I've never done anything to him, just existed. I don't know why he hates me so much. Maybe he resents me because my mother loved me. Maybe he hated being stuck with a wife and child. Maybe tis because I left. My thoughts are interrupted by his vile words.

"Ye filthy whore, move and I'll rid ye of that filthy bastard mongrel ye've growing inside of ye, Darcie."

The hatred spewing from his voice, tis how he spoke to my mammy too. I close my eyes and will away the tears. I think of Denny. My beautiful, strong Denny who believed he wasn't worthy of love for all those years. Why didn't I listen? Why didn't I let Joseph come with me? My own stubbornness is going to be the reason I die, the reason my baby won't get to meet his wonderful daddy. I feel the sting of tears in my eyes and can't push them away now, so I let them fall over my cheeks. He ushers me into a beat-up old car and laughs when I put my seatbelt on.

"I wouldn't worry about ya safety, whore. Ye won't be needing to in a wee while anyway."

My head whips around to him, he has one hand on the steering wheel and the other holding the knife against my bump still.

"What does that mean? What are ye going to do? Please, don't hurt my baby, please. I'll do anyting. Denny has money, he'll give ye some and ye can do what ye want, just please, don't hurt us." I beg him. Willing to bargain my way out of this situation and to keep my boy safe from this monster. But he looks straight ahead and laughs maniacally as he drives at a ridiculous speed in the opposite direction of where Joseph and my family are waiting for me. I try to keep myself calm and get him to talk. I reason with myself if I can get him distracted enough I can maybe crash the car, and as I'm wearing a seatbelt and he isn't, it could work in my favour.

"Daddy, why are ye doing this? Why don't we forget this and try to build a relationship for the sake of your grandson?" I stare at him, willing him to slow down and come to his senses, but instead he sneers at me, his face contorting in hatred.

"Don't! I'm not ya daddy. Ya mammy was a filthy whore too, and ye are a bastard mongrel she tricked me into having in my home for all years. That mongrel inside of ye isn't anyting to do wit me, whore." He swerves into the other lane and I scream whilst he laughs at me once again. My head is reeling from what he's just said. Is he telling the truth? Is he not my daddy? Is that why my mammy stayed because he would've told everyone she was a 'whore'?

"Ye aren't my real father? How do ye know this? When did ye find out?" I don't want to ask him anything, but I need to know more.

"When ye were fecking four. I found ya whore

mammy's love notes. Confessing her love and telling him about his precious baby girl." Scorn is dripping off his words and my head is spinning. She lied to me. All those years and she lied to me. "Ye all ruined my fecking life. Don't worry. I ruined ya real daddy's life, I ruined hers, and now I'll do the same to ye. Ye should tank me. Ya mongrel would just grow up to hate ye anyway. No more talking now, ye filthy, fecking whore."

He pushes the knife into my belly more and I flinch back. All it would take is a bump in the road and the knife could slice through my skin. I try not to even breathe in case it hurts my boy, and for the first time in a long time I pray to whoever can hear me, 'please keep my boy safe.'

Tears stream down my face as we drive in silence for the rest of the journey. I don't know how long we drive for or where we're going, but my thoughts flit between, 'Thank God, I'm not related to this monster' and 'we're going to die, and poor Denny'll be left all alone.'

The car comes to an abrupt stop, and he forces me out of the passenger side, telling me if I try to run he'll kill me slowly and make my baby suffer more. I stand frozen at the passenger side door until he rounds the car and stands next to me again. He smirks and keeps the knife aimed at my bump as I scan my surroundings trying desperately to formulate an escape plan. We're on some cliffs. The light's fading but I can see the edge of the cliff through the oncoming darkness. I can hear the sea below us and to the right is a pathway. No one's around. Tis pouring rain and we're alone. Goosebumps form all over my body as I realise what his plan is. He's going to push me off the cliff. He's going to get rid of me and my boy. My heart thumps in my chest so loudly I'm certain he can hear it as well. I need to get away. I have to save my boy.

I try to remember all the self-defence classes I took when I first came to London, but my mind is blank. All I can see is Denny. Does he know I'm missing? Is he looking for me? How will he take the news our boy is dead? Will he blame me? That thought terrifies me more than anything. The idea of Denny hating me is too much to think about. I have to escape.

A rumbling of a car in the distance gives me the courage I need to take my only chance. As he tries to drag me closer to the edge, I pretend to stumble. With the knife firmly away from my stomach and up by my shoulder as I bend over, I lunge up and wedge my shoulder into his groin with all the strength I have. He shouts out and stumbles backward, letting go of my arm. And I run.

I run as fast as I can. I don't look back to see where he is, but I know he's behind me and I know he's close. I run toward the direction of the car I heard earlier. The rain's pelting me in the face so hard, I can't see through it. I run straight into what feels like a wall and I scream and try to run around it. Hands are gripping me. Stopping me from moving anymore and I kick and thrash about to get free. I have to save our baby. Furiously, I look up and I'm overwhelmed by the most beautiful blue eyes I've ever seen in my life.

"Denny." I whisper at him as relief washes over my entire being and safety consumes me. He gives me a quick kiss on the head, then turns his attention back over my shoulder, suddenly aware of the shouting and swearing. It doesn't sound like tis right behind me though, and when I turn I see Lewis and the others on the cliff side. Lewis is squaring off against the man I used to call daddy. I can't even call him a sperm donor anymore as he isn't even that. I watch the glint of the knife glittering in the car's headlights, but tis in Lewis's hand and fear grips me. I wriggle out of Denny's hold and run back over to stand by Lewis's side. His body's shaking with rage, eyes icy and distant, mouth contorted into a grimace, his entire being ready to pounce. I can't lose him. We need him, Denny needs him. I won't let that man take another person I love away.

"Lewis, he isn't worth it. Call the police. Let's do this the proper way. We need ye here with us. Your son needs ye. I need ye." I scream at him, trying to break the spell this monster has cast over him. Lewis doesn't even look towards me; he doesn't register that I'm there. The need to protect us is evident in his eyes. I grip his arm but he shrugs me off.

Denny comes up on his other side, seconds after me and tells him, "Dad, Darcie's right. We don't want to lose you. Put the knife down. Let the police deal with him. Your grandson needs you too." Denny reaches down to his hand and Lewis whips his head to the side as if he's seeing Denny for the first time. He drops the knife and Denny catches it.

He lifts the knife up to point toward my not-dad and says, "You're going to prison for a long time, you mother-fucker. You won't get to touch Darcie ever again."

He laughs at Denny, a crazy manic laugh, and it sends chills down my spine.

"I'll be let out on good behaviour. And I'll come for her again. And if I can't, I'll get someone else to do it. It'll be even fecking better. I'll get to kill her and ya bastard mongrel she's got inside of her. Maybe I'll let ye watch as the breath leaves them both. Leave ye agonising over this filthy little whore and her fecking mongrel."

An animalistic roar comes from Denny, and I scream, "NO!" at him as I watch someone pounce. Someone from behind me lunges forwards and punches my not-daddy right in his threatening face, and then again in the stomach.

Each blow pushing him closer and closer to the edge of the cliff. He tries to swing and misses, and another punch lands on his chin. He steps back a fraction and falls. No scream comes from him as he drops off the cliff's edge. Just silence. We all stand together, our quick breaths the only sounds until Dan drops to his knees. His head slumped down in defeat. Denny drops the knife and rushes to his brother's side. He's on the ground in front of him, also on his knees, grabbing his brother's head.

"You didn't mean too. You were protecting us. It wasn't your fault. He was threatening your nephew, Dan. He kidnapped Darcie. You didn't mean it. You didn't fucking mean it!" Denny's desperate pleas are all we can focus on. We stand silently and still, daring not to move.

Dan's head snaps up and he stares Denny straight in the eyes as he tells him, "Now we're even. Any self-deprecating thoughts you ever had about yourself, you have to have about me now too. Or you have to let them all go." He gasps a ragged breath and throws his hands against his face, dragging his skin down with his fingers in his shocked state. "Shit, I didn't mean for him to fall."

Denny wraps his arms around his brother, snapping everyone else out of our stupor, and we join their embrace. Except Lewis, who walks over to the edge of the cliff.

He peers over the ledge, spits and then turns to us. "I can't see anything. The son of a bitch isn't clinging onto the side that's for sure, thank fuck." He turns back to face us all and he shrugs at the disapproval on our faces.

"What? He was a waste of space and you all heard what he said. He'd never have stopped. Now he will. We need our stories straight. Den, you're going to phone the old bill in a bit and tell them he's gone over the cliff. Tell them there was a scuffle and Dan did what he did in self-defence. There's nine of us saying the same thing, so hopefully, they won't charge him with anything. We've already reported Darcie as missing, and they know he attacked her before."

"No!" Becs stands up, arms folded across her chest in a warrior pose and faces Lewis. "We aren't risking Daniel. We tell them after Darcie managed to get away, Denny managed to wrestle the knife off him. It's believable, the size of Den compared to him, he stood no chance. Once Den had the knife, we told him we were phoning the police. He lunged at Darcie and *I* pushed him back. I didn't realise how close to the edge he was, and he fell backwards.

"The police aren't going to press charges on me but on Daniel they might. As much as I believe women and men are equal, there are still some points in society that deem us very different. And this is one of those times." She stares Lewis in the eyes and dares him to argue with her. When he inclines his head at her to continue, she does. "The police and CPS are less likely to want to imprison a working mother of three small children than they are a male in his prime who beat up an older man before he fell, aren't they?"

She stands, her hands on hips, and stares at Lewis, willing him to deny she's right. There's more chance of the Police believing her story than Lewis's, simply because she's a woman. Tis one of the times inequality will work in our favour. Daniel stands up and puts his arm around her shoulders.

"Becs you can't do this. They could still charge you. The kids..."

"Enough! They won't charge me; it was self-defence. I'm doing this, Daniel. We will not lose you. You did what any of us would've done. Hell, I was a second behind you. Had you been a touch slower it would've been me throwing him over the cliff. Only difference is I would've meant to do it, so stop."

He stands, gaping at her, then lowers his head and rests his forehead against hers.

"You're a fucking superhero and I love you more than anything."

Lewis walks over to them and squeezes Becs's shoulder in solidarity. He turns to face us all and tells us, "Right, everyone, clear on the story?"

Our heads nod solemnly as a collective.

"Good. Den, phone the old bill."

Chapter 41

Darcie

We all agree home is where we need to be and drive through the night to get there. Denny tried to get me to head to the hospital to make sure the baby was okay, but I managed to assure him he's grand. When he put his hand on my belly and felt an almighty kick from his son, his insistence faded a bit.

I'm trying to keep my eyes open but I'm so tired I fall asleep in the car on our way back to London. Nat and George are following behind us in their car with Joseph and Gloria. Becs, Daniel and Lewis are in our car with us. Lewis decided to drive so Denny could sit with me in the backseat. Daniel is in there with us as Becs sits in the front. I wake up but keep my eyes closed so I can listen to what's being said without everyone trying to sugar coat anything for me. I can hear Becs reassuring Daniel he did the right thing. I don't want them to stop talking about it and I know they will if I'm awake. They seem to think being pregnant has made me unable to bear what we've just lived through, as if I wasn't there, and I want to know whether Daniel, Denny and Becs are truly okay. If I ask, they'll just lie to me and say yes. I know tis a sneaky thing to do but I just need to not be treated with kid gloves for a bit.

"You have nothing to feel guilty about. The police said his house was a big pile of evidence. That he was clearly unhinged, and Darcie was his target. He wouldn't have stopped just because he was in prison. He would've always come after her. You stopped him."

Hearing Becs's words makes me shiver and I have to force myself to regulate my breathing as if I'm still asleep.

"You saved her life and my heart, Dan. You stopped a force of evil, and believe me man, I know what's going through your head right now. But you have to keep silencing it with the fact that, YOU. SAVED. MY. WORLD. I owe you everything."

There's a shuffling sound which I'm assuming is Daniel and Denny embracing, or trying to as much as they can with seatbelts and my supposed sleeping body in between them.

"How hard must it be for Darcie though? She doesn't even know who her dad is now. And growing up with that monster, knowing he was that way because your mum lied, has got to wreck your head a bit. Den, we have to make sure we look after her properly when we get home."

Before Denny can respond to Daniel, Becs is cutting in. "Don't give us those evils and go all caveman on us 'my wife, my job, grunt'. She's not just yours. We're claiming her as ours as much as yours, so there. I'll even fight you for her, and you know I can throw a fucking mean right hook just like my husband."

I can feel Denny's chest vibrate with a chuckle and he holds me closer to him.

"We take care of our own Becs, and I love that you've claimed her as one of us. I'll share with you, no fisticuffs needed."

If I weren't pretending to be asleep right now, I'd be

crying my eyes out. These people have claimed me. They're willing to fight - not physically, well maybe in Becs's case - over who gets to look after me the most. They've taken me in as one of them and I couldn't be happier.

"So Becs," Lewis clears his throat before he continues, "you've claimed Darcie and Nat as one of you guys, anyone else you want to, you know, officially claim?"

I haven't heard Lewis sound so nervous before. He dealt with the police and lawyers and has basically handled the whole shoddy mess with confidence, charisma and swagger. But now, asking Becs if she sees him as one of them, has left him vulnerable. I silently urge Becs, who can be such a hard-head at times, to take him in, let him be one of us. Not because I think it has any semblance on any of our relationships with him, but because he needs it more than anything.

"I suppose George has slipped into our little group easily as well, so yeah I'll claim him as one of us too." Becs replies nonchalantly and my heart sinks for Lewis.

"What? The one who can't follow a simple ban on social media? You've got to be fucking kidding me!"

Lewis's frustration is evident in his voice, as is Becs's sarcasm in her snort laugh.

"Oh, Lewis, don't be a baby. Of course, you're one of us. I don't need to claim you. You automatically became one of us the day you found us. But if you ever call me a hysterical woman again, I'll wear your balls as earrings. Understand?"

The car erupts into laughter, and I take that as my cue to 'wake up'.

"Well, we all sound like we're getting along in here." I say trying to make my voice sound sleepy but not doing a very convincing job. Luckily everyone is laughing so they haven't taken any notice.

"Sorry, Darcie. I'm just teasing Lewis. I didn't mean to wake you up."

I shake my head at Becs and tell her not to worry.

Denny squeezes my hand and asks me, "You okay?" I nod my head at him and smile.

"Ye know I think I'm grander now than I have been in a long time. I'm free. No more worrying or looking over my shoulder. Thank ye, Daniel." I squeeze his hand and he looks at me with relief in his eyes and smiles at me.

"Anything for you, sis."

When he squeezes my hand back, I grin at him and put my head on Denny's shoulder.

He kisses my temple, inhales my hair and tells me, "I love you more than you will ever know, and so do they. Even if Becs thinks I'm going to share, you're still mine."

My breath stutters in my throat and I sigh as I tell him. "Always old man, always."

We all end up in Becs's kitchen again. Tea's being made and my favourite people, except the kids, are all in one room. When I look around at everyone's tired eyes, guilt flashes through me, but I force it away. For too long now I've carried guilt unnecessarily and I won't do it anymore. These people walked into my life and chose me, they love me, accept me and in some cases worship me. I snuggle into Denny a wee bit more and his arm wraps around me tighter. Nat sits opposite me with George at her side, whilst Becs and Dan follow and take the empty chairs next to them. Joseph, with Gloria on his heels, stands behind Nat and George as Lewis places two steaming cups in front of Denny and me. He sits next to me. I look up at him, smile my thanks for the tea and he winks at me.

Nat breaks the silence, of course. "So, me old mucker, how you doing?"

I smile and shake my head at her. "I'm grand, honestly. I'm surrounded by my favourite people in the world, except for the kids, what more could I want."

I see a few nervous glances go around the table and hear Becs clear her throat. "Darcie, what about the news about your dad?"

I smile at her and sweetly ask her, "What news? That I have two dads? I've known that for a while now." I see the confusion on everyone's faces as they try to understand what I'm saying, thinking I knew about HIM not being my biological dad. Before they can question me anymore, I continue. "As I said, I've known for a while I have two dads, one's sitting right next to me, and the other's opposite. My real family. If they'll have me that is."

Denny's hand squeezes my shoulder. Realisation and then love flows through Joseph's face. "I couldn't be prouder to have you as my own, my girl."

Tears prick my eyes at Joseph's declaration, and I turn my head a little to look at the man sitting next to me. Lewis looks down at me, eyes guarded so I can't read them, a blank expression on his face. I want to look away but instead, I sit up straighter and look him straight in the eyes, my face blushing furiously. He narrows his eyes slightly and then his icy cold pools turn warmer and clear, and I can read everything in them. Love, acceptance and admiration.

"If you have to ask, I haven't done a good enough job of showing you just how much I love you. Come here, freckles." He leans over to me and wraps me in a hug, and I hold him so tightly, never having had a hug from a paternal figure before. A few tears escape my eyes and wet his shirt.

"Alright, alright, give her back to me now. I've done enough sharing." Everyone chuckles at Denny, who looks completely confused as to why everyone's laughing seeing as he was being deadly serious.

I snuggle into him as Nat says, "Man, I feel for you and Becs, you too, G. You have four Blanc men suffocating you now."

Denny looks at Daniel, then they look at Joseph and Lewis. They all cross their arms over their chests, narrow their eyes, and focus on her.

Nat shifts in her seat. "What?" She asks them nervously.

Lewis tilts his head at her and hits her with one of his glares.

"Just wondering, why you feel for them when you have four Blanc men that'll be suffocating you just as much? You see Nat, when you're family, you're family, and you my girl, are a Blanc in everything but name."

For the first time in a long time, Nat just stares at them all speechless. Tis a fecking miracle, that.

"Damn. You made me speechless there for a second. I fucking love you all so much."

She doesn't see it coming, we all do, but she doesn't.

Gloria's hand flies gracefully through the air and slaps her upside her head.

"OW, G!"

Gloria looks at her with a frown on her face. "Stop swearing Nat..."

"IT DOESN'T BECOME YOU." We all chorus together, as we smile and look around the table that's filled with love, compassion, loyalty, strength and family. A family of choice. A family that's mine, always.

Epilogue - Denny

A *few months later...*

"No. Nope. Nuh uh. Not happening."

I look over at Darcie with a grin on my mouth. She has a pair of pyjama bottoms on, slung low on her hips, a vest top rolled up over her huge belly, and straps attached to her to monitor little man's heartbeat and her contractions. She's shaking her head and pacing about in the small room, talking with Nat and Becs on a videocall. We're only allowed two people in the birthing suite and she couldn't decide between them; they agreed to be on the call instead.

"I'm afraid you'll have to, Darcie; you don't really have a choice." Becs's voice rings out clearly at about the same time a woman screams nearby.

"I'm splitting in twoooooooooo." Darcie's face goes deathly pale, as does Nat's as she informs us she's never having kids and walks away from the screen, as Becs smiles smugly on. Darcie looks at me, panic streaking through her eyes. I stand up and walk over to her.

"Irish, you're the strongest woman I've ever met. You

can, and you will, do this. You'll be fucking amazing. You'll bring our son into the world and I'll wait on you hand and foot for the rest of time to say thank you, and it still won't be enough."

She smiles a soft smile at me and then her face contorts in pain. She doubles over and breathes whilst I rub her back. "Just breathe, Darcie, breathe in and out."

I try to get my voice to go all soothing like the teacher in our Lamaze class, but Darcie blows out a big breath and sternly tells me, "I am fecking breathing, Denny. If I wasn't, I'd be dead. Now stop fecking telling me what to dooooooooo. Owwwwwwww." As the contraction reaches its peak Darcie stops talking. She rocks back and forth, breathing I might add, and rides out the last of it.

She leans back into my chest and carries on talking to Becs as if nothing happened. "Why did ye do this again, woman? Ye must be mad."

Becs laughs at her and a wistful look takes over her face. "Darcie, once you hold your baby, you forget all about the pain and all you'll be able to see is him. You wait for it. There's no better feeling in the world. Call me when it gets really going or if you need me for anything. Darcie, you can do this." She blows a kiss at the screen and then it goes black. Darcie leans back and I kiss the top of her head.

We've overcome so much in our short time together. We've gone from two damaged, commitment-afraid souls without a parent between us, to two married people, madly in love, having a baby with so many grandparents around him he won't know what to do with them. Lewis is so excited about being a pops, and is adamant he isn't to be called granddad as it makes him sound old. Joseph and Gorgeous are just as excited at being Grams and Grandpa Jo. And even Becs's parents and George's mum are equally excited about being extended grandparents to our little boy. Let alone the uncles and aunties and cousins this kid has; he's going to be so loved and wanted it's unreal. That feeling makes me happier than I can explain. We've overcome violence, kidnapping, attempted murders and accidental deaths. The police didn't charge Becs, they believed it was an accident and didn't suspect Dan had anything to do with it. I think they were happy he wasn't around to cause them further problems, to be honest.

We're free to be a normal, happy, loving couple, about to welcome our baby into the world. And it feels fucking fantastic. The darkness has disappeared and all that's there is light. Darcie's light. It shines through me now and the cloud that was looming over me is no more.

Darcie moans again and sways on her feet as a midwife comes in to check the reports from the monitors.

"You're doing really well, Darcie. Once this contraction is over, I'm going to examine you as they're coming quite quickly now, aren't they?" Darcie manages to nod, and I smile tightly at the midwife.

"I feel like a fucking jack arse standing around and not being able to do anything to help." I half mumble to myself whilst Darcie silently rocks into me, and the midwife smiles at me kindly.

"At least you feel like that. You don't even want to know how many men I have in here playing on their phones or moaning about how bored they are whilst their partners are in agony over in the corner. You're one of the good ones, I can tell." I give her a little smile and Darcie smiles too. She zones out when she's having a contraction and as soon as they stop it's like she comes back to me.

"He is one of the good ones. My very own Adonis."

I kiss her head again and she moves to get on to the bed.

I turn away from the midwife and look into Darcie's eyes whilst she does her checks.

I'm completely thrown off guard when she says, "You're about nine-ten cm dilated, Darcie. The next contraction, if you get the urge to push, go with it my lovely. You're almost there now."

Darcie beams up at me but the fear flashes through her eyes again.

"You can do this, Darcie Blanc. I know you fucking can." I grab the phone and quickly dial Becs and prop her onto the table next to me, pointing at Darcie's head obviously. She's squealing and squeaking but I'm focussed solely on Darcie.

The next contraction comes and Darcie pushes, she holds my hand as tightly as she can, and her eyes lock with mine. The midwife tells her to breathe. The next one comes in seconds and again Darcie is pushing her hardest. The overwhelming pride I have in her is threatening to wash over me, but I swallow it down and focus on her.

"And that's his head, the next push he'll be here, Darcie."

I mouth 'mine' at her and before she can reply with 'always,' another contraction comes and Darcie pushes. Her eyes never leave mine and we're locked in our own little world.

Noise breaks through our little spell. So much noise. I hear 'congratulations', 'it's definitely a boy' and 'look at him', but I can't focus on anything but the tiny bundle of pink skin and jet-black hair on Darcie's chest. She smiles up at me and I smile back. I look down at our son, the most beautiful and perfect little boy that has ever been born, and I look at Darcie in complete awe. "Thank you. Thank you. Mine, you're both mine."

She smiles up at me and tilts her head to me, so I reach down and kiss her as she says, "always," against my lips.

Epilogue Darcie

A *few hours later...*

"Dae Lewis Joseph Blanc, meet your family..."

As the Blanc family, including Nat and George, files into our room on the labour recovery ward my heart is content and so happy. I sit in bed, surrounded by people who love and adore me, people who've risked their lives and freedom for me, and I'm completely, overwhelmingly happy. I watch as the reality of his names dawns on not only Joseph but on Lewis too. He's so choked up with emotion he can't even speak. I watch the three generations of Blanc men. Oldest to newest. They huddle together, forming a protective circle around our tiny bundle. The love flows through them all welcoming the newest member of the clan. I laugh when Denny shows them the babygrow Dae is wearing and his matching t-shirt that says, 'like father like son.' And I laugh even harder when both Joseph and Lewis unzip their jackets and show him their matching t-shirts too. I watch as he embraces his dads, and a happy tear escapes my eye when all three men have a group hug with Dae too.

Nat and Becs come over to me, one on each side.

"They're hogging him, Darcie, it's not fair. I've been here all of five minutes and haven't gotten to hold him yet at all." I grin at Nat who's looking longingly over at Dae.

"You'll be waiting even longer too because I'm next, Nat, I called it." Becs gives a satisfied smirk at her and Nat wails.

"That's not fair, you can't call it. I didn't know you could call it." Nat folds her arms over her chest and pouts, but I can see the laughter on her lips too.

"Yeah, I'm grand by the way girls, ye know. I just gave birth and all but yeah, sure, ye argue over who gets to hold Dae first why don't ye." I roll my eyes at them, and they give each other a mischievous look over my head, then they both pounce on me, hugging me tightly from each side and placing a kiss on each of my cheeks until I laugh out loud with happiness.

"Okay, okay, you're forgiven." I exclaim as they let me go.

Becs dances over to the boys and says, "Gimme my nephew, I need snuggles and sniffs."

For a split-second Daniels face flashes terror at the idea of Becs wanting to sniff a new-born in case she gets broody, but then he looks down at Becs holding Dae and his face crumples into a mix of love, desire and want.

I can't help but laugh as Denny sidles up to the space Becs has vacated next to me.

"I'm not sure Dae's going to be the youngest for a lot longer than nine months, Irish." He kisses me on the cheek, and I put my head on his shoulder.

"Right, I'm going in. I might have to use my feminine wiles on you Becs, be ready girl." Nat gets up from the bed.

Becs rolls her eyes at her. "What are you going to do? Seduce him out of my arms?"

I sigh and Denny looks down at me concerned. "Are you okay? Is this too much?"

I shake my head at him.

"Tis perfect, well almost perfect as the kids aren't here. But this is everything I never knew I wanted or needed before I met ye."

He puts his arm around my shoulders and kisses my head as we settle back onto the bed.

"It's everything I dreamed of but never thought I was worthy of until I met you, Irish. You gave me light, instead of darkness, hope instead of despair, happiness instead of sadness, and love instead of hate. I'm forever indebted to you, but I promise you, I'll spend the rest of forever loving you. Mine, Darcie, always were and always will be."

I tilt my head up to him and kiss him. He's right. There's no more darkness, no more sadness, no more hate. Just love, hope and happiness. We may have had to drag ourselves up from the gutter at different times in our lives and for different reasons, but we did it. As I look around this hospital room filled with love, I can't help feeling sad my mammy isn't here to share in the joy. That she didn't know it was possible to fall in love and not lose yourself, but find who you were meant to be. To not be dependent on a man and rely on them, but to choose to share your entire being with them because without them you're incomplete. She didn't deserve her lot in life. I don't resent her. Without her I wouldn't have found Denny. I wouldn't have been the woman he fell in love with, and I wouldn't be here in this room with my amazing family and our beautiful son.

"I think he's getting hungry, Darcie, he needs his mummy." Gloria walks over to my bed and hands Dae to me.

Denny places a hand on his head and squeezes my shoulder. "Right, everyone, get lost so my beautiful wife can feed our perfect son." Denny grins at them all. As they file out, we tell them all we love them, and we'll see them at home.

Alone and with a fussy baby, I look up at Denny. "Always, old man."

His eyes twinkle and he smiles back at me. "Mine. Always."

He kisses me. A slow, passionate kiss and just as he bites down gently on my lip, Dae lets out an almighty cry.

"Jeez alright son, but remember she was mine first."

I grin up at Denny and he smiles back at me. I feed Dae with Denny sitting next to me, his arm wrapped around my shoulders. His arm that's adorned with my name, surrounded by beautiful colourful flowers to continue his family tattoo, a space next to it for Dae's name to be added as well. Happiness radiates off me and a tranquil calm consumes my soul now. I was always meant to wind up here. With Denny and our son. A smile creeps onto my face and I turn my head to see Denny watching me.

He grins and tells me, "Mine." He leans over and brushes a kiss on my forehead.

I murmur back, "Always." And I mean it. My heart will always belong to my blue-eyed Adonis.

THE END

Freebie alert: Mine, finally.

A spin off novella

Do you want to see if Nat and George get their happily ever after? Click the link below and read the novella for free.

You may meet an interesting character from my new series that's coming soon as well...

https://dl.bookfunnel.com/4um95dy6pa

Acknowledgments

First and foremost, thank you to you. The readers. Thank you for giving Denny and Darcie a go. Thank you for taking a chance on a new author and their debut book. It really means the world to me. You've helped me to achieve a dream I've had since childhood and I'm immensely grateful for that.

I need to thank my family too. My mum and dad for letting me be the bookworm I am and for never discouraging it. My sister for badgering me into publishing and for telling me when something just wasn't right. And for being BRUTALLY honest, I wouldn't have done it without you. Thank you.

To my husband, who has been by my side and listened to me talk through plots and characters when he has no idea about romance and books and would rather be watching football. Always and forever more, bubs.

To my beautiful girls who let mummy write when they wanted to play and who tell me they're proud of me every single day. I love you.

I need to thank Valerie. The best book bestie I have ever met, even if it is only virtually. I don't have the words to express how much you mean to me. If it wasn't for your encouragement and voice of reason, I wouldn't have had the confidence to show anyone my work, let alone publish it. You have given me so much support and strength from a whole other country and I am so grateful to have you in my life. Thank you for sending me that message! I love you, twinny.

Thank you, Melanie. You've been telling me to publish my stories since we were 12 years old and I finally listened! Thank you for being there for me, every step of the way.

To my betas, thank you for reading the even longer versions of this book and for always being truthful with me. You all rock. And to my arc readers - thank you for answering the call and being bloody amazing!

To the authors and PA's of Romancelandia, thank you for being so embracing, encouraging and for helping a newbie out when she needed it. I'm forever grateful and so glad I can live in this amazing land with you all.

And lastly, I want to say a special thank you to Michelle Fewer. You have given me courage, confidence and faith in myself. When I doubted I could do it, you picked me up and told me I was wrong. You reached out to me, gave me encouragement and scoured through this book with me, helping to whip it into shape. I'm honoured to work with you but even more honoured to call you my friend. Thank you.

About the Author

Koko Heart is a romance writer who lives in London, United Kingdom with her husband and their four daughters. She writes from her heart and has always been fascinated with happily ever afters. She still believes in fairytales but likes them a little bit dirtier now.

Sarum Chronicle

recent historical research on Salisbury & district

Issue 23: 2023

ISBN 978-1-9161359-6-3 ISSN: 1475-1844

Copies of current editions of *Sarum Chronicle* are available from the following Salisbury retailers: Waterstones Salisbury, Waitrose Salisbury, the Rocketship Bookshop, the History Bookshop, Salisbury Cathedral shop and Salisbury Museum shop.

To submit material for consideration in future editions contact Emily Naish at e.naish@salcath.co.uk

See www.sarumchronicle.wordpress.com for information on back issues of *Sarum Chronicle* and *Sarum Studies.*

Designed and typeset by John Chandler

Contents

Editorial

Welcome to the latest edition of *Sarum Chronicle*. It contains a wide range of articles exploring different aspects of the history of Salisbury and its surrounds. I will resist the temptation to list them here but a quick read of the contents page will hopefully identify many articles of interest to you, and we hope that the Chronicle will provide many happy hours of reading.

Sarum Chronicle is produced by a very small band of volunteers. Its cover price includes the cost of printing – which is not insubstantial – and funds the ever-popular annual lecture. We are always on the lookout for people who would like to join. If this is of interest to you, then you would be joining a very friendly group. The work load is not excessive and very enjoyable. If you are interested please contact any of the Chronicle board members.

We have decided that for 2024 we will extend the geographical focus of the Chronicle to cover a wider area than just Salisbury and its immediate surrounds. So if you have research material on the rest of Wiltshire, Dorset or Hampshire, do make contact if you would like us to consider it for publication.

Occasionally we publish *Sarum Studies* which contain in-depth research on a local area or topic. Our last *Sarum Studies* celebrated the 800th anniversary of the beginnings of the current Salisbury Cathedral. It was a great success and is now completely sold out.

A few months ago we started work on a new *Sarum Studies* about the churches of Salisbury and its surrounds. It will cover all Christian denominations. For each church there will be a short history of the church and an explanation on why it's worth a visit plus some really excellent photographs. We don't have a fixed publication date yet but it is likely to be published in 2024.

Thank you for buying this edition of the *Sarum Chronicle* and thereby helping to maintain the tradition of an annual journal and lecture. Thank you also for having read this editorial. We hope you enjoy reading *Sarum Chronicle* 2023.

John Elliott

Fig 1: Augustus Pugin circa 1840 *(reproduced by kind permission of National Portrait Gallery, London).*

Pugin's Salisbury Period

Malcolm Sinclair

Introduction

> there is a vast deal of rage excited among certain parties by the publication of this work and I am a marked man here at Salisbury . . . I am quite ready for all comers and will not abate one Line.[1]

Writing these words in 1836, from his home near Alderbury, just outside Salisbury, Augustus Welby Northmore Pugin's career, reputation and notoriety were reaching heights that no one, not even he himself, could have anticipated two years earlier when he decided to move to Wiltshire with his family.

Pugin's life was relatively brief, as he died at the age of forty years, in 1852 (Fig. 1). The moments of those years spent connected to Salisbury were briefer still. He lived there from the spring of 1835 to the late summer of 1837, initially staying in the city itself then moving close to Alderbury nearby. Throughout that time, he would refer to Salisbury or Sarum as his place of residence, but he often travelled away, across England and abroad, as well as working in London. After his 1837 departure, he only visited the area occasionally.

There have been many rigorous scholarly and biographical studies of the ground-breaking influence that Pugin had on architecture, in Britain, Ireland and abroad, and his re-introduction of Medieval Gothic design to a wide range of artisan work. Yet it is notable that the time he spent living in Salisbury, and the connections he had in the local area, have rarely been looked at separately from other periods and locations where he took up residence and worked.

During the time he spent in Salisbury, Pugin lived in his first designed and built residence, changed faith to Roman Catholicism, worked on competition-winning plans for the new Houses of Parliament, and published the first edition of what was to be his most controversial and influential book, *Contrasts.* As will be shown, his achievements during his time there were so significant that they merit consideration as being more explicitly identified as a defined period of his work: Pugin's Salisbury Period.

Early Salisbury connections

The first recorded Pugin visit to Wiltshire occurred in the mid 1820s. At the age of thirteen, he was taken off to the country by his mother for convalescence after a period of illness. They went to Christchurch in Dorset and then to Salisbury, both of which impressed him, due to the Augustinian Priory of the former and the grand old gothic cathedral of the latter.

In 1832, Pugin's father, Auguste, arranged to take his family on what was to be a last trip together. Ever since 1818, when his son was just six, Auguste had organised annual family tours, for weeks on end, to towns and cities across England and sometimes to the continent, to see, and then draw or paint, the structure and fabric of notable old buildings. The highlights of these trips were old churches and castles, and it was clear from the very first tour that father and son were equally enamoured with the medieval gothic styles they discovered. The final family tour was to be to the West Country. It was commenced by mother and son in Salisbury in late summer 1832.

Little detail is known of the time spent in the Wiltshire city in that year, yet it was clearly significant. Pugin struck up a friendship with a stonemason there, William Osmond, who was to become a close collaborator in local building projects and initially welcomed Pugin and his family when he moved to the city three years later. Osmond was mason for the cathedral in Salisbury, and his work had included a memorial there to the late Bishop John Fisher in 1828, of an elaborate table tomb surmounted by cushion, Bible and crozier.

Learning his drawing skills and artistic appreciation through pupillage with his father, himself an architectural draughtsman, Pugin would have come across regular mentions of Salisbury Cathedral in his youth. Not only was the building recognised as one of the greatest Gothic achievements in the country, but it had become notorious architecturally due to alterations which had been undertaken at the end of the eighteenth century by James Wyatt, in the name of improvement, destroying much of the internal structure, such as two chapels, two porches, the medieval screen, and large amounts of stained glass, as well as a large bell tower outside the cathedral (Fig 2).

Pugin had no time for 'the Villain Wyatt',[2] and gravitated towards the views expressed by the Reverend John Milner, whose work he republished in the 1840s, and whose other writings he credited for influencing his Catholicism. Milner had produced, initially in 1798, *A Dissertation on the Modern Style of Altering Antient Buildings as Exemplified in the Cathedral Church of Salisbury,* which had excoriated Wyatt and his destructive changes.[3]

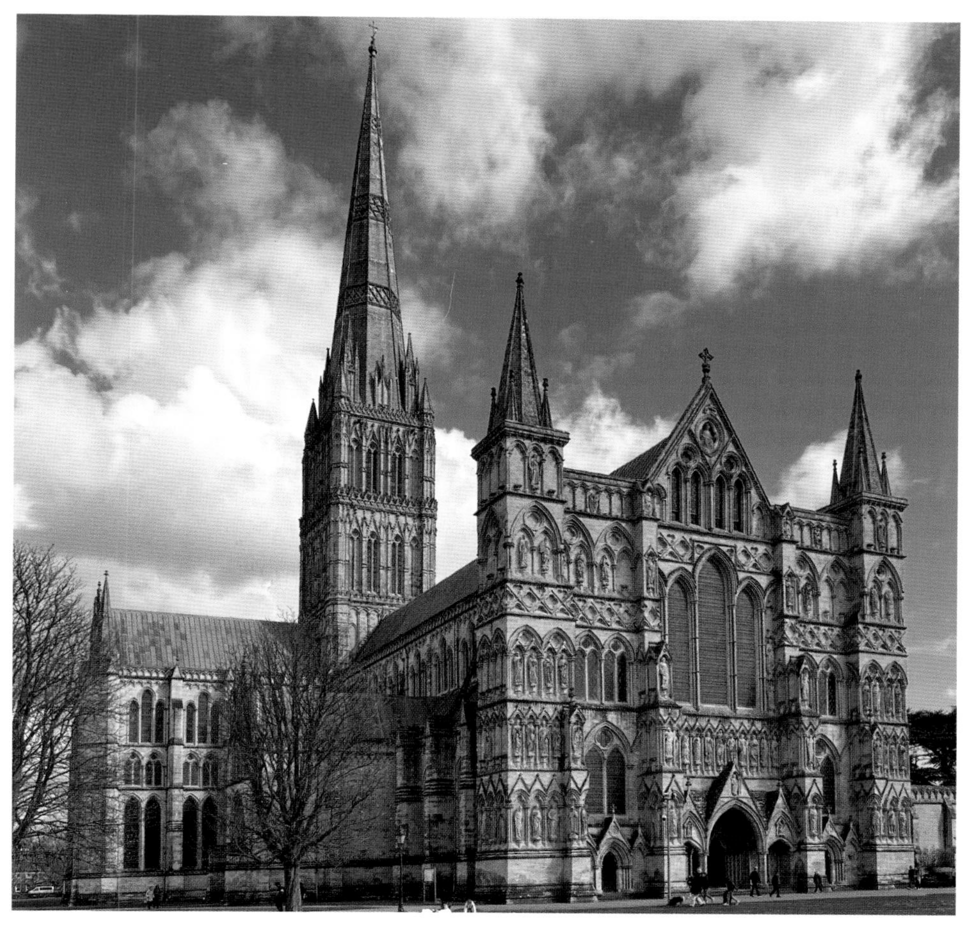

Fig 2: Salisbury Cathedral *(Malcolm Sinclair, 2023).*

Benjamin Ferrey, who had been a fellow pupil in Auguste Pugin's drawing school, described, in his 1861 biography of Pugin, how Augustus responded to Wyatt's work once he was living in Salisbury:

> now was first manifested his indignation at the wanton havoc which had been made in Salisbury Cathedral, where, under the plausible guise of improvements or restorations, most reprehensible changes were effected.[4]

Arrival in Salisbury

In the early 1830s, Pugin lost those dearest to him. His first wife Anne died days after childbirth, and then his parents passed away: his father Auguste followed by his mother Catherine Welby. By 1834, all that was left of close family was his young daughter Anne from his first marriage, his aunt, Selina Welby, and

Fig 3: The entrance to the Hall of Sir John Halle, New Canal, Salisbury *(Malcolm Sinclair, 2021).*

his second wife, Louisa Button, who he had married a year after he became a widower. Initially, Louisa and Anne lived with him in a cottage in St Lawrence near Ramsgate where his aunt lived, although Pugin spent long periods away on his tours around England and France. These travels were refining Pugin's views not only of good and bad architecture, but also of spiritual matters, with hints, in a letter to William Osmond, about the possibility of entering the Catholic Church.[5]

In March 1834, his son, Edward Welby Pugin, was born in Ramsgate. Then, in September, his Aunt Selina died, leaving her nephew enough funds to improve his family's life. Soon after, he decided to move to the place about which, only a few months earlier in his letter to Osmond he had written: 'in all my travels I have never seen a pleasanter city than Salisbury.'

Welcomed into the city by the family of his stonemason friend Osmond, Pugin planned to invest his aunt's money in the building of a new property, but, before he completed that, it is thought that his first work was to help renovate a medieval building, The Hall of Sir John Halle.

Nowadays one of the entrances to the Odeon Cinema, this hall is situated on New Canal, in the centre of Salisbury. The building is named after Sir John Halle, its owner in the fifteenth century, a wool merchant in the city and four times its mayor. In 1834, a China Merchant, Sampson Payne, commissioned work to renovate the old building to become a shop. A history of the Hall, published at that time, describes how Payne:

> at considerable expense removed the modern partitions and renovated the curious hall which is now to be seen in its original size and proportions.[6]

In 1861, Benjamin Ferrey stated that Pugin was involved in this work:

> Pugin with his own hands executed in colour the coat-of-arms supported by an angel in the end wall of the apartment, and decorated the chimney piece and other parts of the hall (Fig 3).[7]

Another book mentioning the Hall, published at the end of the nineteenth century, described a large oak screen with elaborate carvings, which still exists within the property today, and stated that above the screen was:

> a painting representing an angel crowned and holding a scroll inscribed "This Hall built 1470 restored 1834" . . . The illumination is by the ready hand of the late A.W. Pugin who began and finished it at once, having continued at his gratuitous labour of love for six hours without intermission.[8]

The painting no longer can be seen on the screen and the fading painted fireplace is all that now exists of Pugin's work in the Hall. The main restoration work there has been attributed to Frederick Fisher in 1833, undertaken a year before Pugin arrived in the city, with stained glass installations ascribed to the Salisbury glazier John Beare in 1833–34.[9]

St Marie's Grange

In early 1835, with the money inherited from his aunt, Pugin decided to construct his own home and build it from scratch, buying half an acre of land for £150, on the outskirts of Alderbury, just south-east of Salisbury. He wrote about it to a friend:

> It is a most beautiful piece (sic) of grounds close to Salisbury comanding (sic) a magnificent view of the cathedral and city with the river avon winding through the beautiful valley.[10]

The land that he had bought was on sloping ground with the higher part of it affording a clear view of the cathedral, more than a mile away. The name he chose for the property, St Marie's Grange, reflected his imminent Catholic conversion, but it was the style of the design which was to stand out. It was a three-storey building, with the side facing the Southampton Road, and therefore visible to passers-by, being a blank wall devoid of windows. Access to the property was via the first floor, with a dry moat defending it from visitors who had to cross a drawbridge to gain entrance.

Internally, the building had a library, chapel with bellcote, and a stair tower. In some ways it was thoroughly modern, such as being red brick, having casement windows and containing water closets on each floor. In other ways, its owner's love of medieval gothic was plain to see, with its towers, drawbridge, stained glass, carvings, and engravings on doorways and interior walls. Pugin chiselled out some of the stone himself, and displayed his own coat of arms, adding the phrase *en avant* (meaning 'forward') to the shield design. Some stained glass windows were installed, including those above the current front door which remain in place to this day. The windows were prepared by John Beare, and it is thought that Pugin may well have participated in staining some of the glass (Fig 4).[11]

Described in 1945 by the painter John Piper as 'more remarkable than beautiful', the significance of St Marie's Grange as Pugin's first building cannot be overstated. Piper suggested that it was the grandfather of so many Gothic villas which were to be built across the country later that century (Fig 5).[12]

Fig 4: Stained glass window at St Marie's Grange, Alderbury *(Malcolm Sinclair, 2022).*

Pugin initially enjoyed living in Salisbury, developing a good range of contacts in the city linked to his growing design and building interests, and using the good local postal connections to communicate with those further afield. He undertook some of his most important early work whilst residing at St Marie's Grange, and to support this he had made what has been termed the 'piece of furniture most associated with his creative life': his architectural drawing table. This was designed for standing use only, specifically measured to match his height of five foot two inches.[13]

Fig 5: St Marie's Grange, near Alderbury *(Roy Bexon, 2016).*

Conversion to Roman Catholicism

Alongside proximity to the cathedral, the most significant aspect of living in Salisbury for Pugin was his connection to the Catholic community there. In 1836, after several years of internal reflection, he decided to convert.

Raised as a Protestant, Pugin's own writings reflect his experiences as a child, under his mother's aegis, of exposure to fervent Presbyterian preaching. However, as he got older, and visited more and more medieval sites constructed before the Reformation, he was drawn towards the Catholic Church.

The position of Catholicism in the country had been problematic for many years. England was a Protestant nation and over the preceding century, Jacobitism, unrest in Ireland and the recent war against France, had fuelled anti-Catholic sentiments. The Anglican Church had been aligned with the landowning, mainly Tory, power within England, to resist change, but reform was coming. Progress was achieved through a series of legislative changes culminating in the passing of the Catholic Emancipation Act in 1829. Even though still in a minority and often criticised faith, Catholics were finally being allowed back into national life, whilst the control that the Anglican Church had imposed on the leadership of the country was being reduced.

The Catholic community in and around Salisbury was a small but cohesive one. For many years it had relied on the patronage of the wealthy Arundell family who lived at Wardour, fifteen miles west of the city, in a great classical house with its own chapel, next to a ruined medieval castle. In 1828, the city's active worshippers had signed a parliamentary petition seeking Catholic Emancipation. The original petition remains in Wiltshire and records that:

> The Petitioners most respectfully but earnestly implore the removal of these civil disabilities under which they so undeservedly labour.

It goes on to indicate how it felt to be Catholic at that time:

> The Petitioners are thus made to appear as objects of suspicion and distrust, and unworthy of the blessings of equal laws, to which as British subjects they are entitled.[14]

The Petition was sent to the Earl of Radnor, who represented Salisbury in the House of Commons and was a strong advocate of social and electoral reform. A letter accompanying the Petition was signed by a key figure in the Salisbury Catholic community, John Peniston. An architect by trade, Peniston had for several years hosted the Mass at his own house.

Once living in Salisbury, Pugin engaged through Peniston with the local Catholic community, including Frederick Fisher, a surveyor, and John Lambert, a solicitor. Initially, he took communion at the cathedral, but on 6 June 1835, in a room converted into a chapel within a former Inn on St Martin's Lane, Pugin entered formally into the Catholic Church.

Soon after, he wrote how his conversion did not go down well with the local ecclesiastical authorities: 'the bishop published a most infamous circular to his clergy denouncing us as apostates'.[15]

Worse still, a year later, Bishop Burgess banned Pugin from sketching the cathedral:

> Would you believe it I am not to be allowed to draw inside the cathedral anymore and I suppose my name is to be posted everywhere as a person who is not to be suffered to sketch anywhere.[16]

Designing the new Palace of Westminster.

The old Houses of Parliament had been destroyed in the Palace of Westminster fire in October 1834. Pugin had witnessed this, shortly before moving to Salisbury, stating afterwards that 'the spread of the fire was truly astonishing'.[17] Such was the level of destruction that a national competition was launched in 1835 to rebuild the country's seat of government. During the submission period, Pugin met with the Commissioners who were to judge the competition and he was reported as advocating 'the Gothic in opposition to the classic style "of the dry and monotonous temples of Athens".[18] He also published a pamphlet in Salisbury arguing against the classical approach, and favouring the Gothic:

> Those who study this sublime style in all its ramifications – who seek it from the stupendous cathedral to the simple station chapel – from the massive crypt to the elaborate and gorgeous chantry – from the towering castle to the gabled and turreted mansion, – these feel its beauties, and learn to practise them.[19]

During the competition, Pugin worked on two entries, one with his friend, the Scottish architect, James Gillespie Graham, and the other with the English architect and builder, Charles Barry. On 29 February 1836, the submission by Barry was announced as the winner.

It is clear from Pugin's diary that he worked repeatedly on drawings for both entrants during the latter half of 1835, with regular records of such designing in 'Sarum' and specifically at 'St Marie's Grange' where he 'first drew' on 11 September 1835 for Barry.[20] William Osmond later described this work in a letter to Pugin's son:

> The designs for Mr Graham by your father, for the Houses of Parliament, were mostly done in my premises at Salisbury, and whilst they were in progress Sir Charles (then Mr) Barry came to Salisbury and spent the evening at my house with your father. He came again the following morning and breakfasted with us: we then, all three, went and had a thorough look at our Cathedral, after which Mr. Barry went with your father to St. Mary's Grange. I believe that no drawings were made for Mr. Barry in Salisbury, but at the Grange.[21]

In 1836, after the initial competition win, Pugin continued detailed designing, in Salisbury and London, on what were termed Estimate Drawings, for Charles Barry. His diaries indicate work at St Marie's Grange that year, particularly from September onwards. Decades later, Pugin's son Edward, in arguing that 'my father was in very deed strictly the Art Architect of the Houses of Parliament', wrote that he was 'making the competition drawings at Salisbury all through that year'.[22]

Publication of *Contrasts*

The publication, in 1836, of the book *Contrasts,* printed in Salisbury, was the moment in which Pugin truly announced himself to the world.

The book's alternative title was: *A Parallel Between the Noble Edifices of the Middle Ages and Corresponding Buildings of the Present Day Shewing the Present Decay of Taste.*[23] As well as several chapters of text, the book contained drawing plates illustrating Pugin's architectural polemic, symbolising the title of *Contrasts.* Most plates were arranged in twos: one being a contemporary example of deplorable architecture, mainly classical in form, contrasted with a parallel example of a medieval, or medievally inspired, alternative which was held up to be superior.

Fig 6: Contrasted Tombs drawn by Pugin in *Contrasts*, published in Salisbury *(Pugin, 1836, Contrasts).*

For example, in a contrast involving Salisbury Cathedral, a drawing of a plain, simply decorated tomb of the Earl of Malmesbury, fenced off in the cathedral, was juxtaposed on the same page with a drawing of a far more ornate, pointed, and accessible Gothic tomb, that of Admiral Gervase Alard at Winchelsea Church (Fig 6).

Contrasts exhibited a remarkable strength of feeling and moral judgement about the value of medieval buildings and the woeful destruction that occurred to them from the Reformation onwards. Much of this emotional power was drawn from the parallel and interlinked central planks of Pugin's life, the love of the Gothic and his now unshakeable belief in the value of the Catholic Church.

For a twenty-first century viewer steeped in a world of visual imagery and social media, *Contrasts* strikes a strangely familiar tone. Images of 'good' and 'bad' are mixed with vehement commentary on contemporary and historical themes. In the early nineteenth century, such an intermingling of words and pictures was not unusual in historical books. What made *Contrasts* stand out was its moral tone and the strength of the prose to promote Gothic design and denigrate Classical (he termed this Pagan) styles. The book was Pugin's architectural manifesto. He really did take no prisoners, neither in text nor in drawings.

If anything, Pugin's greatest censure was reserved for those who had made recent changes to ancient buildings. These people were 'so vile, so mercenary, and so derogatory'. Top of the list, unsurprisingly, was James Wyatt, 'of execrable memory', for his destruction of the belltower at Salisbury Cathedral, the pulling down of chapels there and mutilation of tombs.

Once published, the book caused considerable controversy, locally and nationally. An anonymous letter, from A.F., in the *Salisbury and Winchester Herald,* attacked *Contrasts* and its author. Pugin responded in detail in the *Salisbury and Winchester Journal,* a rival newspaper to that publishing the original attack. He soon found out that the anonymous author was a local cleric, Reverend Arthur Fane. For the next month they continued further correspondence in their respectively favoured Salisbury newspapers, with Pugin concluding matters by stating that he would not waste his time continuing to convince Fane or 'other persons who feel annoyed at having their darling opinions attacked'.[24]

Contrasts was reprinted in a London second edition five years later, with a similar style but a less critical description of the role that the Reformation had played in architectural changes and more focus on damage caused during the Renaissance. This version of the book also raised social as well as religious issues, for example through a drawing contrasting the living conditions of the poor in a hospitable and protected town environment of 1440 compared to a more industrialised, multi denominational version of the town in 1840s with ruined spires symbolic of the loss of faith, caring and beauty. Other major works by Pugin were to follow, with equally vehement arguments regarding pointed Christian architecture, but none were to surpass the impact of *Contrasts.* At the end of his life, he was to state that his writings had revolutionised the taste of England. This started in 1836 with the first edition of *Contrasts.*

Pugin's design work in Wiltshire

Whilst the building of St Marie's Grange, the conversion to Roman Catholicism, the development of designs for Westminster, and the publication of *Contrasts,* were by far the most important individually, let alone collectively, they were not Pugin's only achievements in Wiltshire. A number of very different designs by him are still in existence today.

Firstly, close to his home near Alderbury, he designed and oversaw the building of a small gatehouse, Clarendon Lodge, in 1836–37, for a wealthy neighbour, Sir Frederick Hervey-Bathurst, who was redesigning the Clarendon estate. This lodge is more symmetrical and much less medieval gothic than most of Pugin's subsequent work, although Holden suggests that 'the adjacent gate peers, with reduced tops and chamfered corners, perhaps give some hint of the Gothic Pugin was to return to' (Fig 7).[25]

Fig 7: Clarendon Lodge *(Malcolm Sinclair, 2023).*

Secondly, a few years after leaving Salisbury, Pugin returned to design an ornate tomb in the Church of St John the Baptist, in Bishopstone. This commemorated a deceased Anglican clergyman and antiquary, Reverend George Montgomery, who had become his good friend. The stonework was undertaken by Pugin's preferred stonemason, George Myers, and was the first major monument that Myers produced for him (Fig 8).

Fig 8: Memorial to Reverend Montgomery in Bishopstone Church *(Malcolm Sinclair, 2022).*

Thirdly, there is also a small Memorial in Salisbury Cathedral, in the Chapel of St Lawrence within the South Transept, to Lieutenant William Fisher, a stone Gothic quatrefoil made by William Osmond with a brass insert by John Hardman of Birmingham to Pugin's design, dated 1849 (Fig 9). The Lieutenant was a great nephew of a previous Bishop of Salisbury, John Fisher, whose memorial by William Osmond is in the same chapel.

Fourthly, on a memorial in St Mary's Church, Calne, in North Wiltshire, Pugin designed a brass cross, made by John Hardman, to commemorate Markham Heale, a cloth factory owner in Quemerford near Calne, with strong links to the local church. He died in 1845.

Fig 9: Memorial to William Fisher in Salisbury Cathedral *(Malcolm Sinclair, 2023).*

In addition to these extant works, Pugin undertook further commissions, no longer in existence. These range from a fountain produced on behalf of a Colonel Baker for his garden in St Ann's Street, Salisbury, in 1835, which can now only be seen on paper through a Pugin sketch,[26] to reputed plans for alterations to the exterior of Longford Castle, which have now disappeared.

Also no longer visible is the initial chapel Pugin decorated around the time of his conversion in 1835. This was in the former World's End Inn, St Martin's Lane, Salisbury, utilised by the local Catholic community 1811–48. The space where the chapel used to be is now part of a Refectory for Wiltshire College.[27]

St Osmund's Church

Most significant of all Pugin's work in Salisbury itself is the church he designed for the city in the 1840s, St Osmund's.

After his departure, Pugin had kept in touch with his friends in the area, particularly those in the Catholic community. In 1839 the Salisbury Herald reported that he had made a liberal distribution of a religious pamphlet in the city.[28] Three years after that, it was said that he was planning to build a place of worship there.[29] By 1846, the plans had come to fruition and the press announced that a 'Romish Chapel' was to be constructed (Fig 10).[30]

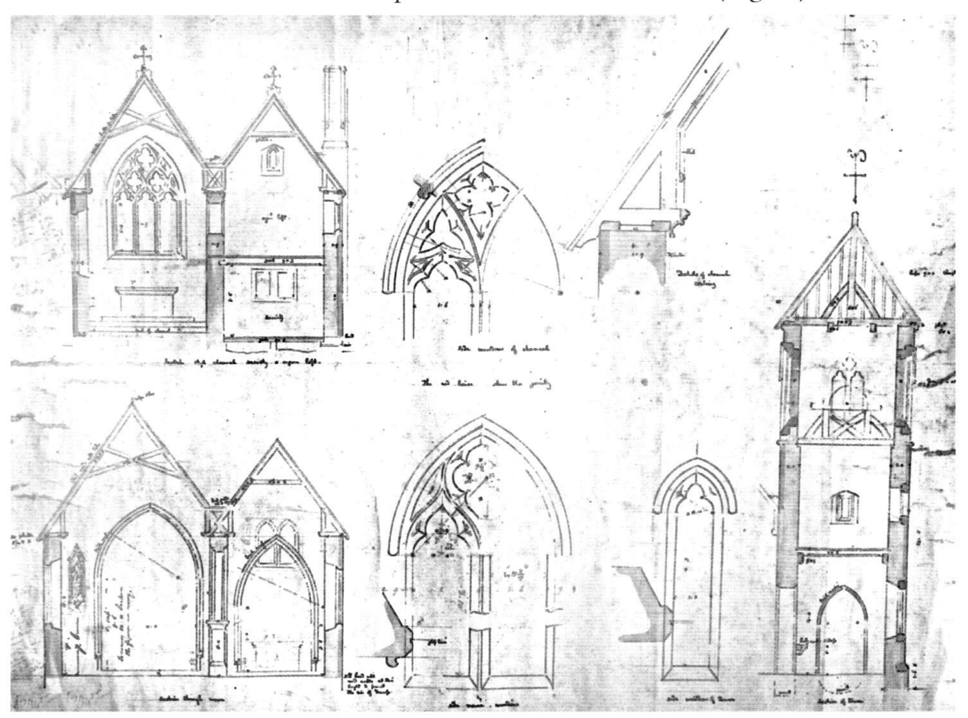

Fig 10: Pugin plans for St Osmund's Church, Salisbury *(Malcolm Sinclair, 2021).*

Built on land provided by the stalwart of the local Catholic community, John Peniston, the new church was funded locally by John Lambert. Peniston died before the completion of the church, but its bells were able to be rung, for the very first time, to mark his funeral.[31]

On 6th September 1848, the building was consecrated, and the first formal Mass was held there the next morning. The Journal described the church as

Fig 11: St Osmund's Church, Salisbury *(Roy Bexon, 2016).*

being 'in the style of the fourteenth century' and reported that the 'architect, as before stated, was Mr. Pugin', but he did not attend the opening (Fig 11).[32]

From the outside, the church has a simple flint and stone exterior. Its overall design is asymmetrical, reflecting Pugin's emerging thinking about small town church design, with a tower and porch adjoining the south aisle rather than the nave.[33] Inside, Pugin's handiwork is evident, although it is not as elaborately decorated as some of his work elsewhere in the country. This probably reflects the financial position of the church's funder.

St Osmund is the saint most associated with Salisbury and the remnants of his shrine lie within the cathedral. His images are central to the internal design of the Church, with his statue in the centre of niches at the front of the Altar and his picture being in the middle of the East Window, made by Pugin's close friend and collaborator John Hardman of Birmingham, who produced most of his metalwork and stained glass designs at that time. On either side of St Osmund are St Thomas and St Martin, the saints of the two medieval churches within Salisbury.

One of the last two complete churches which Pugin was to build, St Osmund has one stylistic variation which is of particular note. This is the position of the chancel arch, which is noticeably off-centre. At this late stage in his career, Pugin was introducing new and often axially asymmetric aspects to his architecture, and St Osmund's chancel is 'deliberately (and somewhat disconcertingly) misaligned with the nave' (Fig 12).[34]

The adjoining Church Hall was designed by Pugin's son, Edward Welby Pugin, in 1867. In the 1890s a number of major changes were made to the church by local architect Edward Doran Webb, including the addition of a new North Aisle, rebuilding of the South Wall and Arcade, and new stained glass by Mayer & Co in the West Window facing the road. Further changes were made in the 1960s including the addition of a second altar, and in the 1980s the walls were repainted to reflect Pugin's original style.[35]

In 2020, several items from the Church were discovered in a collapsing shed

Fig 12: Nave, St Osmund's Church, Salisbury – note the offset Chancel Arch *(Roy Bexon, 2016).*

in the garden to the priest's house. Some of these (a crucifix, statues of Mary and St. John, and parts of a wooden screen), indicated that Pugin included a medievally inspired rood screen in the original construction.[36]

The completion of St Osmund's gave Catholic worship a previously unknown stability in Salisbury. Two years after its opening, there was one major anti-Catholic demonstration attended by over five thousand people, but its march chose to avoid the church — perhaps the simplicity of its exterior design protected it from becoming an anti-Catholic target. The year after that, John Lambert, Pugin's friend and supporter and the main funder of St Osmund's, became the city's first Roman Catholic mayor since the Reformation.[37]

The church still stands today, its entrance looking out towards the cathedral. Alongside St Marie's Grange, it is the most tangible representation of Pugin's legacy in all of Wiltshire.

More written publications in Salisbury

Pugin produced three books other than *Contrasts* whilst living at St Marie's Grange. In 1836 he published one on *Iron and Brass Work,* and another on *Gold and Silversmiths.* Both exhibited exceptional draughtsmanship of everyday household items as well as of altar furnishings used during worship.[38] These were followed in 1837 by a book of drawings of *Antient Timber Houses* in France from his tours there in the preceding years.[39] These three publications gain less appreciation than Pugin's major works such as *Contrasts,* but in their respective fields they were all significant. They demonstrate his growing confidence in promoting what he felt to be the best style in building and artisan work.

Whilst in Salisbury, Pugin also ensured the completion of his late father's series, started in the 1820s, *Examples of Gothic Architecture.* The second volume of this commenced with an introduction written by Pugin from 'St Mary's Grange, July 1836'.[40] The book contained detailed drawings and designs of churches, castles and other buildings across England. Following this publication, Pugin passed future work on the series over to Thomas Larkins Walker, one of his father's former pupils. Walker's final volume of *Examples* focused mostly on Wiltshire, with detailed sections of text and drawings of manor houses at South Wraxall and Great Chalfield, as well as a smaller mention of St Bartholomew's Church in Corsham.[41]

Expanding horizons

Whilst Salisbury was eventually to prove too isolated a place from which to be based, it was whilst still living there that Pugin really started to spread his wings. Through his fellow Westminster competition entrants, he continued work further afield, such as, with Charles Barry, furnishing Birmingham Grammar School and designing the front of Manchester's Unitarian Chapel, and, with James Gillespie Graham, continuing already commenced work in Edinburgh on St Margaret's Convent Chapel and George Heriot's Hospital, and starting designs for restorations at Holyrood Palace, Taymouth Castle and Glasgow Cathedral.[42]

But it was *Contrasts* which was to prove the real springboard for his career after Salisbury. The connections he developed from the book's publication, and his growing reputation within both the architectural and Catholic communities across the country, brought opportunities which would shape his future. Many of these came from three new partnerships he forged, the foundation of each occurring whilst Pugin was still residing in Salisbury.

One was with John Talbot, Earl of Shrewsbury, a major future patron through whom Pugin would go on to design Shrewsbury Cathedral, Alton Towers and his pièce de resistance, St Giles Church at Cheadle.
The second was with the collector Charles Scarisbrick for whom Pugin, in the largest domestic commission of his career, was to turn Scarisbrick Hall in Southport into another Gothic masterpiece. He started work on the interior of Scarisbrick in early to mid 1837.

The third was with the Catholic Seminary at Oscott, near Birmingham, where Pugin became in 1837 Professor of Ecclesiastical Antiquities and prepared plans for a new chapel there.

Leaving Salisbury

However initially proud Pugin was of his first constructed house and the relationships he had developed within the local community, having a main base for work and family in St Marie's Grange was soon to become less satisfactory. By 1837, due to the growth in his reputation after the achievements described above, his main working connections were mostly in London and further north. His wife Louisa was finding the situation unhealthy, and the family, with another baby, Agnes, born in October 1836, was too large for a two bedroomed house. In September 1837, the entire family abandoned St Marie's Grange and Pugin returned to London for them to take up lodgings in Chelsea.

He kept the house, but, by 1839, he was writing that:

> I have several large churches to do in Ireland, and five near Birmingham, so that I am almost worked to death, and all my business, excepting Downside Priory, lies quite wide of Salisbury. I do not see the probability of my being able to reside there for years. I must do something regarding my house.[43]

He stated in that letter that he did not want to sell St Marie's Grange, but this view was not to last. In 1841, the house was put up for sale. Some alterations were made around that time. Advertised in the national press, part of the description was:

> The stone chimney-pieces are carved with heraldic ornaments, the ceilings are of wainscot panels laid in moulded oak beams and joints, and the roof over the room designed for a chapel is of the ancient high pitch, with open framing and bracing. Mr. Pugin planned and built this house as a retired residence for himself. His extended professional engagements deny him living so far from the metropolis.[44]

The same year, St Marie's Grange was sold for £500 to a Mr Staples, from whom Pugin had originally purchased the land on which he built the house.

Conclusion

The young Augustus Pugin who arrived in Salisbury in early 1835 had left Ramsgate after his aunt's death, had been a member of the Anglican Church, and had only produced a small amount of literature and a few architectural commissions. In defining his next two and a half years of achievements as a Salisbury Period, it is important to recognise that much of his time and work was spent elsewhere, particularly in late 1836 and 1837. But, for the first time in his life, Pugin owned a family home which he had designed and to some degree built with his own hands, complete with chapel, library and architect's table. In a sense, he found himself during this time, domestically, professionally and religiously, and that was what enabled him to spread his wings to such great effect.

He wrote in January 1835 of the beautiful situation of St Marie's Grange, his good local connections, and the fact that he could carry out business anywhere that the post could reach him. He was able to collaborate with Barry and Graham, in London and Salisbury, travel in Britain and abroad to research and sketch for *Contrasts,* and have a home to come back to that was religious as well as familial. Ironically, the only place he could not sketch was Salisbury Cathedral, but the friendships he made, the partnerships he forged, and the sense of spiritual wholeness he gained from Catholic worship in the small chapel in Salisbury, were far more important to him than the reaction of the authorities there.

Being banned from the cathedral may have kept him away from Wyatt's destruction, but Pugin could see the spire every day he was in his home. The symbolism of this, the immense beauty of its medieval gothic structure which had been, for him, so brutally degraded just decades earlier, must have inspired and enraged him equally. He was not able to rectify Wyatt's work in Salisbury, and indeed he left only a small architectural footprint locally. But by the time of his departure to Chelsea in 1837, his world had changed forever. Over the next fifteen years, until his death in 1852, he would go on to be the architect of one hundred and fifty buildings and the author of thirty books and tracts, placing at the heart of all his design work, with increasing intricacy, elaboration and beauty, many of the ideals and principles of the Roman Catholic medieval world. The foundation for so many of these achievements was built in Salisbury.

Where we live does not always define us, but it can, for a time, help give direction and meaning to our lives. In Pugin's case, the period 1835–37 launched his career and undoubtedly defined the rest of his life. This really was his Salisbury Period.

Acknowledgements

This paper is a summary of a Dissertation, originally entitled 'Augustus Pugin's Wiltshire Period', which was awarded a Distinction in 2023 by the University of Wales Trinity St David for the Degree of Master of Arts in Medieval Studies. My thanks go to my Supervisor, Dr Alexander Scott. Of particular help locally, I would also like to thank John Elliott of the Pugin Society, Gina Higgins of St Marie's Grange, and the staff of St Osmund's Church, Salisbury.

Bibliography

Atterbury, Paul, and Wainwright, Clive (eds), 1994, *Pugin, A Gothic Passion,* Yale University Press.

Belcher, Margaret, 1987, *A study of Contrasts and other writings of A.W.N. Pugin in relation to the medievalist tradition in Victorian literature,* Doctoral Thesis, University of Canterbury, New Zealand.

Belcher, Margaret, 2001, *The Collected Letters of A.W.N. Pugin, Volume 1, 1830–1842,* Oxford University Press.

Brittain-Catlin, Timothy, 2004, *A.W.N. Pugin's English Residential Architecture in its Context,* Doctoral Thesis, University of Cambridge.

Brown, 1895, *Illustrated Guide to Salisbury and Neighbourhood,* Brown and Co.

Duke, Edward, 1837, *Essays Illustrative of the Halle of Sir John Halle, Citizen and Merchant of Salisbury in the Reign of Henry VI and Edward IV,* W.B. Brodie.

Elliott, John, 2000, 'Pugin, St Osmund and Salisbury', *Ecclesiology Today* 22, 2–8.

Elliott, John, 2002, 'Pugin, St Osmund and Salisbury', *Sarum Chronicle* 2, 45–53.

Elliott, John, 2020, 'Check Your Garden Shed', *Pugin Society E-Newsletter* 9, 1–5.

Ferrey, Benjamin, 1861, *Recollections of A.W.N. Pugin and his father Augustus Pugin,* The Scolar Press Limited, 1978.

Hill, Rosemary, 1999, 'Reformation to Millennium: Pugin's Contrasts in the History of English Thought', *Journal of the Society of Architectural Historians* 58(1), 26–41.

Hill, Rosemary, 2003, 'Pugin's Small Houses', *Architectural History* 46, 147–74.

Hill, Rosemary, 2006, 'Pugin's Churches', *Architectural History* 49, 179–205.

Hill, Rosemary, 2008, *God's Architect, Pugin and the Building of Romantic Britain,* Penguin Books.

Holden, James, 2018, *Wiltshire Gate Lodges,* Hobnob Press.

Holliday, Kathryn, 2012 'Beginnings and Endings: Phoebe Stanton on Pugin's Contrasts', *Journal of Architectural Education* 65(2), 106–116.

Hyland, Gerard, 2018, *Beyond Puginism,* Spire Books & The Pugin Society.

Kerney, Michael, 2012, 'John Beare of Salisbury (1785–1837) and the Hall of John Halle; With Some Remarks on the Revival of Canted Lettering in 19th Century Glass', *The Journal of Stained Glass* 36, 38–55.

MacAulay, James, 1984, 'The Architectural Collaboration between J. Gillespie Graham and A. W. Pugin', *Architectural History* 27, 406–20.

Milner, John, 1798, *A Dissertation on the Modern Style of Altering Antient Cathedrals as Exemplified in the Cathedral Church of Salisbury,* James Robbins, 1811.

Newman, Ruth, 2021, 'Catholics and Protestants in Mid-Nineteenth Century Salisbury: Uneasy Bedfellows', *Sarum Chronicle* 21, 57–70.

Orbach, Julian, Pevsner, Nicholas and Cherry, Bridget 2021, *The Buildings of England, Wiltshire,* Yale University Press.

Piper, John and Buchanan, Peter 1945, 'St Marie's Grange by Augustus Pugin', *The Architectural Review,* Reprinted August 2010.

Pugin, Augustus, 1836, *Contrasts, or, a Parallel between the Noble Edifices of the Fourteenth and Fifteenth Centuries, and similar buildings of the present day; shewing the present decay of taste,* St Marie's Grange.

Pugin, Augustus, 1836, *Designs for iron and brass work in the style of the xv and xvi centuries,* Ackermann.

Pugin, Augustus, 1836, *Designs for Gold and Silversmiths,* Ackermann.

Pugin, Augustus, 1837, *Details of Antient Timber Houses of the 15th and 16th centuries, selected from those existing at Rouen, Caen, Beauvais, Gisors, Abbeville, Strasbourg etc. drawn on the spot & etched by A Welby Pugin,* Ackermann.

Pugin, Auguste, and Pugin, Augustus 1836, *Examples of Gothic Architecture Selected from various Ancient Edifices in England,* Henry George Bohn.

Pugin, Edward, 1867, *Who was the Art Architect of the Houses of Parliament? A Statement of Fact founded on the Letters of Sir Charles Barry and the Diaries of Augustus Welby Pugin,* Longmans, Green & Co.

Stanton, Phoebe, 1971, *Pugin,* Thames and Hudson.

Trappes-Lomax, Michael, 1933, *Pugin, A Mediaeval Victorian,* Sheed and Ward.

Walker, Thomas Larkins, 1836, *The history and antiquities of the Manor House and Church at Great Chalfield, Wiltshire, forming part 2 of Examples of Gothic architecture, 3rd series,* T.L. Walker.

Notes

1 Belcher, 2001, 62, Pugin, 'Letter to Edward Willson, 5 September 1836'.
2 Belcher, 2001, 35, Pugin, 'Letter to William Osmond, May 1834'.
3 Milner, 1798, 8.
4 Ferrey, 1861, 73.
5 Belcher, 2001, 24. Pugin 'Letter to William Osmond, 30 January 1834'.
6 Duke, 1837, v-viii.
7 Ferrey, 1861, 100.
8 Brown, 1895.
9 Kerney, 2012, 46.
10 Belcher, 2001, 45 Pugin, 'Letter to Edward Willson, 1 January 1835'.
11 Kerney, 2012, 46.
12 Piper & Buchanan, 1945, 92.
13 Wainwright, Clive 'Furniture', in Atterbury & Wainwright, 1994, 138.
14 *The Humble Petition of the Undersigned Roman Catholics of Salisbury to the Honorable the Commons of the United Kingdom of Great Britain and Ireland in Parliament Assembled,* 1828, Wiltshire and Swindon History Centre, Papers Relating to Roman Catholic Chapels, 451/391.
15 Belcher, 2001, 50, Pugin 'Letter to Edward Willson, 16 August 1835'.
16 Belcher, 2001, 76, Pugin, 'Letter to Edward Willson, 13 October 1836'.
17 Belcher, 2001, 76, Pugin, 'Letter to Edward Willson, 6 November 1834'.
18 *The Architectural Magazine,* 1835, reported in *The Cheltenham Chronicle,* 12 November 1835.
19 Belcher, 2001, 52, Pugin, 'Letter to Arthur Hakewill, 18 August 1835'.
20 Trappes-Lomax, 1933, 82.
21 Pugin, Edward, 1867, 13, Osmond, 'Letter to Edward Welby Pugin, 2 October 1867'.
22 Pugin, Edward, 1867, 30.
23 Pugin, 1836, *Contrasts.* The drawings are on unnumbered pages at the end of the book.
24 *Salisbury & Winchester Journal (SWJ),* 17 October 1836. Pugin letter, 'To Mr Arthur Fane'.
25 Holden, 2018, 54.
26 Wiltshire and Swindon History Centre, 164/13/3, Pugin, Augustus, 1835, *Letter (copy) with Design for Fountain.*

27 Elliott, 2002, 47–48.
28 *Salisbury Herald,* 4 February 1839, reported in the *Berkshire Chronicle,* 23 February 1839.
29 *SWJ,* 16 March, *and* 17 March 1842.
30 *Hampshire Advertiser,* 19 December 1846 'Romish Chapel in Salisbury'.
31 *SWJ,* 1 July 1848.
32 *SWJ,* 9 September 1848 'Opening of St Osmund's Church, Salisbury'.
33 O'Donnell, Roderick, 1994, 'Pugin as a Church Architect', in Atterbury & Wainwright, 1994, 68.
34 Hyland, 2018, 45.
35 Elliott, 2000, 5–7
36 Elliott, 2020, 1–5.
37 Newman, 2021, 64–66.
38 Pugin, 1836.
39 Pugin, 1836.
40 Pugin and Pugin, 1836.
41 Walker, 1837.
42 MacAulay, 1984, 408–413.
43 Belcher, 2001, 119, Pugin, 'Letter to Frederick Fisher, 29/30 June 1839'.
44 *Morning Herald* (London), 16 June 1841.

Phillip Read: a Wealthy Apothecary

Robina Rand

Introduction

Phillip Read bought a leather-bound book, inscribing 'Mr Phillip Read, His book 1681' on the back (Fig 1) (subsequently referred to as his 'Book' in the text). On the inside page he made a few notes of income received from the supply of medicines and rents. Phillip entered no more in the front of the book but in the last five pages at the back he gives an account of his trip to Scotland in 1697 and of demands made by his second wife, from whom he was separated.

After Phillip died in Salisbury in January 1698 his 'Book' somehow came into the hands of Edmund Abbott, born in 1679, and a member of a well-known Salisbury family. He used it as a commonplace book between the years of 1747 and 1753 when he was married and living in Winterbourne Dauntsey. Phillip could well have known the young Edmund and in the knowledge that his life was nearing its end, it is possible that he gave him the almost empty 'Book' as a gift.

The 'Book' was given to the author by its then owner, who lived near Malvern

Fig 1: The back cover of the 'Book' with Phillip's inscription (*Sue Haslam, 2023*).

Fig 2: The church of St. Peter and St. Paul, Longbridge Deverill, where Phillip and his siblings were baptised (*Roy Bexon, 2023*).

in Worcestershire. Wishing to make sure it would eventually be returned to Wiltshire, the author was put in touch with John Chandler, former editor of the *Sarum Chronicle.* It was he who suggested this article should be written.

Longbridge Deverill and Wells

Phillip Read, son of Samuell, was baptised in the church of St. Peter and St. Paul (Fig 2) in the Wiltshire village of Longbridge Deverill on the 1 May 1637 the youngest of five surviving children.[1] His mother's name is not recorded.

Before the Reformation the manor of Longbridge Deverill was held by the Abbey of Glastonbury.[2] Sir John Thynne acquired the manor and had built Longleat House by 1580.[3] The Read family were prosperous clothiers.[4] In 1651 Samuell brought an action in Chancery against Sir James Thynne for restoration of a copyhold estate in Longbridge Deverill.[5] In 1639 Samuell had paid Sir Thomas Thynne £220 to hold the estate for the term of his life and life of an unnamed son, but Sir Thomas died before it was entered in the court rolls. Samuell had the use of the estate for a few years before it was claimed by Sir Thomas's widow and appropriated by her son. A final case in 1657 ruled against Samuell.[6] Doubtless very angry, Samuell moved to Wells in Somerset where he flourished as a clothier and died in 1681.[7]

Apprenticeship in Bristol

Whether it was Phillip's choice is not known but he was sent to Bristol to serve an apprenticeship to become an apothecary. This could have been in 1653 when Phillip was sixteen and Samuell was embroiled in the court case. Bristol suffered severe damage in the Civil War and Phillip would have experienced its recovery as an important port and city.

The first record of Phillip is in *The Bristol Burgess Book* where William Martin is listed as the apprentice master of Phillip Read. William had died by 1659 and Phillip 'served out his time with Elinor Martin widow and relict of the sayd William'.[8] Elinor leased [9] 4 Broad Street West in 1659 and paid Hearth Tax for eight hearths.[10] It is almost certain that Phillip served his apprenticeship living at this address.

Most Bristol Apothecaries, licensed following completion of their apprenticeship, were later elected as Burgesses. This gave both full municipal rights as a Bristol citizen and social status. In 1679 Phillip is listed as having an apprentice, Samuel Jacob.[11]

The work of apothecaries

In the Middle Ages apothecaries were making and selling drugs and medicines, and could be regarded as early pharmacists. Before 1615 they were often members of the Grocers Company both selling spices, herbs and drugs.[12] Over the next hundred years the work of an apothecary became more specialised, preparing medicines from the prescription of a physician. Gradually they made diagnoses and supplied medicine or drugs as well as preparing them. A useful side-line was the provision of chests of medicines for ships' surgeons.[13] In 1617 the Worshipful Society of Apothecaries was established. The Society set examinations and issued licences, and improved working relationships with physicians and surgeons led to the apothecaries having the role that became the general practitioner of today.

Physicians charged high fees and accumulated large fortunes, but in London in the later seventeenth century a top apothecary could earn £2,000 a year if he had a good working relationship with a successful physician.[14]

The Hall of the Society of Apothecaries was destroyed in the Great Fire of London in 1666, but a new Hall was soon built in Blackfriars Lane. In 1673 the Society acquired land to create a Physic Garden in Chelsea.[15] Apothecaries generally wore black and their shops sold a huge variety of goods, including love charms.

Career and first marriage

By 1676 Phillip must have established his own business and become successful to be elected as a Burgess. It is unfortunate he never became a member of the Society of Apothecaries, whose records would have yielded more information about his work.[16] One of the very few references is when Rosemary O'Day writes 'In the early 1670's Phillip Read worked alongside Dr. Martin in Bristol'.[17]

Phillip remained a bachelor until he was forty years old, by which time he would have become a respected member of Bristol society. It is likely Phillip had also made contacts and established a business outlet in London. After the Great Fire of 1666, a massive programme of rebuilding took place, so there was new property, new shops to buy or rent and new markets. The first reference to London is in 1681 when Phillip records in his 'Book' a receipt of a 'halfe year's rent of £27.15.00 from John Cook'. 1681 is the year he purchased his leather 'Book' and this is the first entry on the inside page. Much later, in 1691 and 1692 he receives 'in my studdy in London' payments totalling £126 in settlement of bills. As no property in London is left to his son in 1698 it has to be assumed this one was rented.

On the 2 October 1677 Phillip married Susanna Rosewell in All Hallows Church, London Wall.[18] Susanna, was born in Salisbury in May 1656.[19] Her mother was the daughter of John Strickland, a well-known Salisbury Minister and her father, Thomas Rosewell, a Non-Conformist Minister. Susanna's mother died in 1661, and a year later her father was ejected from his living. In 1672 suffering from severe depression, Thomas moved to London presumably taking Susanna with him; a difficult and disruptive time for a teenager. He recovered and became the minister for Rotherhithe church in May 1674 where he remained until his death in 1692.[20]

Where Phillip met Susanna is not known, but marriage may have been spurred on by the fact that Thomas Rosewell married a widow, Anne Godsalve, in January 1677.[21] After their marriage in October 1677 Phillip and Susanna returned to Bristol, but their happiness was short lived as Susanna was buried on the 25 March 1679 'with child' in St. James church in Bristol.[22]

After Susanna's death Thomas Rosewell became famous for an unusual reason. In 1684 he was charged with the offence of High Treason for allegedly preaching sermons against King Charles I and Charles II. He was tried and found guilty by the infamous Judge Jeffreys, Lord Chief Justice. On appeal it was proved he was found guilty on entirely false evidence. He was pardoned by Charles II and released from prison on the 28 January 1685. Thomas was buried in the Bunhill Fields Non-Conformist cemetery in London, where his headstone can still be seen.[23]

Second marriage

Working in Bristol Phillip would have met Abell Kelly, a grocer. Although the Worshipful Society of Apothecaries had been founded in 1617, links with grocers in provincial cities and towns remained strong. Abell Kelly had amassed sufficient wealth, possibly because he profited by supplying essential goods during the Civil War, that in May 1668 he and another merchant bought the Manor of Clifton on the west side of Bristol.[24]

On the 28 May 1672 Abell Kelly had married Elizabeth Cole in the church of St. Augustine the Less in Bristol.[25] Elizabeth was the eldest of the three daughters of Mary Cole, who lived in St. Augustine's Back. Her sisters, Mary and Martha, both married merchants. Mary first to Edmund Baugh, a glover. She later married Richard Bayley, a soap boiler.[26] Martha married a William Davies.

Mary Cole was a wealthy widow. Mary made her will on the 20 May 1682, stating she was 'sick in body'.[27] She appointed 'the Sum of ffifty pounds to be expended on my funeral', set aside fifty pounds apiece for her three grandsons and £100 for her then unmarried daughter, Martha. The residue of £750 was to be divided equally between her three daughters, with Mary and Martha to be executors. There was a catch: Mary went on to say that Elizabeth's share should not be paid to her, but invested for her to deploy the interest as she should think fit 'separate from her husband'. Abell Kelly was still alive in May 1682 and married to Elizabeth; they had one surviving son, also Abell.[28]

Abell Kelly must have died soon after Mary Cole made her will as within a year Phillip Read married Elizabeth Kelly! They obtained a Licence Bond on the 9 June 1683 before a Notary in All Saints Church, Clifton.[29] It would be interesting to know why they married on the 21 June 1683 in London, at All Hallows on the Wall, where Phillip had married Susanna.[30] Elizabeth nearly died having twins in 1684. Within a short time both babies had died.[31]

Phillip and Elizabeth challenged her mother's will with an action in Chancery in February 1687 against her two sisters as executors and the Overseer of the Will, Thomas Edwards.[32] The complaint was that Elizabeth's share of £250 had been invested but she had received none of the interest due. She had been persuaded to make available £100 of the £250 to pay some of the debts of her late husband, Abell.

Later in 1687 Elizabeth had a daughter, Elizabeth, who was baptised on the 15 September in St. Mary Matfelon church in Whitechapel.[33]

In 1688 Phillip and Elizabeth submitted further pleadings to Chancery to seek restitution of the £150, the remainder of Elizabeth's share under her mother's will. Phillip argued Mary Cole's wish to keep the money 'separate from her husband' only applied to Abell Kelly who was regarded as a 'careless and unthrifty person'. The response by Richard Bayley, Mary's husband, denies any wrongdoing and asks the Judge for a demurrer in law offering to pay any costs. As there is no further case this suggests some liability was accepted.[34]

On the 23 January 1690 Phillip and Elizabeth's son, Kelly is baptized in St. Mary Matfelon church. His father is cited as 'Dr. Phillip Read' and at last an address is given: 'Goodmans Court'.[35] Goodman's Court still exists near Fenchurch Street station. This could be Phillip's London address since 1681, when he recorded on the first page of his 'Book' a receipt of a 'halfe year's rent of £27.15s from a John Cook. The rest of the entries on the first page are rents received 'in my study in London; between December 1690 and June 1692, totalling a massive £108. As Kelly is not left any London property in his father's will of 1698 it is not clear where or what these rents were for.

Were Phillip and Elizabeth living in London on a more permanent basis after their marriage? It may be relevant that Abell, Elizabeth's son, became apprenticed to Richard Springate, a London apothecary on the 3 June 1690.[36]

Marriage breakdown

What caused the clearly acrimonious break-up between Phillip and Elizabeth is not known, but the court cases against her sisters may have been a factor.

The final entry in Phillip's 'Book' is about a demand received from his wife in early 1695 for various items of jewellery, linen and cutlery, which he lists, to be returned to her (Fig 3). He had also received a threatening letter from his step-son Abell Kelly, then apprenticed to the apothecary in London. Phillip is writing in his 'Book' after 1697 and says he had left the 'noate', in Salisbury. This suggests he had acquired a property in Salisbury by 1697. He wrote back to her in 1695 to ask if she considered the items were hers by a deed of gift given before their marriage. Receiving no reply after two years, he consulted his lawyers in London in March or April 1697, and they were prepared to take the matter to court. Whether Elizabeth and Kelly were still living with their mother in 1695 is not known.

Journey to Scotland

In March 1697 Phillip set off on a round trip of about 1,600 miles to Scotland. Did he decide to go because his marriage had failed? Or it may have been a present to himself to celebrate his 60th birthday. When he returns he writes up the routes and expenditure in detail at the end of his 'Book' but there is no diary to accompany it and very few personal observations other than his account of the witches' trial in Paisley. He writes:

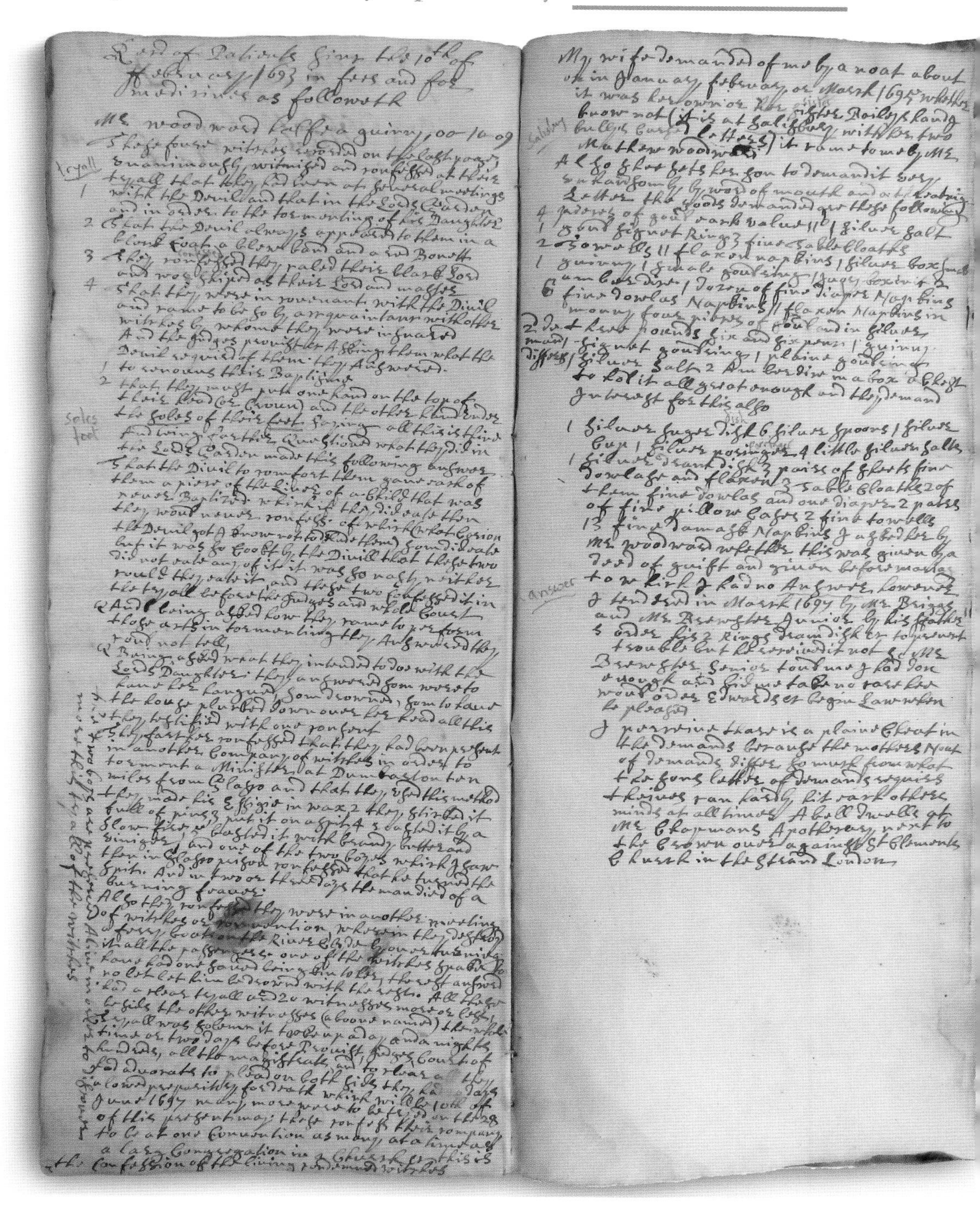

Fig 3: The final entry in the 'Book' concerns the breakdown of Phillip's marriage to Elizabeth, listing the items she has demanded (*Sue Haslam, 2023*).

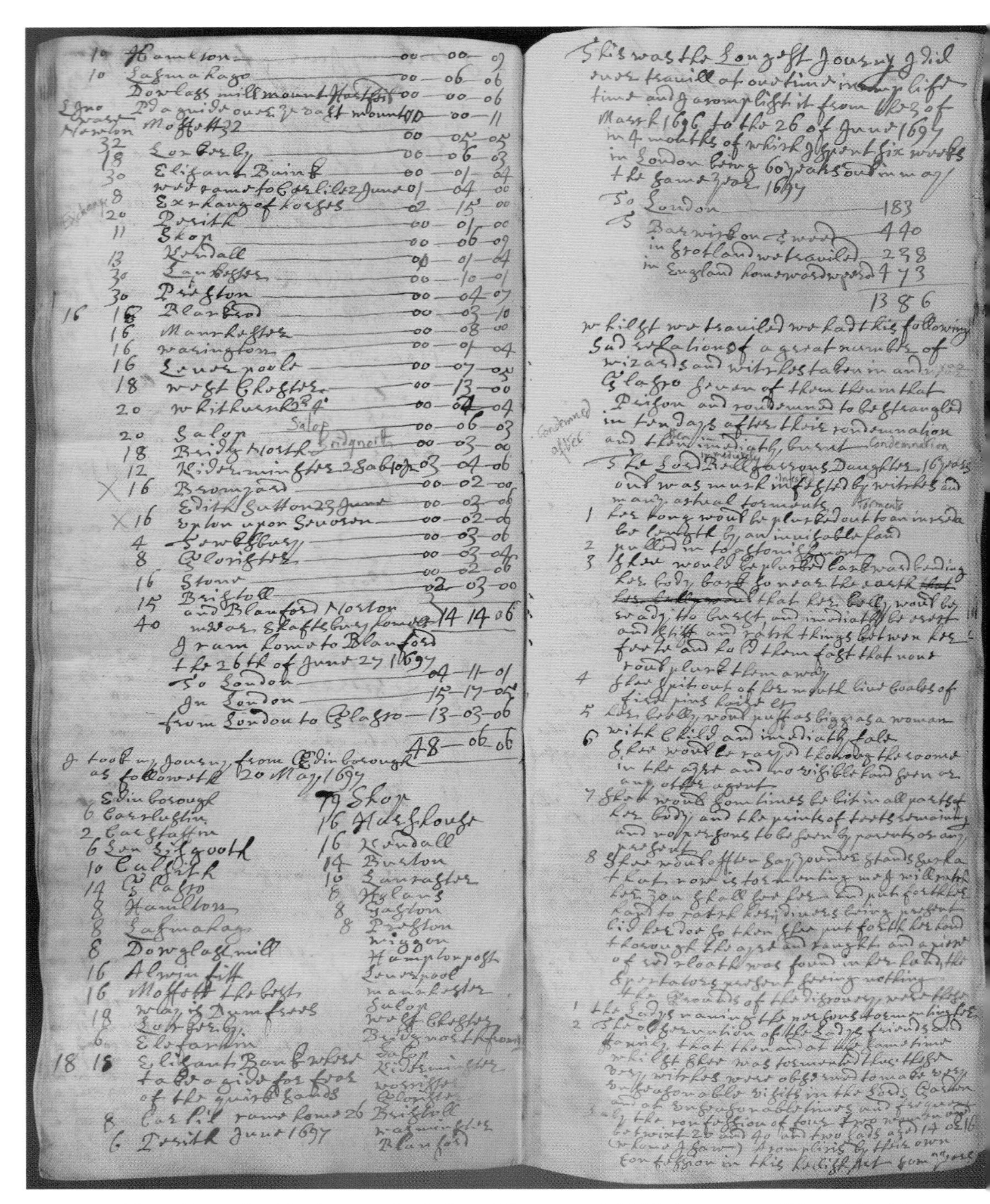

Fig 4: Record of the journey back from Glasgow and Phillip's account of the trial of the Paisley witches (*Sue Haslam, 2022*).

> This was the longest journey I did ever travill of one time in my life time and I accomplist it from the 3 March 1697 to the 26 June 1697 in 4 months of which I spent six weekes in London being 60 years old in May the same year 1697.

The journey must have taken a long time to plan. There is no indication as to why Phillip set out from Blandford Forum. His route to London took him through New Sarum and Chichester.[37] In Lewes, he hired a guide for 1s, which it might be safe to assume was to show him around the site of the Battle of Lewes, where Simon de Montfort defeated Henry III in 1264. After Lewes Phillip headed north to his base in London. He added this entry in his notes:

> I came into London 15 of March 1697 and stayed there about great business till 15 of Aprill 1697 in which time I spent in doeing my business on Lawers and on all other unavoidable charges. I left London 15 Aprill 1697 and went on to Barnet.

From London Phillip heads through Biggleswade to Stamford where a stop for two nights costs £3 5s 4d. Unaccountably he then turns due west and goes to Leicester, arriving on the 28 April. If this is a correct date it has only taken 12 days to get to Leicester from London. Even if the roads were dry, long hours in the coach must have been uncomfortable and tiring.

After the ravages of the Civil War the highways, still unmetalled roads, were improved, starting with an Ordinance issued by Oliver Cromwell in 1654 requiring every parish to appoint a surveyor to raise a rate and oversee repairs to local roads.[38] By 1697 coaches were running between major cities by regular timetables between April and October. A coach from London to York took four days and there was even a fortnightly coach to Edinburgh.[39]

Phillip went from Leicester to Derby before going to Nottingham, yet Nottingham is due north of Leicester so why the diversion? He arrived in Newark on the 1 May before going on to York where he remained for five days. Continuing along the east coast to Berwick-on-Tweed he spends an extra night there before crossing the border, then along the coast to Dunbar and finally to Edinburgh. Phillip's stay in Edinburgh cost him 18s 10d so he may have been there for at least three nights.

Paisley witches and the Bargarran Trial

On the fifty mile journey to Glasgow Phillip learned that an important witch trial had ended in Paisley. This would have been of considerable interest to him and on his return home he recorded in his 'Book' his visit to Glasgow prison and an account (not always accurate) of the trial (Fig 4). If he left Edinburgh on about the 20 May he just missed the end of the trial. He departed for home on the 9 June, the day before the witches were executed.

Witch hunts thrived in times of crisis. In 1696 Scotland was suffering failed harvests, the threat of a French invasion and political and religious unrest. The massacre in Glencoe had taken place in 1672. It was surprising that an Englishman such as Phillip Read was welcomed.

In August 1696 Christian Shaw, the eleven-year-old daughter of the laird of Bargarran, then a village in what is now Paisley, was cursed by a servant. Shortly after she spoke to an elderly lady who came to the house to beg and the following day she began to have fits and talk to people she said were devils. She saw a doctor, there was a short respite but in November she started to cough up bundles of hair, pins and feathers. Her father sought help from the Sheriff; Christian said the servant and beggar had bewitched her and named another twenty-two people as witches who had tormented her.[40]

The trial took place between the 13 April and 19 May 1697. Of the twenty-four accused eighteen were released on lack of evidence, but the remaining seven, three men and four women were convicted. Two of the men were teenage brothers. All seven were to be strangled before being burnt on the 10 June.[41] The brothers may have been reprieved, which Phillip suggests at the end of his account: 'the two boys are preserved alive in order to discover more of this tryall of the witches'.

Phillip says he was able to speak to one of the boys and writes that the witches were accused of two other offences; burning an effigy of a Dumbarton minister on a spit, and causing a ferry boat to sink. The boys confessed to turning the spit. Phillip adds a chilling comment: 'the minister died within a few days of a burning fever'!

Journey home

On the way to Moffat a guide was paid 11d to lead them over the 'vast mount', eventually reaching Carlisle safely. In Carlisle there is the only mention of horses with £2 15s 0d being paid for 'exchange of horses'. In midsummer the scenery passing through Penrith, over Shap Fell to Kendal and Lancaster must have been magnificent. In Manchester Phillip turned west to visit Liverpool whence a ferry would take him across the Mersey to Chester.

In Shrewsbury Phillip embarks on another curious diversion. Instead of following the main road through Ludlow he goes through Bridgnorth to Kidderminster, where he spends another two nights. Was this to visit Hartlebury Castle, the seat of the Bishop of Worcester? The next stop is Bromyard in Herefordshire, a difficult journey along country lanes. If he did go to Bromyard he would have to skirt round the north end of the Malvern Hills to reach his next stop at Upton-on-Severn. There he probably stayed at the White Lion, the 'Inn at Upton' immortalised by Henry Fielding in his novel *Tom Jones.*

He may not have gone to Bromyard in that Worcester is included in a second untidily written list, repeating his journey back from Glasgow (Fig 4). It is a straight road from Kidderminster through Worcester to Upton.

His final accounts add up to £54: today this would be about £9,500.

Phillip Read's will

Having survived the arduous trip to Scotland, Phillip presumably returned to Salisbury and made his last will, which is dated 14 January 1698/9.[42] It opens with a statement that his mind is clear but his body frail, but unusually has no reference to God. It goes straight into the arrangements for his property, starting with his estate and windmill in Little Sodbury in Gloucestershire, which on the 1 January he had signed over to his executors by an Indenture.

Elizabeth, then only eleven years old, is left a purse of gold containing over two hundred pounds in value, together with jewellery and household items, all to be given to her when she is of age or when she is married, if earlier. The household goods include one third of his books and 'the best Bed I now lye in at Sarum'.

Kelly, aged eight, is bequeathed his father's property. Two houses in St. Augustine's Back in Bristol, where Kelly's grandmother Mary Cole lived. House and lands in King's Weston which is to the west of Clifton, the manor purchased by Abell Kelly in 1672. The income from King's Weston was to pay for Kelly's education. The will refers to a house in College Green which Phillip presumably owned as it has been used to secure £100 on a mortgage. College Green lies on the north side of Bristol Cathedral, in the late 17th century a prestigious address.

£150 is set aside, the interest on which is also to pay for Kelly's education. This £150 refers back to the share Elizabeth should have received from her mother's estate, the subject of the court cases contesting her will. Does what Phillip writes mean the £150 was handed over or that he gave it himself? He writes:

> in lieu of the Summe of One hundred and fifty pounds which was formerly given by Mrs Mary Cole deceased to my said wife Elizabeth in the lifetime of her former husband and now by me and my said wife assigned to my said son or such of my children by her as I shall think fit.

Philip's feelings about his wife are clear when he says:

> And I then leave the care and custody guardianship education and disposal of my said Son and Daughter to my Executors hereafter named and the Survivor of them earnestly desiring them to take upon them the same and that they may never come under the direction or government of my said Wife.

If Kelly dies before he is of age, everything goes to Elizabeth. If she then dies before she is of age, everything is left to the eldest son of Phillip's brother, Thomas.[43]

The will was made just in time before he died. Phillip was buried where he wished, by his first wife Susanna in St. James' church, Bristol on the 27 January.[44]

Kelly and Elizabeth

Kelly became an Upholder or Upholsterer in London, living in the parish of St. Vedast alias Foster. By 1709 his health was failing and he made his will on 1 January 1712.[45] He leaves everything to Elizabeth and wishes to be buried in Bunhill Fields, the Non-Conformist cemetery. He died later that year.

Elizabeth was aged twenty and living in the parish of St. Ethelburga, Bishopsgate in London in 1707. Her guardian Samuel Hedges gave consent for her to marry Benedict Winch, aged about twenty six, of the neighbouring parish of St. Botolph.[46] A licence was then obtained for Elizabeth and Benedict to marry on the 7 August 1707 in All Hallows-on-the-Wall.[47] Benedict came from a Bedford farming family and he and Elizabeth may have settled there. Benedict was still alive when Elizabeth's brother Kelly died in 1712, but he died not long after as Elizabeth remarried in 1717. The two deaths so close together must have been a great blow for her.

Elizabeth married Henry Whitbread, a gentleman and widower who farmed in Cardington, a village near Bedford, on the 22 December 1717 in St. John's church in Bedford. In the register she is recorded as 'Elizabeth Read daughter of Philip Read of New Sarum MD'.[48]

Henry was aged fifty-two and had four surviving children, Elizabeth was thirty. She bore three children in three years, Henry in 1719, Samuel in August 1720 and Elizabeth in October 1721. Sadly Elizabeth was widowed for the second time on the 13 October 1727, left with three small children. Ive, the youngest of Henry's children was twenty seven and already a successful merchant Upholsterer in London. Elizabeth did have the advantage of being a very wealthy widow, having inherited all her father's property from her brother Kelly.

Elizabeth's husband Henry had made a will in 1727, leaving most of his estate to his wife Elizabeth but substantial bequests to his children and family.[49] He appointed his cousin John Howard, a London Upholder, as an executor. John's son, also John, became the famous prison reformer, after whom the Howard League for Penal Reform is named.

Elizabeth was buried on the 19 January 1746/7, aged 59, in Cardington church with her husband (Fig 5). In her short will of the 14 August 1745 the

Fig 5: The church of St Mary, Cardington, where Elizabeth and Henry Whitbread are buried. (*Robina Rand, 2022*).

family farm in Cardington is left to her daughter Elizabeth, and the residue of her estate to be shared between Elizabeth and Samuel, who are also to be her executors. There is no mention of her son, Henry, who must have died.[50]

The story has a happy ending. In 1736, aged sixteen, Samuel was apprenticed to a leading Brewer in London, John Wightman, for the large sum of £300.[51] In December 1742, using an inheritance of £2,000, money from the sale of the farm and windmill in Little Sodbury and other loans, he and two partners, Godfrey and Thomas Shewell, bought a small brewery and brewhouse.[52] This prospered and became the famous Whitbread's Brewery of today and Samuel died a multi-millionaire. Phillip Read would have been very proud of his grandson!

Bibliography

Barrett, William, 1789, *The History and Antiquities of the City of Bristol.*

Chandler, John, 1983, *Endless Street: A History of Salisbury and Its People,* Hobnob Press, Salisbury.

Jones, Donald, 1992, *A History of Clifton,* Phillimore, Guildford.

Martin, Lois, 2016, *The History of Witchcraft,* Oldcastle Books, Harpenden.

Porter, Roy (ed), 1996, *The Cambridge Illustrated History of Medicine,* Cambridge University Press.

Waller, Maureen, 2000, *1700: Scenes from London Life,* Hodder and Stoughton, London.

Notes

1 Wiltshire& Swindon History Centre (WSHC) *Parish registers and Bishops' Transcripts,* Longbridge Deverill, 1607–1837. Phillip took the date of his baptism as his birthday.

2 Wiltshire Federation of Women's Institutes, 1999, *The Wiltshire Village Book,* Newbury, 145.

3 Pevsner, Nickolaus, (revised Cherry, Bridget), 1975, *Wiltshire (Pevsner Architectural Guides: Buildings of England),* 308–313.

4 WSHC PI/R/35, *Will of Thomas Read, clothier, 1616.* His inventory lists a mill on the river Wylye.

5 The National Archives (TNA) C8/311/125. *Read v Sir James Thynne.*

6 TNA, C 7/294/20. *Read v Sir James Thynne, Lewis and Others.* Lady Catherine's dower rights upheld.

7 TNA, PROB 4/8471. No Will. *Inventory for Reade, Samuel, of Wells, 1681.* Describes a large house with out-buildings for cloth production.

8 Rawlings, F.H. (ed), n.d., *A Chronological Index of Apothecaries in the Bristol Burgess Books,* Bristol Archives, Pamphlet 317, 228.

9 Leech, Roger, 1997, *The Topography of Mediaeval and Early Modern Bristol,* Bristol Records Society, vol.47, 31.

10 Dresser, Madge, Leech, Roger, Barry, Jonathan (eds) 2018, *The Bristol Hearth Tax 1662–73,* Bristol Record Society, 70, 81.

11 Rawlings, n.d., 300.

12 Ross, Catherine, Clark, John, 2008, *London, The Illustrated History,* Museum of London, Allen and Lane, London, 348.

13 Picard, Liza, 2004, *Restoration London. Everyday Life in London 1660–1670,* Weidenfeld and Nicholson, London, 87.

14 Inwood, Stephen, 1999, *A History of London,* McMillan, London, 267.

15 Minter, Sue, 2000, *The Society of Apothecaries Garden,* Sutton Publishing, Stroud, 12.

16 Correspondence with the Society's librarian confirmed this.

17 O'Day, Rosemary, 2014, *The Professions in Early Modern England 1450–1800,* Routledge, London, 209. This William Martin was the son of Phillip's master, William.

18 London Metropolitan Archives (LMA), Parish Registers. Allhallows on the Wall.

19 Matthew, H.C.G. and Harrison, Brian (eds) 2004, *Oxford Dictionary of National Biography* (ODNB), Oxford University Press, 53, 784.

20 ODNB 53, 785.

21 ODNB 53, 785.

22 Bristol Archives (BA), *Bristol Church of England Parish Registers,* St. James Church.

23 Light, Alfred W. 1913, *Bunhill Fields,* Farncombe and Sons Ltd, London, 102.

24 BA, 6609(11), *The Conveyance of the Manor of Clifton, 4 May 1668.*

25 BA, P/St. Aug/R/1/b, *Bristol Church of England Parish Registers,* St. Augustine the Less.

26 BA, 36826/2, Articles of Agreement 1687. These deal with Edmund's estate when Mary plans to marry Richard Bayley.

27 https://www.ancestry.co.uk, accessed 12 March 2022, subscription site.
28 Abell is named and given £50 in Mary Cole's will.
29 BA, P/AS/R/1/b, *Bristol Church of England Parish Registers,* All Saints.
30 LMA, Parish Registers, All Hallows London Wall.
31 Register of one baby not found, but extensive reference is made to the birth in the Chancery Cases.
32 TNA, C 6/259/84. Read v Davies.
33 LMA, P93/MRY1-1, *Parish Records,* St. Mary Matfelon.
34 TNA, C 6/261/88, *Read v Davies, Bayley and Edwards.*
35 LMA, P93/MRY, Parish Records, St. Mary Matfelon.
36 Webb, Cliff, 2006, *London Livery Company Apprenticeship Registers 1670–1800,* vol.42. Society of Apothecaries, London.
37 He spent the large sum of £2 10s 0d. in Salisbury, possibly to arrange for his house to be looked after and settle debts.
38 Darby, Henry Clifford, 1936, *Historical Geography of England before AD1800,* Cambridge University Press, 427.
39 Darby, 1936, 429.
40 Wasser, Michael, 2002, 'The Western Witch-Hunt of 1697–1700: the last major witch-hunt in Scotland' in Goodare, Julian (ed) *The Scottish Witch-Hunt in Context,* Manchester University Press, 146–150.
41 Maxwell-Stuart, P.G., 2014, *The British Witch: The Biography,* Amberley Publishing, Stroud, 350–352.
42 TNA, PROB 11/449 *Prerogative Court of Canterbury 1694–1700, Philip Read 1699.*
43 Thomas probably was living in Salisbury when Phillip died.
44 BA, P.St_JB/R/1/b. *Bristol Church of England Parish Registers,* St. James,
45 TNA, PROB 11/529/14, *Kelly Read 1712.* Prerogative Court of Canterbury, Wills 1701–1715.
46 Benedict Winch swears his intention of marrying Elizabeth Read, aged 20, having her guardians' consent.
47 Licence granted for their marriage in All Hallows-on-the-Wall, London.
48 Bedfordshire Archives: *Parish Registers for St. John's church, Bedford.*
49 TNA, PROB 11/619/28 *Will of Henry Whitbread, gent.*
50 TNA, PROB 11/752/285 *Will of Elizabeth Whitbread.*
51 Whitbread, Samuel, Charles, 2007, *Plain Mr. Whitbread: Seven Centuries of a Bedfordshire Family,* The Book Castle, Dunstable, 11.
52 Richmond, Lesley, and Turton, Alison, 1990, *The Brewing Industry in England 1700–1830,* Manchester University Press, 18.

Fig 1: A self portrait of Margaret Thomas in her studio in London's Pimlico. She is seen working on an unknown male portrait surrounded by her brushes and artistic bric-a-brac (*reproduced by permission of North Hertfordshire Museum*).

Margaret Thomas 1843–1929: Salisbury Cathedral's First Female Sculptor

David Richards

For centuries, during the medieval period in Salisbury Cathedral, decorative features and images of people were carved in stone by un-named stonemasons. With the advent of the Renaissance in Europe, professional named sculptors and artists began to emerge. Some of these gradually came to England and stimulated the development of a school of English art.[1] They were however, almost entirely male. Women were conspicuous by their absence. It was not until 1892 that Salisbury Cathedral acquired its first work by a woman, the Australian sculptor, Margaret Thomas (Fig 1). This was a bust of Richard Jefferies, the Wiltshire writer. This paper will examine her life and work in Australia and England.

Margaret Thomas was born in Croydon in 1842. Ten years later, in 1852, her parents emigrated to Australia where they settled in Melbourne.[2] Margaret was artistically precocious and by the age of 12 was being tutored by the local sculptor Charles Summers, an emigrant from Somerset. She became the first woman to study sculpture in the state of Victoria.

At the age of fifteen, in 1857, she exhibited a portrait medallion at the inaugural exhibition of the Victorian Society of Fine Arts. She went on to exhibit two sculptures at the 1861 Intercolonial Exhibition in Melbourne (which were also sent to the 1862 London International Exhibition), and five paintings, one sculpture and a medallion at the 1866 Melbourne Intercolonial Exhibition.[3] Her portrait of Charles Summers was presented to the National Gallery of Victoria in 1881.

In her twenties in 1867 she decided to return to England to further her studies and spent a few months at the South Kensington School of Art. The following year, she travelled to Rome where Charles Summers had set up a studio and produced numerous bronze sculptures for Australian clients. She remained in Rome with her friend, Henrietta Pilkington (Fig 2), for nearly three years, studying and copying ancient works of art. In 1871 she returned to England and was admitted as a student to the Royal Academy Schools. A year later she became the first woman to be awarded a silver medal for modelling in clay.[4] In 1874 'she had her greatest success when six of her portraits (including one of Henrietta Pilkington) were hung 'on-the-line' at the Royal Academy annual exhibition.[5] Four years later her tutor, to whom she owed her success, died, and it was left to Margaret to execute the memorial bust of Charles Summers, which today adorns the Shire Hall of his native place, Taunton.[6]

Fig 2: Portrait of Henrietta Pilkington by Margaret Thomas (*reproduced by permission of North Hertfordshire Museum*).

In total she sculpted five busts in Taunton including one of Henry Fielding[7], who had Salisbury connections. It was unveiled with considerable publicity by the American Ambassador, John Lowell, in August 1883. One of the speakers said 'to Miss Thomas the utmost praise was due for the faithfulness and love of her work'.[8]

Nearly 10 years later her reputation was such that Arthur Kinglake (who had been involved with the commissioning of the Taunton busts) wrote in relation to a memorial to Richard Jefferies: 'It may be of interest to your readers to learn that this unrivalled delineator of county life is no longer to remain unhonoured.[9] A wish has been expressed of late by many that some memorial of Richard Jefferies should be erected, and inasmuch as he was a native of Wiltshire, and fond of his county, Salisbury Cathedral appeared to be the most appropriate spot for the purpose'.[10]

The Bishop of Salisbury agreed and the execution of the project was entrusted to Margaret Thomas for a fee of £150. When the bust was unveiled in 1893 some of the local press praised the Cathedral authorities for allowing it to be placed in the cathedral (Fig 3), and went on to say that:

Fig 3: Bust of Richard Jefferies by Margaret Thomas in Salisbury Cathedral (*Roy Bexon, 2023*).

> in doing honour to Richard Jefferies the Cathedral dignitaries have also done honour to themselves, and enriched the sacred shrine with yet another memorial of departed worth. They have not asked themselves whether he was an ecclesiastic, an orthodox Churchman or Christian disciple. Richard Jefferies was a Wiltshire genius; therefore, he has a claim to have his bust placed in the edifice to which men of all and no faiths come.[11]

Readers of this report would have been aware of its subtext.[12] A bitter controversy had been raging for some time about Jefferies's religious beliefs (or disbeliefs), and whether therefore he should be commemorated in a cathedral. His first biographer, Walter Besant, had invented a death-bed conversion to appease the Jefferies family, and admitted as much to Henry Salt, his second biographer, who with great vehemence scorned this 'Christianizing process which is often carried on with boundless effrontery by "religious" writers after the death of free-thinkers'.

It seems clear that the artist's original intention was to mount the bust on a copy of *The Story of my Heart*, the spiritual autobiography in which Jefferies effectively proclaimed his rejection of conventional religion. The plaster cast of the bust in the National Portrait Gallery includes the book, but this was clearly too much for the cathedral authorities, and Thomas diplomatically removed it from her Salisbury commission. The wording of its accompanying inscription, by Kinglake not by Thomas, 'observing the works of Almighty

Richard Jefferies 1848-87

Richard Jefferies was born on a small farm in the village of Coate, near Swindon in Wiltshire. As a young boy and teenager he roamed freely across the local downs and woods. He became captivated by the beauty and wonder of the natural world and fascinated by his surrounding agricultural communities. His friendship with a local gamekeeper on a large estate gave him further insights.

As a seventeen year old he started work as a reporter on the *North Wiltshire Herald* based in Swindon. At about this time he contracted tuberculosis which would tragically end his life some twenty years later. Over the next few years he published articles in *Fraser's Magazine*. 1874 was to be a significant year when he published his first novel, *The Scarlet Shawl*, and married Jessie Baden, the daughter of a local farmer. In 1877 the family moved to Tolworth near London where he continued to produce novels (including, in 1882 *Bevis*, one of his best), as well as publishing articles on Wiltshire life in the *Pall Mall Gazette*.

As his health declined Jefferies moved to various locations in southern England before settling in Goring-by-Sea where he died in 1887. He was buried in Worthing.

The 175th anniversary of his birth on 6 November 2023 was commemorated by a 150 mile walk from his grave to his birthplace at Coate.

God with a poet's eye', only added fuel to the flames. As Edward Thomas caustically commented more than twenty years later: 'If Jefferies had to be commemorated in a cathedral, it was unnecessary to drag in Almighty God'.

Another newspaper recording the unveiling of the bust by Bishop Wordsworth gave criticism and faint praise to Margaret Thomas saying that:

> the Bishop then unveiled the marble bust, which has been executed by Miss Margaret Thomas, an artist of acknowledged ability, who has produced a face, though perhaps slightly idealised, a likeness of the gifted and unfortunate subject. Whether, in the treatment of the head, refinement has not been at some little sacrifice to expressiveness is a matter of opinion: but there can be no doubt of the very considerable artistic merits of the bust which render it a valuable addition to the monuments in the Cathedral.[13]

Unfortunately, Margaret missed the unveiling ceremony because the time of the event was omitted on the invitation. In 1897 she gave a plaster copy of her Richard Jefferies bust to the National Portrait Gallery in London.

In the late 1860s in Australia, Margaret had met a fellow artist, Henrietta Pilkington. From the 1880s it seems that Henrietta Pilkington and Margaret Thomas lived and travelled together.[14] On Pilkington's death she wrote this epitaph to her: 'The sweetest soul that ever looked with human eyes. Friends for sixty years.'[15] Thomas later bequeathed a portrait of Henrietta to Letchworth Museum.

Fig 4: Young Danish girl by Margaret Thomas (*reproduced by permission of North Hertfordshire Museum*).

Margaret, apart from sculpture, had other strings to her artistic bow. After leaving the Royal Academy she set up a studio in Pimlico and became a successful portrait painter. The income from this gave her the independence to indulge her other passions for travel and writing.

She visited northern and southern Europe as well as the Middle East and recorded her experiences in books that she also illustrated (Fig 4).[16] She eventually retired to live in the village of Norton, near Letchworth where she died in 1929 aged 86 (Fig 5). She left

Fig 5: Margaret Thomas's grave in Norton Church, Hertfordshire (*David Richards, 2023*).

25 of her works to Letchworth Museum. They have since been transferred to the North Hertfordshire Museum in Hertford.

Margaret's bust of Jefferies was her last major sculptural work and after its unveiling in 1893 she gradually faded from public consciousness in Salisbury. In 2018 she was re-assessed in Australia, concluding that 'while today she is an almost forgotten figure with few of her works in public collections, Thomas is nevertheless one of the most interesting Australian artists of the second half of the nineteenth century.[17] After over 100 years since her work in Salisbury in the 1890s, it is perhaps now appropriate to acknowledge her role as a pioneering, English born, Australian artist who became the first woman to produce a piece of sculpture in Salisbury Cathedral.

Notes

1 Henry VII commissioned Pietro Torrigiano to produce a bust of him. Torrigiano was later to create Henry VII's magnificent funerary monument in Westminster Abbey. Henry VIII employed Holbein to paint iconic images of himself and his courtiers.

2 Tipping, Marjorie, J, 1976, *Australian Dictionary of Biography,* Vol. 6.

3 Taylor, Elena, 2018, *The Art Journal of the National Gallery of Victoria,* Vol. 56.

4 Modelling is the process of adding increasing amounts of material to create a work of art as opposed to sculpting where material is progressively removed.

5 Taylor, 2018, and exhibiting with the Royal Society of British Artists (1872–81), the Royal Hibernian Academy (1873–95), the Royal Glasgow Institute (1878) and the Society of Women Artists (1874–80).

6 *The British Australasian,* Thursday October 19, 1899.

7 Henry Fielding married Charlotte Craddock from Salisbury Close in 1734.

8 *The Western Times*, September 5, 1883.

9 The following books were published during Jefferies' lifetime: 1874 *The Scarlet Shawl,* 1875 *Restless Human Hearts,* 1877 *World's End,* 1878 *The Gamekeeper at Home,* 1879 *Wild Life in a Southern County,* 1879 *The Amateur Poacher,* 1880 *Greene Ferne Farm,* 1880 *Hodge and His Masters,* 1880 *Round About a Great Estate,* 1881 *Wood Magic,* 1882 *Bevis: the Story of a Boy,* 1883 *Nature Near London,* 1883 *The Story of My Heart: An Autobiography,* 1884 *Red Deer,* 1884 *The Life of the Fields,* 1884 *The Dewy Morn,* 1885 *After London; Or, Wild England,* 1885 *The Open Air,* 1887 *Amaryllis at the Fair.*

10 *The Salisbury Times and South Wilts Gazette* (*ST&SWG*), Saturday July 26, 1890.
11 *ST&SWG*, Friday March 11, 1892.
12 This and the following paragraph, contributed by John Chandler, are derived from a much fuller account of the artist's life and the Jefferies bust than is presented here, by Kedrun Laurie, published in the *Richard Jefferies Society Journal*, no. 13 (2004), pp. 10-24. See also Chandler, J, *The Reflection in the Pond* (2009), 143-4.
13 *The Salisbury and Winchester Journal*, Saturday March 12, 1892.
14 https://northhertsmuseum.org/north-hertfordshire-museum/collections/object-details/184358/, accessed 15 January 2022.
15 https://www.artuk.org and Margaret Thomas's portrait of Miss Pilkington in the North Hertfordshire Museum.
16 Margaret Thomas' books include: 1892 *A Scamper through Spain and Tangier,* 1899 *Two Years in Palestine and Syria,* 1902 *Denmark Past and Present,* 1906 *How to Judge Pictures,* 1908 *A Painter's Pastime,* 1911 *How to Understand Sculpture.*
17 Taylor, 2018.

Fig 1: Little Durnford Manor, with flint and stone chequerwork (*Roy Bexon 2022; by kind permission of Lady June Chichester*).

Fig 2: Peter Bradshaw at the Devenish Nature Reserve 2004 (*Copyright of Peter Bradshaw*).

Fig 3: Portrait of Thomas Whitty, founder of the Axminster carpet factory in 1755 (*by kind permission of the Axminster Heritage Centre*).

Peter M Devenish Bradshaw: a 21st-Century Benefactor

Ruth Newman

with tributes from Richard Death, Adrian Green, Ben Parker, Penny Theobald, and Jane Wilkinson

Introduction

Much has been written in *Sarum Chronicle* about Peter Bradshaw's family, especially at Little Durnford Manor in the early 20th century.[1]

This tribute is to look briefly at Peter as a contemporary philanthropist.[2] How is it that an eminent Canadian geologist has become a major benefactor to the Salisbury district? The answer lies in his family background with his mother, Dorothy Grace Whitty Devenish, her parents, H Noel and Agnes Devenish, and Peter's great grandfather Matthew H Whitty Devenish living at and owning Little Durnford Manor (Fig 1).

Peter has devoted an extraordinary amount of energy supporting projects in and around Salisbury. The Devenish Nature Reserve was a personal project as a favourite spot of his mother's (Fig 2). Laverstock water meadows appealed to his green credentials and The Salisbury Museum has proved a very special cause. During a time of financial difficulties he saw a way of helping the Museum realise its imaginative *Past Forward* plans while perpetuating his family story with its local connections.

His benevolence in England also extends outside the Salisbury area. One of his underlying aims has been to give something back to each specific community and we see this clearly in his response to his ancestral connection with Thomas Whitty of Axminster.

Peter M Devenish Bradshaw: A brief biography and Canadian background

Peter was born in Hamilton, Ontario in September 1938, son of Dorothy G Whitty (née Devenish) and Dr John Bradshaw.[3] He was raised in Campbell's Bay, Quebec, a poor rural outback. Here his Canadian father, John, set up a general medical practice in 1948, while Dorothy became an X-ray technician, and together they ran an informal adoption agency. Later, between 1962 and 1965 Peter did his PhD in economic geology and geochemistry at Durham University, where he met Maggie his wife.[4] Meanwhile his parents in Canada had retired, returning to Wiltshire, and by 1960 were living in the Hermitage at Little Durnford, a stark contrast to the medical practice in the outlying regions of Quebec. For Peter this was home until his marriage in October 1966.[5]

Peter and Maggie Bradshaw have lived in Canada since 1968 with a brief interlude in Fiji and later for five years with all six children in Australia. Since 1986 their home has been in British Columbia. In 1987 Peter co-founded the Mineral Deposit Research Unit at the University of British Columbia (UBC). Canadian tributes to him are extensive. 'Crossing boundaries' has been a theme of Peter's career and his work has taken him around the world. As a result of significant mineral discoveries and working with indigenous people in three continents he was inducted into the Canadian Mining Hall of Fame in 2015 and is the recipient of several other awards. In 2016 at UBC he founded the Bradshaw Research Institute on Minerals and Mining (BRIMM).

Peter is the last of this branch of the Devenish family and wishes to provide a heritage for future generations where residents, volunteers and the wider public can appreciate and continue his work while perpetuating the family name.

Axminster

After his mother died in 1991 Peter inherited an old cardboard box containing family documents relating to genealogy collected by his great grandfather, Salisbury banker, Matthew.[6] Amongst these were papers demonstrating his relationship to Thomas Whitty (1716–1792). In 2005 Peter and Maggie Bradshaw were invited to visit Axminster, Devon to take part in celebrations marking the 250th anniversary of the world famous carpet industry launched by Thomas Whitty in 1755. Peter, as a direct descendant, learnt that there was no known portrait of the founder. On his return to Canada he discovered that the portrait hanging in his Vancouver home was in fact of his ancestor, the entrepreneur and clothier who established the world famous company (Fig 3).[7] Mary Devenish, née Whitty (1774–1842) married Samuel Devenish (1782–1826) in Axminster in 1805. Samuel's 'residence' was given as 'Salisbury St Edmund'.[8]

In 2015 the portrait of Thomas Whitty was returned from Canada to Axminster to be personally presented by Peter and Maggie to the trustees of the Heritage Centre where it now hangs in the original carpet factory, the restored Thomas Whitty House. Chairman of the Trustees, John Church, summed up the feeling of excitement when he stated that:

> The timing is perfect. We have already successfully purchased Whitty's original carpet factory in Silver Street, this portrait of its founder can take pride of place in his historic building.[9]

Peter also offered generous financial support for the new Centre and the current building now includes the Bradshaw Meeting Room, a community space much appreciated and used by local residents and groups.

In 2019, after 20 years of planning, Axminster's new Heritage Centre was officially opened by Peter Bradshaw with celebrations in the streets and the Minster bells ringing in celebration as they did for his illustrious ancestor in 1775.[10]

The Devenish Nature Reserve

The Devenish Nature Reserve in Little Durnford, lies alongside the superb Beech Walk, and is located just north of Little Durnford Manor, on the east side of the Woodford Valley. The reserve 'offers a wonderful mix of young woodland, mature beech woodland, chalk downland and meadow'.[11]

The chalk downland part of the reserve was given to the Wiltshire Wildlife Trust by Dorothy Bradshaw (née Devenish) and her son Peter in 1989, the latter also donating the woodland in 1995 (Fig 4).

What is today often simply known as The Devenish is a narrow strip of downland. It was a magical place for the young Dorothy Devenish (1912–1991), growing up in the nearby manor house. The brow or 'Hilltop' was left uncultivated with little spinneys and hiding places to create hidden dens. As recorded in her book *A Wiltshire Life, w*hen her parents were away a special treat was to take a picnic to the 'Hilltop' with nanny and the elderly Great Aunt Alice who also needed to conquer the steep climb with no helping steps in the 1920s. Here they made:

> elaborate tablecloths on the ground for our meal out of gay little flowers that grew in the short grass . . . Each spinney had its own individuality: one was dark and

mysterious and slippery underfoot with pine needles, another was light and fairy-like with the tracery of beech leaves.[12]

Fig 4: Memorial stone with Peter and Maggie Bradshaw 2004. The inscription on the plaque is reproduced in the box below (*Copyright of Peter Bradshaw*).

THE DEVENISH WOODS
In memory of
Matthew Henry Whitty Devenish 1841 to 1913
Henry Noel Devenish 1874 to 1934
Dorothy Grace Whitty Bradshaw née Devenish 1912 – 1991
Who were long time residents of Little Durnford
"We always called it somewhat parochially the Hilltop. On the Hilltop were a number of little spinneys . . . each . . . had its own individuality . . ."
from A Wiltshire Home, a Study of Little Durnford by Dorothy Devenish
Donated by Peter Martin Devenish Bradshaw 1995

Even in her later years having returned to the Hermitage nearby, Dorothy used to go up to the 'Hilltop' and pull ragwort (Fig 5).[13]

Fig 5: Peter Bradshaw and his mother often walked up to the 'Hilltop' appreciating the view and tranquillity of looking across the River Avon and the Woodford Valley (*Photograph by kind permission of Richard Death*).

Fig 6: Welsh Balwen sheep at The Devenish (*by kind permission of the Stratford sub Castle village web site, https://www.stratfordsubcastle.org.uk*).

Richard Death, Volunteer Warden for The Devenish describes his 'special place' through the seasons (Fig 6).
It is difficult to imagine a greater gift that anyone could offer than some beautiful land, allowing the public to enjoy it forever. Peter's and his mother's donation to Wiltshire Wildlife Trust secured this magical place for the public to enjoy, and for nature to thrive. The Devenish nature reserve has been a significant part of my life for the last 15 years or so, and I have seen how it has provided peace and solitude and enjoyment for so many people over the years. Within a few minutes of any visit to this site, I can feel any tension ebbing away from me. As a direct result of the mixed habitats on site, it is wonderful at all times of the year (Fig 7).

Fig 7: Volunteers work enthusiastically to maintain the site; previous year's hazel coppicing with new growth, April 2018 (*by kind permission of the Stratford sub Castle village web site, https://www.stratfordsubcastle.org.uk*).

In spring, the first signs of life from the leaf and flower buds lift the spirit, and the views over the Woodford valley are fantastic. The birds become more active as they start nest-building. Summer is probably the favourite season for most people, as the wild flowers on the grassy slopes attract huge numbers of butterflies and other pollinators. Autumn is gentler but still enchanting, as the trees and bushes display their seeds. My particular favourite is the spindle tree, with its bright orange seeds initially hidden inside their shocking pink cases, and gradually emerging as the case cracks. Autumn is also a peak period for fungi, less dramatic, but a joy to discover. Winter has so many lovely attributes. It is generally rather quieter and a walk can be so peaceful. The frosts or snow give everywhere a wonderland sheen and the occasional floods in the water meadows in the valley change the view delightfully. Although some birds have migrated to warmer climes, many do remain. My favourites have to be the chattering long-tailed tits skittering from tree to tree.

The Covid pandemic encouraged many more people to get out and appreciate the benefits of the peaceful outdoors, and the reserve has played a

Fig 8: The Devenish steps with autumn leaves, October 2022 (*by kind permission of the Stratford sub Castle village web site, https://www.stratfordsubcastle.org.uk*).

significant part in helping the sense of well-being for its many visitors, although it rarely feels crowded. The Devenish has recently become a regular destination for several Forest School groups, and the young children genuinely appear to be having a brilliant time. 'Lovely' seems such an inadequate word, but it is the one that is on the tip of my tongue whenever I visit. It is truly a lovely place and I am so grateful to Peter and his family for their kind bequest that has bequeathed this gift to me, and everyone else (Fig 8).

The Laverstock Water Meadows and the Devenish Bradshaw Charitable Trust

Peter Bradshaw's generous donation making possible the purchase of 60 acres of meadow land at Laverstock has meant a 'green corridor' between the village and Salisbury and should prevent any harmful development of the site (Fig 9). Above all it has provided enormous benefits for local residents and visitors alike.[14]

The value of the water meadows[15] alongside the chalk streams of the Wiltshire countryside has long been recognised; grazed by the sheep and cows enjoying the 'early bite' of rich grass which was then harvested for hay. In Laverstock there is evidence of the importance of the water meadow system and Manor Farm buildings included a 'drowner's houfe' as early as 1799.[16] Today little remains of the infrastructure of the irrigation ditches or the hatches and sluices which were operated by a drowner, who controlled them for the 'floating of the fields'. The remains of a brick bridge and the

Fig 9: The Laverstock Water Meadows (*Roy Bexon*, 2023).

ditches which drained the water are still in place. A recent study using historic map analysis has suggested that only Narrow Field, River Meadow and the northern sections of Bridge Field are likely to have been floated or flooded (Fig 10).[17] The floated water meadows declined from the later 19th century as new methods of farming evolved but the wet grassland today is still valuable for both hay and livestock. The Devenish Bradshaw Trustees aim 'to restore the site as a wildflower, rich floodplain meadow which will have great agricultural, biodiversity and cultural value.'

The following tributes from trustees indicate the continuing importance of the water meadows and the joy they bring.

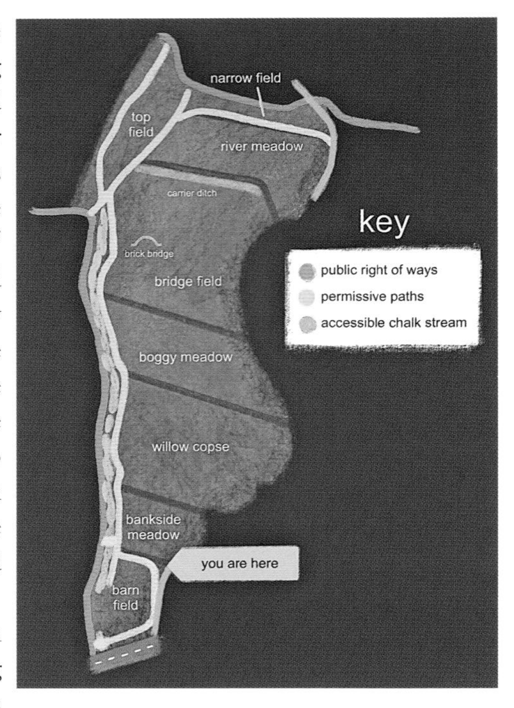

Fig 10: Stylised map of Laverstock water meadows by Emma de Silva (*Devenish Bradshaw Charitable Trust* ©).

Benjamin Parker, MBE, Chairman, River Bourne Community Farm Community Interest Company (CIC)

I first met Peter Bradshaw some six years ago when he was introduced to the farm by Laverstock and Ford Parish Council. Peter explained that he wished to invest in the Laverstock community and as he said, 'Give something back'. The Council had suggested that providing the farm with support was the best thing for the parish and after discussion, that the purchase of the 60 acres of water meadows would be by far the best thing for farm and community. Not only would the farm have the facility for educational and environmental purposes, but the community would secure a 'green lung' separating Laverstock village from the city of Salisbury (Fig 11).

The purchase was completed in 2019 and The Devenish Bradshaw Charitable Trust was formed to protect the interests of the water meadows for all, and for all time. The value to the farm and to the community is beyond measure and a stunning contribution from our benefactor, Peter Bradshaw. We are all so grateful.

Fig 11: From left: Sir Christopher Benson, Patron of River Bourne Community Farm, Ben Parker, Peter Bradshaw, Maggie Bradshaw in the water meadows with Millie, 2018 (*River Bourne Community Farm* ©).

Fig.12: The water meadows with Laverstock schools and Cockey Down in background. Trustees in the foreground (*Devenish Bradshaw Charitable Trust* ©).

Jane Wilkinson, Chair of the Devenish Bradshaw Charitable Trust

Jane works tirelessly for the organisation and 'is proud to be Chair of such a great project'.

There are not many accessible water meadows left in the country and it is a great pleasure to have been given the opportunity to restore the Laverstock meadows to flower rich grassland for the community to enjoy in perpetuity. When properly looked after the meadows attract a vast array of plant life, insects, mammals and birds. The Trust has attracted funding over the last few years to replace all dilapidated fencing with new stock fencing, spread green hay on the meadows, improve access, provide seating and signage and to refurbish the river dipping platform. Our hard working trustees and volunteer work parties are committed to an ongoing programme of restoration and maintenance as recorded by Penny Theobald, a valued special advisor to the Trust (Fig 12).

Penny Theobald, biodiversity advisor to the Trust

The water meadows and permissive paths, which are cared for by the Trust are being enhanced through energy and drive. Trustees and volunteer leaders organise Saturday morning work parties every week for volunteers of all ages, including Duke of Edinburgh award students. The Trust also hosts additional work parties for Scouts, a local school, and other community groups (Fig 13).

Fencing, scrub and litter clearance, tree and wild-flower planting, recording of wildlife, maintenance of paths and installation of new gates – the jobs keep coming!

A Nature Discovery Area is being developed for families with children, including a play area, wild flowers, bird feeders, nest boxes and bug/bee hotels.

Fig 13: Scouts from 1st Laverstock Scout Group transporting a willow log to the Nature Discovery Area, (*Devenish Bradshaw Charitable Trust* ©).

All this is enjoyed by many walkers, especially those with dogs where they can normally run free in the fields. School groups coming to learn about the farm animals, also acquire an understanding of the environment. Giant Steps Nursery tots can be seen out in all weathers, while adult groups appreciate the natural environment.

And all made possible through the generosity of Peter and Maggie Bradshaw.

Fig 14: The King's House, Salisbury Museum, 2020 (*by kind permission of The Salisbury Museum* ©).

The Salisbury Museum

Salisbury Museum (Fig 14) has proved an exciting cause for Peter's philanthropy, especially during the financial difficulties caused by the Covid pandemic. His comprehensive involvement has been of huge benefit to the museum while also perpetuating his family story with its local connections. The museum has accepted his family portraits, photographs and other artefacts so that future generations will understand both the story of the Devenish Bradshaw family and the link between a Canadian geologist and Salisbury.

His great-grandfather, Matthew, became managing director of the Wilts and Dorset Bank in Blue Boar Row, taken over by Lloyds in 1914 and still on the original site. Through wise investments he was able to buy Little Durnford Manor in 1896 just three miles from Salisbury, which became the family home for 40 years. Matthew's granddaughter and Peter's mother, Dorothy, wrote the story of that family home in *A Wiltshire Home: A Study of Little Durnford* which became a minor classic.

Past Forward: Salisbury Museum for Future Generations

The Past Forward project is continuing the recent changes and progress at the museum, following the creation of the Wessex Gallery in 2014. This redevelopment of the museum is essential for people to appreciate and understand the city's history and its sense of community. The museum moved to the King's House in 1981 and this fine Grade 1 listed building dates back to the 13th century when the Cathedral was constructed. A major restoration of this superb building is part of the Past Forward project and will provide a sympathetic showcase for the new galleries and event spaces. With the involvement of local people and hundreds of volunteers, a high quality museum of a consistent standard will be created. These improvements are vital to the museum's ability to increase visitor numbers, both local and from further afield, and to generate the revenue to succeed in the future.[18]

Adrian Green, the director of The Salisbury Museum has written a warm tribute acknowledging both Peter's generosity and his importance in contributing to the Museum at a vital time.

Peter Bradshaw approached Salisbury Museum in 2020 to donate some of his family heirlooms from Little Durnford to the collection. We explained at the time that we were planning to redevelop our Salisbury history gallery as part of our Past Forward Salisbury Museum project so his offer was very timely and we felt we would be able to include some of his items in the new displays. We had originally planned to meet in person in September 2020 but the Covid pandemic put an end to that. We therefore met on Zoom instead. During

Fig 15: New door to Salisbury Gallery into rear courtyard (*Metaphor* ©).

the meeting we discussed Peter's connections with the Salisbury area and the donation of his family portraits, photographs and other personal effects. We also discussed Past Forward. At the time the overall costs of our project were £4.4 million, we were seeking £3.2 million from the National Lottery Heritage Fund (NLHF) and needed to raise match funding of £1.2 million.

It was still early days with the fundraising, and our match funding had not got that far. We needed a 'game changing' donation to put the fundraising on a firm footing and make Past Forward a reality–and that is exactly what Peter appreciated. During the call he offered to make a significant financial donation that it is no exaggeration to say made the project a reality. His contribution unlocked the support of the NLHF and many other trusts and foundations.

In recognition of his generosity one of our new galleries will be called *The Devenish Bradshaw Salisbury History Gallery* (Fig 15). Here you will be able to

Fig 16: View of Little Durnford Manor from Camp Hill (undated). Wilfred de Glehn RA, (1870— 1951) (*by kind permission of Peter Bradshaw and The Salisbury Museum* ©).

see some of the items he kindly donated including an oil painting of Little Durnford by English Impressionist artist Wilfrid Gabriel de Glehn (Fig 16) alongside the family portraits and personal items. We are planning to open the new gallery in the spring of 2024.

Conclusion

This article is not history in the sense that is normally understood in *Sarum Chronicle* but it is 'history in the making'. Peter's donations to the Salisbury area are significant with long lasting implications. His extraordinary generosity and modesty should thus be recorded and preserved as part of local history. Significantly for the future, his involvement has benefited and will continue to enhance the well-being of the communities involved.

Acknowledgements

A very special thanks to Peter and Maggie Bradshaw for advice with the article. Thanks also to the contributors who have paid very special tributes to Peter: Richard Death, Adrian Green, Ben Parker, Penny Theobald, Jane Wilkinson; Roy Bexon for expert photography, John Church from the Axminster Heritage Centre, David Burton and John Loades for help and advice with the Laverstock Water Meadows, and to members of the Stratford sub Castle village web site.

Notes

1 Newman, Ruth, 2022, A Wiltshire Home: the Devenish family at Little Durnford Manor, *Sarum Chronicle (SC)* 22, 92–104 *passim*.
2 See separate biography.
3 John Bradshaw met Dorothy Devenish in Germany where he was studying diseases of the blood. They married in the summer of 1935 in Great Durnford moving to Hamilton, Ontario in 1936. John Bradshaw served with the Second Field Transfusion Unit in Italy in the Second World War before returning to Canada. *SC* 22 102–4, endnote 32.
4 The author and Maggie Bradshaw (née Dalpra) met at the Windsor Girls' Grammar School, where they spent seven years of their life together.
5 Newman, 2022, 103–104; 110–111.
6 Newman, 2022, 92–7. Matthew Devenish became General Manager of the Wilts & Dorset Bank and bought Little Durnford Manor in 1894.
7 Peter Bradshaw is a great, great, great, great, great, grandson of Thomas Whitty.
8 Mary Whitty was Thomas Whitty's granddaughter. The Devenish link with Salisbury is clear. Samuel Devenish had been apprenticed in 1798 to Everett & Mitchell of the Salisbury Company of Woollen Manufacturers and became a clothier; The National Archives: Series IR 1; Class: IR 1; Piece: 37, https://www.ancestry.com. UK, Register of Duties Paid for Apprentices' Indentures, 1710–1811, accessed March 2023, subscription site. As a Dissenter his children were listed in the Non Conformist registers. (Wiltshire

Non Conformist Baptism, Marriages & Burials 1810–1987, https://www.ancestry.com, accessed March 2023.) By the time of his death he had become The Rev Samuel Devenish of Sydling Dorset. Mary and Samuel's son, Matthew was born in Salisbury and their grandson Matthew H Whitty Devenish became the Salisbury banker who bought Little Durnford Manor.

9 Information from Axminster Heritage Centre website: https://axminsterheritage.org; accessed February 2023, *Midweek Herald,* 31 March, 2015.

10 https://wwwdevonhistorysociety.org.uk, accessed February 2023.

11 The Devenish, *Wiltshire Wildlife Trust* (The Devenish Reserve leaflet).

12 Devenish, Dorothy, 1948, *A Wiltshire Home; A Study of Little Durnford,* Batsford, 61.

13 Information from Peter Bradshaw.

14 Management Plan for the Laverstock Water Meadows (Devenish Bradshaw Charitable Trust) January 2023–February 2028 (David Burton, Jane Wilkinson et al).

15 The term 'water meadow' is open to interpretation. A true 'water meadow' in southern Wiltshire was one which was deliberately irrigated and involved the flooding or 'floating' of low lying meadows to increase production. A broader terminology of water meadows includes low lying meadows beside a chalk stream. Laverstock water meadows contain both floated and non-floated meadows.

16 *Salisbury Journal,* 20 May 1799.

17 Map research by John Loades. The majority of flood waters on the meadows come from springs rising to the west of the meadows by Bridge Field. (Management Plan, 2023 1.8).

18 Adapted from the Salisbury Museum website, http://www.salisburymuseum.org.uk, accessed March 2023.

The Origin and First 50 Years of Downton Band

Ed Green

The origins of many English village bands are lost in time. Downton Band is fortunate in that it can pinpoint the date of its formation to a short piece in an 1889 edition of *Downton Parish Magazine (DPM)*. Until recently, it was mistakenly thought that the current band had been founded in 1873 and was therefore due to celebrate its 150th anniversary in 2023. Original research has uncovered the facts.

The current band was not the first brass band in the village. The earliest known reference to a Downton band dates from a 100-word news item in the 2 July 1853 edition of the *Salisbury and Winchester Journal (SWJ)*.[1] Ironically, it's about bad weather causing the non-appearance of the band on the holiday celebrating the anniversary of Queen Victoria's coronation.

Press coverage during this original band's existence is scant. Nevertheless, it does include the band's prestigious role in the Wiltshire Friendly Society's grand festival in 1859[2] and, five years later, playing at the ceremony which began construction of the railway line from Salisbury to West Moors, which would include a station at Downton.[3] The final mention in a local newspaper is a short piece in the *SWJ*, about a picnic in Barford Park arranged by the Downton Branch of the Church of England Temperance Society in the summer of 1880.[4] There's no further reference of a Downton band in the *SWJ* until the start of 1890, some months after the formation of the current band.

By the mid-1880s, the Woodfalls Band had young men from Downton among its players. Its earliest known surviving photograph shows two such Downtonians who were to become founder members of the current Downton Band: Henry Eastman and John Smith (Fig 1). Born in 1870, Eastman was a wicker chair, table and basket maker who lived in The Borough; Smith, born in Gravel Close in 1864, worked as a journeyman tanner.

Fig 1: The Woodfalls Temperance Band, c.1884–87. John Smith is back, far right with sousaphone. Charles Mitchell, co-founder of the Woodfalls Temperance Band is in the centre of the picture (with moustache) leaning on a bass. Henry Eastman is side drummer (front right) (*Reproduced by kind permission of Wiltshire and Swindon History Centre 4499/1/3*).

When the Rev Arthur Du Boulay Hill became vicar of Downton in October 1882, he was quick to start a monthly *DPM* from January of the following year. A mine of information, it contains short items and information about St Laurence's Church, as well as a write-ups of village events, many of which were accompanied by brass bands. From its pages, there's mention of the: St Edmund's Church Band,[5] Redlynch Drum and Fife Band,[6] 1st Wilts Rifle Volunteers (Salisbury) Band, Fisherton Asylum Band, and most of all, the Woodfalls Band (then known as the Woodfalls Temperance Band or the South of England Temperance Band) taking part in events in Downton. But there's never a 'Downton Band'.

The August 1889 issue of the *DPM* informs us: 'A Brass Band has been formed by some of the young men of Downton, who have begun their practices under the tuition of Mr Davis . . . '. The original band had been inactive for so long that the new outfit's instruments had to be bought from scratch, as the piece stated that Band members wished 'to thank those who have kindly contributed to enable them to purchase their instruments.'[7] The vicar played an important role in the new band, acting as treasurer.

The new band's first mention in the local press came a few months later. In its short Downton news column, the *SWJ* of 4 January 1890 briefly covers a Tea and Entertainment story about a 'Parish Tea held on New Year's Day in the National School. Three hundred people were supplied with tea at 6d per head.' Almost in passing, it reports that the 'newly-formed Downton Band played outside'.[8]

There is no known photograph of the band within a year of its formation, but there is a surviving image of a village social event at which the band played on Wednesday and Thursday 25–26 June 1890 (Fig 2). Billed as 'A Grand Bazaar and Open-Air Fete' in the grounds of The Moot, the event was a fund-raiser to clear the outstanding debt on the new heating system in St Laurence's Church.[9]

A long report covering the event at The Moot in that week's *SWJ*, gives two references to the band, stating that 'in the evening the newly-formed Downton brass band played after seven o'clock'. Its performance 'gave great satisfaction, considering that it had only been in existence for such a short period'.[10]

Other early mentions of the band come at the harvest thanksgiving service in September of that year,[11] and local press coverage of the sudden death and funeral of George Batchelor, landlord of the King's Arms in July 1891.[12] Batchelor, a member of both the band, and the Ancient Order of Foresters friendly society, had left a widow and nine young children.[13]

Fig 2: Grand bazaar and open-air fete in the grounds of The Moot, June 1890 (*Reproduced by kind permission of Wiltshire and Swindon History Centre 4499/1/3*).

By coincidence, in the Downton column of the *Salisbury Times (ST),* immediately above the announcement of Batchelor's death, is a short piece headed 'The Charm of Music'. It strongly praises the band:

> The occasional performances on the green by the Band, which comprises a number of capable musicians, are greatly appreciated. Downton being a large and important village rightly leads the way in this laudable attempt to raise the people just above the daily round and the common task of life. Other villages should follow the example . . . [13]

In its quaint late 19th century turn of phrase, the *ST* summarises what the new band was all about. The band wasn't part of a friendly society or had been founded to support a social movement such as a temperance society, a political organisation or trade union. It was simply for the sheer enjoyment of making music, socialising and having a brass band in the village.

Friendly societies, Whitsun and bands

Bands in Downton, as elsewhere, had long associations with friendly societies and Whitsun holiday activities. It's difficult to overestimate the importance that friendly societies and benefit clubs played in the lives of ordinary Downton workers, as membership of a society or club was the only means of receiving access to sick pay and pensions, and to escaping the horrors of the poor law and workhouse. But their importance went even further, as they created a long-lasting strong identity and bonds among members. For instance, when processions marched in Downton to united church services celebrating jubilees and coronations in the late 19th/early 20th century, the parades were led by a band but followed by secular friendly society grouping, not by Christian denomination.[14]

Friendly societies' annual anniversaries or 'club days' were a major part of village holiday leisure right up until 1914. Most societies and clubs celebrated their anniversaries with great pomp and pageantry, starting with a parade to a service at St Laurence's Church, followed by a meal, the all-important society or club business meeting, then would come games or sports, finishing with an evening of dancing and drinking.

By the early 1890s the village-based clubs had amalgamated into larger concerns and a regular Monday-to-Wednesday Whitsun routine had emerged which was to continue right up until the First World War:

- Whit Monday – parade and church service of the Wiltshire Friendly Society, followed by the Downton branch's annual meeting, dinner and social events, usually in the grounds of The Moot.
- Whit Tuesday – parade and church service of the Ancient Order of Foresters,

Fig 3: The Band heads a parade of the Ancient Order of Foresters, outside the Public Hall in 1919 or 1920. Double-bass player John Smith is immediately behind the man carrying the leading banner. Frank Bundy (moustache and trilby) is in the centre of the picture behind the trombone player. William Charles 'Churby' Bundy is the furthest to the right of the picture of all those carrying instruments. He is wearing a bowler hat and has the DCM medal pinned to his waistcoat. Immediately in front of him is another cornet player Bert 'Pec' Fulford (*Reproduced by kind permission of Wiltshire and Swindon History Centre 4499/1/1*).

followed by the Court Radnor's annual meeting, dinner, sports and social events, usually on Barford Down.

- Whit Wednesday – the Whitsun Sunday school treat, featuring a parade, church service and tea and games on the Downton vicarage lawn.

Local bands played an important role leading each friendly society's parade (Fig 3). The Downton Band played at its first Whitsun festivity on Monday 18 May 1891, heading the Wiltshire Friendly Society's parade and performing the remainder of the day's events.[15] This was also the band's first major event in uniform.

Although the bands hired for the friendly societies' parades and social events varied over the years, during this period in the 25 Whit Wednesdays between its formation and the First World War, the Downton Band performed at every Whit Wednesday Sunday school treat parade and event. The annual treat was for members of Downton, Morgan's Vale and Nunton Sunday schools and up to 200 children would attend. An afternoon parade headed by the band, took the children to a short service at St Laurence's Church.[16] This was followed by tea and games on the vicarage lawn. The band played for dancing until nine o'clock in the evening when the children went home.

At their peak in about 1907, both local friendly society branches each had approximately 250 members, the Wiltshire Friendly Society being slightly larger than the Ancient Order of Foresters.[17] Earl Nelson of nearby Trafalgar House, was not only a member of the Downton branch of the Wiltshire Friendly Society, but also President of the entire Wiltshire Friendly Society. The Ancient Order of Foresters' local branch, Court Radnor 7021, had been founded in 1883.[18] Despite the name 'Foresters', it had nothing to do with New Forest foresters, for unlike the Wiltshire Friendly Society, it was part of a national organisation with a membership approaching a million.[19]

By the eve of the First World War however, the friendly society Whitsuntide tradition in Downton had started to wane. The societies themselves were losing membership due to the introduction of national insurance. On Whit Monday, 1 June 1914, the Wiltshire Friendly Society's festivities at The Moot went ahead as usual, but the Ancient Order of Foresters did not stage their annual parade and events the following day. To fill the Whit Tuesday vacuum, both the Downton Band and the Woodfalls Band performed in the village for much of the day – the Downton Band in the grounds of Long Close House, and the Woodfalls Band at the Moot. The *SWJ* reported that of the two, the Downton Band, which was raising money for Downton Cricket Club, had the largest attendance.[20] A belated, and poorly attended Ancient Order of Foresters' event took place over a fortnight later, on Wednesday 17 June, with the Downton Band heading their parade.[21]

All Whitsuntide friendly society events were suspended for the duration of the War. But at the first Whitsun week following the cessation of hostilities, the annual festivities were not re-established in Downton. Instead, on Whit Monday 9 June 1919, the grounds of The Moot opened to the public, with the Woodfalls Band playing there in the evening.[22] Although friendly society-related marches and events still took place at other times of year, the strong bond of members had gone. In the immediate post-war era, the Downton Band was more likely to be leading marches of ex-servicemen who felt a connection as members of the newly-formed organisation Comrades of the Great War, than as members of a friendly society.[23]

Another tradition rendered defunct by the welfare state, this time by the creation of the NHS in 1948, was the 'Hospital Sunday'. Communities up and down the country hosted these and similar events to raise funds for local hospitals and district nursing funds. In the 1890s, the Downton harvest festival was billed as a 'Harvest Festival and Hospital Sunday'. As with the Whitsun festivities, the two major friendly societies paraded behind brass bands: the

Wiltshire Friendly Society always behind the Downton Band, the Ancient Order of Foresters behind the Woodfalls Band.[24]

Charles Fanner

The popular Salisbury musician, Charles Fanner was to have a decade-long association with the Downton Band as its trainer and conductor. His first known involvement was conducting at a soirée at the British School (later the Public Hall, then the Memorial Hall) on 3 April 1891, a fund-raising event to buy uniforms for the new band.[25] The event was evidently a success, because in his speech at the annual Wiltshire Friendly Society meeting a couple of months later, the Earl of Radnor 'congratulated the Band on the smart appearance they presented in their new uniforms'.[26]

Fanner was born in Ringwood in 1847, the son of a bricklayer.[27] His early military career included being a bugle major in Prince Albert's Light Infantry, serving with the regiment for nine years in South Africa. On arriving back in England, he volunteered for service with the 44th Essex Regiment in India and became drum major, the rank with which he was discharged on completing his services. Fanner married Ellen Fanell in Trimulgherry, Secunderabad in 1876,[28] their eldest daughter Ellen was born in Burma a couple of years later.

Once returned to England, Fanner founded the Fisherton House Asylum Band which was made up of staff from the Asylum, which was later known as the Old Manor Hospital. The Asylum's superintendent, Dr William Corbin Finch appointed Fanner deputy chief attendant at the Asylum, a post he held for three years.

Fanner was offered the post of bandmaster of the Band of the Salisbury Volunteers a position he retained for 18 years, eight of which he was also bandmaster of the 1st Wilts Volunteer Battalion. During part of that time, he had also held the post of Bandmaster to the Western Counties' Brigade.

Locally, as well as his work with the Downton, Fisherton Asylum, and Volunteer Battalion bands, Fanner's quadrille band was in popular demand throughout the 1890s, performing at dances, theatre and other events.[29] He also composed music for his bands and arranged popular songs of the time for brass bands.[30]

Fanner was no stranger to Downton, as his bands had performed at village events throughout the 1880s before the current Downton Band was founded. He took the new Band under his wing, even providing members of his other bands to make up the numbers and assist the young band at performances during his first couple of years in charge. For instance, at the Hospital Sunday/Harvest Festival events in October 1891 and September 1892, the band was strengthened by musicians from Fanner's 1st Wilts Volunteer Battalion Band.[31]

Under Fanner's leadership informal soirée concerts became popular. A December 1894 edition of the *ST* is gushing in its praise for one such event, stating that 'the gentlemen who were the prime movers must be highly gratified that the fruits of their indefatigable labours were so complete and satisfactory'.[32] About 50 couples were present, and dancing continued until 4am, and this was on a weekday night.

In the autumn of 1900, continuing ill health forced Fanner to announce his resignation as Bandmaster of the 1st Wilts Volunteer Battalion.[33] It also forced him to step down from other commitments, including his leadership of the Downton Band. With a sole source of income, a pension of 1s 8d per day, Fanner was only a few short steps away from the workhouse. But such was his popularity in South Wiltshire, that in November 1900, a public subscription was launched to raise money to support him and show appreciation for all the work he had put into the 1st Wilts Volunteer Band, as well as his contribution to local musical life in general.[34]

Fanner died at his home in Salisbury on 6 July 1901, aged 54. He is buried at the Devizes Road cemetery.[35] Four members of the 1st Wilts Volunteer Band carried his coffin at the funeral. Among the many mourners were Major MacGill, Hon Major Hodding, Bandmaster Carter, Drum-Major Bungay and ten bandsmen from the 1st Wilts Volunteer Band; the vicar of Downton, Rev Plumptre; and members of the Downton Band.[36]

Performances prompted by national events

Within the first quarter century of the Downton Band's existence, the band played an active part in Downton's celebrations of four royal events: a royal wedding (1893), a diamond jubilee (1897) and two coronations (1902 and 1911). Not only that, but due to unforeseen circumstance – the King's appendicitis, and heavy rain – both coronation celebrations ended up being performed twice.

As well as the expected, planned royal commemorative events in Downton, in which the Band played a part, there were also more spontaneous ones, triggered by patriotism, jingoistic fervour or political events.

During the Boer War, news of the Relief of Mafeking reached Downton on Saturday 19 May 1900. At 7pm the Downton Band paraded through the streets. They were later joined by the Woodfalls Band who marched through the village to the Borough Cross, playing to a large crowd. According to the *ST,* the significance of one piece *One More River to Cross* was greatly appreciated and its rendition was followed by 'hearty cheers'.[37] The Band then marched back up to the High Street, concluding with *God Save the Queen.*

Politically, there's evidence of the band playing at a Liberal Party meeting in the Public Hall in 1902,[38] as well as marching in support of both Tories and trade unions. On news of Conservative Charles Bathurst's victory at the polls in the January 1910 general election, a torch-light procession started at Major Francis's House at the top of Lode Hill and, headed by the Band, marching through the village along the Salisbury Road to Charlton-All-Saints and back.[39] Bathurst had gained the constituency from the Liberals.

A previous political engagement, Downton Band members probably wished they'd not taken up, was on the evening of 14 November 1907 at the defeated Salisbury Tory MP Sir Walter Palmer's first public meeting since his adoption as candidate for the South Wilts constituency. The Band led a parade of supporters from The Moot to the Public Hall which rapidly filled to overcapacity. The *ST* described the scenes as 'lively', as constant laughter and heckling severely interrupted Palmer's speech.[40]

On Saturday 17 May 1919, the band took part in a march of between 300 and 400 trade unionists from the railway arch to the Borough Cross.[41] Here, members of the Agricultural Labourers' and Rural Workers' Union discussed the living wage and the employment of non-union labour.

John Northover

Following Fanner's resignation as bandmaster and trainer in late 1900, Walter Bailey stepped in as caretaker, but by May of the following year, the band had a new conductor, George Chalk. His first known engagement conducting the band was at the 1901 Whit Wednesday Sunday School Treat.[42] Chalk also conducted the band during the 1902 coronation events.

The start of the Edwardian era was a challenging time for the band. As well as still reeling from the loss of the talented, long-serving Fanner, it now had direct competition within the village from the Downton String Band, which had been founded in 1901 and was popular during the Edwardian era.[43] Although fife and drum and whistlepipe bands had been set up in Downton before, they were merely temporary, to celebrate royal jubilees and coronations. Reports in the *SWJ* and *ST* show the String Band was increasingly being hired for events which might otherwise have been taken by the Downton Band.[44] It can't have helped matters when, in November 1902, the Downton Coronation Committee decided to divide its remaining funds between the district nurses' fund and the String Band.[45]

Fortunately, the Downton Band's next conductor was up to the challenge, as he came with plenty of musical experience and even more local connections. He was headmaster of Downton Council School, John George Reid Northover. Unlike Fanner, who had been a professional musician, it's amazing that Northover found enough spare time to train and conduct the Band, a position he was to hold for over 20 years. Born in Southampton, Northover came to

Downton from the Wallops in the summer the Band was founded, 1889, to take over as headmaster of the British School.[46] He remained there until the new Downton Board School opened in Gravel Close in 1896.[47] Northover lived in a cottage in The Borough at the corner of Gravel Close and would hold teachers' social events in his back garden. He was an active member, and former president of the Salisbury and District Teachers' Association (National Union of Teachers).[48]

Northover's involvement in village life was intense. On the musical side, as well as being trainer and conductor of the Band, he had been organist, choirmaster and bell ringer at Charlton-All-Saints Church, and later, choirmaster at St Laurence's Church. He was also conductor of the Downton Choral Society,[49] and director of the Downton Unionist (Conservative) Club Male Voice Choir.[50]

Away from music, Northover served as lieutenant, and later as captain of the old Downton Fire Brigade. He was a freemason and given a 'knighthood' by the Royal Antediluvian Order of Buffaloes (RAOB), of which he was branch secretary. He was also secretary of the Downton Cricket Club, captain of the Church Lads' Brigade, and secretary of the Downton Pig Insurance Club.[51]

Early repertoire, band contests and other challenges

Press coverage of three consecutive annual band concerts at the Public Hall provide a flavour of the band's early repertoire. The first of three consecutive annual concerts held to raise money for band funds, took place in March 1905. According to reports in the *SWJ* and *ST,* repertoire at these concerts included:[52]

> *Friday 3 March 1905*
> 'March No. 2; selections, "Old England" and "Recollections of Flotow"; morceau, "The Turkish Patrol"; song, "The Better Land"; descriptive fantasia, "Rustic Scenes"; overture "Victoria Cross"; fantasia, "The Smithy in the Wood"; and "Patriotic Airs."'
> *Tuesday 27 February 1906*
> 'March, "Under the Double Eagle" (Wagner); overture, "Latona" (Ham); fantasia, "Reminiscences of England" (F Godfrey); cake walk, "Mumbling Moss" (Douglas); descriptive fantasia, "A Hunting Scene" (Bucalossi); descriptive fantasia, "The Smithy in the Wood" (Michaelis); and "The Hallelujah Chorus" (Handel).'
> *Wednesday 17 April 1907*
> 'Hall's "Vanguards," Handel's "Largo," Round's "Lortzing," Balfe's "Bohemian Girl,", Kimmer's "Gems of Song" [. . .], Donizetti's "Anna Bolena," Jones' "Geisha," and the selection "John O'Gaunts."'

In each report of the concerts Northover was praised for his ability and the marked improvements the band had achieved under his leadership. There is scarcely any description of how the band performed however, other than in the *SWJ's* 1905 piece which states:

> They were all rendered with great intelligence, much attention being paid to light and shade. Perhaps the best interpreted were the descriptive fantasia, "Rustic Scenes," and "The Smithy in the Wood." The tempo of the various pieces was well marked and the quality of the tone musical, although at times a little too loud for the room. The music would gain effect by the addition of two clarionets.

In light of the band's general improvement, in the same year as the first annual concert, Northover felt confident enough to enter the band for its first competition, a contest open to all village bands in South Wiltshire.[53] The contest took place at Tisbury Flower Show on 2 August 1905. Ten bands participated: Ansty, Berwick St John, Broad Chalke, West Cholderton, Downton, Fovant, Odstock, Steeple Langford, Tisbury, and Wylye. The contest adjudicator was Mr T Morgan of the Coldstream Guards. There were four prizes of £10 (won by Broad Chalke), £5 (Tisbury), £4 (West Cholderton) and £3 (Berwick St John), with a silver medal for the conductor of the winning band. Downton may have been placed last in its first contest, but of the ten bands that took part, only the Downton Band survives today.

The following year's contest took place on Bank Holiday Monday 6 August, as part of the Wilton Horticultural Show. This time, the event was more sophisticated and included a marching contest–from the Market Square to Wilton Park, and prizes for instrumental solos. The judge was Mr W Short, LRAM (*The King's Trumpeter*), and the test piece, *Latona* by Lewis Ham, which the Downton Band had performed as far back as its concert in the Public Hall in February that year.

The third South Wilts Band Contest took place in Salisbury in July 1907, as part of the Harnham Horticultural Show (Fig 4). By now, such was the popularity of the contest that it helped the show attract a record number of spectators. On this occasion the bands marched from Salisbury Station to Bishop's School Sports Field. The competitors were Berwick St John, Broad Chalke, Downton, Fovant, Odstock, Tisbury, and Woodfalls. The test piece, *Gems of Song,* had been arranged by William Rimmer. The South of England Temperance (Woodfalls) Band, the winner of the cornet solo at the previous year's contest, marched off with all the prizes bar one: Downton took the so-called 'additional prize' of £2 which was awarded to 'the best band which had not won a prize in the contest of 1905, 1906 or 1907'.[54]

Fig 4: The Band, probably taken at the South Wilts Band Contest, Harnham, 24 July 1907. *Back:* Jack Bailey, Jim Moody, George Bailey, Charlie Chalk, Ernest Bailey, Frank Noble, Fred Blake, Charles Victor 'Smith' (Charlie) Moody, John Smith. *Middle:* Sam Senior, Walter Bailey, [?], Frank (Edwin Frank) Bundy, Harry Michael Winton. *Front:* Sam Durdle (child), Bert Smith, ? Harrington, Ralph Bundy, ? Harrington (*Reproduced by kind permission of Wiltshire and Swindon History Centre 4499/1/3*).

The names on the 1907 photograph of the band were identified by John Smith's daughter, Mabel Kelly. Cross-referencing them with the 1901 and 1911 census returns, it's possible to get a picture of what the typical Downton Band member did for a living during the Edwardian era.

As might be expected, tan yard (tannery) labourer and agricultural labourer were the most common occupations. But the band also had bakers, bricklayers, carters, gardeners, a basket maker, a carpenter, a coal porter, and a shepherd.

Downton did not compete in the 1908 contest, or in the early band contests of the newly-formed South Wilts Brass Band Association. In fact, the band appears to have entered a period of instability. Although taking part in some events in 1908, the annual village band concert is no longer a fixture.

A short piece of news about a summer promenade concert in the grounds of The Moot to raise money for the church bells repair fund, provides a clue as to what's been happening. The *SWJ* reported that the band 'played some charming selections of music in good style, notwithstanding the fact that their numbers had been recently depleted by death and other causes'.[55]

A death the *SWJ* alludes to was that of 16-year-old band member, Bertram Charles Marks who had drowned at Weir Gaps less than three weeks before.[56] Marks, an assistant at Farris's butcher's shop in the village, was the son of Wilson Marks a labourer from Slab Lane. Members of the Downton Band attended the funeral in uniform. By tragic coincidence, Marks' eight-year-old brother, Percy had drowned six weeks before. Whilst throwing stones at a can floating in the river outside the Tan Yard. Percy overbalanced and was carried under the mill where his head had become caught in a hatch.[57]

As well as the fall in membership, there were other challenges for the band–not one string band, but two. The Downton String Band was still popular but from 1908 C R King's String Band started playing at several village events. It was directed by Redford King, the young organist at Landford Church who also led the Cadnam String Band as well as various other local musical groups.[58] In 1911 King formed the Downton Orchestral Band.[59] An accompanist at the new outfit's first concert to raise funds for Downton Football Club was Oswald Coppock, who was to continue the orchestra into the 1920s.[60]

If all that competition from other bands wasn't enough, the development of technology few would have predicted as a threat when the band had been founded 20 years before was also cutting opportunities to be hired and perform. The novelty of playing gramophone records during the interval or conclusion of a meeting,[61] or even as part of an indoor concert meant a live band was no longer required. Why pay for a band when a more modest programme of entertainment could be a balance of records, piano, violin and vocals?

And of course, there was the ever-present friendly rivalry from neighbouring Woodfalls. Although the band had not entered further contests, the Woodfalls Temperance Band had competed in more, coming first at the Wilton and Salisbury contests in 1911.[62] As if to rub salt into Downton's wounds, in October that year, a magnanimous Northover invited the Woodfalls Band to perform a concert in the Public Hall with their trophies on full display. Despite not having conducted a prize-winning band himself, Northover even had the temerity to give a brief talk to the audience on 'band contests and their usefulness', before congratulating Woodfalls on their success, complimenting their conductor John Green and professional advisor, Arthur Muddiman of Southampton.[63]

War and peace

An Edwardian village band comprised of so many young men was bound to be affected by the impact of the First World War. When war was declared in August 1914, a group of young men and lads from Downton marched several miles to the nearest recruiting office. They truly thought it would be the war to end all wars, believing all the propaganda they'd seen and heard.

The band fell silent for much of the War with several of its members away fighting. Less than a month after the start of the conflict, the band and the Woodfalls Band headed the Civilian Service Corps as they marched to the Public Hall where a recruiting drive was taking place.[64]

One of these eager young volunteers was 21-year-old band member Harry Winton from Lode Hill. He was the son of Ellen Elizabeth Winton, a widow. In the 1911 census Winton's occupation is listed as a baker.[65] Winton joined the 5th Battalion, Wiltshire Regiment, part of Kitchener's New Army, consisting of inexperienced soldiers who had joined up shortly after war was declared. He was to face the terrors of Chunuk Bair in the disastrous Gallipoli campaign. On 10 August 1915, the defenceless Wiltshires (their arms and equipment stacked) were attacked by the Turks. The Battalion was all but wiped out. Lance Corporal Winton died of his wounds two days later.[66] He is commemorated on the Helles Memorial in Gallipoli.

Although there is no access to a list of band members from 1914, taking the names from the 1907 group photograph of the band, it's possible to trace one other fatality of the War, Ralph Bundy. Twenty-three-year-old Private Ralph Bundy, 2nd Battalion, Wiltshire Regiment died of his wounds in the early days of the Battle of the Somme on 8 July 1916.[67] He is commemorated on the Thiepval Memorial in France.

Other names from that 1907 band photograph who served in the War include Ralph Bundy's elder brother, Frank, who also served in the 2nd Battalion, Wiltshire Regiment and had been one of the first local volunteers to join up in 1914. Another Bundy – Walter, Wiltshire Regiment, had been wounded at the First Battle of Aisne in September 1914. His younger brother Bob (19), who had been fighting by his side, was wounded on 14 September and killed in action six days later.[68] Bandsman William Harrington, again of the Wiltshire Regiment and again, an early recruit, was injured in the fighting at the Battle of Gaza, Palestine in November 1917.[69]

The band played a prominent part in both Downton's peace celebration events. The first was at the celebrations of the signing of the Armistice in November 1918. A procession of the band under Ernest Bailey marched through the village to the East Green, where children took part in an afternoon of sports events. At 8pm, an effigy of the Kaiser was burned on a large bonfire in a meadow near Mould's Bridge to cheers from the large crowd while the band played patriotic music.[70] By Christmas that year, more band members had returned home, including Private Walter Bundy, Wiltshire Regiment who, on Boxing Day, although straight out of hospital, joined the Band in playing in the village streets.[71]

The second, a planned day of activities took place on Saturday 19 July 1919. At 10.30am, the Band headed a procession of returned soldiers and sailors from the railway arch to St Laurence's Church for a united service. Following the service, the procession resumed and continued through the village to The Headlands. At noon, a meal was served to 164 Downton servicemen and ex-servicemen in the Public Hall.[72] Although several of the day's events – a parade of decorated vehicles, events in the grounds of The Moot, sports, a bonfire and firework display – were postponed until the following Saturday, the band gave a concert in the Public Hall for dancing in the evening.

On 19 December 1919, the band was present at an event in the Public Hall during which almost 200 servicemen and officers from the War were presented with cigarette cases on behalf of the inhabitants of Downton.[73]

Earlier that year, on 28 April, Band member, ex-Sergeant William Charles Bundy, Wiltshire Regiment, was presented with the DCM by Colonel Sir Arthur Holbrook KBE at a ceremony in the Public Hall. The event began with a procession headed by the band and the local post of Comrades of the Great War. Sergeant Bundy (known as 'Churby' Bundy) had returned home to Downton from hospital on crutches during the 1918 Christmas holidays.[74]

In the early 1920s the band took part in ceremonies to dedicate two of the three war memorials dedicated to the men of Downton who lost their lives in the War. The band also participated in the dedication of the Bonvalot Memorial Gardens (Fig 5).

Fig 5: The Band in the Bonvalot Memorial Gardens, c.1922. *Back:* [?], Charlie Moody, Reg Smith, [?], Bert Giles, [?], [?], [?], Frank Bundy. *Middle:* Jim Moody, Frank Noble, John Smith, Ernest Bailey, John Northover (conductor), Ern Barter, [?], [?]. *Front:* Percy Chalk, [?], Bert 'Pec' Fulford (*Reproduced by kind permission of Wiltshire and Swindon History Centre 4499/1/1*).

Sad notes

The 1920s would be looked back on with sadness by band members too, due to the tragic death of one of its youngest members and the loss of its long-serving conductor. Eighteen-year-old Reggie Marks died following a workplace accident at the Tannery.[75] On 8 September 1921, Marks fell into a tanning pit after the rope attached to some hides had slipped. The pit contained about six feet of tan liquor.[76]

Marks was immediately pulled out of the pit but astonishingly, despite having swallowed some of the tanning liquid, was not taken to hospital but treated at home. This was presumably because of the cost of hospital admission. It was not until the following day that he was admitted to Salisbury Infirmary. On the Saturday, he was operated on due to severe swelling to the upper part of his abdomen. Four pints of dark liquid were removed but he died the following morning.

The funeral took place at St Laurence's Church on the afternoon of Wednesday 14 September. It was largely attended and work at the tannery was suspended. The vicar Rev George Salmon officiated. A large number of wreaths were received, including ones from the Band and Tannery employees and directors. Marks was the younger brother of Percy and Band member Bertram Charles Marks, who had died within weeks of each other in drowning accidents 13 years before.

In 1925, the band had another solemn task to undertake, playing at the funeral of conductor and trainer John Northover. He had died on 20 July, aged 62. The lengthy funeral cortege was headed by the band under Ernest Bailey which played the *Death March* on route to St Laurence's Church. Next came the RAOB in their regalia, followed by the coffin, mourners, members of the Ancient Order of Foresters, friends, representatives of institutions and public bodies, former school pupils, school children, teachers and general mourners. After the service, the band again played the *Death March* at the graveside in Downton churchyard.

As the *SWJ* so aptly put it, 'death has removed from the public and social life of Downton one of its worthies'.[77] As well as all the voluntary work he had been involved with in the life of the village, Northover had served as head teacher at Downton Council School in Gravel Close, from the day it opened until his retirement, seven weeks before his death. The school was closed on the day of the funeral as a mark of respect.

Bandmasters 1889–1939

Mr Davis	1889–1890(?)
Charles Fanner	1891–1900
Walter Bailey	1900–1901
George Chalk	1901–c.1903
John Northover	c.1904–1925
Ernest Bailey	1925–1926
Jack Beese	1926–1930
Harry Hayter	1930–(1939)

Longstanding band member Ernest Bailey took over the role of bandmaster until October of the following year. He had conducted the band on many occasions in previous decades, standing in for Northover as early as at the Ancient Order of Foresters' Whit Tuesday parade in 1906,[78] and at other more recent events ranging from the dedication of the war memorial at the Memorial Hall,[79] to the annual Downton charity comic football match.[80] It was during Bailey's leadership that Downton had the honour of hosting its first band contest in September 1925.

Unfortunately, torrential rain and a cold, driving wind stopped many spectators from attending the event, and those who did sought sanctuary on the refreshment marquee. Some of the local bands which had taken part in previous Wessex Brass Band Association contests dropped out of the event, but their places were filled by Somerset bands. The contest started with a march from the Borough Cross to Wick, to *London Pride.* The test piece for second section bands was *Hiawatha,* whereas senior section bands were permitted to play a selection and march chosen by their respective conductors. As the *Western Gazette (WG)* points out, 'the variation would doubtless have added much to the enjoyment of an audience'.[81]

Fifty summers on

Bailey stepped down as bandmaster in October 1926.[82] The new bandmaster was Jack (John) Beese, the landlord of the *Three Horseshoes* Inn in The Borough.[83] He had moved to Downton from Bristol and had a good musical knowledge, particularly of brass bands.

In a group photograph of the band in the grounds of The Moot, taken in about 1927, a contented looking Beese sits in the centre of the musicians (Fig 6). This is the third of four formal group shots of the band in this short history, all of which date from before 1935. From the faces that have been identified, it's interesting to pick out the Downton family names: Bailey, Bundy, Chalk, Eastman, Moody, Smith–and the longevity of some of the Band members. At

Fig 6: The Band in the grounds of The Moot, c.1927. *Back:* Gilbert Eastman, 'Dappy' Bundy, [?], Walt Bailey, Bert Giles, Reg Smith, Reg Forder, Ern Barter (deputy bandmaster), [?], [?], Bill Moody, Charlie Chalk, Charl Compton. *Middle:* Frank Noble, John Smith, Jack Beese (bandmaster), George Sherwood, Jack Sherwood, Frank Bundy. *Front:* William Charles 'Churby' Bundy, Percy Chalk (*Reproduced by kind permission of Wiltshire and Swindon History Centre 4499/1/1*).

least three Band members appear in all four group photos (c1907, c1922, c1927 and c1933): Frank Bundy, Frank Noble and John Smith.

Beese entered the band into its first competition in over 20 years, at the Tisbury Band Contest on Wednesday 14 August 1929.[84] Only two other bands took part. Although Downton came third for both the march and the selection, Charlie Chalk received an individual award for horn solo: the Band's first success in a contest.

The final photo, taken in 1933–4 shows the band with bandmaster Harry (Henry) Hayter, to the right of founder member John Smith. Harry's son, Charlie (Charles Henry) is on the far right of the back row (Fig 7). Hayter, a Chelsea Pensioner, was almost 70 when he took over as bandmaster in 1930. He lived to be 96.

In the early to mid-1930s, the band briefly billed itself as the 'Downton Prize Band', following a band contest success under Hayter in 1931. The Amesbury Contest on Saturday 30 June was part of the town's Midsummer Carnival. This time there was a large number of entries, and the contest was divided into four sections.[85] The band participated in Section C, coming second to Lockerley Band (who had taken part in their first band contest at Downton in 1925), in

Fig 7: Harry Hayter and the Band, c.1933–4. *Back:* Jack Moody, Reg Smith, Les Forder, Ern Bailey, Jim Thomas, Ted Amor, Charlie Hayter. *Middle:* Gilbert Eastman, Walt Bailey, Reg Forder, Bert Giles, Frank Bundy, Charlie Chalk, Joey Eastman. *Front:* George Sherwood, 'Dappy' Bundy, John Smith, Henry Hayter (bandmaster), Frank Noble, Bill Moody, Ernest Barter. (*Reproduced by kind permission of Wiltshire and Swindon History Centre 4499/1/3*).

both the march and the test piece *Sea Songs.*

King George V and Queen Mary's Silver Jubilee celebrations took place nationwide on Monday 6 May 1935. The royal couple's wedding, 42 years before, had been the first royal event celebrated by the band. Downton's 1935 celebrations began with a united service at St Laurence's Church. Before the service the band headed a procession from the Borough Cross to the Church. At the service band members accompanied some of the hymns and performed what the *SWJ* described as 'a fine trumpet voluntary'.[86]

The festivities reconvened at 1.30pm with a fancy-dress parade from the Railway Arch to the Memorial Gardens (Fig 8). Members of the band led the way, followed by the comically-dressed Downton 'Ding Dong' Boys, some of whom played band instruments. Conductor Harry Hayter marched alongside the band and, according to the *SWJ,* a large part of the day's success was down to him.

Fig 8: The Band under Harry Hayter (right) march down the High Street, passing the corner of Moot Lane, as they lead Downton's King George V silver jubilee parade, 6 May 1935 (*Reproduced by kind permission of Wiltshire and Swindon History Centre 4499/1/1*).

From 1925 to 1938,[87] the band hosted an annual village summer fete which, from 1932, included a gymkhana at New Court Farm.[88] The event later incorporated a football[89] and darts tournaments.[90] In August 1939, 50 summers on from when the band was founded, members looked forward to their usual annual fete advertised to take place on Saturday 9 September. This was of course not to be, as six days earlier Prime Minister Neville Chamberlain had announced that Britain was at war with Germany. In the England and Wales Register, taken on 29 September that year, Hayter has proudly recorded his occupation as band tutor.

1873 and all that: the mix-up behind the Band's founding myth

By the 1970s the origin of the Downton Band had been long forgotten. The Band's President, 83-year-old Bert Giles set about trying to find the answer.[91] Giles, from Charlton-All-Saints, had joined the band in 1912. He reasonably assumed that the band had been founded at about the same time as the Woodfalls Band (1874), so visiting the offices of the *Salisbury Journal,* he began reading through old editions of the newspaper, working forwards from 1870.

Any 'Downton Band' news items Giles came across related to the original band not the current one. The first reference he stumbled on was a Whitsun 1874 piece about the band heading the procession of the King's Arms Friendly Society.[92] He also found another Whitsun piece, this time from 1870, about a band of music from the White Horse Friendly Society heading a parade.[93] Giles then conflated the bits of information, assuming that the band of the White Horse Friendly Society had somehow become the Downton Band. And, as the first mention he found of a Downton Band was in 1874, he just guessed it had been founded sometime during the previous year.

Researching this history of Downton Band has turned up information that the Woodfalls Band was actually founded five years earlier than it claims. A short piece in an 1872 edition of the *WG* mentions the Woodfalls Temperance Band,[94] and a small ad from an 1880s *SWJ* says the Band was founded in 1869.[95] But that's for someone else to investigate.

Notes

1 *Salisbury and Winchester Journal (SWJ)*, 2 July 1853, 3.
2 *SWJ*, 24 September 1859, 6.
3 *SWJ*, 6 February 1864, 6.
4 *SWJ*, 7 August 1880, 6.
5 *Downton Parish Magazine (DPM)*, July 1886, July 1889.
6 *DPM*, September 1883.
7 *DPM*, July 1889.
8 *SWJ*, 4 January 1890, 6.
9 *Western Chronicle (WC)*, 20 June 1890, 5.
10 *SWJ*, 28 June 1890, 5.
11 *Salisbury Times (ST)*, 27 September 1890, 5.
12 *ST*, 18 July 1891, 8.
13 *SWJ*, 11 July 1891, 7.
14 *SWJ*, 26 June 1897, 9; 27 May 1911, 2.
15 *SWJ*, 23 May 1891, 6.
16 *SWJ*, 25 May 1907, 8.
17 *SWJ*, 25 July 1907, 7.
18 *SWJ*, 4 July 1885, 7.
19 *SWJ*, 1 June 1901, 7.
20 *SWJ*, 6 June 1914, 7.
21 *SWJ*, 20 June 1914, 7.
22 *SWJ*, 14 June 1919, 6.
23 *SWJ*, 23 November 1918, 7.
24 *ST*, 27 September 1890, 5.
25 *SWJ*, 11 April 1891, 8.
26 *SWJ*, 23 May 1891, 6.
27 1851 Census The National Archives (TNA) HO 107/1667 f359.
28 Marriage certificate, Trimulgherry, Madras, 27 April 1876.
29 *SWJ*, 22 February 1890, 7; 15 January 1898, 8; *ST*, 8 January 1892, 8; 20 May 1892, 6; 27 April 1894, 5.
30 *SWJ*, 27 August 1887, 8.
31 *SWJ*, 17 October 1891, 6; 24 September 1892, 6.
32 *ST*, 11 December 1894, 8.
33 *SWJ*, 3 November 1900, 5.
34 *SWJ*, 1 December 1900, 5.
35 *ST*, 12 July 1901, 8.
36 *SWJ*, 13 July 1901, 5.
37 *ST*, 25 May 1900, 10.
38 *SWJ*, 13 December 1902, 6.
39 *SWJ*, 29 January 1910, 7.
40 *ST*, 22 November 1907, 8.
41 *SWJ*, 24 May 1919, 5.
42 *SWJ*, 1 June 1901 7.

43 *SWJ,* 4 January 1902, 8.
44 *SWJ,* 15 August 1903 7; 9 January 1904, 6; 13 February 1904, 8; 27 August 1904, 6.
45 *ST,* 7 November 1902, 8.
46 *DPM,* September 1889.
47 *SWJ,* 15 February 1896, 6.
48 *ST,* 21 December 1900, 8.
49 *ST,* 9 October 1908, 5.
50 *SWJ,* 24 July 1925, 5.
51 *ST,* 28 February 1908, 5.
52 *SWJ,* 11 March 1905, 6; 3 March 1906, 8; *ST,* 19 April 1907, 8.
53 *SWJ,* 5 August 1905, 6.
54 *SWJ*, 27 July 1907, 6.
55 *SWJ,* 18 July 1908 8.
56 *ST,* 10 July 1908, 8.
57 *Western Gazette (WG),* 22 May 1908, 2.
58 *Hampshire Advertiser (HA),* 25 August 1906, 6.
59 *SWJ,* 11 February 1911 8.
60 *HA,* 5 January 1924, 11.
61 *SWJ,* 18 January 1908, 8; 17 October 1908, 6.
62 *SWJ,* 22 April 1911, 5; 9 September 1911, 2.
63 *SWJ,* 14 October 1911, 2.
64 *SWJ,* 5 September 1914, 2.
65 1911 Census TNA RG14/12096 Sch 81.
66 *SWJ,* 11 September 1915, 2.
67 *SWJ,* 26 August 1916, 3.
68 *SWJ,* 17 October 1914, 2.
69 *SWJ,* 8 December 1917, 6.
70 *SWJ,* 23 November 1918 7.
71 *SWJ,* 4 January 1919, 8.
72 *SWJ,* 26 July 1919, 7.
73 *SWJ,* 27 December 1919, 7.
74 *SWJ,* 4 January 1919, 8.
75 *HA,* 17 September 1921, 8.
76 *Wiltshire Times (WT),* 24 September 1921, 4.
77 *SWJ,* 24 July 1925, 5.
78 *SWJ,* 9 June 1906, 7.
79 *SWJ,* 1 April 1921, 7.
80 *HA,* 20 May 1922, 3.
81 *WG,* 25 September 1925, 12.
82 *WG,* 15 October 1926, 7.
83 *Kelly's Directory,* Wiltshire 1927, 111.
84 *SWJ,* 16 August 1929, 8.
85 *SWJ,* 26 June 1931, 3.
86 *SWJ,* 10 May 1935, 5.
87 *SWJ,* 7 June 1929, 8.
88 *HA,* 6 August 1932, 11.
89 *HA,* 1 September 1934, 14.
90 *HA,* 11 September 1937, 3.
91 *Salisbury Journal (SJ),*16 June 1977, 16.
92 *SWJ,* 30 May 1874, 7.
93 *SWJ,* 11 June 1870, 8.
94 *WG,* 2 August 1872, 7.
95 *SWJ,* 7 May 1887, 5.

William Naish's 1716 and 1751 Maps of Salisbury

Christopher Daniell

Introduction

The first detailed and accurate map of Salisbury was surveyed and drawn by William Naish in 1716.[1] A further edition was published in 1751 which included major changes. Whilst both maps are well known amongst archaeologists and historians of the city, this article gives details about William Naish and the significance of the maps.

William Naish

William was born to Thomas and Mary Naish and baptised on 19 January 1673 at St Martin's church, Salisbury.[2] William's father, Thomas Naish, senior, became the Clerk of Works to the Cathedral. William's brother, Thomas, became the sub-dean of the Cathedral and kept a diary which has been edited by Slatter.[3] William's other siblings were John and Richard. William's father, Thomas, died on the 27 December 1727, aged 80 (therefore born 1647) and his will survives with probate being given the 19 October 1728.[4] Thomas, senior, describes himself as one of the Vicars' Choral of the Cathedral, and he was admitted as a lay singer in 1689. It was reported that he 'sang a good bass' and helped with the music in the Cathedral.[5] He left his children substantial amounts of money and property: to Richard £350 of South Sea Bubble stock annuities; to William, his tenement in the High Street and £100. John is described in the will as 'late deceased'.[6]

William's first documented job was in 1696 when he was a surgeon's mate on HMS Royal Oak and he may have followed the path of his brothers, John and Richard, into the Navy.[7] However, William soon left the Navy and on 22 June 1697 he married Anne Kent from Romsey. William was 25 years old and Anne was 30. The marriage took place in the Cathedral by licence and his bondsman was his father Thomas, 'clerk, Salisbury Cathedral'. On the licence William's occupation is given as 'apothecary' and he was living in the Close. William and Anne had two children (Mary b 1701 and William b 1703) who were baptised in St Thomas's church.

A few details are known of William's life. On the 7 November 1700 he rented the 'corner tenement sometimes two tenements with the appurtenances' (sic) in Fish Row, with an annual rent of £4 4s. He continued to rent the property for many years, the last surviving lease being dated 1743, and it was probably the same property which his brother, Thomas, then took over several decades later.[8] In 1746 William made a lease for the Black Bear in Castle Street, but the surviving document is described as a 'draft unexecuted' so whether this transaction took place is now unknown.[9] The Black Bear Inn is referenced in the will of his father Thomas: 'Item I leave to my cousin John Naish, Innholder, now living at the Black Bear in Sarum, £20' and tangentially in the will of William when he gives £10 to his spinster cousin Sarah, Innholder, who was the daughter of John Naish. It may have been the intention of William to buy the Black Bear in order to give Sarah the capital.

William was very successful in his trade, taking on five apprentices between 1711 and 1729, for which he was paid in total by the apprentice families £280.[10] He became an alderman in 1714 and Mayor in 1715.[11] It was whilst as mayor that William part funded a church bell for St Thomas's church.[12] William appears to have been very well regarded as a medical practitioner and was possibly the best in Salisbury as in November 1688 he was called upon to tend to royalty.[13] It was at a momentous time in national politics. William, Prince of Orange, had landed his forces at Torbay on the 5 November and was steadily advancing through the south west. King James II raised his army which had rendezvoused at Salisbury and on the 19 November James arrived at the Bishop's Palace. As part of an intricate plot, John Churchill had persuaded James to travel to Warminster. Although Churchill denied any treachery, it was rumoured that en-route Churchill was either going to kidnap or kill James. However, as James was about to leave for Warminster, and the coach was at the Palace door, James's nose began to bleed uncontrollably. The nose bleed lasted for two days which prevented him from travelling. At this critical point in English history James was forced to stay in Salisbury. The diarist John Aubrey described what happened: 'When James II was at Salisbury, his nose bled for near two days, and after many essays in vain, was stopped by sympathetic ash which Mr Wm Nash, a chirurgeon at Salisbury, applied'. The ash was the wood from the tree and Aubrey describes how it was made: 'Cut an ash of one, two or three years' growth at the very hour and minute of the Sun's entry into Taurus. A chip of this will do it'.[14] Despite the slight variation in the spelling of the surname, this is undoubtedly William Naish the apothecary. His description as a 'chirurgeon' (*ie* surgeon) may also be an echo of when William was an apprentice surgeon in the Navy. If William had been called sooner the history of England may have been very different.

William's father, Thomas, was the Clerk of Works and as early as 1681, when William was just eight years old, he was assisting him. Both worked together to determine whether the spire was leaning. The outcome was that Thomas Naish concluded that whilst the spire leaned, it was not getting worse. In 1710 a serious incident occurred that could have affected William's career as Bishop Burnet of Salisbury prosecuted William for spreading scandal about an (unnamed) great personage of the realm as William had stated the Bishop had preached lies. The Bishop won the case and William was fined £100.[15] This incident does not seem to have affected William's career and William became Deputy Clerk of Works under his father, Thomas, in 1717.[16] On Thomas's death in 1727, William became Clerk of Works, a position he held for 17 years until 1744.[17] In 1736 William performed the same experiment with the spire and discovered that there was no change.[18] There are several surviving yearly account books made by Thomas and then William when they were Clerk of Works.[19] A 'Day Book' held by the Cathedral Archives contains a memorandum about William resigning as Clerk of the Fabric in 1744 and the appointment of Francis Price in his place in 1745.[20] As well as the dispute with the Bishop, William was involved with several other legal disputes or processes. In 1743 he was the plaintiff against the Dean of Salisbury in a 'Bill and Answer' case (which must have been awkward for his brother Thomas, the sub-dean).[21] In 1728 William took William Goddard to court[22] and in 1741 William was a Trustee for John Naish, deceased, conveyancing (by lease and release) a large amount of land in Somerset for the sum of £1000 to four people, one of whom was his nephew John Sweet Naish.[23]

William Naish died in 1751 and was buried on the 10 July. His will survives at The National Archives.[24] It was written 26 November 1746 and probate was granted on the 16 August 1751. He described himself as an 'Apothecary' and asked to be buried in St Edmund's churchyard, Salisbury, 'in the same grave as my dearly beloved wife lately deceased'. William's first personal bequest was for £10, to his cousin 'Sarah Naish, spinster, daughter of my Cousin John Naish late of this City, Innholder'. The second was to his brother Thomas, subdean of Sarum, and his wife Joanna. The amount is not specified, but then follows bequests to a long list of cousins all of whom (including Thomas) received 'one gold ring' to the value of one guinea.[25.] William also leaves £20 to his servant Sarah Emblen. William left his lands, tenements and hereditaments, along with his goods and chattels to his son in law Thomas Bucknall and daughter Mary Bucknall, whom William later describes as his 'beloved children'. Although not specifically named as such, Mary seems to have been the lead Executor as she was named in the notification of probate in August.

From a St Edmund's church history William mentions in his will an interesting aspiration:

> Imprimis whereas there has been a design talked of for many years past and there is at present a Schem upon the 'Tapis' for enlarging the parish Church of St Edmund's by removing the Wall and Great Window behind the Communion Table 40 (sic) or fifty feet (be the same more or less) more Eastwardly and errecting side walls and Roofing the same.

If the scheme was finished in seven years then William left £40, but if not completed then this bequest was to be void. There was a small amount of work undertaken in 1766 but none between 1751–1758 so the bequest became void.[26] One reason that William may have been keen to be involved with St Edmunds was that his brother, Thomas Naish, had been appointed rector in 1694 so there was a close family association with the church.[27] If the aspiration had been Thomas's when rector, William may have been part funding Thomas's own dream.

The 1716 Edition Map of Salisbury

Before William's first map of Salisbury he had surveyed and mapped the manor of Stratford Tony for Thomas Jervoise in 1706. A small black and white portion of the map has been published and shows the village and the ridge and furrow surrounding it. The surviving survey is hand drawn in a relatively loose freehand, but shows the individual plots within the fields and the distribution of houses.[28] It may have been the same style that William drew his original Salisbury map, which was then engraved. Whether William undertook any other surveys outside Salisbury is unknown, but the map of Stratford Tony had given him the experience he needed for the Salisbury undertaking.

The 1716 map is the first scaled and accurately surveyed map of the city of Salisbury (Fig 1). This makes it a really important source of Salisbury's history and development in its own right. One hundred and five years earlier Speed had surveyed and mapped the first depiction of the city but the map has many errors and its quality is of disputable value. How accurate William's map is not at present known. Chandler is silent on the issue, whilst the RCHME volume for Salisbury states that the map is 'a fairly accurate portrayal of the density and distribution of buildings.'[29] Given that the scale of recording is in 'Feet' on the maps, it is likely to be accurate. Ultimately the accumulation of

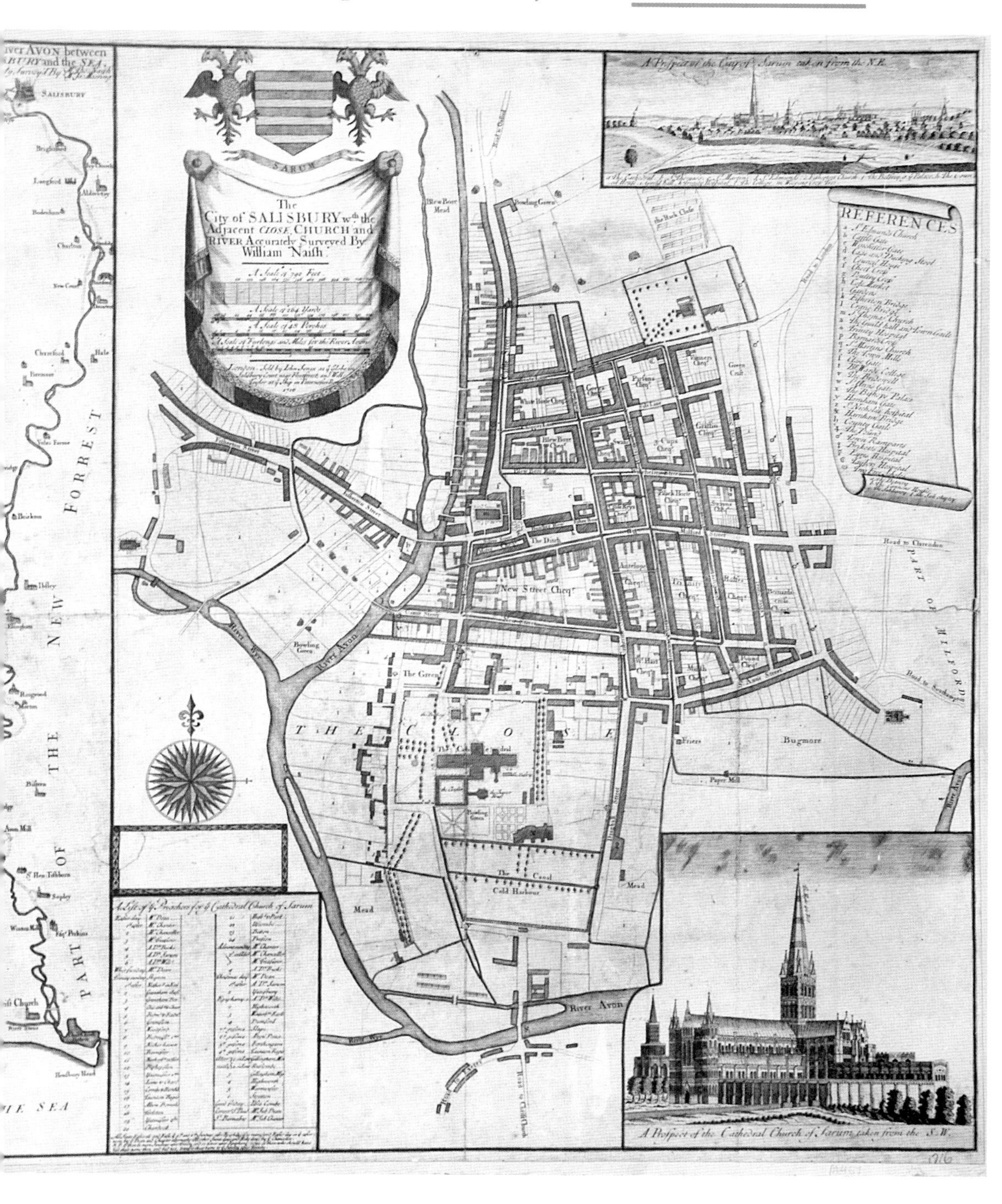

Fig 1: Naish's 1716 map (*Roy Bexon, 2023—map courtesy of Wiltshire Museum*)

archaeological evidence will determine the precise accuracy of elements of the map.

There is no record of how long William took to survey or draw Salisbury, but William's first map of the city was published in 1716. Whilst other towns and cities had been accurately surveyed, in particular London, William's map was innovative for Salisbury.[30] The streets are defined by the buildings within each chequer and the buildings are shown as black rectangular blocks sometimes with wall divisions between them. Interestingly the mapping of the rear ranges and extensions within the chequers indicates he had extensive access, either through official authority, or his own local connections.

As well as the streets of the city, other elements are included. In the top right hand corner is a prospect of the city from the North-East (with identifiable landmarks detailed), and a large picture of the Cathedral (bottom right). In between is a box of 'References', which are listed in a long scroll design and locate prominent elements within the city, such as the 'Cole Market', 'The Bridewell' and the 'County Gaile'. These are all indicated on the map by lower case letters a to z, then by a series of eight symbols, before starting again with a repetition of the smaller lower case letters a to d. The last letters and references are tightly packed into the last curl of the scroll, almost as an afterthought, which they may be as they all refer to buildings in the Close (the Deanery, the Canon's Houses, the Subdeanery and the Sub Chapters) probably as a recognition of his brother Thomas's position and contacts. It is puzzling why letters and symbols were used, rather than numbers, as the repetition of letters allows for potential confusion.

There are several elements on the left. On the far left hand side is a panel showing 'The River Avon between Salisbury and the Sea' Surveyed by Mr Tho Naish & Mr Jas Mooring.'[31] James Mooring of Christ Church appears as the first personal entry in Thomas's will, and he describes him along with the Reverend Mr Thomas Holland minister of Amesbury as 'my old friends.'[32] Thomas and James were paid £20 for making a map of the river on 30 Aug 1675.[33] Thomas was an accomplished surveyor in his own right and he mapped the manor of Britford in 1703.[34] Thomas's interest in surveying and geography is reflected in his will, when he left his grandson, John Sweet Naish, a globe. It is possible that William Naish either copied his father's map of the Avon which was in the Council archives, or there was a copy in the family home. As the original is now lost, William's depiction is the only surviving example of the original map.

Next to the survey, bottom left, is the preaching rota in the Cathedral. This is laid out from Easter to Easter with the ecclesiastical date (festival or saint's day) and then the preacher. Preachers are either specified by position

(Mr Dean, Mr Chanter), or by church: a preacher from Durnford church preached on the 4th Sunday after Epiphany. Churches were chosen from across the counties of Wiltshire and Dorset which made up the diocese. Mr Dean preached on the most important festivals of Easter and Christmas. Above the preaching rotas is an empty box – in later editions this was used for a dedication – with a compass rose above.

The most eye-catching feature is the cartouche (upper-left) which has the city coat of arms under which is stated 'The City of Salisbury wth the Adjacent Close, Church and River Accurately Surveyed by William Naish'. There are then scales of feet, yards, perches and furlongs. The final written element of the cartouche states that it was sold by John Senex and William Taylor in London and the date (see below) (Fig 2).

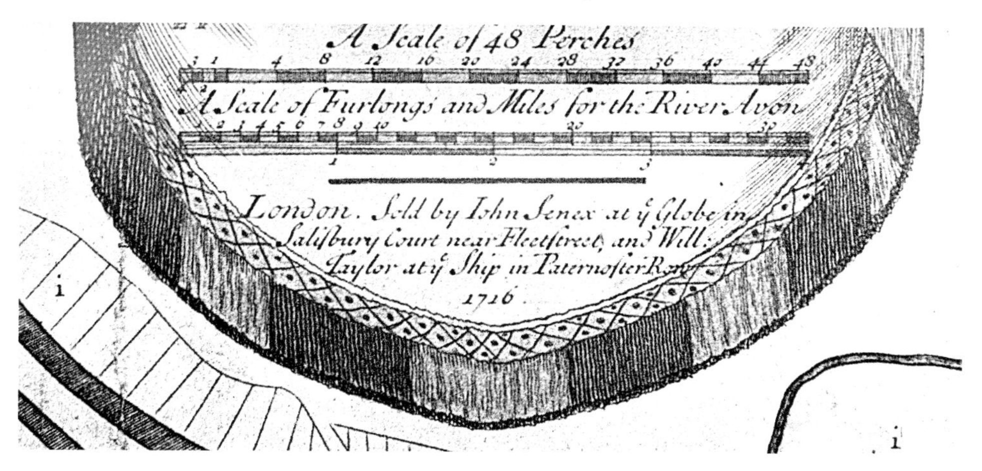

Fig 2: 1716 Print sellers (Senex and Taylor) and date
(*Roy Bexon, 2023—map courtesy of Wiltshire Museum*)

It is not clear why William Naish created the map, but most maps in the 18th century were produced as a commercial venture on the part of the map maker. Whilst he would have surveyed and drawn the map and images, the actual engraving on the brass plate would have been undertaken by an engraver. As John Senex was an engraver the likely process was that William Naish drew the map and sent it to John Senex in London to be engraved. John Senex probably engraved, printed and then sold the map, with William Taylor also selling the map.

Two copies of the Senex/Taylor map have been located, the first in Salisbury Museum and the second in Wiltshire Museum, Devizes. The Salisbury version is coloured, but it is not clear whether the original print was a coloured version, or that it was coloured in later. A second edition, just citing

Senex, was also produced. The few surviving copies probably indicate that the 1716 edition was a small print run. Whilst it is hoped that William got a good return for his painstaking work, the financial reward is unknown.

John Senex and William Taylor

The two editions of the 1716 map are individually identifiable because of the cited sellers: John Senex and William Taylor for the first 1716 edition and just John Senex for the second. The wording of the first edition is: 'London Sold by John Senex at ye Globe in Salisbury Court near Fleetstreet and Will Taylor at ye Ship in Paternoster Row'.[35] Both Senex and Taylor were well known book sellers in London, but it is Senex who had the experience and knowledge to engrave and produce the map. Senex was born in 1678 and became a prominent mapmaker, engraver, globemaker and publisher, and the geographer to Queen Anne. He started his trade engraving plates for almanacs and scientific books, but then specialized in engraving maps, charts and making globes.[36] He obtained professional premises in 1710 at the Globe and which, thereafter, he cited on his maps.[37]

William Taylor was principally known as a bookseller and he was the first publisher of Robinson Crusoe.[38] One of his catalogues has survived entitled: 'Books printed for William Taylor at the Ship in Paternoster Row', compiled in 1716. The catalogue contains over 150 books, ranging from medicine, astronomy, geography, midwifery, magic, Shakespeare, religion and poetry. There was even a book by John Love which would have been pertinent to William Naish's undertaking: 'No 25 The whole Art of Surveying and Measuring Land made easy'. Taylor died of a 'violent fever' in May 1724 and left an estate reputedly worth between £40–50,000. His business and premises, The Ship, was bought by Thomas Longman, the founder of the Longman publishing dynasty, for £2,282 9s 6d.[39]

The second 1716 edition is imprinted 'London. Sold by John Senex at ye Globe agst St Dunstan's Church Fleet street.'[40] As there is no mention of William Taylor, who died in 1724, the map was probably changed and sold after this date. For the two editions of the 1716 map no Salisbury seller is listed.

The '1726' Edition Map of Salisbury

In Rogers's article of 1963 he wrote 'there may be an edition of 1726. What purported to be one was published in Thomas Sharp's *Newer Sarum* but the reproduction is not clear enough to read the date certainly.'[41] On enquiry by Rogers, the reply from Sharp and his publishers was that they had no record of the whereabouts of the map that was used. Sharp's *Newer Sarum* was written in 1949 as a blue print for the second half of the 20th Century for Salisbury.[42]

Fig 3: Front cover of Thomas Sharp's *Newer Sarum* (*Roy Bexon, 2023*)

Fig 4: Date on Naish's map within *Newer Sarum* (p 12) (*Roy Bexon, 2023*)

Naish's map occurs three times in the book: on the front cover (Fig 3), on the back cover (negative image) and on page 12. Unfortunately, as Rogers states, it is not clear enough to definitively determine the date: the '1' of '16' can be mis-interpreted as a '2' (Fig 4). There is no other evidence that there was a 1726 version and it is likely it is simply a miss-reading of '1716'.

The 1751 Edition Map of Salisbury

Then, for 35 years, Naish's 1716 map went into abeyance before it was re-printed, with additions and updates, in 1751 (Fig 5). Once again it was probably a commercial venture. There were some immediate differences in the production of the map. The first is that it was dedicated to John, Bishop of Salisbury. This would have been in the expectation, or actuality, of sponsorship. The second change was that the London sellers were replaced in the cartouche by Benjamin Collins – the locally and regionally important printer in Salisbury who published the *Salisbury Journal* (*SJ*).[43] A more local audience was now being targeted. The *SJ* was also used as an advertising platform and the revised map was announced as 'This Day Published' on the 1 July 1751. The advert states that the map is 'Printed and sold by Benjamin Collins, on the Canal, in Salisbury; and R Baldwin, Bookseller, in Paternoster Row, London'. The map was then sporadically advertised until 1752 although the format of the maps changes. The initial advertisements state that the map is 'printed on a large Imperial Paper' (1 July 1751 and, for example 23 September 1751) and on the 11 May 1752, and thereafter, the advertisement gives more options: 'Price 2s plain and 2s 6d colour'd'.[44] On each advertisement the title is 'This Day is Published'. If this equates to the actual printing of the map then it was printed at least seven times (1 July 1751,

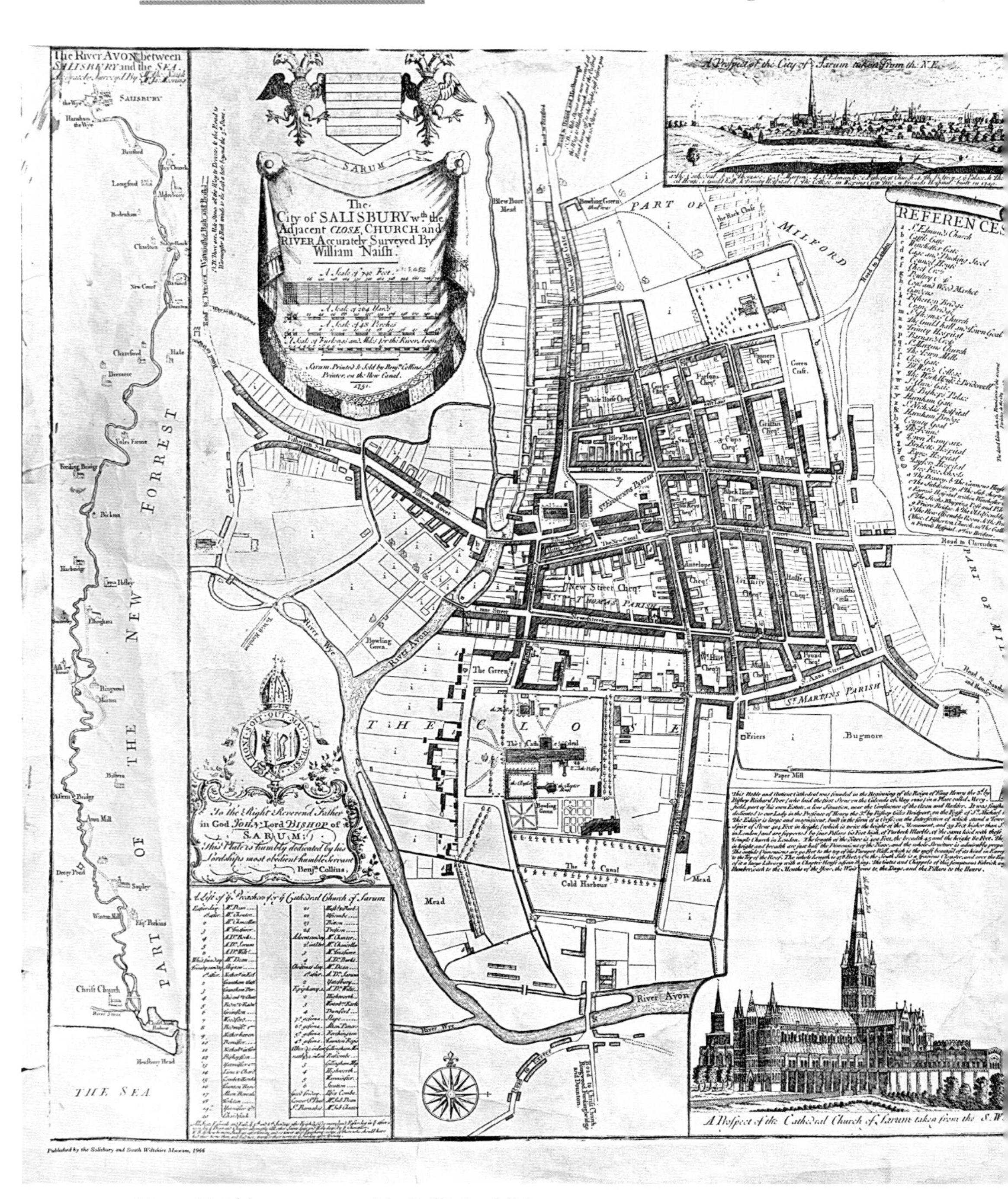

Fig 5: Naish's 1751 map with Collin's additions
(*Roy Bexon, 2023—map courtesy of Salisbury Library*)

23 September 1751, 16 May 1752, 27 July 1752, 17 August 1752, 31 August 1752, 27 August 1752).

Whilst the advertisement mentions R. Baldwin, his name does not appear on any of the maps so far seen. However, the link between Collins and Baldwin was far from a casual acquaintance.[45] When Richard Baldwin was fifteen years old he was sent from London to Salisbury to serve as an apprentice to Benjamin Collins. Benjamin Collins was originally born in Faringdon, Berkshire where Robert Baldwin, an apothecary, and others of the Baldwin family also lived. Furthermore, Benjamin's elder brother William, was also a Salisbury bookseller and printer and he had formed partnerships with Richard's father, also called Richard. The Baldwin-Collins connections ran deep. Benjamin Collins obviously trusted the younger Richard, as he entrusted the running of his Isle of Wight business to-Richard in 1743, when Richard was just 18 years old. In 1746 Richard left the Isle of Wight and set up his own business in London, where he printed the *London Magazine*. Baldwin's connections with Salisbury remained and he printed Francis Price's work about the Cathedral in 1774.[46] Baldwin's business thrived and he took on a number of apprentices, including John Staples of Salisbury, and later John's brother, Moses.[47]

The number of maps per printing is not known, but the seven print runs would explain why there are so many copies of the 1751 map in existence, including two in George III's map collection, whilst so far only three copies of the 1716 map have been found.[48] The 1751 map was, in addition, republished by Salisbury and South Wiltshire Museum in 1966 and in the 21st century reproductions of an original 1751 map are being produced, further increasing the number.[49] However, even within the 1751 map editions a subtle change occurs – for a number of the maps are undated with the '1751' being deleted. This may simply be to keep the map relevant and not seen to be 'yesterday's map'.

Before strict copyright laws the de-facto ownership of maps was vested in the physical copper plate that the map was engraved upon.[50] There are two possible explanations as to how Collins received the copper plate. The first is that at some point after the 1716 printing William acquired the engraved plate from John Senex and then kept it. By 1751 the scheme to re-publish the map had started. As Collins was now the printer, William would have passed, or sold, the engraved plate of the map to Collins for changes to be made. A second explanation is that Collins acquired the copper plate via Baldwin and his London contacts, thereby by-passing William altogether, in which case all profits would have flowed to Collins. This is the scenario portrayed by 'H.P', the commentator who described Collins in the margin of a 1751 map as 'The thief Collins . . .'.[51]

Fig 6: Collin's additions to the dedication box on the 1751 map
(*Roy Bexon, 2023—map courtesy of Salisbury Library*)

On the 1 July 1751 Collins advertised the 1751 map for the first time in his newspaper, *The Salisbury Journal*. Just ten days later, on the 10 July 1751, St Edmund's parish register recorded the burial of William Naish. There are three possible scenarios. The first is that William had sold Collins the map and the timing was a coincidence. The second is that Collins printed the map just before William's death as a monument to William's work, though as Collins personally dedicated the map to the Bishop this mitigates this theory, or, thirdly, that Collins was a thief and assumed William was so close to death that he could not take action against him. It is notable that the majority of the printings (five of the seven) took place in 1752, as if Collins was making as much money as he could as quickly as he could. Four of the 1752 printings were produced between May and August, and the last and final printing was in November 1752. The market had been flooded. Thirteen years later Collins advertised the 'plan', with other books, in the *Salisbury Journal* in July and August 1765.[52] Naish is not mentioned and the advertisement gives the appearance of Collins selling off old stock rather than a new printing. The number of print runs, compared to the initial two 1716 small print-runs also explains the much greater survival of the 1751 version.

The changes

The core of the 1751 map showing the buildings and streets of Salisbury is substantially unchanged from the 1716 map, though there were two deletions of sections of watercourses – the watercourse along St Anne's Street and the watercourse from the New Street to St Anne's Gate. As the same engraved plate was used this must have been a deliberate change, though whether the original 1716 map was incorrect or the watercourses changed is unknown.[53] The only change to buildings within the chequers was the addition of 'n Froud's Hospital' in Parson's Chequer which was built in 1750.[54]

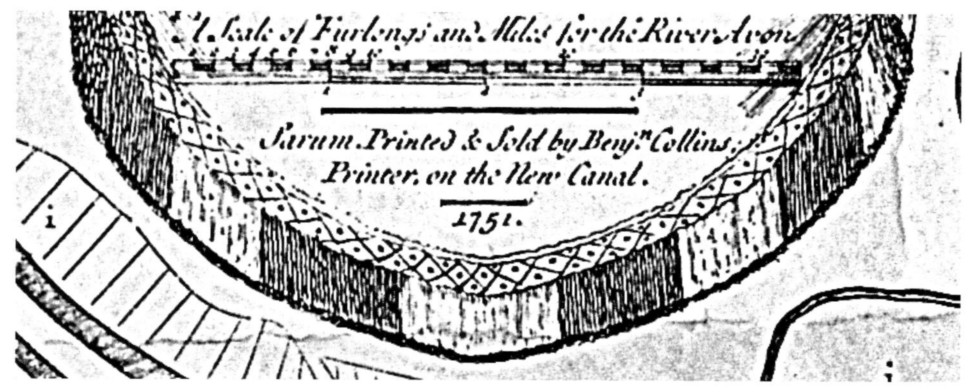

Fig 7: Collin's name and date on Naish's 1751 map
(*Roy Bexon, 2023—map courtesy of Salisbury Library*)

The additional information outside of the streets and chequers is more substantial and there is noticeable increase in the wording and small details. The three largest and most obvious changes are: the new dedication and embellished decoration (Fig 6); the additional text and the change from Senex and Taylor to Benjamin Collins (Fig 7).

The largest textual change (above the bottom left Cathedral picture) is in the form of a 13 line description of the Cathedral, which states:

> This Noble and Ancient Cathedral was founded in the Beginning of the Reign of King Henry the 3d by / Bishop Richard Poor (who laid the first Stone on the Calends of May 1220) in a Place called Mery-/field, part of his own Estate, a low Situation, near the Confluence of the Avon and Nadder. It was finished and / dedicated to our Lady in the Presence of Henry the 3d by Bishop Giles Bridport, on the Feast St Michael 1258. / The Edifice is large and magnificent, built in the form of a Cross: on the Intersection of which stand a Tower and / Spire of Stone 404 feet in height (which is twice the height of the Monument and 39 Feet higher than St Pauls / in London) and are supported by four Pillars 60 Feet high, of Purbeck Marble, of the same kind with those in the Temple Church in London. The length of the Nave is 400 Feet, the breadth 45 and the height 80 Feet. The side Isle in height and breadth are just half the dimensions of the Nave, and the whole Structure is admirably proportioned. / The outside Dimensions are 90 Feet to the top of the Parapet Wall, which is the most beautiful of its kind in Europe & in / to the Top of the Roof. The whole Length is 478 Feet. On the South Side is a spacious Cloister, and over the East Part of it a large Library with a Chapter House adjoining. The Gates and Chappels of this sumptuous Fabrick answer in / Number, each to the Months of the Year, the Windows to the Days, and the Pillars to the Hours.

Most of the detail about the dimensions and fabric would have been known to William as part of his Clerk of Works role, which implies a collaboration with Collins, though Collins could have got the information from the new Clerk of Works, Francis Price. The references to the three London buildings imply at least a passing knowledge of London landmarks amongst the intended audience. Following the 1666 Great Fire of London, the new St Paul's Cathedral was consecrated in 1697, and the Monument to the Fire of London, finished in 1677, made them relatively recent additions to London's skyline. The specific information regarding Purbeck marble in the Temple Church may indicate that William had personal knowledge of the building, or that he (or Collins) knew a barrister who had trained at the Temple and had relayed the information.

The references to the date of the laying of foundation stone on the Calends of May 1220, and that the field was called Meryfield, were possibly the first time that the information had been printed and made accessible to a wider Salisbury audience.[55]

Whilst the description of the Cathedral is the longest new piece of text, the new 1751 map included more text about milestones along the main roads from Salisbury. On the road to Devizes, Warminster, Bath and Bristol (1751 map top left by cartouche) there is the new text: 'N.B. There are Mile Stones all the way to Devizes, & the Road to Warminster & Bath winds to the Left

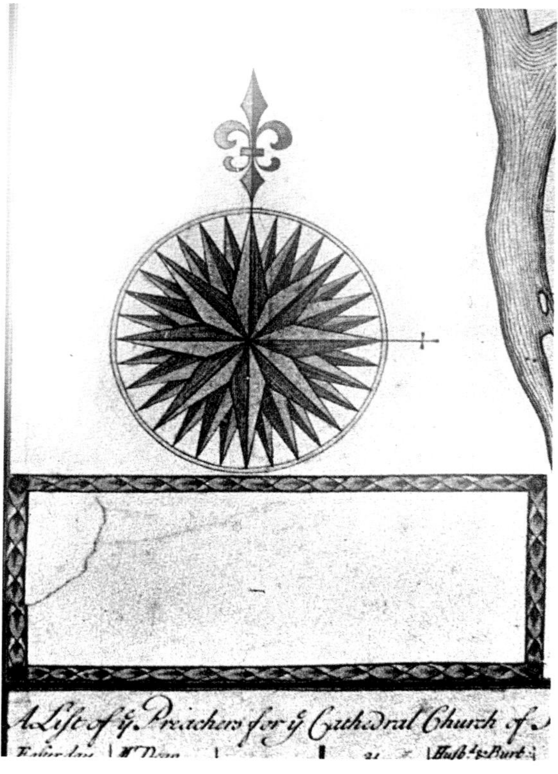

Fig 8: Empty dedication box on Naish's 1716 map (*Roy Bexon, 2023—map courtesy of Wiltshire Museum*)

a little beyond the 5th Stone' and the text regarding the road to Oxford and Marlborough (top middle) reads: 'N.B. Mile stones are now erected all the Way to Marlborough and the Oxford Road turns off to the Right just before you come to the 10th stone'. But the increase and change in wording also have the effect of changing the 'ownership' of the map from Naish to Collins. Collins still states that William Naish surveyed the city, something that Collins could not do, but in other respects he not only cites himself as the only printer and seller of the map (ignoring Baldwin in London), but it is Collins (not Naish) who dedicates the map to the Bishop of Salisbury. The dedication reads 'To the Right Reverend Father in God John Lord Bishop of Sarum, This Plate is humbly dedicated by his Lordships most obedient humble servant Benjn Collins'. The difference between the empty dedication box in 1716 (Fig 8) and the decorative 1751 dedication box (Fig 6) shows the difference in style. As a former Clerk of Works, it is quite possible that William Naish knew the Bishop personally as John Gilbert was bishop between 1748 to 1757. Collins adds some eye-catching designs to the dedication, changing the previous 1716 compass rose to the arms of the Bishop of Salisbury.[56] The original empty rectangular box has been completely altered with a new wavy design round the outside with leaves and tendrils. Furthermore, Collins further emphasizes the new dedication in his newspaper advertisements where, in large letters, the map is described as 'dedicated to the Lord Bishop of Sarum'

From a local viewpoint there are three sets of useful changes. The first is an increase in the number of 'References' (Figs 9 and 10). The end curl of the scroll design has been removed and new references (from 'e' to 'o', missing out 'j') have been inserted and also placed in the appropriate locations on the

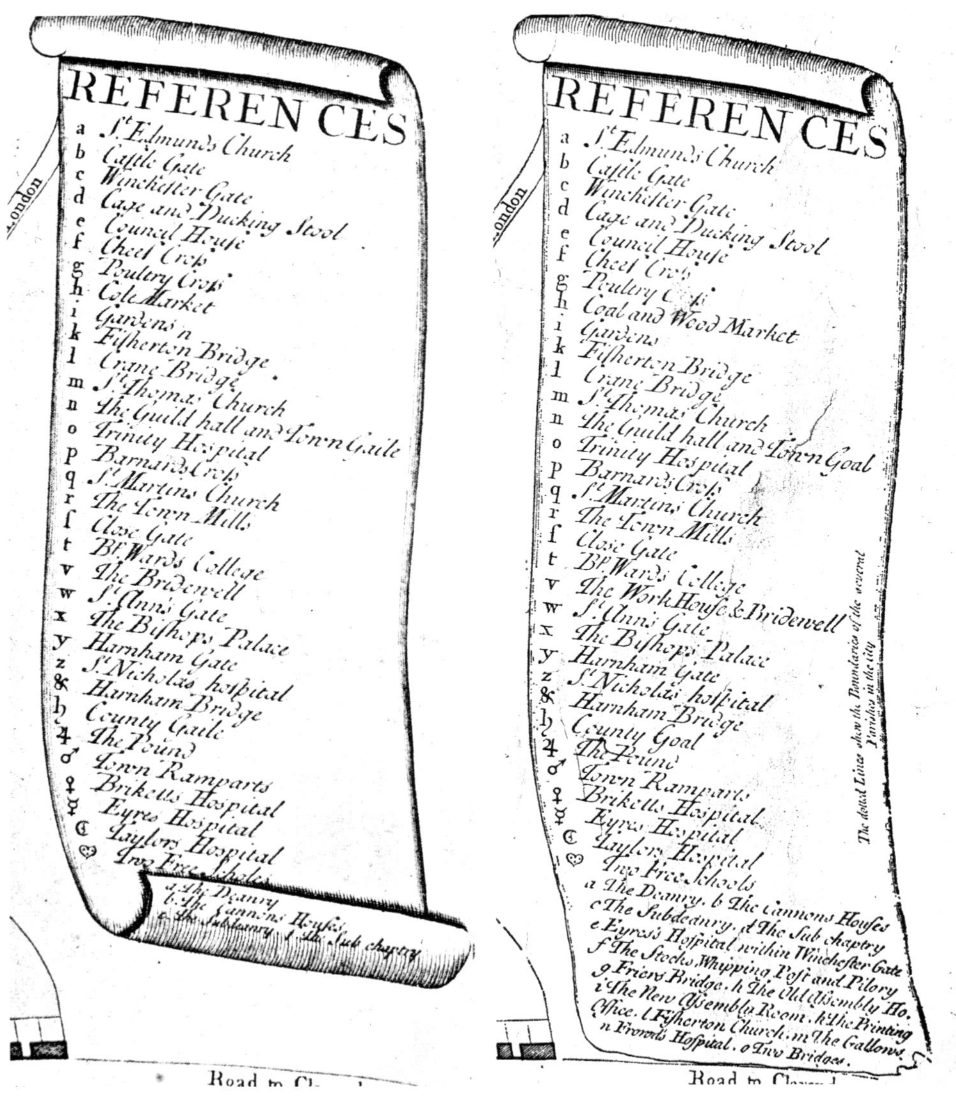

Fig 9: The Reference scroll on the 1716 map (*Roy Bexon, 2023—map courtesy of Wiltshire Museum*)

Fig 10: The Reference scroll on the 1751 map (*Roy Bexon, 2023—map courtesy of Salisbury Library*)

map. These include 'i The New Assembly Rooms' and 'm The Gallows'. Some of the pre-existing references have been amended so 'h' changes from 'Cole Market' to 'The Coal and Wood Market' and 'The Bridewell; changes to 'The Work House and Bridewell'. The second is that vertically along the right hand side of the 'References the explanation is given 'The dotted lines show the Boundaries of the several Parishes of the city'. This is the first time that the

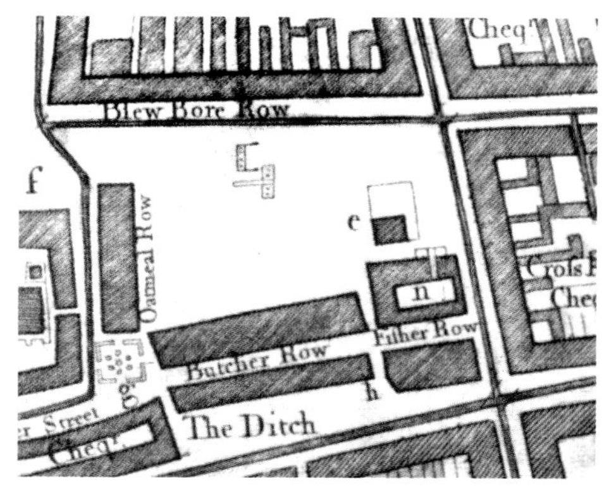

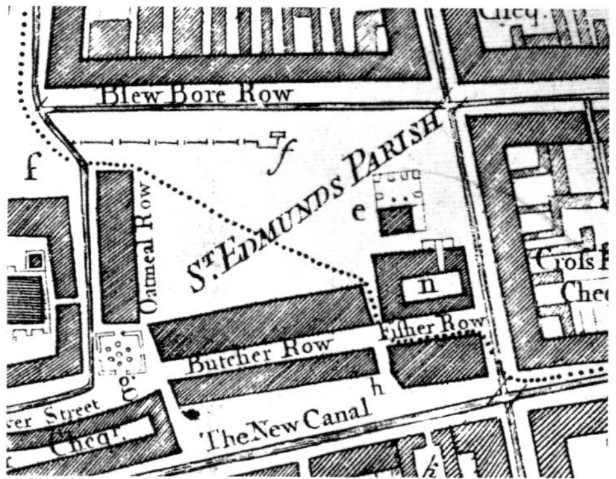

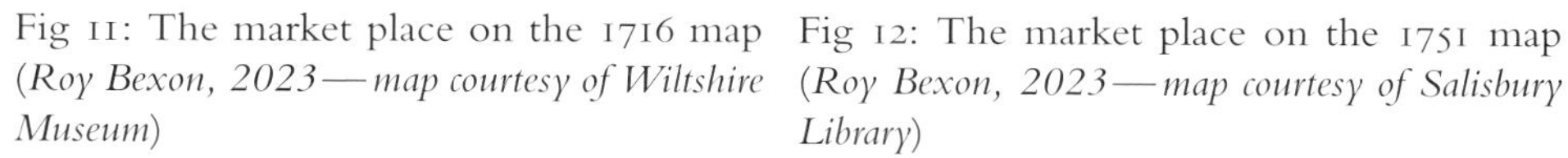
Fig 11: The market place on the 1716 map (*Roy Bexon, 2023—map courtesy of Wiltshire Museum*)

Fig 12: The market place on the 1751 map (*Roy Bexon, 2023—map courtesy of Salisbury Library*)

parish boundaries have been mapped.[57] There is one change which is difficult to interpret. In the middle of the market place the stocks, shown on the 1716 map (Fig 11), have been replaced by a segmented line, running right to left, which ends at a rectangle. The left hand end stops at a water course, so could it be a water channel, perhaps for a water trough? (Fig 12).[58]

However, there is one error which is so obvious that it is difficult to explain. As mentioned the parish boundaries have been drawn in on the 1751 map, and the parish boundary between St Thomas's parish and St Edmund's parish correctly crosses the market place on a diagonal slant (Fig 12). However the label of 'St Edmunds' crosses the parish boundary – indicating that the whole of the market place is in St Edmund's parish, whereas the market place is actually divided between St Thomas's and St Edmund's parishes. William Naish and Benjamin Collins, both local people with great knowledge of the city, must have known this was wrong. One explanation might be that when the changes were being described to the engraver, the labelling in this instance was unclear. The correct label would have been 'The Market Place'. That this error was allowed to stay, rather than being corrected, probably indicates that there was only one substantial amended edition to the 1716 map (though the minor change of the date being removed did occur later).

The after-life of the map

The last advertised printing of the map by Benjamin Collins was in 1752 but thereafter it was very rarely discussed. There were a few references to the map by 19th century historians (for example Henry Penistone's letter in *The Salisbury and Winchester Journal* of 3 September 1887) though it is puzzling that Benson and Hatcher do not mention such an important source. If Naish was mentioned at all it is usually in relation to his cure of James II's nose bleed.[59] In 1949 the map was used by Thomas Sharp as the front cover – and as an image of Salisbury – on his plan for Salisbury called *Newer Sarum*. Whilst this has caused some confusion, in that he stated it was from a 1726 map (see above), it brought the map to prominence once again. In 1966 the Salisbury and South Wiltshire Museum reprinted the dated 1751 version, and the map was frequently used thereafter as an image in publications such as the Royal Commission on the Historical Monuments of England (RCHME) volume (1716 edition) and Chandler's *Endless Street* (1751 edition).[60]

As well as a visual representation of the city, the changes to the 1751 map may have performed another function (though possibly unintentionally): as a proto guide-book to the city. It is not outside the bounds of possibility that maps could have been sent to friends and relations about to visit the city to give them a literal and 'tourist' overview. Furthermore, in 1751 there were no guidebooks to Salisbury for visitors or tourists. The first guidebook to Salisbury, called *The Salisbury Guide* was written by James Easton in 1769 proved to be incredibly popular. The second edition was brought out just two years later in 1771 and between 1769 and 1825 there were twenty five editions of the book, with the nineteenth edition being printed in 1797, 1799, 1800 and 1805. *The Salisbury Guide* also used some of the same types of information found on Naish's 1751 map – in particular the description of the Cathedral and the distances to nearby places.

Conclusion

The importance of the maps is not only that they are the first scaled and accurate maps of Salisbury, but also in their many precise details that are included. That there was a ducking stool in Milford Street is well known, but it is only the 1716/1751 maps that allow it to be precisely located. There are significant differences between the two maps, and the changes made to the 1751 map indicate that it was being made more attractive to a local or regional audience. The new text along the roads records mileages and milestones for inhabitants leaving Salisbury, and also for tourists and visitors arriving in Salisbury. Similarly details about the Cathedral are given (in 13 lines of closely written text) as if for visitors.

Unlike Speed's inaccurate and deeply problematic 1611 map of Salisbury, William Naish's two maps gave the citizens a literal and accurate overview of their city for the first time. Both have stood the test of time and even today are used by historians and archaeologists alike to reveal or confirm aspects of the landscape of the city in the 18th century.

Bibliography

Aubrey, John, 1972, *Three Prose Works,* Centaur Press, London.

Benson, Richard, and Hatcher, Henry, 1843, *Old and New Sarum or Salisbury,* John Bowyer Nichols and Son, London.

Chandler, John, 1983, *Endless Street: a history of Salisbury and its people.* Hobnob Press, Gloucester.

Cox, Harold, and Chandler, John E., 1925, *The House of Longman: With a Record of Their Bicentenary Celebrations, 1724–1924,* Longmans Green, London.

Cross, Don, 2003 'Salisbury as a Seaport', *Sarum Chronicle* 3, 35–44.

Dale, Christabel, 1961, *Wiltshire Apprentices and their Masters, 1710–1760,* Wiltshire Archaeological Society Records Series, 17.

Ferdinand, Christine, and Ferdinand, C.Y., 1997, *Benjamin Collins and the Provincial Newspaper Trade in the Eighteenth Centre,* Clarendon Press, Oxford.

Ferdinand, C.Y., 1989, 'Richard Baldwin, Junior Bookseller', *Studies in Bibliography,* 42, 254–264.

Haycock, Lorna, 1988, 'Wiltshire and the Revolution of 1688', *Wiltshire Archaeological and Natural History Magazine* (*WANHM*), 82, 160–164.

Price, Francis, 1774, *A description of that admirable structure, the cathedral church of Salisbury,* Printed for R. Baldwin, London.

Royal Commission on the Historical Monuments of England (RCHME), 1980, *The Ancient and Historical Monuments in the City of Salisbury,* HMSO, London.

Rogers, K. H., 1963 'Naish's Map of Salisbury', *WANHM,* 211, 453–454.

Rogers, Pat (ed), 2014, *Robinson Crusoe,* Routledge, London.

Sharp, Thomas, 1949, *Newer Sarum,* Salisbury City Council, Architectural Press.

Skelton R., 1970, *County Atlases of the British Isles 1759–1703,* Carta Press, London.

Slatter, Doreen (ed), 1965, *The Diary of Thomas Naish,* Wiltshire Archaeological and Natural History Society Records Branch, 20, Devizes.

Notes

1 The first map of Salisbury was John Speed's 1611 map of Salisbury, but it has major inaccuracies and is of dubious value for historians and archaeologists.

2 Wiltshire & Swindon Archives (WSA) 1899/2 (register) and BT/S/SM/1 (bishop's transcript). He was named after an older sibling, baptised 24 December 1671, who was buried a week later, on 1 January 1672. William was the third eldest surviving son, after John (born 1666), Thomas (born 1669), with a younger sibling Richard (born 1675). I am very grateful to John Chandler for resolving the issue of William's birth.

3 Slatter, 1965, 1–12 where Thomas Naish's immediate family is described. Thomas became sub-dean of the Cathedral.

4 The National Archives (TNA), PROB 11/625/171.

5 Slatter, 1965. Thomas was also instrumental in drawing up an inventory of Cathedral communion plate and other goods (see Robert Beddard, 1971, 'Cathedral Furnishings of the Restoration Period: A Salisbury Inventory of 1685', *WANHM,* 66, 147–155).

6 The lives of the brothers are given in Slatter 1965, 4–7.

7 Slatter, 1965, 6–7. John was in Chatham, Ireland, Sheerness, Harwich and Woolwich. He finished his career as a master shipwright in Portsmouth. He bought a property

at Babcary in Somerset, and left 'draughts of ships and optic glasses' to his brother Richard. He had no children and was buried in St Edmund's church, Salisbury. Richard was based in Plymouth, Chatham and Woolwich.

8 Salisbury Cathedral Archives (SCA), CO/CH/5/1/27/15, lease of 1700; CO/CH/5/1/27/18 lease of 1705; CO/CH/5/1/26/22, lease of 1726; CO/CH/5/1/26/23, lease of 1740; CO/CH/5/1/27/22, lease of 1743. William's brother, 'Thomas Naish the younger, clerk' also leased a corner tenement in Fish Row (CO/CH/5/1/27/24), which may have been the same property as William's. Trying to precisely locate the property is made more difficult as it is located by the neighbours surrounding it, who might themselves move or die, as well as missing leases or documents.

9 WSA, 212B/5954.

10 Dale, 1961, 17. Apprentice references are at nos 243 (John Bishop, 1711, £50 paid to William), 357 (Henry Bishop, 1728–9, £70), 739 (Joseph Edgar, 1713, £50), 1226 (Charles Hooton, 1719, £60), 1532 (Daniel Martin, 1720–1, £50).

11 The road to becoming an alderman was not straightforward and William, as part of a group, had a major dispute over election procedures, 10th October 1706. (Benson and Hatcher 1843, 503).

12 RCHME, 1980, 29.

13 Whilst well known, William does not seem to have had his own token, see T D Whittet, 1987, 'Wiltshire Apothecaries' Tokens and their issuers, *WANHM,* 81, 74–9.

14 Aubrey, 1972, 88 cited in Haycock, 1988.

15 Slatter, 1965, 7. The case received some public comment, being mentioned by Narcissus Luttrell in his *Historical Relation of State Affairs*, and some comic verse 'The Whigs new Toast to the B- of S-y'.

16 Slatter, 1965, 7.

17 Slatter, 1965, 6–7.

18 Slatter, 1965, 3. Price 1774, 33–31.

19 1736–1737 (SCA, FA/1/1/84); 1743–1744 (SCA, FA/1/1/91).

20 Anon, Day Book 1744/5 (SCA, FA/1/3/4).

21 TNA, C 11/552/44. The National Archives describes a Bill and Answer as 'A petition or bill (also known as a pleading) from the plaintiff would be submitted to the court laying out their grievance. A response from the defendant, known as an 'answer'.

22 TNA, C 11/1140/35.

23 Somerset Heritage Centre: DD\BC/171,172. John Sweet Naish was the son of the diarist Thomas Naish and his wife Joan (née Sweet). The diary records 1717, 2 Aug 'My wife was delivered of a son, and I gave it a private baptism, Aug the 8th, and named it John Sweet' (Slatter, 1965, 75).

24 TNA, PROB 11/789/402.

25 The cousins were: John Sweet Naish, Thomas Naish of Bath and his wife, Richard (W?)ing of 'Wincanuto' (presumably Wincanton) and his wife, John Chiddiock Kent of Romsey, Ruth Barker, (Jeboe?) Book 'both of the same (*ie* Romsey)), Giles Rook of London and his wife, Jos Peirce of Linnington and his wife, 'and lastly to my esteemed friend and cousin Sir James Collier of the Bank of England'. The last

reference is particularly interesting as it shows that William moved in prosperous and very well connected London society.

26 RCHME, 1980, 36–7.

27 Slatter, 1965, 8.

28 WSA, 776/922: The Mannor of Stratford Toney in the County of Wilts, survey'd for Thomas Jervoise Esq by William Naish. Stratford Tony is 5 miles south-west of Salisbury. Detail in J Bettey, (ed), 2005, *Wiltshire Farming in the Seventeenth Century,* Wiltshire Record Society 57, xli.

29 Chandler, 1983, 49, 51, 53: RCHME 1980 xlviii.

30 John Ogilby and William Morgan surveyed map of London was published in 1676. In 1751 maps, authorized by Act of Parliament, were also produced for Birmingham and Wolverhampton.

31 For a brief history of the navigation see Cross, 2003, 35–44: Cross, 1970, 'The Salisbury Avon Navigation', *WANHM,* 65, 172–6.

32 James died on 9 March 1728, aged 82 and there is a plaque to him in Priory Church Christchurch.

33 Benson and Hatcher, 1843, 471. A reference in the *Catalogue of the Library of the Wiltshire Archaeological and Natural History Society,* 1894, 52 gives a date for the survey of 1660 (*ie* 15 years before payment). This date cannot be correct as Thomas was born in 1647, which would make him 13 when he surveyed the river. It is not known where this date derives from as it is not on the maps.

34 Hampshire Archives and Local Studies, HRO, 44M69/P1/116. I am very grateful to Hadrian Cook for this information. It is very likely that William helped him in this enterprise and he may have learnt his mapping skills from his father whilst undertaking the Britford map.

35 A note in *WANHM* for 1963 by K H Rogers records 'The only located copy of this belongs to St Thomas's School, Bemerton Heath, Salisbury. There must, however, be at least one more in existence, for it was used by Miss Kathleen Edwards when she wrote her article 'Houses of Salisbury Close in the 14th Century' *Jnl Brit Arch Assoc* (3rd ser) iv 54–115. Miss Edwards believes that she saw a copy of this edition at the British Museum, but it does not appear in the catalogue of maps, and the officials of the map room could not suggest its whereabouts (Rogers, 1963, 53, 453). The online British Library catalogue only has two versions of the 1751 map. The two extant copies found by the author are at Salisbury Museum and Wiltshire Museum.

36 Given the connections, it is possible that the globe left by Thomas to his grandson John Sweet Naish was a Senex globe.

37 https://content.libraries.wsu.edu/digital/collection/senex, accessed March 2023.

38 Rogers, 2014, 10.

39 https://www.oakknoll.com/resources/bookexcerpts/096667.pdf, accessed March 2023; Cox and Chandler, 1925.

40 Only a single copy is known to exist (Wiltshire Museum, DZSWS: Map.407.1).

41 Rogers, 1963, 453–4.

42 Sharp, 1949. For a short biography of Sharp see https://www.ncl.ac.uk/apl/alumni/graduates/thomas-sharp/, accessed March 2023.

43 Ferdinand and Ferdinand, 1997: Ferdinand, C.Y, 1989, 'Richard Baldwin, Junior Bookseller', *Studies in Bibliography,* 42, 254–64. The title of *The Salisbury Journal* changed

to *The Salisbury and Winchester Journal* on the 7 December 1772 (No 1801).

44 The 'large Imperial paper' paper size is not specific enough to identify the editions. The paper size of a map in Wiltshire Museum (DZSWS.Map.218.1) measures 29 inches by 26 inches (74 cms by 66 cms) which does not equate with a standard named Imperial paper size. A more common paper size for the maps is 29 inches by 25.75 inches (31 cms by 53 cms), for example maps DZSWS.Map.218.6, and DZSWS.Map.374, but again these do not equate to named Imperial paper sizes. There are two coloured 1751 Naish maps known. The coloured map in the Wiltshire and Swindon History Centre has been hand coloured at a later date (Ref G/23/1/164PC). The 1751 map in the bar of the Pembroke Arms, Wilton, appears to be an original coloured map, though analysis was restricted.

45 Ferdinand, 1989, 42, 254–64.

46 Ferdinand, 1989, 256–8: Price, 1774.

47 Ferdinand, 1989, 259, and Note 35.

48 George III's maps are now housed in the British Library: British Library Cartographic Items Maps BLL01004925523 and BLL01017158828.

49 A copy of the 1966 map can be viewed in Salisbury City Library.

50 Skelton, 1970, 231.

51 The note is by 'H P' (or possibly 'H R') who wrote in light pencil down the side of an undated (1751 edition) map, Wiltshire Museum DZSWS: Map.218.1.

52 *Salisbury Journal*, 15, 22 July, 19 August 1765

53 The watercourses were a dynamic system which could be changed and altered, for example in Exeter Street in 1819.

54 RCHME, 1980, 58 (building 33).

55 The name 'Meryfield' was well known in the Middle Ages through the various legends, see Chandler, 1983, 12–15.

56 The compass rose was relocated to the bottom of the map.

57 The parish boundaries shown on Naish's depiction are assumed to be the medieval parish boundaries.

58 I am grateful to Geoff Lang for discussions on this aspect of the market place.

59 Benson and Hatcher, 1843. William only appears twice in the index, the first under the James II account (491) and secondly in the 1710 dispute about electing aldermen (503).

60 RCHME, 1980, plate 16: Chandler, 1983, 49. Both maps have cropped the River Avon map.

'The Star-Spangled Scotchman': Andrew Carnegie and Salisbury Public Library 1890–1910

Monte Little

The first public library

Salisbury's first public library occupied a former Congregational chapel above Messrs Webb & Co, Upholsterers and Furniture Removers, at 9 Endless Street. It measured 60 × 40 ft with a cork tile floor, hot water heating and lighting appropriate to a furniture store. The premises was on a five-year rental with an annual rent of £50 plus 50% of rateable value. The Library had one member of staff – George Walter Atkinson – formerly of Rotherham Public Library, on an annual salary of £60. It had been opened on Wednesday 10 December 1890 by the Rt Hon M E Grant Duff (1829–1906), former Governor of Madras and former Winchester MP, together with the Mayor & Corporation in full regalia[1] (Fig 1).

Fig 1: Rt Hon M E Grant Duff (1829–1906). Vanity Fair, 2 October 1869 by "Ape" (Carlo Pellegrini) (*Reproduced by permission of National Portrait Gallery*).

Salisbury Town Council were now faced with the reality of the new library. The Council had delegated powers to a Library Committee and in August 1890 the committee comprised ten members–7 elected councillors and 3 co-opted members–with the Mayor as chairman.[2]

The Public Libraries Acts were only adopted in the city by the smallest of majorities, against strong opposition, and the product of a penny rate (the maximum allowed by law) was only £220 pa of which the rent and the librarian's modest salary took over half. The library had no books, little furniture, and a premises soon to be described as '. . . dingy, inaccessible, dark and inhospitable . . .'. It is impossible not to sympathise with the council as they groped their way forward in the dark and with little practical experience nationally to guide them and no idea whatsoever how the public in Salisbury would respond to their efforts.[3]

On 11 December 1890, the Reading Room opened for the first time with 16 daily newspapers, 34 weekly newspapers and 23 monthly magazines.[4] The first Lending Library followed on 23 April 1891 with a stock of 1,000 books–mostly donated along with the shelves, furniture, clocks and everything else–as the committee found the restrictions of the 'penny rate' very severe. By November 1893, the library had 1,652 members and 1,943 books.[5]

Early proposals

The inadequacy of the Endless Street Library was quickly evident and in 1892 the *Salisbury and Winchester Journal* (*SWJ*)–no friend to the rate-supported library–attempted to re-visit the 1877 proposal that the library might be combined with Salisbury College of Art in New Street.[6] Neither committee nor council were interested in re-visiting this scheme but by December 1894, the Mayor (Mr E F Pye-Smith)–amidst growing complaints over Endless Street and the 5-year lease on the premises drawing closer–suggested that the Guildhall would make a fine library with new Courts being relocated elsewhere.[7] This was the first of a great many such suggestions which included the Pig Market (1903), the Literary & Scientific Institution (1877), the Fire Station (1903), the City Workhouse (1880), the Assembly Rooms (1903) and the Salisbury and South Wiltshire Museum (1897). The town council's most favoured sites were the old Technical Education Building on Brown Street (1904) and a derelict piano store on Butcher Row (1903) with arguments over their respective merits continuing for many years and involving an increasingly exasperated Local Government Board (LGB).[8]

In 1897, to commemorate the Diamond Jubilee of Queen Victoria, the Mayor (Arthur Whitehead) called a public meeting on 30 March to discuss how the city might mark the occasion. The council favoured a 'Jubilee Library' along with fireworks, bonfires, concerts, and the usual events. However, it had not considered the views of the *SWJ* which–without any reference to the local authority–launched its own Jubilee Appeal for "The Salisbury Infirmary & Victoria Nurses Home Shilling Fund." This was extremely popular for a much-loved institution founded in 1766 and in perpetual debt. The 'Shilling Fund' was quickly adopted at the public meeting and the council managed to retain some credibility by adopting the lesser project of the Victoria Park for civic purposes.[9]

History repeated itself in 1902 when the council proposed a 'Coronation Library' to mark the accession of King Edward VII, setting a target of £1,000 by public subscription but only receiving £385-9-6d! The 'Coronation Library' was abandoned but the money was deposited on behalf of the library and would soon prove significant.[10]

The boundary extension

In December 1903, the Council announced that they wished to incorporate the Parishes of Fisherton Anger Without, East Harnham, Milford Without, Britford and West Harnham into the City. This required a public enquiry which was held from 2 to 4 March 1904 under the chairmanship of Major C E Norton, Royal Engineers, acting on behalf of the LGB. The council was successful, and the population of Salisbury increased from 17,000 to 21,000 with an increase of one-third in the rateable value. The implications for Salisbury Public Library were considerable. With seven wards in the 'new' city–each with an alderman and three councillors–the workload on elected members increased dramatically and they could no longer manage their library in such great detail, leading to greater delegation to both committee and their librarian. Of more immediate impact, however, there was a 23% increase in the value of the 'penny rate' from £332 (1903/04) to £407 (1904/05). Both of these factors allowed real progress to be made prior to the outbreak of the Great War.[11]

The 'Proper Library'

John Alfred Folliott served as Mayor during 1901–02 and, as such, was Chairman of Salisbury Library Committee. As virtually his last function before handing over the office, he wrote to Andrew Carnegie (Fig 2) 'calling his attention to the position of Salisbury Free Library' and setting forth in detail the financial situation to 'assist Mr Carnegie in forming an opinion.' He advised Carnegie that the library committee already had a site in mind–the premises used as a piano warehouse by Messrs Aylward and Spinney in Butcher Row near the Council House.[12]

On 14 February 1903, a letter arrived from Andrew Carnegie in New York offering to donate £4,000 for the building of a new library in Salisbury with two main conditions:

- that the town council provide the site – free of all encumbrances and not from the library rate;
- that the town council adopt the Public Libraries Acts and levy the maximum permissible rate of 1d in the £1.

Fig 2: Andrew Carnegie (1835–1919) (*Reproduced by permission of National Portrait Gallery*).

Additionally, the letter made clear that the £4,000 grant was only for a library building, not for books, and that any overspending must be met by the authority. The grant was given based on plans and estimates being approved before work commenced. The library committee met on 20 February 1903 to examine the offer and expressed delight at Mr Carnegie's generosity. The committee decided to seek the advice of a special meeting of the town council on Monday 23 February 1903. The *SWJ* – in an unusual surge of enthusiasm – recommended a purpose-built library rather than a conversion, but this support was short-lived because later that month the paper was advocating incorporation of the library into the municipal offices on the grounds of economy:

> . . . with taxes and rates what they are, and with the cost of living greater than it used to be, there could hardly be a worse time than the present to ask the people of Salisbury to find £1,000 or more to buy a site for a Free Library. They will not do it . . .[13]

The *SWJ* was also very aware of the need for speed in reaching a decision because Carnegie (68 years old in 1903) was in poor health and had gone to Florida to recover. Worried in case he died before the offer was ratified, the paper observed deferentially:

> There is not another millionaire like MR CARNEGIE and not only America, but the whole world would be poorer for the loss of such a man.[14]

The special town council meeting accepted Mr Carnegie's offer, expressing some concern at the condition that the site should not be a burden on the library rate. The next six months would be spent on wrangling over the sites, and it is not being too unjust to Salisbury Town Council to suggest a considerable streak of pedantry in their approach and in the advice given by successive town clerks. This indecisiveness could have continued for an indefinite period–despite Carnegie's health issues–and it is therefore fortunate for posterity that in September 1903, a coachbuilder called Edward J West died in his 65th year. He owned an extensive property at 25 Chipper Lane with the adjacent property (No 23) formerly owned by Miss S A Lawrence now empty.[15]

The town council, in the meantime, accused the library committee of 'dragging their feet'. They felt that the library committee were being unduly slow in reaching a decision over the library site. The most popular site for many Councillors was the Technical Education Building in Brown Street. The Brown Street site was jointly owned by the new Wiltshire County Council and Salisbury Town Council but had a debt of £720 13s 1d owed to the Wilts & Dorset Bank (plus interest since the Spring of 1903) and a further £254 5s 1d owed to Messrs Pye-Smiths for legal work. The town council asked the library committee to make it clear if they would accept the responsibility for raising the money–with Carnegie's restrictions–but at no point told the library committee whether they would be required to clear the debt, buy out the County Council's interest or merely meet the site costs. There can be no surprise that the library committee were "dragging their feet". The LGB was twice contacted by the town council over this problem. Ultimately, the library committee acted with speed and resolution in the new circumstances and by mid-September 1903 had an option on 23–25 Chipper Lane and launched an Appeal.[16]

Andrew Carnegie (1835–1919)

Andrew Carnegie was born in Dunfermline, Scotland, second of two sons to William, a handloom weaver, and Margaret, who sewed for local shoemakers. In 1848, the family emigrated to the USA and settled in Allegheny City (now part of Pittsburgh). Andrew was employed as a 'bobbin-boy' in the local mill earning $1.20 per week. He had various jobs including a messenger in a telegraph office and secretary to the telegraph operator for the Superintendent of the Pennsylvania Railroad in 1859. He avoided involvement in the American Civil War by paying $850 for a substitute (a common practice allowed by the US Conscription Act, 1863) and became the railroad superintendent himself, making profitable investments in coal, iron, oil and the manufacture of railroad sleeping cars. He left railroads in 1865 and founded the Keystone Bridge Company and his own telegraph company, using his special knowledge and insider contacts. In 1870, he visited Britain selling bonds in his various companies and saw the Bessemer steel process for the first time. On returning to the USA, he used the process in his first steel company near Pittsburgh. In 1892 his holdings were consolidated into the 'Carnegie Steel Company' and in 1901, Carnegie sold his company to the banker, John Pierpont Morgan (1837–1913) for $480 million and–merged with others–it became the US Steel Corporation, the first multi-billion corporation in the world.

Carnegie's philanthropy came from his belief that 'The man who dies rich, dies disgraced' and that life should be lived in three parts–the first one-third to acquire education; the second one-third to make money; and the final one-third to give it away. Public libraries were amongst his favourite causes because he believed that anyone with access to books and a desire to learn could educate themselves to be successful and founding a community library

Fig 3: Mrs Louise Carnegie, Miss Margaret Carnegie and Andrew Carnegie at unknown event 1910–15 (*Reproduced by permission of the US Library of Congress, Bain Collection*).

was a way to achieve that. To this end, he spent $55 million on public libraries throughout the world and 2,811 premises are attributed to his generosity.

Carnegie's mother, Margaret, was a major influence and lived with him until her death in 1886. In the following year, he married Louise Whitfield (1857–1946), and they had one daughter, Margaret (1897–1990) (Fig 3). In 1898, Carnegie bought Skibo Castle and 28,000 acres in Sutherland, Scotland, for £85,000 to keep Margaret in touch with her heritage. The family spent each summer there and the winter in their New York mansion.[17]

Carnegie's first grant in the United Kingdom was to his native town of Dunfermline in 1879 but it was not until 1897 that the business of "library-giving" was – as Carnegie put it – on a 'wholesale' as opposed to a 'retail' basis. This led to the famous quip by George Bernard Shaw that 'when Mr Carnegie rattled his millions in his pockets, all England became one rapacious cringe . . . '.[18]

The second public library

The immediate response to the September 1903 Appeal in Salisbury were encouraging. The Bishop gave £50, Lady Hulse, Walter Palmer MP, and the prospective MP (E F Tennant) all gave £25 and with smaller donations, the sum of £300 was quickly raised. With a sense of relief, the town council endorsed the decision of the library committee over Chipper Lane and invited 'a deputation from the Free Library Committee' to attend the October council meeting and give their views on the choice of site before the final decision was made. This deputation comprised two co-opted members – Arthur Russell Malden (the Cathedral Librarian) and Canon Benjamin Whitefoord (Principal of Salisbury Theological College) – with the latter acting as spokesman. This was an excellent choice. Canon Whitefoord had been one of the most outspoken and influential supporters of the public library movement in the city. He summarised the history of the Endless Street library – "dingy, inaccessible, dark and inhospitable" – observing that with a stock never exceeding 3,000 volumes, the library had managed to loan some 400,000 since 1890. It was 'no ornament to the City' and continuing delays might well cost them the Carnegie grant. He noted that £1,100 needed to be raised for the site, of which £700 ('Coronation Library' plus Appeal monies) had been received and only £400 was required. The final council debate was a foregone conclusion with only four councillors preferring the Butcher Row site and the remainder endorsing Chipper Lane. The Town Clerk was asked to contact Andrew Carnegie to see if the site met with his approval.[19]

Salisbury Town Council did not appreciate that Carnegie had little interest in such matters. By 1903, the procedures for the giving of Carnegie grants to libraries had become standardised. A Carnegie grant could be spent on library furniture but his Private Secretary, James Bertram (1872–1934), tended not to make this clear. Bertram, with Carnegie's treasurer, Robert Franks, and clerical help were the only employees dealing with the matter.[20]

On 19 October 1903, the town council received a letter from Robert Franks of the Home Trust Company, Hoboken, New Jersey, confirming the grant of £4,000 for 'the erection of library buildings in Salisbury' payable by instalments of £500-£1,000 on the certificate of the architect as the work progressed. The letter was read to the council by the town clerk, William Charles Powning (1843–1904), who also advised them that he had conveyed the site to the council, free of charge, as his personal contribution. Some discussion took place over a concern that the verbatim reports in the press of their proceedings might be monitored by Carnegie employees and show the council in an unfavourable light![21] The council decided not to hold an architectural competition for the new library on the grounds that 'few architects wished to enter.' On the subject of money for the site, the council quickly reaffirmed delegation to the library committee and urged them to 'deal with the matter'![22]

Fig 4: William Boyd-Carpenter, Bishop of Ripon (1841–1918). Photograph by Francis Henry Hart (no date) (*Reproduced by permission of National Portrait Gallery*).

This is precisely what the library committee did. They invited the Bishop of Ripon, the Rt Rev William Boyd-Carpenter (1841–1918), to come and address a fund-raising meeting on Friday 6 May 1904 (Fig 4). The occasion proved to be an outstanding success and his words were quoted by the local press for months afterwards and a considerable sum of money raised. Canon Whitefoord – on behalf of the committee – announced at this time that Thomas Hardy had agreed to come and open the new library (which he never did) and that a mere £408 was required. Canon Whitefoord suggested that the *SWJ* be asked to run a 'Shilling Subscription Fund,' as they had done for the Infirmary in 1897. The *SWJ*, however, were unobliging, claiming that 'if they had been asked in the first place, they might have opened a shilling subscription, but as the matter has been in hand for so long, they did not feel like adopting the suggestion now . . .'[23]

In August 1904, the Mayor (Charles Woodrow) announced that a total of £923–3–6d was in the bank or promised. Various town councillors had been asked in May 1904 to canvass the city wards for contributions towards the new library. The results were–to say the least–unspectacular. The Close contributed £2–16–0d; St Martin's Ward £3–17–8d ('very hard work' it was reported); St Mark's Ward £6–18–4d and St Thomas' Ward, '. . . for various reasons the parishioners seemed opposed to the scheme . . .', nothing. The City Librarian had received four donations (a guinea, 5s, 2s 6d and 12s). The canvassing in total raised less than £50, to which was added 25 guarantors (£1 each now, £1 when the foundation stone was laid and £2 when the library opened) and a further £50 for the building materials on the cleared library site in Chipper Lane.[24]

The following month, September 1904, the library at last had a stroke of luck. The town clerk advised that in 1891 the sum of £82 8s 5d had been collected by the Finance Committee towards the foundation of the 'Salisbury Scholarship' to send a child from the city to the Royal College of Music. The idea had allegedly originated with a visit to Salisbury in 1882 by HRH Prince Leopold of Belgium but no action had been taken other than to transfer the money to a deposit account at Pinckneys Bank. By 1904, however, such a scholarship would cost £3,000 and the Finance Committee therefore proposed that the money (£102 with interest) be used for the new library. The target had now been reached (a mere £20 unaccounted for) and building could proceed, with a collective sigh of relief from the library committee![25]

Alfred Champney Bothams (1861–1931)

The question of who designed the new library was already a 'hot topic' nationally, but Salisbury had decided not to have an architectural competition and to employ existing staff. Alfred C Bothams was the son of John Bothams (1822–1903). The Bothams had an architectural practice at 33 Chipper Lane and by 1904 Alfred Bothams was a part-time employee of Salisbury Town Council and paid the substantial salary of £325 per annum. At least 51 Carnegie libraries in the UK were designed by council employees–sometimes called 'City Architect' but more often 'Surveyor' or 'Engineer' and members of the Institution of Civil Engineers.[26]

Fig 5: 4 November 1904. Laying of Foundation for Carnegie Library in Chipper Lane (*Personal Collection*).

The foundation stone

On Friday 4 November 1904, the foundation stone was laid by the MP for Salisbury (now Sir Walter Palmer) and the retiring Mayor of Salisbury (Charles Woodrow). Sir Walter Palmer made some fulsome and pertinent remarks before passing the trowel to the Mayor who laid that stone inscribed 'This stone was laid on November 4th, 1904, by Charles John Woodrow, Mayor of Salisbury' (still to be seen in Chipper Lane). Carnegie's generosity was praised, Canon Whitefoord proposed a vote of thanks and–not missing a trick–a collection was taken which raised £20 for library funds matched by Sir Walter Palmer. In mid-November, the *SWJ* confirmed that the target had been reached.[27] (Fig 5, Fig 6 and Fig 7).

As work proceeded rapidly on the new library with the contractors, Messrs Harris of Dews Road, Salisbury, under the watchful eye of Alfred Bothams, excitement mounted in the city with letters to the press extolling the 'handsome new building' and 'very little to complain about in the way that the Salisbury Free Library is conducted.' In August 1905, it was announced that the new library would be officially opened on Monday 2 October 1905 at 3pm by Lord Avebury (formerly Sir John Lubbock MP) as a prominent supporter of the public library cause in Parliament. The Opening would be preceded by a Civic Lunch in the Council Chamber at 3s 6d per head 'exclusive of wine'.[28]

left Fig 6: Sir Walter Palmer (1858–1910), MP for Salisbury. Photograph by Benjamin Stone, August 1902 (*Reproduced by permission of National Portrait Gallery*).

above Fig 7: Foundation Stone (*Roy Bexon, 2023*).

The opening of the Chipper Lane Library

At 1.30pm on that day, following the civic lunch:

> . . . the Mayor and Corporation, with Lord Avebury, the City Magistrates, and other officials, marched in procession to the new Library, where they were received by Mr S R Atkins (the Chairman) and other members of the Library Committee. Mr Atkins asked Lord Avebury to open the doors of the Library, and handed his Lordship a silver key, which bore the following inscription: 'Presented to the Rt Hon the Lord Avebury, October 2nd, 1905, to open the new Public Library building'. Lord Avebury having opened the doors of the Library; the company entered the premises and inspected the new building . . .

The official party then went the short distance to the County Hall Vaudeville Theatre on the corner of Endless Street and Chipper Lane where the Mayor, James Dowden (1861–1916), praised the architect, the builders and 'a very excellent librarian' (Joseph Jones) before introducing Lord Avebury (Fig 8) who praised libraries for bringing 'universities to the homes of them all' and dismissed the cost noting that 'ignorance a deal more expensive than education' with the smallest additional burden placed on the rates. After further apt remarks, a vote of thanks was passed, and Andrew Carnegie praised by the Mayor for his great generosity. In true library tradition, the meeting closed with a collection towards furniture from those assembled.[29]

The library building

Alfred Bothams' designs for Salisbury Library—described architecturally as 'free Cotswold Tudor-Jacobean'—made the most of the limited grant and avoided many of the mistakes made by his contemporaries. 'Mr Carnegie, always a firm believer in home rule . . . left the matter of plans entirely to those managing the affair locally . . .' Salisbury received no criticism for Botham's designs—unlike Middlesborough which was 'excessively embellished' or Burton-on-Trent for spending too much money on football, according to James Bertram, Carnegie's Secretary. This 'home rule' principle precluded Carnegie (or Bertram) from any subsequent interference in the running of the local library. The library had a Bath stone 'gothic' front and large window to maximise the natural light. A pitch pine wood block floor was used throughout to minimise noise and it was entirely lit by electricity (unusual in 1905). It was heated by a low-pressure boiler hot water system using 'one general boiler'—fed by coke or coal—with convection to radiators throughout the building. Ventilation was by air inlets behind each radiator. The ground floor comprised an entrance hall, large Reading Room and Lending Library designed for 'Closed Access.' An 'attendants counter' provided supervision and a 'cement concrete staircase, with a wrought-iron ornamental balustrade' gave access to the first floor. Here there was a small 'Ladies Room' with toilet and the Reference Library 'simply fitted . . . with a counter and a small number of shelves . . .'[30] (Fig 9).

Fig 8: Sir John Lubbock (Lord Avebury) (1834–1913). Vanity Fair, 23 February 1878 by "Spy" (Sir Leslie Ward) (*Reproduced by permission of National Portrait Gallery*).

'The Star-Spangled Scotchman'

Many tributes to Andrew Carnegie had been paid prior to the opening of the new library. The town council were now faced with the problem of how to acknowledge this in a more tangible form. After some discussion, it was

Fig 9: Salisbury's Carnegie Library (1906–75). The original Library was to the right of the door with the Edwin Young Gallery added in 1915 (left of door) *http://claystreet.co.uk)*.

decided to offer him the Freedom of the City. This was one of the most cherished and jealously guarded honours that the Corporation could bestow. Past recipients were few and in recent years included Lord Nelson (1800), the Earl of Pembroke (1829) and William George Maton, the Salisbury-born physician to Princess (later Queen) Victoria (1827). Since the passing of the Honorary Freedom of the Borough Act in 1895 only Sir Edward Hulse MP had been thus honoured.[31] Andrew Carnegie genuinely enjoyed receiving the Freedom of any city and would eventually accrue 57 such honours (a record even unsurpassed by Winston Churchill) but Salisbury remained unaware that communities bestowing this honour were often presented with an extra cash award!

In October 1905 Carnegie replied 'I am highly honoured by the action the Town Council have taken . . . Pray convey to the Mayor and Town Council my thanks for their action and believe me, Very Truly Yours, Andrew

Carnegie.' There followed some difficulty in fixing the precise date with James Bertram, but Tuesday 6 June 1906 was finally agreed. The council agreed to spend a considerable sum (£33 12s 0d) on a 'casket . . .', to stage a civic lunch in his honour, followed by a public meeting at which the presentation would be made.[32] Seven local silversmiths were invited to compete for the 25-guinea casket with the winner being Messrs W Carter & Son of Minster Street. The 'engrossment'–on vellum and costing 7 guineas–was the work of Frank Highman of 23 Catherine Street.[33]

The great day arrived and Carnegie, accompanied by James Bertram, arrived at Salisbury Station on the 12.32pm train from London. They were met by the Mayor (Mr F Baker) and the Town Clerk (Francis Hodding) and driven straight to the library for a brief tour. Carnegie expressed himself as being 'very pleased' with what he saw and–after an equally brief tour of the Cathedral–was whisked off to lunch at the White Hart Hotel. Guests at this lunch included the Deputy Mayor (Mr Dowden), Alderman Haskins and Mr Pye-Smith–though the City Librarian, Joseph Jones, was conspicuously absent.

After lunch, the party moved to the Council Chamber and Carnegie was presented with the Freedom of the City. The casket had four panels with representations of the Cathedral, Poultry Cross, Library and a fourth inscribed 'City of New Sarum. Presented with the Freedom of the City to Andrew Carnegie, Esq., LLD, 6 June 1906' with Carnegie's initials in blue enamel on the lid and the Freedom scroll inside.[34]

In the speeches that followed it was unfortunate that Salisbury was unaware that by 1906 Carnegie had grown rather tired of philanthropy and sought 'a mission in life more challenging to his intellect and talents' turning to pacifism as the solution. On behalf of the town council, Samuel Atkins delivered the keynote speech almost entirely drawn from one of Carnegie's own books–'Round the World'–and quoted to an attentive audience the Carnegie dictum that 'There is only one source of true blessedness in wealth, and that comes from giving it away for things that tend to elevate our brothers and enable them to share it with us . . .'.[35] Carnegie appeared irritated at having a dictum quoted in which he no longer believed, and this led him to make a rather tactless and inconsequential reply. He remarked that he had received the freedom of 'six or seven boroughs in almost as many days' but noted that there was, of course, 'only one Salisbury.' Carnegie spoke of the fascination that the city had for him and a visit he made to it twenty years ago in the company of Matthew Arnold–'the most charming man.'[36] He then delivered his own version of American and British history and the Anglo-Saxon love of evolution as opposed to revolution–observing with great tactlessness that in such matters the British 'did not make a frontal attack as their troops foolishly did so often in South Africa.' This was an observation to an audience who had lost friends and relatives in the Boer Wars and in an area where since 1897 the War Office had been extensively acquiring chalk downland for military training. He thanked the Council for the casket–'felt humbled'–and after a few more remarks sat down to polite but unenthusiastic applause. A vote of thanks was proposed by William Hammick and three cheers given before Carnegie departed for a brief tour of the Salisbury and South Wiltshire Museum and the return to London on the late afternoon train.[37] The occasion was not a success and evidence for this can be seen in the refusal of the town council to participate in events during 1911 and 1913 to honour Andrew Carnegie.[38]

Conclusion

Carnegie's benefactions were to total $62 million over his lifetime. He died from bronchial pneumonia on 11 August 1919 at his home in Lenox, Massachusetts, and was buried in the Sleepy Hollow Cemetery in New York.

This is really the beginning of the story of Salisbury's Carnegie Library. The building continued to provide a valuable community service until 1975 when it was required to move to the former Market House, the present location. The former Carnegie Library in Chipper Lane was awarded Grade 2 listing in 1972 and is currently a commercial office premises.

This article is drawn from an unpublished thesis for London University: B M Little, 1981, *A History of Libraries in Salisbury, 1850–1922.*

Notes

1 Little, Monte, 2022, *Josiah Saunders and the Public Library Movement in Salisbury,* Sarum Chronicle, 22, 18–37. Four librarians cover this period: George Walter Atkinson (1890–94); Oliver Langmead (1894–1904); Joseph Jones (1904–07) and Albert E Butcher (1907–22). Oliver Langmead was appointed from Newport Public Library and lived at 5 St Marks Road, Salisbury. His professional abilities were challenged in 1895 over the second public library catalogue–'a hotch-potch of authors and titles' (*The Library,* 7, 192). In 1904, Langmead was held responsible for the committee decision to 'delete all news relative to horse racing . . .' with an ink roller. Quickly reversed after an outcry and pending local elections in November, Langmead resigned his post in September 1904 and quit librarianship.

2 *Salisbury & Winchester Journal (SWJ)* 9 August 1890; *Wiltshire & Swindon History Centre (WSHC)* Salisbury Council Minutes 1889–1904, G23/100/8. George Nodder (1832–

1903) was senior partner in a firm of solicitors; Mr S M Parker, a town councillor; Henry Brown (1832–1911) was the proprietor of the largest bookselling, commercial library, stationery and printing business in the City; Joseph William Lovibond was a chemist; Arthur Russell Malden (1850–1913) was a solicitor and Salisbury Cathedral Librarian; George Fullford (1843–1919) was a baker and grocer; Benjamin Whitefoord (1848–1910) was Principal of Salisbury Theological College; Joseph Berry Gullett (1849–1921) was a clerk and local Liberal Party agent; Edward Foulgar Pye-Smith (1853–1927) was a solicitor.

3 When Canon Whitefoord addressed the town council in October 1903 and described Salisbury Public Library in Endless Street as 'a premises which they would be quite ashamed to show a visitor', this was not just a figure of speech. The Library Association organised 'The Second International Library Conference' in London during July 1897 to mark Queen Victoria's Jubilee. On Saturday 17 July 1897, sixty distinguished delegates from the Conference arrived in Salisbury. They were given a civic lunch at the Guildhall, a tour of the City, tea with the Bishop and a visit to Stonehenge before returning to London on Monday on the 8.25am train. The one place that they did not see was Salisbury Library – very conveniently closed for "interior redecoration" at the time. *SWJ*, 24 July 1897.

4 *SWJ*, 31 January 1891.

5 *SWJ*, 11 November 1893. Donors included the Salisbury Co-operative Society – for further reading on this important movement: Kelly, Thomas, 1977, *History of Public Libraries in Great Britain, 1845–1977*, Library Association, 2nd edition.

6 *SWJ*, 19 November 1892; Little, 2022, 26–27. The Local Government Act of 1888 had created County Councils in England and one of the first tasks of Wiltshire County Council was to implement the Technical Instruction Act of 1889 which enabled the local authority to levy a rate of 1d in the £ to provide technical education. It is not clear why the indebtedness of the Technical Education Building remained unknown until August/September 1903.

7 *SWJ*, 5 January 1895. Other suggested sites (in order of inclusion) *SWJ*, 28 February 1903; *SWJ*, 7 March 1903; *SWJ*, 11 December 1890; *Salisbury Times* (*ST*), 26 August 1960 *and* 2 September 1960; *SWJ*, 11 March 1911; *SWJ*, 20 March 1897; *SWJ*, 6 March 1897; *SWJ*, 25 June 1904; *SWJ*, 11 July 1903 and many, many, more!

8 The Local Government Board (LGB) was the result of a 'Sanitary Commission' Report from 1868–71. This advocated an effective system of central control over local government and led to the Local Government Board Act of 1871, steered through Parliament by a former Salisbury solicitor, Sir John Lambert (1815–92), who became the LGB's first Permanent Secretary.

9 *SWJ*, 3 April 1897. John Leith Veitch was editor of the *SWJ* from 1895–1904. He was described as a young Scot 'of retiring disposition' who authored novels, articles, and short stories under the pseudonym of 'Leith Derwent.' *SWJ*, 13 March 1897 includes a strong leader attacking the principles of 'public libraries': 'All over England people may differ on the claims of free libraries to public support, and Salisbury is no exception to the rule . . . Here, as elsewhere, the free readers of novels and newspapers are in the majority . . . No doubt the Salisbury Free Library has done good work in the past and may do more in the future; but we are afraid that the superabundant consumption of light literature which characterises it, in common

with other similar institutions, will be a sore point with a good many people and may hinder them from subscribing to a fund for providing a new building . . .'.

10 *SWJ*, 15 November 1902.

11 *SWJ*, 31 December 1903; *SWJ*, 17 September 1904; *SWJ*, 5 November 1904. *WHSC*, Librarian: Reports to Committee 1893–1958, G23/892/1.

12 *SWJ*, 21 February 1903.

13 *SWJ*, 28 February 1903. Under the editorship of Mr W S Martin (d. October 1880) the policy of the Salisbury Journal towards rate-supported libraries changed from wholehearted support to one of "cautious antipathy" under Mr C Osborne (editor 1880–95) and John Leith Veitch (see above). The change was out of character for the newspaper which, for example, was courageous in defending the rights of working men to drink in a public house on a Sunday and supporting the 'Half-Day Closing Association' which sought to improve conditions in the retail trade, despite the tide of influential public opinion being strongly against both causes. The Journal's antipathy to the free library movement was the cause of many local difficulties, not the least of which was the constraining effect it had on Salisbury MP (1880–85) and the greatest library philanthropist in England (after Carnegie), John Passmore Edwards. Further reading: *Little.* Sarum Chronicle, 22, 18–37.

14 *SWJ*, 28 *February 1903.*

15 *SWJ*, 19 September 1902; *Western Gazette*, Langmead & Evans Directory of Salisbury, 1897–98.

16 *SWJ*, 19 September 1903.

17 Wall, Joseph Frazier, 1970, *Andrew Carnegie*, Oxford University Press (first edition) with a second edition, 1989, University of Pittsburgh Press. All references relate to the first edition unless otherwise stated. Skibo Castle remained in the Carnegie Family until 1982 and is now a very smart, members-only, resort hotel–the 'Carnegie Club'–extensively used by 'A List' celebrities. For example, in December 2000 Madonna's wedding to Director, Guy Ritchie, was held there.

18 Shaw, George Bernard, 1902, preface to *Man & Superman.*

19 *SWJ*, 26 September 1903.

20 Smith, Anne Judith, 1974, *Carnegie Library Buildings in Great Britain: An Account, Evaluation and Survey*, unpublished thesis for the Library Association, 29–32, 221, 84.

21 Smith, 32 notes an article appearing in a Twickenham newspaper in 1903 criticising delays in receiving a grant promised for their library. Immediately afterwards, the Chairman of Twickenham Library Committee received a letter from Carnegie asking for details and the grant was paid within two weeks.

22 *SWJ*, 31 October 1903.

23 *SWJ*, 7 May 1904.

24 *SWJ*, 13 August 1904.

25 *WSHC*, G23/100/8; *SWJ*, 3 September 1904. This is something of a mystery–there is a town council reference to 'HRH Prince Leopold of Belgium' visiting Salisbury in 1882. King Leopold II, King of Belgium, had only one son–the Duke of Brabant–who died of pneumonia in January 1869, aged 10. All his other children were girls: Louise, Stephanie, and Clementine.

26 Library Association Record, April 1905, and May 1905, 7, Adams, M B, *Public Libraries, their Buildings and Equipment: A Plea for State Aid*, 166–177 (April) and 220–

226 (May). 'Bothams, Brown & Dixon' flourished in Chipper Lane until the late 20th century.

27 Sir Walter Palmer (1858–1910) was the son of the founder of "Huntley & Palmer Biscuits" and represented Salisbury from 1900–06. Created baronet by Edward VII in 1904 (*SWJ*, 25 June 1904). Lost his seat by 41 votes in 1906.

28 *SWJ*, 12 August 1905; *SWJ*, 25 September 1905 with tickets for the lunch on sale from Messrs Brown & Co, Booksellers.

29 *SWJ*, 7 October 1905; *SWJ*, 7 October 1905. The speech was apt, light, and accomplished. Lord Avebury declared that giving prizes to children and opening public libraries were "the two most pleasant ceremonies which public men are called upon to fulfil." Joseph Jones was librarian of Salisbury from 1904–07. He was recruited from Cardiff Public Library, organised the move to Chipper Lane and Carnegie's visit in 1906. In February 1907, he became the first librarian of Torquay Public Library.

30 *SWJ*, 5 November 1904; *SWJ*, 7 October 1905 for design details. *A Manual of the Public Benefactions of Andrew Carnegie*, 1919, Carnegie Endowment for International Peace, 298.

31 *SWJ*, 11 November 1905. Sir Edward Hulse (1859–1903) was MP for Salisbury from 1886–97 and was a late 'convert' to the public library cause.

32 *SWJ*, 7 April 1906; *SWJ*, 5 May 1906. The Finance Committee established the basic details of Carnegie's visit on 28 May 1906 with only the Mayor and the Town Clerk meeting him at Salisbury Station, all members Council to wear their civic robes for the public meeting and so forth (*WSHC*, Salisbury Town Council: Finance Committee Minutes 1906–08, G23/110/.8)

33 Seven local silversmiths were invited to tender for the 25-guinea casket: Mr E A Carse; Messrs Carter & Sons; Messrs Gator & Sons; Messrs J Macklin & Son; Mr J S Rambridge; Mr J Rumbold and Mr T Sly. William and his son, Frank Highman were responsible for most of the civic presentation documents throughout this period.

34 *SWJ*, 9 June 1906.

35 Wall, 1970, 881 & 887. 'Round the World' (1884) was based on a trip by Carnegie and his friend, John Vandervort, between October 1878 and May 1879 (http//www.goodreads.com, accessed, 3 July 2023).

36 Carnegie visited Salisbury in 1884 as part of a six-week coaching trip around Britain. His party consisted of William Black, an author who coined the phrase 'Star-Spangled Scotchman' (Carnegie took great pride in the title); Edwin A Abbey, US painter and illustrator; Matthew Arnold, poet, with his wife and daughter; the son and daughter of Prime Minister William Ewart Gladstone and Carnegie's favourite radical politician, Samuel Storey, MP for Newcastle on Tyne. Wall, Joseph Frazier, 1989, *Andrew Carnegie,* Oxford University Press (second edition), University of Pittsburgh Press, 435–436.

37 *SWJ*, 9 June 1906. Carnegie was strongly opposed to both American imperialism and British colonialism. He joined the American Anti-Imperialist League in 1898 and opposed the US acquisition of Puerto Rico, the Philippines, Guam, and Cuba. In 1910, he founded the 'Carnegie Endowment for International Peace' and in 1914, the 'Church Peace Union' (now the 'Carnegie Council for Ethics in International Affairs (CEIP)') and was heartbroken at the failure of his efforts over the Treaty of Versailles in 1919. Further reading–CEIP, 1919, *A Manual of the Public Benefactions of Andrew*

Carnegie, CEIP, Washington, 298.

38 *SWJ,* 29 March 1913. The events were in Dunfermline (1911) and London (1913). Councillor Josiah Saunders criticised Salisbury Town Council over the whole event because of what Andrew Carnegie represented – a capitalist of the most pronounced kind – and would not have accepted the new library (*SWJ, 28 October 1905*). In a postscript to the event, His Majesty's Inland Revenue in 1908 pointed out that the stamp duty had not been paid on Carnegie's Freedom of the City and that £3 was owing but agreed to waive the fine on this omission!

A History of Salisbury Cathedral in 27 Cushion Designs

Beatrice King

Introduction

We are so used to finding out about our history through words, pictures and online sources that other ways of discovering the past can easily be overlooked. Few visitors to the Morning Chapel of Salisbury Cathedral pause to give even a cursory glance at another source of information – 22 embroidered seat cushions which are part of an original design scheme of 27 initially conceived in the run up to the 700th anniversary of the completion and consecration of Salisbury Cathedral in 1958. There are 15 of these cushions laid out in the right-hand chapel, St Catherine's (Fig 1) and seven in the left-hand chapel, St Martin's (Fig 2). Although the seven cushions in St Martin's Chapel are of a later creation,

Fig 1: St Catherine's Chapel showing the first group of cushions worked in the 1950s (*Roy Bexon, 2023).*

Fig 2: St Martin's Chapel showing the second group of cushions worked in the 1970s (*Roy Bexon, 2023*).

they are easily recognisable as part of the set. The whereabouts of the remaining five are unknown at the time of writing.

In contrast to ecclesiastical embroidery, which had a particularly English expression as *opus anglicanum* and was famous throughout the Western mediaeval world, ecclesiastical tapestry, the art of the needlepoint working of cushions and kneelers, is a relatively modern concept. According to Lucy Judd the first large-scale ecclesiastical tapestry scheme in England in modern times was in the Winchester Diocese in 1931 under the leadership of Louisa Pesel.[1] In 1937 the Salisbury Cathedral Embroiderers' Guild (interestingly no mention of tapestry in the name of this group) was founded, with a view to furnish embroidered cushions and stools for the Quire and Trinity Chapel as the first part of a project which would eventually include seat cushions for the Morning Chapel. The leaders of this group were Florence Alcock[2], Mrs Daniell-Bainbridge and Annie Morris.

After the death of Florence Alcock in 1951 a new committee of embroiderers took over and began to plan, design, and execute a project for Morning Chapel seat cushions illustrating the origins and history of the cathedral. The two leading lights in this group were the co-ordinator and moving spirit, Lady Jeane Petherick (née Playdell-Bouverie) (Fig 3) and Monica Sanctuary, the designer of the cushions.

Lady Jeane Petherick's (1892–1976) father was the 6th Earl of Radnor.[3] Her grandmother the gifted Helen (1846–1929), who was married to the 5th Earl, was both musician and artist. In 1894 Helen commissioned her close friend Hubert Parry, who had married into the Herbert family of Wilton House, to write the 'Lady Radnor's Suite' and she also helped design the stained-glass window in the cathedral's North Quire Aisle as a memorial to her husband. The Earls of Radnor have left their mark on the cathedral from the 1770s. The 2nd Earl in particular was both a generous donor and influential advisor in the decisions of Bishop Shute Barrington and James Wyatt when they reordered the cathedral in the 1790s. In 1778/9 the Earl was permitted to move parts of the now demolished Hungerford chantry chapel to its present position in the chancel by claiming descent from the Hungerfords through his wife, and this remains the Hungerford/Radnor pew to this day. He also donated the Moses window high above the East window in 1781.[4] This is a rare surviving example of Georgian painted glass executed by James Pearson and even Wyatt did not dare remove it. In 1914 Lady Jeane married Major George Gerald Petherick and moved to Winchester. Here she became involved in the Winchester Cathedral embroidery work: she had been trained from a young age by Mrs Newall of Fisherton de la Mere.[5] Between 1938 and 1942 Lady Jeane was Chief Commandant of the Auxiliary Territorial Service (ATS).[6] She brought back some of the needlework ideas she had picked up in Winchester when she moved to Salisbury in 1947 after the death of her husband.

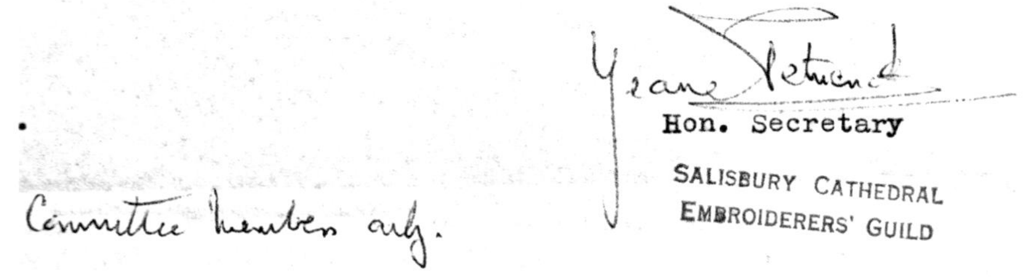
Annual General Meeting will be held at 4.15. It is hoped that & Associates of the Guild will be able to come.

Jeane Petherick
Hon. Secretary

SALISBURY CATHEDRAL
EMBROIDERERS' GUILD

Committee member only.

Fig 3: Lady Jeane Petherick's signature taken from documents in Salisbury Cathedral Archive (*Roy Bexon, 2023*).

The designer of the Morning Chapel seat cushions, Monica Sanctuary (1886–1980), was born in Fordington, Dorset in 1886.[7] The family moved to Salisbury in 1898 when Monica's father Charles Lloyd Sanctuary became Rector of St Thomas's Church. By the time of the 1911 Census[8] she was a trained nurse in the Sussex County General Hospital in Brighton. Between 1915 and 1920 the hospital was taken over by the War Office and used to accommodate sick and wounded Indian soldiers. In 1916 Monica's brother, Captain Charles Lloyd Sanctuary, died of wounds received after the capture of Thieval, aged 28 years. A copper plaque near the south porch door in St Thomas' Church, Salisbury, commemorates him. The description of Monica Sanctuary as a masseuse in Judd[9] sounds somewhat surprising but can be explained. At the turn of the 20th century, medical massage and electrical therapy were an important part of a nurse's training as there were relatively few medical treatments available then. To address the issue of the questionable implications of the term 'masseuse' the Society of Massage and Medical Gymnasts was founded in 1894, incorporated in 1900 and granted a royal charter in 1920. Monica qualified in 1916 and we can trace her membership of the Society between 1916 and 1946 through the Physiotherapy and Masseuse Registers 1895–1980.[10] In 1934 the Society became known as the Chartered Society of Physiotherapists and the terms 'masseuse' and 'medical gymnasts' were dropped from the title to reflect the broader range of skills now being practised. Monica also spent a short time as a Red Cross Volunteer in 1918.[11] In the 1920s Monica moved to Sherborne where she continued to practise professionally but also developed her growing interest in art. She joined the Sherborne Arts Club and, in this context, she is mentioned throughout the 1930s and 1940s in the *Western Gazette.* In the late 1940s she moved back to Salisbury and enrolled in an arts course at Salisbury College of Art.

The first group of Morning Chapel cushions was made in the 1950s, and from the themes of some of them (*eg* Charter Fair 1958) it appears that they were designed with the 700th anniversary of the consecration of the Salisbury Cathedral in 1958 in mind. Five of the best embroiderers were asked to work the central medallions which depicted the main design on each cushion and 15 of the 27 cushions were completed and made up between March 1957 and April 1959.[12] The scheme was abruptly halted in 1959 and the group disbanded following an unspecified disagreement with the cathedral dignitaries.[13]

During the 1970s Dean Fenton Morley and his wife Marjorie decided to reinstate the work on the design scheme[14] and a further group of cushions was made. We only have records of how the first group of cushions was made, and it seems that those in this second later group were made in a similar way. The central medallions were made by the five most skilled embroiderers in very fine needlepoint. This was not only technically difficult as the artwork of the designs made no concessions to the challenges of representing the design in needlepoint, but the fine scale of the work was very challenging to the eyes. Several records of the work of individual embroiderers are marked as being unable to continue due to failing health and eyesight. The medallions themselves were worked on 20 threads to the inch Glamis linen and when completed were applied to coarser Winchester canvas and blue borders worked round them in varieties of cross stitch using crewel wools. The golden 'Winchester strapwork' designs surrounding the medallions were based on designs by Louisa Pesel (1870–1947), leader of the Winchester Embroiderers Group, a great friend of Lady Jeane Petherick and one of the leading embroiderers of her generation. The stone benches around the edges of the right-hand chapel, St Catherine's (then called the Baptistry), were to be covered with the worked seat cushions each measuring about 24ins x 14ins so laid out as to provide a continuous band of colour on either side.[15] When completed the cushions were professionally made up by Southons of Salisbury.[16]

How do the cushions depict the history of Salisbury Cathedral?

The list (Fig 4) as conceived by Monica Sanctuary is broadly accurate, with only a few errors or ambiguities though some details need updating due to new information or the passage of 70 years since the cushions were designed.

The origins of the Salisbury Diocese

The complex origins of the Salisbury Diocese can be dated from the time of St Birinus (cushion 1), who re-established Christianity in Wessex in the seventh century, until the founding of the Diocese of Sarum (Salisbury) in 1058. St Aldhelm (c.639–709 AD) is perhaps better known than Birinus, as he became the first Bishop of Sherborne (cushion 2). By the tenth century there were also Bishops of Ramsbury, the most well-known being Odo, Siric and Aelfric (cushion 3), all with local connections (Fig 5).

In 1058 the Diocese of Salisbury was finally

Design scheme for the 27 historic cushions in Salisbury Cathedral

Cushions marked * were either never worked or are now lost

1. St Birinus c.600-650AD
2. St Aldhelm c.639-709AD
3. Bishops Odo, Siric and Aelfric of Ramsbury
4. St Osmund, d. 1099
5. Bishop Richard Poore, bishop 1217-28
6. Elias of Dereham, d.1246
7. St Edmund of Abingdon c.1174-1240
8. Mason, Carpenters, Smiths and Glaziers
9. Magna Carta 1215
10. Ela, Countess of Salisbury 1187-1261
11. Henry III 1207-72
12. Salisbury Fair
13. * Friars
14. Nicholas of Ely and Richard of Farleigh, Master Masons
15. Edward III 1312-1377
16. Bishop Richard Beauchamp c.1421-81
17. Cardinal Bishop Campeggio, bishop 1524-35
18. Bishop John Jewel 1522-71
19. George Herbert, Rector of Bemerton 1630-33
20. * Isaac Walton 1651-1719
21. Bishop Seth Ward 1617-1689
22. * Music at the cathedral
23. Sir Christopher Wren1632-1723
24. * Bishop Wordsworth, 1843 -1911
25. Friends of the Cathedral
26. The Army
27. * The Church Overseas

Fig 4: The original list of cushions (*Roy Bexon, 2023*).

Fig 5: Cushion 3 Bishops Odo, Siric and Aelfric (*Roy Bexon, 2023*).

Fig 6: Cushion 10 Ela Countess of Salisbury (*Roy Bexon, 2023*).

constituted by uniting Sherborne and Ramsbury bishoprics. The new diocese was initially based at Sherborne but after the Norman Conquest the seat of the diocese moved to what became known as Old Sarum in 1075 under the leadership of Bishop Herman, the first bishop of the newly formed diocese, and the construction of a stone cathedral began in 1078.

The cathedral at Old Sarum and the founding of the cathedral at New Sarum

This period of the story of the diocese is better documented. The saintly Bishop Osmund (bishop 1078–99) (cushion 4) saw the completion of the first cathedral in 1092. Osmund was a man of learning; he revised the old service books and founded the cathedral library and the song school. In recognition of this, his cushion depicts a mitre, a page of music, Old Sarum Cathedral and books from his library. However, over time it was realised that conditions were increasingly difficult at the cathedral on Old Sarum; relations between cathedral and castle had broken down, water was scarce, the winds strong and the whiteness of the chalk blinding. So, during Bishop Poore's (cushion 5) time a decision was made to move the cathedral to a more congenial spot two miles away then called Myrfield. Permission was sought in 1217 from the Pope to move the cathedral and given in 1218.[17] The foundation stones were laid in 1220. Some of the key players in the building of the new cathedral were Elias of Dereham (cushion 6), and the cathedral's treasurer Edmund Rich (1222–33) who was canonised in 1246 (cushion 7). The Church of St Edmund (1269) in Salisbury (now the Arts Centre) was dedicated to him (cushion 7). The workers who physically built the cathedral, the masons, carpenters, smiths and glaziers are remembered by the masons' marks cushion (cushion 8). The master masons Nicholas of Ely, who worked alongside Elias of Dereham, and Richard of Farleigh are also celebrated (cushion 14). Ela, Countess of Salisbury (cushion 10) laid one of the Cathedral's foundation stones in 1220 (Fig 6). She was one of the most remarkable women of her time and she is the only woman remembered in these cushions. Among Salisbury Cathedral's most treasured possessions, one of four surviving original copies of the 1215 Magna Carta originally received at the Old Sarum cathedral, is given a cushion to itself (cushion 9) (Figs 7 and 8).

Cathedral and city in the Middle Ages

The city of New Sarum quickly developed alongside the new cathedral and during the Middle Ages grew as Salisbury's prosperity increased. Its position as a leading town of the area was enhanced by Henry III (cushion 11) granting a charter in 1227 conferring borough status on the city and permission to hold a weekly, later twice weekly, market[18] (Fig 9). The right to hold a fair in October was granted in 1270 and the fair held in 1958 is depicted in cushion 12 (Fig

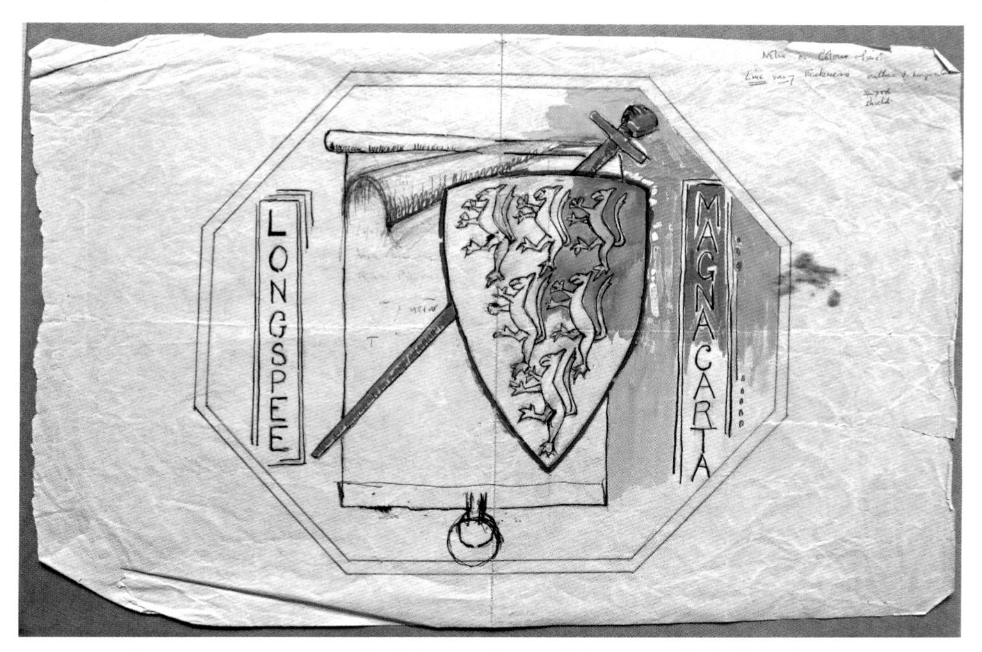

Fig 7: Cushion 9 Magna Carta, draft design from Salisbury Cathedral Archive (*Roy Bexon, 2023*).

Fig 8: Cushion 9 Magna Carta, as worked (*Roy Bexon, 2023*).

Fig 9: Cushion 11 1227 Charter granted by King Henry III (*Roy Bexon, 2023*).

Fig 10: Cushion 12 Salisbury's Charter Fair in 1958 (*Roy Bexon, 2023*).

Fig 11: Cushion 18, Bishop John Jewel (*Roy Bexon, 2023*).

10). In 1327 Edward III (cushion 15) gave the bishop permission to build a stone wall round the Close and to use some of the stone from the abandoned cathedral at Old Sarum. Apart from the cathedral and its clergy there were other religious institutions and communities living in Salisbury. Prominent among these were the Franciscans and Dominicans, remembered in a cushion either never worked or now lost (cushion 13). Notable bishops of the fifteenth century include Richard Beauchamp whose cushion (cushion 16) reminds us of his work in improving the building and finally achieving the canonisation of St Osmund in 1457.

The cathedral in the sixteenth century

The sixteenth century was a time of turbulence nationally and Salisbury was no exception. Cardinal Lorenzo Campeggio's (bishop 1524–35) cushion (number 17) commemorates a bishop who is remembered for two things – he never once visited his diocese and he opposed Henry VIII's divorce from Katherine of Aragon. We are reminded of happier times in celebrating Bishop John Jewel (cushion 18) who had been in exile but returned from abroad when Queen Elizabeth I came to the throne (Fig 11). His great theological work *An Apology for the Church of England*[19] helped to lay the foundations of, and give the theological basis for, a 'reasonable Protestantism' which has formed the basis for Anglican theology to this day.

The seventeenth century

Events in the seventeenth century are celebrated in cushions 19–23. Firstly, there is George Herbert (cushion 19), Rector of Bemerton, near Salisbury from 1630 to 1633. Twice weekly he walked across the meadows to the cathedral where he worshipped and played music with his friends. He was one of the greatest poets of his time. Seth Ward, bishop from 1671 to 1689, did much to repair and re-establish the cathedral administration and services following the Civil War and end of the Commonwealth. His interest in science and astronomy is referenced in his cushion (cushion 21). In 1688 Bishop Seth Ward invited his friend Sir Christopher Wren (cushion 23) to undertake a structural survey of the cathedral (Figs 12 and 13). Canon Isaac Walton (1651–1719), the son of the writer of the same name (but spelt Izaak), is remembered in cushion 20, now lost. The last cushion (number 22) in this group known to have been worked

Fig 12: Cushion 21, Bishop Seth Ward (*Roy Bexon, 2023*).

Fig 13: Cushion 23, Sir Christopher Wren (*Roy Bexon, 2023*).

but is now also lost. It celebrated the musical tradition in the cathedral, which dates back to St Osmund himself and continues to this day.

The cathedral in modern times

It would appear, if just relying on the cushions to tell the tale, that nothing at all happened between the life and times of Sir Christopher Wren (cushion 23) and cushion 24 commemorating Bishop John Wordsworth, who died in 1911. Bishop Wordsworth's cushion was probably never worked, though he made a significant contribution to the life of the cathedral in several fields, notably theology and education.

An important cushion is number 25 which celebrates the contribution that supporters of the cathedral have made over the centuries. In the late 14th century a Confraternity of the Benefactors of the Cathedral was formed[20]. Membership was taken very seriously, with a special service of admittance and sharing in cathedral prayers. The original design for this cushion had five crests representing: John of Gaunt, his son John Beaufort, Keith Wedgewood the cathedral succentor who contributed much to cathedral life in the mid-twentieth century, the co-ordinator of the cushion scheme Lady Jeane Petherick and the designer Monica Sanctuary.[21] The cushion as finally worked omitted the crest of John Beaufort.

Given Salisbury's long-standing links with the military, a cushion commemorating this link would be expected, and indeed this is the case with cushion number 26 called The Army. When the scheme was drawn up, the Wiltshire Regiment (the Duke of Edinburgh's) crest was depicted on the cushion although now several regiments have been amalgamated to form The Rifles. The final design of the series called at the time The Church Overseas (cushion 27) was designed very much with the 700th anniversary celebrations of 1958 in mind. The cushion theme was not intended to represent the work of the wider Church overseas but rather churches in overseas towns and cities also called Salisbury such as Salisbury in South Australia. This cushion was also probably never worked or has been lost.

Conclusion

Why are these cushions important in the life of the cathedral and why go to the trouble of researching their story? Firstly, they are beautifully made and provide a welcome spot of colour in the cathedral. They acknowledge the contribution of a group of craftspeople often overlooked but none the less important. Secondly, there are several puzzles connected with them. Why 27 cushions? They clearly would not all fit in their intended places and although there is no evidence for such a discussion, disagreement about where they should go could be the reason why the group disbanded before the set was completed. Thirdly, as a group they do not flow as a narrative story of the cathedral; at best they provide an adjunct to it. Why was Bishop Campeggio (bishop 1524–35) included when he did not visit Salisbury even once? Why was there such a long gap between the cushion of Isaac Walton (1651–1719) and that of Bishop John Wordsworth (1843–1911). Did nothing happen in the life of the cathedral between these dates? Of course not. For example, we need only consider the controversial but important reordering of James Wyatt in the 1790s, and the campaigning work by Thomas Burgess (bishop 1825–37) on the anti-slavery debate. There is the cathedral's contribution to higher education in the nineteenth century, by founding the pioneering teacher training college in 1841 and the theological college 20 years later.

The story told by these cushions draws attention to the fact that history can never be purely objective and will always reflect the context and viewpoint of the historian.[22] The concerns and interests of the 1950s may not be the same as what we would consider important today. Indeed, seventy years have passed since the cushions were designed, in which time the life of the cathedral has moved on. It has been a pioneer in being the first to include girls in the cathedral choir (1991), appointed the first female Dean to an English medieval cathedral (June Osborne in 2004) and was the first to achieve a Gold Eco-Church Award in 2021. It has installed inspiring modern art, for example the Prisoner of Conscience Window (Gabriel Loire 1980) at the East End, the 'Walking Madonna' statue (Elizabeth Frink 1981) in the Close and the Font (William Pye 2008). There are hundreds of volunteers who welcome visitors and keep the cathedral running smoothly. In 2021 it became a much-appreciated Covid-19 vaccination centre. All these have encouraged people to visit, to worship, to appreciate the beauty or to find peace and solace in one of the most glorious medieval cathedrals.

Bibliography

Naish, Emily and Elliott, John (eds), 2020, *Salisbury Cathedral: 800 Years of People and Place,* Sarum Studies 7, Sarum Chronicle.

Tatton-Brown, Tim and Crook, John, 2009, *Salisbury Cathedral, the Making of a Medieval Masterpiece,* Scala Publishers, London.

Notes

1 Judd, Lucy & Sanctuary, Monica, undated but c.1970s, *Embroidery in Salisbury Cathedral, Misericordia Updated,* Friends of Salisbury Cathedral, 2–3.
2 Not the wife of the well-known organist Walter Alcock (1861–1947).
3 https://www.thepeerage.com/p3435, accessed 5 October 2022.
4 Brown, Sarah, 1999, *Sumptuous and Richly Adorn'd— The decoration of Salisbury Cathedral,* HMSO, 41–3.
5 Judd, Lucy, 1980, *Embroideries in Salisbury Cathedral,* Friends of Salisbury Cathedral, 6.
6 https://www.thepeerage.com/p3435, accessed 5 October 2022.
7 General Register Office (GRO), reference 1886 D Quarter in DORCHESTER Vol 05A p. 317.
8 GRO, reference 1911/RG14/05119/0091.
9 Judd, 1980, 6.
10 https://www.ancestry.com.UK, 'Physiotherapy and Masseuse Registers 1895–1980', accessed October 2022.
11 https://www.search.findmypast/search-world-Records/british-army-british-red-cross-society-volunteers-1914-1918, accessed October 2022.
12 Salisbury Cathedral Archive, Card Index of Embroiderers' Work, VL/EG/2/5.
13 Judd & Sanctuary, 6.
14 Judd & Sanctuary, 7.
15 Judd, 1980.
16 Judd & Sanctuary, 6 & 8.
17 Tatton-Brown, Tim and Crook, John 2009, *Salisbury Cathedral: The Making of a Masterpiece,* Scala Publishers, London, 21.

18 Chandler, John, 1983, *Endless Street: a History of Salisbury and its People,* Hobnob Press, Gloucester, 26, 95 & 158.
19 Jewel, John, 1562, reprinted 2020, *An Apology for the Church of England,* Davenant Press, London.
20 Wordsworth, John, 1901, *Processions and Ceremonies of the Cathedral Church of Salisbury,* Cambridge University Press, Cambridge, 146.
21 Judd & Sanctuary, 22.
22 This debate is currently very important in the context of the part played by present-day Ukraine in the founding of Russia. For a fascinating discussion on the topic see Figes, Orlando, 2022, *The Story of Russia,* Bloomsbury Publishing, London, Introduction & Chapter 1.

The 1923 General Election in the Salisbury Division

Jane Howells

One hundred years ago, on 6 December 1923, voters in the United Kingdom went to the polls for the second of three general elections held in consecutive years. The result was the last time the Salisbury constituency had a member of parliament who was not a Conservative.[1]

The years following the coalition landslide in 1918 were a period of increasing difficulty for the Prime Minister David Lloyd George. Both major parties were divided between those supporting the coalition, and separate factions of Conservatives under Bonar Law and Austen Chamberlain, and Liberals led by H H Asquith. Domestic and international circumstances, as well as party issues, forced Lloyd George's resignation in October 1922. The election that followed in November 1922 resulted in a clear Conservative majority. Andrew Bonar Law held the office of Prime Minister for only six months. His health deteriorated and he was succeeded by Stanley Baldwin in May 1923.

There was no need for an immediate election, but Baldwin argued that protectionist policies should be introduced to support home industries and therefore to help relieve unemployment, and the electorate should be consulted over this significant change.[2]

By modern standards the election timetable was tight. Parliament was dissolved on 16 November, three days after the election had been announced. Nominations closed on 26 November, and polling day was 6 December. After a Christmas and New Year break, Parliament would then assemble on 8 January 1924.

In the Salisbury Division constituency the sitting MP was Hugh Morrison (1868–1931) (Fig 1), who had held the seat since 1918. Morrison was a very wealthy landowner who lived at Fonthill, some 15 miles west of the city.

Fig 1: Hugh Morrison
(*reproduced by permission of Lord Margadale and the Trustees of the Fonthill Estate*).

Speaking at Britford in early November 1923 he predicted 'unless the situation in foreign affairs took a graver turn, there might be an appeal to the country within the next few weeks'.[3]

Once the election was confirmed, for a while it was thought Morrison would be returned unopposed. Ernest Brown who had stood for the Liberals in the previous two elections was fighting a safer seat in Rugby.[4] However, the Salisbury Liberal Party found a candidate in Hugh Fletcher Moulton (1876–1962) (Fig 2). It is unclear from the local newspapers how this came about; the *Salisbury and Winchester Journal* (*SWJ*) commented 'a Liberal candidate appeared and was unanimously adopted . . . there was no other choice'.[5] The *Salisbury Times* (*ST*) gave a brief biography:

> Major Fletcher Moulton is a barrister of the Middle Temple. He was educated at Eton and King's College Cambridge . . . He served in the Artillery for three years in France during the war, and won the Military Cross. He is a prolific writer on legal and other subjects, and since the Armistice has published several books, including a life of his father and a volume on the Peace Treaty. For six years he served on the London Education committee.[6]

In 1902 he had married Isabel Tredwell Houghton, who was actively involved in his campaign in Salisbury.

At one point the *SWJ* speculated that the city might see a three-cornered fight for the first time, but then reported that Labour had decided not to put up a candidate 'owing to lack of funds'. The local Labour Party was growing and the women's section was busy with a variety of activities. Annie Townley, appointed in 1920 as women's organiser for the south-west, wrote about what her work involved, describing the vast distances she covered and the number of people she met. She visited Salisbury several times, for example in April 1923 when she gave an address on organisation.[7] However, it was not until the following year that the local electorate first had the option of voting Labour.

Nomination papers for the candidates were published in the local newspapers, so the names of those who had supported each party in this way were made public. Unsurprisingly, in both cases, officials of the local party associations seem to have begun the process.[8]

The first of 57 papers for Hugh Morrison was proposed by George Nicholson, chairman of the Salisbury Division Unionist Association, and seconded by John Clark. Amongst the eight assenters were Firmin Bradbeer of the Haunch of Venison,[9] Harry Carpenter, Precentor and Archdeacon of Sarum[10] and Francis Wort, builder. The proposer of the second paper was Beatrice Countess of Pembroke;[11] others named there included Sir Cosmo

Fig 2: Hugh Fletcher Moulton, photograph Bassano Ltd, 15 January 1924, (*reproduced with permission ©National Portrait Gallery, London*).

Gordon Antrobus, of Amesbury Abbey, and Henry Clarke JP of Brigmerston House. As discussed elsewhere,[12] nominators were often grouped by family, work and particularly location, a likely result of a combination of 'networks' and the need to secure the nominations in less than two weeks. A few examples will suffice: names on paper 31 for Morrison all came from Harnham, including neighbours on Harnham Road, licensees at both the Rose & Crown, and the Three Crowns, and Agnes and Eleanor Warre of Parsonage Farm.[13] Paper 32 came from Laverstock, signed by, amongst others, James and Jessie Keevil of Manor Farm, Jessie Young at The Hall, and John and Lilian Adlam who ran the carpenter's shop.[14]

A total of 28 nomination papers were submitted for Hugh Fletcher Moulton. Chairman of the Salisbury Division Liberal Association (SDLA) was the first proposer, John Catterell Hudson. He lived at Times House on Dews Road and would be mayor of Salisbury 1926–7. Several residents of Devizes Road were also on that list, Henry and Sarah Dart, shopkeeper Lilian Allen, and three Bartletts. Also included was Lavinia Hardy, geography lecturer at the Training College, and an originator of The Courts, a pioneering social housing scheme whose flats can still be seen on the corner of Ashley Road and Coldharbour Lane. Rev Geoffry Hill of Harnham proposed the second paper, followed by Gideon Hancock, vice-chairman of the SDLA (who would be mayor 1932–33). Eliza Robertson Hudson, wife of the chairman, was an assentor. For the Liberals as well as Conservatives, some papers came from a specific place, number 10 from Dinton, numbers 11 and 12 from Wilton, 13 from Bemerton, 14 Porton and 15 Amesbury.

With polling day such a short time away, the campaign got under way enthusiastically. Both candidates published their election addresses to voters[15] and set about holding meetings in the city and villages. For example 'Mr Morrison has had a busy time in the constituency during the week. On Monday he addressed meetings at Teffont, Chilmark and Fonthill Bishop; on Tuesday at Steeple Langford and Wylye; on Wednesday at Hindon, Semley and the Donheads; and last night at Stoford, Woodford, Stratford sub Castle and Dinton.'[16] Major Fletcher Moulton was as energetic; for example 'On Saturday–in addition to speaking at the meeting in Salisbury Market Place in the afternoon–he spoke in the evening at Bodenham, Coombe Bissett, Stratford-sub-Castle and Winterslow, also at the Wilton Road Liberal Club in Salisbury. On Monday morning he paid visits to electors in Stratford-sub-Castle, Woodford, Netton, Bulford and Figheldean; in the afternoon he spoke at the women's meeting in the New Theatre in Salisbury, while in the evening he addressed meetings at Bowerchalke, Ebbesbourne Wake, Semley, Donhead St Mary, Tisbury and Hindon'.[17] As polling day approached the timetable of meetings got even more hectic.

Free Trade or Protectionism, the relationship of that with unemployment and the implications for agriculture, were, as predicted, the central issues raised. According to the *SWJ's* leader of 30 November 'Mr Morrison and Major Fletcher Moulton have taken every means of making their views known . . . their . . . respective attitudes [are] in keeping with those of the leaders of the Conservative and Liberal parties'.[18] Here is a brief quote from both sides as examples of what the audiences were hearing. The Liberals arguing for Free Trade, Major Moulton's letter to electors:

> Think what it will mean for every household if clothes, boots, utensils and many other articles cost half as much again or more. Think what it will mean to the farmer if feeding stuffs, agricultural machinery etc etc rise in the same way.[19]

The Conservatives supporting Protectionism, Edith Olivier speaking at Bemerton:

> The price of passenger motors before the war was £300, but now as the result of the tariff the cost was only £135 . . . gramophones and fabric gloves had become cheaper under the tariff, the home industries concerned had greatly benefited.[20]

Both parties held meetings especially for women, and addressed them directly within general meetings, recognising the numbers of women in the electorate and the importance their votes carried (Fig 3). Conservative agent, Major Turner pointed out the numbers: 'Women electors were a very important factor in the Division, for out of the total number of electors of 30,000 there were 17,000 men and 13,000 women . . . they must not be forgotten'.[21] Women speakers were conspicuous on many platforms. Mrs Moulton attended with her husband throughout the campaign, and also took part in meetings on her own. Another notable example was Viscountess Grey of Fallodon, wife of the Liberal statesman. Speaking at a 'Great Liberal Rally', she expressed the hope that 'the women of Salisbury would work better than ever they had done for the Liberal candidate'.[22]

FREE TRADE MEETINGS
In Support of the Candidature of
MAJOR FLETCHER MOULTON, M.C.
SATURDAY, at 3.
Market Place, Salisbury.
MONDAY, at 2.45.
WOMEN'S MEETING,
NEW THEATRE, CASTLE ST.
FINAL RALLY.—Wednesday, at 8.
VICTORIA HALL
(Rollestone Street).
For full particulars see bills.
[4545

Fig 3: Advertisement for some Liberal election meetings (*Salisbury Times 30 November 1923, 7*).

The weather on 6 December was described as 'fine but dull, and so was fairly favourable to a large poll'.[23] Indeed the turnout was over 80%, only slightly down on the previous year. The *SWJ* reported:

> Compared with the last election there was a marked increase in activity in both camps. In Salisbury itself there was a prolific display of party colours by pedestrians and enthusiasm was not lacking among the juvenile element . . . In the afternoon Lady Mary Morrison visited Salisbury, and in a motor car which also contained Miss Morrison and Mr John Morrison, led a procession of cars containing the leading supporters of the Conservative candidate around the principal streets of the city. The vehicles were decorated with blue streamers and the occupants waved flags and party colours. . . .[24]

Morrison supporters were said to have more cars at their disposal for transporting voters to the polling stations, though 'there never has been in recent years a greater display of the Liberal colour . . . '.[25]

When the result was declared the excitement amongst the Liberals and the disappointment of Conservatives was clear. 12,375 votes were cast for Hugh Fletcher Moulton and 11,710 for Hugh Morrison giving a Liberal majority of 665, more than double the majority Morrison had over Brown in 1922 (Fig 4). Both sides held meetings of their supporters, and discussed the outcome. The *SWJ* said 'we share the regret that the constituency has lost – temporarily we hope – the services in Parliament of Mr Hugh Morrison'.[26] The *ST* commented that:

> Fletcher Moulton's legal experience should stand the city and the division in good stead . . . and he will be a genial and sympathetic representative, who would be assisted to the utmost by his wife who has won golden opinions from those she has come into contact with in her short but extremely busy fortnight in the constituency.[27]

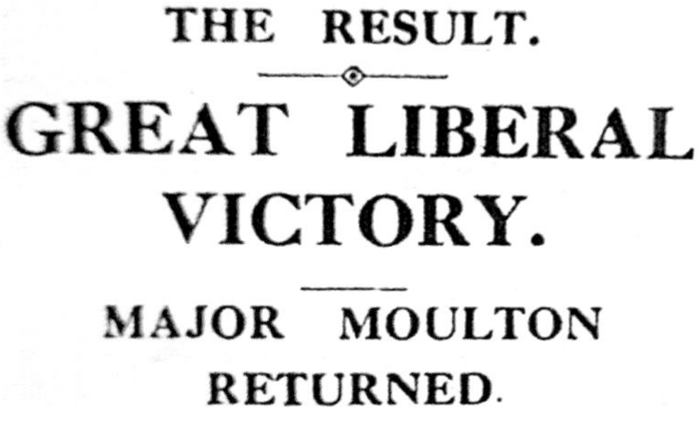

THE RESULT.

GREAT LIBERAL VICTORY.

MAJOR MOULTON RETURNED.

Fig 4: Headline when the result was published (*Salisbury Times 7 December 1923, 8*).

Mrs Moulton herself remarked that she was 'wearing a smile that would not come off'! It seems to have been agreed that, as the *SWJ* put it 'local Labourists threw their weight upon the side of the Free Trade candidate'. Lord Pembroke, writing to the paper the following week as Chancellor of the Primrose League said 'Conservatives and Primrose Leaguers will overhaul their machinery of organisation and will remove whatever impedes its efficiency . . . We shall continue our work with redoubled energy'.[28]

The Liberal Party gained seats across the south west of England, from Cornwall, Devon and Somerset and into Wiltshire, according to the *SWJ*, 'born of the fear of high prices'.[29] Nationally the Conservatives won 258 seats, Labour 192 and Liberals 159, resulting in a 'hung parliament' in which any two parties could outvote the third. So there was no clear mandate for Protectionism that Baldwin had wanted. He resigned in January. The King sent for Ramsay MacDonald as leader of the next largest party, and the first Labour Government was formed. Despite the difficulties of being 'in office but not in power', they were able to demonstrate that they were fit to govern. But the next general election was less than 12 months away. In October 1924 Stanley Baldwin was again Prime Minster and Hugh Morrison returned as Salisbury's Member of Parliament.

General references

There are numerous political history books which will provide the background to this short article, including:

Marr, Andrew, 2009, *The Making of Modern Britain*, Pan Books (book, BBC documentary series and DVD).
Pearce, Robert, 1992, *Britain: Domestic Politics 1918–1939*, Hodder & Stoughton.
Robbins, Keith, 1983, *The Eclipse of a Great Power: Modern Britain 1870–1970*, Longman.

Invaluable for statistics is: Craig, F W S, 1976, *British Electoral Facts 1885–1975*, Macmillan.

Many biographies have been written of the main individuals in national politics at this time; G M Young on Stanley Baldwin, 1952, is old-fashioned in style, but an enjoyable read. Roy Jenkins tackled the same subject in 1987.

The government website contains much history of government, parliament and politicians, and has an interesting collection of blogs at https://history.blog.gov.uk/about-this-blog/

Notes

1 In 1918 not only had women over 30 been given a parliamentary vote, but there were also changes to constituency boundaries. Salisbury was no longer a parliamentary borough, but the centre of a large area covering much of the southern part of the county, known as the Salisbury Division, containing small neighbouring towns such as Wilton, Downton and Amesbury and many villages.

2 See brief list of references for further information. Protectionism involves implementing government policies to protect domestic industries by restricting international trade, often by imposing tariffs on imported goods; other methods include subsidies, quotas

and embargoes. Free trade policies have no such barriers to trade.

3 Quotation from *Salisbury Times* (*ST*), 9 Nov 1923, 8. See also *Sarum Chronicle* (*SC*), 13, 80.

4 *SC*, 19, 28.

5 *Salisbury & Winchester Journal* (*SWJ*), 23 Nov 1923, 12.

6 *ST*, 23 Nov, 1923, 8. His father was Lord John Fletcher Moulton 1844-1921, MP, FRS, barrister and mathematician. Hugh also had two interesting siblings, step-sister Elspeth Thomson, wife of Kenneth Grahame, who wrote *Wind in the Willows,* and half-sister barrister Sylvia May Fletcher Moulton.

7 Townley, Annie, 1937, 'South-West women's work in the districts', *Labour Woman,* Aug 1937; Townley, Annie, 1943, Organising in the South West 1920-1943, *Labour Woman,* Sept 1943. *ST,* 27 April 1923, 8.

8 *SWJ,* 30 Nov 1923, 5 and *ST,* 30 Nov 1923, 2. A nomination paper required a proposer, a seconder and eight assenters, so 10 signatures. To sign a nomination paper it was necessary to be on the electoral register. Wiltshire & Swindon History Centre archives A1/355/231 Electoral Registers Salisbury Division 1923.

9 Moody, Ruby Vitorino, 2022, *The Haunch of Venison, Salisbury,* Hobnob Press, Gloucester, 23.

10 Ross, Christopher, 2000, *The Canons of Salisbury,* Dean & Chapter of Salisbury Cathedral, 68.

11 Foster, Ruscombe E and Michaela S G, 2022, *The Women of Wilton,* Hobnob Press, Gloucester, 152.

12 *SC,* 19, 28–31.

13 Alexander, William, 2013, in Howells, Jane (ed) *Harnham Historical Miscellany,* Sarum Studies 4, chapter 8.

14 Laverstock & Ford *Chapters from Local History,* 2019, Sarum Studies 6, 86, 137.

15 *SWJ,* 23 Nov 1923, 7 and *ST,* 23 Nov 1923, 5.

16 *SWJ,* 16 Nov 1923, 11.

17 *ST,* 7 Dec 1923, 8.

18 *SWJ,* 30 Nov 1923, 12.

19 *ST,* 22 Nov 1923, 5.

20 *SWJ,* 30 Nov 1923, 10.

21 *SWJ,* 16 Nov 1923, 5.

22 Perhaps better known as Pamela Wyndham, then Pamela Tennant, Lady Grey had local connections having been born at Clouds House; she died in 1928 at Wilsford Manor. *ST,* 30 Nov 1923, 8.

23 *ST,* 7 Dec 1923, 8.

24 *ST,* 7 Dec 1923, 9.

25 *ST,* 7 Dec 1923, 8.

26 *ST,* 14 Dec 1923, 12.

27 *ST,* 14 Dec 1923, 2.

28 *SWJ,* 21 Dec 1923, 11. The Primrose League was founded in 1883 to promote Conservative ideas throughout the country, it was wound up in 2004.

29 *SWJ,* 14 Dec 1923, 12.

Fig 1: St Thomas, exterior view of the western end *(Roy Bexon, 2023)*.

Pubs and Churches: Salisbury City Centre

John Elliott

For this edition of *Sarum Chronicle* I have chosen three city-centre medieval churches – St Martin, St Thomas and St Edmund – and the Haunch of Venison pub.

St Thomas Becket, St Thomas Square

St Thomas was the merchants' church in the medieval period. It stands at the northern end of the High Street while the north gate to the Cathedral Close is at the south end. It is adjacent to the market place and its position proclaims the city's commercial status which acts as a counter balance to the cathedral (Fig 1).

The city of Salisbury, or New Sarum as it was called, was created shortly after work on building the cathedral began around 1220. The new city was laid out in building plots and these were leased so that houses could be built on the sites. Many merchants were attracted to the new city with its spacious market place. Quickly a thriving market trade developed on Tuesdays and Saturdays drawing in produce from the surrounding areas and from within the city. A thriving import-export trade also developed through Southampton Dock which could be reached in a day. In the process the city became very prosperous, and the bishop as the landowner accumulated much of the profits, so much so that a great animosity developed between the merchants and the bishop until the early 1600s when the city gained its freedom (Fig 2).

The church of St Thomas is a fifteenth century rebuilding of an earlier thirteenth century church, and the scale and magnificence of its interior evidences the wealth of the merchants who created it (Fig 3). Today it is the main parish church of Salisbury and also a tourist 'hotspot', mostly because of its late fifteenth or early sixteenth century Doom painting which shows an

Fig 2: St Thomas, exterior view from the north *(Roy Bexon, 2023)*.

Fig 3: St Thomas, interior *(John Elliott, 2023)*.

ale-wife and a bishop leading the way to hell–such was the level of animosity between the city and its landlord (Fig 4).

Plans to reorder the church were formulated a few years ago. Initially the great wooden entrance doors were replaced in 2018 by glass doors which were designed by Anthony Feltham-King of St Ann's Gate Architects. This made the inside of the church visible to passers-by. The nave altar was then created in 2020 by Matthew Burt, a very distinguished furniture maker from Hindon just to the west of Salisbury.

Fig 4: St Thomas, The Doom painting *(John Elliott, 2023).*

The Doom painting was restored by Peter Martindale, a conservation specialist from Fovant which is also just to the west of Salisbury. Much of the paintwork had become detached from the wall and its conservation was a real challenge. Also conserved are panels depicting the first three decades of the joyful mysteries of the Rosary—a very rare find (Fig 5). These are located in the chapel at the east end of the south aisle. From the middle of the fifteenth century this became the Lady Chapel, and the wall paintings presumably originate from this date. If so the panels depicting the two remaining decades of the Joyful mysteries would most probably have been at the eastern end of north arcade of the chapel, with the five decades of the Sorrowful mysteries on the south side and a stained glass depiction of the Assumption of the Virgin Mary in the east end window. This latter was largely destroyed during the Reformation and then obliterated by the installation of the huge memorials which are still in situ.

Previously the nave was dominated by Victorian bench pews which were both uncomfortable and impossible to move. These have now been replaced by 88 beautiful stacking pews which were made from European Oak. They were designed and made by Luke Hughes whose workshop is close to the Old Wardour Castle which yet again is just to the west of Salisbury. Luke

Fig 5: St Thomas, the Annunciation Rosary panel *(John Elliott, 2023).*

Fig 6: St Thomas, stacking benches by Luke Hughes *(John Elliott, 2023).*

is responsible for similar work in several other major English cathedrals and in the Washington National Cathedral in the USA (Fig 6).

It is no real surprise that the reordering has been recognised with an award. It is of the highest order, and throughout utilised the skills of very talented local craftsmen. The church authorities deserve great applause for their vision, as do the architects who started the process of turning the dreams into reality. It really is a magnificent production.

St Martin, St Martin's Church Street

A church existed on this site before the cathedral was built and before the medieval city was created. The church remained outside what became the medieval city. Some Norman fragments were discovered in 1886 and evidence of Saxon burials which were unearthed in 2003 (Fig 7).

Fig 7: St Martin, exterior *(John Elliott, 2023).*

Fig 8: St Martin, interior and rood screen *(John Elliott, 2023)*.

The current church is the result of additions and adaptions which have been made over many centuries. The chancel and some other parts date from the twelfth century – it seems that the structure was partly refaced in the fourteenth century when parapets and a spire were added. The vault is largely from the fifteenth century and a western porch with a chapel (now the Parish Office) were added in the sixteenth century. The south aisle vault was replaced in 1886.

Over the centuries there have been significant restorations. The font dates from the thirteenth century and the lectern from 1471–1513. In 1849 the structure was given a major restoration by T H Wyatt, and again in 1886 by Crickmay & Sons, and by C E Ponting in 1918–19 when the magnificent rood screen was installed (Fig 8). In 2006 Antony Feltham-King restored the chancel area in particular and made it more sacramental – of especial note is the new altar that was added.

St Edmund, Bedwin Street

A very large collegiate church was built here in 1269 as the city expanded to the north. A chancel and aisles, or replacements, were added in 1407. There

Fig 9: St Edmund, now the Salisbury Arts Centre, exterior *(John Elliott, 2023)*.

was a central tower but it fell down in 1653 and the nave was demolished at the same time leaving the large area at the west of the current church which became part of the graveyard (Figs 9 & 10).

A new chancel was built in 1766 but replaced by G G Scott as part of his major restoration in 1865–7 when he also added the existing tower. Everything is in the perpendicular gothic style which developed in England during the fifteenth century.

The church was decommissioned in 1973 and eventually became the Arts Centre. An office and meeting room extension to the north was added in 2003–5.

The Haunch of Venison, Minster Street

This is one of the famous British pubs, the structure dating from the middle of the fifteenth century. It continues to exhibit evidence of being a typical medieval city building, with lots of timbering showing, especially inside, and it is jettied outside. Like most of the other medieval buildings in Salisbury it was given a Georgian 'make-over', though it escaped the mathematical tile façade

Fig 10: St Edmund, now the Salisbury Arts Centre, exterior *(John Elliott, 2023)*.

that many other Salisbury buildings suffered as they were made to look like brick structures rather than half-timbered medieval ones (Fig 11).

Originally pubs were organised into a number of separate rooms in which the drinkers gathered as distinct from the open bar plan that is currently used. This original arrangement is still visible in the Haunch of Venison,

Fig 11: The Haunch of Venison in Minster Street *(John Elliott, 2023).*

making it particularly valuable as a historic pub. For those who want to learn more about historic pubs look for *Licensed to Sell: The History and Heritage of the Public House* by Geoff Brandwood, Andrew Davison and Michael Slaughter which was published by English Heritage in 2004.

Aspects of Bishopsdown Farm in the Late 19th Century

Part 1: A tenancy dispute

Heather Adeley

Historically Salisbury Cathedral owned many farms in the Diocese. One of these was Bishopsdown Farm, which today is the site of a large housing development on the north east of Salisbury, off the London Road.

In August 1881 a lease was drawn up between the Cathedral and John Thomas Gay (Fig 1). The terms and conditions of the lease are recorded in great detail

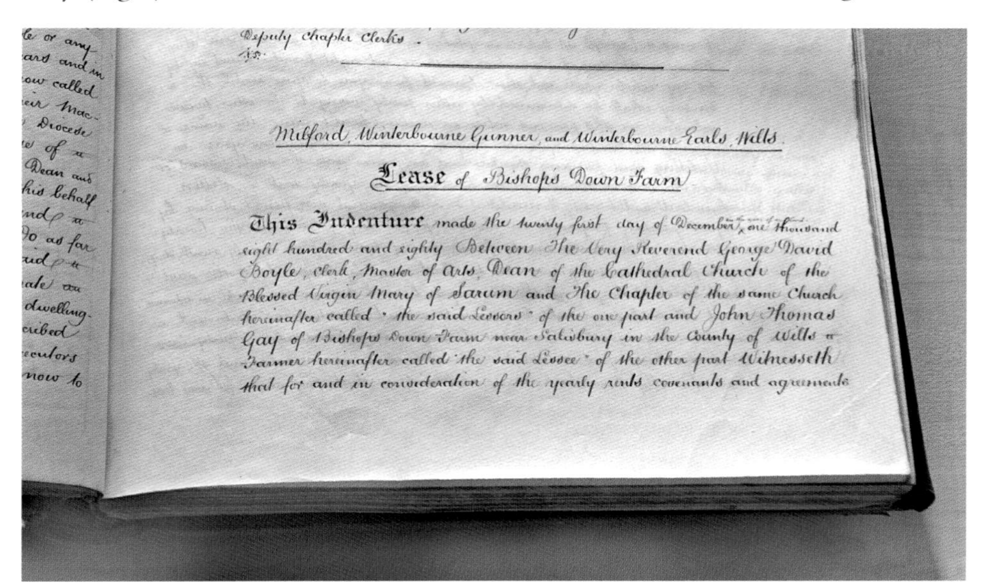
Deputy Chapter Clerks

Milford, Winterbourne Gunner, and Winterbourne Earls, Wilts.

Lease of Bishop's Down Farm

This Indenture made the twenty first day of December, one thousand eight hundred and eighty Between The Very Reverend George David Boyle, clerk, Master of Arts, Dean of the Cathedral Church of the Blessed Virgin Mary of Sarum and The Chapter of the same Church hereinafter called "the said Lessors" of the one part and John Thomas Gay of Bishops Down Farm near Salisbury in the County of Wilts Farmer hereinafter called "the said Lessee" of the other part Witnesseth that for and in consideration of the yearly rents covenants and agreements

Fig1: Record of Lease of Bishopsdown Farm to John Thomas Gay in the Contracts Register 1877–1889, Salisbury Cathedral Archive CH/13/26 (*Roy Bexon, 2023*).

in the Cathedral Contract Book 1877–89.[1] There are also references in the Draft Chapter Minutes 1866–1881 and 1881–1891 and Notes of Leases 1875–1955.[2]

At the time John Gay was aged 24.[3] He was the son of a local farmer and his wife Emily was from a family living in Salisbury.[4] The farm consisted of approximately 484 acres, leased at an annual rent of £727 6s 6d, together with a tithe of over £200, both to be paid in quarterly instalments. A farmhouse and buildings were included. In addition to the newlywed couple, the farm provided employment for six men, two boys and four women.[5]

The terms and conditions imposed were onerous–conditions that were similar to those for all the farms owned and leased by the Cathedral at this time. The control that the Cathedral Dean and Chapter had over the lessee would seem untenable to modern tenants. It is possible that the level of quarterly payments and the other onerous conditions might have made it hard for Mr Gay to make a living, although he might just be self-sufficient.

The Lease that John Gay signed ran for a year and was renewable but required 12 months' notice from either side if it was to be terminated. Rent was paid quarterly, but the final two payments in the last year of tenancy had to be paid in advance, and all had to be surrendered in good order and well cultivated. In addition, the incoming tenant had the right to till, and cultivate one eighth of the land and to occupy a portion of the farmhouse and buildings during the outgoing tenant's final year.

The Dean and Chapter reserved the right to retain all timber, all quarried minerals, clay for bricks and tiles, gravel *etc.* They also reserved the right to erect machine sheds, saw pits and warehouses and reserved the right for themselves, their agents and workmen free access to the premises at all reasonable times to mark, cut down and grub up trees, to dig and search for clay, minerals, *etc* and to carry them away.

The tenant was required to pay all local parish taxes and he had to repair the walls, gates, stiles, bridges, hedges and ditches. If any tillage of land took place without licence or consent then a fine of £50 per acre was to be imposed. In addition, the tenant was not allowed to plough or convert into tillage any new land without consent.

The land had to be cultivated and managed in a certain way and all thistles and weeds had to be removed. The buildings, walls, gates, stiles, *etc* had to be kept in good repair. Hedging and ditching were to be carried out at least annually. The woodwork used in the farmhouse and buildings was to be re-painted outside every three years and inside every five years with 'good paint'. The tenant was not allowed to dispose of any premises–except sub-letting to his farm labourers–without consent. The penalty for this was for the annual rent to double.

Trees, saplings and hedges had to be looked after. If any were damaged by cattle or by inappropriate pruning *etc* then a fine of £10 per tree was to be imposed. Mangelwurzels (a root crop used for feeding animals), other root crops, grasses, hay, straw, dung or manure were not to be removed from the farm. Seed and turnips were not to be left on the land except enough to re-crop but only for two years after which rotation was to take place.

Hay and straw were to be stacked and the corn threshed. The hay and straw were not to be removed from the farm but used for fodder. If any straw was removed it had to be replaced by manure.

Manure was to be spread on the fields at least once every four years and manure was to be stored during the last year of tenancy. If it was destroyed by fire it was to be replaced by the tenant purchasing artificial fertiliser.

The Dean and Chapter, or their agents, were to have free access to the farm and buildings at any time during the day without due warning. If anything was not satisfactory, three months' notice was to be given for the situation to be rectified, otherwise outside workmen would be employed and all the costs would be charged to the lessee.

The Lease was intended to ensure good farming practice was followed – maintaining hedges and ditches, repairing and maintaining the fabric and general husbandry. The potential problems come with the prescriptive nature of planting and managing a farm and the draconian sanctions that could be imposed.

There are a few references to livestock in the lease; therefore, the farmer seemingly must supplement his living from livestock, hens and garden produce. Much else appears to be monitored closely by the Dean and Chapter.

Very early on in John Gay's tenancy he must have had a change of mind because as early as October 1881, one month after signing the lease, he gave notice that he intended to leave the farm at Michaelmas (29 September) 1882 thus giving one year's notice as required.

On 3 January 1882 the Dean and Chapter noted that Mr Gay had sent a letter offering to remain on the farm but at a reduced rent plus tithe of £744 per annum, a reduction of approximately 20%, but this was refused. Four months later the matter was still not resolved though the Dean and Chapter did continue with Mr Gay farming the land but required him to pay rent arrears as had previously been agreed, but with a discount of 15% which was conditional on him withdrawing his notice to quit.

On 16 June 1882 there is a note in the Dean and Chapter minutes that an application had been made by a prospective new tenant who was being vetted. Presumably this came to nothing and on 3 October a letter from the Diocese's land agent, Mr Rigden, dated 29 September was considered by the Dean and Chapter. This stated that the only offer Mr Gay had made was to continue but with the quarterly rental reduced by £200 a year, though the Dean and Chapter were told that Mr Gay had already advertised his stock for sale (Fig 2).[6] Either way the break-up of the farm had already started. Fifty acres had already been let to a Mr Bowle (tithe free) at an annual rent of £150 and a further forty-two acres to a Mr Yates at £73 and another small plot for £1.

TUESDAY, 26th SEPTEMBER, 1882.
BISHOP DOWN FARM, SALISBURY,
About One Mile from the City.

MESSRS. WATERS AND RAWLENCE are instructed by Mr. [illegible] T. Gay (whose lease expires at Michaelmas next), to SELL by AUCTION, on the Premises, on TUESDAY, 26th SEPTEMBER, at HALF-PAST TWO O'CLOCK in the Afternoon, the undermentioned

VALUABLE LIVE STOCK,
Viz.:
230 Well-bred HAMPSHIRE DOWN EWE LAMBS
22 Capital DAIRY COWS, forming a regular running Dairy, many being due to calve before Christmas
4 In-calf HEIFFERS, 7 WEANLERS, 1 BULL
5 Breeding SOWS, 1 BOAR
40 Store PIGS
10 Active and powerful CART HORSES
Catalogues may be obtained of the Auctioneers, Canal, Salisbury. [8207

Fig 2: Advertisement for the sale on 26 September 1882 of John Gay's livestock (*Salisbury Journal, 9 September 1882, 4*).

The present rent from the land totalled £727 6s 6d but the tithe rent of £202 3s 4d had to be added giving a total of £929 9s 10d. It was clearly going to be hard for the Dean and Chapter to cover the earlier rental with these multiple smaller rentals which totalled just £224, leaving a balance of £705 9s 10d. The Dean and Chapter had however received an enquiry from a sheep farmer for a reduced acreage and an offer that he would pay £600 a year.

The problem with Mr Gay rumbled on. The Dean and Chapter offered to spend £100 rearranging the water meadows but this did not resolve the issue. Finally, on 11 October the Dean reported that it had been impossible to reach an agreement with Mr Gay, and the Dean and Chapter instructed its agents to seek a new tenant. An advertisement appeared in the Salisbury Journal three days later (Fig 3).[7]

Then on 17 October 1882 it was decided that the Dean would meet Mr Gay the following day. What was discussed is not recorded but on 20 October they wrote to Mr Gay demanding a half year's rental and formally rejecting his offers.

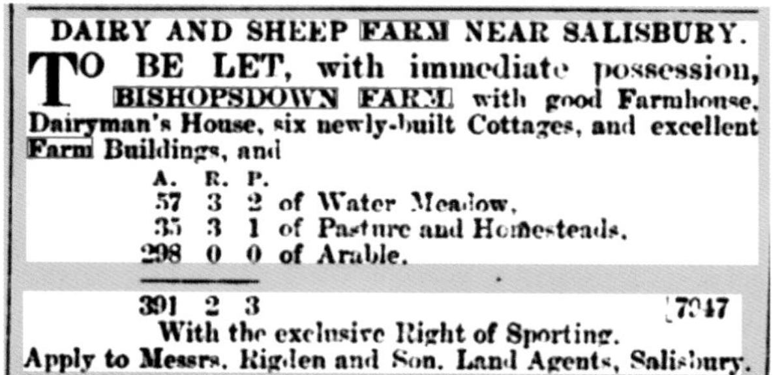

DAIRY AND SHEEP FARM NEAR SALISBURY.

TO BE LET, with immediate possession, BISHOPSDOWN FARM with good Farmhouse, Dairyman's House, six newly-built Cottages, and excellent Farm Buildings, and

A.	R.	P.	
57	3	2	of Water Meadow,
35	3	1	of Pasture and Homesteads,
298	0	0	of Arable.
391	2	3	

With the exclusive Right of Sporting.
Apply to Messrs. Rigden and Son, Land Agents, Salisbury. [7347

Fig 3: Advertisement for farm to let 'with immediate possession', October 1882 (*Salisbury Journal, 14 October 1882, 4*).

So it seems the whole sorry tale of John Gay's tenancy drew to an end approximately one year and one month after signing the original lease. Presumably Mr Gay had to abide by the terms of his original lease, but whether or not he was given one year's or six months' notice, or not, is not clear. No doubt the final part of his tenancy must have been challenging.

While it is unclear what motivated John Gay to exit from the Bishopsdown Farm lease, it seems likely that the onerous conditions would have been a factor.

We do not know when John Gay left the farm but we do know that in 1883 a lease was signed between the Dean and Chapter and William John Cross and Herbert Steer to rent part of Bishopsdown Farm, all the usual terms and conditions were still in place. It referred to land tenanted by the 'late Mr Gay' so he must have left by then. Once again this was underlining the break-up of the farm as a whole.

Where John Gay moved to immediately after he left Bishopsdown Farm is not recorded but the 1891 Census records him living at Parsonage Farm, Stockton, Warminster with his wife and one servant; they had no children.[8] He must have settled there and run a successful farm because according to the 1901 census he was still there with his wife and two servants but no children.[9] John Thomas Gay died from a sudden stroke in March 1910 in Stockton, Wylye Valley, Wiltshire aged 53. In an obituary, he is described as 'of a kindly and genial disposition, and most charitable'. He had served as Chairman on the Warminster Board of Guardians and the Rural District Council as well as being a local magistrate. He was also active in local farming associations and 'took a deep interest in all agricultural matters . . . The people of Stockton and surrounding villages will lose in him a kind and sympathetic neighbour'.[10]

Postscript - farm tenancies

Change in tenancies was slow to arrive and in the 1930s depression a farmer in Devon was reprimanded for shooting or catching a hare. He and all the other farmers on the estate gave their notice and moved to other farms not far away. At that time farmland had almost no value and tenancies were easy to get!

By the end of the 20th century, farm tenancies were less draconian, but still included some ancient restrictions and requirements. Annual renewable farm leases had finished, but were still in place for parcels of land. A typical tenancy had no hunting or shooting rights, but the farmer could not stop the local hunt from riding through the farmyard and disturbing the animals. Nor could he stop the landlord's shoot from firing guns over the animals, when they were in open yards in the winter.

A newspaper article in 2002 states that one third of the land in Britain was tenanted, although this will be for the number of farms rather than their total acreage.[11] Another authority in 2002 found some tenant farmers living on the 'margins of existence'.[12] They did not own the houses where they lived, and it was noted that they often had huge overdrafts and no exit strategy, mostly caused by falling incomes and rising rents.

The Tenant Farmers Association attributed some of their plight to the outdated tenant/landlord legislation which drew a strict definition of agriculture that prevented many tenants from following Government advice to use their land and the buildings they rented to diversify into other businesses.[13]

The Government listened sympathetically and concluded that changes in the tenancy legislation might be needed 'to remove the constraints on the tenant farmer (and) allow them to respond positively to the challenges the industry was facing'.[14] The Agricultural Tenancies Act 1995 s.38 defined agriculture as including:

> horticulture, fruit growing, seed growing, dairy farming, and livestock breeding and keeping, the use of land as grazing land, meadow land, osier land, market gardens and nursery gardens, and the use of land for woodlands where it is ancillary to the farming of land for other agricultural purposes.

This definition now precludes horses, unless they are kept for farm work, meat or hides.

Examples of typical farm tenancies can be found advertised on the internet and provide an illustration of modern tenancies. On reading the particulars, the Lease is generally to be for ten years, with a break clause at five years, available to either landlord or tenant. Rent reviews take place every three years at the market rate, in accordance with the provision of the Agricultural Tenancies Act 1995. In the 20th century a farm tenancy often ran for the life of the farmer, as long as he lived there 'with his family and servants'. Rent was generally paid twice a year, at Michaelmas and on Lady Day.

Maintenance of the outside of the farmhouse was the landlord's responsibility but was not often undertaken. The inside was the tenant's responsibility and might often not be carried out. A barn roof had to be repainted every eight years. By the terms of a standard agricultural tenancy, the landlord could not erect sheds, but could take timber. However, the tenant was not allowed to cut timber or to quarry stone.

While this list is not exhaustive, some of the terms and conditions have a vaguely familiar ring about them, although not as onerous as those of the Salisbury Cathedral Dean and Chapter in 1881. Nowadays, big landowners tend to amalgamate small farms, and to have farm managers rather than tenants.

Bibliography
Wade Martins, Susanna, 2004, *Farmers, Landlords and Landscapes,* Windgather Press.
Offer, Avner, 1991, *Farm tenure and land values in England c.1750–1950,* The Economic History Review, 44 (1) February.
Woodman, Mark, *Modern Farming Tenancies,*
https://www.das/law.co.uk/blog/farmingtenancies-what-you-need-to-know, accessed February 2023.

Part 2: A South Wiltshire Farmer at Bishopsdown and Ford

John Loades

George Gay (1826–1908)

George Gay came from a Wiltshire farming family and is recorded as farming on the north eastern outskirts of Salisbury over a period spanning some 20 years during the 1860s and 1870s. Specifically, he was the tenant of Ford Farm and then Bishopsdown Farm, as well as leasing Ford Mill for a brief period.

He was born in the Chippenham area in March 1826, son of farmer William Gay who subsequently farmed near Downton during George's boyhood. George was part of a large family, one of six brothers all having 'the distinction of being six-footers'.[15]

He gained experience of farming on his own account at Whiteparish where he is recorded in the 1851 census, together with his wife Sarah and where their two sons and a daughter were born.[16] Early in the 1860s, the family moved to Ford Farm in the parish of Laverstock, on the eastern side of the River Bourne and about two miles from Salisbury.[17] He would remain in this vicinity for the next twenty years before moving to another Wiltshire farm near Orcheston on Salisbury Plain.

By 1871, George was tenant farmer at the adjacent Bishopsdown Farm, on the western side of the Bourne River while his elder son, George Frank Gay (1852–1935), was living at Ford Farm together with his sister Fanny (1856–1924). This arrangement seems to have created a family enterprise, jointly holding two adjacent farms in the Bourne Valley. For a brief period, George also took the tenancy of Ford Mill from the Dean and Chapter of Salisbury Cathedral. He signed a lease agreement in September 1874 and gave one year's notice to quit by 29 September 1879.[18] Simultaneously, he served as a member of the Highways Board of Salisbury for nearly 20 years.[19]

By 1881, George had recently moved to Orcheston while his younger son, John Thomas Gay (1857–1910), was continuing the family connection as tenant farmer at Bishopsdown Farm.[20] John Gay's brief tenancy there is explored in more detail in the previous section of this article.

George lived to the age of 82, dying in Wylye to where he had retired in his final years. From a contemporary obituary, it is indicated that 'he belonged to the old school of farmers and was very highly respected. He was of a most generous disposition.'[21]

Ford Farm

This farm was located in the Bourne Valley in the northern section of the parish of Laverstock, covering around 370 acres with a farmyard, farmhouse and labourer's cottage. This land area included some 18 acres of water meadows in the valley bottom on the eastern banks of the River Bourne, as well as areas of downland on Ford Down on the higher ground east of the valley. Over 300 acres was recorded as being arable land, providing the opportunity to grow a variety of both cash and fodder crops. The combination of water meadows, corn production and downland would have been suitable to support a sizeable sheep flock, following the 'sheep and corn' system of grazing the water meadows followed by 'folding' the flock progressively across arable fields to manure the soil.

It was a tenanted farm with the landowner being the Wyndham and subsequently Campbell-Wyndham family. The 1861 census records that farmer George Gay employed ten men and three boys on the farm, with specific identification of the shepherd, Noah James.[22]

During the 1850s, the London and South Western Railway Company constructed a rail line from London to Salisbury *via* Andover, which passed on an embankment through Ford Farm's water meadows before bridging the Bourne River.

Bishopsdown Farm

This farm is also located along the Bourne Valley, to the western side of the river, with fields directly adjacent to Ford Farm and then extending north west to the downlands. It fell within the parish of Milford (Salisbury St Martin) and consisted of some 479 acres, again with a mix of water meadow, arable fields, pastures and downland. The southern extent of the farm was traversed by the London Road where St Thomas's Bridge provides passage across the Bourne River. This highway was a toll road operated by the Sarum and Ealing Turnpike Trust during the period 1753 to 1871, with a tollhouse 'Lopcombe Gate' located on the road near the farm's entrance. The farmhouse and yard

Fig 4: Bishopsdown Farm and farmyard in 2023. The original barn is top centre with three bay openings. The granary structure is at right angles to the right-hand side of the barn, with the farmhouse across the yard. The buildings are now converted into residences. (*Google Earth data SIO, NOOA, U. S. Navy, NGA, GEBCO IBCAO Landsat / Copernicus, 2023*).

were situated along a driveway leading off London Road with a terrace of labourers' cottages on the corner of the drive and highway. The farmhouse, barn, granary and cottages have survived, although modernised and now surrounded by the Bishopsdown Estate residential area (Fig 4).[23]

Like Ford Farm, Bishopsdown Farm was traversed by the Andover to Salisbury rail line, constructed in the 1850s and crossing over the farm's water meadow channels leading off the Bourne River. The brick culvert work to carry the channels under the railway embankment can still be seen from the A30 London Road on the St Thomas's Bridge side of the arched viaduct where the railway crosses the road (Fig 5).

As its name suggests, the farm's landowner was the Bishop of Salisbury, a grant that probably dates back to the early 12th century following the establishment of a Salisbury diocese at Old Sarum. The Bishop's Manor of Milford (Milford *Episcopi*) was created and included most of the land in the parish of St Martin.[24] The earliest lease of land specifically referred to as Bishopsdown is recorded in 1523 to Anthony Erneley, formerly of the Bishop's household. He was granted a 40-year lease of 'all the demesne lands, meadows and pastures of the new ditch, with the grange and fold at the sheephouse commonly called the farm

Fig 5: Bishopsdown Farm's water channel culverts under the railway. The two channels then crossed beneath the London Road to 'float' the farm's adjacent water meadows (*John Loades, 2023*).

of Bishopsdown'.[25] He is commemorated on a brass plaque in St Andrew's Church, Laverstock where his brother William had been vicar (Fig 6). By the 19th century, the farm remained tenanted, being administered by the Dean and Chapter of Salisbury Cathedral who, in turn, appointed a land agent to supervise the tenant farmers.

Over the centuries, there are indications that the landlord and successive tenants combined to adopt progressive agricultural practices. Bishopsdown Farm is recorded as developing some of the earliest water meadows in Wiltshire *c*1650.[26] Mr Colbourne, tenant farmer at Bishopsdown in 1830, had been an

Fig 6: Commemorative brass plaque to Anthony Erneley (Ernley), first recorded tenant of Bishopsdown Farm, located in St Andrew's Church, Laverstock. (*Roy Bexon, 2019*).

early adopter of a small threshing machine, probably horse powered. His farm and equipment were the target that year of a mob of Swing rioters, who destroyed the threshing machine before proceeding towards the city.[27]

Ford Mill

George Gay took the lease on the corn mill for five years while he was also the tenant farmer at Bishopsdown Farm (Fig 7).[28] The mill is located on the Bourne River just upstream from where the original Roman Road, connecting Old Sarum and Winchester, crossed the river.[29] While the millhouse includes a date stone 1783, it is possible that a mill had existed at this location for some considerable time prior to this date.

Fig 7: Ford Mill *c*1900. It would have looked very similar in the late 1870s when George Gay held the tenancy of the mill and cottages (*from a contemporary postcard, with an original picture held by Wiltshire and Swindon History Centre*).

At the time of Laverstock's Tithe Apportionments in 1843, Ford Mill's landowner is recorded as Thomas Blake with Thomas Blake Junior as the occupier. It seems that the Church Commissioners may have acquired the mill and associated properties from the Blake descendants, possibly widow Ann Blake after she died in 1874.

Ford Farm's farmhouse and yard were nearby with fields adjacent to the mill property. The lease included two cottages, outbuildings, a yard, and two small water meadows downstream – Great Mill Meadow and Little Mill Meadow

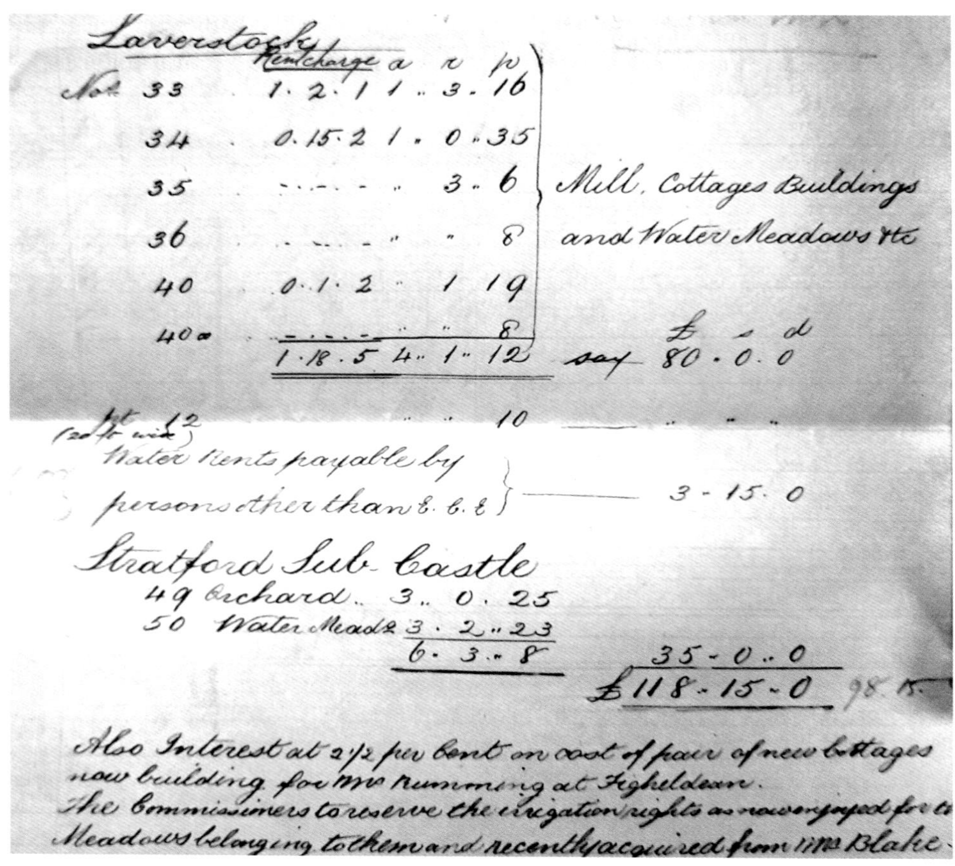

Laverstock

	Rentcharge	a	r	p	
No. 33	1 . 2 . 11	1	3	16	
34	0 . 15 . 2	1	0	35	
35			3	6	Mill, Cottages Buildings
36				8	and Water Meadows &c
40	0 . 1 . 2		1	19	
40a				8	£ s d
	1 . 18 . 5	4	1	12	say 80 . 0 . 0
pt 12 (part with?)				10	

Water Rents payable by persons other than E. C. E. — 3 - 15 - 0

Stratford Sub Castle

49 Orchard .. 3 .. 0 . 25
50 Water Meads 3 . 2 .. 23
6 . 3 .. 8 — 35 - 0 .. 0

£118 - 15 - 0 98.15

Also Interest at 2½ per Cent on cost of pair of new Cottages now building for Mr Rumming at Figheldean.
The Commissioners to reserve the irrigation rights as now enjoyed for the Meadows belonging to them and recently acquired from Mr Blake.

Fig 8: Ford Mill tenancy proposal of September 1874, with references to plot number and area details from the tithe map (*Image courtesy of Wiltshire and Swindon History Centre, D24/18/7*).

which together covered about three acres. An initial annual rent of £80 was proposed by the land agent (Fig 8). After agreeing some structural alterations to the building and the installation of a flour dressing machine, the annual rental was set at £65 with a further £3 15s 0d payable in water rents.[30] Since the Gay family members would have been producing corn from the arable areas of both their nearby farms, the mill would have provided them with a useful value addition activity. George Gay gave one year's notice of his intention to terminate the tenancy, effective 28 September 1879 (Fig 9).

Gay Family Enterprise in the Bourne Valley

By the mid-1870s, George Gay together with both his sons were operating two substantial and adjoining farms covering some 850 acres as well as the nearby corn mill.

This significant family enterprise did not survive for long, with the family members dispersing to other locations by 1882. George Gay senior relocated to a farm in the Till valley around 1879 while his younger son John Thomas Gay surrendered the Bishopsdown Farm lease in 1882 when he moved to a farm in Stockton in the Wylye valley. The elder son, George Frank, having married a farmer's daughter in Wylye parish church in 1880, appears in the 1881 census as a dairy farmer at the hamlet of Great Bathampton in Steeple Langford parish.[31] By 1901, the couple had moved again to the Manor Farm, Winterbourne Gunner in the Bourne valley.[32]

There is no clear indication of what prompted this shift away from the Salisbury area. However, there are circumstances which may have contributed. Wiltshire agriculture experienced a period of relative prosperity in the early 1870s,[33] which may have encouraged the Gay family to expand their operations. Farmers then suffered a recession in prices of cereal crops during the late 1870s. The harvests for 1878 through to 1880 were poor due to climatic factors, while cereal imports were starting to increase from new cornlands in the United States, resulting in reduced prices. This combination of low yield and low prices squeezed farm incomes.

To Mr Rigden

Sir

I hereby give you Notice of my Intention to quit and deliver up on the 29th September 1879 all that Mill and Premises together with the two Cottages and Land I now rent of the Dean & Chapter of Salisbury Cathedral, situate at Ford in the Parish of Laverstock in the County of Wilts

Dated this 28th September 1878

George Gay

Fig 9: George Gay's 1878 letter of termination of his Ford Mill tenancy (*Image courtesy of Wiltshire and Swindon History Centre, D24/18/7*).

> The depression was associated with a prolonged run of disastrously unfavourable seasons, with delayed growth in the spring, and with wet and late harvests, which themselves had a cumulatively adverse effect by producing late and difficult ploughing and sowing conditions. Moreover, the excessive wetness was a prime factor in causing the sheep rot, which ravaged the flocks of southern Wiltshire . . . the price of store lambs took a downward turn in 1879 and 1880, as did that of wool.[34]

Tenant farmers were particularly exposed to these fluctuations in income as the need to cover the fixed annual costs of rent and tithe resulted in diminishing net returns to the farmer. There is also evidence that investment in the sheep-corn system had intensified in order to gain efficiencies.[35] Many farmers following this system may have committed working capital to improving the farm's livestock and equipment, possibly by resorting to commercial loans.

With this tight economic background, it appears possible that the Gay family, among others, may have decided to rationalise and downsize their agricultural operations to release working capital in order to survive these lean years and to clear any outstanding creditors and loans. Such moves were a feature in Wiltshire at that time, leading to a gradual downward adjustment in agricultural rents by as much as 40% over the succeeding twenty years to the end of the century. Analysis has also indicated that the average length of an agricultural tenancy declined over this period.[36]

Conclusion

The mixed fortunes of the Gay family while farming in the Salisbury area during the second half of the 19th century is probably typical of the experiences of many tenant farmers, both locally and nationally. By its nature, agriculture was prone to fluctuations both in weather and in produce prices. When these combined factors shifted against a tenant, their income was reduced whilst the landlord remained protected in the short term through fixed rents.

Probably challenged by this combination of adverse events, the members of the Gay family seem to have found a way to continue farming in other locations, in the hope of better times. George Gay and both his sons managed to relocate to other farms in South Wiltshire and are recorded as subsequently enjoying sustained tenure and apparent success. George Gay had come from a large Wiltshire farming family and succeeded in seeing his two sons established in their own right. Disappointingly, there is no evidence of a further generation continuing the family farming tradition, as subsequent census data indicate that whilst both sons and the daughter married, none of them are recorded with children.

Acknowledgements

My thanks to Ruth Newman for her assistance and for locating newspaper cuttings on the Gay family. Thanks also to Roy Bexon for his help in preparing the illustrations.

Notes

1 Salisbury Cathedral Archives (SCA), CH/13/26, Cathedral Contract Book 1877–89.

2 SCA, CH/5/17–18, Draft Chapter Minutes 1866–1881 and 1881–1891 and Notes of Leases 1875–1955.

3 He was baptised on 13 July 1856. His parents were George and Sarah Gay who were living at Tichbourne Farm, Whiteparish; Wiltshire and Swindon History Centre

(WSHC) 2274/1 *Parish Registers of Whiteparish All Saints, Baptisms 1855–1943.*

4 She had previously lived in Endless Street, Salisbury. Her father was George Brown and declared himself to be a gentleman. She and John Gay were married on 31 March 1880 at St Edmund's Church and she stated that she was living in Exeter Street; WSHC, 1901/20, *Parish Registers of Salisbury St Edmund's Marriages, 1859–1880.*

5 1881 Census, The National Archives (TNA) RG 11/2070 f66, 22.

6 *Salisbury Journal* (*SJ*), 9 September 1882, 4.

7 *SJ*, 14 October 1882, 4.

8 1891 Census, TNA RG 12/1611 f57, 1.

9 1901 Census, TNA RG 13/1945 f61, 14.

10 *SJ*, 12 March 1910, 3.

11 *The Guardian*, 7 September 2002, 'Farmers who are stuck in a feudal furrow', article by Peter Hetherington, available online at https://www.theguardian.com/uk/2002/sep/07/ruralaffairs.peterhetherington, accessed March 2023.

12 *The Guardian*, 7 September 2002, Hetherington article quoting the Tenant Farmers' Association chief executive, George Dunn.

13 Agricultural Tenant Act 1995, details of which can be found at https://www.legislation.gov.uk, accessed April 2023.

14 *The Guardian*, 7 September 2002, Hetherington article quoting the agriculture minister, Lord Whitty.

15 *Salisbury Times* (*ST*), 4 September 1908, 3, obituary.

16 1851 Census, TNA HO 107/1846 f111, 13.

17 1861 Census, TNA RG 9/1315 f122, 14.

18 WSHC, D24/18/7, letter from George Gay dated 28 September 1878 to land agent Rigden.

19 *ST*, 4 September 1908, 3, obituary.

20 1881 Census, TNA RG11/2070 f66, 22.

21 *ST*, 4 September 1908, 3, obituary.

22 1861 census, TNA RG9/1315 f122, 14.

23 The barn and granary are designated Grade II Listed Buildings. Details appear on the Historic England website https://www.historicengland.org.uk, accessed April 2023.

24 Durman, Richard, 2007, *Milford*, Sarum Studies 1, Sarum Chronicle.

25 Crittall, Elizabeth (ed), 1962, *Victoria County History Wiltshire* (VCH Wilts) Volume 6 Salisbury; the Expansion of the City; Rural Milford, 92–3.

26 Aubrey, John, 1862, *Wiltshire Topographical Collections*, ed Jackson, John Edward 1862, Devizes,104.

27 Newman, Ruth, 2019, 'The Swing Riots of 1830', in Evans, Bryan et al, 2019, *Laverstock and Ford, Chapters from Local History,* Sarum Studies 6, Sarum Chronicle, 82.

28 WSHC, D24/18/7, correspondence between 1874 and 1879 between land agent Rigden and George Gay.

29 The mill with millhouse are Grade II Listed Buildings. Details appear on the Historic England website: https://historicengland.org.uk/listing/the-list/list-entry/1355735?section=official-list-entry, accessed April 2023.

30 WSHC, D24/18/7, letter dated 18 September 1875 from land agent Rigden to George Gay.

31 1881 census, TNA RG 11/2074 f38, 11; WSHC 521/46.

32 1901 census, TNA RG13/1950 f47, 11.
33 Thompson, Francis Michael Longstreth, 1959, 'Agriculture since 1870' in Crittall, Elizabeth (ed), *VCH Wilts Volume 4*, VCH London. This paper includes summaries from *Minutes of Evidence before and the Report of the Royal Commission on the Depressed Condition of the Agricultural Interests 1881.*
34 Thompson, 1959, 92–114.
35 Thompson, 1959, 92–114.
36 Thompson, 1959, 92–114.

Music Festivals and the Infirmary in 18th-Century Salisbury

Nigel Wyatt

As a member of the Salisbury Baroque orchestra I have been able to devise concert programmes that are informed by historical research - recreating some of the performances our 18th century Salisbury counterparts enjoyed. I became intrigued by the published lists of those who attended the annual music festivals in the city and decided to look into them a little further...

Introduction

On Wednesday 24 September 1766, the first day of the annual two day music festival in Salisbury, a committee was formed at the Vine Inn whose purpose was the establishment of a new infirmary in Salisbury. At the meeting the Earl of Pembroke was nominated as the visitor and the Earl of Radnor the president. Earlier in the day, after the morning concert, there was a collection at the cathedral door in support of the new hospital. The infirmary accounts show that this raised the large sum of £36 9s 1½d. The following year, in September 1768, the annual music festival grew to three days, Wednesday to Friday, with the insertion of a performance of Messiah in the cathedral on the middle morning. The advert in the *Salisbury and Winchester Journal (SWJ)* again linked the festival to the project to build the infirmary declaring that:

> It is proposed, in order to encourage the Salisbury Infirmary, that a third part of the neat Profits of the several Days above mentioned should be applied to the Use of that most beneficial and humane Institution.[1]

This newly established pattern of an annual three day music festival was to continue through the 1770s until the death of James Harris in 1780. The festivals, which had begun as celebrations of St Cecilia's Day with largely amateur players and singers, had now become three day events featuring some of the greatest singers and instrumentalists of the period. I have written elsewhere about the history of the festivals and the central role that author and MP James Harris played in their success.[2] In this article I want to explore the connections between these two flourishing civic projects in Salisbury, the annual music festivals and the building of the infirmary, and the cooperative efforts of the members of local notable families that underpin them both. This will provide a more broadly based explanation of the success of the festivals during this period.

The annual music festivals and the local aristocracy

It is striking to the modern reader that reports of the annual music festivals in the *Salisbury and Winchester Journal* from 1767 onwards list the members of the aristocracy who attended - devoting almost as much space to this as to the reports of the music that was performed. So to take an example from 1770:

> *Salisbury and Winchester Journal, 8 October, 1770*
> This week was celebrated our Annual Musical Festival-------on Wednesday evening was performed, at the Assembly room, the musical drama of HERCULES, composed by Mr. Handell. On Thursday morning, in the cathedral, a new ANTHEM, composed by Mr. Norris, and the oratorio of the MESSIAH. Friday morning, in the cathedral, a new overture, by Bach, with a repetition of Mr. Norris's ANTHEM. In time of service was introduced a JUBILATE, selected from some capital Italian masters; and, after the service, the grand CORONATION ANTHEM by Mr. Handell. In the evening, the celebrated STABAT MATER of Pergolese, and many select pieces from the admired oratorio of Jomelli, called LA PASSIONE. Between the acts, on Friday evening, Mr. Stanley favoured the company with an organ concerto, which was received with that admiration and applause the performance of that gentleman always deserve; and Messrs. Malchair, Simpson, Richards and Lates, displayed their taste and execution in playing two elegant quartettos, composed by Mr. Bach [J. C. Bach]. The performances in general were executed with the greatest spirit and accuracy; Mr. Tenducci and Miss Linley did justice to the masterly composition of Mr. Norris's anthem, and in their respective parts at the assembly-room gave the highest pleasure to a numerous and brilliant audience, by the elegance of their taste, and the uncommon powers of their voices. Amongst many other persons of fashion who were present on this occasion were, the Duke and Dutchess of Queensbury, Earl and Countess of Pembroke, Earl and Countess of Radnor, Earl of Ancram, Viscount Folkestone, Viscount Dunkelling, Lady Mary Hume, Lady Amelia Duburgh, Lord and Lady Arundel, Lady Ranelagh, Marquis Adrianoli, Hon. Mr and Mrs. Howard, Hon. Mr. Bouverie, Hon. Mr. Arundel and two Mrs. Arundels, Hon. Mr. Wallop,

Hon. Miss Duncombes, Sir William and Lady Hanham, Lady Hulse, Sir Thomas and Lady Champneys, Sir John and Lady Alleyn, Sir Alexander and Lady Powell, Mrs. Moss, Mrs. Pechell, Miss Hales, Miss Elwell, Miss Hulse, General Clavering, Mr Pennington, &c. &c. &c. The ball was opened the first evening by the Countess of Pembroke and Lord Folkestone, and on Friday by the Countess of Pembroke and the Earl of Ancram, and the county-dances lasted till about four o'clock each morning.

It is unusual to have a list of those attending a public concert in the 18th century – so even this partial list gives a valuable insight into the make-up of the audience. From the Harris family letters in the Hampshire Record Office it is clear that James Harris and his wife, Elizabeth, saw the attendance of the aristocracy as an important measure of success:

29 October 1760. James Harris, Salisbury, to William Young, Antigua
The first compliments being over, you ask me, what news? Salisbury, I reply, was never more brilliant than at our late St Cecilia [festival] ... all our neighbours of the first quality, the Queensbury, the Pembroke, the Shaftesbury, the Folkstone, the Feversham families, with the Duke of York at their head, did us the honour of their company. The Ball was opened the first night by the Duke of York & Lady Pembroke: the second by Mr Arundel & Lady Shaftesbury: and for country [dances] at least fifty couple in two parallel rows filled the whole area, which soon grew so warm, as would have made Antigua winter.[3]

10 October 1767. From Elizabeth Harris, Salisbury, to James Harris jr, Warsaw
Our St Cecilia [festival] ended last night or more properly this morning, for I did not get home till after four. The music went well both at church & the [assembly] room: a most excellent instrumental band, vocal better than I expected. We had very good company though not so numerous as usual for numbers were kept away because they could not get their mourning...We had 24 persons of quality.... Gertrude got applause by her dancing both minuets & country dances.[4]

I have analysed in Table 1 the lists of those attending the annual festivals published in the *SWJ* between 1771 and 1777 (when the music festivals were at their high point).

Given the connection between the festival of 1766 and the committee formed to build the new infirmary, I thought it would be interesting to see how many of these members of the aristocracy were also founding benefactors and subscribers of the new infirmary.

The development of the Salisbury Infirmary and the role of the aristocracy

Outbreaks of smallpox had led to several meetings in 1763 to consider the provision of a smallpox hospital. The sum of £300 was quickly raised for the

	1771	1772	1773	1774	1775	1776	1777
Duke and Duchess of Queensberry *Amesbury*	Y	Y	Y		Y	Y	
Earl and Countess of Radnor *Longford*	Y	Y	Y	Y	Y	Y	Y
Hon Mr Bouverie *Longford*	Y				Y		Y
Miss Harriet Bouverie *Longford*		Y	Y				
Mr Bertie Bouverie *Longford*		Y			Y		
Mr Edward Bouverie *Longford*		Y	Y	Y	Y		Y
Hon Mr Bartholomew Bouverie *Longford*			Y	Y			
Lord Viscount Folkestone *Longford*	Y	Y		Y	Y		
Hon Miss Anne Duncombe *Barford*	Y			Y	Y		
Bishop of Salisbury *Salisbury*				Y			
Lady Mary Hume *Salisbury*	Y		Y	Y	Y	Y	Y
Sir Alexander Powell *Salisbury*	Y	Y	Y	Y		Y	Y
Henry Dawkins *Standlynch*		Y					
Lady Juliana Dawkins *Standlynch*	Y		Y			Y	
Lord Herbert, Earl of Pembroke *Wilton*	Y	Y	Y		Y	Y	Y
Lady Elizabeth Herbert *Wilton*	Y	Y	Y		Y	Y	Y
Sir John Elwill *West Dean*		Y					
Lady Ranelagh *West Dean*	Y	Y	Y		Y	Y	
Sir Eyre and Lady Coote *West Park, Rockbourne*	Y	Y		Y	Y		Y
Colonel and Mrs Bathurst *Clarendon*		Y					
Hon Mr Fox *Winterslow*	Y	Y	Y	Y			
Mr Fox and Lady Mary Fox *Winterslow*		Y	Y	Y			
Hon Mrs Arundell *Wardour*	Y		Y				Y
Hon Mr and Mrs Everard Arundell *Berwick St John*	Y		Y	Y	Y		Y
Sir Edward and Lady Hulse *Breamore*		Y	Y	Y	Y		Y

Table 1: Local notable families who attended the annual music festivals between 1771 and 1777.

project, including a contribution of £200 from Colonel Peter Bathurst of Clarendon Park. When Anthony Duncombe, Lord Faversham of Barford and MP for Downton, died in 1763 he left a legacy of £500 towards the first hospital to be built in Wiltshire within five years of his death. By 1766 time was pressing if the new infirmary was to benefit from Lord Faversham's legacy and this acted as the spur to the meeting at the Vine Inn in September 1766. Within a month a site was purchased between the Bull Inn and the County Gaol on Fisherton

Street and the existing houses were adapted and opened for patients on 2 May 1767. The first surgeon, Mr John Tatum, was appointed in 1767 (Fig 1). On 11 August 1767 the *Salisbury and Winchester Journal* reported that an 'ingenious Plan for an Infirmary' by Mr Wood of Bath had been accepted by the building

Fig 1: Pastel portrait of Dr Tatum by artist Margaret King dated c.1782 *(Roy Bexon, 2023. Kindly provided by ArtCare, Salisbury District Hospital).*

committee. There was sufficient land to allow for the new building behind the houses used as a temporary hospital.[5]

The grand procession through the city from the Council House to the cathedral to mark the laying of the foundation stone of the new Salisbury Infirmary on 23 September 1767 was one of the most important civic events in Salisbury of the second half of the 18th century. The next day Elizabeth Harris wrote to her son in Warsaw to report on the occasion:

> *23-24 September 1767. Elizabeth Harris, Durnford, to James Harris jr, Warsaw*
> Wednesday September 23rd. The greatest event we have had in Salisbury was the grand march of the subscribers to the Infirmary from the Council House to the Cathedral. They made a fine procession down the High Street. The Corporation with Lord Radnor in his gold gown were the foremost, then followed music, then the Duke of Queensberry & Lord Pembroke, then the clergy of the city & country; next Messrs Howe & Fox, then Ned Young & your father, & so on till it came down to butchers, bakers &c.[6]

A large banner led the procession with a motto devised by the Dean and James Harris, "The Sick and Needy shall not always be forgotten" (Fig 2).[7] The collection taken at the cathedral after the service raised the substantial sum of £50 7s 6d.

The first set of published accounts for the infirmary covering the year September 1766 to September 1767 were presented later that day, together with a full list of the subscribers and benefactors. The accounts reveal that at the end of this first year there were 325 subscribers who each paid at least one guinea raising a total of £668 15s, and that the benefactors had given a total of £4,020 9s 0d which included contributions of £500 from the Earl of Radnor, £200 from the Earl of Pembroke and £31 10s from James Harris.

Fig 2: Modern nurses' badge with motto devised by the Dean and James Harris *(Nigel Wyatt, 2023. Kindly provided by ArtCare, Salisbury District Hospital).*

This published list of subscribers and benefactors from 1767 (Table 2) allows us to see which of those in the list of regular supporters of the annual music festivals were also supporters of the new infirmary. The considerable overlap between Tables 1 and 2 shows the close involvement of key local families in the success of both projects.

	Benefactor	Subscriber
Duke and Duchess of Queensberry *Amesbury*	£200	£10 10s
Earl of Radnor *Longford*	£500	£21
Countess of Radnor *Longford*		£5 5s
Miss Harriet Bouverie *Longford*	£6 6s	£3 3s
Mr Edward Bouverie *Longford*		£5 5s
Bishop of Salisbury *Salisbury*	£105	£10 10s
Sir Alexander Powell *Salisbury*	£42	£3 3s
James Harris	£31 10s	£3 3s
Henry Dawkins *Standlynch*	£50	£5 5s
Lady Juliana Dawkins *Standlynch*		£3 3s
Lord Herbert, Earl of Pembroke *Wilton*	£200	£25
Lady Elizabeth Herbert *Wilton*		£10
Hon Mr Fox *Winterslow*	£50	£5 5s
Lady Mary Fox *Winterslow*		£2 2s
Lord Henry and Mrs Arundell *Wardour*	£50	£3 3s
Hon Mr and Mrs Everard Arundell *Berwick St John*	£21 2s	£2 2s
Sir Edward Hulse *Breamore*		£5 5s
Lady Hulse *Breamore*		£3 3s

Table 2: Members of local notable families who were supporters of the new infirmary.

The newly finished infirmary opened in 1771 (Fig 3). In August brief reports of admissions to the Infirmary began to appear in the *Salisbury and Winchester Journal*:

> *5 Monday August 1771*
>
> Salisbury Infirmary. Casualties admitted last week: Samuel Lodge, of Downton, for a fractured clavicle, by the tread of a horse; John Oak, of this city, a fractured scapula, by a fall from a waggon; and William Porter, of the same, wounded by a bull.

> *12 Monday August 1771*
>
> Salisbury Infirmary. Casualties admitted last week: Aeneas Potticary of Boyton for a fractured thigh; Mary Hibberd, of this city, for a fractured arm; and William Price, much bruised by a wall, which he was removing, suddenly giving way.

Then in the following week the formal announcement of the opening of the new building appeared – setting out the conditions for those recommended for admission by a subscriber or benefactor:

Fig 3: Front Elevation of Salisbury General Infirmary. Ink drawing dated 1819 by T Atkinson *(Roy Bexon, 2023. Kindly provided by ArtCare, Salisbury District Hospital).*

> SALISBURY INFIRMARY, Aug. 17. 1771.
> NOTICE IS HEREBY GIVEN,
> That the new building is now opened for the reception of patients; and that as wards are large and commodious, all subscribers and benefactors may be assured no persons, recommended as in-patients, will, for the future, be either rejected or made out-patients, unless in the cases excluded by rule 34, which is as follows:
>
> *That no woman big with child, no child under seven years of age (except in very extraordinary cases, such as fractures, and the stone in the bladder, or where couching, trepanning, or amputation, or other operations, which are necessary to be performed at the infirmary), none who are disordered in their senses, suspected to have the small pox, itch, or other infectious distempers, having habitual ulcers in the legs, obstinate scrophulous or leperous cases, cancers not admitting operation, consumptions or dropsies in their last stages, epileptic or other fits, in a dying condition, or judged incurable, be admitted as in-patients, or (if inadvertently admitted) be suffered to continue.*
>
> By order of the Committee
> RADNOR, President
> John Turner, Secretary.[8]

The statutes and rules of the infirmary (Fig 4) make it clear in Rule 4 that 'no Patient shall be admitted but by Recommendation of a Subscriber or

Benefactor, unless in Cases which admit of no Delay....'. This is explained further in Rule 5:

> That for every Guinea subscribed and every Twenty-five Pounds given in Benefaction, the Subscriber or Benefactor shall have a Right of recommending from the Town or Parish which such Subscriber has any Dwelling or Property, one in-Patient in the Year.... Out-Patients shall be recommended by the Subscribers without limitation of Place or Number....[9]

The annual procession to the cathedral in 1771 was particularly splendid and the SWJ reported, 'The public thanks of the meeting were ... to the Countess of Radnor and Lady Mary Hume, for their good office in making a collection at the church-door, for the benefit of this laudable institution, which amounted to 65l. 7s.'[10]

THE
STATUTES
AND
RULES,
For the GOVERNMENT of the
GENERAL INFIRMARY,
AT
The City of SALISBURY,
FOR THE
Relief of the Sick and Lame POOR,
FROM
Whatever COUNTY recommended.

SALISBURY:
Printed by BENJAMIN COLLINS.
MDCCLXVII.

Fig 4: Frontispiece – Statutes of the Salisbury Infirmary 1767 *(Roy Bexon, 2023).*

Support for the theatre in Salisbury

Alongside the flourishing annual music festivals between 1765 to 1780, Salisbury was also able to support regular seasons of plays at the theatre at the Vine Inn presented by touring groups of actors.[11] In part this was due to the regular support of many of the same local members of the aristocracy. During each season the notices in the *Salisbury and Winchester Journal* describe a number of performances as being 'by the desire of' a local notable figure. As Hare points out, it was the support of many of these families that underpinned the regular performances in the Salisbury theatre:

> The Countess of Radnor, The Countess of Pembroke, Lady Ranelagh, Lady Knatchbull, Lady Julia Dawkins, Lady Webb, Lady Mary Fox, Hon. Mrs Howe, Hon. Benson Earle, Miss Furber, Mrs Hermes Harris, Mrs Penruddocke Wyndham – are among the names of the local gentry 'bespeaking' performances during the early years of the Salisbury companies. .... The players courted their

> favour and their financial support, both as sponsors, and as subscribers to the boxes.[12]

In most years the players would also present a performance for the benefit of the poor (Fig 5). To take one example, a performance benefitting the poor was advertised on 30 December 1768 (which was reported the following week to have raised £28 10s).

On Saturday evening the comedy of *Meaſure for Meaſure*, and the farce of the *Deuce is in him*, were performed at our theatre, for the benefit of the Poor of this city; to which the Earl of Radnor and the Hon. Mr. Fox gave five guineas each :--- Mr. Fox gave alſo 25l. more, for the immediate relief of the moſt indigent at this inclement ſeaſon, to be diſtributed at the diſcretion of the Mayor.

Fig 5: Theatre performance for the benefit of the poor – *SWJ* advert 21 Jan 1771 *(Nigel Wyatt, 2023).*

The notice given in the *Salisbury and Winchester Journal* on 13 January 1772 makes clear the role of the mayor of Salisbury in these performances for the benefit of the poor:

> The Mayor of Salisbury presents his respectful compliments to the nobility and gentry of the city, Close, and neighbourhood, and desires the favour of their company at the Theatre in this city, this present evening, when a comedy called, the English Merchant, with the Padlock, will be acted, for the benefit of the poor.

Just as the music festivals had done, the players also put on performances for the benefit of the new infirmary. A performance of *The Busybody* and *High Life Below Stairs* on 9 March 1771 was given for the benefit of the Salisbury Infirmary. We learn from the published Infirmary Annual Report for the period September 1770 to September 1771 that 'Mr Collins, Comedian' gave £13 12s 5d to the infirmary following the performance. In the previous year's accounts Mr Collins gave £6 0s 4d.

Benefits to the local economy

The presence of so many members of the aristocracy drew others to the annual music festivals which had other beneficial effects locally. In 1772 the festival began on 30 September. The *Salisbury and Winchester Journal* of 28 September 1772 carried adverts from three hairdressers - Grindley and Ball from Soho, Donaldson from London and Woollard and Davis from Bath – offering punctual attention to ladies requesting their services during the festival. Other adverts promote what would appear to be sales of new china, hats or fabrics timed to coincide with the festival period. So, for example, in the same edition of the *SWJ* there is an advert promoting both the sale of china and rooms to let for the duration of the festival:

> *28 September 1772*
>
> Now selling off, under the original Cost, at the China-shop in Endless-street, the remaining part of the CHINA, DELPH, Yellow and White STONEWARE...
>
> To be let during St. Caecilia's Festival, a dining-room, parlour, and three genteel bed-chambers.

Clearly the influx of people to the city for the music festivals also had a positive effect on the local economy.

Conclusion

It seems clear, then, that the involvement of the local notable families was an important factor in the flourishing of music and theatre in Salisbury at this time and that this went hand in hand with their cooperative efforts to support the establishment of the new infirmary. This allows us to provide a more broadly based explanation for the artistic success of the music festivals in the 1770s. As I have written previously, James Harris undoubtedly played the key role in attracting some of the greatest musicians of the day to perform in Salisbury – a period that came to an abrupt end at his death in 1780. However, it is evident that it was also the cooperative engagement of local families, cemented by the efforts to establish the new infirmary from 1766 onwards, which created the circumstances in which the annual festivals could flourish.

Bibliography

The letters of the Harris family are held in the Malmesbury collection at the Hampshire Record Office (HRO) starting with reference 9M73. There are two published selections from the collection:

Harris, James, 1st Earl of Malmesbury, 1870, *A series of letters of the first Earl of Malmesbury, his family and friends from 1745 to 1820*, vol. 1, R. Bentley, London.

Burrows, Donald and Dunhill, Rosemary (eds.), 2002, *Music and Theatre in Handel's World: The Family Papers of James Harris, 1732-1780*, Oxford University Press, Oxford.

Salisbury Infirmary, 1767, *The Statutes and Rules for the Government of the General Infirmary at the City of Salisbury 1767,* printed by Benjamin Collins.

Hare, Arnold, 1958, *The Georgian Theatre in Wessex,* Phoenix House, London.

Haskins, Charles, 1922, 'The history of Salisbury Infirmary, founded by Anthony Lord

Feversham A.D. 1766', *Salisbury Times*, Salisbury.

Shemilt, Philip, 1992, *Salisbury 200 – Salisbury Infirmary bicentenary review 1766-1966.* Salisbury Infirmary (privately printed).

Woodall, T. J, 1893, *Records of the Salisbury Infirmary, 1766-1893.*

Notes

1 *Salisbury and Winchester Journal (SWJ), 26 September 1768.*

2 See previous articles concerning James Harris and his role in the musical life of 18th century Salisbury: Wyatt, Nigel, 2016, 'The Salisbury subscription concerts in the 18th century'. *Sarum Chronicle*, Issue 16, 79-89; Wyatt, 2018, 'Salisbury's Lost Opera: The Spring or Daphnis and Amaryllis by James Harris', *The Consort*, Dolmetsch Foundation, Vol 74, 79-95; Wyatt, 2020, 'The annual music festivals of 18th century Salisbury', *Sarum Chronicle,* Issue 20, 23-40;Wyatt, 2021, 'Elizabeth Harris', *Sarum Chronicle*, Issue 21, 157-172.

3 Hampshire Record Office (HRO), 9M73/0345/60.

4 HRO, 9M73/01254/29. The requirement to wear mourning for the Duke of York, who succumbed to 'maleary fever' and died on 17 September 1767 in Monaco, had apparently discouraged some people from attending the public events of the festival.

5 The infirmary building was in use as a hospital until 1991 and finally closed 1993. The building was converted for residential use in 1997.

6 HRO, 9M73/01254/28.

7 The annual processions continued until 1993 – led by a banner with the motto devised by James Harris and the Dean. The motto has been used on the nurses' badge into the 20th century and in the crest and badge of the Salisbury Group of Hospitals.

8 *SWJ*, 17 August 1771.

9 *The Statutes and Rules for the Government of the General Infirmary at the City of Salisbury 1767,* printed by Benjamin Collins, page 24/5.

10 *SWJ,* 30 September 1771.

11 The Vine Inn (sometimes referred to as The New Playhouse in early adverts) occupied the corner of the Cheese Market opposite St Thomas' churchyard (currently Dinghams and Jordan & Mason Estate Agents).

12 See Hare, 1958, *The Georgian Theatre in Wessex*, Phoenix House, London. Mrs Hermes Harris here is Elizabeth, wife of James Harris who was commonly known as 'Hermes Harris' after his most famous book *Hermes, or, A Philosophical Inquiry Concerning Universal Grammar,* published in 1751.

Author Biographies

Heather Adeley

After having had a career in teaching, speech therapy and theatre in Cambridge and Sussex, Heather and her husband retired to the Salisbury area. Since then, she has been a volunteer with Salisbury Cathedral's education team and at the Cathedral Library. Heather is also involved in her local village community and the Churches Conservation Trust (CTT).

Christopher Daniell

Christopher Daniell has various degrees from the University of York and worked as an archaeologist and historian for York Archaeological Trust for many years. He currently works as the Senior Historic Buildings Advisor for the Ministry of Defence, advising on the Ministry's one thousand listed buildings across the UK. He has written extensively, including the book *Death and Burial in Medieval England,* 1066-1550, and an article for *World Archaeology* on historic graffiti. His current specialisms are St Thomas's church, the foundation of New Sarum and early maps of the city.

John Elliott

Now retired and living near Salisbury, John used to teach art and architectural history at Reading University and at Royal Holloway College which is part of London University. For many years he was director of Spire Books and has contributed chapters to various books on architectural history. He edited *Salisbury Cathedral: 800 years of People and Place* with Emily Naish as well as contributing several chapters. He is a member of the *Sarum Chronicle* editorial board.

Ed Green

Ed Green is a London-based freelance editor and writer with a background in economics and history. His interest in social history has led to previous publications on Downton and the First World War, as well as a biography on the 1820s millennial religious figure, John Wroe. Ed is currently researching aspects of the development of mass democracy in England and Wales.

Jane Howells

Jane Howells is a member of the standing committee of the West of England and South Wales Women's History Network, and this article arises from her involvement with their Study Group on 'Women's political and civic engagement in the 1920s. Long retired from teaching, she has recently retired after many years as editor of *Local History News* for the British Association for Local History. See below for Ruth Newman and Jane Howells' joint authored publications on Salisbury local history.

Monte Little

Monte Little has lived in the Salisbury area since 1969 and was a senior librarian for Wiltshire Library service based in Wilton, Salisbury and Trowbridge. He was awarded a Fellowship of the Library Association in 1973 and a Master's degree from London University in 1981. He specialises in the history of local libraries as part of Wiltshire social history and has published several articles and monographs.

Beatrice King

Beatrice has lived in Salisbury since 2010 and retired from paid employment in 2019. Since then she has been pursuing her interests in local history and needlework, including combining both interests in restoring a set of historical cushions in Salisbury Cathedral and researching their background and history.

John Loades

John is Treasurer for *Sarum Chronicle* and an amateur local historian. He contributed several sections to the volume *Laverstock and Ford; Chapters in Local History,* Sarum Studies 6, 2019.

Ruth Newman

Ruth is a past editor of *Sarum Chronicle* and the co-author with Jane Howells of *Salisbury Past.* In 2011 they edited and transcribed William Small's *Cherished Memories and Associations* for the Wiltshire Record Society. They have also written *Women in Salisbury Cathedral Close*, Sarum Studies 5, 2014. She is a Salisbury Cathedral guide.

Robina Rand

Robina grew up in the village of Hanley Castle in south Worcestershire and went to school in Worcester. She read law at Leeds University but thereafter trained as a psychiatric social worker. She worked at The Retreat hospital in York and then for Social Services. Having married and living in Reading, she returned to University to complete a degree in archaeology and an MA in mediaeval studies, followed by a range of different jobs. Robina and her husband returned to Worcestershire in December 2014 after they had both retired. She has since enjoyed researching local history and working as a volunteer at Upton-on-Severn library.

David Richards

David Richards is a retired dental surgeon who is now a Blue Badge Guide with a particular interest in the history of the people and buildings of the Salisbury area.

Malcolm Sinclair

After a career in the NHS in London and southern England, Malcolm is using retirement to pursue his first love of history. In 2023 he was awarded a Master of Arts in Medieval Studies, with Distinction, by the University of Wales Trinity St David, which included a dissertation on Augustus Pugin. Now living just outside Melksham, he is pursuing a number of writing projects related to his main interests of the gothic, stained glass, memento mori and the historical treatment of madness. Originally a Clinical Nurse Specialist & Trainer in Addictions, he spent 15 years as an NHS Director in Wiltshire, Bristol and Gloucestershire, which included work leading to the building and opening of Fountain Way in Salisbury to replace the Old Manor Hospital. He is a member of the *Sarum Chronicle* editorial board.

Nigel Wyatt

Nigel completed a degree in philosophy at Lancaster University and an MA in Contemporary Philosophy at Southampton University. After teaching in the West Midlands and Suffolk, he was appointed Headteacher of a middle school in Salisbury. He then worked as an education consultant supporting and advising headteachers and developing education materials, and is currently Executive Officer of the National Middle Schools forum. He performs with a number of local orchestras and choirs, including Salisbury Baroque. In recent years Nigel has been researching the musical life of Salisbury in the 18th century.

One of the Sarum Chronicle team

Alan Castle has been a member of the Sarum Chronicle team since 2020. His main task is as a proof reader responsible for the editing process from initial article submission to final typeset proofs. Alan was a Principal Lecturer in Radiography at the University of Portsmouth until he retired in 2013, after a teaching career spanning over 30 years. Following a period in the merchant navy, he qualified as a diagnostic radiographer in 1974 and worked as a clinical radiographer in the UK and Australia before becoming a lecturer. He holds a Bachelor's, Master's and a PhD in Education from the University of Southampton. Alan has volunteer roles as a guide at Salisbury Cathedral and with English Heritage at Stonehenge. He is a keen walker and, together with his wife, has walked the coastline of England and Wales and completed many National and International Trails but has yet to tackle Scotland!

BACK ISSUES

Availability and prices

Sarum Chronicle

Since the first issue was published in 2001, *Sarum Chronicle* has built an enthusiastic following of readers and contributors. Each issue contains articles, shorter notes, and book reviews. The content is scholarly but accessible, significant but concise. Coverage demonstrates the huge variety of topics of interest to local historians, and the wealth of sources they use.

Further information about *Sarum Chronicle*, including contact details for enquiries and orders, can be found at *www.sarumchronicle.wordpress.com*

Back issues are available as follows (excluding postage):

- **Issue 2** is now out of print.
- **Issue 1 and Issues 3 – 10** are available at £3 each.
- OR as a special offer: the first **NINE** available issues (as above) together for £20 plus postage while stocks last.

Issue 11 onwards are more substantial with colour illustrations:

- **Issues 11 and 12** have been reprinted and are now available at £8.95 each.
- **Issues 13 to 21** at £5.00 each.
- **Issue 22** at £13.50.

A contents list for each issue can be accessed by selecting the relevant issue from the 'Back Issues' page of the *Sarum Chronicle* website: *www.sarumchronicle.wordpress.com*

Sarum Studies

In addition to the annual Sarum Chronicle, the editorial team produces independent publications on specific aspects of Salisbury's history, entitled Sarum Studies.
To date, seven titles have been published and are available as follows (excluding postage):

Sarum Studies 1. **Milford** by Richard Durman, 2007 at £5.95 each.
Sarum Studies 2. **Harnham Mill** by Michael Cowan, 2008 at £4.95 each.
Sarum Studies 3. **The Harnham Water Meadows** by Hadrian Cook, Michael Cowan and Tim Tatton-Brown, 2008 at £5.95 each.
Sarum Studies 4. **Harnham Historical Miscellany** edited by Jane Howells, 2013 at £8.95 each.
Sarum Studies 5. **Women in Salisbury Cathedral Close** by Jane Howells and Ruth Newman, 2014 at £8.95 each.
Sarum Studies 6. **Laverstock & Ford: Chapters from Local History** by Laverstock and Ford Local History research group, 2019 at £10.00 each.
Sarum Studies 7. **Salisbury Cathedral: 800 Years of People and Place** edited by Emily Naish and John Elliott, June 2020, now out of print.

Further information about each publication can be accessed by selecting the 'Sarum Studies' page of the *Sarum Chronicle* website. *www.sarumchronicle.wordpress.com*